The best American mystery stories of the nineteenth century

THE BEST AMERICAN
MYSTERY STORIES
OF THE 19TH CENTURY

THE BEST AMERICAN MYSTERY STORIES OF THE 19TH CENTURY

EDITED AND WITH AN INTRODUCTION BY

OTTO PENZLER

HOUGHTON MIFFLIN HARCOURT
BOSTON • NEW YORK
2014

For information about permission to reproduce selections from this book,
write to Permissions, Houghton Mifflin Harcourt Publishing Company,
215 Park Avenue South, New York, New York 10003.

www.hmhco.com

Library of Congress Cataloging-in-Publication Data is available.
ISBN 978-0-544-30222-8

Printed in the United States of America
DOC 10 9 8 7 6 5 4 3 2 1

For Nelson DeMille

*A wonderful writer and dear friend,
with thanks for helping to
change my life — for the better!*

CONTENTS

INTRODUCTION

Mystery fiction has been the most successful literary genre in the English-speaking world for a century and a half, and when examining its significant elements, there should be no surprise in understanding why that is true.

Virtually all mystery fiction dramatizes one of the simplest and purest components of human existence and behavior: the battle between the forces of Good and those of Evil. God versus Satan. The killer versus the savior. The detective versus the criminal. Since the majority of civilized society prefers good to evil, a great pleasure, or at least comfort, may be found in the mystery story, in which it is prevalent for righteousness to emerge triumphant.

There is a theory—one that carries some validity—that detective fiction became popular late in the nineteenth century, coinciding with a decline in unwavering adherence to religion, wherein the sense of guilt that is ingrained in all of us had been somewhat relieved through the agency of some divine or apotheosized being. When religion loosened its hold upon our hearts, another outlet for our guilt had to be invented, and this occurred in the creation of mystery fiction.

It often has been noted that the detective novel has as strict a composition as a sonnet (which may be a trifle exaggerated, but you get the idea), yet it is even more true that it is as formalized as a religious ritual. There is a necessary sin (in most mystery novels and stories, this takes the form of murder), a victim, of course, a high priest (the criminal) who must be destroyed by a higher power—the detective. Having inevitably identified to some degree with the light and dark sides of his own nature, the detective and the criminal, the reader seeks absolution and redemption. Thus the denouement of the mystery will be analogous to the Day of Judgment, when all is made clear and the soul is cleansed

— and the criminal, through the omnipotent power of the detective, is caught and punished.

It is important to understand what a mystery story is. It is common for most readers and people connected to the literary world to assume that mystery stories are detective stories. Some are, but there are many other subgenres, too. Fiction told from the point of view of a criminal, whether a bank robber or a gentleman jewel thief, falls into the mystery category, though the detectives tend be less significant characters. The thriller, in which the fate of the world or nation or another significant entity is at risk, also falls into the mystery category. Just because a murderer (or group of murderers) wants to kill a large number of people rather than have a single target does not make him less of a murderer, just as the detective — again, whether an individual or a group of people attempting to thwart a nefarious scheme, such as a police department or the Federal Bureau of Investigation — is no less defined as the heroic protagonist merely because he is hunting numerous villains rather than just one.

The definition of the mystery that I have used for many years and that serves well is that it is any work of fiction in which a crime, or the threat of a crime, is central to the theme or the plot. Thus such books as *Crime and Punishment* and *To Kill a Mockingbird* should be regarded as mysteries, because lacking the underlying crimes, there can be no book. On the other hand, *The Great Gatsby* and *The House of the Seven Gables,* in which murder and other crimes occur, do not qualify, as those crimes are not the essential elements of the narratives; the books could still exist without the violence.

The evolution of the mystery is long and complicated. Because it has become such a successful genre, both critically and commercially, it naturally has many fathers. Arguments have been made for innumerable works as being the first mystery novel or the first mystery short story. The murder of Abel by his brother Cain in the Old Testament has a legitimate claim to being the first crime story, but it is not, of course, a mystery, as the culprit was immediately known. There were, you see, so few possible suspects. Other stories of crime without detection abound in literature, notably in *Tales of the Arabian Nights* (under its many different titles) and in the dramas of William Shakespeare, such as *Hamlet, Julius Caesar,* and *Macbeth,* just as there are some excellent examples of detection without crime, as in Voltaire's *Zadig,* in which the eponymous hero, in the episode titled "The Dog and the Horse," has made studies of nature that have enabled him to discern "a thousand differences where other men see nothing but uniformity." As a result, he makes deductions so precisely that he is able to describe the queen's missing spaniel and a runaway horse with incredible accuracy, though he has never seen either. He is suspected of sorcery, but his method of scientific reason makes the exercise seem elementary, as Sherlock Holmes would say.

> I observed the marks of a horse's shoes, all at equal distance. This must be a horse, said I to myself, that gallops excellently. The dust on the trees on a narrow road that was but seven feet wide was a little brushed off, at the distance of three feet and a half from the middle of the road. This horse, said I, has a tail three feet and a half long, which, being whisked to the right and left, has swept away the dust. I observed under the trees that form an arbor five feet in height, that the leaves from the branches were newly fallen, from whence I inferred that the horse had touched them, and that he must therefore be five feet high. As to his bit, it must be of gold of twenty-three carats, for he had rubbed its bosses against a stone which I knew to be a touchstone, and which I have tried. In a word, from a mark made by his shoes on flints of another kind, I concluded that he was shod with silver eleven deniers fine.

While one would be prepared to state that this is a somewhat implausible sequence of deductions, it is nonetheless not unfair to describe Zadig as the first systematic detective in literature.

Once the case has been made for murder stories without detection and for detection without crime, it becomes necessary to identify the first true detective in mystery fiction, and it can be none other than C. Auguste Dupin, who made his first appearance in 1841 in Edgar Allan Poe's milestone of modern literature, "The Murders in the Rue Morgue."

To state it simply and superfluously, there was very little likelihood of a detective appearing in fiction until there were such things in real life, and there were no detectives until the creation of the Bow Street Runners in London in 1749 by the author Henry Fielding (though it numbered only six members and was eventually superseded by Scotland Yard) and the Sûreté in Paris (1811), created by Eugène François Vidocq, who was, incredibly enough, a notorious criminal. These organizations formalized to some degree the apprehension of criminals and were responsible for turning them over to the courts for a trial and fairly measured-out punishment. While the administration of justice was not always as prevalent as the ideal, it was far superior to the previous system, which generally relied on state-sponsored torture during the interrogation process.

When Poe created his detective, an amateur, he found it expedient to set the story in Paris. In this way, Dupin could show off his observational skills and deductive-reasoning genius as a counterpoint to the ineptitude of the official Parisian police. This established one of the tropes of the detective story. While many protagonists in detective fiction are members of an official police force, readers have long held a special place in their hearts for the romantic figure who is either a gifted amateur or a privately hired investigator. If he is a professional policeman in whatever agency he may be employed by, he is generally a maverick who prefers to work on his own and outside the rules that otherwise would restrict his behavior.

In America, this figure, this lone protector of law and order, derives from the most romantic hero of the country's history: the solitary gunfighter, sheriff, or U.S. marshal who singlehandedly helped defend honest citizens from the depredations of the outlaws in the West as the country expanded from its East Coast beginnings. Such names as Wyatt Earp, Wild Bill Hickok, Doc Holliday, and Kit Carson still resonate, though many of their exploits and positive character traits were exaggerated by newspapers, which welcomed increased sales to Easterners titillated by the thrilling stories about these larger-than-life figures. To an even greater degree, the dime novels of the day made celebrities and legends out of the drunken Calamity Jane, the lecherous Hickok, the diminutive (five-foot-four) Carson, the card cheat Earp, and the William Cody who became famous for slaughtering 4,300 buffalo in eighteen months for no particular reason, earning him the nickname Buffalo Bill.

Nevertheless, the legends had enough truth in them and were powerful enough to help form Americans' notion of who they were as a nation. What was prized was the strength and values of the individual to protect the ordinary citizen. After the West was essentially tamed, readers looked for new heroes for whom to root, and they came along in detective fiction. They may not have been as swashbuckling as the lone gunman riding into town to clean it up, but they had their virtues. Instead of a six-shooter, they used their brains.

Poe's Dupin was the archetypical detective of the nineteenth century and remained so until the creation of the hard-boiled American private eye shortly after the end of World War I. Most American fiction until Poe's invention had been some variations of folk tales and legends (by Washington Irving and his followers) and western adventures by James Fenimore Cooper, whose Leatherstocking saga became enormously popular. There were sea stories, romance stories, and attempts at the equivalent of gothic fiction, but it was a new country that didn't have much time to write or read — and, with a still-developing educational system, many people couldn't do either.

Having created such a significant figure in his first detective story, then following it with two others about Dupin, Poe would have been expected to continue his unique, pioneering series, but he did not — nor did anyone else. There was general apathy to this new literary genre, and few writers decided to follow in his footsteps in America. It took twenty-five years after the publication of "The Murders in the Rue Morgue" for a detective novel to be written, the now completely forgotten *The Dead Letter* (1866), by Seeley Regester (the pseudonym of Metta Victoria Fuller Victor).

England was a different story, and the idea of detective fiction took hold fairly quickly when Charles Dickens wrote *Bleak House* (1852–1853), thus creating the first significant police detective in literature with Inspector Bucket. Most of Dickens's ensuing novels involved crime and mystery, culminating with *The Mystery of Edwin Drood* (1870), regrettably left unfinished when he died after six chapters (of a planned twenty) were published. His friend and sometime collaborator, Wilkie Collins, entered the field as well, producing such masterpieces as *The Woman in White* (1860) and *The Moonstone* (1868), described by T. S. Eliot as "the first, the longest, and the best" detective novel ever written. The fact that he was wrong on all three counts does not diminish Collins's achievement in any way.

Although pure tales of ratiocination (the word made up by Poe to describe the rational deductions derived from the detective's keen observations) were not part of the American literary scene before or immediately after Poe's groundbreaking work, other types of crime stories enjoyed success, though some of them stretch the definition of mystery that pertains to the genre as defined above. Tales posing such mysteries as "How many angels can dance on the head of a pin?" and "What do women want?" need not concern us here. The detective cerebral enough to answer these questions has yet to be created, and they are beyond the scope of this collection.

Riddle stories are the foundation of the detective story and have existed since the first narratives were created to entertain the reader. In a riddle story, the reader is presented with a series of baffling situations and is challenged to arrive at a rational explanation for these unusual circumstances. The author reserves the solution to these confusing occurrences until the conclusion of the tale. While this may sound like a detective story, authors in the pre-Poe era largely resorted to explanations other than those employed in what may be regarded as the modern mystery. Supernatural entities like ghosts may make a sudden appearance to explain a mystery, or a character's alter ego or subconscious may provide a solution. Coincidence may play a major role, or, to the discredit of all writers who did it, a character may wake from a dream to find that we were not connected to reality in the first place. While stories of this nature may often have some value, they are unsatisfying to a more discerning readership. The invention of the detective was needed to bring order to the chaos of the amorphous riddle story (although there are exceptions, such as the highly accomplished examples in this collection).

Since it has been made clear that the detective story began with "The Murders in the Rue Morgue," it may seem eccentric to begin this chronological compilation with several stories that preceded Poe. However, as defined earlier, the mystery genre includes a great deal of fiction that is neither about detectives nor is restricted to tales of ratiocination.

Washington Irving's brutal little crime story, truly as horrific today as when it was composed nearly two centuries ago, requires no detective to inform us of what happened, or why, or by whom. Indeed, it might be said that it is precisely this kind of story, and the kind of crime it illustrates, that required the creation of detectives, both in real life and in fiction, to bring the villainous perpetrators to justice.

The almost unknown and rarely reprinted (in spite of its historical significance and readability) William Leggett story, "The Rifle," is the greatest leap forward in the evolution of the detective story. It is an excellent suspense story that displays a very early use of an element frequently employed in modern mystery stories: the accusation, capture, and imminent punishment of an innocent man for a murder he did not commit. The sophisticated storytelling technique of providing evidence of the protagonist's innocence to the reader while concealing it from the other characters in the story became the mainstay of many of Alfred Hitchcock's motion pictures as well as numerous suspense novels, notably the classic *Phantom Lady,* written by Cornell Woolrich under the pseudonym William Irish.

Also groundbreaking in "The Rifle" is the amount of pure detective work described and the significance tied to the forensics of ballistics. This may seem rather straightforward and simplistic in a century intimately familiar with the techniques of modern police laboratories and the geniuses of *CSI,* but if we look back at the analysis today, it was dazzling for its time — the early years of an America that had just begun to inch westward from the Atlantic coast.

Many of the stories in this comprehensive collection succeed as literature while failing the test of purity in the realm of detective fiction. Crime stories are strongly represented here, as are riddle stories, and several romans à clef that purport to be true crime journalism but are in fact honed to present their central figure in a brighter light than their actual activities might have warranted.

The shortage of what may ironically (considering the era under discussion) be termed old-fashioned detective stories should come as a surprise to no one. After Poe failed to inspire a raft of followers, magazine editors saw no urgent need to induce others to follow in his footsteps, so, as inevitable as crime itself seems to be, writers avoided this new and unrewarded literary genre.

In France, detective fiction had achieved popularity at the hands of Émile Gaboriau, whose series character, Monsieur Lecoq, a member of the Sûreté, appeared in numerous novels and short stories in the 1860s and 1870s. Lecoq's adventures were closely patterned after the real-life career of Eugène François Vidocq, whose four-volume *Memoires* (1828–1829) contained far more fiction than actual memoir. Lecoq was the first significant detective of fiction to employ disguises to shadow a suspect, develop the use of plaster to make casts of footprints, and even invent a test to determine when a bed had been slept in. The success of Gaboriau's books encouraged scores of French hacks to produce books about detectives, all of whom had the same high level of frenetic activity as Lecoq, scurrying around to find clues, chase suspects, and even engage in physical confrontations.

It was not until 1887 and Arthur Conan Doyle's creation of Sherlock Holmes in England that the pure cerebral methodology of Dupin was combined with the energy of Lecoq to give the public a detective about whom it wanted to read stories on a regular basis. And, it should be noted, even then it was not an instantaneous response, as the first novel, *A Study in Scarlet,* was followed in 1890 by *The Sign of Four* without a noticeable stir in the reading public. It was not until July 1891, with the publication of the first Holmes short story, "A Scandal in Bohemia," in the *Strand Magazine,* that a large readership was found, and the publication of *The Adventures of Sherlock Holmes* (1892) sealed the deal.

Inevitably, the staggering success of Holmes brought out copycats who attempted to emulate the formula that Doyle so successfully maintained. A somewhat eccentric detective, his slightly dim sidekick, a sensational crime, a baffled police department, and a startling denouement based on keen observation and brilliant deductive reasoning — that was the formula. It had all been invented by Poe, as already noted, but Dupin was not nearly as interesting as Holmes, nor were the hundreds of detectives who followed in his wake.

The sudden popularity of mystery fiction induced many writers to try their hands at it. Some, predictably, were the ungifted who would produce, on demand, whatever editors were looking for to fill the pages of their magazines, gift annuals, and newspapers. This sort of pedestrian writing, in every genre and of every type, has a long history that has caused the destruction of uncountable evergreens to produce the paper on which so much undistinguished prose was offered to a largely undiscerning public.

However, many first-rate authors took their pens in hand and decided that they, too, could add something worthwhile to the genre. While this was more true in the twentieth century, after the literary genre had been established for a while, it also pertained in the previous century, when such luminaries as Mark Twain, Frank Stockton, Jack London, Edith Wharton, Ambrose Bierce, Stephen Crane, and Ellen Glasgow produced short stories involving crime, mystery, and murder. Curiously, so did such highly successful writers of books for young readers as L. Frank Baum, Thomas Bailey Aldrich, and Louisa May Alcott.

All of these authors, major contributors to American letters in the 1800s, will be found in this collection. Some of their stories will be familiar to many readers and have enjoyed the success of being often reprinted and anthologized.

There also rest between these covers authors whose works were unheralded in their own lifetimes and whose names have receded into the unforgiving, vast darkness of time. Their names and the stories they wrote are unknown to all but a few antiquarians, just as they have been for a century or more. Obscure or not, they have much to recommend them, even if they do not quite sparkle to the same degree as their more famous contemporaries. They still have good stories to tell, and the best of them crack open a door for a peek at another time and people who otherwise would not have been met.

This anthology covers virtually the entire nineteenth century, offering the best work in the mystery genre produced during those years. The range is from the greatest and most famous writers of the century to the most obscure. The length varies from a short-short of less than two pages to works that might almost qualify as novellas. Every type of mystery is included, from crime to detective to suspense to riddle, and from humorous to blindingly dark.

A great deal more crime fiction was produced in the twentieth century than in the nineteenth, and much of it may well be superior to all but the best of that earlier era. Still, the later works could not have been produced without the groundbreaking creativity of the earliest practitioners of this demanding form. The stories in this collection are more than pioneering efforts being offered merely to illustrate the roots of the genre. They are superb examples of American fiction that will endure as long as stories are told and written, and as long as they are heard and read.

Otto Penzler
January 2014

THE BEST AMERICAN
MYSTERY STORIES
OF THE 19TH CENTURY

1824

WASHINGTON IRVING

THE STORY OF THE YOUNG ROBBER

Noted for their charm and simplicity, the stories, sketches, and full-length books by WASHINGTON IRVING (1783–1859) earned him the title of "Father of American Literature," as the first author of significance to marry American literature with the literature of the world. His life abroad, mainly in Spain, Italy, and England, heavily influenced his work in the formative years of nineteenth-century America.

The easy grace of his narratives and their gentle humor endeared him to the reading public, and he enjoyed great success with such works as *A History of New-York* (under the byline Diedrich Knickerbocker, 1809), generally regarded as the first American work of humorous fiction, and especially *The Sketch Book of Geoffrey Crayon, Esq.* (1819–1820), which contained the immortal tales known by all American schoolchildren, "Rip Van Winkle" and "The Legend of Sleepy Hollow."

In 1824 he wrote *Tales of a Traveller* under the Geoffrey Crayon byline, hoping to recreate the success of *The Sketch Book,* though some elements are very different in tone and this is now regarded as a minor work. While his early stories were noted for their sentimental, romantic views of life and (the word cries out to be used again) their charm, many of the little sketches in *Tales of a Traveller* are downright shocking, especially "The Story of the Young Robber." Whereas Irving's many warm and kindly stories of love and marriage portrayed lovely young maidens and their suitors in syrupy, conventional terms of ethereal, pure devotion and bliss, the unfortunate heroine and the young man who loves her in this short tale appear to have been pulled from the pages of the most melodramatic examples of gothic horror.

The titular character narrates the story in the first person with a peculiar detachment that belies the violence and tragedy that it depicts. The chapter of *Tales of a Traveller* titled "The Story of the Young Robber" actually contains more than one tale, but this episode is complete as offered here. It is not a detective story in any way, nor even a mystery, but it is a crime story of such unusual brutality that it cannot be surprising to know that it, like so many of Irving's stories, influenced many American writers of the nineteenth century.

"The Story of the Young Robber" was first published in *Tales of a Traveller* (London: John Murray, 1824, two volumes); the first American edition was published later in 1824 in Philadelphia by H. C. Carey & I. Lea.

• • •

I WAS BORN AT the little town of Frosinone, which lies at the skirts of the Abruzzi. My father had made a little property in trade, and gave me some education, as he intended me for the church, but I had kept gay company too much to relish the cowl, so I grew up a loiterer about the place. I was a heedless fellow, a little quarrelsome on occasion, but good-humored in the main, so I made my way very well for a time, until I fell in love. There lived in our town a surveyor, or land bailiff, of the prince's who had a young daughter, a beautiful girl of sixteen. She was looked upon as something better than the common run of our townsfolk, and kept almost entirely at home. I saw her occasionally, and became madly in love with her, she looked so fresh and tender, and so different from the sunburnt females to whom I had been accustomed.

As my father kept me in money, I always dressed well, and took all opportunities of showing myself off to advantage in the eyes of the little beauty. I used to see her at church; and as I could play a little upon the guitar, I gave a tune sometimes under her window of an evening; and I tried to have interviews with her in her father's vineyard, not far from the town, where she sometimes walked. She was evidently pleased with me, but she was young and shy, and her father kept a strict eye upon her, and took alarm at my attentions, for he had a bad opinion of me, and looked for a better match for his daughter. I became furious at the difficulties thrown in my way, having been accustomed always to easy success among the women, being considered one of the smartest young fellows of the place.

Her father brought home a suitor for her, a rich farmer from a neighboring town. The wedding day was appointed, and preparations were making. I got sight of her at her window, and I thought she looked sadly at me. I determined the match should not take place, cost what it might. I met her intended bridegroom in the market-place, and could not restrain the expression of my rage. A few hot words passed between us, when I drew my stiletto and stabbed him to the heart. I fled to a neighboring church for refuge, and with a little money I obtained absolution, but I did not dare to venture from my asylum.

At that time our captain was forming his troop. He had known me from boyhood, and hearing of my situation, came to me in secret, and made such offers that I agreed to enlist myself among his followers. Indeed, I had more than once thought of taking to this mode of life, having known several brave fellows of the mountains, who used to spend their money freely among us youngsters of the town. I accordingly left my asylum late one night, repaired to the appointed place of meeting, took the oaths prescribed, and became one of the troop. We were for some time in a distant part of the mountains, and our wild adventurous kind of life hit my fancy wonderfully, and diverted my thoughts. At length they returned with all their violence to the recollection of Rosetta. The solitude in which I often found myself gave me time to brood over her image, and as I have kept watch at night over our sleeping camp in the mountains, my feelings have been roused almost to a fever.

At length we shifted our ground, and determined to make a descent upon the road between Terracina and Naples. In the course of our expedition, we passed a day or two in the woody mountains which rise above Frosinone. I cannot tell you how I felt when I looked down upon the place, and distinguished the residence of Rosetta. I determined to have an interview with her; but to what purpose? I could not expect that she would quit her home, and accompany me in my hazardous life among the mountains. She had been brought up too tenderly for that; and when I looked upon the women who were associated with some of our troop, I could not have borne the thoughts of her being their companion. All return to my former life was likewise hopeless; for a price was set upon my head. Still I determined to see her; the very hazard and fruitlessness of the thing made me furious to accomplish it.

About three weeks since, I persuaded our captain to draw down to the vicinity of Frosinone, in hopes of entrapping some of its principal inhabitants, and compelling them to a ransom. We were lying in ambush towards evening, not far from the vineyard of Rosetta's father. I stole quietly from my companions, and drew near to reconnoiter the place of her frequent walks. How my heart beat when among the vines I beheld the gleaming of a white dress! I knew it must be Rosetta's, it being rare for any female of the place to dress in white. I advanced secretly and without noise, until, putting aside the vines, I stood suddenly before her. She uttered a piercing shriek, but I seized her in my arms, put my hand upon her mouth, and conjured her to be silent. I poured out all the frenzy of my passion; offered to renounce my mode of life, to put my fate in her hands, to fly with her where we might live in safety together. All that I could say or do would not pacify her. Instead of love, horror and affright seemed to have taken possession of her breast. She struggled partly from my grasp, and filled the air with her cries.

In an instant the captain and the rest of my companions were around us. I would have given anything at that moment had she been safe out of our hands, and in her father's house. It was too late. The captain pronounced her a prize, and ordered that she should be borne to the mountains. I represented to him that she was my prize, that I had a previous claim to her; and I mentioned my former attachment. He sneered bitterly in reply; observed that brigands had no business with village intrigues, and that, according to the laws of the troop, all spoils of the kind were determined by lot. Love and jealousy were raging in my heart, but I had to choose between obedience and death. I surrendered her to the captain, and we made for the mountains.

She was overcome by affright, and her steps were so feeble and faltering that it was necessary to support her. I could not endure the idea that my comrades should touch her, and assuming a forced tranquillity, begged that she might be confided to me, as one to whom she was more accustomed. The captain regarded me for a moment with a searching look, but I bore it without flinching, and he consented. I took her in my arms; she was almost senseless. Her head rested on my shoulder; her mouth was near to mine. I felt her breath on my face, and it seemed to fan the flame which devoured me. Oh, God! to have this glowing treasure in my arms, and yet to think it was not mine!

We arrived at the foot of the mountain. I ascended it with difficulty, particularly where the woods were thick; but I would not relinquish my delicious burthen. I reflected with rage, however, that I must soon do so. The thoughts that so delicate a creature must be abandoned to my rude companions maddened me. I felt tempted, the stiletto in my hand, to cut my way through them all, and bear her off in triumph. I scarcely conceived the idea before I saw its rashness; but my brain was fevered with the thought that any but myself should enjoy her charms. I endeavored to outstrip my companions by the quickness of my movements, and to get a little distance ahead, in case any favorable opportunity of escape should present. Vain effort! The voice of the captain suddenly ordered a halt. I trembled, but had to obey. The poor girl partly opened a languid eye, but was without strength or motion. I laid her upon the grass. The captain darted on me a terrible look of suspicion, and ordered me to scour the woods with my companions, in search of some shepherd who might be sent to her father's to demand a ransom.

I saw at once the peril. To resist with violence was certain death; but to leave her alone, in the power of the captain! — I spoke out then with a fervor inspired by my passion and my despair. I reminded the captain that I was the first to seize her; that she was my prize; and that my previous attachment to her ought to make her sacred among my companions. I insisted, therefore, that he should pledge me his word to respect her; otherwise I should refuse obedience to his orders. His only reply was to cock his carbine, and at the signal my comrades did the same. They laughed with cruelty at my impotent rage. What could I do? I felt the madness of resistance. I was menaced on all hands, and my companions obliged me to follow them. She remained alone with the chief — yes, alone — and almost lifeless! —

Here the robber paused in his recital, overpowered by his emotions. Great drops of sweat stood on his forehead; he panted rather than breathed; his brawny bosom rose and fell like the waves of a troubled sea. When he had become a little calm, he continued his recital.

I was not long in finding a shepherd, said he. I ran with the rapidity of a deer, eager, if possible, to get back before what I dreaded might take place. I had left my companions far behind, and I rejoined them before they had reached one-half the distance I had made. I hurried them back to the place where we had left the captain. As we approached, I beheld him seated by the side of Rosetta. His triumphant look, and the desolate condition of the unfortunate girl, left me no doubt of her fate. I know not how I restrained my fury.

It was with extreme difficulty, and by guiding her hand, that she was made to trace a few characters, requesting her father to send three hundred dollars as her ransom. The letter was dispatched by the shepherd. When he was gone, the chief turned sternly to me. "You have set an example," said he, "of mutiny and self-will, which if indulged would be ruinous to the troop. Had I treated you as our laws require, this bullet would have been driven through your brain. But you are an old friend; I have borne patiently with your fury and your folly. I have even protected you from a foolish passion that would have unmanned you. As to this girl, the laws of our association must have their course." So saying, he gave his commands, lots were drawn, and the helpless girl was abandoned to the troop.

Here the robber paused again, panting with fury, and it was some moments before he could resume his story.

Hell, said he, was raging in my heart. I beheld the impossibility of avenging myself, and I felt that, according to the articles in which we stood bound to one another, the captain was in the right. I rushed with frenzy from the place. I threw myself upon the earth, tore up the grass with my hands, and beat my head, and gnashed my teeth in agony and rage. When at length I returned, I beheld the wretched victim, pale, disheveled, her dress torn and disordered. An emotion of pity for a moment subdued my fiercer feelings. I bore her to the foot of a tree, and leaned her gently against it. I took my gourd, which was filled with wine, and applying it to her lips, endeavored to make her swallow a little. To what a condition was she reduced! She, whom I had once seen the pride of Frosinone, who but a short time before I had beheld sporting in her father's vineyard, so fresh and beautiful and happy! Her teeth were clenched; her eyes fixed on the ground; her form without motion, and in a state of absolute insensibility. I hung over her in an agony of recollection of all that she had been, and of anguish at what I now beheld her. I darted round a look of horror at my companions, who seemed like so many fiends exulting in the downfall of an angel, and I felt a horror at myself for being their accomplice.

The captain, always suspicious, saw with his usual penetration what was passing within me, and ordered me to go upon the ridge of woods to keep a look-out over the neighborhood and await the return of the shepherd. I obeyed, of course, stifling the fury that raged within me, though I felt for the moment that he was my most deadly foe.

On my way, however, a ray of reflection came across my mind. I perceived that the captain was but following with strictness the terrible laws to which we had sworn fidelity. That the passion by which I had been blinded might with justice have been fatal to me but for his forbearance; that he had penetrated my soul, and had taken precautions, by sending me out of the way, to prevent my committing any excess in my anger. From that instant I felt that I was capable of pardoning him.

Occupied with these thoughts, I arrived at the foot of the mountain. The country was solitary and secure, and in a short time I beheld the shepherd at a distance crossing the plain. I hastened to meet him. He had obtained nothing. He had found the father plunged in the deepest distress. He had read the letter with violent emotion, and then calming himself with a sudden exertion, he had replied coldly, "My daughter has been dishonored by those wretches; let her be returned without ransom, or let her die!"

I shuddered at this reply. I knew, according to the laws of our troop, her death was inevitable. Our oaths required it. I felt, nevertheless, that, not having been able to have her to myself, I could become her executioner!

The robber again paused with agitation. I sat musing upon his last frightful words, which proved to what excess the passions may be carried when escaped from all moral restraint. There was a horrible verity in this story that reminded me of some of the tragic fictions of Dante.

We now came to a fatal moment, resumed the bandit. After the report of the shepherd, I returned with him, and the chieftain received from his lips the refusal of the father. At a signal, which we all understood, we followed him some distance from the victim. He there pronounced her sentence of death. Every one stood ready to execute his order, but I interfered. I observed that there was something due to pity as well as to justice. That I was as ready as anyone to approve the implacable law which was to serve as a warning to all those who hesitated to pay the ransoms demanded for our prisoners, but that, though the sacrifice was proper, it ought to be made without cruelty. The night is approaching, continued I; she will soon be wrapped in sleep; let her then be dispatched. All that I now claim on the score of former fondness for her is, let me strike the blow. I will do it as surely, but more tenderly, than another.

Several raised their voices against my proposition, but the captain imposed silence on them. He told me I might conduct her into a thicket at some distance, and he relied upon my promise.

I hastened to seize my prey. There was a forlorn kind of triumph at having at length become her exclusive possessor. I bore her off into the thickness of the forest. She remained in the same state of insensibility and stupor. I was thankful that she did not recollect me, for had she once murmured my name, I should have been overcome. She slept at length in the arms of him who was to poniard her. Many were the conflicts I underwent before I could bring myself to strike the blow. But my heart had become sore by the recent conflicts it had undergone, and I dreaded lest, by procrastination, some other should become her executioner. When her repose had continued for some time, I separated myself gently from her, that I might not disturb her sleep, and seizing suddenly my poniard, plunged it into her bosom. A painful and concentrated murmur, but without any convulsive movement, accompanied her last sigh. So perished this unfortunate!

1827

WILLIAM LEGGETT

THE RIFLE

It has been well established that the true inventor of the detective short story is Edgar Allan Poe, who defined most of the major tropes of the genre with his very first effort in the literary form, "The Murders in the Rue Morgue" (1841).

Nonetheless, it would be unfair to deny WILLIAM LEGGETT (1801–1839) the recognition he deserves for having produced a story fourteen years earlier that anticipates so many of the elements that the far more gifted Poe honed to such excellence in his story.

Leggett, like the hero in "The Rifle," was an Easterner who moved to the wilds of Illinois early in the nineteenth century before moving to New York permanently in 1822. A critic and journalist, he founded several journals (all of which failed very quickly) but enjoyed some success when he was hired by William Cullen Bryant to write for the *New York Evening Post,* adding political columns to his literary and drama reviews. A staunch Jeffersonian Democrat, he was a powerful advocate of laissez-faire and the rights of individuals to be left alone by the government, a sentiment that moved him to the front of the antislavery movement. He died very young from complications of the yellow fever he had contracted while in the navy.

The suspense in "The Rifle" derives from wondering if the innocent man accused and convicted of murder will be set free and the true culprit apprehended. There is a certain amount of true detective work, and the story may boast literature's first use of ballistics in the solution to a mystery.

"The Rifle" was first published anonymously in *The Atlantic Souvenir, Christmas and New Year's Offering* for 1827. It was first collected in *Tales and Sketches by a Country School Master* (New York: Harper, 1829). The story as published here has been cut by the great American cultural critic Jacques Barzun for his anthology *The Delights of Detection* (1961). Having compared it with the original text, I believe the reader should be grateful for Professor Barzun's efforts.

• • •

THE TRAVELER WHO passes, during the summer or autumn months of the year, through the States of our union that lie west of the Ohio river, Indiana and Illinois in particular, will often pause in his journey, with feelings of irrepressible admiration, to gaze upon the ten thousand beauties which nature has spread through these regions with an uncommonly liberal hand. The majestic mountain, upholding the heavens on its cloudy top, does not, to be sure, arrest his astonished eye; and the roaring cataract, dashing from a dizzy height, and thundering down into whirling depths below, then rising again in upward showers, forms no part of the character of their quiet scenes. But the wide-spread prairie, level as some waveless lake, from whose fertile soil the grass springs up with a luxuriance unparalleled in any other part of our country, and whose beautiful green is besprinkled with myriads and myriads of flowers, ravishing the sight with their loveliness, and filling the air with their sweets; and, again, on either side of these immense savannas, standing arrayed, "like host to host opposed," the leafy forests, whose silence has not often been broken by the voice of man, and through whose verdant recesses the deer stalk in herds, with the boldness of primeval nature, —these are some of the scenes that call forth a passing tribute of praise from every beholder. Such is their summer aspect; but when winter "has taken angrily his waste inheritance," not even the painter's pencil can convey a just conception of the bleakness and desolation of the change. Then those extensive plains, lately covered with the infinitely diversified charms of nature, become one white unvaried waste; through the vistas of the naked trees, nothing meets the glance but snow; and if from the chilly monotony of earth, the wearied eye looks up to heaven, thick and heavy clouds, driven along upon the wind, seem overcharged to bursting, with the same frigid element. It was during the latter season that the incidents of our story took place.

About the middle of December, some ten or twelve years ago, before Illinois was admitted a sister State into the union, on the afternoon of a day that had been uncommonly severe, and during the morning of which there had occurred a light fall of snow, two persons were seen riding along one of the immense prairies, in a northern direction. The elder seemed advanced in years, and was dressed in the usual habiliments of the country. He wore a cap made of the skin of the otter, and a hunting-shirt of blue linsey-wolsey covered his body, descending nearly to the knees, and trimmed with red woolen fringe. It was fastened round the waist by a girdle of buckskin, to which was also appended a bullet pouch, made of the same material with the cap. His feet were covered with buckskin moccasins, and leggings of stout cloth were wrapped several times round his legs, fastened above the knee and at the ankle with strings of green worsted. The horse he bestrode was so small, that his rider's feet almost draggled on the ground, and he had that artificial gait, which is denominated rocking. The old man's hair fell in long and uncombed locks beneath his cap, and was white with the frosts of many winters; while the sallowness of his complexion gave proof of a long residence in those uncultivated parts of the country where the excessive vegetable decay, and the stagnation of large bodies of water, produce perennial agues. His companion was a young man, dressed according to the prevailing fashion of the cities of the eastern States, and his rosy cheeks, and bright blue eyes, evinced that he had not suffered from the effects of climate. He was mounted on a spirited horse, and carried in his hand, the butt resting on his toe, a heavy looking rifle.

"Well, Doctor Rivington," said the elder person, "I should no more ha' looked to see one of you Yankees taking about wi' you a rail Kentuck rifle, than I should ha' thought I'd be riding myself without one. If I didn't see it in your hands, I could almost swear that it's Jim Buckhorn's."

"You have guessed correctly, Mr. Silversight," replied the young physician; "I believe you know almost every rifle in this part of the territory."

"Why, I have handled a power of 'em in my time, Doctor," said the old man, "and there a'n't many good ones atwixt Sangano and the Mississip', that I don't know the vally on. I reckon, now, that same rifle seems to you but a clumsy sort of shooting-iron, but it's brought down a smart chance of deer, first and last. That lock's a rail screamer, and there a'n't a truer bore, except mine, that I left down in the settlement, to get a new sight to — no, not atwixt this and Major Marsham's. It carries just ninety-eight, and mine a little over ninety-four to the pound. Jim has used my bullets often, when we've been out hunting together."

"I was unacquainted with the worth of the gun," resumed Charles Rivington; "but stepping into the gunsmith's this morning, I heard him lament that he had missed a chance of sending it out to Jimmy Buckhorn's; so, intending to come this way, I offered to take charge of it myself. In this wilderness country, we must stand ready to do such little offices of friendship, Mr. Silversight."

"'Twas no doubt kindly meant, Doctor, and Jim will be monstrous glad to git his piece agin," said the hunter. "But my wonderment is, and I don't mean no harm by it, how that tinker would trust such a screamer as that 'ere with a Yankee doctor. Do give it to me; I can't 'bide seeing a good rifle in a man's hand that don't know the vally on it."

Doctor Rivington resigned the weapon with a good-humored smile; for he had been some time in the country, and partly understood the love which a hunter always feels for a piece, of the character of that he had been carrying; he knew, too, though the old man's manners were rough, there was nothing like roughness in his heart. Indeed, the very person who was loath to trust his young companion with a gun, intrinsically worth but a trifle, would nevertheless, as we shall presently see, have unhesitatingly placed in his charge, without witness or receipt, an uncounted or unlimited amount of money. The term Yankee, which we have heard him applying, in rather a contemptuous manner, was then, and for years after, used indiscriminately in reference to all such as emigrated from the States east of the Alleghany mountains. Handing his rifle across his horse to the old hunter, Charles Rivington observed, "I am glad you have offered to take it, Mr. Silversight, for there appears to be a storm coming up, and as I wish to reach Mr. Wentworth's to-night, I can make the distance shorter, by crossing through the timber into the other prairie, before I get to Buckhorn's."

"Will you be going to town, to-morrow, Doctor?" asked Silversight.

"I shall."

"Well, then, you can do me a good turn. Here," said the old man, handing a little leathern bag, "is fifteen dollars in specie; and the rest, four hundred and eighty-five in Shawnee-town paper, is wrapped in this bit of rug. Want you to pay it into the land-office, to clear out old Richly's land: I was going to take it in; but you'll do just as well, and save me a long ride."

The physician promised to attend to the business, and they kept on together, conversing about such subjects as the nature of the scene suggested, until they reached the place where the path, dividing, pursued opposite directions.

"This is my nearest way, I believe?" said Charles.

"It is," answered the old man. "This first track, that we noticed a while ago, lies on my route; so I'll push my nag a little, soon as I load this rifle, and it may so be, that I'll overtake company. Doctor, look here, and you'll know how an old hunter loads his piece — it may stand you in stead some day; I put on a double patch, because my bullets are a leetle smaller than Jim's, you mind I told you. There," said he, as he shoved the ball into its place, and carefully poured some priming into the pan, "it's done in quick time by them what have slept, year in and year out, with red Indians on every side of 'em. Good night to ye, Doctor; you needn't lift the certificates — the register may as well keep 'em till old Richly goes in himself."

So saying, the two travelers parted, each urging his horse to greater speed, as the night threatened to set in dark and stormy. The old hunter, acknowledging to himself in mental soliloquy, that the doctor was "a right nice and cute young fellow, considering he was raised among Yankees," rode briskly along the path. He had proceeded about four or five miles further on his way, when he perceived that the track he before observed turned aside: "So, so," said he, "Slaymush has been out among the deer, to-day; I was in hopes 'twas some one going up to the head-waters"; and he kept rocking along the road, when, directly, the report of a musket was heard reverberating through the night, and the old man, writhing and mortally wounded, fell from his horse, which, scared by the occurrence, ran wildly over the prairie. A form was seen a few minutes after, cautiously approaching the place, fearful lest his victim should not yet be dead; but apparently satisfied in this particular, by his motionless silence, he advanced, and proceeded immediately to examine the pockets of the deceased.

"Damnation!" muttered he at length, when a fruitless search was finished, "the old curmudgeon hasn't got the money after all; and I've put a bullet through his head for nothing. I'm sure, I heard him say, in Brown's tavern, down in the settlement, that old Richly give it to him to carry; well, it's his own fault, for telling a bragging lie about it; and the gray-headed scoundrel won't never jeer me again, for using a smooth-bore, before a whole company of Kentuck-squatters—it carried true enough to do his business. I'm sorry I dropped that flask, any how; but this powder-horn will make some amends," grumbled the wretch, as he tore the article he spoke of from the breast, where it had hung for forty years. "What the devil have we here!" said he again, as he struck his foot against the rifle that the murdered man had dropped; "ho, ho," discharging it into the air, "if the worst comes to worst, they'll think his piece went off by accident, and shot him. But there's no danger—it will snow by day light, and cover the trail; and the prairie-wolves will finish the job."

Thus muttering, the ruffian remounted the animal he held by the bridle, and trotted across the prairie, nearly at right angles with the path, along which the unfortunate hunter had been traveling.

It was in a log-house, larger, and of rather more comfortable construction, than was usually seen in that wilderness country, beside a fire that sent a broad and crackling flame half way up the spacious chimney, that there was seated, on the evening of this atrocious murder, in addition to its ordinary inmates, the young physician from whom we have lately parted. His great-coat, hat, and overalls were laid aside, and he was conversing with that agreeable fluency, and pleased expression of countenance, which denoted that he was happy in the society around him. Opposite, and busily employed in knitting, sat a beautiful girl of eighteen. From her work, which seemed to engross an unusual portion of her attention, she every now and then would send a furtive glance to their guest, thus telling, in the silent language of love, the tale she never could have found words to utter. We say she was beautiful; and if a complexion so clear, that

> The eloquent blood spoke through her cheek, and so distinctly wrought,
> That we might say of her, her body thought;

if laughing blue eyes, lighted up by intelligence and affection; if smooth and glossy auburn ringlets; teeth white as the snow around her father's dwelling, and a person which, though not tall, was well formed and graceful;—if all these traits combined, constitute a claim to the epithet, it certainly belonged to her. She was modestly attired in a dress of no costly material; and the little feet that peeped from underneath it, were clothed in white stockings of her own fabrication, and in shoes of too coarse a texture ever to have been purchased from the shelves of a fashionable city mechanic. Yet that same form had been arrayed in richer apparel, and had been followed by glances of warmer admiration, than perhaps ever fell to the share of those, who are ready to condemn her on account of her simple garb.

Catharine Wentworth was the daughter (at the time of our story, the only one), of a gentleman who had formerly been a wealthy merchant in the city of New York; but to whom misfortune in business had suddenly befallen, and had stripped him of all his fortune. While surrounded by affluence, he had been considered remarkably meek and affable; but became proud and miserable in adversity: and not caring to remain among scenes that continually brought to mind the sad change in his condition, he emigrated, with his whole family, to the wilds of Illinois. He was actuated in part, no doubt, by a higher and better motive. At that time he was the father of another daughter. Louisa, older than Catharine, was fast falling a victim to that disease, which comes over the human form, like autumn over the earth, imparting to it additional graces, but too truly whispering that the winter of death is nigh. The medical attendant of the family, perhaps to favor the design which he knew Mr. Wentworth entertained, intimated that a change of climate was their only hope. The change was tried and failed, and the fair Louisa reposed beneath the turf of the prairie.

How strangely does the human mind accommodate itself to almost any situation! The man who had spent his life hitherto in a sumptuous mansion, surrounded by all those elegances and means of enjoyment, which, in a large city, are always to be procured by fortune, now experienced, in a log cabin, divided into but four apartments, and those of the roughest kind, a degree of happiness that he had never known before. And well he might be happy; for he was rich, not in money, but in a better, a more enduring kind of wealth. His wife, two hardy and active sons, and his remaining daughter, Catharine, were all around him, smiling in contentment, and ruddy with health. We can only estimate our condition in this life by comparison with others; and his plantation was as large, and as well cultivated, his crops as abundant, his stock as good as any of the settlers on that prairie. He had still a better source of consolation: Louisa's death, the quiet of the country, and the natural wish of every active mind to create to itself modes of employment, had led him more frequently to read and search the sacred scriptures, than he had found leisure to do before; and this was attended, as it always is, with the happiest result, a knowledge and love of Him, "whom to know is life eternal." But we are digressing.

The family of Mr. Wentworth, with the addition of Charles Rivington (whom, indeed, we might almost speak of as one of its members, for, on the coming New Year's Day, he was to receive the hand of their "saucy Kate," as the happy parents fondly called her), were gathered round the fireside, conversing cheerfully on every topic that presented itself, when a light tap was heard at the door, and Mr. Rumley, the deputy-sheriff of the county, entered the apartment. He apologized for his intrusion, by saying, that having had business to attend to at a cabin farther up the prairie, which detained him longer than he expected, he should not be able, on account of the darkness of the night, to return to town until the following morning; he therefore hoped that he might be accommodated with a bed. His request was, of course, readily complied with.

He was a tall, dark person, dressed much in the manner of the unfortunate hunter, except that his leggings were of buckskin. He had lost an eye when a young man, in a scuffle with an Indian, two of whom sprung upon him from an ambush; this, with a deep scar upon his forehead, received in a tavern-brawl at New Orleans, two or three years before, and the wrinkles that age, or more likely, his manner of life, had plowed, gave to his countenance a sinister and disagreeable expression. At this time, the haggard appearance of his face was increased, either from having been a long while exposed to the cold, or from some latent sickness working on him, for his lip quivered, and was of a bloodless hue, and he was remarkably pale. Charles Rivington, who often met him in his rides, was the first to notice the change from his usual appearance.

"You look pale and fatigued, Mr. Rumley; I hope you are not unwell?"

"No, sir — that is — yes, I do feel a little sickish; and should be glad to go to bed, if it's convenient," answered Mr. Rumley.

"Perhaps there is something we can do for you, sir?" said the maternal Mrs. Wentworth.

"No, ma'am, I thank ye. I reckon a good night's sleep will be best for me; it's what cures all my ailings."

And in compliance with his wish the guest was shown to his apartment.

One by one the different members of this peaceful family sought their pillows, till soon Charles Rivington and the blushing Catharine were left sole occupants of the room.

But though alone, they were not lonely; he had many an interesting tale to whisper into the maiden's ear (for it was almost a week since they met), and she, though something of a chatterbox, when none but her mother and brothers were present, on this occasion betrayed a wonderful aptitude for listening. The hours glided happily away, and the gray morning was already advancing, when the happy young man, imprinting a good-night kiss upon her cheek, left her to those sweet dreams which slumber bestows only on the young and innocent.

It was late in the afternoon of the following day, that Charles Rivington, being returned to the town where he resided, was seated in his office, employed in counting a roll of notes, a pile of dollars lying, at the same time, on the table before him, when three men abruptly entered the apartment.

"You are our prisoner," cried the foremost of the party. "By heavens, Jim! Look there; there's the very money itself. I can swear to that pouch."

And here he rudely seized our hero by the collar.

"Stand back, sir, and lay hold of me at your peril," returned Charles Rivington, sternly, as, shaking the man from him, he gave him a blow that sent him to the other side of the office; "What is it that you have to say? If I am to be made prisoner, produce your warrant."

"You may as well submit quietly, Doctor Rivington," said another of the party, who was a constable. "You perhaps can explain every thing; but you must come with us before Squire Lawton. This is my authority (showing a paper), and it is only necessary to say that suspicion rests on you, as the murderer of old Silversight, who was found shot through the head, on the road this morning."

"Is it possible?—poor old man! has he really been killed! When I parted from him last night he was not only well, but seemed in excellent spirits," said the doctor.

"He parted from him last night! mark that, Buckhorn," said the one who had just received so severe a repulse from our hero, and whose name was Carlock. "He left him in excellent spirits! mark what the villain says!"

"There needs no jeering about it," replied Buckhorn. "Doctor Rivington, you tended me in my bad fever last spring, and again when I had the chills in the fall, and you stuck by me truer than any friend I've had since my old mother died, except this ere rifle; and I am monstrous sorry I found it where I did. It may so be that you've got a clear conscience yet; but whether or no, though old Silversight and me has hunted together many and many's the day, you shall have fair play any how, damn me if you sha'n't. That 'ere money looks bad; if it had been a fair fight, we mought a hushed it up somehow or 'nother."

Our hero, while Buckhorn was speaking, had time to reflect that if Silversight were indeed dead, circumstances would really authorize his arrest. The rifle, which he was known to have carried with him from town, had been found, it seems, beside the murdered body. The money that the unfortunate man had entrusted to him, was discovered in his possession; and how could it be proved for what purpose it had been given to him? As these thoughts rushed rapidly through his mind, he turned to the officer, and observed,

"Mr. Pyke, I yield myself your prisoner. I perceive there are some circumstances that cause suspicion to rest on me. I must rely, for a while upon the character which, I trust, I have acquired since my residence among you, for honor and fair dealing, until I shall be enabled to prove my innocence, or till heaven places in the hands of justice the real perpetrator of the deed."

So saying, he gathered up the money from the table, and departed with the officer and his companions, to the house of Mr. Lawton, who, being a justice of the peace, had issued a warrant for his apprehension.

"I have always been glad to see you heretofore, Doctor Rivington," said the magistrate, politely, on the appearance of that person before him, "and should be so now, were it not that you are charged with a crime, which, if proved, will call down the severest vengeance of the law. I hope and believe, however, that you can establish your innocence. Where were you, sir, on the afternoon of yesterday?"

"I went out to visit some patients, meaning to continue my ride as far as Mr. Buckhorn's; and took his rifle with me, from the gunsmith's, with the intention of stopping and leaving it; but I met with old Mr. Silversight at the cross-roads, who was going up from the New Settlements, and he offered to take charge of it. I gave it to him. We parted at the Fork, and I crossed over to Mr. Wentworth's."

"Did Mr. Silversight continue on his journey, having Jim Buckhorn's rifle with him?" asked the justice.

"Yes, sir; but before we separated he gave me this money," (handing the notes and specie to the magistrate), "requesting me to pay it into the land-office to-day, to clear out Mr. Richly's land. He said there were five hundred dollars in all, and I was counting it when arrested."

"There is a most unfortunate coincidence of circumstance against you, Doctor. The man is found murdered, the rifle which you were known to have carried laying near him, and you arrived in town on the next day, with the money of the deceased in your possession. The poor old man's horse going home without his rider, excited alarm; Buckhorn and Carlock, with other neighbors, set out upon the track; they found the murdered victim, stark and bloody, lying on the snow, which was scarcely whiter than his aged head; they divided—some bearing the body back, while the others followed on the trail; it led them to Mr. Wentworth's, where you acknowledge you passed the night; they there inquired what person made the track which they had followed, and were answered it was you; they continued on your trail until they arrived in town; they make affidavit of these facts, and procure a warrant for your arrest; when, to complete the chain of evidence, you are found counting the spoils of the murdered man. Now, sir, what answer can you make to these appalling circumstances?"

"They are appalling, indeed, sir," said our hero; "and I can only reply to them—I am innocent. If the poor man was murdered, the one who did it must certainly have left tracks; and I fear they have fallen upon his trail and taken it for mine. But it is in my power to prove that I had no weapons with me, except that unlucky rifle, and the gunsmith will testify that he gave me no balls with it."

"The gunsmith has already been before me," said Mr. Lawton, "for I was loath to have you apprehended, except on an application backed by such proof as could not be rejected. He states that when he gave you the gun, the lock had been repaired and polished, and that since that time it has certainly been discharged. I am sorry to do it, but my duty compels me to commit you."

He came into court, arm in arm with the attorney, who was employed to plead his cause; and slightly bowing to those whose friendly salute indicated that they believed him innocent, he passed through the crowd, and took a seat behind the lawyers within the bar. From the high and exemplary character which he had sustained invariably, from his first settling in the place until the present black suspicion rested on him, a degree of intuitive respect was accorded by all, that must have been highly gratifying to his feelings. A plea of not guilty was entered, and the examination of witnesses commenced.

George Carlock was the nephew of the deceased. On the night of the sixteenth of December, he was surprised to see the horse of his uncle arrive, with saddle and bridle on, but without a rider. He thought that the deceased had stopped, perhaps, for a while at Buckhorn's, who lived a mile or so further down the timber; but, as the night passed away without his returning home, he started early in the morning with the intention of tracking the horse. He called for Buckhorn, and they got upon the trail, and followed it till they found the dead body. It led them to Mr. Wentworth's. They inquired if any person had been there, that crossed over from the other side of the stream. They were answered that Doctor Rivington had crossed the stream, and remained the night with them. That Mr. Rumley, the deputy-sheriff, had also remained the night, but that he had come from farther up on the same side. They followed on the trail till they arrived in town. Being informed, by Mr. Drill, the gunsmith, that Doctor Rivington had taken Buckhorn's rifle out with him, they immediately procured a warrant for his apprehension. They found him employed in counting the identical money, which had been taken from the unfortunate Silversight.

James Buckhorn's testimony was in full corroboration of the preceding. He mentioned, in addition, that he examined the lock and barrel of his rifle, on finding it lying near the murdered man, and discovered that it certainly had been discharged but a short time before.

The gunsmith deposed to his having given the rifle to the prisoner, on his offering to carry it out to Buckhorn, and that it had been discharged since.

"Mr. Drill," said Lawyer Blandly, who was counsel for our hero, "you mention having given the gun to Doctor Rivington; did you also give him a bullet that would fit the bore?"

"I did not."

"Did he exhibit any anxiety to obtain the weapon?" again asked the lawyer.

"By no means," replied the gunsmith; "I considered, at the time, that the doctor's offer was one of mere kindness; and he had previously mentioned he was going out that way to visit his patients."

"The bore of this rifle, Mr. Drill," continued the sagacious lawyer, "is very small. I presume that you are familiar with the size and qualities of all that are owned on the road out to Mr. Buckhorn's. Is there any house at which Doctor Rivington could have stopped, and procured a ball of sufficient smallness?"

"John Guntry's rifle," answered Mr. Drill, "carries eighty-seven or eight to the pound, and one of his bullets, with a thick patch, would suit Buckhorn's pretty well. That is the only one any where near the size."

The attorney for the people here asked another question.

"For what purpose did the prisoner go into your shop, on the morning of the sixteenth of December?"

"I was employed in repairing a pair of pocket pistols for him, and fitting a bullet mold to them. He came in, I believe, to inquire if they were finished."

"Please to note that answer, gentlemen of the jury," said the prosecuting attorney. "Mr. Drill, you may stand aside."

Samuel Cochrane was next called. He was one of the young men, who had returned with the body of Silversight. On his way back, and about two hundred yards from the place where the murder had been committed, he found a copper powder flask, (which was shown to him, and he identified it), the letters C. R. M. D. being cut upon one of its sides, apparently with a knife. There was but one more witness on the part of the people, Mr. Lawton, the magistrate before whom the unfortunate prisoner had been examined. He testified as to the facts which were deposed before him, together with the acknowledgment of Doctor Rivington, that he had been in company with Mr. Silversight, etc. But we may pass over these circumstances, as the reader is already acquainted with them. The prisoner was now put on his defense, and all that talent or ingenuity could devise, was done by his skillful counsel. The witnesses were cross-examined, and re-cross-examined; but their answers were uniformly the same. A large number of respectable persons came forward to testify to the excellence of our hero's general character; but their evidence was rendered unnecessary by the attorney for the people admitting, in unequivocal terms, that previous to this horrid occurrence, it had been exemplary in a high degree. At length, wearied by his exertions and distressed at the result, Mr. Blandly discontinued his examination: he had one more weapon to try in behalf of his client—the powerful one of eloquence; and it was used by a master of the art; but, alas! was used in vain. He dwelt much on the fact that his unfortunate client had wished his route to be trailed from the village, and that Buckhorn had started for the purpose, when the disastrous snowstorm occurred, and took away the only hope he had of proving his innocence. He cited many cases to the jury, in which circumstances, even stronger than these, had been falsified, when their victim, murdered by the laws, was slumbering in his grave. He appealed to them as parents, to know if they would believe, that a son, who had been so filial, whose character had previously been without stain or blemish, could suddenly turn aside from the path of rectitude and honor, to commit such an atrocious crime? But it were useless to recapitulate the arguments that were made use of on this interesting occasion—they were ineffectual. The attorney for the prosecution summed up very briefly. He assured the jury that the evidence was so clear in its nature, so concatenated, so incontrovertible, as to amount to moral certainty. Near the body of the murdered man, a powder flask, such as the eastern people principally use, had been found, with the initials of the prisoner's name and medical degree, engraved upon it—C. R. M.D.—Charles Rivington, Doctor of Medicine. The trail is pursued, and it leads them to the house of Mr. Wentworth, where the prisoner arrived on the evening of the bloody deed, and remained all night. They continue on the trail, till at last they find him, with greedy eyes, bending over the plunder he had torn from his gray-haired victim. "Such," concluded he, "is a rapid outline of the facts; and deeply as I deplore the wretched young man's guilt, yet, believing him guilty, it is my sacred duty to display his enormity; but further than the imperious call of justice requires, I will not go, I cannot go."

The charge of the judge, who was evidently very much affected, occupied but a few minutes; and the jury retired to make up their verdict. We have already told the reader that the prisoner was pale, in consequence of sickness, produced by his exposed situation in prison; but the appalling events of the trial had caused no alteration in his appearance. He sat firm and collected; and there was a melancholy sweetness in the expression of his countenance, which told that all was calm within.

The assembled crowd was still anxiously awaiting the return of the verdict, when the mother of Charles Rivington, leaning on the arm of Catharine Wentworth, entered the courthouse of Edgarton. A passage was instantly opened for them, with that intuitive respect which almost all men are ready to yield to misfortune, even when accompanied by guilt. They had not been long seated in the part of the room, where they could be most screened from observation, when the jury returned, and, handing a sealed verdict to the clerk, resumed their places. The clerk arose, and read in a faltering voice, "We find the prisoner, Charles Rivington, guilty." The words had scarcely left his lips, when a piercing shriek ran through the apartment, and Catharine Wentworth fell lifeless on the floor. Not so with that Christian mother; with an unwonted strength she darted through the assembly, till she reached her child.

"My boy!" she cried, "my boy! be of good cheer; your heavenly Father knows your inmost soul, and sees that you are guiltless. We shall lie down together, for think not I can survive you. We shall lie down together, to wake with the Lord! My boy! my boy! little did I think to see this bitter day!"

Exhausted nature could endure no more, and the mother fainted in the arms of her son.

We shall not attempt to describe the situation of our unhappy hero, for words are inadequate to the task. The insensible forms of his mother and his beloved Catharine, were conveyed from the scene; and when some degree of silence was restored among the sympathizing multitude, the judge proceeded to pronounce sentence upon him. He had nothing to say to avert it, except a reiterated declaration of his innocence; and he besought the court that the time previous to his execution might be as brief as possible, in mercy to his bereaved parent, who would be but dying a continual death while he survived. It was accordingly fixed to take place on that day three weeks.

It was near midnight of that important day — the busy throng which the trial had collected together were dispersed, and the moon, high in heaven, was wading on her silent course, through the clouds of a wintry sky, when Charles Rivington, startled from unquiet slumber, by a noise at the door of his prison, and sitting up in bed, that he might more intently listen, heard his own name whispered from the outer side.

"Will you wake, Mr. Charles?" was softly uttered in the sweet accents of our little Irish acquaintance, Judy. "Was there iver the like," continued she, "and he asleeping at that rate, when his friends are opening the door for him?"

"Be quiet, Judy," responded a masculine voice, but modulated to its softest tone, "and stand more in the shadow, the doctor'll awake fast enough, as soon as I get this bolt sawed out; but if ye git that tavern-keeper's dog a-barking, there's no telling but it may wake the jailer instead of the doctor."

"And you're right, Jimmy dear," responded Judy; "there now, leave go with your fingers, man, you can't pull it off that ere way. Here, take this bit of a stake for a pry—and now, that's your sort," continued she, adding her strength to his, and a large end of the log, to which the fastenings of the door were appended, fell to the ground: "Now, one more pull, Jimmy, and the day's our own."

They accordingly made another exertion of united strength, when the prison door flying open, Buckhorn and Judy stood before the prisoner.

"There, Mister Charles, say nothing at all, at all about it; but jist take Jimmy's nag, that's down in the hollow, and git clare as well as ye can. There's a steam-boat, Jimmy says, at St. Louis going right down the river; and here's all the money we could git, but it's enough to pay your passage any how," said the affectionate girl, tears standing in her eyes as she reached to her respected, and, as she firmly believed, guiltless master, all her own hoardings, together with the sum which Buckhorn had been accumulating, ever since he became a suitor for her hand.

"You are a kind and excellent girl," answered Rivington, sensibly affected by the heroism and attachment of his domestic, "and you are a noble fellow, Buckhorn; but you forget that by flying I should only confirm those in the belief of my guilt who are wavering now; besides, I could hardly expect to escape; for my life being forfeit to the laws, a proclamation would be immediately issued, and apprehension and death then, as now, would be my doom. No, no, my good friends, you mean me well, but I cannot consent to live, unless I can live with an unsullied fame."

"Ah, dear doctor," sobbed out poor Judy, whose heart seemed almost broken; "what's the use of spaking about it? If you stay, you've but a few days to live; and if you take your chance now, who knows but the rail murderer may be found out, and then you might come back, Mr. Charles, and all would go well again."

"That is a powerful argument, Judy; but my trust is in him who beholds all my actions," returned our hero; "and I must confess that I cannot divest myself of the hope that the truth will yet be brought to light before I die the death of a felon."

"Doctor Rivington," said Buckhorn, going up to him, and taking him warmly by the hand, "I've been wavering all along about you; but I'm sartin now. The man that murdered Silversight in cold blood, wouldn't be agoing to stand shilly-shally, and the jail door wide open. I always was dub'ous about it, though the proof seemed so sure. My nag is down in the hollow, with saddle bags on him, and Judy has filled 'em full of your clothes; you may take him, Doctor, if ye will; you may take the money and welcome — but I that come here to set you clear, advise you to stay; and if I don't find out somethin' to turn the tables before hanging day, it shan't be because I don't try."

Our hero exchanged with the honest hunter one of those warm pressures of the hand, which may be termed the language of the soul, and conveyed to him, by the eloquent action, more than he could readily have found words to express. They were now alarmed by the report of two rifles near them, fired in quick succession, and two persons issuing from the shadow of a neighboring horse shed, at the same moment made directly towards the door of the jail, crying out in a loud voice, "The prisoner has broke out! the prisoner has broke out!" Our friends, Judy and Buckhorn, were enabled to make good their retreat, as the object of the alarm seemed more to secure the prisoner than to arrest his intended deliverers. It was not many minutes before a considerable number of the idle and curious were collected by this clamor around the insufficient place of confinement, and effectual means were devised to prevent any danger of a further attempt at rescue.

The glimmer of hope which had been lighted up in our hero's heart by the last words of Buckhorn, and the confident manner in which they were uttered, gradually declined as day after day rolled by, and no trace could be discovered of the real perpetrator of the crime. To add to the anguish of his situation, he learned that his beloved Catharine was confined by a wasting fever to her bed, and that his mother, though she still bore up and uttered not a murmur against the Almighty's will, was fast sinking with a broken heart into the grave. The evening previous to the fatal day which was to terminate his earthly career at length arrived, but brought no cheering promise with it, and the unhappy young man, therefore, humbling himself before the throne of heaven, and beseeching that mercy there which he could no longer hope for on earth, devoted the greater part of the night to prayer.

It was on the same evening, in a little mean looking cabin, called "Brown's Tavern," in the place which we have before had occasion to speak of as the New Settlements, that two men were sitting at a table, with a bottle of whiskey between them, conversing on the general topic, the execution that was to take place on the morrow, when a third person entered, and, calling for a dram, took a seat at some distance from them. He was a tall, dark man, dressed in a hunting frock and buckskin leggings, and held in his hand one of those mongrel weapons, which partaking of the characters both of rifle and musket, are called smooth bores by the hunters of our western frontier, who, generally speaking, hold them in great contempt. The apartment of the little grocery, or tavern, where these three persons were assembled, was lighted, in addition to the blaze of a large wood fire, by a single long-dipped tallow candle, held in an iron candlestick; and its only furniture consisted of the aforementioned table, with the rude benches on which the guests were seated. The conversation had been interrupted by the entry of the third person, but was now resumed.

"For my part, as I was saying," observed one of the persons, in continuation of some remark he had previously made, "I think the thing's been too hasty altogether. The doctor's character, which every body respected, should have made 'em more cautious how they acted; especially as he wanted 'em to go right out on his trail, and said they'd find he'd kept straight on to Mr. Wentworth's. Now he wouldn't a told 'em that if it wasn't so; and I am half a mind to believe that he's not guilty after all."

"That's damned unlikely," said the stranger, in a gruff voice.

"Why bless me, Mr. Rumley," continued the first speaker, "I didn't know it was you, you set so in the dark. How have you been this long time? Let me see, why, yes, bless me, so it was — it was you and I that was talking with poor old Silversight the day he started from here with the money. I haven't seen you since. Why, a'n't you a going to be over in Edgarton to see the doctor hung tomorrow?"

"I don't know whether I shall go or not," replied Rumley.

"Well, I've a great notion to ride over there, though I'm monstrous sorry for the poor man."

"Sorry — the devil! hang all the cursed Yankees, say I," responded the amiable deputy-sheriff.

"Come, that's too bad — though I like to see you angry on account of the old man's murder, because ye wasn't very good friends with him when he was alive — but bless me, Mr. Rumley, that powder-horn looks mighty like old Silversight's," taking hold of it to examine it, as he said so.

"Stand off!" cried Rumley; "what do you s'pose I'd be doing with the old scoundrel's powder-horn? It's not his — it never was his — he never seen it."

"It's a lie!" cried a person, who had glided in during the foregoing conversation, and had obtained a view of the horn in question, as the deputy-sheriff jerked it away from the other. "It's a lie! — I know it well — I've hunted with the old man often; I know it as well as I do my own. Bill Brown, and you, John Gillam," addressing himself to the one who first recognized the horn, "I accuse Cale Rumley of old Silversight's murder — help me to secure him."

The deputy-sheriff stood motionless for a moment; and turned as pale as death (from surprise, perhaps), then suddenly recovering his powers, he darted across the room, and seizing his gun, before any one was aware of his intention, leveled and fired at his accuser. The apartment became instantly filled with smoke, which, as it slowly rolled away, discovered to the astonished beholders the stiff and bleeding form of Caleb Rumley, stretched at full length upon the floor. As soon as he discharged his piece, the infuriated man had sprung towards the door, designing to make an immediate escape; but the motion was anticipated by our friend Jimmy Buckhorn (for it was he who charged his fallen antagonist with murder, and who luckily was not touched by the ball that was meant to destroy him), and with one blow of his powerful arm he felled the scoundrel to the earth. He now rapidly explained to the wondering trio the nature of the proof he had obtained of Rumley's guilt; and succeeded in satisfying them that he ought to be made prisoner, and immediately conveyed to Edgarton.

The morning which our hero believed was to be the last of his earthly existence, rose with unwonted brightness; and throngs of males and females came pouring into the little village, impelled by the mysterious principle of our nature, which incites us to look on that we nevertheless must shudder to behold. But no sounds of obstreperous merriment, no untimely jokes, were uttered, as they passed along the road, to grate upon the ear of the unfortunate Charles, and break him off from his communion with heaven: on the contrary, many a tear was shed that morning by the bright eyes of rustic maidens, who were "all unused to the melting mood"; and many a manly breast heaved a sigh of sympathy for the culprit, who was that day to make expiation to the offended laws. Indeed, since the sentence of the court was passed, a wonderful change had been wrought among the ever-changing multitude, by various rumors that were whispered from one part of these wide prairies to another, and spread with almost incredible velocity. A thousand acts of unasked benevolence were now remembered, in favor of him, who was soon to suffer. Here was an aged and afflicted woman, whom he had not only visited without hope of reward, but upon whom he had conferred pecuniary, as well as medical comforts. There was an industrious cripple, who had received a receipt in full from the young physician, when creditors to a less amount were levying upon his farm. And many similar acts of bounty were proclaimed abroad, by the grateful hearts on which they had been conferred; all helping to produce the change of sentiment which was manifestly wrought. Still the general impression seemed to be unshaken, (so strong had been the proofs), that, in an evil hour, he had yielded to temptation, and embrued his hands in a fellow-creature's blood.

The hour at last arrived when Charles Rivington was to suffer the sentence of the law. A rude gallows was erected at about a quarter of a mile from the public square; and thither the sad procession moved. He was decently dressed in a black suit, and walked to the fatal place with a firm step. He was very pale; but from no other outward sign might the spectators guess that he shrunk from the horrors of such a death; for his eye had a calm expression, and the muscles of his face were as motionless as an infant's in slumber. They reached the spot: a prayer, a solemn prayer was offered up to heaven for the murderer's soul; in which every hearer joined with unaccustomed fervor. The sheriff's attendant stood in waiting with the fatal cord, while the agonized mother, vainly endeavoring to emulate the firmness of her heroic son, approached with trembling steps, to bid a last farewell—when hark! a shout was heard; all eyes were turned to catch its meaning; another shout, and the words "Stop, stop the execution!" were distinctly audible. In less than an instant after, the death-pale form of Jimmy Buckhorn tumbled from his horse with just sufficient strength remaining to reach towards the sheriff, with an order from the judge to stay the execution.

Reader, our tale is nearly at an end. Jimmy Buckhorn had been faithful to his word: he had sought for some clue to the real murderer, with an earnestness, which nothing but a firm conviction of our hero's innocence, superadded to his love for Judy, could possibly have enkindled. For some time he was unsuccessful. At length the thought struck him, that the track on the side of the stream where Mr. Wentworth resided, might have been caused by a traveler passing along, on the morning after the fatal deed, and the deputy-sheriff, in that case, might be the real culprit. He immediately set out to visit every cabin above Mr. Wentworth's, to see if his story that he had been further up the stream was correct. This took a considerable time; but the result satisfied him that that tale was false. He then procured the assistance of a surgeon, imposing upon him secrecy, until the proper time for disclosure; and proceeded to disinter the body of Silversight. This was more successful than he had even dared to hope: the ball had lodged in a cavity of the head; and being produced, Buckhorn pronounced at once, from its great size, that it could have been discharged only from Rumley's smooth-bore. He set out directly for Edgarton, choosing to go by the way of the New Settlements, for a two-fold reason. He had heard that Rumley was in that neighborhood; and to get possession of him or of his gun, at any rate, he deemed very essential. Besides, that route would take him by the house of the judge, and from him it would be necessary to procure an order to delay the proceedings. We have seen the result. But the chain of evidence was not yet complete.

A wild and dissipated young man, by the name of Michael Davis, who had just returned up the river from New Orleans, entered the office of the clerk of the county, on his way back to the tavern, from the place where the execution was to have taken place, in order to while away an hour, until the time for dinner should arrive. The powder-flask, which had been brought in evidence against our hero, was lying on the table, the graven side downwards. There is a restless kind of persons in the world, who can never be easy, let them be sitting where they will, without fingering and examining whatever is in their reach—and such an one was Michael Davis: he accordingly took up the flask in a careless manner, and turning it over in his hand, his eye fell upon the letters.

"Why, halloo! what the devil are you doing with my powder-flask?" asked he.

"I wish the unlucky article had been yours, or any body's, except the unfortunate Dr. Rivington's," returned the clerk, who was a friend of our hero, and deeply deplored the circumstances that had lately transpired.

"Unfortunate devil's," reiterated Michael; "I tell you it's my flask, or article, as you prefer calling it; or rather it was mine and Cale Rumley's together. We bought it when him and me went down to New Orleans—let's see, that's three years, come spring. I ought to know the cursed thing, for I broke a bran new knife in scratching them letters on it."

The clerk started from his seat—he snatched the flask out of the hand of Davis—he gazed at it a moment intently—then, the truth suddenly flashing on his mind, he rushed out into the road, forgetting his hat, forgetting every thing but the letters on the flask. The magistrate, who grieved as much as any one, at the supposed dereliction of their young friend, the physician, was amazed to see the clerk enter his apartment in such a plight.

"There!" cried he, as he threw down the flask on the table, "C. R. M.D. spells something beside Rivington. Send your servant out of the room."

As soon as he was gone, and the door carefully closed, the clerk continued in a low, confidential tone, "That flask is Caleb Rumley's, and Caleb Rumley is the murderer (no wonder he has kept himself away all this while). It belonged to him, and that imp of Satan, Mich. Davis, together, and Mich. Davis told me so, with his own mouth, not three minutes ago—and Charles Rivington's an honest man—huzza! huzza! huzza!" concluded he, as he danced and skipped about the apartment, with the delirious joy true friendship inspired. The magistrate was a man of middle age, and very large and corpulent, but a mountain of flesh could not have kept him down, when such thrilling news tingled in his ears, and he, too, began to dance a jig, that shook the tenement to its foundation.

It became the duty of the worthy magistrate, to commit, in the course of that very day, our respected friend, Caleb Rumley, Esq., deputy-sheriff of the county of —— to the same capacious tenement which Dr. Rivington had lately inhabited; he, with the consent of the judge, being more safely disposed of in the prison of his own house. A bill was immediately found by the Grand Jury, and the trial of the real murderer came on shortly after. For a long time he obstinately denied any knowledge of the death of Silversight; but as proofs after proofs were disclosed against him, he first became doggedly silent, then greatly intimidated, and at last made a full disclosure of his crime. He was found guilty, and executed on the same gallows that had been erected for our calumniated hero.

The sickness of Catharine Wentworth was long and severe; but our friend Charles was her physician, and the reader will not wonder that it yielded at last to his skill. The Christian parent of our hero had been condemned, at different periods of her life, to drink deeply of the cup of affliction, and she had bowed with a noble humility to the decree of heaven; it was thence she now derived support in this more trying hour of joy. Spring had gone forth, warbling with her thousand voices of delight, over these wide-extended prairies, and the flowers had sprung into a beautiful existence at her call, when the hand of the blushing Catharine, herself a lovelier flower, was bestowed in marriage on the transported Charles Rivington. Never did there stand before the holy man, a happier, a more affectionate pair. Their hearts had been tried — severely tried; they had been weighed in the balance, and not found wanting. The house of Mr. Wentworth was the scene of their union; and, on the same evening, and by the same hand that had bound her dear "Mister Charles" to his blooming bride, our little Irish friend Judy was united to the worthy Buckhorn, who had been prevailed upon, reluctantly, to lay aside his hunting shirt and leather leggings on the joyful occasion. The evening glided rapidly away, urged along by tales of mirth, and song, and jest; and it was observed, that though Charles and Catharine took but little share in the rattling conversation of the hour, they appeared to enjoy the scene with happiness that admitted of no increase. Indeed, often did the tender blue eyes of the beautiful bride become suffused with crystal drops of joy, as she raised them in thankfulness to her heavenly Father, who had conducted them safely through all the perils of the past, and at last brought them together under the shelter of his love.

"The whole trouble come out of your being so kind, Dr. Rivington," said the manly, though, in his new suit, rather awkward-looking Buckhorn; "it was all of your kindness to offer to bring out my plaguy rifle. If it hadn't been for that, suspicion wouldn't a lighted on you at all."

"Now hould your tongue, Jimmy dear," answered his loquacious little wife; "I thought so myself, till Mister Charles explained it to me, and then I found out how 'twas the wisdom of the Almighty put it into his head to carry your gun; for how would you iver got on the true scent, if the big bullet hadn't a tould ye for sartain that it was niver the small-bored rifle that kilt him. No, blessed be his name, that made then, as he always will, goodness its own reward, and put it into the heart of my dear, kind master, to carry out a great clumsy gun, to an old ranger like you, Buckhorn. And, under heaven, the cause of all our present happiness, take my word for it, is THE RIFLE."

1834

NATHANIEL HAWTHORNE

MR. HIGGINBOTHAM'S CATASTROPHE

In the years before Edgar Allan Poe clearly defined the detective story, most mysteries generally were known as "riddle stories," and few authors wrote them as well as the one frequently ranked at or near the top of every list of the greatest American novelists, NATHANIEL HAWTHORNE (born Hathorne) (1804–1864). He endowed most of his major work with classic elements of mystery, superstition, allegory, horror, and the supernatural, and the present story is no exception.

Born in Salem, Massachusetts, the great-grandson of a judge in the Salem witch trials, Hawthorne was extremely solitary as a child, a state that endured throughout most of his life. His masterpiece, *The Scarlet Letter* (1850), is filled with such fantastic elements as a great glowing *A* in the sky and another apparently burned into the chest of the cowardly minister. *The House of the Seven Gables* (1851) also contains numerous, if nuanced, overtones of gothic fantasy, including a well in which the water turns foul when an injustice is done, the hereditary curse of a wizard, a skeleton with a missing hand, and a portrait that seems to change expressions. In his short stories, especially those collected in *Twice-Told Tales* (1837; expanded in 1842), *Mosses from an Old Manse* (1846), and *The Snow Image and Other Twice-Told Tales* (1852), otherworldly creatures such as ghosts, demons, witches, and so on abound, though they are often rationalized or made to seem as no more than entities in dreams. In his finest short story, "Young Goodman Brown," the title character encounters a witch, a coven attended by virtually everyone he knows, and the Devil himself—or in fact he encounters no one but has either fantasized the episode or dreamed it; Hawthorne does not resolve whether it really occurred, leaving it to the reader to decide. While he is not normally thought of as a master of humor, some of the scenes in "Mr. Higginbotham's Catastrophe," as well as those in other stories, are so broad as to be downright slapstick.

"Mr. Higginbotham's Catastrophe" was first published in the December 1834 issue of *New England Magazine;* it was first collected in *Twice-Told Tales* (Boston: American Stationers Co., John B. Russell, 1837).

A YOUNG FELLOW, A tobacco pedlar by trade, was on his way from Morristown, where he had dealt largely with the Deacon of the Shaker settlement, to the village of Parker's Falls, on Salmon River. He had a neat little cart, painted green, with a box of cigars depicted on each side panel, and an Indian chief, holding a pipe and a golden tobacco stalk, on the rear. The pedlar drove a smart little mare, and was a young man of excellent character, keen at a bargain, but none the worse liked by the Yankees; who, as I have heard them say, would rather be shaved with a sharp razor than a dull one. Especially was he beloved by the pretty girls along the Connecticut, whose favor he used to court by presents of the best smoking tobacco in his stock; knowing well that the country lasses of New England are generally great performers on pipes. Moreover, as will be seen in the course of my story, the pedlar was inquisitive, and something of a tattler, always itching to hear the news, and anxious to tell it again.

After an early breakfast at Morristown, the tobacco pedlar, whose name was Dominicus Pike, had travelled seven miles through a solitary piece of woods, without speaking a word to anybody but himself and his little gray mare. It being nearly seven o'clock, he was as eager to hold a morning gossip as a city shopkeeper to read the morning paper. An opportunity seemed at hand when, after lighting a cigar with a sunglass, he looked up, and perceived a man coming over the brow of the hill, at the foot of which the pedlar had stopped his green cart. Dominicus watched him as he descended, and noticed that he carried a bundle over his shoulder on the end of a stick, and travelled with a weary, yet determined pace. He did not look as if he had started in the freshness of the morning, but had footed it all night, and meant to do the same all day.

"Good morning, mister," said Dominicus, when within speaking distance. "You go a pretty good jog. What's the latest news at Parker's Falls?"

The man pulled the broad brim of a gray hat over his eyes, and answered, rather sullenly, that he did not come from Parker's Falls, which, as being the limit of his own day's journey, the pedlar had naturally mentioned in his inquiry.

"Well, then," rejoined Dominicus Pike, "let's have the latest news where you did come from. I'm not particular about Parker's Falls. Any place will answer."

Being thus importuned, the traveler — who was as ill looking a fellow as one would desire to meet in a solitary piece of woods — appeared to hesitate a little, as if he was either searching his memory for news, or weighing the expediency of telling it. At last, mounting on the step of the cart, he whispered in the ear of Dominicus, though he might have shouted aloud and no other mortal would have heard him.

"I do remember one little trifle of news," said he. "Old Mr. Higginbotham, of Kimballton, was murdered in his orchard, at eight o'clock last night, by an Irishman and a nigger. They strung him up to the branch of a St. Michael's pear tree, where nobody would find him till the morning."

As soon as this horrible intelligence was communicated, the stranger betook himself to his journey again, with more speed than ever, not even turning his head when Dominicus invited him to smoke a Spanish cigar and relate all the particulars. The pedlar whistled to his mare and went up the hill, pondering on the doleful fate of Mr. Higginbotham, whom he had known in the way of trade, having sold him many a bunch of long nines, and a great deal of pigtail, lady's twist, and fig tobacco. He was rather astonished at the rapidity with which the news had spread. Kimballton was nearly sixty miles distant in a straight line; the murder had been perpetrated only at eight o'clock the preceding night; yet Dominicus had heard of it at seven in the morning, when, in all probability, poor Mr. Higginbotham's own family had but just discovered his corpse, hanging on the St. Michael's pear tree. The stranger on foot must have worn seven-league boots to travel at such a rate.

"Ill news flies fast, they say," thought Dominicus Pike; "but this beats railroads. The fellow ought to be hired to go express with the President's Message."

The difficulty was solved by supposing that the narrator had made a mistake of one day in the date of the occurrence; so that our friend did not hesitate to introduce the story at every tavern and country store along the road, expending a whole bunch of Spanish wrappers among at least twenty horrified audiences. He found himself invariably the first bearer of the intelligence, and was so pestered with questions that he could not avoid filling up the outline, till it became quite a respectable narrative. He met with one piece of corroborative evidence. Mr. Higginbotham was a trader; and a former clerk of his, to whom Dominicus related the facts, testified that the old gentleman was accustomed to return home through the orchard about nightfall, with the money and valuable papers of the store in his pocket. The clerk manifested but little grief at Mr. Higginbotham's catastrophe, hinting, what the pedlar had discovered in his own dealings with him, that he was a crusty old fellow, as close as a vice. His property would descend to a pretty niece who was now keeping school in Kimballton.

What with telling the news for the public good, and driving bargains for his own, Dominicus was so much delayed on the road that he chose to put up at a tavern, about five miles short of Parker's Falls. After supper, lighting one of his prime cigars, he seated himself in the bar room, and went through the story of the murder, which had grown so fast that it took him half an hour to tell. There were as many as twenty people in the room, nineteen of whom received it all for gospel. But the twentieth was an elderly farmer, who had arrived on horseback a short time before, and was now seated in a corner, smoking his pipe. When the story was concluded, he rose up very deliberately, brought his chair right in front of Dominicus, and stared him full in the face, puffing out the vilest tobacco smoke the pedlar had ever smelt.

"Will you make affidavit," demanded he, in the tone of a country justice taking an examination, "that old Squire Higginbotham of Kimballton was murdered in his orchard the night before last, and found hanging on his great pear tree yesterday morning?"

"I tell the story as I heard it, mister," answered Dominicus, dropping his half-burnt cigar; "I don't say that I saw the thing done. So I can't take my oath that he was murdered exactly in that way."

"But I can take mine," said the farmer, "that if Squire Higginbotham was murdered night before last, I drank a glass of bitters with his ghost this morning. Being a neighbor of mine, he called me into his store, as I was riding by, and treated me, and then asked me to do a little business for him on the road. He didn't seem to know any more about his own murder than I did."

"Why, then it can't be a fact!" exclaimed Dominicus Pike.

"I guess he'd have mentioned, if it was," said the old farmer; and he removed his chair back to the corner, leaving Dominicus quite down in the mouth.

Here was a sad resurrection of old Mr. Higginbotham! The pedlar had no heart to mingle in the conversation any more, but comforted himself with a glass of gin and water, and went to bed, where, all night long, he dreamed of hanging on the St. Michael's pear tree. To avoid the old farmer (whom he so detested that his suspension would have pleased him better than Mr. Higginbotham's), Dominicus rose in the gray of the morning, put the little mare into the green cart, and trotted swiftly away towards Parker's Falls. The fresh breeze, the dewy road, and the pleasant summer dawn revived his spirits, and might have encouraged him to repeat the old story, had there been anybody awake to hear it. But he met neither ox team, light wagon, chaise, horseman, nor foot traveler, till, just as he crossed Salmon River, a man came trudging down to the bridge with a bundle over his shoulder, on the end of a stick.

"Good morning, mister," said the pedlar, reining in his mare. "If you come from Kimballton or that neighborhood, may be you can tell me the real fact about this affair of old Mr. Higginbotham. Was the old fellow actually murdered two or three nights ago, by an Irishman and a nigger?"

Dominicus had spoken in too great a hurry to observe, at first, that the stranger himself had a deep tinge of negro blood. On hearing this sudden question, the Ethiopian appeared to change his skin, its yellow hue becoming a ghastly white, while, shaking and stammering, he thus replied: "No! no! There was no colored man! It was an Irishman that hanged him last night, at eight o'clock. I came away at seven! His folks can't have looked for him in the orchard yet."

Scarcely had the yellow man spoken, when he interrupted himself, and though he seemed weary enough before, continued his journey at a pace which would have kept the pedlar's mare on a smart trot. Dominicus stared after him in great perplexity. If the murder had not been committed till Tuesday night, who was the prophet that had foretold it, in all its circumstances, on Tuesday morning? If Mr. Higginbotham's corpse were not yet discovered by his own family, how came the mulatto, at above thirty miles' distance, to know that he was hanging in the orchard, especially as he had left Kimballton before the unfortunate man was hanged at all? These ambiguous circumstances, with the stranger's surprise and terror, made Dominicus think of raising a hue and cry after him, as an accomplice in the murder; since a murder, it seemed, had really been perpetrated.

"But let the poor devil go," thought the pedlar. "I don't want his black blood on my head; and hanging the nigger wouldn't unhang Mr. Higginbotham. Unhang the old gentleman! It's a sin, I know; but I should hate to have him come to life a second time, and give me the lie!"

With these meditations, Dominicus Pike drove into the street of Parker's Falls, which, as every body knows, is as thriving a village as three cotton factories and a slitting mill can make it. The machinery was not in motion, and but a few of the shop doors unbarred, when he alighted in the stable yard of the tavern, and made it his first business to order the mare four quarts of oats. His second duty, of course, was to impart Mr. Higginbotham's catastrophe to the hostler. He deemed it advisable, however, not to be too positive as to the date of the direful fact, and also to be uncertain whether it were perpetrated by an Irishman and a mulatto, or by the son of Erin alone. Neither did he profess to relate it on his own authority, or that of any one person; but mentioned it as a report generally diffused.

The story ran through the town like fire among girdled trees, and became so much the universal talk that nobody could tell whence it had originated. Mr. Higginbotham was as well known at Parker's Falls as any citizen of the place, being part owner of the slitting mill, and a considerable stockholder in the cotton factories. The inhabitants felt their own prosperity interested in his fate. Such was the excitement, that the Parker's Falls Gazette anticipated its regular day of publication, and came out with half a form of blank paper and a column of double pica emphasized with capitals, and headed HORRID MURDER OF MR. HIGGINBOTHAM! Among other dreadful details, the printed account described the mark of the cord round the dead man's neck, and stated the number of thousand dollars of which he had been robbed; there was much pathos also about the affliction of his niece, who had gone from one fainting fit to another, ever since her uncle was found hanging on the St. Michael's pear tree with his pockets inside out. The village poet likewise commemorated the young lady's grief in seventeen stanzas of a ballad. The selectmen held a meeting, and, in consideration of Mr. Higginbotham's claims on the town, determined to issue handbills, offering a reward of five hundred dollars for the apprehension of his murderers, and the recovery of the stolen property.

Meanwhile, the whole population of Parker's Falls, consisting of shopkeepers, mistresses of boarding houses, factory girls, millmen, and schoolboys, rushed into the street and kept up such a terrible loquacity as more than compensated for the silence of the cotton machines, which refrained from their usual din out of respect to the deceased. Had Mr. Higginbotham cared about posthumous renown, his untimely ghost would have exulted in this tumult. Our friend Dominicus, in his vanity of heart, forgot his intended precautions, and mounting on the town pump, announced himself as the bearer of the authentic intelligence which had caused so wonderful a sensation. He immediately became the great man of the moment, and had just begun a new edition of the narrative, with a voice like a field preacher, when the mail stage drove into the village street. It had travelled all night, and must have shifted horses at Kimballton, at three in the morning.

"Now we shall hear all the particulars," shouted the crowd.

The coach rumbled up to the piazza of the tavern, followed by a thousand people; for if any man had been minding his own business till then, he now left it at sixes and sevens, to hear the news. The pedlar, foremost in the race, discovered two passengers, both of whom had been startled from a comfortable nap to find themselves in the centre of a mob. Every man assailing them with separate questions, all propounded at once, the couple were struck speechless, though one was a lawyer and the other a young lady.

"Mr. Higginbotham! Mr. Higginbotham! Tell us the particulars about old Mr. Higginbotham!" bawled the mob. "What is the coroner's verdict? Are the murderers apprehended? Is Mr. Higginbotham's niece come out of her fainting fits? Mr. Higginbotham! Mr. Higginbotham!!"

The coachman said not a word, except to swear awfully at the hostler for not bringing him a fresh team of horses. The lawyer inside had generally his wits about him even when asleep; the first thing he did, after learning the cause of the excitement, was to produce a large, red pocket book. Meantime, Dominicus Pike, being an extremely polite young man, and also suspecting that a female tongue would tell the story as glibly as a lawyer's, had handed the lady out of the coach. She was a fine, smart girl, now wide awake and bright as a button, and had such a sweet pretty mouth, that Dominicus would almost as lief have heard a love tale from it as a tale of murder.

"Gentlemen and ladies," said the lawyer to the shopkeepers, the millmen, and the factory girls, "I can assure you that some unaccountable mistake, or, more probably, a wilful falsehood, maliciously contrived to injure Mr. Higginbotham's credit, has excited this singular uproar. We passed through Kimballton at three o'clock this morning, and most certainly should have been informed of the murder had any been perpetrated. But I have proof nearly as strong as Mr. Higginbotham's own oral testimony, in the negative. Here is a note relating to a suit of his in the Connecticut courts, which was delivered me from that gentleman himself. I find it dated at ten o'clock last evening."

So saying, the lawyer exhibited the date and signature of the note, which irrefragably proved, either that this perverse Mr. Higginbotham was alive when he wrote it, or—as some deemed the more probable case, of two doubtful ones — that he was so absorbed in worldly business as to continue to transact it even after his death. But unexpected evidence was forthcoming. The young lady, after listening to the pedlar's explanation, merely seized a moment to smooth her gown and put her curls in order, and then appeared at the tavern door, making a modest signal to be heard.

"Good people," said she, "I am Mr. Higginbotham's niece."

A wondering murmur passed through the crowd on beholding her so rosy and bright; that same unhappy niece, whom they had supposed, on the authority of the Parker's Falls Gazette, to be lying at death's door in a fainting fit. But some shrewd fellows had doubted, all along, whether a young lady would be quite so desperate at the hanging of a rich old uncle.

"You see," continued Miss Higginbotham, with a smile, "that this strange story is quite unfounded as to myself; and I believe I may affirm it to be equally so in regard to my dear uncle Higginbotham. He has the kindness to give me a home in his house, though I contribute to my own support by teaching a school. I left Kimballton this morning to spend the vacation of commencement week with a friend, about five miles from Parker's Falls. My generous uncle, when he heard me on the stairs, called me to his bedside, and gave me two dollars and fifty cents to pay my stage fare, and another dollar for my extra expenses. He then laid his pocket book under his pillow, shook hands with me, and advised me to take some biscuit in my bag, instead of breakfasting on the road. I feel confident, therefore, that I left my beloved relative alive, and trust that I shall find him so on my return."

The young lady courtesied at the close of her speech, which was so sensible and well worded, and delivered with such grace and propriety, that everybody thought her fit to be preceptress of the best academy in the State. But a stranger would have supposed that Mr. Higginbotham was an object of abhorrence at Parker's Falls, and that a thanksgiving had been proclaimed for his murder; so excessive was the wrath of the inhabitants on learning their mistake. The millmen resolved to bestow public honors on Dominicus Pike, only hesitating whether to tar and feather him, ride him on a rail, or refresh him with an ablution at the town pump, on the top of which he had declared himself the bearer of the news. The selectmen, by advice of the lawyer, spoke of prosecuting him for a misdemeanor, in circulating unfounded reports, to the great disturbance of the peace of the commonwealth. Nothing saved Dominicus, either from mob law or a court of justice, but an eloquent appeal made by the young lady in his behalf. Addressing a few words of heartfelt gratitude to his benefactress, he mounted the green cart and rode out of town, under a discharge of artillery from the schoolboys, who found plenty of ammunition in the neighboring clay pits and mud holes. As he turned his head to exchange a farewell glance with Mr. Higginbotham's niece, a ball, of the consistence of hasty pudding, hit him slap in the mouth, giving him a most grim aspect. His whole person was so bespattered with the like filthy missiles, that he had almost a mind to ride back, and supplicate for the threatened ablution at the town pump; for, though not meant in kindness, it would now have been a deed of charity.

However, the sun shone bright on poor Dominicus, and the mud, an emblem of all stains of undeserved opprobrium, was easily brushed off when dry. Being a funny rogue, his heart soon cheered up; nor could he refrain from a hearty laugh at the uproar which his story had excited. The handbills of the selectmen would cause the commitment of all the vagabonds in the State; the paragraph in the Parker's Falls Gazette would be reprinted from Maine to Florida, and perhaps form an item in the London newspapers; and many a miser would tremble for his money bags and life, on learning the catastrophe of Mr. Higginbotham. The pedlar meditated with much fervor on the charms of the young schoolmistress, and swore that Daniel Webster never spoke nor looked so like an angel as Miss Higginbotham, while defending him from the wrathful populace at Parker's Falls.

Dominicus was now on the Kimballton turnpike, having all along determined to visit that place, though business had drawn him out of the most direct road from Morristown. As he approached the scene of the supposed murder, he continued to revolve the circumstances in his mind, and was astonished at the aspect which the whole case assumed. Had nothing occurred to corroborate the story of the first traveler, it might now have been considered as a hoax; but the yellow man was evidently acquainted either with the report or the fact; and there was a mystery in his dismayed and guilty look on being abruptly questioned. When, to this singular combination of incidents, it was added that the rumor tallied exactly with Mr. Higginbotham's character and habits of life; and that he had an orchard, and a St. Michael's pear tree, near which he always passed at nightfall; the circumstantial evidence appeared so strong that Dominicus doubted whether the autograph produced by the lawyer, or even the niece's direct testimony, ought to be equivalent. Making cautious inquiries along the road, the pedlar further learned that Mr. Higginbotham had in his service an Irishman of doubtful character, whom he had hired without a recommendation, on the score of economy.

"May I be hanged myself," exclaimed Dominicus Pike aloud, on reaching the top of a lonely hill, "if I'll believe old Higginbotham is unhanged till I see him with my own eyes, and hear it from his own mouth! And as he's a real shaver, I'll have the minister or some other responsible man for an indorser."

It was growing dusk when he reached the toll house on Kimballton turnpike, about a quarter of a mile from the village of this name. His little mare was fast bringing him up with a man on horseback, who trotted through the gate a few rods in advance of him, nodded to the toll gatherer, and kept on towards the village. Dominicus was acquainted with the tollman, and, while making change, the usual remarks on the weather passed between them.

"I suppose," said the pedlar, throwing back his whiplash, to bring it down like a feather on the mare's flank, "you have not seen anything of old Mr. Higginbotham within a day or two?"

"Yes," answered the toll gatherer. "He passed the gate just before you drove up, and yonder he rides now, if you can see him through the dusk. He's been to Woodfield this afternoon, attending a sheriff's sale there. The old man generally shakes hands and has a little chat with me; but to-night, he nodded,—as if to say, "Charge my toll"—and jogged on; for wherever he goes, he must always be at home by eight o'clock."

"So they tell me," said Dominicus.

"I never saw a man look so yellow and thin as the squire does," continued the toll gatherer. "Says I to myself, to-night, he's more like a ghost or an old mummy than good flesh and blood."

The pedlar strained his eyes through the twilight, and could just discern the horseman now far ahead on the village road. He seemed to recognize the rear of Mr. Higginbotham; but through the evening shadows, and amid the dust from the horse's feet, the figure appeared dim and unsubstantial; as if the shape of the mysterious old man were faintly moulded of darkness and gray light. Dominicus shivered.

"Mr. Higginbotham has come back from the other world, by way of the Kimballton turnpike," thought he.

He shook the reins and rode forward, keeping about the same distance in the rear of the gray old shadow, till the latter was concealed by a bend of the road. On reaching this point, the pedlar no longer saw the man on horseback, but found himself at the head of the village street, not far from a number of stores and two taverns, clustered round the meeting-house steeple. On his left were a stone wall and a gate, the boundary of a woodlot, beyond which lay an orchard, farther still, a mowing field, and last of all, a house. These were the premises of Mr. Higginbotham, whose dwelling stood beside the old highway, but had been left in the background by the Kimballton turnpike. Dominicus knew the place; and the little mare stopped short by instinct; for he was not conscious of tightening the reins.

"For the soul of me, I cannot get by this gate!" said he, trembling. "I never shall be my own man again, till I see whether Mr. Higginbotham is hanging on the St. Michael's pear tree!"

He leaped from the cart, gave the rein a turn round the gate post, and ran along the green path of the woodlot as if Old Nick were chasing behind. Just then the village clock tolled eight, and as each deep stroke fell, Dominicus gave a fresh bound and flew faster than before, till, dim in the solitary centre of the orchard, he saw the fated pear tree. One great branch stretched from the old contorted trunk across the path, and threw the darkest shadow on that one spot. But something seemed to struggle beneath the branch!

The pedlar had never pretended to more courage than befits a man of peaceful occupation, nor could he account for his valor on this awful emergency. Certain it is, however, that he rushed forward, prostrated a sturdy Irishman with the butt end of his whip, and found—not indeed hanging on the St. Michael's pear tree, but trembling beneath it, with a halter round his neck—the old, identical Mr. Higginbotham!

"Mr. Higginbotham," said Dominicus tremulously, "you're an honest man, and I'll take your word for it. Have you been hanged or not?"

If the riddle be not already guessed, a few words will explain the simple machinery by which this "coming event" was made to "cast its shadow before." Three men had plotted the robbery and murder of Mr. Higginbotham; two of them, successively, lost courage and fled, each delaying the crime one night by their disappearance; the third was in the act of perpetration, when a champion, blindly obeying the call of fate, like the heroes of old romance, appeared in the person of Dominicus Pike.

It only remains to say, that Mr. Higginbotham took the pedlar into high favor, sanctioned his addresses to the pretty schoolmistress, and settled his whole property on their children, allowing themselves the interest. In due time, the old gentleman capped the climax of his favors, by dying a Christian death, in bed, since which melancholy event Dominicus Pike has removed from Kimballton, and established a large tobacco manufactory in my native village.

1841

EDGAR ALLAN POE

THE MURDERS IN THE RUE MORGUE

Among his numerous accomplishments, significant enough to cause numerous critics to regard him as the greatest American writer of the nineteenth century, EDGAR ALLAN POE (1809–1849) is widely recognized as the inventor of the detective story. His poems are among the most often read, quoted, enjoyed, and parodied by any American poet of the nineteenth century; he was a monumentally influential literary critic and editor; and his short stories are relentlessly anthologized and remain popular pleasure reading to the present day, especially his tales of the macabre and supernatural. Even schoolchildren are familiar with such masterpieces as "The Pit and the Pendulum," "The Black Cat," "The Cask of Amontillado," "The Fall of the House of Usher," and "The Tell-Tale Heart," often, perhaps, because so much of his work has served as the basis (albeit very loosely) for scores of horror films.

The detective short story was born with "The Murders in the Rue Morgue," regardless of the many significant elements of the genre evident in William Leggett's "The Rifle." Within a single story, Poe produced virtually all the significant tropes of the detective story. In C. Auguste Dupin, of course, he gave us the first eccentric genius detective (perfected by Arthur Conan Doyle forty-six years later when Sherlock Holmes burst upon the scene). The anonymous narrator of the story serves as the stand-in for the reader, marveling at his friend's brilliance while asking the questions that the reader would otherwise ask. Poe gave us the seemingly impossible crime, the bungling police, the astute observations of clues invisible to others, and the deductions made from them. He called this story (and the two others featuring Dupin) tales of ratiocination (a word he created). Note that he did not call Dupin a detective—because the word did not exist, nor did the position.

Only three Dupin stories were written because the little interest they garnered was attributed by Poe to their original flavor rather than their literary excellence and because he quickly tired of the form. The second Dupin story, "The Mystery of Marie Roget" (1842), is a lengthy, rather dull description (mainly newspaper accounts) of the real-life murder of Mary Rogers, moved from New York to Paris by the author.

"The Murders in the Rue Morgue" bears little resemblance to the motion pictures it has inspired, including the 1932 horror film it became when Bela Lugosi used his pet ape to kidnap prostitutes for his lab experiments.

"The Murders in the Rue Morgue" was originally published in the April 1841 issue of *Graham's Magazine.* It was later published in 1843 in a slim pamphlet as a single story, *The Prose Romances of Edgar A. Poe, No. 1,* one of the rarest and most precious volumes of American literature. It was first collected in *Tales* (New York: Wiley and Putnam, 1845).

• • •

> What song the Syrens sang, or what name Achilles assumed when he bid himself among women, although puzzling questions, are not beyond all conjecture.
>
> —*Sir Thomas Browne*

THE MENTAL FEATURES discoursed of as the analytical, are, in themselves, but little susceptible of analysis. We appreciate them only in their effects. We know of them, among other things, that they are always to their possessor, when inordinately possessed, a source of the liveliest enjoyment. As the strong man exults in his physical ability, delighting in such exercises as call his muscles into action, so glories the analyst in that moral activity which *disentangles.* He derives pleasure from even the most trivial occupations bringing his talent into play. He is fond of enigmas, of conundrums, of hieroglyphics; exhibiting in his solutions of each a degree of *acumen* which appears to the ordinary apprehension preternatural. His results, brought about by the very soul and essence of method, have, in truth, the whole air of intuition.

The faculty of re-solution is possibly much invigorated by mathematical study, and especially by that highest branch of it which, unjustly, and merely on account of its retrograde operations, has been called, as if *par excellence,* analysis. Yet to calculate is not in itself to analyze. A chess-player, for example, does the one without effort at the other. It follows that the game of chess, in its effects upon mental character, is greatly misunderstood. I am not now writing a treatise, but simply prefacing a somewhat peculiar narrative by observations very much at random; I will, therefore, take occasion to assert that the higher powers of the reflective intellect are more decidedly and more usefully tasked by the unostentatious game of draughts than by all the elaborate frivolity of chess. In this latter, where the pieces have different and *bizarre* motions, with various and variable values, what is only complex is mistaken (a not unusual error) for what is profound. The *attention* is here called powerfully into play. If it flag for an instant, an oversight is committed, resulting in injury or defeat. The possible moves being not only manifold but involute, the chances of such oversights are multiplied; and in nine cases out of ten, it is the more concentrative rather than the more acute player who conquers. In draughts, on the contrary, where the moves are *unique* and have but little variation, the probabilities of inadvertence are diminished, and the mere attention being left comparatively unemployed, what advantages are obtained by either party are obtained by superior *acumen*. To be less abstract, let us suppose a game of draughts where the pieces are reduced to four kings, and where, of course, no oversight is to be expected. It is obvious that here the victory can be decided (the players being at all equal) only by some *recherché* movement, the result of some strong exertion of the intellect. Deprived of ordinary resources, the analyst throws himself into the spirit of his opponent, identifies himself therewith, and not unfrequently sees thus, at a glance, the sole methods (sometimes indeed absurdly simple ones) by which he may seduce into error or hurry into miscalculation.

Whist has long been known for its influence upon what is termed the calculating power; and men of the highest order of intellect have been known to take an apparently unaccountable delight in it, while eschewing chess as frivolous. Beyond doubt there is nothing of a similar nature so greatly tasking the faculty of analysis. The best chess-player in Christendom *may* be little more than the best player of chess; but proficiency in whist implies a capacity for success in all these more important undertakings where mind struggles with mind. When I say proficiency, I mean that perfection in the game which includes a comprehension of *all* the sources whence legitimate advantage may be derived. These are not only manifold but multiform, and lie frequently among recesses of thought altogether inaccessible to the ordinary understanding. To observe attentively is to remember distinctly; and, so far, the concentrative chess-player will do very well at whist; while the rules of Hoyle (themselves based upon the mere mechanism of the game) are sufficiently and generally comprehensible. Thus to have a retentive memory, and proceed by "the book," are points commonly regarded as the sum total of good playing. But it is in matters beyond the limits of mere rule that the skill of the analyst is evinced. He makes, in silence, a host of observations and inferences. So, perhaps, do his companions; and the difference in the extent of the information obtained, lies not so much in the validity of the inference as in the quality of the observation. The necessary knowledge is that of *what* to observe. Our player confines himself not at all; nor, because the game is the object, does he reject deductions from things external to the game. He examines the countenance of his partner, comparing it carefully with that of each of his opponents. He considers the mode of assorting the cards in each hand; often counting trump by trump, and honor by honor, through the glances bestowed by their holders upon each. He notes every variation of face as the play progresses, gathering a fund of thought from the differences in the expression of certainty, of surprise, of triumph, or of chagrin. From the manner of gathering up a trick he judges whether the person taking it can make another in the suit. He recognizes what is played through feint, by the air with which it is thrown upon the table. A casual or inadvertent word; the accidental dropping or turning of a card, with the accompanying anxiety or carelessness in regard to its concealment; the counting of the tricks, with the order of their arrangement; embarrassment, hesitation, eagerness, or trepidation — all afford, to his apparently intuitive perception, indications of the true state of affairs. The first two or three rounds having been played, he is in full possession of the contents of each hand, and thenceforward puts down his cards with as absolute a precision of purpose as if the rest of the party had turned outward the faces of their own.

The analytical power should not be confounded with simple ingenuity; for while the analyst is necessarily ingenious, the ingenious man is often remarkably incapable of analysis. The constructive or combining power, by which ingenuity is usually manifested, and to which the phrenologists (I believe erroneously) have assigned a separate organ, supposing it a primitive faculty, has been so frequently seen in those whose intellect bordered otherwise upon idiocy, as to have attracted general observation among writers on morals. Between ingenuity and the analytic ability there exists a difference far greater, indeed, than that between the fancy and the imagination, but of a character very strictly analogous. It will be found, in fact, that the ingenious are always fanciful, and the *truly* imaginative never otherwise than analytic.

The narrative which follows will appear to the reader somewhat in the light of a commentary upon the propositions just advanced.

Residing in Paris during the spring and part of the summer of 18 —, I there became acquainted with a Monsieur C. Auguste Dupin. This young gentleman was of an excellent, indeed of an illustrious family, but, by a variety of untoward events, had been reduced to such poverty that the energy of his character succumbed beneath it, and he ceased to bestir himself in this world, or to care for the retrieval of his fortunes. By courtesy of his creditors, there still remained in his possession a small remnant of his patrimony; and, upon the income arising from this, he managed, by means of a rigorous economy, to procure the necessities of life, without troubling himself about its superfluities. Books, indeed, were his sole luxuries, and in Paris these are easily obtained.

Our first meeting was at an obscure library in the Rue Montmartre, where the accident of our both being in search of the same very rare and very remarkable volume, brought us into closer communion. We saw each other again and again. I was deeply interested in the little family history which he detailed to me with all that candor which a Frenchman indulges whenever mere self is the theme. I was astonished, too, at the vast extent of his reading; and, above all, I felt my soul enkindled within me by the wild fervor, and the vivid freshness of his imagination. Seeking in Paris the objects I then sought, I felt that the society of such a man would be to me a treasure beyond price; and this feeling I frankly confided to him. It was at length arranged that we should live together during my stay in the city; and as my worldly circumstances were somewhat less embarrassed than his own, I was permitted to be at the expense of renting, and furnishing in a style which suited the rather fantastic gloom of our common temper, a time-eaten and grotesque mansion, long deserted through superstitions into which we did not inquire, and tottering to its fall in a retired and desolate portion of the Faubourg St. Germain.

Had the routine of our life at this place been known to the world, we should have been regarded as madmen—although, perhaps, as madmen of a harmless nature. Our seclusion was perfect. We admitted no visitors. Indeed the locality of our retirement had been carefully kept a secret from my own former associates; and it had been many years since Dupin had ceased to know or be known in Paris. We existed within ourselves alone.

It was a freak of fancy in my friend (for what else shall I call it?) to be enamored of the Night for her own sake; and into this *bizarrerie,* as into all his others, I quietly fell; giving myself up to his wild whims with a perfect *abandon.* The sable divinity would not herself dwell with us always; but we could counterfeit her presence. At the first dawn of the morning we closed all the massy shutters of our old building, lighting a couple of tapers which, strongly perfumed, threw out only the ghastliest and feeblest of rays. By the aid of these we then busied our souls in dreams — reading, writing, or conversing, until warned by the clock of the advent of the true Darkness. Then we sallied forth into the streets, arm in arm, continuing the topics of the day, or roaming far and wide until a late hour, seeking, amid the wild lights and shadows of the populous city, that infinity of mental excitement which quiet observation can afford.

At such times I could not help remarking and admiring (although from his rich ideality I had been prepared to expect it) a peculiar analytic ability in Dupin. He seemed, too, to take an eager delight in its exercise — if not exactly in its display — and did not hesitate to confess the pleasure thus derived. He boasted to me, with a low chuckling laugh, that most men, in respect to himself, wore windows in their bosoms, and was wont to follow up such assertions by direct and very startling proofs of his intimate knowledge of my own. His manner at these moments was frigid and abstract; his eyes were vacant in expression; while his voice, usually a rich tenor, rose into a treble which would have sounded petulant but for the deliberateness and entire distinctness of the enunciation. Observing him in these moods. I often dwelt meditatively upon the old philosophy of the Bi-Part Soul, and amused myself with the fancy of a double Dupin — the creative and the resolvent.

Let it not be supposed, from what I have just said, that I am detailing any mystery, or penning any romance. What I have described in the Frenchman was merely the result of an excited, or perhaps of a diseased, intelligence. But of the character of his remarks at the periods in question an example will best convey the idea.

We were strolling one night down a long dirty street, in the vicinity of the Palais Royal. Being both, apparently, occupied with thought, neither of us had spoken a syllable for fifteen minutes at least. All at once Dupin broke forth with these words:

"He is a very little fellow, that's true, and would do better for the *Théâtre des Variétés.*"

"There can be no doubt of that," I replied unwittingly, and not at first observing (so much had I been absorbed in reflection) the extraordinary manner in which the speaker had chimed in with my meditations. In an instant afterward I recollected myself, and my astonishment was profound.

"Dupin," said I, gravely, "this is beyond my comprehension. I do not hesitate to say that I am amazed, and can scarcely credit my senses. How was it possible you should know I was thinking of ——?" Here I paused, to ascertain beyond a doubt whether he really knew of whom I thought.

"—— of Chantilly," said he, "why do you pause? You were remarking to yourself that his diminutive figure unfitted him for tragedy."

This was precisely what had formed the subject of my reflections. Chantilly was a *quondam* cobbler of the Rue St. Denis, who, becoming stage-mad, had attempted the *rôle* of Xerxes, in Crébillon's tragedy so called, and been notoriously Pasquinaded for his pains.

"Tell me, for Heaven's sake," I exclaimed, "the method—if method there is—by which you have been enabled to fathom my soul in this matter." In fact, I was even more startled than I would have been willing to express.

"It was the fruiterer," replied my friend, "who brought you to the conclusion that the mender of soles was not of sufficient height for Xerxes *et id genus omne.*"

"The fruiterer!—you astonish me—I know no fruiterer whomsoever."

"The man who ran up against you as we entered the street—it may have been fifteen minutes ago."

I now remembered that, in fact, a fruiterer, carrying upon his head a large basket of apples, had nearly thrown me down, by accident, as we passed from the Rue C—— into the thoroughfare where we stood; but what this had to do with Chantilly I could not possibly understand.

There was not a particle of *charlatânerie* about Dupin. "I will explain," he said, "and that you may comprehend all clearly, we will first retrace the course of your meditations, from the moment in which I spoke to you until that of the *rencontre* with the fruiterer in question. The larger links of the chain run thus—Chantilly, Orion, Dr. Nichols, Epicurus, Stereotomy, the street stones, the fruiterer."

There are few persons who have not, at some period of their lives, amused themselves in retracing the steps by which particular conclusions of their own minds have been attained. The occupation is often full of interest; and he who attempts it for the first time is astonished by the apparently illimitable distance and incoherence between the starting-point and the goal. What, then, must have been my amazement when I heard the Frenchman speak what he had just spoken, and when. I could not help acknowledging that he had spoken the truth. He continued:

"We had been talking of horses, if I remember aright, just before leaving the Rue C——. This was the last subject we discussed. As we crossed into this street, a fruiterer, with a large basket upon his head, brushing quickly past us, thrust you upon a pile of paving-stones collected at a spot where the causeway is undergoing repair. You stepped upon one of the loose fragments, slipped, slightly strained your ankle, appeared vexed or sulky, muttered a few words, turned to look at the pile, and then proceeded in silence. I was not particularly attentive to what you did; but observation has become with me, of late, a species of necessity.

"You kept your eyes upon the ground — glancing, with a petulant expression, at the holes and ruts in the pavement (so that I saw you were still thinking of the stones), until we reached the little alley called Lamartine, which has been paved, by way of experiment, with the overlapping and riveted blocks. Here your countenance brightened up, and, perceiving your lips move, I could not doubt that you murmured the word 'stereotomy,' a term very affectedly applied to this species of pavement. I knew that you could not say to yourself 'stereotomy' without being brought to think of atomies, and thus of the theories of Epicurus; and since, when we discussed this subject not very long ago, I mentioned to you how singularly, yet with how little notice, the vague guesses of that noble Greek had met with confirmation in the late nebular cosmogony, I felt that you could not avoid casting your eyes upward to the great *nebula* in Orion, and I certainly expected that you would do so. You did look up; and I was now assured that I correctly followed your steps. But in that bitter *tirade* upon Chantilly, which appeared in yesterday's *'Musée,'* the satirist, making some disgraceful allusions to the cobbler's change of name upon assuming the buskin, quoted a Latin line about which we have often conversed. I mean the line

Perdidit antiquum litera prima sonum.

I had told you that this was in reference to Orion, formerly written Urion; and, from certain pungencies connected with this explanation, I was aware that you could not have forgotten it. It was clear, therefore, that you would not fail to combine the two ideas of Orion and Chantilly. That you did combine them I saw by the character of the smile which passed over your lips. You thought of the poor cobbler's immolation. So far, you had been stooping in your gait; but now I saw you draw yourself up to your full height. I was then sure that you reflected upon the diminutive figure of Chantilly. At this point I interrupted your meditations to remark that as, in fact, he *was* a very little fellow — that Chantilly — he would do better at the *Theâtre des Variétés.*"

Not long after this, we were looking over an evening edition of the

"Gazette des Tribunaux," when the following paragraphs arrested our attention.

"EXTRAORDINARY MURDERS.—This morning, about three o'clock, the inhabitants of the Quartier St. Roch were aroused from sleep by a succession of terrific shrieks, issuing, apparently, from the fourth story of a house in the Rue Morgue, known to be in the sole occupancy of one Madame L'Espanaye, and her daughter, Mademoiselle Camille L'Espanaye. After some delay, occasioned by a fruitless attempt to procure admission in the usual manner, the gateway was broken in with a crowbar, and eight or ten of the neighbors entered, accompanied by two *gendarmes.* By this time the cries had ceased; but, as the party rushed up the first flight of stairs, two or more rough voices, in angry contention, were distinguished, and seemed to proceed from the upper part of the house. As the second landing was reached, these sounds, also, had ceased, and everything remained perfectly quiet. The party spread themselves, and hurried from room to room. Upon arriving at a large back chamber in the fourth story (the door of which, being found locked, with the key inside, was forced open), a spectacle presented itself which struck every one present not less with horror than with astonishment.

"The apartment was in the wildest disorder—the furniture broken and thrown about in all directions. There was only one bedstead; and from this the bed had been removed, and thrown into the middle of the floor. On the chair lay a razor, besmeared with blood. On the hearth were two or three long and thick tresses of gray human hair, also dabbled with blood, and seeming to have been pulled out by the roots. Upon the floor were found four Napoleons, an ear-ring of topaz, three large silver spoons, three smaller of *métal d'Alger,* and two bags, containing nearly four thousand francs in gold. The drawers of a *bureau,* which stood in one corner, were open, and had been, apparently, rifled, although many articles still remained in them. A small iron safe was discovered under the *bed* (not under the bedstead). It was open, with the key still in the door. It had no contents beyond a few old letters, and other papers of little consequence.

"Of Madame L'Espanaye no traces were here seen; but an unusual quantity of soot being observed in the fire-place, a search was made in the chimney, and (horrible to relate!) the corpse of the daughter, head downward, was dragged therefrom; it having been thus forced up the narrow aperture for a considerable distance. The body was quite warm. Upon examining it, many excoriations were perceived, no doubt occasioned by the violence with which it had been thrust up and disengaged. Upon the face were many severe scratches, and, upon the throat, dark bruises, and deep indentations of finger nails, as if the deceased had been throttled to death.

"After a thorough investigation of every portion of the house, without farther discovery, the party made its way into a small paved yard in the rear of the building, where lay the corpse of the old lady, with her throat so entirely cut that, upon an attempt to raise her, the head fell off. The body, as well as the head, was fearfully mutilated — the former so much so as scarcely to retain any semblance of humanity.

"To this horrible mystery there is not as yet, we believe, the slightest clew."

The next day's paper had these additional particulars:

"*The Tragedy in the Rue Morgue.* — Many individuals have been examined in relation to this most extraordinary and frightful affair," [the word "*affaire*" has not yet, in France, that levity of import which it conveys with us] "but nothing whatever has transpired to throw light upon it. We give below all the material testimony elicited.

"*Pauline Dubourg,* laundress, deposes that she has known both the deceased for three years, having washed for them during that period. The old lady and her daughter seemed on good terms — very affectionate towards each other. They were excellent pay. Could not speak in regard to their mode or means of living. Believed that Madame L. told fortunes for a living. Was reputed to have money put by. Never met any persons in the house when she called for the clothes or took them home. Was sure that they had no servant in employ. There appeared to be no furniture in any part of the building except in the fourth story.

"*Pierre Moreau,* tobacconist, deposes that he has been in the habit of selling small quantities of tobacco and snuff to Madam L'Espanaye for nearly four years. Was born in the neighborhood, and has always resided there. The deceased and her daughter had occupied the house in which the corpses were found, for more than six years. It was formerly occupied by a jeweller, who under-let the upper rooms to various persons. The house was the property of Madame L. She became dissatisfied with the abuse of the premises by her tenant, and moved into them herself, refusing to let any portion. The old lady was childish. Witness had seen the daughter some five or six times during the six years. The two lived an exceedingly retired life — were reputed to have money. Had heard it said among the neighbors that Madame L. told fortunes — did not believe it. Had never seen any person enter the door except the old lady and her daughter, a porter once or twice, and a physician some eight or ten times.

"Many other persons, neighbors, gave evidence to the same effect. No one was spoken of as frequenting the house. It was not known whether there were any living connections of Madame L. and her daughter. The shutters of the front windows were seldom opened. Those in the rear were always closed, with the exception of the large back room, fourth story. The house was a good house — not very old.

"*Isidore Musèt, gendarme,* deposes that he was called to the house about three o'clock in the morning, and found some twenty or thirty persons at the gateway, endeavoring to gain admittance. Forced it open, at length, with a bayonet — not with a crowbar. Had but little difficulty in getting it open, on account of its being a double or folding gate, and bolted neither at bottom nor top. The shrieks were continued until the gate was forced — and then suddenly ceased. They seemed to be screams of some person (or persons) in great agony — were loud and drawn out, not short and quick. Witness led the way up stairs. Upon reaching the first landing, heard two voices in loud and angry contention — the one a gruff voice, the other much shriller — a very strange voice. Could distinguish some words of the former, which was that of a Frenchman. Was positive that it was not a woman's voice. Could distinguish the words '*sacré*' and '*diable*.' The shrill voice was that of a foreigner. Could not be sure whether it was the voice of a man or of a woman. Could not make out what was said, but believed the language to be Spanish. The state of the room and of the bodies was described by this witness as we described them yesterday.

Henri Duval, a neighbor, and by trade a silver-smith, deposes that he was one of the party who first entered the house. Corroborates the testimony of Musèt in general. As soon as they forced an entrance, they reclosed the door, to keep out the crowd, which collected very fast, notwithstanding the lateness of the hour. The shrill voice, this witness thinks, was that of an Italian. Was certain it was not French. Could not be sure that it was a man's voice. It might have been a woman's. Was not acquainted with the Italian language. Could not distinguish the words, but was convinced by the intonation that the speaker was Italian. Knew Madame L., and her daughter. Had conversed with both frequently. Was sure that the shrill voice was not that of either of the deceased.

"—— *Odenheimer, restaurateur.* This witness volunteered his testimony. Not speaking French, was examined through an interpreter. Is a native of Amsterdam. Was passing the house at the time of the shrieks.

They lasted for several minutes — probably ten. They were long and loud — very awful and distressing. Was one of those who entered the building. Corroborated the previous evidence in every respect but one. Was sure that the shrill voice was that of a man — of a Frenchman. Could not distinguish the words uttered. They were loud and quick — unequal — spoken apparently in fear as well as in anger. The voice was harsh — not so much shrill as harsh. Could not call it a shrill voice. The gruff voice said repeatedly, '*sacré*,' '*diable*,' and once '*mon Dieu*.'

"*Jules Mignaud*, banker, of the firm of Mignaud et Fils, Rue Deloraine. Is the elder Mignaud. Madame L'Espanaye had some property. Had opened an account with his banking house in the spring of the year —— (eight years previously). Made frequent deposits in small sums. Had checked for nothing until the third day before her death, when she took out in person the sum of 4000 francs. This sum was paid in gold, and a clerk sent home with the money.

"*Adolphe Le Bon*, clerk to Mignaud et Fils, deposes that on the day in question, about noon, he accompanied Madame L'Espanaye to her residence with the 4000 francs, put up in two bags. Upon the door being opened, Mademoiselle L. appeared and took from his hands one of the bags, while the old lady relieved him of the other. He then bowed and departed. Did not see any person in the street at the time. It is a by-street — very lonely.

"*William Bird*, tailor, deposes that he was one of the party who entered the house. Is an Englishman. Has lived in Paris two years. Was one of the first to ascend the stairs. Heard the voices in contention. The gruff voice was that of a Frenchman. Could make out several words, but cannot now remember all. Heard distinctly '*sacré*' and '*mon Dieu*.' There was a sound at the moment as if of several persons struggling — a scraping and scuffling sound. The shrill voice was very loud — louder than the gruff one. Is sure that it was not the voice of an Englishman. Appeared to be that of a German. Might have been a woman's voice. Does not understand German.

"Four of the above-named witnesses, being recalled, deposed that the door of the chamber in which was found the body of Mademoiselle L. was locked on the inside when the party reached it. Everything was perfectly silent — no groans or noises of any kind. Upon forcing the door no person was seen. The windows, both of the back and front room, were down and firmly fastened from within. A door between the two rooms was closed but not locked. The door leading from the front room into the passage was locked, with the key on the inside. A small room in the front of the house, on the fourth story, at the head of the passage, was open, the door being ajar. This room was crowded with old beds, boxes, and so forth. These were carefully removed and searched. There was not an inch of any portion of the house which was not carefully searched. Sweeps were sent up and down the chimneys. The house was a four-story one, with garrets (*mansardes*). A trap-door on the roof was nailed down very securely—did not appear to have been opened for years. The time elapsing between the hearing of the voices in contention and the breaking open of the room door was variously stated by the witnesses. Some made it as short as three minutes—some as long as five. The door was opened with difficulty.

"*Alfonzo Garcio,* undertaker, deposes that he resides in the Rue Morgue. Is a native of Spain. Was one of the party who entered the house. Did not proceed up stairs. Is nervous, and was apprehensive of the consequences of agitation. Heard the voices in contention. The gruff voice was that of a Frenchman. Could not distinguish what was said. The shrill voice was that of an Englishman—is sure of this. Does not understand the English language, but judges by the intonation.

"*Alberto Montani,* confectioner, deposes that he was among the first to ascend the stairs. Heard the voices in question. The gruff voice was that of a Frenchman. Distinguished several words. The speaker appeared to be expostulating. Could not make out the words of the shrill voice. Spoke quick and unevenly. Thinks it is the voice of a Russian. Corroborates the general testimony. Is an Italian. Never conversed with a native of Russia.

"Several witnesses, recalled, here testified that the chimneys of all the rooms of the fourth story were too narrow to admit the passage of a human being. By 'sweeps' were meant cylindrical sweeping-brushes, such as are employed by those who clean chimneys. These brushes were passed up and down every flue in the house. There is no back passage by which any one could have descended while the party proceeded upstairs. The body of Mademoiselle L'Espanaye was so firmly wedged in the chimney that it could not be got down until four or five of the party united their strength.

"*Paul Dumas,* physician, deposes that he was called to view the bodies about daybreak. They were both then lying on the sacking of the bedstead in the chamber where Mademoiselle L. was found. The corpse of the young lady was much bruised and excoriated. The fact that it had been thrust up the chimney would sufficiently account for these appearances. The throat was greatly chafed. There were several deep scratches just below the chin, together with a series of livid spots which were evidently the impressions of fingers. The face was fearfully discolored, and the eye-balls protruded. The tongue had been partially bitten through. A large bruise was discovered upon the pit of the stomach, produced, apparently, by the pressure of a knee. In the opinion of M. Dumas, Mademoiselle L'Espanaye had been throttled to death by some person or persons unknown. The corpse of the mother was horribly mutilated. All the bones of the right leg and arm were more or less shattered. The left *tibia* much splintered, as well as all the ribs of the left side. Whole body dreadfully bruised and discolored. It was not possible to say how the injuries had been inflicted. A heavy club of wood, or a broad bar of iron — a chair — any large, heavy, and obtuse weapon would have produced such results, if wielded by the hands of a very powerful man. No woman could have inflicted the blows with any weapon. The head of the deceased, when seen by witness, was entirely separated from the body, and was also greatly shattered. The throat had evidently been cut with some very sharp instrument — probably with a razor.

"*Alexandre Etienne,* surgeon, was called with M. Dumas to view the bodies. Corroborated the testimony, and the opinions of M. Dumas.

"Nothing farther of importance was elicited, although several other persons were examined. A murder so mysterious, and so perplexing in all its particulars, was never before committed in Paris — if indeed a murder has been committed at all. The police are entirely at fault — an unusual occurrence in affairs of this nature. There is not, however, the shadow of a clew apparent."

The evening edition of the paper stated that the greatest excitement still continued in the Quartier St. Roch — that the premises in question had been carefully re-searched, and fresh examinations of witnesses instituted, but all to no purpose. A postscript, however, mentioned that Adolphe Le Bon had been arrested and imprisoned — although nothing appeared to criminate him beyond the facts already detailed.

Dupin seemed singularly interested in the progress of this affair — at least so I judged from his manner, for he made no comments. It was only after the announcement that Le Bon had been imprisoned, that he asked me my opinion respecting the murders.

I could merely agree with all Paris in considering them an insoluble mystery. I saw no means by which it would be possible to trace the murderer.

"We must not judge of the means," said Dupin, "by this shell of an examination. The Parisian police, so much extolled for *acumen,* are cunning, but no more. There is no method in their proceedings, beyond the method of the moment. They make a vast parade of measures; but, not infrequently, these are so ill-adapted to the objects proposed, as to put us in mind of Monsieur Jourdain's calling for his *robe-de-chambre —pour mieux entendre la musique*. The results attained by them are not unfrequently surprising, but for the most part, are brought about by simple diligence and activity. When these qualities are unavailing, their schemes fail. Vidocq, for example, was a good guesser, and the persevering man. But, without educated thought, he erred continually by the very intensity of his investigations. He impaired his vision by holding the object too close. He might see, perhaps, one or two points with unusual clearness, but in so doing he, necessarily, lost sight of the matter as a whole. Thus there is such a thing as being too profound. Truth is not always in a well. In fact, as regards the more important knowledge, I do believe that she is invariably superficial. The depth lies in the valleys where we seek her, and not upon the mountain-tops where she is found. The modes and sources of this kind of error are well typified in the contemplation of the heavenly bodies. To look at a star by glances — to view it in a sidelong way, by turning toward it the exterior portions of the *retina* (more susceptible of feeble impressions of light than the interior), is to behold the star distinctly — is to have the best appreciation of its lustre — a lustre which grows dim just in proportion as we turn our vision *fully* upon it. A greater number of rays actually fall upon the eye in the latter case, but, in the former, there is the more refined capacity for comprehension. By undue profundity we perplex and enfeeble thought; and it is possible to make even Venus herself vanish from the firmament by a scrutiny too sustained, too concentrated, or too direct.

"As for these murders, let us enter into some examinations for ourselves, before we make up an opinion respecting them. An inquiry will afford us amusement," [I thought this an odd term, so applied, but said nothing] "and besides, Le Bon once rendered me a service for which I am not ungrateful. We will go and see the premises with our own eyes. I know G——, the Prefect of Police, and shall have no difficulty in obtaining the necessary permission."

The permission was obtained, and we proceeded at once to the Rue Morgue. This is one of those miserable thoroughfares which intervene between the Rue Richelieu and the Rue St. Roch. It was late in the afternoon when we reached it, as this quarter is at a great distance from that in which we resided. The house was readily found; for there were still many persons gazing up at the closed shutters, with an objectless curiosity, from the opposite side of the way. It was an ordinary Parisian house, with a gateway, on one side of which was a glazed watch-box, with a sliding panel in the window, indicating a *loge de concierge.* Before going in we walked up the street, turned down an alley, and then, again turning, passed in the rear of the building—Dupin, meanwhile, examining the whole neighborhood, as well as the house, with a minuteness of attention for which I could see no possible object.

Retracing our steps, we came again to the front of the dwelling, rang, and, having shown our credentials, were admitted by the agents in charge. We went up stairs—into the chamber where the body of Mademoiselle L'Espanaye had been found, and where both the deceased still lay. The disorders of the room had, as usual, been suffered to exist. I saw nothing beyond what had been stated in the "Gazette des Tribunaux." Dupin scrutinized everything—not excepting the bodies of the victims. We then went into the other rooms, and into the yard; a *gendarme* accompanying us throughout. The examination occupied us until dark, when we took our departure. On our way home my companion stepped in for a moment at the office of one of the daily papers.

I have said that the whims of my friend were manifold, and that *Je les ménagais:*—for this phrase there is no English equivalent. It was his humor, now, to decline all conversation on the subject of the murder, until about noon the next day. He then asked me, suddenly, if I had observed anything *peculiar* at the scene of the atrocity.

There was something in his manner of emphasizing the word "peculiar," which caused me to shudder without knowing why.

"No, nothing *peculiar,*" I said; "nothing more, at least, than we both saw stated in the paper."

"The 'Gazette,'" he replied, "has not entered, I fear, into the unusual horror of the thing. But dismiss the idle opinions of this print. It appears to me that this mystery is considered insoluble, for the very reason which should cause it to be regarded as easy of solution—I mean for the *outré* character of its features. The police are confounded by the seeming absence of motive—not for the murder itself—but for the atrocity of the murder. They are puzzled, too, by the seeming impossibility of reconciling the voices heard in contention, with the facts that no one was discovered upstairs but the assassinated Mademoiselle L'Espanaye, and that there were no means of egress without the notice of the party ascending. The wild disorder of the room; the corpse thrust, with the head downward, up the chimney; the frightful mutilation of the body of the old lady; these considerations, with those just mentioned, and others which I need not mention, have sufficed to paralyze the powers, by putting completely at fault the boasted *acumen,* of the government agents. They have fallen into the gross but common error of confounding the unusual with the abstruse. But it is by these deviations from the plane of the ordinary, that reason feels its way, if at all, in its search for the true. In investigations such as we are now pursuing, it should not be so much asked 'what has occurred,' as 'what has occurred that has never occurred before.' In fact, the facility with which I shall arrive, or have arrived, at the solution of this mystery, is in the direct ratio of its apparent insolubility in the eyes of the police."

I stared at the speaker in mute astonishment.

"I am now awaiting," continued he, looking toward the door of our apartment—"I am now awaiting a person who, although perhaps not the perpetrator of these butcheries, must have been in some measure implicated in their perpetration. Of the worst portion of the crimes committed, it is probable that he is innocent. I hope that I am right in this supposition; for upon it I build my expectation of reading the entire riddle. I look for the man here—in this room—every moment. It is true that he may not arrive; but the probability is that he will. Should he come, it will be necessary to detain him. Here are pistols; and we both know how to use them when occasion demands their use."

I took the pistols, scarcely knowing what I did, or believing what I heard, while Dupin went on, very much as if in a soliloquy. I have already spoken of his abstract manner at such times. His discourse was addressed to myself; but his voice, although by no means loud, had that intonation which is commonly employed in speaking to someone at a great distance. His eyes, vacant in expression, regarded only the wall.

"That the voices heard in contention," he said," by the party upon the stairs, were not the voices of the women themselves, was fully proved by the evidence. This relieves us of all doubt upon the question whether the old lady could have first destroyed the daughter, and afterward have committed suicide. I speak of this point chiefly for the sake of method; for the strength of Madame L'Espanaye would have been utterly unequal to the task of thrusting her daughter's corpse up the chimney as it was found; and the nature of the wounds upon her own person entirely precludes the idea of self-destruction. Murder, then, has been committed by some third party; and the voices of this third party were those heard in contention. Let me now advert—not to the whole testimony respecting these voices—but to what was *peculiar* in that testimony. Did you observe anything peculiar about it?"

I remarked that, while all the witnesses agreed in supposing the gruff voice to be that of a Frenchman, there was much disagreement in regard to the shrill, or, as one individual termed it, the harsh voice.

"That was the evidence itself," said Dupin, "but it was not the peculiarity of the evidence. You have observed nothing distinctive. Yet there was something to be observed. The witnesses, as you remarked, agreed about the gruff voice; they were here unanimous. But in regard to the shrill voice, the peculiarity is — not that they disagreed — but that, while an Italian, an Englishman, a Spaniard, a Hollander, and a Frenchman attempted to describe it, each one spoke of it as that *of a foreigner.* Each is sure that it was not the voice of one of his own countrymen. Each likens it — not to the voice of an individual of any nation with whose language he is conversant — but the converse. The Frenchman supposes it the voice of a Spaniard, and 'might have distinguished some words *had he been acquainted with the Spanish.*' The Dutchman maintains it to have been that of a Frenchman; but we find it stated that '*not understanding French this witness was examined through an interpreter.*' The Englishman thinks it the voice of a German, and '*does not understand German.*' The Spaniard 'is sure' that it was that of an Englishman, but 'judges by the intonation' altogether, '*as he has no knowledge of the English.*' The Italian believes it the voice of a Russian, but '*has never conversed with a native of Russia.*' A second Frenchman differs, moreover, with the first, and is positive that the voice was that of an Italian; but, *not being cognizant of that tongue,* is, like the Spaniard, 'convinced by the intonation.' Now, how strangely unusual must that voice have really been, about which such testimony as this *could* have been elicited! — in whose *tones,* even, denizens of the five great divisions of Europe could recognize nothing familiar! You will say that it might have been the voice of an Asiatic — of an African. Neither Asiatics nor Africans abound in Paris; but, without denying the inference, I will now merely call your attention to three points. The voice is termed by one witness 'harsh rather than shrill.' It is represented by two others to have been 'quick and *unequal.*' No words — no sounds resembling words — were by any witness mentioned as distinguishable.

"I know not," continued Dupin, "what impression I may have made, so far, upon your own understanding; but I do not hesitate to say that legitimate deductions even from this portion of the testimony — the portion respecting the gruff and shrill voices — are in themselves sufficient to engender a suspicion which should give direction to all farther progress in the investigation of the mystery. I said 'legitimate deductions';

but my meaning is not thus fully expressed. I designed to imply that the deductions are the *sole* proper ones, and that the suspicion arises *inevitably* from them as the single result. What the suspicion is, however, I will not say just yet. I merely wish you to bear in mind that, with myself, it was sufficiently forcible to give a definite form — a certain tendency — to my inquiries in the chamber.

"Let us now transport ourselves, in fancy, to this chamber. What shall we first seek here? The means of egress employed by the murderers. It is not too much to say that neither of us believe in preternatural events. Madame and Mademoiselle L'Espanaye were not destroyed by spirits. The doers of the deed were material and escaped materially. Then how? Fortunately, there is but one mode of reasoning upon the point, and that mode *must* lead us to a definite decision. Let us examine, each by each, the possible means of egress. It is clear that the assassins were in the room where Mademoiselle L'Espanaye was found, or at least in the room adjoining, when the party ascended the stairs. It is, then, only from these two apartments that we have to seek issues. The police have laid bare the floors, the ceiling, and the masonry of the walls, in every direction. No *secret* issues could have escaped their vigilance. But, not trusting to *their* eyes, I examined with my own. There were, then, *no* secret issues. Both doors leading from the rooms into the passage were securely locked, with the keys inside. Let us turn to the chimneys. These, although of ordinary width for some eight or ten feet above the hearths, will not admit, throughout their extent, the body of a large cat. The impossibility of egress, by means already stated, being thus absolute, we are reduced to the windows. Through those of the front room no one could have escaped without notice from the crowd in the street. The murderers *must* have passed, then, through those of the back room. Now, brought to this conclusion in so unequivocal a manner as we are, it is not our part, as reasoners, to reject it on account of apparent impossibilities. It is only left for us to prove that these apparent 'impossibilities' are, in reality, not such.

"There are two windows in the chamber. One of them is unobstructed by furniture, and is wholly visible. The lower portion of the other is hidden from view by the head of the unwieldy bedstead which is thrust close up against it. The former was found securely fastened from within. It resisted the utmost force of those who endeavored to raise it. A large gimlet-hole had been pierced in its frame to the left, and a very stout nail was found fitted therein, nearly to the head. Upon examining the other window, a similar nail was seen similarly fitted in it; and a vigorous attempt to raise this sash failed also. The police were now entirely satisfied that egress had not been in these directions. And, *therefore,* it was thought a matter of supererogation to withdraw the nails and open the windows.

"My own examination was somewhat more particular, and was so for the reason I have just given — because here it was, I knew, that all apparent impossibilities must be proved to be not such in reality.

"I proceeded to think thus — *à posteriori.* The murderers *did* escape from one of these windows. This being so, they could not have refastened the sashes from the inside, as they were found fastened; — the consideration which put a stop, through its obviousness, to the scrutiny of the police in this quarter. Yet the sashes *were* fastened. They *must,* then, have the power of fastening themselves. There was no escape from this conclusion. I stepped to the unobstructed casement, withdrew the nail with some difficulty, and attempted to raise the sash. It resisted all my efforts, as I had anticipated. A concealed spring must, I now knew, exist; and this corroboration of my idea convinced me that my premises, at least, were correct, however mysterious still appeared the circumstances attending the nails. A careful search soon brought to light the hidden spring. I pressed it, and, satisfied with the discovery, forbore to upraise the sash.

"I now replaced the nail and regarded it attentively. A person passing out through this window might have reclosed it, and the spring would have caught — but the nail could not have been replaced. The conclusion was plain, and again narrowed in the field of my investigations. The assassins *must* have escaped through the other window. Supposing, then, the springs upon each sash to be the same, as was probable, there *must* be found a difference between the nails, or at least between the modes of their fixture. Getting upon the sacking of the bedstead, I looked over the head-board minutely at the second casement. Passing my hand down behind the board, I readily discovered and pressed the spring, which was, as I had supposed, identical in character with its neighbor. I now looked at the nail. It was as stout as the other, and apparently fitted in the same manner — driven in nearly up to the head.

"You will say that I was puzzled; but, if you think so, you must have misunderstood the nature of the inductions. To use a sporting phrase, I had not been once 'at fault.' The scent had never for an instant been lost. There was no flaw in any link in the chain. I had traced the secret to its ultimate result, — and that result was *the nail.* It had, I say, in every respect, the appearance of its fellow in the other window; but this fact was an absolute nullity (conclusive as it might seem to be) when compared with the consideration that here, at this point, terminated the clew. 'There *must* be something wrong,' I said, 'about the nail.' I touched it; and the head, with about a quarter of an inch of the shank, came off in my fingers. The rest of the shank was in the gimlet-hole, where it had been broken off. The fracture was an old one (for its edges were incrusted with rust), and had apparently been accomplished by the blow of a hammer, which had partially imbedded, in the top of the bottom sash, the head portion of the nail. I now carefully replaced this head portion in the indentation whence I had taken it, and the resemblance to a perfect nail was complete — the fissure was invisible. Pressing the spring, I gently raised the sash for a few inches; the head went up with it, remaining firm in its bed. I closed the window, and the semblance of the whole nail was again perfect.

"This riddle, so far, was now unriddled. The assassin had escaped through the window which looked upon the bed. Dropping of its own accord upon his exit (or perhaps purposely closed), it had become fastened by the spring; and it was the retention of this spring which had been mistaken by the police for that of the nail, — farther inquiry being thus considered unnecessary.

"The next question is that of the mode of descent. Upon this point I had been satisfied in my walk with you around the building. About five feet and a half from the casement in question there runs a lightning-rod. From this rod it would have been impossible for any one to reach to the window itself, to say nothing of entering it. I observed, however, that the shutters of the fourth story were of the peculiar kind called by Parisian carpenters *ferrades* — a kind rarely employed at the present day, but frequently seen upon very old mansions at Lyons and Bordeaux. They are in the form of an ordinary door (a single, not a folding door), except that the lower half is latticed or worked in open trellis — thus affording an excellent hold for the hands. In the present instance these shutters are fully three feet and a half broad. When we saw them from the rear of the house, they were both about half open — that is to say, they stood off at right angles from the wall. It is probable that the police, as well as myself, examined the back of the tenement; but, if so, in looking at these *ferrades* in the line of their breadth (as they must have done), they did not perceive this great breadth itself, or, at all events, failed to take it into due consideration. In fact, having once satisfied themselves that no egress could have been made in this quarter, they would naturally bestow here a very cursory examination. It was clear to me, however, that the shutter belonging to the window at the head of the bed, would, if swung fully back to the wall, reach to within two feet of the lightning-rod. It was also evident that, by exertion of a very unusual degree of activity and courage, an entrance into the window, from the rod, might have been thus effected. By reaching to the distance of two feet and a half (we now suppose the shutter open to its whole extent) a robber might have taken a firm grasp upon the trellis-work. Letting go, then, his hold upon the rod, placing his feet securely against the wall, and springing boldly from it, he might have swung the shutter so as to close it, and, if we imagine the window open at the time, might even have swung himself into the room.

"I wish you to bear especially in mind that I have spoken of a very unusual degree of activity as requisite to success in so hazardous and so difficult a feat. It is my design to show you, first, that the thing might possibly have been accomplished: — but, secondly and *chiefly,* I wish to impress upon your understanding the *very extraordinary* — the almost prӕternatural character of that agility which could have accomplished it.

"You will say, no doubt, using the language of the law, that to make out my case, I should rather undervalue than insist upon a full estimation of the activity required in this matter. This may be the practice in law, but it is not the usage of reason. My ultimate object is only the truth. My immediate purpose is to lead you to place in juxtaposition, that *very unusual* activity of which I have just spoken, with that *very peculiar* shrill (or harsh) and *unequal* voice, about whose nationality no two persons could be found to agree, and in whose utterance no syllabification could be detected."

At these words a vague and half-formed conception of the meaning of Dupin flitted over my mind. I seemed to be upon the verge of comprehension, without power to comprehend — as men, at times, find themselves upon the brink of remembrance, without being able, in the end, to remember. My friend went on with his discourse.

"You will see," he said, "that I have shifted the question from the mode of egress to that of ingress. It was my design to convey the idea that both were effected in the same manner, at the same point. Let us now revert to the interior of the room. Let us survey the appearances here. The drawers of the bureau, it is said, had been rifled, although many articles of apparel still remained within them. The conclusion here is absurd. It is a mere guess — a very silly one — and no more. How are we to know that the articles found in the drawers were not all these drawers had originally contained? Madame L'Espanaye and her daughter lived an exceedingly retired life—saw no company—seldom went out—had little use for the numerous changes of habiliment. Those found were at least of as good quality as any likely to be possessed by these ladies. If a thief had taken any, why did he not take the best—why did he not take all? In a word, why did he abandon four thousand francs in gold to encumber himself with a bundle of linen? The gold *was* abandoned. Nearly the whole sum mentioned by Monsieur Mignaud, the banker, was discovered, in bags, upon the floor. I wish you, therefore, to discard from your thoughts the blundering idea of *motive,* engendered in the brains of the police by that portion of the evidence which speaks of money delivered at the door of the house. Coincidences ten times as remarkable as this (the delivery of the money, and murder committed within three days upon the party receiving it), happen to all of us every hour of our lives, without attracting even momentary notice. Coincidences, in general, are great stumbling-blocks in the way of that class of thinkers who have been educated to know nothing of the theory of probabilities—that theory to which the most glorious objects of human research are indebted for the most glorious of illustration. In the present instance, had the gold been gone, the fact of its delivery three days before would have formed something more than a coincidence. It would have been corroborative of this idea of motive. But, under the real circumstances of the case, if we are to suppose gold the motive of this outrage, we must also imagine the perpetrator so vacillating an idiot as to have abandoned his gold and his motive altogether.

"Keeping now steadily in mind the points to which I have drawn your attention—that peculiar voice, that unusual agility, and that startling absence of motive in a murder so singularly atrocious as this—let us glance at the butchery itself. Here is a woman strangled to death by manual strength, and thrust up a chimney, head downward. Ordinary assassins employ no such mode of murder as this. Least of all, do they thus dispose of the murdered. In this manner of thrusting the corpse up the chimney, you will admit that there was something *excessively outré*—something altogether irreconcilable with our common notions of human action, even when we suppose the actors the most depraved of men. Think, too, how great must have been that strength which could have thrust the body *up* such an aperture so forcibly that the united vigor of several persons was found barely sufficient to drag it *down!*

"Turn, now, to other indications of the employment of a vigor most marvellous. On the hearth were thick tresses—very thick tresses—of gray human hair. These had been torn out by the roots. You are aware of the great force necessary in tearing thus from the head even twenty or thirty hairs together. You saw the locks in question as well as myself. Their roots (a hideous sight!) were clotted with fragments of the flesh of the scalp — sure tokens of the prodigious power which had been exerted in uprooting perhaps half a million of hairs at a time. The throat of the old lady was not merely cut, but the head absolutely severed from the body: the instrument was a mere razor. I wish you also to look at the *brutal* ferocity of these deeds. Of the bruises upon the body of Madame L'Espanaye I do not speak. Monsieur Dumas, and his worthy coadjutor Monsieur Etienne, have pronounced that they were inflicted by some obtuse instrument; and so far these gentlemen are very correct. The obtuse instrument was clearly the stone pavement in the yard, upon which the victim had fallen from the window which looked in upon the bed. This idea, however simple it may now seem, escaped the police for the same reason that the breadth of the shutters escaped them — because, by the affair of the nails, their perceptions had been hermetically sealed against the possibility of the windows having ever been opened at all.

"If now, in addition to all these things, you have properly reflected upon the odd disorder of the chamber, we have gone so far as to combine the ideas of an agility astounding, a strength superhuman, a ferocity brutal, a butchery without motive, a *grotesquerie* in horror absolutely alien from humanity, and a voice foreign in tone to the ears of men of many nations, and devoid of all distinct or intelligible syllabification. What result, then, has ensued? What impression have I made upon your fancy?"

I felt a creeping of the flesh as Dupin asked me the question. "A madman," I said, "has done this deed — some raving maniac, escaped from a neighboring *Maison de Santé.*"

"In some respects," he replied, "your idea is not irrelevant. But the voices of madmen, even in their wildest paroxysms, are never found to tally with that peculiar voice heard upon the stairs. Madmen are of some nation, and their language, however incoherent in its words, has always the coherence of syllabification. Besides, the hair of a madman is not such as I now hold in my hand. I disentangled this little tuft from the rigidly clutched fingers of Madame L'Espanaye. Tell me what you can make of it."

"Dupin!" I said, completely unnerved; "this hair is most unusual — this is no *human* hair."

"I have not asserted that it is," said he; "but, before we decide this point, I wish you to glance at the little sketch I have here traced upon this paper. It is a *facsimile* drawing of what has been described in one portion of the testimony as 'dark bruises and deep indentations of finger nails' upon the throat of Mademoiselle L'Espanaye, and in another (by Messrs. Dumas and Etienne) as a 'series of livid spots, evidently the impression of fingers.'

"You will perceive," continued my friend, spreading out the paper upon the table before us, "that this drawing gives the idea of a firm and fixed hold. There is no *slipping* apparent. Each finger has retained —possibly until the death of the victim—the fearful grasp by which it originally imbedded itself. Attempt, now, to place all your fingers, at the same time, in the respective impressions as you see them."

I made the attempt in vain.

"We are possibly not giving this matter a fair trial," he said. "The paper is spread out upon a plane surface; but the human throat is cylindrical. Here is a billet of wood, the circumference of which is about that of the throat. Wrap the drawing around it, and try the experiment again."

I did so; but the difficulty was even more obvious than before. "This," I said, "is the mark of no human hand."

"Read now," replied Dupin, "this passage from Cuvier."

It was a minute anatomical and generally descriptive account of the large fulvous Ourang-Outang of the East Indian Islands. The gigantic stature, the prodigious strength and activity, the wild ferocity, and the imitative propensities of these mammalia are sufficiently well known to all. I understood the full horrors of the murder at once.

"The description of the digits," said I, as I made an end of the reading, "is in exact accordance with this drawing. I see no animal but an Ourang-Outang, of the species here mentioned, could have impressed the indentations as you have traced them. This tuft of tawny hair, too, is identical in character with that of the beast of Cuvier. But I cannot possibly comprehend the particulars of this frightful mystery. Besides, there were *two* voices heard in contention, and one of them was unquestionably the voice of a Frenchman."

"True; and you will remember an expression attributed almost unanimously, by the evidence, to this voice,—the expression, '*mon Dieu!*' This, under the circumstances, has been justly characterized by one of the witnesses (Montani, the confectioner) as an expression of remonstrance or expostulation. Upon these two words, therefore, I have mainly built my hopes of a full solution of the riddle. A Frenchman was cognizant of the murder. It is possible—indeed it is far more than probable — that he was innocent of all participation in the bloody transactions which took place. The Ourang-Outang may have escaped from him. He may have traced it to the chamber; but, under the agitating circumstances which ensued, he could never have recaptured it. It is still at large. I will not pursue these guesses — for I have no right to call them more — since the shades of reflection upon which they are based are scarcely of sufficient depth to be appreciated by my own intellect, and since I could not pretend to make them intelligible to the understanding of another. We will call them guesses, then, and speak of them as such. If the Frenchman in question is indeed, as I suppose, innocent of this atrocity, this advertisement, which I left last might, upon our return home, at the office of 'Le Monde' (a paper devoted to the shipping interest, and much sought by sailors), will bring him to our residence."

He handed me a paper, and I read thus:

> CAUGHT — In the Bois de Boulogne, early in the morning of the —— inst. (the morning of the murder), a very large, tawny Ourang-Outang of the Bornese species. The owner (who is ascertained to be a sailor, belonging to a Maltese vessel) may have the animal again, upon identifying it satisfactorily, and paying a few charges arising from its capture and keeping. Call at No. —— Rue ——, Faubourg St. Germain — au troisiême.

"How was it possible," I asked, "that you should know the man to be a sailor, and belonging to a Maltese vessel?"

"I do *not* know it," said Dupin. "I am not *sure* of it. Here, however, is a small piece of ribbon, which from its form, and from its greasy appearance, has evidently been used in tying the hair in one of those long *queues* of which sailors are so fond. Moreover, this knot is one which few besides sailors can tie, and is peculiar to the Maltese. I picked the ribbon up at the foot of the lightning-rod. It could not have belonged to either of the deceased. Now if, after all, I am wrong in my induction from this ribbon, that the Frenchman was a sailor belonging to a Maltese vessel, still I can have done no harm in saying what I did in the advertisement. If I am in error, he will merely suppose that I had been misled by some circumstance into which he will not take the trouble to inquire. But if I am right, a great point is gained. Cognizant although innocent of the murder, the Frenchman will naturally hesitate about replying to the advertisement — about demanding the Ourang-Outang. He will reason thus: — 'I am innocent; I am poor; my Ourang-Outang is of great value — to one in my circumstances a fortune of itself — why should I lose it through idle apprehensions of danger? Here it is, within my grasp. It was found in the Bois de Boulogne—at a vast distance from the scene of that butchery. How can it ever be suspected that a brute beast should have done the deed? The police are at fault—they have failed to procure the slightest clew. Should they even trace the animal, it would be impossible to prove me cognizant of the murder, or to implicate me in guilt on account of that cognizance. Above all, *I am known.* The advertiser designates me as the possessor of the beast. I am not sure to what limit his knowledge may extend. Should I avoid claiming a property of so great value, which it is known that I possess, I will render the animal at least, liable to suspicion. It is not my policy to attract attention either to myself or to the beast. I will answer the advertisement, get the Ourang-Outang, and keep it close until this matter has blown over.'"

At this moment we heard a step upon the stairs.

"Be ready," said Dupin, "with your pistols, but neither use them nor show them until at a signal from myself."

"The front door of the house had been left open, and the visitor had entered, without ringing, and advanced several steps upon the staircase. Now, however, he seemed to hesitate. Presently we heard him descending. Dupin was moving quickly to the door, when we again heard him coming up. He did not turn back a second time, but stepped up with decision, and rapped at the door of our chamber.

"Come in," said Dupin, in a cheerful and hearty tone.

A man entered. He was a sailor, evidently,—a tall, stout, and muscular-looking person, with a certain dare-devil expression of countenance, not altogether unprepossessing. His face, greatly sunburnt, was more than half hidden by whisker and *mustachio.* He had with him a huge oaken cudgel, but appeared to be otherwise unarmed. He bowed awkwardly, and bade us "good evening," in French accents, which, although somewhat Neufchatelish, were still sufficiently indicative of a Parisian origin.

"Sit down, my friend," said Dupin. "I suppose you have called about the Ourang-Outang. Upon my word, I almost envy you the possession of him; a remarkably fine, and no doubt very valuable animal. How old do you suppose him to be?"

The sailor drew a long breath, with the air of a man relieved of some intolerable burden, and then replied in an assured tone:

"I have no way of telling—but he can't be more than four or five years old. Have you got him here?"

"Oh, no; we had no conveniences for keeping him here. He is at a livery stable in the Rue Dubourg, just by. You can get him in the morning. Of course you are prepared to identify the property?"

"To be sure I am, sir."

"I shall be sorry to part with him," said Dupin.

"I don't mean that you should be at all this trouble for nothing, sir," said the man. "Couldn't expect it. Am very willing to pay a reward for the finding of the animal — that is to say, any thing in reason."

"Well," replied my friend, "that is all very fair, to be sure. Let me think! — what should I have? Oh! I will tell you. My reward shall be this. You shall give me all the information in your power about these murders in the Rue Morgue."

Dupin said the last words in a very low tone, and very quietly. Just as quietly, too, he walked toward the door, locked it, and put the key in his pocket. He then drew a pistol from his bosom and placed it, without the least flurry, upon the table.

The sailor's face flushed up as if he were struggling with suffocation. He started to his feet and grasped his cudgel; but the next moment he fell back into his seat, trembling violently, and with the countenance of death itself. He spoke not a word. I pitied him from the bottom of my heart.

"My friend," said Dupin, in a kind tone, "you are alarming yourself unnecessarily — you are indeed. We mean you no harm whatever. I pledge you the honor of a gentleman, and of a Frenchman, that we intend you no injury. I perfectly well know that you are innocent of the atrocities in the Rue Morgue. It will not do, however, to deny that you are in some measure implicated in them. From what I have already said, you must know that I have had means of information about this matter — means of which you could never have dreamed. Now the thing stands thus. You have done nothing which you could have avoided — nothing, certainly, which renders you culpable. You were not even guilty of robbery, when you might have robbed with impunity. You have nothing to conceal. You have no reason for concealment. On the other hand, you are bound by every principle of honor to confess all you know. An innocent man is now imprisoned, charged with a crime of which you can point out the perpetrator."

The sailor had recovered his presence of mind, in a great measure, while Dupin uttered these words; but his original boldness of bearing was all gone.

"So help me God!" said he, after a brief pause, "I *will* tell you all I know about this affair;—but I do not expect you to believe one half I say—I would be a fool indeed if I did. Still, I am innocent, and I will make a clean breast if I die for it."

What he stated was, in substance, this. He had lately made a voyage to the Indian Archipelago. A party, of which he formed one, landed at Borneo, and passed into the interior on an excursion of pleasure. Himself and a companion had captured the Ourang-Outang. This companion dying, the animal fell into his own exclusive possession. After great trouble, occasioned by the intractable ferocity of his captive during the home voyage, he at length succeeded in lodging it safely at his own residence in Paris, where, not to attract toward himself the unpleasant curiosity of his neighbors, he kept it carefully secluded, until such time as it should recover from a wound in the foot, received from a splinter on board ship. His ultimate design was to sell it.

Returning home from some sailors' frolic on the night, or rather in the morning, of the murder, he found the beast occupying his own bedroom, into which it had broken from a closet adjoining, where it had been, as was thought, securely confined. Razor in hand, and fully lathered, it was sitting before a looking-glass, attempting the operation of shaving, in which it had no doubt previously watched its master through the keyhole of the closet. Terrified at the sight of so dangerous a weapon in the possession of an animal so ferocious, and so well able to use it, the man, for some moments, was at a loss what to do. He had been accustomed, however, to quiet the creature, even in its fiercest moods, by the use of a whip, and to this he now resorted. Upon sight of it, the Ourang-Outang sprang at once through the door of the chamber, down the stairs, and thence, through a window, unfortunately open, into the street.

The Frenchman followed in despair; the ape, razor still in hand, occasionally stopping to look back and gesticulate at his pursuer, until the latter had nearly come up with it. It then again made off. In this manner the chase continued for a long time. The streets were profoundly quiet, as it was nearly three o'clock in the morning. In passing down an alley in the rear of the Rue Morgue, the fugitive's attention was arrested by a light gleaming from the open window of Madame L'Espanaye's chamber, in the fourth story of her house. Rushing to the building, it perceived the lightning-rod, clambered up with inconceivable agility, grasped the shutter, which was thrown fully back against the wall, and, by its means, swung itself directly upon the headboard of the bed. The whole feat did not occupy a minute. The shutter was kicked open again by the Ourang-Outang as it entered the room.

The sailor, in the meantime, was both rejoiced and perplexed. He had strong hopes of now recapturing the brute, as it could scarcely escape from the trap into which it had ventured, except by the rod, where it might be intercepted as it came down. On the other hand, there was much cause for anxiety as to what it might do in the house. This latter reflection urged the man still to follow the fugitive. A lightning-rod is ascended without difficulty, especially by a sailor; but when he had arrived as high as the window, which lay far to his left, his career was stopped; the most that he could accomplish was to reach over so as to obtain a glimpse of the interior of the room. At this glimpse he nearly fell from his hold through excess of horror. Now it was that those hideous shrieks arose upon the night, which had startled from slumber the inmates of the Rue Morgue. Madame L'Espanaye and her daughter, habited in their night clothes, had apparently been occupied in arranging some papers in the iron chest already mentioned, which had been wheeled into the middle of the room. It was open, and its contents lay beside it on the floor. The victims must have been sitting with their backs toward the window, and, from the time elapsing between the ingress of the beast and the screams, it seem probable that it was not immediately perceived. The flapping-to of the shutter would naturally have been attributed to the wind.

As the sailor looked in, the gigantic animal had seized Madame L'Espanaye by the hair (which was loose, as she had been combing it), and was flourishing the razor about her face, in imitation of the motions of a barber. The daughter lay prostrate and motionless; she had swooned. The screams and struggles of the old lady (during which the hair was torn from her head) had the effect of changing the probably pacific purposes of the Ourang-Outang into those of wrath. With one determined sweep of its muscular arm it nearly severed her head from her body. The sight of blood inflamed its anger into phrensy. Gnashing its teeth, and flashing fire from its eyes, it flew upon the body of the girl, and imbedded its fearful talons in her throat, retaining its grasp until she expired. Its wandering and wild glances fell at this moment upon the head of the bed, over which the face of its master, rigid with horror, was just discernible.

The fury of the beast, who no doubt bore still in mind the dreaded whip, was instantly converted into fear. Conscious of having deserved punishment, it seemed desirous of concealing its bloody deeds, and skipped about the chamber in an agony of nervous agitation; throwing down and breaking the furniture as it moved, and dragging the bed from the bedstead. In conclusion, it seized first the corpse of the daughter, and thrust it up the chimney, as it was found; then that of the old lady, which it immediately hurled through the window headlong.

As the ape approached the casement with its mutilated burden, the sailor shrank aghast to the rod, and, rather gliding than clambering down it, hurried at once home—dreading the consequences of the butchery, and gladly abandoning, in his terror, all solicitude about the fate of the Ourang-Outang. The words heard by the party upon the staircase were the Frenchman's exclamations of horror and affright, commingled with the fiendish jabberings of the brute.

I have scarcely any thing to add. The Ourang-Outang must have escaped from the chamber, by the rod, just before the breaking of the door. It must have closed the window as it passed through it. It was subsequently caught by the owner himself, who obtained for it a very large sum at the *Jardin des Plantes.* Le Bon was instantly released, upon our narration of the circumstances (with some comments from Dupin) at the *bureau* of the Prefect of Police. This functionary, however well disposed to my friend, could not altogether conceal his chagrin at the turn which affairs had taken, and was fain to indulge in a sarcasm or two, about the propriety of every person minding his own business.

"Let him talk," said Dupin, who had not thought it necessary to reply. "Let him discourse; it will ease his conscience. I am satisfied with having defeated him in his own castle. Nevertheless, that he failed in the solution of this mystery, is by no means that matter for wonder which he supposes it; for, in truth, our friend the Prefect is somewhat too cunning to be profound. In his wisdom is no *stamen.* It is all head and no body, like the pictures of the Goddess Laverna—or, at best, all head and shoulders, like a codfish. But he is a good creature after all. I like him especially for one master stroke of cant, by which he has attained his reputation for ingenuity. I mean the way he has *'de nier ce qui est, et d'expliquer ce qui n'est pas.'"* [Rousseau—Nouvelle Heloise.]

1845

EDGAR ALLAN POE

THE PURLOINED LETTER

"The Murders in the Rue Morgue" was the first pure detective story, with which Edgar Allan Poe (1809–1849), although he didn't know it at the time, opened the door to the most important literary genre of the ensuing two centuries. His mystery masterpiece, however, was "The Purloined Letter." While his first story was rather melodramatic and his second broke ground as the first story to feature an armchair detective, when C. Auguste Dupin solved the crime merely by the use of ratiocination, his third combined the strength of both previous tales. It remains one of the handful of classic detective stories that can be used to illustrate the qualities of the perfect tale.

Edgar Poe was born in Boston and orphaned at the age of two, when both his parents died of tuberculosis in 1811. He was taken in by a wealthy merchant, John Allan, and his wife; although never legally adopted, Poe nonetheless took Allan for his name. He received a classical education in England from 1815 to 1820. After returning to the United States, he published his first book, *Tamerlane and Other Poems* (1827). It and his next two volumes of poetry were financial disasters.

He won a prize for "Ms. Found in a Bottle" and began a series of jobs as editor and critic of several periodicals, and while he dramatically increased their circulations, his alcoholism (or, at any rate, perceived alcoholism, as it is theorized today that Poe reacted powerfully to even a single glass of wine), strong views, and arrogance enraged his bosses, costing him one job after another. He married his thirteen-year-old cousin, Virginia, and lived in abject poverty for many years with her and her mother (who certain scholars believe Poe viewed with greater affection than he did her daughter). Lack of money undoubtedly contributed to the death at twenty-four of Poe's wife.

Influenced by the English Romantic poets, Poe was unrivaled by his contemporaries. The most brilliant literary critic of his time, the influential magazine editor, the master of horror stories, the poet whose work remains familiar and beloved to the present day, and the inventor of the detective story died a pauper.

"The Purloined Letter" was first published in *The Gift: A Christmas, New*

Year, and Birthday Present (Philadelphia: Carey and Hart, 1845); it was first published in book form in *Tales* (New York: Wiley and Putnam, 1845).

• • •

Nil sapientiæ odiosius acumine nimio.

—*Seneca*

At Paris, just after dark one gusty evening in the autumn of 18—, I was enjoying the twofold luxury of meditation and a meerschaum, in company with my friend C. Auguste Dupin, in his little back library, or book-closet, *au troisiême, No. 33, Rue Dunôt, Faubourg St. Germain.* For one hour at least we had maintained a profound silence; while each, to any casual observer, might have seemed intently and exclusively occupied with the curling eddies of smoke that oppressed the atmosphere of the chamber. For myself, however, I was mentally discussing certain topics which had formed matter for conversation between us at an earlier period of the evening; I mean the affair of the Rue Morgue, and the mystery attending the murder of Marie Rogêt. I looked upon it, therefore, as something of a coincidence, when the door of our apartment was thrown open and admitted our old acquaintance, Monsieur G——, the Prefect of the Parisian police.

We gave him a hearty welcome; for there was nearly half as much of the entertaining as of the contemptible about the man, and we had not seen him for several years. We had been sitting in the dark, and Dupin now arose for the purpose of lighting a lamp, but sat down again, without doing so, upon G.'s saying that he had called to consult us, or rather to ask the opinion of my friend, about some official business which had occasioned a great deal of trouble.

"If it is any point requiring reflection," observed Dupin, as he forbore to enkindle the wick, "we shall examine it to better purpose in the dark."

"That is another of your odd notions," said the Prefect, who had a fashion of calling everything "odd" that was beyond his comprehension, and thus lived amid an absolute legion of "oddities."

"Very true," said Dupin, as he supplied his visitor with a pipe, and rolled towards him a comfortable chair.

"And what is the difficulty now?" I asked. "Nothing more in the assassination way, I hope?"

"Oh no; nothing of that nature. The fact is, the business is very simple indeed, and I make no doubt that we can manage it sufficiently well ourselves; but then I thought Dupin would like to hear the details of it, because it is so excessively *odd*."

"Simple and odd," said Dupin.

"Why, yes; and not exactly that, either. The fact is, we have all been a good deal puzzled because the affair *is* so simple, and yet baffles us altogether."

"Perhaps it is the very simplicity of the thing which puts you at fault," said my friend.

"What nonsense you *do* talk!" replied the Prefect, laughing heartily.

"Perhaps the mystery is a little *too* plain," said Dupin.

"Oh, good heavens! who ever heard of such an idea?"

"A little *too* self-evident."

"Ha! ha! ha!—ha! ha! ha!—ho! ho! ho!" roared our visitor, profoundly amused, "oh, Dupin, you will be the death of me yet!"

"And what, after all, *is* the matter on hand?" I asked.

"Why, I will tell you," replied the Prefect, as he gave a long, steady, and contemplative puff, and settled himself in his chair. "I will tell you in a few words; but, before I begin, let me caution you that this is an affair demanding the greatest secrecy, and that I should most probably lose the position I now hold, were it known that I confided it to anyone."

"Proceed," said I.

"Or not," said Dupin.

"Well, then; I have received personal information, from a very high quarter, that a certain document of the last importance, has been purloined from the royal apartments. The individual who purloined it is known; this beyond a doubt; he was seen to take it. It is known, also, that it still remains in his possession."

"How is this known?" asked Dupin.

"It is clearly inferred," replied the Prefect, "from the nature of the document, and from the nonappearance of certain results which would at once arise from its passing *out* of the robber's possession;—that is to say, from his employing it as he must design in the end to employ it."

"Be a little more explicit," I said.

"Well, I may venture so far as to say that the paper gives its holder a certain power in a certain quarter where such power is immensely valuable." The Prefect was fond of the cant of diplomacy.

"Still I do not quite understand," said Dupin.

"No? Well; the disclosure of the document to a third person, who shall be nameless, would bring in question the honor of a personage of most exalted station; and this fact gives the holder of the document an ascendancy over the illustrious personage whose honor and peace are so jeopardized."

"But this ascendancy," I interposed, "would depend upon the robber's knowledge of the loser's knowledge of the robber. Who would dare—"

"The thief," said G., "is the Minister D——, who dares all things, those unbecoming as well as those becoming a man. The method of the theft was not less ingenious than bold. The document in question—a letter, to be frank—had been received by the personage robbed while alone in the royal *boudoir.* During its perusal she was suddenly interrupted by the entrance of the other exalted personage from whom especially it was her wish to conceal it. After a hurried and vain endeavor to thrust it in a drawer, she was forced to place it, open as it was, upon a table. The address, however, was uppermost, and, the contents thus unexposed, the letter escaped notice. At this juncture enters the Minister D——. His lynx eye immediately perceives the paper, recognizes the handwriting of the address, observes the confusion of the personage addressed, and fathoms her secret. After some business transactions, hurried through in his ordinary manner, he produces a letter somewhat similar to the one in question, opens it, pretends to read it, and then places it in close juxtaposition to the other. Again he converses, for some fifteen minutes, upon the public affairs. At length, in taking leave, he takes also from the table the letter to which he had no claim. Its rightful owner saw, but, of course, dared not call attention to the act, in the presence of the third personage who stood at her elbow. The minister decamped; leaving his own letter—one of no importance—upon the table."

"Here, then," said Dupin to me, "you have precisely what you demand to make the ascendancy complete—the robber's knowledge of the loser's knowledge of the robber."

"Yes," replied the Prefect; "and the power thus attained has, for some months past, been wielded, for political purposes, to a very dangerous extent. The personage robbed is more thoroughly convinced, every day, of the necessity of reclaiming her letter. But this, of course, cannot be done openly. In fine, driven to despair, she has committed the matter to me."

"Than whom," said Dupin, amid a perfect whirlwind of smoke, "no more sagacious agent could, I suppose, be desired, or even imagined."

"You flatter me," replied the Prefect; "but it is possible that some such opinion may have been entertained."

"It is clear," said I, "as you observe, that the letter is still in possession of the minister; since it is this possession, and not any employment of the letter, which bestows the power. With the employment the power departs."

"True," said G.; "and upon this conviction I proceeded. My first care was to make thorough search of the minister's hotel; and here my chief embarrassment lay in the necessity of searching without his knowledge. Beyond all things, I have been warned of the danger which would result from giving him reason to suspect our design."

"But," said I, "you are quite *au fait* in these investigations. The Parisian police have done this thing often before."

"Oh yes; and for this reason I did not despair. The habits of the minister gave me, too, a great advantage. He is frequently absent from home all night. His servants are by no means numerous. They sleep at a distance from their master's apartment, and, being chiefly Neapolitans, are readily made drunk. I have keys, as you know, with which I can open any chamber or cabinet in Paris. For three months a night has not passed, during the greater part of which I have not been engaged, personally, in ransacking the D—— Hotel. My honor is interested, and, to mention a great secret, the reward is enormous. So I did not abandon the search until I had become fully satisfied that the thief is a more astute man than myself. I fancy that I have investigated every nook and corner of the premises in which it is possible that the paper can be concealed."

"But is it not possible," I suggested, "that although the letter may be in possession of the minister, as it unquestionably is, he may have concealed it elsewhere than upon his own premises?"

"This is barely possible," said Dupin. "The present peculiar condition of affairs at court, and especially of those intrigues in which D—— is known to be involved, would render the instant availability of the document—its susceptibility of being produced at a moment's notice—a point of nearly equal importance with its possession."

"Its susceptibility of being produced?" said I.

"That is to say, of being *destroyed,*" said Dupin.

"True," I observed; "the paper is clearly then upon the premises. As for its being upon the person of the minister, we may consider that as out of the question."

"Entirely," said the Prefect. "He has been twice waylaid, as if by footpads, and his person rigorously searched under my own inspection."

"You might have spared yourself this trouble," said Dupin. "D——, I presume, is not altogether a fool, and, if not, must have anticipated these waylayings, as a matter of course."

"Not *altogether* a fool," said G., "but then he's a poet, which I take to be only one remove from a fool."

"True," said Dupin, after a long and thoughtful whiff from his meerschaum, "although I have been guilty of certain doggerel myself."

"Suppose you detail," said I, "the particulars of your search."

"Why the fact is, we took our time, and we searched *everywhere.* I have had long experience in these affairs. I took the entire building, room by room; devoting the nights of a whole week to each. We examined, first, the furniture of each apartment. We opened every possible drawer; and I presume you know that, to a properly trained police agent, such a thing as a *secret* drawer is impossible. Any man is a dolt who permits a 'secret' drawer to escape him in a search of this kind. The thing is *so* plain. There is a certain amount of bulk — of space — to be accounted for in every cabinet. Then we have accurate rules. The fiftieth part of a line could not escape us. After the cabinets we took the chairs. The cushions we probed with the fine long needles you have seen me employ. From the tables we removed the tops."

"Why so?"

"Sometimes the top of a table, or other similarly arranged piece of furniture, is removed by the person wishing to conceal an article; then the leg is excavated, the article deposited within the cavity, and the top replaced. The bottoms and tops of bedposts are employed in the same way."

"But could not the cavity be detected by sounding?" I asked.

"By no means, if, when the article is deposited, a sufficient wadding of cotton be placed around it. Besides, in our case, we were obliged to proceed without noise."

"But you could not have removed — you could not have taken to pieces *all* articles of furniture in which it would have been possible to make a deposit in the manner you mention. A letter may be compressed into a thin spiral roll, not differing much in shape or bulk from a large knitting-needle, and in this form it might be inserted into the rung of a chair, for example. You did not take to pieces all the chairs?"

"Certainly not; but we did better — we examined the rungs of every chair in the hotel, and, indeed, the jointings of every description of furniture, by the aid of a most powerful microscope. Had there been any traces of recent disturbance we should not have failed to detect it instantly. A single grain of gimlet-dust, for example, would have been as obvious as an apple. Any disorder in the gluing — any unusual gaping in the joints — would have sufficed to insure detection."

"I presume you looked to the mirrors, between the boards and the plates, and you probed the beds and the bed-clothes, as well as the curtains and carpets."

"That of course; and when we had absolutely completed every particle of the furniture in this way, then we examined the house itself. We divided its entire surface into compartments, which we numbered, so that none might be missed; then we scrutinized each individual square inch throughout the premises, including the two houses immediately adjoining, with the microscope, as before."

"The two houses adjoining!" I exclaimed; "you must have had a great deal of trouble."

"We had; but the reward offered is prodigious."

"You include the *grounds* about the houses?"

"All the grounds are paved with brick. They gave us comparatively little trouble. We examined the moss between the bricks, and found it undisturbed."

"You looked among D——'s papers, of course, and into the books of the library?"

"Certainly; we opened every package and parcel; we not only opened every book, but we turned over every leaf in each volume, not contenting ourselves with a mere shake, according to the fashion of some of our police officers. We also measured the thickness of every book-cover, with the most accurate measurement, and applied to each the most jealous scrutiny of the microscope. Had any of the bindings been recently meddled with, it would have been utterly impossible that the fact should have escaped observation. Some five or six volumes, just from the hands of the binder, we carefully probed, longitudinally, with the needles."

"You explored the floors beneath the carpets?"

"Beyond doubt. We removed every carpet, and examined the boards with the microscope."

"And the paper on the walls?"

"Yes."

"You looked into the cellars?"

"We did."

"Then," I said, "you have been making a miscalculation, and the letter is *not* upon the premises, as you suppose."

"I fear you are right there," said the Prefect. "And now, Dupin, what would you advise me to do?"

"To make a thorough re-search of the premises."

"That is absolutely needless," replied G——. "I am not more sure that I breathe than I am that the letter is not at the hotel."

"I have no better advice to give you," said Dupin. "You have, of course, an accurate description of the letter?"

"Oh yes!" — And here the Prefect, producing a memorandum-book, proceeded to read aloud a minute account of the internal, and especially of the external appearance of the missing document. Soon after finishing the perusal of this description, he took his departure, more entirely depressed in spirits than I had ever known the good gentleman before.

In about a month afterwards he paid us another visit, and found us occupied very nearly as before. He took a pipe and a chair and entered into some ordinary conversation. At length I said, —

"Well, but G——, what of the purloined letter? I presume you have at last made up your mind that there is no such thing as overreaching the Minister?"

"Confound him, say I — yes; I made the reexamination, however, as Dupin suggested — but it was all labor lost, as I knew it would be."

"How much was the reward offered, did you say?" asked Dupin.

"Why, a very great deal — a *very* liberal reward — I don't like to say how much, precisely; but one thing I *will* say, that I wouldn't mind giving my individual check for fifty thousand francs to anyone who could obtain me that letter. The fact is, it is becoming of more and more importance every day; and the reward has been lately doubled. If it were trebled, however, I could do no more than I have done."

"Why, yes," said Dupin, drawlingly, between the whiffs of his meerschaum, "I really — think, G——, you have not exerted yourself — to the utmost in this matter. You might — do a little more, I think, eh?"

"How? — In what way?"

"Why — puff, puff — you might — puff, puff — employ counsel in the matter, eh? — puff, puff, puff. Do you remember the story they tell of Abernethy?"

"No; hang Abernethy!"

"To be sure! hang him and welcome. But, once upon a time, a certain rich miser conceived the design of sponging upon this Abernethy for a medical opinion. Getting up, for this purpose, an ordinary conversation in a private company, he insinuated his case to the physician, as that of an imaginary individual.

" 'We will suppose,' said the miser, 'that his symptoms are such and such; now, doctor, what would *you* have directed him to take?'

" 'Take!' said Abernethy, 'why, take *advice,* to be sure.' "

"But," said the Prefect, a little discomposed, "I am *perfectly* willing to take advice, and to pay for it. I would *really* give fifty thousand francs to anyone who would aid me in the matter."

"In that case," replied Dupin, opening a drawer, and producing a check-book, "you may as well fill me up a check for the amount mentioned. When you have signed it, I will hand you the letter."

I was astounded. The Prefect appeared absolutely thunderstruck. For some minutes he remained speechless and motionless, looking incredulously at my friend with open mouth, and eyes that seemed starting from their sockets; then, apparently recovering himself in some measure, he seized a pen, and after several pauses and vacant stares, finally filled up and signed a check for fifty thousand francs, and handed it across the table to Dupin. The latter examined it carefully and deposited it in his pocket-book; then, unlocking an *escritoire,* took thence a letter and gave it to the Prefect. This functionary grasped it in a perfect agony of joy, opened it with a trembling hand, cast a rapid glance at its contents, and then, scrambling and struggling to the door, rushed at length unceremoniously from the room and from the house, without having uttered a syllable since Dupin had requested him to fill up the check.

When he had gone, my friend entered into some explanations.

"The Parisian police," he said, "are exceedingly able in their way. They are persevering, ingenious, cunning, and thoroughly versed in the knowledge which their duties seem chiefly to demand. Thus, when G—— detailed to us his mode of searching the premises at the Hotel D——, I felt entire confidence in his having made a satisfactory investigation — so far as his labors extended."

"So far as his labors extended?" said I.

"Yes," said Dupin. "The measures adopted were not only the best of their kind, but carried out to absolute perfection. Had the letter been deposited within the range of their search, these fellows would, beyond a question, have found it."

I merely laughed — but he seemed quite serious in all that he said.

"The measures, then," he continued, "were good in their kind, and well executed; their defect lay in their being inapplicable to the case, and to the man. A certain set of highly ingenious resources are, with the Prefect, a sort of Procrustean bed, to which he forcibly adapts his designs. But he perpetually errs by being too deep or too shallow, for the matter in hand; and many a schoolboy is a better reasoner than he. I knew one about eight years of age, whose success at guessing in the game of 'even and odd' attracted universal admiration. This game is simple, and is played with marbles. One player holds in his hand a number of these toys, and demands of another whether that number is even or odd. If the guess is right, the guesser wins one; if wrong, he loses one. The boy to whom I allude won all the marbles of the school. Of course he had some principle of guessing; and this lay in mere observation and measurement of the astuteness of his opponents. For example, an arrant simpleton is his opponent, and, holding up his closed hand, asks, 'are they even or odd?' Our schoolboy replies, 'odd,' and loses; but upon the second trial he wins, for he then says to himself, 'the simpleton had them even upon the first trial, and his amount of cunning is just sufficient to make him have them odd upon the second; I will therefore guess odd';—he guesses odd, and wins. Now, with a simpleton a degree above the first, he would have reasoned thus: 'This fellow finds that in the first instance I guessed odd, and, in the second, he will propose to himself, upon the first impulse, a simple variation from even to odd, as did the first simpleton; but then a second thought will suggest that this is too simple a variation, and finally he will decide upon putting it even as before. I will therefore guess even'—he guesses even, and wins. Now this mode of reasoning in the schoolboy, whom his fellows termed 'lucky,'—what, in its last analysis, is it?"

"It is merely," I said, "an identification of the reasoner's intellect with that of his opponent."

"It is," said Dupin; "and, upon inquiring of the boy by what means he effected the *thorough* identification in which his success consisted, I received answer as follows: 'When I wish to find out how wise, or how stupid, or how good, or how wicked is anyone, or what are his thoughts at the moment, I fashion the expression of my face, as accurately as possible, in accordance with the expression of his, and then wait to see what thoughts or sentiments arise in my mind or heart, as if to match or correspond with the expression.' This response of the schoolboy lies at the bottom of all the spurious profundity which has been attributed to Rochefoucauld, to La Bougive, to Machiavelli, and to Campanella."

"And the identification," I said, "of the reasoner's intellect with that of his opponent, depends, if I understand you aright, upon the accuracy with which the opponent's intellect is admeasured."

"For its practical value it depends upon this," replied Dupin; "and the Prefect and his cohort fail so frequently, first, by default of this identification, and, secondly, by ill-admeasurement, or rather through non-admeasurement, of the intellect with which they are engaged. They consider only their *own* ideas of ingenuity; and, in searching for anything hidden, advert only to the modes in which *they* would have hidden it. They are right in this much — that their own ingenuity is a faithful representative of that of *the mass;* but when the cunning of the individual felon is diverse in character from their own, the felon foils them, of course. This always happens when it is above their own, and very usually when it is below. They have no variation of principle in their investigations; at best, when urged by some unusual emergency — by some extraordinary reward — they extend or exaggerate their old modes of *practice,* without touching their principles. What, for example, in this case of D——, has been done to vary the principle of action? What is all this boring, and probing, and sounding, and scrutinizing with the microscope, and dividing the surface of the building into registered square inches — what is it all but an exaggeration *of the application* of the one principle or set of principles of search, which are based upon the one set of notions regarding human ingenuity, to which the Prefect, in the long routine of his duty, has been accustomed? Do you not see he has taken it for granted that *all* men proceed to conceal a letter, — not exactly in a gimlet-hole bored in a chair-leg — but, at least, in *some* hole or corner suggested by the same tenor of thought which would urge a man to secrete a letter in a gimlet-hole bored in a chair-leg? And do you not see also, that such *recherchés* nooks for concealment are adapted only for ordinary occasions, and would be adopted only by ordinary intellects; for, in all cases of concealment, a disposal of the article concealed — a disposal of it in this *recherché* manner, — is, in the very first instance, presumable and presumed; and thus its discovery depends, not at all upon the acumen, but altogether upon the mere care, patience, and determination of the seekers; and where the case is of importance — or, what amounts to the same thing in the policial eyes, when the reward is of magnitude, — the qualities in question have *never* been known to fail. You will now understand what I meant in suggesting that, had the purloined letter been hidden anywhere within the limits of the Prefect's examination — in other words, had the principle of its concealment been comprehended within the principles of the Prefect — its discovery would have been a matter altogether beyond question. This functionary, however, has been thoroughly mystified; and the remote source of his defeat lies in the supposition that the Minister is a fool, because he has acquired renown as a poet. All fools are poets; this the Prefect *feels;* and he is merely guilty of a *non distributio medii* in thence inferring that all poets are fools."

"But is this really the poet?" I asked. "There are two brothers, I know;

and both have attained reputation in letters. The Minister I believe has written learnedly on the Differential Calculus. He is a mathematician, and no poet."

"You are mistaken; I know him well; he is both. As poet *and* mathematician, he would reason well; as mere mathematician, he could not have reasoned at all, and thus would have been at the mercy of the Prefect."

"You surprise me," I said, "by these opinions, which have been contradicted by the voice of the world. You do not mean to set at naught the well-digested idea of centuries. The mathematical reason has long been regarded as *the* reason *par excellence.*"

" '*Il y a à parier,*' " replied Dupin, quoting from Chamfort, " '*que toute idée publique, toute convention reçue, est une sottise, car elle a convenu au plus grand nombre.*' The mathematicians, I grant you, have done their best to promulgate the popular error to which you allude, and which is none the less an error for its promulgation as truth. With an art worthy a better cause, for example, they have insinuated the term 'analysis' into application to algebra. The French are the originators of this particular deception; but if a term is of any importance — if words derive any value from applicability — then 'analysis' conveys 'algebra' about as much as, in Latin, '*ambitus*' implies 'ambition,' '*religio*' 'religion,' or '*homines honesti,*' a set of *honorable* men."

"You have a quarrel on hand, I see," said I, "with some of the algebraists of Paris; but proceed."

"I dispute the availability, and thus the value, of that reason which is cultivated in any especial form other than the abstractly logical. I dispute, in particular, the reason educed by mathematical study. The mathematics are the science of form and quantity; mathematical reasoning is merely logic applied to observation upon form and quantity. The great error lies in supposing that even the truths of what is called *pure* algebra, are abstract or general truths. And this error is so egregious that I am confounded at the universality with which it has been received. Mathematical axioms are *not* axioms of general truth. What is true of *relation* — of form and quantity — is often grossly false in regard to morals, for example. In this latter science it is very usually *un*true that the aggregated parts are equal to the whole. In chemistry also the axiom fails. In the consideration of motive it fails; for two motives, each of a given value, have not, necessarily, a value when united, equal to the sum of their values apart. There are numerous other mathematical truths which are only truths within the limits of *relation*. But the mathematician argues, from his *finite truths,* through habit, as if they were of an absolutely general applicability—as the world indeed imagines them to be. Bryant, in his very learned 'Mythology,' mentions an analogous source of error, when he says that 'although the Pagan fables are not believed, yet we forget ourselves continually, and make inferences from them as existing realities.' With the algebraists, however, who are Pagans themselves, the 'Pagan fables' *are* believed, and the inferences are made, not so much through lapse of memory, as through an unaccountable addling of the brains. In short, I never yet encountered the mere mathematician who could be trusted out of equal roots, or one who did not clandestinely hold it as a point of his faith that $x^2 + px$ was absolutely and unconditionally equal to q. Say to one of these gentlemen, by way of experiment, if you please, that you believe occasions may occur where $x^2 + px$ is *not* altogether equal to q, and, having made him understand what you mean, get out of his reach as speedily as convenient, for, beyond doubt, he will endeavor to knock you down.

"I mean to say," continued Dupin, while I merely laughed at his last observations, "that if the Minister had been no more than a mathematician, the Prefect would have been under no necessity of giving me this check. I knew him, however, as both mathematician and poet, and my measures were adapted to his capacity, with reference to the circumstances by which he was surrounded. I knew him as a courtier, too, and as a bold *intriguant.* Such a man, I considered, could not fail to be aware of the ordinary policial modes of action. He could not have failed to anticipate—and events have proved that he did not fail to anticipate—the waylayings to which he was subjected. He must have foreseen, I reflected, the secret investigations of his premises. His frequent absences from home at night, which were hailed by the Prefect as certain aids to his success, I regarded only as *ruses,* to afford opportunity for thorough search to the police, and thus the sooner to impress them with the conviction to which G——, in fact, did finally arrive—the conviction that the letter was not upon the premises. I felt, also, that the whole train of thought, which I was at some pains in detailing to you just now, concerning the invariable principle of policial action in searches for articles concealed—I felt that this whole train of thought would necessarily pass through the mind of the Minister. It would imperatively lead him to despise all the ordinary *nooks* of concealment. *He* could not, I reflected, be so weak as not to see that the most intricate and remote recess of his hotel would be as open as his commonest closets to the eyes, to the probes, to the gimlets, and to the microscopes of the Prefect. I saw, in fine, that he would be driven, as a matter of course, to *simplicity,* if not deliberately induced to it as a matter of choice. You will remember, perhaps, how desperately the Prefect laughed when I suggested, upon our first interview, that it was just possible this mystery troubled him so much on account of its being so *very* self-evident."

"Yes," said I, "I remember his merriment well. I really thought he would have fallen into convulsions."

"The material world," continued Dupin, "abounds with very strict analogies to the immaterial; and thus some color of truth has been given to the rhetorical dogma, that metaphor, or simile, may be made to strengthen an argument, as well as to embellish a description. The principle of the *vis inertiæ,* for example, seems to be identical in physics and metaphysics. It is not more true in the former, that a large body is with more difficulty set in motion than a smaller one, and that its subsequent *momentum* is commensurate with this difficulty, than it is, in the latter, that intellects of the vaster capacity, while more forcible, more constant, and more eventful in their movements than those of inferior grade, are yet the less readily moved, and more embarrassed and full of hesitation in the first few steps of their progress. Again: have you ever noticed which of the street signs, over the shop doors, are the most attractive of attention?"

"I have never given the matter a thought," I said.

"There is a game of puzzles," he resumed, "which is played upon a map. One party playing requires another to find a given word — the name of town, river, state or empire — any word, in short, upon the motley and perplexed surface of the chart. A novice in the game generally seeks to embarrass his opponents by giving them the most minutely lettered names; but the adept selects such words as stretch, in large characters, from one end of the chart to the other. These, like the over-largely lettered signs and placards of the street, escape observation by dint of being excessively obvious; and here the physical oversight is precisely analogous with the moral inapprehension by which the intellect suffers to pass unnoticed those considerations which are too obtrusively and too palpably self-evident. But this is a point, it appears, somewhat above or beneath the understanding of the Prefect. He never once thought it probable, or possible, that the Minister had deposited the letter immediately beneath the nose of the whole world, by way of best preventing any portion of that world from perceiving it.

"But the more I reflected upon the daring, dashing, and discriminating ingenuity of D——; upon the fact that the document must always have been *at hand,* if he intended to use it to good purpose; and upon the decisive evidence, obtained by the Prefect, that it was not hidden within the limits of that dignitary's ordinary search — the more satisfied I became that, to conceal this letter, the Minister had resorted to the comprehensive and sagacious expedient of not attempting to conceal it at all.

"Full of these ideas, I prepared myself with a pair of green spectacles, and called one fine morning, quite by accident, at the Ministerial hotel. I found D—— at home, yawning, lounging, and dawdling, as usual, and pretending to be in the last extremity of *ennui.* He is, perhaps, the most really energetic human being now alive — but that is only when nobody sees him.

"To be even with him, I complained of my weak eyes, and lamented the necessity of the spectacles, under cover of which I cautiously and thoroughly surveyed the apartment, while seemingly intent only upon the conversation of my host.

"I paid especial attention to a large writing-table near which he sat, and upon which lay confusedly, some miscellaneous letters and other papers, with one or two musical instruments and a few books. Here, however, after a long and very deliberate scrutiny, I saw nothing to excite particular suspicion.

"At length my eyes, in going the circuit of the room, fell upon a trumpery filigree card-rack of pasteboard, that hung dangling by a dirty blue ribbon, from a little brass knob just beneath the middle of the mantelpiece. In this rack, which had three or four compartments, were five or six visiting cards and a solitary letter. This last was much soiled and crumpled. It was torn nearly in two, across the middle — as if a design, in the first instance, to tear it entirely up as worthless, had been altered, or stayed, in the second. It had a large black seal, bearing the D—— cipher *very* conspicuously, and was addressed, in a diminutive female hand, to D——, the minister, himself. It was thrust carelessly, and even, as it seemed, contemptuously, into one of the upper divisions of the rack.

"No sooner had I glanced at this letter, than I concluded it to be that of which I was in search. To be sure, it was, to all appearance, radically different from the one of which the Prefect had read us so minute a description. Here the seal was large and black, with the D—— cipher; there it was small and red, with the ducal arms of the S—— family. Here, the address, to the Minister, was diminutive and feminine; there the superscription, to a certain royal personage, was markedly bold and decided; the size alone formed a point of correspondence. But, then, the *radicalness* of these differences, which was excessive; the dirt; the soiled and torn condition of the paper, so inconsistent with the *true* methodical habits of D——, and so suggestive of a design to delude the beholder into an idea of the worthlessness of the document; these things, together with the hyperobtrusive situation of this document, full in the view of every visitor, and thus exactly in accordance with the conclusions to which I had previously arrived; these things, I say, were strongly corroborative of suspicion, in one who came with the intention to suspect.

"I protracted my visit as long as possible, and, while I maintained a most animated discussion with the Minister, on a topic which I knew well had never failed to interest and excite him, I kept my attention really riveted upon the letter. In this examination, I committed to memory its external appearance and arrangement in the rack; and also fell, at length, upon a discovery which set at rest whatever trivial doubt I might have entertained. In scrutinizing the edges of the paper, I observed them to be more *chafed* than seemed necessary. They presented the *broken* appearance which is manifested when a stiff paper, having been once folded and pressed with a folder, is refolded in a reversed direction, in the same creases or edges which had formed the original fold. This discovery was sufficient. It was clear to me that the letter had been turned, as a glove, inside out, redirected, and resealed. I bade the Minister good morning, and took my departure at once, leaving a gold snuff-box upon the table.

"The next morning I called for the snuff-box, when we resumed, quite eagerly, the conversation of the preceding day. While thus engaged, however, a loud report, as if of a pistol, was heard immediately beneath the windows of the hotel, and was succeeded by a series of fearful screams, and the shoutings of a mob. D—— rushed to a casement, threw it open, and looked out. In the meantime, I stepped to the card-rack, took the letter, put it in my pocket, and replaced it by a *fac-simile,* (so far as regards externals,) which I had carefully prepared at my lodgings—imitating the D—— cipher, very readily, by means of a seal formed of bread.

"The disturbance in the street had been occasioned by the frantic behavior of a man with a musket. He had fired it among a crowd of women and children. It proved, however, to have been without ball, and the fellow was suffered to go his way as a lunatic or a drunkard. When he had gone, D—— came from the window, whither I had followed him immediately upon securing the object in view. Soon afterwards I bade him farewell. The pretended lunatic was a man in my own pay."

"But what purpose had you," I asked, "in replacing the letter by a *fac-simile?* Would it not have been better, at the first visit, to have seized it openly, and departed?"

"D——," replied Dupin, "is a desperate man, and a man of nerve. His hotel, too, is not without attendants devoted to his interests. Had I made the wild attempt you suggest, I might never have left the Ministerial presence alive. The good people of Paris might have heard of me no more. But I had an object apart from these considerations. You know my political prepossessions. In this matter, I act as a partisan of the lady concerned. For eighteen months the Minister has had her in his power. She has now him in hers — since, being unaware that the letter is not in his possession, he will proceed with his exactions as if it was. Thus will he inevitably commit himself, at once, to his political destruction. His downfall, too, will not be more precipitate than awkward. It is all very well to talk about the *facilis descensus Averni;* but in all kinds of climbing, as Catalani said of singing, it is far more easy to get up than to come down. In the present instance I have no sympathy — at least no pity — for him who descends. He is the *monstrum horrendum,* an unprincipled man of genius. I confess, however, that I should like very well to know the precise character of his thoughts, when, being defied by her whom the Prefect terms 'a certain personage,' he is reduced to opening the letter which I left for him in the card-rack."

"How? did you put anything particular in it?"

"Why — it did not seem altogether right to leave the interior blank — that would have been insulting. D——, at Vienna once, did me an evil turn, which I told him, quite good-humoredly, that I should remember. So, as I knew he would feel some curiosity in regard to the identity of the person who had outwitted him, I thought it a pity not to give him a clue. He is well acquainted with my MS., and I just copied into the middle of the blank sheet the words —

"'—— —— Un dessein si funeste,
S'il n'est digne d'Atrée, est digne de Thyeste.

They are to be found in Crébillon's 'Atrée.'"

1846

ABRAHAM LINCOLN

REMARKABLE CASE OF ARREST FOR MURDER

Readers of mystery fiction the world over can only rejoice that ABRAHAM LINCOLN (1809–1865) had a legal and political career of some note, as the odds of attaining renown as a writer were slim, to be generous. This story appears to be his only attempt in this difficult and challenging genre and is included in this collection as a curiosity, not as an example of compelling storytelling or distinguished literary style.

Lincoln was known to have read and admired the work of Edgar Allan Poe, and the events narrated in this story, albeit published for the first time five years after they occurred, took place while Lincoln was practicing law and almost precisely at the time of the publication of "The Murders in the Rue Morgue."

In the mid-1800s it was a common practice for lawyers to use their own cases as the basis for lurid "true crime" fiction, embellishing where needed to bring excitement to a case and, not coincidentally, enhance the perception of them as brilliant lawyers and clever detectives. This genre was extremely popular for about a half century, appearing with regularity in newspapers and magazines as well as finding book publication for the most skilled.

Lincoln defended the Trailor brothers, among many others, during his career, and no light has been shed on why he chose to write about this case — apparently the only time he attempted it. He might have been inspired by Poe, or it might have been the truly strange circumstances that inspired him. It is worth noting that the Trailor brothers never paid Lincoln for his defense.

When the story appeared in print on the front page of the *Quincy Whig*, the editor prefaced it with a note:

> The following narrative has been handed to us for publication by a member of the bar. There is no doubt of the truth of every fact stated; and the whole affair is of so extraordinary a character as to entitle it to publication, and commend it to the attention of those at present engaged in discussing reforms in criminal jurisprudence, and the abolition of capital punishment.

The story was reprinted in the March 1952 issue of *Ellery Queen's Mystery Magazine,* retitled "The Trailor Murder Mystery."

"Remarkable Case of Arrest for Murder" was originally published in the April 15, 1846, issue of the *Quincy Whig.*

• • •

IN THE YEAR 1841, there resided, at different points in the State of Illinois, three brothers by the name of Trailor. Their Christian names were William, Henry and Archibald. Archibald resided at Springfield, then as now the seat of Government of the State. He was a sober, retiring and industrious man, of about thirty years of age; a carpenter by trade, and a bachelor, boarding with his partner in business—a Mr. Myers. Henry, a year or two older, was a man of like retiring and industrious habits; had a family and resided with it on a farm at Clary's Grove, about twenty miles distant from Springfield in a north-westerly direction. William, still older, and with similar habits, resided on a farm in Warren county, distant from Springfield something more than a hundred miles in the same north-westerly direction. He was a widower, with several children.

In the neighborhood of William's residence, there was, and had been for several years, a man by the name of Fisher, who was somewhat above the age of fifty; had no family, and no settled home; but who boarded and lodged a while here, and a while there, with the persons for whom he did little jobs of work. His habits were remarkably economical, so that an impression got about that he had accumulated a considerable amount of money.

In the latter part of May in the year mentioned, William formed the purpose of visiting his brothers at Clary's Grove and Springfield; and Fisher, at the time having his temporary residence at his house, resolved to accompany him. They set out together in a buggy with a single horse. On Sunday evening they reached Henry's residence, and stayed overnight. On Monday morning, being the first Monday of June, they started on to Springfield, Henry accompanying them on horseback. They reached town about noon, met Archibald, went with him to his boarding house, and there took up their lodgings for the time they should remain.

After dinner, the three Trailors and Fisher left the boarding house in company, for the avowed purpose of spending the evening together in looking about the town. At supper, the Trailors had all returned, but Fisher was missing, and some inquiry was made about him. After supper, the Trailors went out professedly in search of him. One by one they returned, the last coming in after late tea time, and each stating that he had been unable to discover anything of Fisher.

The next day, both before and after breakfast, they went professedly in search again, and returned at noon, still unsuccessful. Dinner again being had, William and Henry expressed a determination to give up the search, and start for their homes. This was remonstrated against by some of the boarders about the house, on the ground that Fisher was somewhere in the vicinity, and would be left without any conveyance, as he and William had come in the same buggy. The remonstrance was disregarded, and they departed for their homes respectively.

Up to this time, the knowledge of Fisher's mysterious disappearance had spread very little beyond the few boarders at Myers', and excited no considerable interest. After the lapse of three or four days, Henry returned to Springfield, for the ostensible purpose of making further search for Fisher. Procuring some of the boarders, he, together with them and Archibald, spent another day in ineffectual search, when it was again abandoned, and he returned home.

No general interest was yet excited.

On the Friday, week after Fisher's disappearance, the Postmaster at Springfield received a letter from the Postmaster nearest William's residence, in Warren county, stating that William had returned home without Fisher, and was saying, rather boastfully, that Fisher was dead, and had willed him his money, and that he had got about fifteen hundred dollars by it. The letter further stated that William's story and conduct seemed strange; and desired the Postmaster at Springfield to ascertain and write what was the truth in the matter.

The Postmaster at Springfield made the letter public, and at once, excitement became universal and intense. Springfield, at that time, had a population of about 3,500, with a city organization. The Attorney General of the State resided there. A purpose was forthwith formed to ferret out the mystery, in putting which into execution, the Mayor of the city and the Attorney General took the lead. To make search for, and, if possible, find the body of the man supposed to be murdered, was resolved on as the first step.

In pursuance of this, men were formed into large parties, and marched abreast, in all directions, so as to let no inch of ground in the vicinity remain unsearched. Examinations were made of cellars, wells, and pits of all descriptions, where it was thought possible the body might be concealed. All the fresh, or tolerably fresh graves in the graveyard, were pried into, and dead horses and dead dogs were disinterred, where, in some instances, they had been buried by their partial masters.

This search, as has appeared, commenced on Friday. It continued until Saturday afternoon without success, when it was determined to dispatch officers to arrest William and Henry, at their residences respectively. The officers started on Sunday morning; meanwhile, the search for the body was continued, and rumors got afloat of the Trailors having passed, at different times and places, several gold pieces, which were readily supposed to have belonged to Fisher.

On Monday, the officers sent for Henry, having arrested him, arrived with him. The Mayor and Attorney Gen'l took charge of him, and set their wits to work to elicit a discovery from him. He denied, and denied, and persisted in denying. They still plied him in every conceivable way, till Wednesday, when, protesting his own innocence, he stated that his brothers, William and Archibald, had murdered Fisher; that they had killed him, without his (Henry's) knowledge at the time, and made a temporary concealment of his body; that, immediately preceding his and William's departure from Springfield for home, on Tuesday, the day after Fisher's disappearance, William and Archibald communicated the fact to him, and engaged his assistance in making a permanent concealment of the body; that, at the time he and William left professedly for home, they did not take the road directly, but, meandering their way through the streets, entered the woods at the north-west of the city, two or three hundred yards to the right of where the road they should have travelled, entered them; that, penetrating the woods some few hundred yards, they halted and Archibald came a somewhat different route, on foot, and joined them; that William and Archibald then stationed him (Henry) on an old and disused road that ran nearby, as a sentinel, to give warning of the approach of any intruder; that William and Archibald then removed the buggy to the edge of a dense brush thicket, about forty yards distant from his (Henry's) position, where, leaving the buggy, they entered the thicket, and in a few minutes returned with the body, and placed it in the buggy; that from his station he could and did distinctly see that the object placed in the buggy was a dead man, of the general appearance and size of Fisher; that William and Archibald then moved off with the buggy in the direction of Hickox's mill pond, and after an absence of half an hour, returned, saying they had put him in a safe place; that Archibald then left for town, and he and William found their way to the road, and made for their homes.

At this disclosure, all lingering credulity was broken down, and excitement rose to an almost inconceivable height. Up to this time, the well-known character of Archibald had repelled and put down all suspicions as to him. Till then, those who were ready to swear that a murder had been committed, were almost as confident that Archibald had had no part in it. But now, he was seized and thrown into jail; and indeed, his personal security rendered it by no means objectionable to him.

And now came the search for the brush thicket, and the search of the mill pond. The thicket was found, and the buggy tracks at the point indicated. At a point within the thicket, the signs of a struggle were discovered, and a trail from thence to the buggy track was traced. In attempting to follow the track of the buggy from the thicket, it was found to proceed in the direction of the mill pond, but could not be traced all the way. At the pond, however, it was found that a buggy had been backed down to, and partially into the water's edge.

Search was now to be made in the pond; and it was made in every imaginable way. Hundreds and hundreds were engaged in raking, fishing, and draining. After much fruitless effort in this way, on Thursday morning the mill dam was cut down, and the water of the pond partially drawn off, and the same processes of search again gone through with.

About noon of this day, the officer sent for William, returned having him in custody; and a man calling himself Dr. Gilmore, came in company with them. It seems that the officer arrested William at his own house, early in the day on Tuesday, and started to Springfield with him; that after dark awhile, they reached Lewiston, in Fulton county, where they stopped for the night; that late in the night this Dr. Gilmore arrived, stating that Fisher was alive at his house, and that he had followed on to give the information, so that William might be released without further trouble; that the officer, distrusting Dr. Gilmore, refused to release William, but brought him on to Springfield, and the Dr. accompanied them.

On reaching Springfield, the Dr. reasserted that Fisher was alive, and at his house. At this, the multitude for a time, were utterly confounded. Gilmore's story was communicated to Henry Trailor, who, without faltering, reaffirmed his own story about Fisher's murder. Henry's adherence to his own story was communicated to the crowd, and at once the idea started, and became nearly, if not quite universal, that Gilmore was a confederate of the Trailors, and had invented the tale he was telling, to secure their release and escape.

Excitement was again at its zenith.

About 3 o'clock the same evening, Myers, Archibald's partner, started with a two-horse carriage, for the purpose of ascertaining whether Fisher was alive, as stated by Gilmore, and if so, of bringing him back to Springfield with him.

On Friday a legal examination was gone into before two Justices, on the charge of murder against William and Archibald. Henry was introduced as a witness by the prosecution, and on oath reaffirmed his statements, as heretofore detailed; and, at the end of which, he bore a thorough and rigid cross-examination without faltering or exposure. The prosecution also proved, by a respectable lady, that on the Monday evening of Fisher's disappearance, she saw Archibald, whom she well knew, and another man whom she did not then know, but whom she believed at the time of testifying to be William, (then present;) and still another, answering the description of Fisher, all enter the timber at the north-west of town, (the point indicated by Henry,) and after one or two hours, saw William and Archibald return without Fisher.

Several other witnesses testified, that on Tuesday, at the time William and Henry professedly gave up the search for Fisher's body, and started for home, they did not take the road directly, but did go into the woods, as stated by Henry. By others, also, it was proved, that since Fisher's disappearance, William and Archibald had passed rather an unusual number of gold pieces. The statements heretofore made about the thicket, the signs of a struggle, the buggy tracks, &c., were fully proven by numerous witnesses.

At this the prosecution rested.

Dr. Gilmore was then introduced by the defendants. He stated that he resided in Warren county, about seven miles distant from William's residence; that on the morning of William's arrest, he was out from home, and heard of the arrest, and of its being on a charge of the murder of Fisher; that on returning to his own house, he found Fisher there; that Fisher was in very feeble health, and could give no rational account as to where he had been during his absence; that he (Gilmore) then started in pursuit of the officer, as before stated; and that he should have taken Fisher with him, only that the state of his health did not permit. Gilmore also stated that he had known Fisher for several years, and that he had understood he was subject to temporary derangement of mind, owing to an injury about his head received in early life.

There was about Dr. Gilmore so much of the air and manner of truth, that his statement prevailed in the minds of the audience and of the court, and the Trailors were discharged, although they attempted no explanation of the circumstances proven by the other witnesses.

On the next Monday, Myers arrived in Springfield, bringing with him the now famed Fisher, in full life and proper person.

Thus ended this strange affair; and while it is readily conceived that a writer of novels could bring a story to a more perfect climax, it may well be doubted whether a stranger affair ever really occurred. Much of the matter remains in mystery to this day. The going into the woods with Fisher, and returning without him, by the Trailors; their going into the woods at the same place the next day, after they professed to have given up the search; the signs of a struggle in the thicket, the buggy tracks at the edge of it; and the location of the thicket, and the signs about it, corresponding precisely with Henry's story, are circumstances that have never been explained.

William and Archibald have both died since — William in less than a year, and Archibald in about two years after the supposed murder. Henry is still living, but never speaks of the subject.

It is not the object of the writer of this, to enter into the many curious speculations that might be indulged upon the facts of this narrative; yet he can scarcely forbear a remark upon what would, almost certainly, have been the fate of William and Archibald, had Fisher not been found alive. It seems he had wandered away in mental derangement, and, had he died in this condition, and his body been found in the vicinity, it is difficult to conceive what could have saved the Trailors from the consequence of having murdered him. Or, if he had died, and his body never found, the case against them would have been quite as bad, for, although it is a principle of law that a conviction for murder shall not be had, unless the body of the deceased be discovered, it is to be remembered, that Henry testified he saw Fisher's dead body.

1850

DANIEL WEBSTER

THE FATAL SECRET

A talent, or skill, that has largely lost its luster in recent years is that of oratory, but it was highly prized in an earlier era, and few dispute that America's greatest orator was DANIEL WEBSTER (1782–1852). Although his "Second Reply to Hayne" in the Senate in 1830 is regarded as "the most eloquent speech ever delivered in Congress" and first made his reputation, it was Stephen Vincent Benet's famous short story and play, "The Devil and Daniel Webster" (1936), which later was the basis for a motion picture, in which the lawyer wins a debate with Satan, that made his name familiar to generations a century after his powerful address in the Senate. Webster's political career lasted forty years, the first ten as a congressman from New Hampshire, followed by seventeen as a senator representing Massachusetts, and then as secretary of state for three presidents.

Webster's career as a lawyer and statesman did not leave much time for writing outside of those disciplines, and his collected works are mainly the speeches he delivered to Congress and the laws he wrote (one of which settled the border with Canada), as well as his often lengthy and always eloquent letters.

The following story is an anomaly and is included in this collection as a curiosity. Even in its brevity, the power of Webster's language and the lushness of his prose cannot be denied. Is it a story? Well, there is a fictional scenario. Is it a sermon? He was not a man of the cloth. Is it an essay? It is conjecture and fabrication. However it may be defined, it is a florid, superbly crafted piece, grandiloquent in its argument for the religious conscience of New England in the middle of the nineteenth century. And you have never before read it!

"The Fatal Secret" was first published in *The Boston Book. Being Specimens of Metropolitan Literature* (Boston: Ticknor, Reed, and Fields, 1850).

• • •

AN AGED MAN, without an enemy in the world, in his own house and in his own bed, is made the victim of a butcherly murder, for mere pay.

Deep sleep had fallen on the destined victim, and on all beneath his roof. A healthful old man, to whom sleep was sweet, the first sound slumbers of the night held him in their soft but strong embrace. The assassin enters, through the window already prepared, into an unoccupied apartment. With noiseless foot he paces the lonely hall, half lighted by the moon; he winds up the ascent of the stairs, and reaches the door of the chamber. Of this, he moves the lock, by soft and continued pressure, till it turns on its hinges without noise; and he enters, and beholds his victim before him.

The room is uncommonly open to the admission of light. The face of the innocent sleeper is turned from the murderer, and the beams of the moon, resting on the gray locks of his aged temple, show him where to strike.

The fatal blow is given! and the victim passes, without a struggle or a motion, from the repose of sleep to the repose of death!

It is the assassin's purpose to make sure work; and he yet plies the dagger, though it is obvious that life has been destroyed by the blow of the bludgeon. He even raises the aged arm, that he may not fail in his aim at the heart, and replaces it again over the wounds of the poniard. To finish the picture, he explores the wrist for the pulse. He feels for it, and ascertains that it beats no longer.

It is accomplished. The deed is done. He retreats, retraces his steps to the window, passes out through it as he came in, and escapes. He has done the murder. No eye has seen him, no ear has heard him. The *secret* is his own, and it is safe!

Ah! gentlemen, that was a dreadful mistake. Such a secret can be safe nowhere. The whole creation of God has neither nook nor corner where the guilty can bestow it, and say it is safe. Not to speak of that eye which pierces through all disguises, and beholds everything.

True it is, generally speaking, that "murder will out." True it is, that Providence hath so ordained, and doth so govern things, that those who break the great law of heaven by shedding man's blood seldom succeed in avoiding discovery. Especially, in a case exciting so much attention as this, discovery must come . . .

A thousand eyes turn at once to explore every man, every thing, every circumstance, connected with the time and place; a thousand ears catch every whisper; a thousand excited minds intensely dwell on the scene, shedding all their light, and ready to kindle the slightest circumstance into a blaze of discovery.

Meantime, the guilty soul cannot keep its own secret. It is false to itself; or rather it feels an irresistible impulse of conscience to be true to itself. It labors under its guilty possession, and knows not what to do with it. The human heart was not made for the residence of such an inhabitant. It finds itself preyed on by a torment, which it dares not acknowledge to God or man. A vulture is devouring it, and it can ask no sympathy or assistance, either from heaven or earth.

The secret which the murderer possesses soon comes to possess him; and, like the evil spirits of which we read, it overcomes him, and leads him whithersoever it will. He feels it beating at his heart, rising to his throat, and demanding disclosure. He thinks the whole world sees it in his face, reads it in his eyes, and almost hears its workings in the very silence of his thoughts. It has become his master. It betrays his discretion, it breaks down his courage, it conquers his prudence.

When suspicions, from without, begin to embarrass him, and the net of circumstance to entangle him, the fatal *secret* struggles with still greater violence to burst forth. It must be confessed, *it will be* confessed; there is no refuge from confession but suicide, and suicide is confession.

1862

THOMAS BAILEY ALDRICH

THE DANSEUSE

When THOMAS BAILEY ALDRICH (1836–1907) wrote *Story of a Bad Boy* (1870), he and his wife were a popular couple in the literary circle of Boston that included Nathaniel Hawthorne, John Greenleaf Whittier, and James Russell Lowell, leading the eminent William Dean Howells, editor of the prestigious literary journal *The Atlantic Monthly,* to hail the book as the first truly American novel (though readers of James Fenimore Cooper might have disagreed). Aldrich was such a giant figure in American letters in the latter part of the nineteenth century that at his memorial service in 1908, Mark Twain stated that *Story of a Bad Boy,* based on Aldrich's own experiences growing up in Portsmouth, New Hampshire, was his inspiration for Tom Sawyer.

Aldrich was a prolific writer of novels, short stories, poetry, and nonfiction and was extremely popular in his day, though he is almost entirely forgotten today. Among his many works are several that involve mystery fiction, such as *Marjorie Daw and Other People* (1873), a short story collection; *The Stillwater Tragedy* (1880); and his most important contribution to the genre, *Out of His Head* (1862), an episodic novel in which the complete short story "The Danseuse" comprises chapters 11–14.

This self-contained excerpt from the novel reveals the author's debt to Edgar Allan Poe, though he adds significant advances of his own. The plot is clearly derived from "The Murders in the Rue Morgue," but an important element in the development of the detective story is the first American variation of Poe's "locked room" mystery. Also, while Poe's Monsieur Dupin was certainly an eccentric sleuth, Aldrich more than continued the notion (though perhaps to an unusual extreme, as his detective, Paul Lynde, is also a borderline madman who is working on a secret invention known as "the Moon-Apparatus").

"The Danseuse" was first published as chapters 11–14 of *Out of His Head* (New York: Carleton, 1862).

• • •

THE ENSUING SUMMER I returned North, and, turning my attention to mechanism, was successful in producing several wonderful pieces of work, among which may be mentioned a brass butterfly, made to flit so naturally in the air as to deceive the most acute observers. The motion of the toy, the soft down and gorgeous damask-stains on the pinions, were declared quite perfect. The thing is rusty, and won't work now; I tried to set it going for Dr. Pendegrast, the other day.

A manikin musician, playing a few exquisite airs on a miniature piano, likewise excited much admiration. This figure bore such an absurd, unintentional resemblance to a gentleman who has since distinguished himself as a pianist, that I presented the trifle to a lady admirer of Gottschalk.

I also became a taxidermist, and stuffed a pet bird with springs and diminutive flutes, causing it to hop and carol, in its cage, with great glee. But my masterpiece was a nimble white mouse, with pink eyes, that could scamper up the walls, and masticate bits of cheese in an extraordinary style. My chambermaid shrieked, and jumped up on a chair, whenever I let the little fellow loose in her presence. One day, unhappily, the mouse, while nosing around after its favorite aliment, got snapt in a rat-trap that yawned in the closet, and I was never able to readjust the machinery.

Engaged in these useful inventions — useful, because no exercise of the human mind is ever in vain — my existence for two or three years was so placid and uneventful, I began to hope that the shadows which had followed on my path from childhood, making me unlike other men, had returned to that unknown world where they properly belong; but the Fates were only taking breath to work out more surely the problem of my destiny. I must keep nothing back. I must extenuate nothing.

I am about to lift the veil of mystery which, for nearly seven years, has shrouded the story of Mary Ware; and though I lay bare my own weakness, or folly, or what you will, I do not shrink from the unveiling.

No hand but mine can now perform the task. There was, indeed, a man who might have done this better than I. But he went his way in silence. I like a man who can hold his tongue.

On the corner of Clarke and Crandall streets, in New York, stands a dingy brown frame-house. It is a very old house, as its obsolete style of structure would tell you. It has a morose, unhappy look, though once it must have been a blythe mansion. I think that houses, like human beings, ultimately become dejected or cheerful, according to their experience. The very air of some front-doors tells their history.

This house, I repeat, has a morose, unhappy look, at present, and is tenanted by an incalculable number of Irish families, while a picturesque junk-shop is in full blast in the basement; but at the time of which I write, it was a second-rate boarding-place, of the more respectable sort, and rather largely patronized by poor, but honest, literary men, tragic-actors, members of the chorus, and such like gilt people.

My apartments on Crandall street were opposite this building, to which my attention was directed soon after taking possession of the rooms, by the discovery of the following facts:

First, that a charming lady lodged on the second-floor front, and sang like a canary every morning.

Second, that her name was Mary Ware.

Third, that Mary Ware was a danseuse, and had two lovers — only two.

Fourth, that Mary Ware and the page, who, years before, had drawn Howland and myself into that fatal masquerade, were the same person.

This last discovery moved me strangely, aside from the fact that her presence opened an old wound. The power which guides all the actions of my life constrained me to watch this woman.

Mary Ware was the leading-lady at The Olympic. Night after night found me in the parquette. I can think of nothing with which to compare the airiness and utter abandon of her dancing. She seemed a part of the music. She was one of beauty's best thoughts, then. Her glossy gold hair reached down to her waist, shading one of those mobile faces which remind you of Guido's picture of Beatrix Cenci — there was something so fresh and enchanting in the mouth. Her luminous, almond eyes, looking out winningly from under their drooping fringes, were at once the delight and misery of young men.

Ah! you were distracting in your nights of triumph, when the bouquets nestled about your elastic ankles, and the kissing of your castanets made the pulses leap; but I remember when you lay on your cheerless bed, in the blank daylight, with the glory faded from your brow, and "none so poor as to do you reverence."

Then I stooped down and kissed you — but not till then.

Mary Ware was to me a finer study than her lovers. She had two, as I have said. One of them was commonplace enough — well-made, well-dressed, shallow, flaccid. Nature, when she gets out of patience with her best works, throws off such things by the gross, instead of swearing. He was a lieutenant, in the navy I think. The gilt button has charms to soothe the savage breast.

The other was a man of different mold, and interested me in a manner for which I could not then account. The first time I saw him did not seem like the first time. But this, perhaps, is an after-impression.

Every line of his countenance denoted character; a certain capability, I mean, but whether for good or evil was not so plain. I should have called him handsome, but for a noticeable scar which ran at right angles across his mouth, giving him a sardonic expression when he smiled.

His frame might have set an anatomist wild with delight — six feet two, deep-chested, knitted with tendons of steel. Not at all a fellow to amble on plush carpets.

"Some day," thought I, as I saw him stride by the house, "he will throw the little Lieutenant out of that second-story window."

I cannot tell, to this hour, which of those two men Mary Ware loved most — for I think she loved them both. A woman's heart was the insolvable charade with which the Sphinx nipt the Egyptians. I was never good at puzzles.

The flirtation, however, was food enough for the whole neighborhood. But faintly did the gossips dream of the strange drama that was being shaped out, as compactly as a tragedy of Sophocles, under their noses.

They were very industrious in tearing Mary Ware's good name to pieces. Some laughed at the gay Lieutenant, and some at Julius Kenneth; but they all amiably united in condemning Mary Ware.

This state of affairs had continued for five or six months, when it was reported that Julius Kenneth and Mary Ware were affianced. The Lieutenant was less frequently seen in Crandall street, and Julius waited upon Mary's footsteps with the fidelity of a shadow.

Yet — though Mary went to the Sunday concerts with Julius Kenneth, she still wore the Lieutenant's roses in her bosom.

A MYSTERY

ONE DRIZZLY NOVEMBER morning — how well I remember it! — I was awakened by a series of nervous raps on my bed-room door. The noise startled me from an unpleasant dream.

"O, sir!" cried the chambermaid on the landing. "There's been a dreadful time across the street. They've gone and killed Mary Ware!"

"Ah!"

That was all I could say. Cold drops of perspiration stood on my forehead.

I looked at my watch; it was eleven o'clock; I had over-slept myself, having sat up late the previous night.

I dressed hastily, and, without waiting for breakfast, pushed my way through the murky crowd that had collected in front of the house opposite, and passed up stairs, unquestioned.

When I entered the room, there were six people present: a thick-set gentleman, in black, with a bland professional air, a physician; two policemen; Adelaide Woods, an actress; Mrs. Marston, the landlady; and Julius Kenneth.

In the centre of the chamber, on the bed, lay the body of Mary Ware — as pale as Seneca's wife.

I shall never forget it. The corpse haunted me for years afterwards, the dark streaks under the eyes, and the wavy hair streaming over the pillow — the dead gold hair. I stood by her for a moment, and turned down the counterpane, which was drawn up closely to the chin.

"There was that across her throat
Which you had hardly cared to see."

At the head of the bed sat Julius Kenneth, bending over the icy hand which he held in his own. He was kissing it.

The gentleman in black was conversing in undertones with Mrs. Marston, who every now and then glanced furtively toward Mary Ware.

The two policemen were examining the doors, closets and windows of the apartment with, obviously, little success.

There was no fire in the air-tight stove, but the place was suffocatingly close. I opened a window, and leaned against the casement to get a breath of fresh air.

The physician approached me. I muttered something to him indistinctly, for I was partly sick with the peculiar moldy smell that pervaded the room.

"Yes," he began, scrutinizing me, "the affair looks very perplexing, as you remark. Professional man, sir? No? Bless me! — beg pardon. Never in my life saw anything that looked so exceedingly like nothing. Thought, at first, 'twas a clear case of suicide — door locked, key on the inside, place undisturbed; but then we find no instrument with which the subject could have inflicted that wound on the neck. Queer. Party must have escaped up chimney. But how? Don't know. The windows are at least thirty feet from the ground. It would be impossible for a person to jump that far, even if he could clear the iron railing below. Which he couldn't. Disagreeable things to jump on, those spikes, sir. Must have been done with a sharp knife. Queer, very. Party meant to make sure work of it. The carotid neatly severed, upon my word."

The medical gentleman went on in this monologuic style for fifteen minutes, during which time Kenneth did not raise his lips from Mary's fingers.

Approaching the bed, I spoke to him; but he only shook his head in reply.

I understood his grief.

After regaining my chamber, I sat listlessly for three or four hours, gazing into the grate. The twilight flitted in from the street; but I did not heed it. A face among the coals fascinated me. It came and went and came. Now I saw a cavern hung with lurid stalactites; now a small Vesuvius vomiting smoke and flame; now a bridge spanning some tartarean gulf; then these crumbled, each in its turn, and from out the heated fragments peered the one inevitable face.

The *Evening Mirror*, of that day, gave the following detailed report of the inquest:

"This morning, at eight o'clock, Mary Ware, the celebrated danseuse, was found dead in her chamber, at her late residence on the corner of Clarke and Crandall streets. The perfect order of the room, and the fact that the door was locked on the inside, have induced many to believe that the poor girl was the victim of her own rashness. But we cannot think so. That the door was fastened on the inner side, proves nothing except, indeed, that the murderer was hidden in the apartment. That the room gave no evidence of a struggle having taken place, is also an insignificant point. Two men, or even one, grappling suddenly with the deceased, who was a slight woman, would have prevented any great resistance. The deceased was dressed in a ballet-costume, and was, as we conjecture, murdered directly after her return from the theatre. On a chair near the bed, lay several fresh bouquets, and a water-proof cloak which she was in the habit of wearing over her dancing-dress, on coming home from the theatre at night. No weapon whatever was found on the premises. We give below all the material testimony elicited by the coroner. It explains little.

"*Josephine Marston* deposes: I keep a boarding house at No. 131 Crandall street. Miss Ware has boarded with me for the past two years. Has always borne a good character as far as I know. I do not think she had many visitors; certainly no male visitors, excepting a Lieutenant King, and Mr. Kenneth to whom she was engaged. I do not know when King was last at the house; not within three days, I am confident. Deceased told me that he had gone away. I did not see her last night when she came home. The hall-door is never locked; each of the boarders has a latchkey. The last time I saw Miss Ware was just before she went to the theatre, when she asked me to call her at eight o'clock (this morning) as she had promised to walk with 'Jules,' meaning Mr. Kenneth. I knocked at the door nine or ten times, but received no answer. Then I grew frightened and called one of the lady boarders, Miss Woods, who helped me to force the lock. The key fell on the floor inside as we pushed against the door. Mary Ware was lying on the bed, dressed. Some matches were scattered under the gas-burner by the bureau. The room presented the same appearance it does now.

"*Adelaide Woods* deposes: I am an actress by profession. I occupy the room next to that of the deceased. Have known her twelve months. It was half-past eleven when she came home; she stopped in my chamber for perhaps three-quarters of an hour. The call-boy of The Olympic usually accompanies her home from the theatre when she is alone. I let her in. Deceased had misplaced her night-key. The partition between our rooms is of brick; but I do not sleep soundly, and should have heard any unusual noise. Two weeks ago, Miss Ware told me she was to be married to Mr. Kenneth in January next. The last time I saw them together was the day before yesterday. I assisted Mrs. Marston in breaking open the door. [Describes the position of the body, etc., etc.]

"Here the call-boy was summoned, and testified to accompanying the deceased home the night before. He came as far as the steps with her. The door was opened by a woman; could not swear it was Miss Woods, though he knows her by sight. The night was dark, and there was no lamp burning in the entry.

"*Julius Kenneth* deposes: I am a master-machinist. Reside at No. — Forsythe street. Miss Ware was my cousin. We were engaged to be married next — [Here the witness's voice failed him.] The last time I saw her was on Wednesday morning, on which occasion we walked out together. I did not leave my room last evening: was confined by a severe cold. A Lieutenant King used to visit my cousin frequently; it created considerable talk in the neighborhood: I did not like it, and requested her to break the acquaintance. She informed me, Wednesday, that King had been ordered to some foreign station, and would trouble me no more. Was excited at the time, hinted at being tired of living; then laughed, and was gayer than she had been for weeks. Deceased was subject to fits of depression. She had engaged to walk with me this morning at eight. When I reached Clark street I learned that she — [Here the witness, overcome by emotion, was allowed to retire.]

"*Dr. Wren* deposes: [This gentleman was very learned and voluble, and had to be suppressed several times by the coroner. We furnish a brief synopsis of his testimony.] I was called in to view the body of the deceased. A deep incision on the throat, two inches below the left ear, severing the left common carotid and the internal jugular vein, had been inflicted with some sharp instrument. Such a wound would, in my opinion, produce death almost instantaneously. The body bore no other signs of violence. A slight mark, almost indistinguishable, in fact, extended from the upper lip toward the right nostril — some hurt, I suppose, received in infancy. Deceased must have been dead a number of hours, the rigor mortis having already supervened, etc., etc.

"*Dr. Ceccarini* corroborated the above testimony.

"The night-watchman and seven other persons were then placed on the stand; but their statements threw no fresh light on the case.

"The situation of Julius Kenneth, the lover of the ill-fated girl, draws forth the deepest commiseration. Miss Ware was twenty-four years of age.

"Who the criminal is, and what could have led to the perpetration of the cruel act, are questions which, at present, threaten to baffle the sagacity of the police. If such deeds can be committed with impunity in a crowded city, like this, who is safe from the assassin's steel?"

THOU ART THE MAN

I COULD BUT SMILE on reading all this serious nonsense.

After breakfast, the next morning, I made my toilet with extreme care, and presented myself at the sheriff's office.

Two gentlemen who were sitting at a table, busy with papers, started nervously to their feet, as I announced myself. I bowed very calmly to the sheriff, and said, "*I am the person who murdered Mary Ware!*"

Of course I was instantly arrested; and that evening, in jail, I had the equivocal pleasure of reading these paragraphs among the police items of the *Mirror:*

"The individual who murdered the ballet-girl, in the night of the third inst., in a house on Crandall street, surrendered himself to the sheriff this forenoon.

"He gave his name as Paul Lynde, and resides opposite the place where the tragedy was enacted. He is a man of medium stature, has restless gray eyes, chestnut hair, and a supernaturally pale countenance. He seems a person of excellent address, is said to be wealthy, and nearly connected with an influential New England family. Notwithstanding his gentlemanly manner, there is that about him which would lead one to select him from out a thousand, as a man of cool and desperate character.

"Mr. Lynde's voluntary surrender is not the least astonishing feature of this affair; for, had he preserved silence he would, beyond a doubt, have escaped even suspicion. The murder was planned and executed with such deliberate skill, that there is little or no evidence to complicate him. In truth, there is no evidence against him, excepting his own confession, which is meagre and confusing enough. He freely acknowledges the crime, but stubbornly refuses to enter into any details. He expresses a desire to be hanged immediately!

"How Mr. Lynde entered the chamber, and by what means he left it, after committing the deed, and why he cruelly killed a lady with whom he had had (as we gather from the testimony) no previous acquaintance — are enigmas which still perplex the public mind, and will not let curiosity sleep. These facts, however, will probably be brought to light during the impending trial. In the meantime, we await the dénouement with interest."

PAUL'S CONFESSION

On the afternoon following this disclosure, the door of my cell turned on its hinges, and Julius Kenneth entered.

In *his* presence I ought to have trembled; but I was calm and collected. He, feverish and dangerous.

"You received my note?"

"Yes; and have come here, as you requested." I waved him to a chair, which he refused to take. Stood leaning on the back of it.

"You of course know, Mr. Kenneth, that I have refused to reveal the circumstances connected with the death of Mary Ware? I wished to make the confession to you alone."

He regarded me for a moment from beneath his shaggy eyebrows.

"Well?"

"But even to you I will assign no reason for the course I pursued. It was necessary that Mary Ware should die."

"Well?"

"I decided that she should die in her chamber, and to that end I purloined her night-key."

Julius Kenneth looked through and through me, as I spoke.

"On Friday night after she had gone to the theatre, I entered the hall-door by means of the key, and stole unobserved to her room, where I secreted myself under the bed, or in that small clothes-press near the stove — I forget which. Sometime between eleven and twelve o'clock, Mary Ware returned. While she was in the act of lighting the gas, I pressed a handkerchief, saturated with chloroform, over her mouth. You know the effect of chloroform? I will at this point spare you further detail, merely remarking that I threw my gloves and the handkerchief in the stove; but I'm afraid there was not fire enough to consume them."

Kenneth walked up and down the cell greatly agitated; then seated himself on the foot of the bed.

"Curse you!"

"Are you listening to me, Mr. Kenneth?"

"Yes!"

"I extinguished the light, and proceeded to make my escape from the room, which I did in a manner so simple that the detectives, through their desire to ferret out wonderful things, will never discover it, unless, indeed, *you* betray me. The night, you will recollect, was foggy; it was impossible to discern an object at four yards distance — this was fortunate for me. I raised the window-sash and let myself out cautiously, holding on by the sill, until my feet touched on the molding which caps the window below. I then drew down the sash. By standing on the extreme left of the cornice, I was able to reach the tin water-spout of the adjacent building, and by that I descended to the sidewalk."

The man glowered at me like a tiger, his eyes green and golden with excitement: I have since wondered that he did not tear me to pieces.

"On gaining the street," I continued coolly, "I found that I had brought the knife with me. It should have been left in the chamber — it would have given the whole thing the aspect of suicide. It was too late to repair the blunder, so I threw the knife —"

"Into the river!" exclaimed Kenneth, involuntarily.

And then I smiled.

"How did you know it was I!" he shrieked.

"Hush! they will overhear you in the corridor. It was as plain as day. I knew it before I had been five minutes in the room. First, because you shrank instinctively from the corpse, though you seemed to be caressing it. Secondly, when I looked into the stove, I saw a glove and handkerchief, partly consumed; and then I instantly accounted for the faint close smell which had affected me before the room was ventilated. It was chloroform. Thirdly, when I went to open the window, I noticed that the paint was scraped off the brackets which held the spout to the next house. This conduit had been newly painted two days previously—I watched the man at work; the paint on the brackets was thicker than anywhere else, and had not dried. On looking at your feet, which I did critically, while speaking to you, I saw that the leather on the inner side of each boot was slightly chafed, paint-marked. It is a way of mine to put this and that together!"

"If you intend to betray me—"

"O, no, but I don't, or I should not be here—alone with you. I am, as you may allow, not quite a fool."

"Indeed, sir, you are as subtle as—"

"Yes, I wouldn't mention him."

"Who?"

"The devil."

Kenneth mused.

"May I ask, Mr. Lynde, what you intend to do?"

"Certainly—remain here."

"I don't understand you," said Kenneth with an air of perplexity.

"If you will listen patiently, you shall learn why *I* have acknowledged this deed, why *I* would bear the penalty. I believe there are vast, intense sensations from which we are excluded, by the conventional fear of a certain kind of death. Now, this pleasure, this ecstasy, this something, I don't know what, which I have striven for all my days, is known only to a privileged few—innocent men, who, through some oversight of the law, are *hanged by the neck!* How rich is Nature in compensations! Some men are born to be hung, some have hanging thrust upon them, and some (as I hope to do) achieve hanging. It appears ages since I commenced watching for an opportunity like this. Worlds could not tempt me to divulge your guilt, nor could worlds have tempted me to commit your crime, for a man's conscience should be at ease to enjoy, to the utmost, this delicious death! Our interview is at an end, Mr. Kenneth. I held it my duty to say this much to you."

And I turned my back on him.

"One word, Mr. Lynde."

Kenneth came to my side, and laid a heavy hand on my shoulder, that red right hand, which all the tears of the angels cannot make white again.

As he stood there, his face suddenly grew so familiar to me—yet so vaguely familiar—that I started. It seemed as if I had seen such a face, somewhere, in my dreams, hundreds of years ago. The face in the grate.

"Did you send this to me last month?" asked Kenneth, holding up a slip of paper on which was scrawled, *Watch them* — in my handwriting.

"Yes," I answered.

Then it struck me that these few thoughtless words, which some sinister spirit had impelled me to write, were the indirect cause of the whole catastrophe.

"Thank you," he said hurriedly. "I watched them!" Then, after a pause, "I shall go far from here. I can not, I *will* not die yet. Mary was to have been my wife, so she would have hidden her shame — O cruel! she, my own cousin, and we the last two of our race! Life is not sweet to me, it is bitter, bitter; but I shall live until I stand front to front with *him*. And you? They will not harm you — *you* are a madman!"

Julius Kenneth was gone before I could reply. The cell door shut him out forever — shut him out in the flesh. His spirit was not so easily exorcised.

After all, it was a wretched fiasco. Two officious friends of mine, who had played chess with me, at my lodgings, on the night of the 3rd, proved an alibi; and I was literally turned out of the Tombs; for I insisted on being executed.

Then it was maddening to have the newspapers call me a monomaniac.

I a monomaniac?

What was Pythagoras, Newton, Fulton? Have not the great original lights of every age, been regarded as madmen? Science, like religion, has its martyrs.

Recent surgical discoveries have, I believe, sustained me in my theory; or, if not, they ought to have done so. There is said to be a pleasure in drowning. Why not in strangulation?

In another field of science, I shall probably have full justice awarded me — I now allude to the Moon-Apparatus, which is still in an unfinished state, but progressing.

1865

LOUISA MAY ALCOTT

A DOUBLE TRAGEDY: AN ACTOR'S STORY

Before she became famous as the author of *Little Women or Meg, Jo, Beth and Amy* (1868), Louisa May Alcott (1832–1888) had been a hardworking, prolific, and largely unsuccessful author, selling poems, sketches, and melodramatic stories to newspapers and magazines from the age of sixteen as the principal breadwinner of her family. She and her three sisters — the prototypes of the girls in *Little Women,* with Jo, the hopeful writer, very obviously being autobiographical — became accustomed to hard work and drudgery at an early age. During the Civil War, Louisa volunteered to be a nurse in Washington, D.C., far from her home in Concord, Massachusetts, which proved to be ruinous to her health. However, she wrote of her experiences and had her first success, a modest one, with the publication of *Hospital Sketches* (1863). Her publisher prevailed on her to write a book for young readers and she wrote *Little Women,* which changed her fortune, enhanced with *Little Women or Meg, Jo, Beth and Amy, Part Second* (1869) and *Little Men* (1871), which was based on her cousins.

What was unknown until almost a century after Alcott's death is that she wrote numerous thrillers and melodramatic novels and stories anonymously and pseudonymously as A. M. Barnard, and with such skill that her payments were substantially greater than those for the work she produced under her own name. Discovered by Madeleine Stern, a bookseller and scholar, several collections of these previously uncollected ripping yarns were published in the 1970s and 1980s.

The tales were written in the day when melodramatic stage plays were immensely popular and commonly featured beautiful, virtuous young women under threat, handsome and stalwart young men who loved them and were willing to risk everything to save them, and villains so heinous that audiences were encouraged to hiss at them whenever they stepped onto the stage, literally twirling the ends of their mustaches.

"A Double Tragedy: An Actor's Story" is not a stage play, but it easily could have been converted into one, with all the characters and situations slotted into their assigned roles. It is, in fact, surprising that it never was adapted to the stage, as Alcott was devoted to the theater and especially to Shakespeare, as will be seen here. Her work was so professional that her publisher asked her for more and more fiction, even paying her in advance. When this story was delivered to Frank Leslie, he gave it the honor of placing it on the first page of the first issue of his newest publication.

"A Double Tragedy: An Actor's Story" was originally published in the June 3, 1865, issue of *Frank Leslie's Chimney Corner;* it was first collected in *A Double Life: Newly Discovered Thrillers of Louisa May Alcott,* edited by Madeleine B. Stern (Boston: Little, Brown, 1988).

• • •

CHAPTER 1

CLOTILDE WAS IN her element that night, for it was a Spanish play, requiring force and fire in its delineation, and she threw herself into her part with an *abandon* that made her seem a beautiful embodiment of power and passion. As for me I could not play ill, for when with her my acting was not art but nature, and I *was* the lover that I seemed. Before she came I made a business, not a pleasure, of my profession, and was content to fill my place, with no higher ambition than to earn my salary with as little effort as possible, to resign myself to the distasteful labor to which my poverty condemned me. She changed all that; for she saw the talent I neglected, she understood the want of motive that made me indifferent, she pitied me for the reverse of fortune that placed me where I was; by her influence and example she roused a manlier spirit in me, kindled every spark of talent I possessed, and incited me to win a success I had not cared to labor for till then.

She was the rage that season, for she came unheralded and almost unknown. Such was the power of beauty, genius, and character, that she made her way at once into public favor, and before the season was half over had become the reigning favorite. My position in the theater threw us much together, and I had not played the lover to this beautiful woman many weeks before I found I was one in earnest. She soon knew it, and confessed that she returned my love; but when I spoke of marriage, she answered with a look and tone that haunted me long afterward.

"Not yet, Paul; something that concerns me alone must be settled first. I cannot marry till I have received the answer for which I am waiting; have faith in me till then, and be patient for my sake."

I did have faith and patience; but while I waited I wondered much and studied her carefully. Frank, generous, and deep-hearted, she won all who approached her; but I, being nearest and dearest, learned to know her best, and soon discovered that some past loss, some present anxiety or hidden care, oppressed and haunted her. A bitter spirit at times possessed her, followed by a heavy melancholy, or an almost fierce unrest, which nothing could dispel but some stormy drama, where she could vent her pent-up gloom or desperation in words and acts which seemed to have a double significance to her. I had vainly tried to find some cause or explanation of this one blemish in the nature which, to a lover's eyes, seemed almost perfect, but never had succeeded till the night of which I write.

The play was nearly over, the interest was at its height, and Clotilde's best scene was drawing to a close. She had just indignantly refused to betray a state secret which would endanger the life of her lover; and the Duke had just wrathfully vowed to denounce her to the Inquisition if she did not yield, when I her lover, disguised as a monk, saw a strange and sudden change come over her. She should have trembled at a threat so full of terror, and have made one last appeal to the stern old man before she turned to defy and dare all things for her lover. But she seemed to have forgotten time, place, and character, for she stood gazing straight before her as if turned to stone. At first I thought it was some new presentiment of fear, for she seldom played a part twice alike, and left much to the inspiration of the moment. But an instant's scrutiny convinced me that this was not acting, for her face paled visibly, her eyes dilated as they looked beyond the Duke, her lips fell apart, and she looked like one suddenly confronted by a ghost. An inquiring glance from my companion showed me that he, too, was disturbed by her appearance, and fearing that she had over-exerted herself, I struck into the dialogue as if she had made her appeal. The sound of my voice seemed to recall her; she passed her hand across her eyes, drew a long breath, and looked about her. I thought she had recovered herself and was about to resume her part, but, to my great surprise, she only clung to me, saying in a shrill whisper, so full of despair, it chilled my blood—

"The answer, Paul, the answer: it has come!"

The words were inaudible to all but myself; but the look, the gesture were eloquent with terror, grief, and love; and taking it for a fine piece of acting, the audience applauded loud and long. The accustomed sound roused Clotilde, and during that noisy moment a hurried dialogue passed between us.

"What is it? Are you ill?" I whispered.

"He is here, Paul, alive; I saw him. Heaven help us both!"

"Who is here?"

"Hush! not now; there is no time to tell you."

"You are right; compose yourself; you must speak in a moment."

"What do I say? Help me, Paul; I have forgotten every thing but that man."

She looked as if bewildered; and I saw that some sudden shock had entirely unnerved her. But actors must have neither hearts nor nerves while on the stage. The applause was subsiding, and she must speak. Fortunately I remembered enough of her part to prompt her as she struggled through the little that remained; for, seeing her condition, Denon and I cut the scene remorselessly, and brought it to a close as soon as possible. The instant the curtain fell we were assailed with questions, but Clotilde answered none; and though hidden from her sight, still seemed to see the object that had wrought such an alarming change in her. I told them she was ill, took her to her dressing-room, and gave her into the hands of her maid, for I must appear again, and delay was impossible.

How I got through my part I cannot tell, for my thoughts were with Clotilde; but an actor learns to live a double life, so while Paul Lamar suffered torments of anxiety Don Felix fought a duel, killed his adversary, and was dragged to judgment. Involuntarily my eyes often wandered toward the spot where Clotilde's had seemed fixed. It was one of the stage-boxes, and at first I thought it empty, but presently I caught the glitter of a glass turned apparently on myself. As soon as possible I crossed the stage, and as I leaned haughtily upon my sword while the seconds adjusted the preliminaries, I searched the box with a keen glance. Nothing was visible, however, but a hand lying easily on the red cushion; a man's hand, white and shapely; on one finger shone a ring, evidently a woman's ornament, for it was a slender circlet of diamonds that flashed with every gesture.

"Some fop, doubtless; a man like that could never daunt Clotilde," I thought. And eager to discover if there was not another occupant in the box, I took a step nearer, and stared boldly into the soft gloom that filled it. A low derisive laugh came from behind the curtain as the hand gathered back as if to permit me to satisfy myself. The act showed me that a single person occupied the box, but also effectually concealed that person from my sight; and as I was recalled to my duty by a warning whisper from one of my comrades, the hand appeared to wave me a mocking adieu. Baffled and angry, I devoted myself to the affairs of Don Felix, wondering the while if Clotilde would be able to reappear, how she would bear herself, if that hidden man was the cause of her terror, and why? Even when immured in a dungeon, after my arrest, I beguiled the tedium of a long soliloquy with these questions, and executed a better stage-start than any I had ever practiced, when at last she came to me, bringing liberty and love as my reward.

I had left her haggard, speechless, overwhelmed with some mysterious woe; she reappeared beautiful and brilliant, with a joy that seemed too lovely to be feigned. Never had she played so well; for some spirit, stronger than her own, seemed to possess and rule her royally. If I had ever doubted her love for me, I should have been assured of it that night, for she breathed into the fond words of her part a tenderness and grace that filled my heart to overflowing, and inspired me to play the grateful lover to the life. The last words came all too soon for me, and as she threw herself into my arms she turned her head as if to glance triumphantly at the defeated Duke, but I saw that again she looked beyond him, and with an indescribable expression of mingled pride, contempt, and defiance. A soft sound of applause from the mysterious occupant of that box answered the look, and the white hand sent a superb bouquet flying to her feet. I was about to lift and present it to her, but she checked me and crushed it under foot with an air of the haughtiest disdain. A laugh from behind the curtain greeted this demonstration, but it was scarcely observed by others; for that first bouquet seemed a signal for a rain of flowers, and these latter offerings she permitted me to gather up, receiving them with her most gracious smiles, her most graceful obeisances, as if to mark, for one observer at least, the difference of her regard for the givers. As I laid the last floral tribute in her arms I took a parting glance at the box, hoping to catch a glimpse of the unknown face. The curtains were thrown back and the door stood open, admitting a strong light from the vestibule, but the box was empty.

Then the green curtain fell, and Clotilde whispered, as she glanced from her full hands to the rejected bouquet—

"Bring that to my room; I must have it."

I obeyed, eager to be enlightened; but when we were alone she flung down her fragrant burden, snatched the stranger's gift, tore it apart, drew out a slip of paper, read it, dropped it, and walked to and fro, wringing her hands, like one in a paroxysm of despair. I seized the note and looked at it, but found no key to her distress in the enigmatical words—

"I shall be there. Come and bring your lover with you, else—"

There it abruptly ended; but the unfinished threat seemed the more menacing for its obscurity, and I indignantly demanded,

"Clotilde, who dares address you so? Where will this man be? You surely will not obey such a command? Tell me; I have a right to know."

"I cannot tell you, now; I dare not refuse him; he will be at Keen's; we *must* go. How will it end! How will it end!"

I remembered then that we were all to sup *en costume,* with a brother actor, who did not play that night. I was about to speak yet more urgently, when the entrance of her maid checked me. Clotilde composed herself by a strong effort—

"Go and prepare," she whispered; "have faith in me a little longer, and soon you shall know all."

There was something almost solemn in her tone; her eye met mine, imploringly, and her lips trembled as if her heart were full. That assured me at once; and with a reassuring word I hurried away to give a few touches to my costume, which just then was fitter for a dungeon than a feast. When I rejoined her there was no trace of past emotion; a soft color bloomed upon her cheek, her eyes were tearless and brilliant, her lips were dressed in smiles. Jewels shone on her white forehead, neck, and arms, flowers glowed in her bosom; and no charm that art or skill could lend to the rich dress or its lovely wearer, had been forgotten.

"What an actress!" I involuntarily exclaimed, as she came to meet me, looking almost as beautiful and gay as ever.

"It is well that I am one, else I should yield to my hard fate without a struggle. Paul, hitherto I have played for money, now I play for love; help me by being a calm spectator to-night, and whatever happens promise me that there shall be no violence."

I promised, for I was wax in her hands; and, more bewildered than ever, followed to the carriage, where a companion was impatiently awaiting us.

CHAPTER II

We were late; and on arriving found all the other guests assembled. Three strangers appeared; and my attention was instantly fixed upon them, for the mysterious "he" was to be there. All three seemed gay, gallant, handsome men; all three turned admiring eyes upon Clotilde, all three were gloved. Therefore, as I had seen no face, my one clue, the ring, was lost. From Clotilde's face and manner I could learn nothing, for a smile seemed carved upon her lips, her drooping lashes half concealed her eyes, and her voice was too well trained to betray her by a traitorous tone. She received the greetings, compliments and admiration of all alike, and I vainly looked and listened till supper was announced.

As I took my place beside her, I saw her shrink and shiver slightly, as if a chilly wind had blown over her, but before I could ask if she were cold a bland voice said,

"Will Mademoiselle Varian permit me to drink her health?"

It was one of the strangers; mechanically I offered her glass; but the next instant my hold tightened till the slender stem snapped, and the rosy bowl fell broken to the table, for on the handsome hand extended to fill it shone the ring.

"A bad omen, Mr. Lamar. I hope my attempt will succeed better," said St. John, as he filled another glass and handed it to Clotilde, who merely lifted it to her lips, and turned to enter into an animated conversation with the gentleman who sat on the other side. Some one addressed St. John, and I was glad of it; for now all my interest and attention centered in him. Keenly, but covertly, I examined him, and soon felt that in spite of that foppish ornament he *was* a man to daunt a woman like Clotilde. Pride and passion, courage and indomitable will met and mingled in his face, though the obedient features wore whatever expression he imposed upon them. He was the handsomest, most elegant, but least attractive of the three, yet it was hard to say why. The others gave themselves freely to the enjoyment of a scene which evidently possessed the charm of novelty to them; but St. John unconsciously wore the half sad, half weary look that comes to those who have led lives of pleasure and found their emptiness. Although the wittiest, and most brilliant talker at the table, his gaiety seemed fitful, his manner absent at times. More than once I saw him knit his black brows as he met my eye, and more than once I caught a long look fixed on Clotilde,—a look full of the lordly admiration and pride which a master bestows upon a handsome slave. It made my blood boil, but I controlled myself, and was apparently absorbed in Miss Damareau, my neighbor.

We seemed as gay and care-free a company as ever made midnight merry; songs were sung, stories told, theatrical phrases added sparkle to the conversation, and the varied costumes gave an air of romance to the revel. The Grand Inquisitor still in his ghostly garb, and the stern old Duke were now the jolliest of the group; the page flirted violently with the princess; the rivals of the play were bosom-friends again, and the fair Donna Olivia had apparently forgotten her knightly lover, to listen to a modern gentleman.

Clotilde sat leaning back in a deep chair, eating nothing, but using her fan with the indescribable grace of a Spanish woman. She was very lovely, for the dress became her, and the black lace mantilla falling from her head to her shoulders, heightened her charms by half concealing them; and nothing could have been more genial and gracious than the air with which she listened and replied to the compliments of the youngest stranger, who sat beside her and was all devotion.

I forgot myself in observing her till something said by our opposite neighbors arrested both of us. Some one seemed to have been joking St. John about his ring, which was too brilliant an ornament to pass unobserved.

"Bad taste, I grant you," he said, laughing, "but it is a *gage d'amour,* and I wear it for a purpose."

"I fancied it was the latest Paris fashion," returned Keen. "And apropos to Paris, what is the latest gossip from the gay city?"

A slow smile rose to St. John's lips as he answered, after a moment's thought and quick glance across the room.

"A little romance; shall I tell it to you? It is a love story, ladies, and not long."

A unanimous assent was given; and he began with a curious glitter in his eyes, a stealthy smile coming and going on his face as the words dropped slowly from his lips.

"It begins in the old way. A foolish young man fell in love with a Spanish girl much his inferior in rank, but beautiful enough to excuse his folly, for he married her. Then came a few months of bliss; but Madame grew jealous. Monsieur wearied of domestic tempests, and, after vain efforts to appease his fiery angel, he proposed a separation. Madame was obdurate, Monsieur rebelled; and in order to try the soothing effects of absence upon both, after settling her in a charming chateau, he slipped away, leaving no trace by which his route might be discovered."

"Well, how did the experiment succeed? asked Keen. St. John shrugged his shoulders, emptied his glass, and answered tranquilly.

"Like most experiments that have women for their subjects, for the amiable creatures always devise some way of turning the tables, and defeating the best laid plans. Madame waited for her truant spouse till rumors of his death reached Paris, for he had met with mishaps, and sickness detained him long in an obscure place, so the rumors seemed confirmed by his silence, and Madame believed him dead. But instead of dutifully mourning him, this inexplicable woman shook the dust of the chateau off her feet and disappeared, leaving everything, even to her wedding ring, behind her."

"Bless me, how odd! what became of her?" exclaimed Miss Damareau, forgetting the dignity of the Princess in the curiosity of the woman.

"The very question her repentant husband asked when, returning from his long holiday, he found her gone. He searched the continent for her, but in vain; and for two years she left him to suffer the torments of suspense."

"As he had left her to suffer them while he went pleasuring. It was a light punishment for his offense."

Clotilde spoke; and the sarcastic tone, for all its softness, made St. John wince, though no eye but mine observed the faint flush of shame or anger that passed across his face.

"Mademoiselle espouses the lady's cause, of course, and as a gallant man I should do likewise, but unfortunately my sympathies are strongly enlisted on the other side."

"Then you know the parties?" I said, impulsively, for my inward excitement was increasing rapidly, and I began to feel rather than to see the end of this mystery.

"I have seen them, and cannot blame the man for claiming his beautiful wife, when he found her," he answered, briefly.

"Then he did find her at last? Pray tell us how and when," cried Miss Damareau.

"She betrayed herself. It seems that Madame had returned to her old profession, and fallen in love with an actor; but being as virtuous as she was fair, she would not marry till she was assured beyond a doubt of her husband's death. Her engagements would not allow her to inquire in person, so she sent letters to various places asking for proofs of his demise; and as ill or good fortune would have it, one of these letters fell into Monsieur's hands, giving him an excellent clue to her whereabouts, which he followed indefatigably till he found her."

"Poor little woman, I pity her! How did she receive Monsieur De Trop?" asked Keen.

"You shall know in good time. He found her in London playing at one of the great theaters, for she had talent, and had become a star. He saw her act for a night or two, made secret inquiries concerning her, and fell more in love with her than ever. Having tried almost every novelty under the sun he had a fancy to attempt something of the dramatic sort, so presented himself to Madame at a party."

"Heavens! what a scene there must have been," ejaculated Miss Damareau.

"On the contrary, there was no scene at all, for the man was not a Frenchman, and Madame was a fine actress. Much as he had admired her on the stage he was doubly charmed with her performance in private, for it was superb. They were among strangers, and she received him like one, playing her part with the utmost grace and self-control, for with a woman's quickness of perception, she divined his purpose, and knowing that her fate was in his hands, endeavored to propitiate him by complying with his caprice. Mademoiselle, allow me to send you some of these grapes, they are delicious."

As he leaned forward to present them he shot a glance at her that caused me to start up with a violence that nearly betrayed me. Fortunately the room was close, and saying something about the heat, I threw open a window, and let in a balmy gust of spring air that refreshed us all.

"How did they settle it, by duels and despair, or by repentance and reconciliation all round, in the regular French fashion?"

"I regret that I'm unable to tell you, for I left before the affair was arranged. I only know that Monsieur was more captivated than before, and quite ready to forgive and forget, and I suspect that Madame, seeing the folly of resistance, will submit with a good grace, and leave the stage to play 'The Honey Moon' for a second time in private with a husband who adores her. What is the Mademoiselle's opinion?"

She had listened, without either question or comment, her fan at rest, her hands motionless, her eyes downcast; so still it seemed as if she had hushed the breath upon her lips, so pale despite her rouge, that I wondered no one observed it, so intent and resolute that every feature seemed under control,—every look and gesture guarded. When St. John addressed her, she looked up with a smile as bland as his own, but fixed her eyes on him with an expression of undismayed defiance and supreme contempt that caused him to bite his lips with ill-concealed annoyance.

"My opinion?" she said, in her clear, cold voice, "I think that Madame, being a woman of spirit, would *not* endeavor to propitiate that man in any way except for her lover's sake, and having been once deserted would not subject herself to a second indignity of that sort while there was a law to protect her."

"Unfortunately there is no law for her, having once refused a separation. Even if there were, Monsieur is rich and powerful, she is poor and friendless; he loves her, and is a man who never permits himself to be thwarted by any obstacle; therefore, I am convinced it would be best for this adorable woman to submit without defiance or delay—and I do think she will," he added, significantly.

"They seem to forget the poor lover; what is to become of him?" asked Keen.

"*I* do not forget him"; and the hand that wore the ring closed with an ominous gesture, which I well understood. "Monsieur merely claims his own, and the other, being a man of sense and honor, will doubtless withdraw at once; and though 'desolated,' as the French say, will soon console himself with a new *inamorata.* If he is so unwise as to oppose Monsieur, who by the by is a dead shot, there is but one way in which both can receive satisfaction."

A significant emphasis on the last word pointed his meaning, and the smile that accompanied it almost goaded me to draw the sword I wore, and offer him that satisfaction on the spot. I felt the color rise to my forehead, and dared not look up, but leaning on the back of Clotilde's chair, I bent as if to speak to her.

"Bear it a little longer for my sake, Paul," she murmured, with a look of love and despair, that wrung my heart. Here some one spoke of a long rehearsal in the morning, and the lateness of the hour.

"A farewell toast before we part," said Keen. "Come, Lamar, give us a sentiment, after that whisper you ought to be inspired."

"I am. Let me give you—The love of liberty and the liberty of love."

"Good! That would suit the hero and heroine of St. John's story, for Monsieur wished much for his liberty, and, no doubt, Madame will for her love," said Denon, while the glasses were filled.

Then the toast was drunk with much merriment and the party broke up. While detained by one of the strangers, I saw St. John approach Clotilde, who stood alone by the window, and speak rapidly for several minutes. She listened with half-averted head, answered briefly, and wrapping the mantilla closely about her, swept away from him with her haughtiest mien. He watched for a moment, then followed, and before I could reach her, offered his arm to lead her to the carriage. She seemed about to refuse it, but something in the expression of his face restrained her; and accepting it, they went down together. The hall and little anteroom were dimly lighted, but as I slowly followed, I saw her snatch her hand away, when she thought they were alone; saw him draw her to him with an embrace as fond as it was irresistible; and turning her indignant face to his, kiss it ardently, as he said in a tone, both tender and imperious—

"Good night, my darling. I give you one more day, and then I claim you."

"Never!" she answered, almost fiercely, as he released her. And wishing me pleasant dreams, as he passed, went out into the night, gaily humming the burden of a song Clotilde had often sung to me.

The moment we were in the carriage all her self-control deserted her, and a tempest of despairing grief came over her. For a time, both words and caresses were unavailing, and I let her weep herself calm before I asked the hard question—

"Is all this true, Clotilde?"

"Yes, Paul, all true, except that he said nothing of the neglect, the cruelty, the insult that I bore before he left me. I was so young, so lonely, I was glad to be loved and cared for, and I believed that he would never change. I cannot tell you all I suffered, but I rejoiced when I thought death had freed me; I would keep nothing that reminded me of the bitter past, and went away to begin again, as if it had never been."

"Why delay telling me this? Why let me learn it in such a strange and sudden way?"

"Ah, forgive me! I am so proud I could not bear to tell you that any man had wearied of me and deserted me. I meant to tell you before our marriage, but the fear that St. John was alive haunted me, and till it was set at rest I would not speak. To-night there was no time, and I was forced to leave all to chance. He found pleasure in tormenting me through you, but would not speak out, because he is as proud as I, and does not wish to hear our story bandied from tongue to tongue."

"What did he say to you, Clotilde?"

"He begged me to submit and return to him, in spite of all that has passed; he warned me that if we attempted to escape it would be at the peril of your life, for he would most assuredly follow and find us, to whatever corner of the earth we might fly; and he will, for he is as relentless as death."

"What did he mean by giving you one day more?" I asked, grinding my teeth with impatient rage as I listened.

"He gave me one day to recover from my surprise, to prepare for my departure with him, and to bid you farewell."

"And will you, Clotilde?"

"No!" she replied, clenching her hands with a gesture of dogged resolution, while her eyes glittered in the darkness. "I never will submit; there must be some way of escape; I shall find it, and if I do not—I can die."

"Not yet, dearest; we will appeal to the law first; I have a friend whom I will consult to-morrow, and he may help us."

"I have no faith in law," she said, despairingly, "money and influence so often outweigh justice and mercy. I have no witnesses, no friends, no wealth to help me; he has all, and we shall only be defeated. I must devise some surer way. Let me think a little; a woman's wit is quick when her heart prompts it."

I let the poor soul flatter herself with vague hopes; but I saw no help for us except in flight, and that she would not consent to, lest it should endanger me. More than once I said savagely within myself, "I will kill him," and then shuddered at the counsels of the devil, so suddenly aroused in my own breast. As if she divined my thought by instinct, Clotilde broke the heavy silence that followed her last words, by clinging to me with the imploring cry,

"Oh, Paul, shun him, else your fiery spirit will destroy you. He promised me he would not harm you unless we drove him to it. Be careful, for my sake, and if any one must suffer let it be miserable me."

I soothed her as I best could, and when our long, sad drive ended, bade her rest while I worked, for she would need all her strength on the morrow. Then I left her, to haunt the street all night long, guarding her door, and while I paced to and fro without, I watched her shadow come and go before the lighted window as she paced within, each racking our brains for some means of help till day broke.

CHAPTER III

EARLY ON THE following morning I consulted my friend, but when I laid the case before him he gave me little hope of a happy issue should the attempt be made. A divorce was hardly possible, when an unscrupulous man like St. John was bent on opposing it; and though no decision could force her to remain with him, we should not be safe from his vengeance, even if we chose to dare everything and fly together. Long and earnestly we talked, but to little purpose, and I went to rehearsal with a heavy heart.

Clotilde was to have a benefit that night, and what a happy day I had fancied this would be; how carefully I had prepared for it; what delight I had anticipated in playing Romeo to her Juliet; and how eagerly I had longed for the time which now seemed to approach with such terrible rapidity, for each hour brought our parting nearer! On the stage I found Keen and his new friend amusing themselves with fencing, while waiting the arrival of some of the company. I was too miserable to be dangerous just then, and when St. John bowed to me with his most courteous air, I returned the greeting, though I could not speak to him. I think he saw my suffering, and enjoyed it with the satisfaction of a cruel nature, but he treated me with the courtesy of an equal, which new demonstration surprised me, till, through Denon, I discovered that having inquired much about me he had learned that I was a gentleman by birth and education, which fact accounted for the change in his demeanor. I roamed restlessly about the gloomy green room and stage, till Keen, dropping his foil, confessed himself outfenced and called to me.

"Come here, Lamar, and try a bout with St. John. You are the best fencer among us, so, for the honor of the company, come and do your best instead of playing Romeo before the time."

A sudden impulse prompted me to comply, and a few passes proved that I was the better swordsman of the two. This annoyed St. John, and though he complimented me with the rest, he would not own himself outdone, and we kept it up till both grew warm and excited. In the midst of an animated match between us, I observed that the button was off his foil, and a glance at his face assured me that he was aware of it, and almost at the instant he made a skillful thrust, and the point pierced my flesh. As I caught the foil from his hand and drew it out with an exclamation of pain, I saw a gleam of exultation pass across his face, and knew that his promise to Clotilde was no idle breath. My comrades surrounded me with anxious inquiries, and no one was more surprised and solicitous than St. John. The wound was trifling, for a picture of Clotilde had turned the thrust aside, else the force with which it was given might have rendered it fatal. I made light of it, but hated him with a redoubled hatred for the cold-blooded treachery that would have given to revenge the screen of accident.

The appearance of the ladies caused us to immediately ignore the mishap, and address ourselves to business. Clotilde came last, looking so pale it was not necessary for her to plead illness; but she went through her part with her usual fidelity, while her husband watched her with the masterful expression that nearly drove me wild. He haunted her like a shadow, and she listened to him with the desperate look of a hunted creature driven to bay. He might have softened her just resentment by a touch of generosity or compassion, and won a little gratitude, even though love was impossible; but he was blind, relentless, and goaded her beyond endurance, rousing in her fiery Spanish heart a dangerous spirit he could not control. The rehearsal was over at last, and I approached

Clotilde with a look that mutely asked if I should leave her. St. John said something in a low voice, but she answered sternly, as she took my arm with a decided gesture.

"This day is mine; I will not be defrauded of an hour," and we went away together for our accustomed stroll in the sunny park.

A sad and memorable walk was that, for neither had any hope with which to cheer the other, and Clotilde grew gloomier as we talked. I told her of my fruitless consultation, also of the fencing match; at that her face darkened, and she said, below her breath, "I shall remember that."

We walked long together, and I proposed plan after plan, all either unsafe or impracticable. She seemed to listen, but when I paused she answered with averted eyes—

"Leave it to me; I have a project; let me perfect it before I tell you. Now I must go and rest, for I have had no sleep, and I shall need all my strength for the tragedy to-night."

All that afternoon I roamed about the city, too restless for anything but constant motion, and evening found me ill prepared for my now doubly arduous duties. It was late when I reached the theater, and I dressed hastily. My costume was new for the occasion, and not till it was on did I remember that I had neglected to try it since the finishing touches were given. A stitch or two would remedy the defects, and, hurrying up to the wardrobe room, a skillful pair of hands soon set me right. As I came down the winding-stairs that led from the lofty chamber to a dimly-lighted gallery below, St. John's voice arrested me, and pausing I saw that Keen was doing the honors of the theater in defiance of all rules. Just as they reached the stair-foot some one called to them, and throwing open a narrow door, he said to his companion—

"From here you get a fine view of the stage; steady yourself by the rope and look down. I'll be with you in a moment."

He ran into the dressing-room from whence the voice proceeded, and St. John stepped out upon a little platform, hastily built for the launching of an aerial-car in some grand spectacle. Glad to escape meeting him, I was about to go on, when, from an obscure corner, a dark figure glided noiselessly to the door and leaned in. I caught a momentary glimpse of a white extended arm and the glitter of steel, then came a cry of mortal fear, a heavy fall; and flying swiftly down the gallery the figure disappeared. With one leap I reached the door, and looked in; the raft hung broken, the platform was empty. At that instant Keen rushed out, demanding what had happened, and scarcely knowing what I said, I answered hurriedly,

"The rope broke and he fell."

Keen gave me a strange look, and dashed down stairs. I followed, to find myself in a horror-stricken crowd, gathered about the piteous object which a moment ago had been a living man. There was no need to call a surgeon, for that headlong fall had dashed out life in the drawing of a breath, and nothing remained to do but to take the poor body tenderly away to such friends as the newly-arrived stranger possessed. The contrast between the gay crowd rustling before the curtain and the dreadful scene transpiring behind it, was terrible; but the house was filling fast; there was no time for the indulgence of pity or curiosity, and soon no trace of the accident remained but the broken rope above, and an ominous damp spot on the newly-washed boards below. At a word of command from our energetic manager, actors and actresses were sent away to retouch their pale faces with carmine, to restore their startled nerves with any stimulant at hand, and to forget, if possible, the awesome sight just witnessed.

I returned to my dressing-room hoping Clotilde had heard nothing of this sad, and yet for us most fortunate accident, though all the while a vague dread haunted me, and I feared to see her. Mechanically completing my costume, I looked about me for the dagger with which poor Juliet was to stab herself, and found that it was gone. Trying to recollect where I put it, I remembered having it in my hand just before I went up to have my sword-belt altered; and fancying that I must have inadvertently taken it with me, I reluctantly retraced my steps. At the top of the stairs leading to that upper gallery a little white object caught my eye, and, taking it up, I found it to be a flower. If it had been a burning coal I should not have dropped it more hastily than I did when I recognized it was one of a cluster I had left in Clotilde's room because she loved them. They were a rare and delicate kind; no one but herself was likely to possess them in that place, nor was she likely to have given one away, for my gifts were kept with jealous care; yet how came it there? And as I asked myself the question, like an answer returned the remembrance of her face when she said, "I shall remember this." The darkly-shrouded form was a female figure, the white arm a woman's, and horrible as was the act, who but that sorely-tried and tempted creature would have committed it. For a moment my heart stood still, then I indignantly rejected the black thought, and thrusting the flower into my breast went on my way, trying to convince myself that the foreboding fear which oppressed me was caused by the agitating events of the last half hour. My weapon was not in the wardrobe-room; and as I returned, wondering what I had done with it, I saw Keen standing in the little doorway with a candle in his hand. He turned and asked what I was looking for. I told him, and explained why I was searching for it there.

"Here it is; I found it at the foot of these stairs. It is too sharp for a stage-dagger, and will do mischief unless you dull it," he said, adding, as he pointed to the broken rope, "Lamar, that was cut; I have examined it."

The light shone full in my face, and I knew that it changed, as did my voice, for I thought of Clotilde, and till that fear was at rest resolved to be dumb concerning what I had seen, but I could not repress a shudder as I said, hastily,

"Don't suspect me of any deviltry, for heaven's sake. I've got to go on in fifteen minutes, and how can I play unless you let me forget this horrible business."

"Forget it then, if you can; I'll remind you of it to-morrow." And, with a significant nod, he walked away, leaving behind him a new trial to distract me. I ran to Clotilde's room, bent on relieving myself, if possible, of the suspicion that would return with redoubled pertinacity since the discovery of the dagger, which I was sure I had not dropped where it was found. When I tapped at her door, her voice, clear and sweet as ever, answered "Come!" and entering, I found her ready, but alone. Before I could open my lips she put up her hand as if to arrest the utterance of some dreadful intelligence.

"Don't speak of it; I have heard, and cannot bear a repetition of the horror. I must forget it till to-morrow, then—." There she stopped abruptly, for I produced the flower, asking as naturally as I could—

"Did you give this to any one?"

"No; why ask me that?" and she shrunk a little, as I bent to count the blossoms in the cluster on her breast. I gave her seven; now there were but six, and I fixed on her a look that betrayed my fear, and mutely demanded its confirmation or denial. Other eyes she might have evaded or defied, not mine; the traitorous blood dyed her face, then fading, left it colorless; her eyes wandered and fell, she clasped her hands imploringly, and threw herself at my feet, crying in a stifled voice,

"Paul, be merciful; that was our only hope, and the guilt is mine alone!"

But I started from her, exclaiming with mingled incredulity and horror—

"Was this the tragedy you meant? What devil devised and helped you execute a crime like this?"

"Hear me! I did not plan it, yet I longed to kill him, and all day the thought would haunt me. I have borne so much, I could bear no more, and he drove me to it. To-night the thought still clung to me, till I was half mad. I went to find you, hoping to escape it; you were gone, but on your table lay the dagger. As I took it in my hand I heard his voice, and forgot every thing except my wrongs and the great happiness one blow could bring us. I followed then, meaning to stab him in the dark; but when I saw him leaning where a safer stroke would destroy him, I gave it, and we are safe."

"Safe!" I echoed. "Do you know you left my dagger behind you? Keen found it; he suspects me, for I was near; and St. John has told him something of the cause I have to wish you free."

She sprung up, and seemed about to rush away to proclaim her guilt, but I restrained her desperate purpose, saying sternly—

"Control yourself and be cautious. I may be mistaken; but if either must suffer, let it be me. I can bear it best, even if it comes to the worst, for my life is worthless now."

"And I have made it so? Oh, Paul, can you never forgive me and forget my sin?"

"Never, Clotilde; it is too horrible."

I broke from her trembling hold, and covered up my face, for suddenly the woman whom I once loved had grown abhorrent to me. For many minutes neither spoke or stirred; my heart seemed dead within me, and what went on in that stormy soul I shall never know. Suddenly I was called, and as I turned to leave her, she seized both my hands in a despairing grasp, covered them with tender kisses, wet them with repentant tears, and clung to them in a paroxysm of love, remorse, and grief, till I was forced to go, leaving her alone with the memory of her sin.

That night I was like one in a terrible dream; every thing looked unreal, and like an automaton I played my part, for always before me I seemed to see that shattered body and to hear again that beloved voice confessing a black crime. Rumors of the accident had crept out, and damped the spirits of the audience, yet it was as well, perhaps, for it made them lenient to the short-comings of the actors, and lent another shadow to the mimic tragedy that slowly darkened to its close. Clotilde's unnatural composure would have been a marvel to me had I not been past surprise at any demonstration on her part. A wide gulf now lay between us, and it seemed impossible for me to cross it. The generous, tender woman whom I first loved, was still as beautiful and dear to me as ever, but as much lost as if death had parted us. The desperate, despairing creature I had learned to know within an hour, seemed like an embodiment of the murderous spirit which had haunted me that day, and though by heaven's mercy it had not conquered me, yet I now hated it with remorseful intensity. So strangely were the two images blended in my troubled mind that I could not separate them, and they exerted a mysterious influence over me. When with Clotilde she seemed all she had ever been, and I enacted the lover with a power I had never known before, feeling the while that it might be for the last time. When away from her the darker impression returned, and the wildest of the poet's words were not too strong to embody my own sorrow and despair. They told me long afterwards that never had the tragedy been better played, and I could believe it, for the hapless Italian lovers never found better representatives than in us that night.

Worn out with suffering and excitement, I longed for solitude and silence with a desperate longing, and when Romeo murmured, "With a kiss I die," I fell beside the bier, wishing that I too was done with life. Lying there, I watched Clotilde, through the little that remained, and so truly, tenderly, did she render the pathetic scene that my heart softened; all the early love returned strong, and warm as ever, and I felt that I *could* forgive. As she knelt to draw my dagger, I whispered, warningly,

"Be careful, dear, it is very sharp."

"I know it," she answered with a shudder, then cried aloud,

"Oh happy dagger! this is thy sheath; there rust, and let me die."

Again I saw the white arm raised, the flash of steel as Juliet struck the blow that was to free her, and sinking down beside her lover, seemed to breathe her life away.

"I thank God it's over," I ejaculated, a few minutes later, as the curtain slowly fell. Clotilde did not answer, and feeling how cold the cheek that touched my own had grown, I thought she had given way at last.

"She has fainted; lift her, Denon, and let me rise," I cried, as County Paris sprang up with a joke.

"Good God, she has hurt herself with that cursed dagger!" he exclaimed, as raising her he saw a red stain on the white draperies she wore.

I staggered to my feet, and laid her on the bier she had just left, but no mortal skill could heal that hurt, and Juliet's grave-clothes were her own. Deaf to the enthusiastic clamor that demanded our re-appearance, blind to the confusion and dismay about me, I leaned over her passionately, conjuring her to give me one word of pardon and farewell. As if my voice had power to detain her, even when death called, the dark eyes, full of remorseful love, met mine again, and feebly drawing from her breast a paper, she motioned Keen to take it, murmuring in a tone that changed from solemn affirmation to the tenderest penitence,

"Lamar is innocent — I did it. This will prove it. Paul, I have tried to atone — oh, forgive me, and remember me for my love's sake."

I did forgive her; and she died, smiling on my breast. I did remember her through a long, lonely life, and never played again since the night of that DOUBLE TRAGEDY.

1875

ALLAN PINKERTON

THE TWO SISTERS; OR, THE AVENGER

It is entirely likely that the Scottish-born ALLAN PINKERTON (1819–1884) was the single most significant individual in the history of crime fighting in America. After immigrating to the United States in 1842, he soon took a position with Chicago Abolitionist leaders (his home becoming a stop on the Underground Railroad) and, in 1849, became the first detective in Chicago. A few years later, he cofounded the North-Western Police Agency, later named the Pinkerton National Detective Agency, a firm still in business.

As the first private detective in America, Pinkerton developed such now-common practices as surveillance and undercover work and at the time of his death was compiling a national databank of all known criminals, a system vastly magnified and today maintained by the FBI. His agency quickly grew and became famous for catching train and bank robbers and for preventing an assassination attempt on Abraham Lincoln as he was traveling to his inauguration. After Pinkerton's death, the Pinkertons, as his agents were known, became involved with such anti-union efforts as the protection of replacement workers and the property of businessmen.

The company logo was an open eye captioned with "We Never Sleep," lending its symbol to the generations of private eyes who followed, both in real life and in fiction; it appeared on the covers of the many books that appeared under the Allan Pinkerton byline. These extremely popular, frequently reprinted books were compiled to tell the tales of his detectives and the cases purportedly handled by the agency. It is almost certain that they were ghostwritten, with much color and sensationalism added, and were mainly produced as a way of spreading the fame and reputation of the agency. The first of the books was *The Expressman and the Detective* (1874) and an additional seventeen titles followed, including several published years after Pinkerton died.

The story offered here is one of the fictionalized accounts of events that may or may not actually have occurred. These tales were evidently produced by writers whose primary skill was in public relations rather than literary style. Still, they are of such historical importance that they cannot be ignored.

"The Two Sisters; or, The Avenger" was first published in *Claude Melnotte as a Detective and Other Stories* (Chicago: W. B. Keen, Cooke & Co., 1875).

• • •

CHAPTER 1

IN THE EARLY part of April, 1851, I was attending to some business for the United States Treasury Department, under orders from Mr. Guthrie, the Secretary of the Treasury at that time. Having no one to assist me, I was obliged to do an immense amount of work, and to take advantage of every unoccupied moment, to rest and sleep. I was not, then, living in Chicago, but was temporarily boarding at the Sherman House, in that city, my own home being at Dundee, in Kane County, Illinois. One evening, I had retired early, exhausted by a hard day's work, and had just fallen into a sound sleep, when I was awakened by my old friend, William L. Church, the sheriff of Cook County, Illinois. He was accompanied by two other gentlemen, whom he introduced to me, as soon as I could make a hasty toilet and admit them to my room. One was Deputy-Sheriff Green, of Coldwater, Michigan, and the other, William Wells, of Quincy, a small town about six miles north of Coldwater. Mr. Church said that he wished me to listen to the story which Mr. Wells had to tell, and to give my services to aid in capturing two of the worst villains that ever went unhung, as well as to save their victims from their clutches.

Mr. Wells seemed to be about twenty-one years old, and had an erect carriage, which gave him a more manly and determined look than is usual in young men of his age. Drawing around the stove, we listened to his sad, sad story, which, at times, threw him into fits of violent passion, and at others, overwhelmed him with grief. I shall not attempt to tell the story in the disconnected manner in which he gave it to us, but will combine, with his account, the further information which we obtained at the close of my researches in the case. Of course, many of the details here given were unknown to young Wells at the time he called, with Mr. Church, to ask my assistance; but enough was known positively, beside much that was evident inferentially, to make my blood boil as I listened, and to draw tears even from Mr. Church and Mr. Green, accustomed as they were to scenes of agony and sorrow. The following is the story of Mr. Wells, together with many incidents which were developed later.

CHAPTER 2

ERASTUS B. WELLS, William's father, was about fifty-five years of age, and had long been a merchant in Boston. He had been successful in business, and had been a wealthy man, up to less than a year previous, at which time, he had been on the point of retiring from active life and establishing his son in his place. Mr. Wells was well known and highly respected in Boston, and had many friends and acquaintances. He was a man of large heart and generous instincts, so that he had been frequently asked to endorse accommodation paper for his business associates, and had given the use of his name and credit very freely — too freely, as events proved. A very dull season in trade came on, and, although his own business was not seriously affected, his friends went down, one after another, leaving him to meet their debts, for which he had made himself liable. In consequence, Mr. Wells, himself, was called upon to pay the notes which he had endorsed for his friends, and the result was financial ruin. After selling all his property, he found himself stripped of his whole fortune, (except a small sum) with a family dependent upon him for support.

While his affairs prospered, he had been blessed with one of the happiest homes imaginable. His wife was industrious and loving, and his children, of whom he had four, obedient and affectionate. His children's names and ages were as follows: William, twenty-one years; Mary, seventeen years; Alice, fifteen years, and Emma, nine years. Mary was already a well-developed woman. She was tall, but her figure was compact and plump. Her face was almost a perfect oval in shape, and her eyes were large, and expressive, jet black in color, fringed with long, fine lashes. She was noticeable for the beauty of her soft, clear, brunette complexion, which was a rich olive, deepening into a delicate red in her cheeks. She had a small mouth, red, full lips and very regular, pearly teeth. But her greatest charm was her sweet expression, which spoke directly to the hearts of all who met her. She did not belong to the class of sentimental beauties, who look as if a strong wind would blow them away; but, on the contrary, she possessed a glow of health and flow of spirits which added greatly to her attractiveness. Hers was a strong nature, kept in check by firm, religious principles.

Alice had reached the age "where womanhood and childhood meet." She was not as tall as Mary, nor was her figure as fully developed. She had her mother's eyes, dark grey in color, and she almost rivaled Mary in the beauty of her complexion. When she laughed, she showed such pretty teeth, lips and dimples, that many considered her the beauty of the family.

Mrs. Wells was a noble woman, and, in the hour of her husband's distress, she showed a courage superior to all misfortunes. William and the girls, also, were sources of great comfort to their father by the cheerfulness with which they met the change in their circumstances. Mary, as the eldest daughter, felt that it was her duty to take an active part in the struggle against poverty, which was now commencing. Although naturally timid, she had the courage to carry out any plan which she considered right and necessary. The Wells family had not gone into society a great deal; hence, they were spared much of the heartless treatment that is so generally inflicted in fashionable circles upon those whom fate deprives of wealth. Still, there were many among their acquaintances, who dropped them as soon as they became poor. Although they keenly felt these slights, they did not give way to useless repinings, but adapted their habits and mode of life to their changed circumstances, with cheerful resignation and contentment. In a short time, nearly all of Mr. Wells' property had been absorbed in the payment of the debts of his friends, and he had only a small sum left. He pondered for some time as to what would be the best course for him to pursue. Many of his friends advised him to take advantage of the credit which his established reputation for honesty and business capacity would command, and start in business again. But the shock of his losses, although not caused by any neglect of duty on his part, had so unnerved him, that he felt it would be impossible, at his age, to commence at the foot of the ladder, perhaps only to be again dashed to the ground before he could reach a secure position. He, therefore, took a small cottage in Boston, temporarily, while settling his affairs, and moved thither such necessary furniture as he was able to reserve from the sale of his effects.

Having finally satisfied all his creditors, he had remaining only a few hundred dollars. He then decided to go West and purchase a farm in the State of Michigan, which was, at that time, rapidly filling up with New England settlers. The soil was rich, and the country was well wooded and watered, so that farms, which could then be bought from the Government at low rates, would become worth thousands of dollars in a few years. He had money enough to buy a quarter-section of land, and to stock his farm with a few cows and the necessary oxen and farming implements required in breaking and working a new piece of ground. He proposed to put up a comfortable log-house, where, with good health, he hoped that they might soon become independent — for he felt that no one was so truly independent as a successful farmer, owning a well-stocked farm, free from debt.

The girls were quite delighted at the prospect, not only on account of the future pecuniary advantages, but because it would remove them from the probability of contact with those who had known them when wealthy. The undesired pity of their friends was almost as hard to bear as the contemptuous sneers of their enemies; so that they were not sorry to make a decided change of residence. It did not take long to prepare for the journey, and in a few days they were westward bound.

The tracks of the Michigan Southern Railroad had been just laid as far as Laporte, Indiana, and many gangs of men were at work all along the line, ballasting the road and putting it into smooth running order. The opening of the road had made a large area of valuable farming lands easily accessible, and settlers were pouring in fast.

Mr. Wells bought a quarter-section of land (one hundred and sixty acres) near Quincy, Michigan, where he put up a small dwelling-house and barn, investing what little money he had left, in live-stock and farming implements. Quincy was a mere village, consisting of a tavern, two or three stores, two small churches and a few dwelling-houses.

The Wells family soon found that there were many little things required which, having no money, they could not obtain, as Mr. Wells would not go in debt for anything. He could not expect much return from the first year on a new farm, especially as he was comparatively a novice in the business, not having had any experience since he was a boy, working on his father's farm in New England. Both he and William, however, worked very hard, and succeeded in fully realizing their anticipations for the first year's crops, though, of course, the returns were no more than sufficient for their bare subsistence. The prospects for the ensuing year were very bright, provided they could get through the winter safely, as the farm was a fine one, and their late-and-early labor had put it into excellent condition. But, as winter came on, it was evident that it would be difficult to provide the necessaries of life for the whole family until Spring.

Accordingly, as soon as the cold weather put an end to farm-work, William applied for and obtained a place as foreman of a gang of men at work on the railroad, a position he was well qualified to fill. All his wages, he brought home and put into the general family fund, which Mr. Wells disbursed as needed. It also occurred to Mary and Alice that they might contribute something to the family treasury, (beside getting their own living,) by hiring out for the winter to do housework in Coldwater, the nearest town of any size.

In the West, at that time, (and it is so, even now, in the country,) the domestic servant held a much higher place, socially, than at present. She was looked upon more as a companion than as a servant; and the daughters of wealthy farmers often worked out for small wages, rather than remain at home toiling for nothing. Mary's acquaintances in Boston would have probably raised their hands in holy horror, if they had heard that the Wells girls were working out; but it did not in the least affect their social standing in Coldwater. In fact, it rather raised them, as it should have done, in the estimation of their neighbors.

William, therefore, obtained places for them in Coldwater; Mary taking a place as domestic in the family of Mr. Cox, a merchant, while Alice took a similar position in a restaurant at the depot, kept by a man named Blake. Their wages were one dollar and fifty cents for Mary, and one dollar for Alice. The girls soon settled down to their duties, and got along unusually well. Mary generally finished her work earlier than Alice, and then went down to Blake's to assist her. Having completed their daily tasks, they would have a pleasant chat, or take a short walk, but they never received any company. Alice, while waiting on the table, would be polite to all, and would pleasantly answer any questions put to her; but as soon as her duties were finished, she held herself quietly aloof from every one.

Mrs. Blake did a fair share of the work herself, although she had one servant besides Alice. She was a good little woman, of very pleasing appearance, and had been married eight or nine years, though she had no children.

Mr. Blake was a remarkably handsome man. He was six feet in height, and carried himself with a very erect, military air. His features were regular and clear-cut, and he was the picture of good health. His hair and silky moustache were jet black, and his complexion, though dark, was clear and smooth. He was generally dressed in excellent taste, with the exception that he showed a weakness for jewelry. He wore a showy diamond pin, and frequently looked at his watch, a very valuable English, gold hunting-case time-piece, which he carried attached to a massive gold chain. At that time, gold watches were not as common in the West as now, and Blake displayed his very ostentatiously. In general, however, he was very agreeable in his manners. He attended very little to the business of the restaurant, leaving it to his wife, while he went about the country a great deal, driving a fast horse, which he owned. He was away from home most of the time, in fact, going sometimes to Toledo, Detroit, Laporte, and Chicago.

Coldwater lay a quarter of a mile distant from the depot, and Blake rarely went to the town; though he was always very civil and polite to any of the residents who visited his restaurant. About all that was known of him in Coldwater, was that he had kept the restaurant for two years, and seemed to be making money. Stations then were very far apart on the railroad, and travelers frequently drove long distances to take the train, remaining at Blake's over night and leaving by the morning train next day. Blake's business was, therefore, that of a hotel-keeper; his bar-keeper, under Mrs. Blake's superintendence, attended to most of the work in Blake's absence, and accounted to Mrs. Blake every night for the money received.

Although Alice was an inmate of the house, she was engaged in sewing for Mrs. Blake most of the day, and saw nothing of the boarders, except at meal-times. Hence, as far as the girls knew, the restaurant was a highly respectable place, and it was not until I had rent the veil of mystery surrounding it, that they learned the true character of the persons who made it their rendezvous.

Blake, as we subsequently learned, was in reality a most villainous and dangerous man. For twelve years he had been a professional gambler and swindler. He had been in the habit of traveling on the Mississippi and its tributaries, always as a gambler or roper-in. He had been seen in Dubuque; was well acquainted in Keokuk and Cairo; had gone up the Missouri to Independence, and, thence, out on the plains; Natchez, Vicksburg, Memphis, and New Orleans — all were familiar haunts; and, as a cool, desperate villain, he had an extensive reputation, though he had not yet been exposed at Coldwater, where little or nothing was known of him.

His object in following up the line of the new Michigan Southern Railroad, was to take advantage of the men at work on the road, and fleece them of their hard-earned wages, by gambling games. His restaurant, in reality, was a regular gambling den, and was the resort, not only of all the fast men and gamblers of Coldwater, but, also, of many young men, sons of rich farmers in the vicinity. There were a variety of games played; but the gambling portion of the house was removed from the rooms of Mrs. Blake and Alice, and no sound of the games was ever heard outside of the gambling rooms. For experienced gamblers, there were "square" games of poker, faro and roulette, Blake, whenever he was at home, officiating as dealer; at other times the rooms were closed, except for poker and other games not requiring a "banker." For farmers, laborers, and inexperienced young men, Blake had a special faro box, arranged in such a way as to enable the dealer to know every card before slipping it out, and to make it win or lose at his pleasure. He had inveigled so many persons into his clutches, that there were a number of rumors afloat about the character of the house and its proprietor, but they were so vague as never to have reached either William or Mary.

About eleven miles from Coldwater, was the little town of Bronson, situated about half a mile from the railroad station of the same name. The only building at the station, was a tavern, kept by one Harris, a great friend of Blake. It was afterward discovered that, at Burr Oak, six miles from Harris tavern, a gang of counterfeiters were at work; and, in order not to attract attention to Burr Oak, most of the gang stopped with Harris. The latter was a most consummate villain, and his wife was even worse; so that congenial spirits were not wanting among the keepers of the tavern and their guests.

Among the frequenters of Blake's gambling rooms and Harris tavern, was a young man named Sloan, son of a well-to-do farmer near Coldwater. He had lived with his parents, until he had exhausted their patience by his extravagance and dissipation; he had then left home to take a place as stage-driver. At first, he had driven a stage from Coldwater north to Lansing. Soon becoming a most proficient "knight of the whip," he had gone to Chicago to drive for Frink & Walker, the owners of all the stage lines running north, west and south from that city.

In those days, lively scenes could have been witnessed in front of the Tremont House, where all the stages started from every morning. Old drivers would try to see how near they could come to overturning their vehicles without doing so, and green hands, in their efforts at imitation, would come to grief, and be hauled from the ruins of a general smash-up.

Sloan had learned to cut a circle in the street with a four-horse team and a heavy stage, and was as good a driver as could be found. Hence, he had easily obtained a stage on one of the western routes, but had taken leave of absence, and come home to spend the winter with his friends. Up to the time he left Coldwater, Sloan had not been a vicious man; but stage-driving had not been a good school for his morals. He was about five feet nine inches in height, full-faced, dark complexioned, and had dark eyes and hair. He wore heavy side-whiskers, and a Kossuth hat, which he kept on his head, in-doors and out. He would have been very good looking but for his rakish, dissipated appearance. He was well acquainted with Blake and his bar-keeper, Jim Kelly, so that he was quite at home about the restaurant.

I have now presented all of the *dramatis personæ* of the tragedy which was shortly enacted, and will proceed to give the particulars thereof, as they occurred.

CHAPTER 3

MARY WAS IN the habit of calling frequently to see Alice, and soon became well acquainted with Mrs. Blake. While in the latter's rooms, Blake would occasionally meet Mary, and, in this way, he came to know her. He hardly noticed either of the girls, as a rule, though he sometimes spoke to Alice, while she was waiting on him at table. Once or twice, apparently by accident, he overtook Mary and Alice when on their way to town, and walked part way with them. Occasionally, also, he walked with them to Mrs. Cox's, and returned with Alice. He was always very respectful, however, and seemed to pay very little attention to them.

Three months passed quickly away without any incidents of consequence. William came often to see his sisters, and they were allowed to go home once a month, to pass Sunday. Every week they sent their wages home; and their spirits were kept up by frequent letters from their parents, and by the thought that the little sum at home was increasing slowly by their assistance.

About this time, Sloan began to notice Alice, and, in order to see her as much as possible, began to take his meals at the restaurant. While Alice was waiting on him, he used to say sweet things to her; but, though she always waited upon him promptly, she paid no attention to his sweet speeches and loving looks. If he attempted any familiarity, she always walked out of the room.

There were a number of young men, farmers' sons, clerks, and students from Coldwater, who were very anxious to get acquainted with Mary and Alice; but the latter were quietly reserved, and they coldly repelled all advances. The decided manner with which the sisters shunned all gentlemen's society, greatly exasperated these young men, and they talked a great deal about the girls. Sloan was particularly angry, and he tried his best to get introduced into Blake's family, but without success; as Mrs. Blake approved of the girls' conduct, and aided them as much as possible.

In the early part of March, Mrs. Blake decided to pay a visit to her mother, who lived in Ypsilanti. As she would need someone to superintend the restaurant during her absence, it occurred to her that Mary would be just the person for the place. Accordingly, when Mary next visited Alice, Mrs. Blake suggested the plan to her, and urged her warmly to accept the position of house-keeper for two or three months. Mrs. Blake said that the winter's work had completely tired her out, and that she wished to visit her family, in order to get rested. She had full confidence in Mary, who, though so young, was, nevertheless, very systematical and orderly; she was sure that Mary would manage the domestic arrangements of the restaurant as well as she could, herself.

Mary did not like to leave Mrs. Cox. She got along well with the family, and liked her place. On the other hand, Mrs. Blake offered her two dollars a week, to take full charge of everything at the restaurant; and, though she would have more responsibility, it would give her also a more independent position. There were two other important advantages: the increase of wages, and the fact that she would always be with Alice. They had several talks upon the subject, and, finally, Mrs. Blake offered her two dollars and fifty cents a week, and Alice two dollars, if Mary would accept the situation of house-keeper, while Mrs. Blake was away. This decided the matter, and Mary agreed to the terms. She felt that she could not afford to refuse an offer, which was not only advantageous pecuniarily, but which would enable her to live with Alice.

When Mary informed Mrs. Cox of her intentions, that lady was quite displeased; and, in order to induce her to remain, Mrs. Cox repeated a number of the ugly rumors that were afloat with regard to Blake and his restaurant. Among other things, she said that there had been a bowling-alley attached to the restaurant, which had burned down one night, very strangely; and it was strongly suspected that Blake, himself, had fired the building, in order to get the insurance on it, which was very heavy. Mr. Cox came in while they were talking, and said that Mary must not mention what Mrs. Cox had told her, because there was no certainty of the truth of the story; though such were the suspicions of some of the people living in Coldwater. It was, also, publicly reported that Blake kept a gambling-house, and he advised her not to go to such a place. Mary was horrified at these stories; but, at the same time, it seemed strange that Mrs. Cox should not have told her these things before, knowing that her sister was employed in the restaurant, and that she, herself, often went there. She told Alice about the rumors, and asked her whether she had seen anything wrong about Blake, or the restaurant. Alice replied that she had not; but that Blake had always been quiet and gentlemanly in his words and actions; and that the restaurant, though having a bar attached, had been remarkably orderly and well-conducted. They, finally, agreed to lay the matter before William, and abide by his decision.

William was working on the railroad between Coldwater and Quincy, and often visited Coldwater station on business, always stopping to see Alice when he came there. The next time that Alice saw him, she told him about the rumors concerning Blake's restaurant, and asked what he thought of them. He said that he had heard such rumors, and had closely questioned the track-men and others as to the truth of the stories; but they had unanimously pronounced them false. With regard to the charge of setting fire to the bowling-alley, the fact that the insurance had been paid without question, was sufficient evidence of Blake's innocence. William considered Mrs. Blake's offer too good to be refused, and, therefore, advised Mary to accept it. Alice informed Mary of William's decision, the next day, and Mary gave Mrs. Cox notice that she would leave in a week.

At the end of that time, she moved down to Mrs. Blake's, and was given a small but pleasant room with Alice, on the second floor. Mrs. Blake remained a week, in order to instruct Mary in her new duties; and then, feeling that matters would run smoothly without her, she packed her clothes, preparatory to a visit of three months.

Mrs. Blake was rather jealous of her husband, but she knew the purity of the girls' characters so well, that she had no fears of them. What she did fear, however, was that Blake would bring strange women into the house, in her absence; and, to guard against this, she cautioned Mary not to allow any straggling women to stop at the restaurant.

"If any women come 'round," said she to Mary, "you must insist on turning them out. If Blake objects, you write to me. I shall be only sixty miles away, and I will come over and soon oust them. I have all confidence in you, Mary, and so has Blake; and he has agreed to let you have your own way, while I am gone."

Blake then took his wife to Ypsilanti in his light cutter, the sleighing being good, and returned in about a week. He brought a letter from his wife for Mary, and had a long talk with the latter about the business of the house. He asked her a number of questions about the financial and culinary arrangements, but showed no more freedom of manner than when his wife was at home.

Mary and Alice were now very happy. They had good situations, and, as they were always together, began to feel almost as contented as if they were in their own home. Mary had no difficulty in managing the house, and all went on smoothly. Kelly, the bar-keeper, occasionally came in to turn over the money from the bar, and to order extra meals for late passengers; but he was always very respectful to both girls.

Sloan was at the restaurant most of the time, and he used to sit in the dining-room, with other fast young men, every evening, the bar being in the same room. If anything disorderly occurred, Mary would walk into the dining-room to see what was the matter, and immediately the disturbance would cease. It was a strange sight to see the manner in which the worst rowdies cowered before this slight girl of seventeen.

Alice did not possess her sister's power of command, and found it very hard to control some of the customers. Many of the young men tried to make the acquaintance of Alice at table, and several of them sent invitations to parties, etc., to both girls, but no answers were ever returned. In consequence, it was generally conceded that the sisters "put on a good many airs" for girls in their position, and the young men were duly indignant. Sloan was particularly angry at Alice, for whom he had conceived a violent passion, and he never ceased to think about her. Alice became almost afraid of him, and said to Mary, once:

"That man makes me tremble every time he looks at me."

The California gold mines had only recently been discovered, and the "gold fever" was at its height in Coldwater. It seemed as if every one was preparing to start for the "diggings," and farmers were offering their farms for sale at very low prices, to obtain the means to carry them across the plains, to the land of promise in California. The stories of the wealth to be obtained by a few months' work in the mines had affected all classes of people, and even the oldest and steadiest were tempted.

It is not to be wondered, then, that men like Blake and Sloan should have turned toward the new *El Dorado* with longing hearts. Blake was about tired of a settled life, and, moreover, he was aware that his character was becoming known, and that some of his dupes would be apt to bring a hornet's nest about his ears, some day, which might result in still more unpleasant revelations with regard to him. He, therefore, began to make preparations for a move, keeping his intentions perfectly secret from everyone except Sloan, with whom he now became very intimate, indeed.

Blake needed such a man as Sloan for a tool, and so, drew him on to commit the crime which they were then engaged in planning, in order to prepare him for other schemes of villainy, when Blake should require his services. Sloan was greatly flattered at being noticed by Blake, who was much superior in education and intellect to any of the men in that vicinity, besides being a dashing, daring sort of a fellow, with great ability to fascinate his associates. Thus, by flattering Sloan's vanity, Blake obtained a complete mastery over him; and it was only necessary for Blake to say the word, to lead Sloan into any wickedness that might turn up. These two now remained together constantly, making frequent visits to Harris, at Bronson station. Harris would sometimes come back with them, as, also, two men known as Dick and Joe. These latter were a bad lot, and showed their hardened characters in their faces.

Two weeks passed thus very pleasantly to the sisters. Their work was not tiresome, and they were always happy in each other's society. During the day, they were quite busy, but, after seven o'clock, they usually sat down in the sitting-room and read aloud to each other, or talked over past pleasures and future prospects.

All went along quietly at Blake's, until one morning the great equinoctial gales commenced, and brought with them a heavy snow-storm. Very few customers visited the restaurant that day, and those who did brave the storm, went home before evening, leaving only Blake, Kelly, Sloan, and the sisters in the house.

After tea the girls went into the sitting-room, where they sat, listening to the storm, and looking into the fire. In a short time, Blake came in and conversed with them for some minutes. He was dressed with great care, and he made himself very agreeable, yet without showing the least want of respect. He was soon called out by Sloan, who told him that Harris had just come. As Sloan went out, he glanced at Alice with that devilish expression in his eye that always frightened her, and she was so alarmed that she begged Mary to go to bed. Norah had already gone to her room; and, as there was no prospect of any one coming for meals at that hour, Mary agreed, and the sisters prepared to retire.

They went to the back door and glanced out at the storm. The snow almost blinded them, but they saw that there was a light in the stable, and caught a glimpse of Blake, Sloan, and a stranger, moving about, the stranger being Harris. There was nothing unusual in this, so they closed the door and went to bed.

Blake's room was opposite the sitting-room, and, next to it, was the room of Norah, the Irish cook. The sitting-room was between the kitchen and the dining-room; the sisters' bed-room was up-stairs, directly over the main outside entrance to the dining-room.

The girls little thought that at that moment the plot was being planned, and the arrangements made, which should forever blast their lives. As they knelt to ask God's aid and blessing, Blake and his attendant scoundrels were preparing for a crime most foul. But, ignorant of the depravity of these men, the sisters retired in peace, and quiet soon reigned over the house.

CHAPTER 4

About midnight, a loud knocking was commenced at the main entrance, which quickly awoke the girls overhead. After a prolonged pounding, they heard a gruff voice, saying:

"Open the door! I am the sheriff, and I have a warrant to arrest you, Blake, for setting fire to your bowling-alley."

The storm still howled fiercely, and the snow was drifting in immense sheets against the window-panes; but far above the noise of the storm, the terrified girls heard the knocks, and the stern voice commanding the inmates to open, in the name of the law. Not a sound was heard within the house, and again came the voice:

"Open the door! I am the sheriff, and I shall break down the door, if you don't let me in at once."

Then came a heavy thud, and the order:

"Break down the door, boys! I'm bound to have that scoundrel, Blake."

Crash followed crash, the door yielded, and soon a number of heavy footsteps were heard, crossing the dining-room, and rushing about the lower part of the house. The men ran hither and thither, searching the rooms below, and blaspheming in a manner terrible to hear. They entered Norah's room, dragged her out of bed, and demanded where Blake was concealed. Not finding him there, the search was continued. Suddenly, the girls heard a stealthy footstep outside their door, and then, a hasty fumbling at their latch. The door flew open, and Blake, in a voice seemingly choked with terror, said:

"Oh! girls, hide me! hide me! They are going to arrest me!"

Before they could collect their scattered senses, Blake sprang into the bed, and forced himself down between the two girls, who shrank away, powerless and almost fainting from fright. The men in search were close behind Blake, however; and, as he drew the clothes up over his head, they burst into the room with a yell of exultation. The supposed sheriff and his men proved to be Sloan, Harris, Dick, and Joe.

"Ha! ha! ha!" laughed Sloan, fiendishly; "this is where you spend your nights, is it, Blake? You're a sly coon, but we've treed you at last."

As he spoke, he seized the bed-clothes and, with a fling, threw them over the foot of the bed, disclosing Blake, in his night-shirt, lying between the nearly insensible girls.

Blake sprang up and said, in a horrified tone:

"Oh! gentlemen, gentlemen, you have gone too far! I was so frightened — as I really thought you had a warrant — that I rushed in here and begged the girls to hide me. The girls are virtuous, I assure you, but my indiscretion has placed them in an awful position. It is terrible! terrible! Don't, for God's sake, let any one know of this. Come down stairs, and I will treat you to all the whiskey and brandy you want. This affair must be hushed up! The girls are as innocent as babes. It is all my fault."

"Ha! ha!" sneered Sloan; "that you, Alice? Blake is smart, but I never knew he was a Mormon before," and coming to the bed-side, with an insulting remark, he grasped Alice in his arms.

"Quit that sort of business," said Blake. "The girls are as pure as snow, and I won't have them insulted. Go down stairs, and keep quiet about this."

"Well," said Sloan, with an oath, "I'm going to have a kiss anyhow," saying which, he clasped Alice close, and kissed her.

The poor child was powerless to resist, and an attempt to scream died away on her lips. Mary was pale as death, and she lay motionless, with a look of horror on her face, that would have moved less hardened wretches to pity.

"Go down stairs, I say," repeated Blake, and all but Sloan left the room.

The latter again seized Alice, but Blake succeeded in forcing him from the room, and then returned to the door.

"Mary," he said, "I have done you both a great wrong, but those men frightened me so much that I did not know what I was doing. You know that I never wished to do you an injury. Oh! forgive me! please forgive me!"

Mary's mouth was parched and dry, so that she could not speak. She seemed to be the victim of a hideous nightmare, which rendered her will and muscles powerless.

Blake went on speaking:

"Mary, you won't tell this to my wife, will you? She would feel terribly, if she were to know it. I will make it all right with the boys down-stairs. All they want is liquor. Won't you forgive me, and promise not to tell my wife?"

For a time, neither of the girls could speak, but Mary was, at length, able to find her voice.

"Leave the room, and let us alone," she said. "I don't know what I am doing. I am going crazy. Go! go! I pray God I may never see daylight."

Blake saw that any further annoyance might make them desperate, and, therefore, went out. The girls lay in a nervous stupor for some minutes after his departure, but finally Mary got up and closed the door. There was no lock nor bolt upon it; so she motioned Alice to assist her, and, together, they dragged their trunks against it, and barricaded it as well as possible. Neither could speak, but Mary opened her arms and clasped Alice to her bosom in a loving embrace. Their breaking hearts were relieved by a flood of tears, and crawling into bed, they passed the remainder of the night in each other's arms, trembling like leaves at every gust of wind that swept around the house.

After dressing, Blake went into the bar-room; there he found Kelly up, dealing out drinks to the scoundrels, who were laughing over their success in invading the privacy of the poor sisters' chamber. Blake tried to calm them down and induce them to go home; but they were partly intoxicated, and were determined to stay as long as they pleased.

Sloan said, with an oath, that he had never had so sweet a kiss before, and that Alice was bound to be his.

"Shut up, Sloan, you're a fool," said Blake.

"Don't talk to me that way, or I'll put a knife into you," muttered Sloan.

"I tell you, you're a d—d fool," said Blake. "Don't you know how to act your part any better? If you don't take care, we'll go to the penitentiary. If you'll keep your mouth shut and leave matters to me, we shall have a good thing out of this."

"That's so," coincided Dick. "I have done some shrewd things in my time, and I can always do well, if I have a good chum."

By this time, Harris had the sleigh at the door, the party took a parting drink, and in a few minutes, Harris, Dick, and Joe were on the road to Bronson.

When they had gone, Blake turned to Sloan and said:

"Now, Sloan, the time for rough work has not yet come. It will come, bye-and-bye; but, in the meantime, keep cool, don't talk much, and go slow."

"I'll have another drink, at all events," said Sloan, with an oath; "and mind you remember the bargain — Alice is to be mine!"

"Hush up! hush up!" said Blake impatiently. "I wish I had never known you. You're a cursed fool, and will spoil everything by your d—d gas."

Sloan took a deep drink of brandy, and, without another word, started out into the storm, to walk to Coldwater, where he had a room.

"Kelly," said Blake, "be sure to tell Norah that the row to-night was only a spree on the part of the boys, and that they had a mighty fine time. I don't think we shall have any trouble with Mary and Alice, but we must treat them kindly. If they should go home, their father and brother would soon be after us, and we should have to leave the country. If we keep friendly with the girls, we shall be safe; but we must prevent them from running away in the first alarm and excitement. There is no fear of seeing William here to-morrow, as his gang will be busy clearing the snow from the track."

Having settled everything satisfactorily, Blake and Kelly took a "night-cap" of brandy before retiring; and, in a short time, the house was again quiet.

CHAPTER 5

THE OBJECT OF this invasion of the girls' chamber will be readily divined. Blake and Sloan had determined to go to California together, and to take Mary and Alice with them. They were perfectly aware that the consent of the sisters could never be obtained; hence, they had decided to take them by force. This could only be done by so terrifying their victims as to prevent them from making any disturbance while traveling, and this scheme was the preliminary step. The scene which transpired in the bar-room, after Sloan called Blake out of the sitting-room, in the early part of the evening, was narrated to me by Sloan, after his capture; I give it, in order to show the villainous character of the men, and the way in which the plan was carried out.

Blake, Sloan, Harris, and Kelly sat in the bar-room, talking on general topics for about an hour. Blake was restless and nervous, frequently looking at his watch, and muttering:

"I wonder what keeps them."

"They will be here, sure," said Harris. "I never knew Dick to fail. I am afraid he has stopped to play cards, and, if so, it will be hard for him to break away. I never knew a fellow to get bound up in cards as he does."

Blake walked to the outside door, peered out a moment, and then crept noiselessly up to the door of the sisters' room, where he listened a short time. On returning to the bar-room, he said, as he sat down:

"They are sound asleep."

"Give us some whiskey," said Harris, and he poured out drinks for Sloan and himself. Blake neither drank nor spoke, but maintained a moody silence, looking anxious and irritable.

Harris took up a pack of cards and began to deal them.

"No, I don't want to play — I am too much worried," exclaimed Blake, brushing the cards away. "I wish Dick would come!"

For some time, little was done or said. Blake walked up and down uneasily, occasionally opening the door to look out. At length, he asked:

"Harris, how in the world will you ever get home? This storm is the fiercest I have known for some years. Shall you and Dick go home to-night?" Then, without waiting for an answer, he continued: "It is better that you should go, as it might create suspicion, if you stayed here."

"I don't fear the storm," said Harris; "and shall get home all right."

In a short time, Dick and his friend, Joe, walked in, covered with snow. Blake grasped them warmly by the hand, and said to Dick:

"I am so glad to see you! I began to think you had forgotten me."

"No," replied Dick; "I am always on hand in an affair of this sort, though I don't yet know exactly what's wanted of me. I don't mind the snow. When I was sheriff of Butler County, Pennsylvania, I had to go out on a night similar to this, and I tell you, I made money before morning. The boys robbed an old man with lots of money, and I came down on 'em just in time to — make 'em divide! The next morning, the old cuss met me when I had my share in my pocket, and put the case in my hands (being sheriff, you know,) to hunt up the thieves; but I never caught them, ha! ha! ha!" Then, slapping Joe on the shoulder, he added: "I think I can lay my hand on one of the boys that did that job, now," and he burst into a fit of satanic laughter, in which he was joined by all except Blake, who took no notice, whatever.

A whispered consultation was then held between Blake, Sloan, Harris, Joe, and Dick — the bar-keeper being half asleep behind the bar. Blake explained what he wished done and the other ruffians readily coincided. At eleven o'clock, Blake took a glass of brandy, his first drink that evening, and again looked out, down the track. Not a light was to be seen, and the snow was piled in great drifts over the track; it was quite evident that no trains could pass over the line for some time.

"Now is a good time to commence operations, is it not?" said Blake.

"Yes," said Dick. "Harris, hitch up the team, and we'll get ready to start for Bronson."

Blake wished them good night, told Kelly to lock up the house, and went to bed. Sloan, Dick, Harris, and Joe took one more drink, and then went out to the stable. Kelly locked the door and tumbled into bed, at about half past eleven o'clock.

The events of the remainder of that terrible night have already been given, and I now return to the sisters.

CHAPTER 6

ALL THROUGH THE still hours of that gloomy night, the sisters mingled their tears together, almost speechless from physical fear and mental agony.

"What shall we do! what shall we do!" murmured Alice.

"I don't know," said Mary. "What *can* we do?"

What, indeed, could two innocent girls, the oldest but seventeen, do in a struggle with such crafty villains?

Toward daybreak, they fell into a troubled sleep, but by seven o'clock, they again awoke to all the horrors of their situation. After dressing, they remained in their room some time, fearing to go down stairs. They finally mustered up the courage to go into the kitchen, where they found Norah, going on with her work, as if nothing had happened. The sisters glanced at her in a half-frightened way, and she said:

"Shure, Mary, and didn't yees hear the row last night? Faith, thin, they had a foine time playin' their tricks on the masther. Didn't yees hear them, Alice?"

Then was taken the fatal step which placed the sisters in the power of the scoundrels.

"No," said Alice; "was anything going on?"

"There was, indade," replied Norah. "Yees must ha' slept sound the night, not to ha' heerd thim bys that was here about midnight. There was a whole pack of thim, and, d'yees know, they broke in the door to the bar-room. The blaggards came into my room, aven, and axed if the masther was there. But, after all, they was very dacent gintlemin on a bit of a lark, and they spent their money fraly. Kelly spakes well of thim."

"We did not hear anything," said Alice; "at least, I did not; did you, Mary?"

Mary did not answer. She could not decide what to do; but, as Alice had adopted that course, she thought best not to contradict her. She, therefore, pretended not to have heard the question, and walked into the sitting-room. She dusted the furniture mechanically, and then went to the window and looked out. On every side, she saw evidences of the severity of the storm. The snow was two feet deep on a level, and the roads were all blocked by almost impassable drifts. No one would venture out that day, unless compelled by some great necessity.

The girls prepared breakfast as usual; but, when Blake came in, they were unable to look him in the face. He sat down alone with them, as there were no boarders in the house, and talked in a very gentle and sorrowful tone about the unfortunate occurrence of the previous night. He said that he would take care that no harm should come to them. The boys had only tried to have a good joke at his expense, little thinking it would turn out so seriously. He would see that no one should ever hear anything about the matter, and that the girls' reputation should not suffer.

The sisters said nothing, whatever, finishing their breakfast in complete silence. After their work was done, they went into the sitting-room, to talk over what had happened.

"Mary," said Alice, "I want William to take us both home. How I wish he would come up this morning!"

"I do not intend to remain here any longer," said Mary. "I would go home at once, if it were possible; but look at the roads! They are impassable, and the railroad is worse. Kelly says that no trains passed last night, and he thinks none will pass to-day. We cannot go to Coldwater, as we know only Mrs. Cox, and she is angry with me for leaving her. I would not let her know what has happened for the world, as she is a gossip, and would spread the story everywhere. The best course for us to pursue is to give notice that we shall leave at the end of the week. Blake is really sorry for us, and will prevent any one from molesting us until then; and when we get home, father and mother will know what to do, in case the story gets abroad. As soon as William comes, he shall take our trunks home, and we will follow on Saturday."

After further conversation, this plan was adopted; so when Blake came into the room, Mary told him that they were going home permanently on Saturday, as they could not stay in a place where they were subjected to such insults.

Blake expressed his regret at losing them, as they had always been so capable and trustworthy; but, under the circumstances, he could not blame them for leaving. He would guarantee that no one should ever learn the reason of their departure, outside of those engaged in the "joke." He had always admired the purity of their characters, and the thought, that he had been the means of sullying their reputations so irreparably, filled him with sincere sorrow. He could not sufficiently condemn his own conduct.

In this way, while apparently trying to lessen their fears, he was, in reality, working on their feelings in a most alarming manner. The only trouble which the girls anticipated, was the talk which would be made about them, if the story got abroad; but Blake cunningly magnified the scandal which would result, while professing to be able to keep it quiet. By making it appear that their guilt would be universally believed, if the story should ever get out, he made them think that he, alone, could save them from infamy. In this, he fully succeeded, as he was aware of Alice's falsehood to Norah, and, by casually referring to it, he showed them that the best thing for them was to keep the whole affair perfectly quiet. He talked so kindly, and seemed to feel so sorry, as almost to win the girls' respect, and he induced Mary to promise never to tell his wife.

He had now gained the point for which the plot had been laid, and felt confident of success in the whole scheme of abduction. He had sufficiently compromised the girls to accomplish two objects, as he thought. Having taken the first steps in deception, the girls would be afraid to appeal to any one, except their own family, for aid, and he proposed to get them out of the reach of their friends, as quickly as possible. He then intended that Harris, Dick, and Joe should tell the story of having found him in bed with the girls, to blacken their characters, and make their abduction appear like a voluntary flight. The falsehood which Alice had told Norah would, also, play an important part, as corroborating the theory that Blake had actually seduced the girls, before their flight. This would probably prevent pursuit by the officers of the law, while the Wells family would not have the means to hunt for him. The time that would elapse before the affair would become known, and the delay created in the early investigation, would give him such a start as to make his capture impossible, even if the county authorities should conduct the search.

Like all criminals, he was expert in hiding his tracks; but he had forgotten one thing — that crime invariably carries its own punishment, and that there is no escape for the guilty.

CHAPTER 7

DINNER WAS SERVED at the usual hour, and Blake acted in the same kind, gentle manner as before. While the meal was in progress, Sloan entered the room, walked over to Alice, and put his arm around her neck. She sprang away from him in terror, while Blake rushed over to protect her, seemingly in a towering passion.

"Sloan, didn't you do enough harm last night? Get out of this room!" he commanded, as if speaking to a dog.

Sloan turned upon him savagely, but, seeing that Blake was in earnest, he fairly cringed and said, as he crawled out of the room:

"I didn't mean any harm. I'll see you when you come out."

Both the sisters felt the blow, but did not know what to do. They went immediately to their room, and Mary said:

"What is to prevent others from making the same kind of advances that Sloan has made? If William would only come, he would take us away at once; but there are no trains running, and there is no one to help us."

They dropped on their knees and prayed for help, as only those can pray, who are driven to the verge of desperation.

Sloan and Blake had a meeting in the barn.

"You are acting wrong," said Blake. "I had just succeeded in calming down the girls, when you must come in and spoil everything, by taking liberties with Alice."

"Yes, d—n it, isn't she mine?" asked Sloan. "Haven't I a right to kiss her when I please?"

"Pshaw! you're a fool! Don't you understand that we shall have to use strategy? If you act properly, she will be yours bye-and-bye, but if you try to force things, you will find yourself in the penitentiary. I thought you had some common sense. She is young, she is courageous, and if you take liberties with her, the game is up. Many decent people come to my restaurant, and if they should hear her scream, they would burst in on you, and then where would you be? You fool! I wish I never had had anything to do with you. I see my mistake now."

"Well," said Sloan, in a conciliatory manner, "I will do just as you say, provided I am certain of having Alice."

"What do you want to talk about it for? You must keep quiet, or you will get them excited, and they have friends all around to whom they might go. I'll tell you what you must do. It will be a hard job, but it can't be helped. You must go to Bronson, get a double sleigh with plenty of buffalo robes, and come here by eleven o'clock to-night. I will have the girls drugged by that time, and we will carry them off at once." As he spoke, he drew a small phial of laudanum from his pocket.

Sloan touched the laudanum to his tongue and asked:

"Will that put them to sleep?"

"Yes," said Blake; "it is laudanum. We can keep them drugged with it for seven or eight hours, and even longer by renewing the dose."

An expression of brutal admiration came into Sloan's face, as he said:

"Blake, you're a bully fellow! What a fool I have been to kick against you! You're just the man for me!"

"All right; now listen. I am going to carry them off to-night, so you must tell Harris to have a couple of bed-rooms warm and comfortable for us on our arrival. Tell him to have Dick and Joe on hand to carry the girls into the house, as we shall be too numbed by the cold to do anything. Be sure to tell him to have the house quiet, with no outsiders around. Take this money, one hundred dollars, and give it to Harris to pay all expenses, including Dick and Joe."

"I'm your man," said Sloan, and he started off at a rapid pace for Bronson.

At supper, Blake acted in the same manner as at breakfast and dinner, taking pains not to say anything to hurt the feelings of the sisters. He was so kind and reassuring in his conversation, that the girls began to have great confidence in him. He acted his devilish part well.

At nine o'clock, as the girls said good-night and started to go to bed, Blake said:

"Mary, you and Alice must be wholly exhausted from the terrible shock you received last night, and I am afraid you will be so nervous as to be unable to rest well. Let me give you each a glass of wine. It will quiet your nerves and make you sleep."

Mary, at first, declined, but Blake pressed it upon her so urgently, yet politely, that she, at length, consented. The girls were both very weak and faint, as they had not felt like eating anything all day, and Mary thought that perhaps a glass of wine would do them good.

"I will set the wine outside the door of your room," said Blake, "and you need not drink it until you are getting into bed."

The girls then went to their room, and about ten o'clock, Blake came up with two glasses of wine. He set the waiter down on a chair close to the door, knocked, to let them know he had brought the wine, and went down stairs. When he had gone, Mary brought the wine into the room, and, with Alice's assistance, barricaded the door as well as they were able. After saying their prayers, they each drank a glass of the wine and got into bed. They talked a few minutes and then dropped into a peaceful sleep. Care and fear faded out of their minds, and their only dreams were of home and parents. Finally, their sleep became heavier and deeper, until it was evident that the drugged wine had done its work.

CHAPTER 8

SLOAN ARRIVED FROM Bronson shortly after eleven o'clock. He had a wide box-sleigh, provided with movable seats, and filled with hay and buffalo robes. Silently as cats, the two men stole up to the room of the sleeping girls. They easily pushed back the slight barricade against the door, and entered the chamber. Their light revealed to them the two sisters, sleeping in each other's arms. For a moment, even their hardened hearts were touched by the purity of the scene; but they forced back every good feeling, and proceeded with their damnable work. Lifting Alice out of bed, they hurriedly drew some of her clothing over her helpless form, wrapped her in a blanket, and laid her down. They then did the same with Mary. Both sisters were restless, in spite of the laudanum; and Mary, raising herself on one arm, muttered plaintively, as if dreaming:

"Mother! Oh! mother! Why don't you help me!"

This powerful and touching appeal from her unconscious lips, had no effect, except to cause Blake to administer an additional dose of the drug to both girls.

"There," said he, with an oath, "I guess that will quiet them."

He then packed some of the girls' clothing into a carpet-sack and put it into the sleigh. Sloan then lifted Alice in his arms, carried her down to the sleigh, and quickly covered her up completely with blankets and buffalo robes, as he feared that the cold air might revive her. Blake followed with Mary, whom he placed beside Alice. He then seated himself by them to watch, while Sloan sprang to the front seat to drive. The horses were kept at the top of their speed, where the drifts would permit, and, in about two hours, they arrived at Harris' tavern.

As the panting horses dashed up, Dick and Joe came out and assisted Blake and Sloan to carry the unconscious girls to the rooms which had been prepared, and which were separated from each other only by folding doors. Alice was placed in one bed, and Mary in the other, while Blake and Sloan returned to the bar-room to get warm. When thoroughly warmed through, they instructed Harris not to disturb them in the morning, took a drink of brandy, and went to the rooms of the girls.

That night was consummated the crime which sent Blake and Mary to their graves — the guilty and the innocent. Blake had succeeded so far in his villainy, but, ere long, the avenger was to be upon his track.

It was nearly nine o'clock the next morning before Mary began to regain consciousness, and, for a time, she lay in a semi-stupor. Gradually, a dull, throbbing pain in her temples awakened her, and she opened her eyes. Everything was new and strange to her. She must be crazy, she thought, and she said aloud:

"Oh! mother, what is it?"

Then she stretched out her hand, as if to touch Alice beside her, but touched Blake, instead. Her eye followed her hand; and, on seeing Blake, a dazed comprehension of the truth flashed through her mind. She sprang from the bed, hastily drew some of her clothes about her, and rushed to the door, which was locked. Blake also jumped from the bed, and approached her.

"Mary," said he, in a stern, commanding voice, "take care! Remember, that now you are mine! I will do anything for you, if you will only love me. I love you truly. I tried to banish your image from my heart, but could not. I then determined that you should be mine. To accomplish this end, I sent my wife to visit her mother; and then carried out the plan which has placed you in my power. You must yield to me, and love me, or *I will kill you.*"

"Kill me, kill me at once! You are a monster! I know I am ruined, but oh! let me go from here!" Mary answered.

As Blake approached to take hold of her, she shrieked, "Murder! murder!" with all the energy of despair. At the same moment, came a piercing shriek from the adjoining room.

Sloan was a coarser villain than Blake, and, as Alice, on awakening, sprang from his side, with a scream, he struck her a blow that knocked her down. He then lifted her up and put her into bed.

"There, d—n you," said he; "I'll teach you not to put on airs. You're mine, now, and you've got to obey me."

Alice neither moved nor spoke, and Sloan, seeing that she had swooned, became frightened. He rushed down to tell Harris, and the latter sent his wife up. Mrs. Harris was a hardened wretch, who, like many another fallen creature, gloated over the ruin of innocent girls. She was capable of attempting any crime, which would bring in money.

I shall not try to describe the agony of those pure young sisters; it would be impossible for pen to give an adequate idea of their sufferings. Escape was impossible. They were in the hands of as inhuman monsters as ever drew breath; but there was no help for them, and they were forced to submit.

What a fate was theirs! Young, innocent, lovely, and entirely ignorant of the sin and misery of the world, they were dragged away from all that made life dear, and made to suffer cruelly, both mentally and physically. But their future trials were even worse than their present. They still had to pass through the most degrading of ordeals, from which Mary was to find escape only in death. What earthly punishment could be devised severe enough to punish justly the brutes who had debauched them?

Blake and Sloan went down stairs, leaving Dick and Joe to watch the girls, who were not allowed to leave their respective rooms. In the afternoon, Blake drove over to the restaurant, to get the girls' trunks and remaining clothes, which he brought to Bronson about dusk.

In the meantime, the girls had dressed themselves, but they had eaten nothing all day, and they began to be faint and weak. On his return, Blake went in to see Alice, and found her weeping.

"Won't you have some wine?" he asked.

"Oh! yes," said Sloan; "she will take anything I offer her. I have been teaching her to mind me without making a fuss about it."

Blake passed into Mary's room, and asked her if she would take some wine. She was so weak and sick that she could not speak, so she merely nodded her head in assent. He then went down stairs, where he met Sloan.

"It is well they are dressed," said Blake. "We shall not have any bother with them when they start out. Take some wine and cake up to Alice, and I will take some to Mary. We must leave here by the evening train. I have sent word to my wife to come and take charge of the restaurant; telling her that Mary had gone home sick, and that Alice had gone to nurse her. We must strike for the West and keep out of danger. We have got the girls pretty well broken in, but we must watch them, for if they give us the slip, their brother will be after us in no time. We must keep them stupefied with the laudanum, and prevent any one from speaking to them, or seeing their faces. Hurry up! we have no time to lose."

Sloan went up to see Alice, and made her eat some food and drink some wine, while Blake took some wine and cakes to Mary, and left her alone. Mary knelt down before she ate, and prayed her Heavenly Father to deliver her from the power of her enemies.

When the evening train came along, Mary and Alice were sleeping quietly from the effects of a mild dose of laudanum, administered to them in their wine. The train stopped to take wood and water. Blake found one car almost empty, and in this car, the sisters were placed, being half carried in a drowsy stupor by Blake and Sloan. Both girls were heavily veiled and no one could have recognized them, even if any of their acquaintances had been on the train. Blake took a seat by Mary, and Sloan beside Alice, so as to keep control of them. The sisters were so far under the influence of the drug, however, as to fall asleep as soon as they were seated; and, in this way Laporte was reached, without any suspicion having been awakened in the minds of any one. From Laporte, the party went by a connecting line to the Michigan Central Railroad, and thence to Chicago, where all trace of them was lost.

CHAPTER 9

NEARLY A WEEK elapsed before the girls' abduction was discovered. Kelly, the bar-keeper, said nothing in reference to the matter, and Mrs. Blake, on her return, three days later, supposed that Mary had gone home sick, as Blake had stated in his letter. Blake's absence was nothing unusual, as it was his habit to start off suddenly, to be gone, perhaps, for several weeks. William was too busy to go to Coldwater; and, although Mrs. Wells thought it strange that Mary did not write to her, she was not alarmed, supposing that the girls might be too much occupied to write.

When William went to Coldwater, however, and heard the story which Blake had written to Mrs. Blake, all was plain to him in an instant. His anguish was terrible, and he cursed himself for having advised his sisters to go to the restaurant to live. Mrs. Blake was equally affected. She loved her husband, brute as he was, and would not believe that he could have committed a crime. On the contrary, she accused Mary of leading him astray.

William did not know what to think nor do. He knew that his sisters were innocent, and that they must, therefore, have been carried away by force, but he could find no clue as to how or where they had gone. He returned home and gave his parents the sad intelligence that Mary and Alice had mysteriously disappeared. They were frantic with grief, but could suggest no means of recovering the girls. William then went immediately to Coldwater and laid the case before the sheriff. The sheriff was a man of excellent feelings, and his heart was touched at William's story; he, also, fully believed that they had been abducted by force. He at once sent for his deputy, Mr. Green, to whom he gave charge of the case.

"Green," said he, "you must not waste a moment in getting on the trail of these villains and their victims. You must then leave nothing undone to bring them back to Coldwater — the girls to their parents and the scoundrels to jail. It will be a lasting disgrace to our county, if we do not bring the perpetrators of this vile crime to justice."

Green soon learned the particulars of the abduction, up to the time when Blake and Sloan took the girls away from Bronson. William, while at home, had obtained all the money that he could raise, and was ready to accompany Green on his search.

They, accordingly, proceeded west as far as Laporte, where they met the conductor of the train in which Blake had taken the party away from Bronson. The conductor described Blake and Sloan exactly, but could not describe the girls, as their faces had been closely veiled, and they had slept most of the time. He recollected that just before arriving at Laporte, he had seen the taller of the two girls trying to speak to some passengers, as they passed out of the car at Carlyle. The man sitting with her had pulled her down on the seat again, at the same time showing her a knife and apparently saying something harsh to her. The conductor had regarded it, at the time, as merely a family quarrel, with which it would be better for him not to interfere. There had been nothing else, whatever, to arouse any suspicions with regard to the party, and, therefore, no idea of abduction had ever occurred to him.

The party was traced as far as Chicago, the accounts always being the same — that the girls had slept during the whole journey, except when changing cars, when they had seemed only half-awake.

Green and William arrived in Chicago and applied to Sheriff Church for his aid; but, though every effort was made, no trace of the villains could be found. All that could be discovered was that the party they were searching for, had arrived in Chicago, Saturday morning, but there all clue was lost. They were determined to continue the search, however, and Mr. Church, therefore, advised them to put the case in my hands.

It was nearly morning, by the time William had finished the story of the abduction, so far as he then knew it; and, having agreed to undertake the task of discovering the villains, I parted with my visitors and returned to bed.

This form of crime was new to me then, and I never before had heard such a truly painful case. My heart was deeply touched, as I thought of the helpless misery of those pure, young girls, and I lay awake for some time, thinking over the best course to pursue. I had intended to go to my home in Dundee the next day, but I determined not to give up the chase, until I had rescued the girls, and brought to punishment the brutes who had debauched them.

CHAPTER 10

After sleeping a couple of hours, I started out, very early in the morning, on my work of detection. Mary's avenger was now upon Blake's track, never to be shaken off. I had obtained a full description of the whole party from William and Green, so that I felt confident of my ability to follow them up, the moment I should discover any trace of them.

After visiting the depot and several hotels nearby, I walked into the American Hotel, on the corner of Lake street and Wabash avenue. Although I did not live in Chicago, I was well acquainted with the city, and knew Mr. Rossitter, the proprietor of the American Hotel, very well. Accordingly, I described Blake's party to Mr. Rossitter, and asked if any persons answering to their description had stopped at his hotel.

"Yes," he replied, "and I thought there was something strange about them. I did not like the appearance of the tall man. He looked like a gambler, and a desperate one at that. They gave their names as 'Brown and lady,' and 'Snell and lady.' They occupied adjoining rooms, opening into each other, and took their meals there, never once appearing in the dining-room. In fact, the ladies never left their rooms for any purpose, whatever, and looked dull and sleepy all the time. After they had gone, I learned from the chambermaids and waiting-girls that there were a number of suspicious circumstances connected with them. The ladies were evidently afraid of the men, and one of the latter had a small phial which, the chambermaid thought, contained laudanum. The men drank heavily and always had a bottle of wine on the table."

"Do you know where they went?" I asked.

"They went west on the Galena and Chicago Union Railroad, but I don't know where they were bound."

"When did they leave?" I asked, but immediately answered my own question: "Oh! of course they stopped over Sunday and took the train Monday morning. Goodbye, Rossitter," and I hurried over to the sheriff's office.

"Church," I said, "I'm off. Detain young Wells and Deputy-Sheriff Green until you hear from me. It is now Friday; you will probably get a dispatch from me by Monday or Tuesday. Keep them easy, and say that I am on the trail of the scoundrels."

So saying, I went out and hastened to the Galena depot, being just in time for the morning train going west. The conductor, Mr. Wiggins, was an old acquaintance, so I entered into conversation with him, in the course of which, I asked him, casually, whether he had had charge of the train Monday morning, ten days before. He replied that "Deacon" Harvey had taken the train out that morning, the two conductors going out alternately morning and evening.

As I lived on the line of the road, I knew all the conductors, and hoped to get some information from Harvey, if we did not pass him between stations.

I then stretched myself comfortably in my seat, and began to ponder upon the probabilities as to Blake's course. I knew that he was the moving spirit in the whole affair, and that all my calculations must be made upon his probable action. If he were going to California, he was taking a very circuitous route, since it was necessary to go much further south, if he intended to strike across the plains. Still, he might intend waiting somewhere in the interior of Illinois until spring, and then he could go down the Mississippi to St. Louis, or any other point that he might choose. It was not at all likely that he would go into an unsettled country to stay; he was too fond of company and gambling to do that. It was most probable that he would stop in some large town until spring, and then go to St. Louis, thence up the Missouri river to Independence, and from there start across the plains for California.

"Yes," I soliloquized, inaudibly, "there is something probable in that. They will most likely hide in Illinois, but will they stay together? Sloan is a stage-driver, and is well acquainted on all the stage routes; hence, he will be of service in getting passes and reduced rates of fare on the stage lines. He will probably wish to remain east of the Mississippi, and Blake will not go far away. Well, I shall have to feel as I go along, trusting to getting some clue in Belvidere."

The Galena and Chicago Union Railroad, (now absorbed in the Chicago and Northwestern Railroad,) was the first railroad commenced in Illinois, and the only one running west of Chicago. It had been completed only to Belvidere, in Boone county, from which point travelers and immigrants were carried west and north in stages, many of which were in waiting, on the arrival of each train.

At Marengo, John Perkins, the agent of Frink & Walker, got aboard the train to sell tickets to persons wishing to leave Belvidere by any of the numerous stage-lines, all of which were owned by the above-named firm. John was a fine young fellow, who had been promoted to his present place from that of stage-driver. He was a genial, shrewd man, who tried to be on good terms with every one, and generally succeeded. He and I were well acquainted with each other, and I determined to draw him out quietly, as he was just the man to have observed Blake's party, if he had met any of them.

It is my practice never to tell any one what object I have in view, unless it is absolutely necessary that I should do so. Therefore, I did not tell John what the business was which took me to Belvidere. He joined me after he had been through the whole train, and we had a pleasant conversation. At length, I introduced the subject of stage management, upon which John was never tired of talking.

"How many different stage routes start from Belvidere?" I asked, after a few remarks had passed.

"Oh! several," said John, and he went on to tell how many stages there were on each route, the number of times the horses were changed, the average number of passengers, and many other details.

"Do you employ many men to handle baggage?" I asked.

"Yes; we have six men in Belvidere alone, and they have all they can attend to."

"What a number of drivers you must have, John!" I said, carelessly. "How do you ever manage to keep track of them all?"

"That's an easy matter," said he, pulling a memorandum book from his pocket. "This contains an alphabetical list of the names of all the drivers in my division."

"You stage men have brought things down to a wonderful system," said I, as I took the book and casually glanced through it.

I saw that E. Sloan was a driver on the route from Janesville to Madison, and I continued to turn the leaves as I said:

"Oh! so Sloan is driving for you, eh! I used to know him some time ago. He was driving for the Humphries, in Michigan, then, I believe."

"Yes," replied John, "he came to us from them."

"He's a good driver, isn't he?"

"Yes," said John, "very good, indeed."

"Where is he now?" I asked, as I saw that John did not suspect me of having any particular object in my inquiries.

"He and his wife came west about a week ago and went on to Rockford. I gave him a pass to Janesville and told him he could have his old route, but I don't know whether he will take it, as he said he could not decide what he should do for a week or two. He said he might like a southern route."

"I am glad to hear he's doing so well," I replied. "He is an old friend of mine, and I should like to see him."

"You will most likely find him in Rockford; but if he has left there, you can easily find where he has gone."

"So, he has taken a wife, eh?" I said, half musingly. "I wonder whom he married. Did he have any friends with him?"

"Yes; a man and his wife were with him," said John. "I did not like the looks of the man very much; from the 'cut of his jib,' as the sailors say, I took him to be a gambler, and one of the sort who always win."

"Gambling is carried on everywhere just now," I said. "You can find any number of gamblers at Galena, or Rockford. In fact, every little place seems to have its gambling hell. Do you remember his friend's name? I wonder if I know him."

"I have his name here," said John. "I gave him a pass, too."

As he spoke, he drew out a note-book and showed me the entry:

"Blake and lady — Belvidere to Rockford, with pass."

"So, that's the way you do things, is it?" I asked.

"Yes; we are not very particular now. Old Frink tells us to be liberal with the good drivers, and grant them small favors. Good drivers are hard to find, and while business is so brisk, we need all we can get. Hence, we lose nothing by treating them well."

Now, I was close on their track. Blake got a pass to Rockford, and Sloan, to Janesville. It seemed strange that such men did not know enough to get off the beaten routes of travel, and endeavor to hide more effectually. I concluded that they had little fear of detection, and still less of pursuit, and, therefore, proposed to take things easily. I did not imagine for an instant the extent of Blake's villainy, nor his real reason for frequenting the large towns.

On arriving in Belvidere, I went to the American House, as I was well acquainted with the proprietor, Mr. Irish; from him I soon learned that Blake's party had stopped there one day.

"Blake is a pretty good fellow, isn't he, Mr. Irish?" I asked.

"Yes; he seems to be a good fellow. He knows how to play cards; he never lost a game, while here."

"Well, it would be hard to find a man in Belvidere who could get away with him at cards," said I. "Did his wife come down into the parlor and associate with the other ladies?"

"No, indeed. But I must hurry away, as the stages are soon going out. Are you going west?"

"No," I replied; "I may take a buggy and drive out a few miles, but I am not sure what I shall do. Oh! one more question before you go. Did Blake make much money here?"

"I guess he did; and that reminds me—I think King went up to Mrs. Blake's room while Blake was playing," said Irish.

As he spoke, he gave a knowing laugh, and poked me with his finger in the ribs.

"Is it possible!" said I. "How long did he stay?"

"About an hour. You know, King has plenty of money, and I presume he treated the lady liberally. When he came down, he went into the room where Blake was gambling, and ordered drinks for the crowd."

"After King went away, did any one else go to Mrs. Blake's room?" I asked.

"I think not," replied Irish. "It was after eleven o'clock before King came down, and Blake went to bed by midnight. Blake is a good fellow, and I would like to have him for a regular boarder, as he is generous with his cash."

"Well," said I, as Irish moved off, "I believe I'll change my mind, and go on to Galena by the next stage. I shall spend the night at Pecatonica; if there is anything I can do for you, let me know."

What a terrible revelation had been made to me in this short conversation! I knew King well as an infamous libertine. What was the business that kept him in Mary's room for over an hour? I had to shudder at the only answer that could be given. From all I could learn, the girls were kept constantly in a comatose state, which, together with the terror with which Blake and Sloan had inspired them, had prevented them from attempting to escape, or asking assistance. Mary, undoubtedly, had been made wholly insensible, before King was admitted to her room. He was a rich, but unscrupulous brute, fit for any crime, and the more revolting to nature it was, the more he would delight in it.

This terrible discovery filled me with horror, and I determined to lose not a moment in freeing the sisters from their brutal captors.

CHAPTER 11

FIVE STAGES WERE on the point of starting for Rockford, and I took a seat beside the driver of one of them. The night was dark, and the road was none of the best, so that we seemed to creep along at a snail's pace. I was impatient to grasp the villains, and rescue the sisters from their terrible position.

The driver of the stage was a pleasant, genial fellow; in conversation with him, I found that he knew Sloan, but that he had not seen him for a day or two. I was rather disconcerted at this news, as I had hoped to find the whole party in Rockford. It was about half-past eight o'clock when we entered Rockford, and drove up before the Washington House, where the stages usually stopped.

I did not know how I should be received here. Only six months before, I had obtained the necessary evidence to convict some counterfeiters, who had a haunt in Winnebago County. With the assistance of the United States Marshal, I had arrested them and taken them to Chicago. I believed at the time that the landlord of the Washington House was, in some way, in the interest of the gang; hence, I was rather suspicious of him. I determined not to trust him at all, but to take a room, and make my investigations quietly.

Accordingly, I sauntered up to the register, entered my name, and glanced over the list of the arrivals for a few days back. I found that Blake and lady had been given room number five; and Sloan and lady, room number nine. I then ate supper and loitered around the barn, until I met the hostler. I asked him whether he knew Sloan. He said yes; but that he had not seen him for a day or two. Finding that nothing could be done that night, I went to bed, pretty well tired out.

Early the next morning (Saturday), I met the landlord; and, as I shook hands with him, I said, quietly:

"Don't talk with me, nor let any one know who I am. I want to get some more evidence against those counterfeiters, and don't wish any one to know me. I may be here for two or three days; so, please keep mum for the present."

"All right," said he, and after taking a drink with me, he moved off.

I placed more confidence in the clerk than in the landlord, but I thought best to tell him the same story. I then lounged about the hall, and saw every one who came to breakfast; but none of the parties I was seeking made their appearance.

About ten o'clock, I went over to the stage barn, to see what information might be learned about Sloan. After a time, I made the acquaintance of the driver who had taken Sloan and Alice to Janesville. By treating him to whisky and cigars, I succeeded in making him talkative and friendly; then, I ventured to ask after Sloan.

"Oh! Sloan went up to Janesville with me Thursday week," said the driver. "He had a mighty fine girl with him, and she will make him a splendid wife; but, after all, he is a very shiftless fellow, and it is a pity to see such a nice girl throw herself away on him. To my mind, she is sick of her bargain, already. Why, she never spoke to him during the whole trip."

"So, you took them to Janesville, did you?"

"Yes; that's my run. I saw Sloan yesterday, and shall see him the next time I go up. Who shall I say was asking for him?"

I pretended not to hear his question; since, if I should give my real name, Sloan would immediately take the alarm; and, if I gave a fictitious name, it would almost certainly be strange to Sloan, and his suspicions might be excited. I, therefore, tided over the difficulty by asking the driver to take another drink; and, as the dinner hour had arrived, I bade him good-day and walked away.

I ate dinner very slowly and kept my seat until all the other boarders had finished. I carefully scrutinized the features of every one, but saw no one that would correspond to the description of Blake, or Mary.

My reticence and my strict rule against letting any one know my business, made my search slower and more difficult—but, at the same time, more certain—than as if I had taken the landlord or clerk into my confidence. But I was determined not to risk even the possibility of giving Blake the alarm; so, I worked entirely unassisted.

I knew where there was a gambling saloon on the east side of the river, and I decided to pay it a visit. I, accordingly, walked to it, entered the bar-room, and sat down, ordering a glass of whisky and a cigar. There was a crowd in the bar-room, but I sat quietly smoking and listening to the talk around me. The afternoon slipped away without any new developments; and, as it began to grow dark, the crowd gradually thinned out, until I was almost alone.

Finally my patience was rewarded. Shortly after five o'clock, four men came down from the gambling rooms which, I knew, were up stairs. I immediately picked out one of them as Blake. He answered the description perfectly. His fine appearance and showy jewelry were unmistakable, and I knew that the man I was seeking, was before me. He was a representative specimen of the professional gambler. His companions were not professionals, but wealthy men who gambled for amusement. They called for drinks at the bar, and then two of them went out, leaving Blake and the remaining member of the party sipping their liquor, with their backs turned toward me. By this time, I was sitting back, apparently sound asleep; and, though I was quite near them, they took no notice of me, so that I was able to overhear their remarks.

"Call at ten o'clock," said Blake, "and I will have all arranged. She will be asleep by that time."

Good Heavens! could I have heard aright! Blake was deliberately planning to give his pure and innocent victim into the power of another lustful brute!

"By the Eternal! I will end it now!" I muttered, as I started to my feet. But the folly of my course flashed across me instantly, and I sat down again, fortunately unobserved by them. It would not do to act in my then excited state.

"Ten o'clock?" said Blake's companion. "All right; I will be there without fail."

"The door will be locked; but you knock, and I will let you in," said Blake, as his friend went out.*

Blake conversed a few minutes with the bar-keeper, paid for the drinks, and walked out. I allowed him to go some distance ahead of me, and then kept him in sight. He walked to the Washington House and entered the hall door. I quickened my pace and ran up the steps only a moment behind him. I hurried into the bar-room, but he was not there. I then went up stairs and found number five, which was a suite of rooms, with two doors opening into the hall. Before I could get out of the way, Blake opened his door and looked out. I was obliged to walk into a room, the door of which was fortunately unlocked, and pretend that it was my room. I waited there until all was quiet, and then slipped out, noiselessly. It was now nearly six o'clock, and I went to my own room to reflect upon what course to pursue.

At this moment, I recollected that I had no warrant upon which to arrest Blake. I had a justice's warrant, issued in Coldwater, Michigan, for the arrest of Blake and Sloan; but this paper was useless in Illinois. Nevertheless, I had heard the bargain made to let a brute into Mary's room that night, and I determined that that crime should never be permitted. I would arrest Blake or die in the attempt.

I confess that I had never been so excited before. I had been deeply affected by William's story; I had heard of Mary's sale to King in Bel-

---

* By a peculiar coincidence, just at the time that this agreement was made, the nephew of Sheriff Church entered the latter's office in Chicago and said that he had just come in from Rockford. In the course of the conversation, he told Sheriff Church that there was a gambler in Rockford, who was cleaning out all the other gamblers there. He added: "The money that the man doesn't win, in one way, his wife obtains, in another. She is said to be a beautiful woman; but it takes one hundred dollars to make her acquaintance."

Of course, Church did not think of Mary in this connection, as the possibility that the girls might have been separated did not occur to him.

videre; and, now that the incarnate fiend was about to give her over to another man, I was ready to take the law in my own hands, if necessary, to prevent the outrage.

I had no one to assist me in making the arrest. It is true, I had many friends in Rockford; but they all lived across the river, and I had not been in West Rockford during the day. I decided to arrest Blake at once, however, relying on the justice of my case. After supper, therefore, I wrote a note to the sheriff, with whom I was slightly acquainted, asking him to come immediately to the Washington House, on very important business. I sent the note by a safe messenger and then went to my room to get my pistols. I put one in each pocket of my pantaloons and went down stairs, taking a position in front of the hotel. I was now perfectly cool, and was only awaiting the arrival of the sheriff, to assist me in arresting Blake.

CHAPTER 12

THE MINUTES SLIPPED rapidly away, and by half-past eight o'clock, I began to get excited again. Time was precious; Blake's appointment had been made for ten o'clock; but the man might come earlier. I had no overcoat on; so, I went into the hotel, to wait for the sheriff. In a few minutes, I resolved to take some decisive action soon.

I walked upstairs and opened the door of number five. Blake stood in the middle of the room, beside a table, and was engaged in pouring some liquid from a bottle into a tumbler. He had evidently just finished writing a letter, as one lay on the table unsealed. A lady sat in the shadow near the window. As soon as Blake saw me, he walked towards me.

"Oh! I beg pardon," I said; "I was looking for number seventeen."

"It is not here," he said, in a hoarse voice.

"Please excuse me," I added, as I backed out of the room and closed the door.

In a second, I heard him bolt it.

"That is bad," thought I; "but I know they are there, and that Blake's friend has not arrived."

I had just obtained a glimpse of Mary. She looked very haggard, and was terribly changed, as compared with the rosy, beautiful girl who had been described to me.

I then walked down to the street, but could see no signs of the sheriff. I walked as far as the bridge, but could not see him coming.

"I will end the matter now," I muttered; "or he will end me, one of the two. I must have the girl out of danger before ten o'clock."

It was then half-past nine. The landlord was behind his desk, as I entered the office, and I called him to one side.

"I'll tell you what I am here for," I said. "I have some business with Mr. Blake, in number five. You may possibly hear some noise, but don't mind it. If I break anything, I will pay for it. I have sent for the sheriff, and I expect him every minute. When he comes, send him up to the room; but let no one else come up, until I call."

"All right, Pink.," said he; "I know you will do only what is right."

I had a light coat on, and was unencumbered with anything which could place me at a disadvantage in a struggle; so I walked straight up to number five.

I gave a light knock. Blake evidently thought his friend had come, for I heard him moving across the room. The thought flashed into my mind:

"Perhaps Mary is already drugged! I hope not."

Blake opened the door. In a second, I pushed into the room, locked the door, and dropped the key into my pocket. I then pointed my pistol at his head.

"You are my prisoner!" I said, in a stern voice.

The betrayer and the avenger were, now, face to face.

He started back, with an amazed look, and made a quick motion towards his pocket, as if to draw a weapon.

"Raise your hands over your head, and go to the other side of the room," I commanded. "I will kill you if you attempt to draw your pistol."

He did not move.

"Will you go back?" I asked, in a determined tone. "If you don't go this instant, you're a dead man. I know you are armed. Go back!"

He went. From that moment, I knew he was a coward. I had awed him by my commanding tone and resolute look.

As he moved back, Mary rushed toward me.

"Oh! save me! save me!" she exclaimed. "May Heaven protect you! Oh! where is my father! where is my mother!"

As she spoke, she fainted away at my feet; but I could not attend to her then.

"Let me come to her, I will revive her," said Blake; and he dropped his hands by his side.

"Throw your hands over your head and keep them there," I again commanded; he quickly obeyed.

At this instant, I recollected that I had brought no hand-cuffs with me. They are almost indispensable in my business; yet I had forgotten them.

"Blake," I said, "keep your right hand over your head, take out your pistol with your left hand, and lay it on the table. If you make a single suspicious move, I shall kill you. I am a sure shot, and, on the least provocation, a ball will go crashing through your brain."

"Who are you who dare talk to me in this way?" he asked. "This is my room; that lady is my wife; what business have you in here?"

"Pshaw! that lady your wife? That lady is Mary Wells, whom you have abducted, you scoundrel. Lay down your pistol, or take the consequences. One hand only; keep the other over your head," I continued, as he began to lower both hands.

He then slipped his revolver out of his pocket and laid it on the table.

"Back again, now," I said; and he obeyed. I stepped to the table and put his pistol into my pocket.

"You see that I have the advantage of you," I went on; "I have three pistols while you have none."

Then, glancing at Mary, who was just recovering consciousness, I said:

"Raise yourself, Miss Wells; I cannot help you, as I must look out for Blake."

She raised herself and moved toward me.

"Don't touch me, now," I said; "I don't want to give Blake a chance of escape. I will talk to you bye-and-bye."

Mary staggered back and fell into a chair, as a low knock was heard at the door.

"Who is there?" I asked; but there was no answer. "Who is there?" I repeated, thinking it might be the sheriff.

A fiendish expression of delight came into Blake's face, and then, the thought flashed into my mind that it was Blake's friend, who had been told to call at ten o'clock.

"Blake," I said, "that is your friend, to whom you agreed to deliver Mary at ten o'clock. He can come in, if he likes, as I have pistols enough for both of you. You are a beast, not a man."

"How the h—l did you know a man was to have been here at ten o'clock?" he asked, in a surly, but surprised tone.

"Because I heard you make the bargain with him. Mary was to have been asleep."

"How long are you going to keep me with my hands over my head?" he asked.

"Until the sheriff comes to take you to jail; then, Mary, I will be ready to talk to you."

"I may as well give up," he muttered. "Your d—d pistol settled me. If I had got mine out first, it would have been very different; but I admit it was a fair game, and I am caught. I know that I have wronged Mary; that I have ruined her; but I could not help it."

Mary attempted to speak.

"No, Miss Wells," I said; "don't talk now."

Blake continued:

"I will do all in my power to atone for my crime. I have done wrong, indeed. This will kill my wife. I may as well go to jail quietly."

I had given up all hope of the sheriff's arrival; I therefore decided that I had better take Blake to jail myself. It was my intention, then, to come back, to get all the information possible from Mary. I further expected to start for Janesville early the next morning, to rescue Alice and capture Sloan.

I glanced hastily at Mary. Her appearance was pitiable in the extreme; her face was perfectly livid, and she seemed absolutely helpless.

"Blake," I said, "if I thought I could trust you to go quietly, I would take you over to the jail, myself."

"You have the advantage," said he, "and, of course, you will keep it. I shall make no resistance."

"I'll do it," said I; "but mind! Just as surely as you attempt to escape, I will shoot you down, like a dog. I shall have no mercy on you; and if you attempt any treachery, you will be a dead man the next instant; be assured of that."

"I will go peaceably," he said, "there is no use in trying to resist; moreover, I want to keep the affair quiet for the sake of my wife and the girls."

"Get your hat and come along, then."

"Will you allow me to get an overcoat?" he asked.

"Yes," I said, as I knew the more clothing he had on, the more powerless he would be.

On that account, I always have made it a practice to go without an overcoat, and have hardened myself to stand a great deal of cold without suffering.

I stood with my back against the door, while Blake went into the adjoining room to get his overcoat. Mary said, in a quick, excited manner:

"He will make his escape from that room, and he has a knife in his pocket."

I sprang to the door connecting the two rooms, and said:

"Come in here! What knife was that you put in your pocket?"

"It is a lie," he replied; "I did not put a knife in my pocket."

"Lay your coat down on the table," I said.

He did not obey, but looked as if he would like to rebel.

"Blake, lay your coat down and raise your hands above your head."

He saw, by my eye, that I was not to be trifled with, and he obeyed. I examined the coat, but found no knife.

"Blake, what have you done with your knife?" I asked.

"She is a liar; I have no knife," he answered.

Mary raised her head, and said:

"Yes, he has; it is concealed in the pocket of his pants. He means to kill either you or me with it."

"Hand me that knife," I said, firmly, "or I will spatter the room with your brains."

With a sullen oath, he drew a fine bowie-knife from his pocket, and pitched it toward me.

"Have a care, Blake," said I. "You should not throw a knife in that way. I know you wouldn't hurt me for the world, but I advise you to be more polite in future."

I picked up the knife and handed it to Mary.

"Keep that until I come back," I said. "I shall return in three-quarters of an hour, and you had better keep the door locked, while I am gone."

The man whom Blake had agreed to let in, had been gone for some time. I, therefore, apprehended no attempt at a rescue, unless Blake should get help in passing some of the saloons. Many of these drinking holes were still open, it being Saturday night, and only a little after ten o'clock. Still I did not fear any such attempt. Blake then put on his overcoat; I grasped him by the right arm with my left hand, and held my revolver in my right hand, ready to give him the contents, if he attempted to escape. He was a muscular, powerful man, and I did not propose to give him a chance to grapple with me.

We met no one on the stairs, as we went down, but I saw about a dozen persons in the bar-room. The hotel was raised three or four steps above the sidewalk, and, as we passed out of the hall door, Blake went down the steps so quickly as to make me jump the whole distance, in order to keep hold of him.

"If you make another attempt to escape," I said, "you must take the consequences."

"I wasn't trying to escape," he replied; "I don't wish to be seen by any of the boarders."

A short distance down the street, we passed two men, and I heard one of them say:

"The river is rising rapidly, and it will sweep away the bridge before morning."

"Good God!" I thought, "what shall I do, if I can't cross the bridge!"

In a few moments, we came in sight of the bridge; I then saw that two of the spans had already been washed away, and that communication was kept up by a single plank, thrown across from pier to pier. I, afterwards, learned that the two spans had been washed away about two weeks before. This night, however, there was danger that even the foot-planks might be carried off.

CHAPTER 13

As WE NEARED the river I said: "Blake, we cannot cross."

While I was in the act of speaking, Blake swung himself quickly around, facing me, and struck me a tremendous blow between the eyes. I should have fallen, had I not seized the lapel of his coat. Although it tore off, as he darted away, I kept my footing by means of the pull; but, for a second, I could see nothing but fire. Then the shock passed off, and I saw Blake rushing swiftly up the street. I dashed after him, instantly, leaving my hat behind, and shouted:

"Stop thief! stop thief!"

The crowds in the saloons began to pour out, and all was excitement. I was a swift runner, and felt sure of catching my man. He ran due east for a time, and then, turning north, passed through a street lined with trees. He had a good start of me, and was rapidly nearing the woods on the edge of the town. I had a clear view of him, as he ran, so I raised my pistol and shouted:

"Stop! or you are a dead man!"

He did not answer, but kept on running; so, I took a hurried aim and fired.

"Confound it! have I lost that shot!" I muttered. I again sighted at him and fired, as I continued the chase.

Someone at my side said:

"For God's sake! Pinkerton, stop firing! Don't you see that you have killed me?"

Just as Blake said this, he staggered and fell down, close by the fence. I found that my first shot had taken effect; the second, I found in the trunk of a tree, next morning.

"Get up!" I said to Blake, in a harsh tone; "I told you I would shoot you, if you tried to escape, and now I have done it."

He tried to rise, but could not. By this time, the crowd from the saloons had come up. Someone said:

"Blake, who shot you?"

Seeing that there were many of Blake's old chums in the crowd, some of whom were dangerous-looking characters, I raised Blake up and said:

"He is my prisoner."

At this, the crowd fell back; but, at my request, four of them raised him up and conveyed him to a small tavern, nearby, where he was laid on a lounge. He was then insensible, and medical aid was at once called. I remained with him to hear the surgeon's report; and, once, Blake opened his eyes and muttered:

"Pinkerton, I will kill you yet!" to which I made no reply.

In a few minutes, two doctors arrived and probed Blake's wound. It was on the right side of the spine, near the small of the back, and they immediately said that he could not live more than a day or two. By this time, a great crowd had gathered around the tavern door; and, as I passed out, several voices cried out:

"There goes the murderer!"

"Send for the sheriff," I replied; "I will answer to the proper authorities."

I then went back into the tavern and wrote a note to Mr. Holland, a lawyer, asking him to meet me at the Washington House, as soon as possible. Having sent this note, I started for the hotel. The streets were filled with people, all in a state of great excitement, and my situation was neither pleasant nor safe.

On reaching the hotel, I went up to see Mary. I knocked at the door, and she immediately let me in. She was crying quietly, and was, evidently, very weak.

"Mary," I asked, "what is in that phial?" and I pointed to the one I had seen in Blake's hand.

"I don't know," she replied. "Blake always poured a few drops out of it into our wine, when he wished to make us sleep."

"Mary," I said, "you must not get excited at what I am going to tell you. *Blake is shot.* I had to shoot him to prevent his escape. I had no alternative, as he would have got into the woods."

She said nothing, but continued to weep, even more bitterly than before. The thought flashed across me: "Can it be possible that she cared for this handsome scoundrel?" and I said:

"You do not feel angry with me, because I have done this, do you?"

"Oh! no sir; it is not anger that makes me weep; but oh! how horrible it is, to think of him being ushered into eternity with all his sins unrepented of! I have not words to express my gratitude to you for your kindness in rescuing me, and I hope no harm will come to you."

At this moment, the sheriff and several citizens entered the room. I took the sheriff into an adjoining room, closed the door, and told him all that had happened. I then asked him to go over to the tavern and secure the papers on Blake's person; I felt sure that some evidence of his guilt would be found on him. I, also, called Mary into the room and asked her whether she knew where Alice was.

"No, sir; Sloan took her away last Thursday week; but I don't know where they went. Blake was writing a letter to Sloan, this evening, and I think he has it in his pocket, now."

"I know where Alice is," I said; "Sloan took her to Janesville. Sheriff, you would oblige me very much, by getting Blake's papers. You need not fear that I shall run away."

Mr. Holland, my lawyer, came in, at this moment, and I explained my case to him. He shook me warmly by the hand and said:

"It will give me great pleasure to defend you. I, not only, sympathize with you heartily, but wholly approve your course. You will have more friends in Rockford than ever before."

Mr. Holland and the sheriff then went over to obtain Blake's papers. They found the streets crowded with people, as the shooting had been plainly heard, and every one was anxious to learn the cause of the trouble. During the sheriff's absence, I advised the people who had crowded into the hotel, to go away quietly; and they, finally, did so. I induced Mary to lie down to get some sleep, and the landlord, at my request, sent a girl to stay with her.

I was just about to retire, when a gentleman asked to see me. He proved to be the pastor of the Methodist church in Rockford; he stated that, having heard, briefly, from the sheriff, the story of Mary's wrongs, he had come to offer to take her to his own home, until her family should arrive, to take care of her. The hotel was so noisy, and the excitement was so bad for Mary, that I thankfully accepted his kind offer. I, therefore, procured a carriage, and Mary was, at once, conveyed to the minister's house.

Meanwhile, the sheriff had searched Blake's clothing, and the following letter was found:

> FRIEND SLOAN: I am just coining money. Mary has several admirers, and I often have two gentlemen up to see her of a night. She is getting d—d pale, but all the gentlemen pronounce her a regular beauty.
>
> I have my eye on two stunning girls in West Rockford; and we will get them to go out on the plains with us, when we take Mary and Alice to the "diggins." If they won't come willingly, *we know how to make them.*
>
> Are you doing well with Alice? I am making more money out of this speculation than out of any I ever attempted before.
>
> Yours, etc., BLAKE.

The sheriff brought this letter to me, and went off without locking me up; although I advised him to arrest me, as a matter of form.

"After reading that letter," said he, "there is no power on earth that could make me arrest you."

CHAPTER 14

IT WAS NEARLY four o'clock before I went to bed, but by six, I was up. I, at once, sent the following dispatch to Sheriff Church:

> SHERIFF W. L. CHURCH, Chicago:
>
> I arrested Blake last night. He broke away from me and ran for the woods. After a sharp race, I fired two shots at him. The first ball entered his back and passed through his body. The doctors pronounce the wound fatal. A letter to Sloan, found on his person, stated that he had two Rockford girls under his eye, whom he intended to debauch and take to California. Send William and Deputy-Sheriff Green by first train. Sloan and Alice are at Janesville. Will leave for Belvidere as soon as possible. I want Alice here. Fear Mary will be sick. She asks all the time for her father and William.
>
> ALLAN PINKERTON.

Having sent the dispatch, I ate breakfast, and then, paid a visit to all the clergymen on both sides of the river. I narrated the particulars of the outrage that had been perpetrated on the girls; spoke of their innocence and beauty, and of the hellish means used to destroy them; called attention to the letter found on Blake's person, in which he spoke of an intention to debauch two Rockford girls; and, in fact, laid bare the whole vile scheme, which had been successfully carried out, in part.

The clergymen, unanimously, approved of my course. In their morning discourses, they gave their congregations a short sketch of Blake's wicked plots, and offered devout thanks that he had been stopped in his career of crime, before he had had the opportunity to carry out his designs on the two Rockford girls. Prayer was offered up for Mary and Alice; also, for Mr. and Mrs. Wells, that they might be given strength to bear up under their terrible affliction. In this way, Mary's sad story was conveyed to all the church-going people in Rockford, and many ladies called that day at the Methodist parsonage, to offer their services.

During the forenoon, I called to see Mary, and found that she was quite delirious. At times, Blake would appear to her; the fearful events of the first stormy night would float before her; and she would shudder and almost faint with agony. Again, she thought she was on the cars, making the forced trip, and she suddenly startled every one by a piercing cry for Alice. Then she was at home, with her father, mother, and William, and her pleasant smiles showed that all was peace, purity, and happiness.

A physician stayed with her all the time; as I left, he went to the door with me and said that she had no appetite, and was running down fast. He wished that her sister would come, as Alice would have more influence over her, than strangers, although the Rockford ladies were doing everything in their power. She had youth and a good constitution on her side, however, and might pull through.

I returned to the Washington House, and as I passed some of the groggeries, the loafers, congregated in front of them, jeered at me, and called me a murderer. One bloated sot swaggered up to me and said:

"So, you are the murderer, are you? D—n you, I will put a ball through you!"

I turned on him and calmly said:

"I don't know you, nor do I wish to; but if you give me cause, I will shoot you, too. I will show the people of Rockford what kind of a man you are," and I advanced toward him.

He was, evidently, a cowardly braggart, for he slunk away into the crowd, and said no more.

Sunday was a busy day with me, as people came in to see me every minute. All the respectable people of the community were anxious to express to me their approval of my actions.

At seven o'clock in the evening, a carriage drove up, and, to my astonishment, William and Deputy-Sheriff Green jumped out. Immediately on receipt of my dispatch, in Chicago, they had obtained a special train, which had brought them to Belvidere; there, they had hired a carriage, in which they had come to Rockford.

I was delighted to see them, and, after a hasty supper, I took William to see Mary. I impressed upon him the necessity of being perfectly calm, and then led him into her room. Mary was propped up with pillows in a half-reclining position, and was very weak. William's color rose and his eyes flashed, as he saw what a wreck Mary had become; but, in a second, tears filled his eyes, and he almost fell, as he walked carefully across the room, and knelt at the bedside.

"Mary, don't you know me?" he said, in a voice trembling with emotion. "Don't you know William?"

As the familiar tones reached her ear, a look of delight came into her face; she raised herself on her arm, gazed lovingly at William, and tried to speak; but her emotions overcame her, and she dropped back in a swoon. The Doctor, assisted by two ladies who were present, soon revived her, and she was able to speak in a faint voice.

"Oh! William, I am so delighted to see you! Where are father, mother, and Alice? Won't they come to me?"

William took her hand gently, and endeavored in vain, to suppress the sobs that *would* come in spite of himself. His chest heaved convulsively, and his eyes were full of tears. Finally, he mastered his grief with great effort, and said:

"Father is coming as soon as he can. You will meet him in Chicago, if you are strong enough to make the journey."

I will not dwell upon this affecting meeting. Sorrow is the heritage of the whole world, and we all have so much unhappiness in our own lives, that we, naturally, do not desire to contemplate the misery of others, too long.

CHAPTER 15

I LEFT WILLIAM WITH Mary, and returned to the Washington House, to see Deputy-Sheriff Green. Having told him that Sloan was in Janesville, I offered to go there to arrest the villain and get Alice. Mary needed her sister's presence immediately, as the physicians feared the worst.

Green said that I had already done everything, and that I ought to have some rest; so, he would go to Janesville. Accordingly, I gave him a letter of introduction to the sheriff of Rock county, and, in less than an hour, he had hired a buggy and started on his journey.

He reached Janesville at three o'clock in the morning; he then called up the sheriff and asked his assistance in arresting Sloan. The sheriff hurriedly dressed himself and accompanied Green to Sloan's room. Green had not forgotten his handcuffs, and, in an instant, Sloan was a prisoner.

Alice fairly cried for joy at her deliverance, but her joy vanished on hearing of Mary's illness.

Green brought both Sloan and Alice back to Rockford in the buggy he had used in going to Janesville; and, on reaching Rockford, Sloan was lodged in jail, while Alice went to Mary's bedside.

Blake lived through Monday, but died that night. I cared but little for this. I had done only my duty. I had the approval, not only of my own conscience, but, also, of all the law-loving people of Rockford. A death by violence was the natural end of such a life as Blake's. Sooner or later his sin was sure to find him out; in the course of my duty, I was the appointed instrument of vengeance.

The arrival of William and Alice did Mary much good, and she cheered up perceptibly. I thought it would be best to move her to Chicago, and the doctor agreed with me. We, therefore, started Tuesday morning by stage, and took the train at Belvidere. We reached Chicago without accident, and Mary was immediately taken to the Sherman House, where the proprietors, Messrs. Tuttle & Brown, had prepared their best room. The whole community deeply sympathized with the unfortunate family, and Mary received the greatest attention and kindness from every one.

Doctor McVickar was called, and his opinion was awaited with deep anxiety. When he came out from Mary's room, he said that it would be impossible for her to live. She had been poisoned by heavy doses of cantharides, or Spanish fly, administered for a purpose better imagined than described. It had been given to her in such large doses, and had had time to work into her system so thoroughly, that it would be impossible to save her.

Mrs. Wells was quite ill, at home, from the overpowering effects of grief, and Mr. Wells was not in Chicago, on our arrival there. He came on, immediately; but Mary had been dead an hour and a half, when he entered the Sherman House.

Poor Mary! Only a few days before, she had been so full of life, so beautiful—now, she was a corpse. To her, however, death came as a release; and few would have cared to call her back to the suffering, which life would have entailed upon her.

Green obtained the necessary papers, and conveyed Sloan to the jail in Coldwater. He was there tried, convicted, and sentenced to imprisonment, at hard labor, for five years — the longest term allowable by law for his offense, at that time. The villains, Harris, Dick, and Joe, had taken an early alarm, and fled to the wilds of the Far West; so that they escaped, temporarily, from the hands of justice. Their further career was never known, but, in all probability, they were hanged.

CHAPTER 16

Ten eventful years passed away. I had entered into business, on my own account, and was doing well. I had gone into Montcalm County, Michigan, on the track of some parties, who were suspected of stealing goods from the Michigan Central Railroad. Montcalm County was just becoming settled up; and, as I drove along in my buggy, on my way to the little town of Stanton, I began to fear that I had lost my way. It was a very sultry summer day, and my horse jogged along, with drooping head, evidently suffering greatly from the heat. I, therefore, decided to stop at the first farm-house, to water my horse and inquire the way to Stanton.

I soon came in sight of a farm-house, situated in a large clearing. It was, evidently, a well-kept farm. The house was neat and comfortable; the fences and barns were in good order; and the stock looked well-fed and well-cared for. Everything showed thrifty, capable management.

I drove up to the house, and entered the open door. A handsome lady was seated at a table, sewing, and three children were playing around her. I asked her where I could get water for myself and my horse. She gave me a drink, took down a pail, and handed it to me, at the same time pointing to the well.

I thanked her, and made a few remarks about the fine appearance of her farm. She said nothing, but I noticed that she looked at me in a very curious manner. I then went out, watered my horse, and returned to the house with the pail; the lady took it from me, and handed it to a brown-eyed little boy, to take into the house, all the time keeping her eyes fixed upon me. I have always had a great liking for a handsome face, and this lady was, certainly, a beauty; but she gazed at me so steadily that, I must confess, I was somewhat abashed. However, I asked the road to Stanton, which she told me; and I then turned to get into my buggy. At this, she inquired, in a shy, timid way:

"Is your name Pinkerton?"

This question was rather startling, as I did not wish to be known; and Montcalm County having been so recently settled, I had not expected to be recognized there. Still, I could not deceive her, so I said, politely:

"Yes, madam; but you have the advantage of me."

She held out both her hands, and said, smilingly:

"Why, don't you know me, Mr. Pinkerton?"

I looked at her, and then at her three children, but could not recall a single familiar feature; so I was obliged to say:

"No; I do not know you."

"What! not know me! Why, I am Alice Wells," she replied.

"Good gracious! is it possible!" I said. "Well, this *is* a pleasant surprise."

I could hardly realize that it was Alice. She was married to an upright, intelligent farmer, and her husband was then at work in the field. She was determined that I should stay all night, and would not take "no" for an answer.

Finding that I could not get away, I drove my horse into the barn, while she sent for her husband. When he came, Alice told him who I was; as he knew all her previous history, and my connection with it, he received me with great cordiality.

A pleasanter night than the one I spent under their roof, I never passed. They did all in their power to make my stay agreeable, and succeeded perfectly. They were admirably suited to each other, and were evidently as devoted lovers as ever they were in their days of courtship, of which they related to me many amusing and touching anecdotes.

I have heard from them several times since then, and they seem to be as happy as mortals can ever expect to be.

1882

FRANK STOCKTON

THE LADY, OR THE TIGER? and THE DISCOURAGER OF HESITANCY

Mystery is a term that encompasses many types of stories, and one of the earliest kinds was known as riddle stories. The notion of the riddle was carried to an extreme by a writer of humorous children's books and popular fiction, FRANK STOCKTON (1834–1902), who is remembered almost exclusively today for "The Lady, or the Tiger?"

This beloved tale, one of the two most famous riddle stories of all time (the other being "The Mysterious Card," by Cleveland Moffett), was originally titled "The King's Arena" when Stockton read it aloud at a party. It drew such enthusiastic response that he expanded it, changed the title, and sold it to the very popular *Century Magazine.* Two years later, it became the title story of his most successful collection of short stories.

There is no detective in the story. Is there a body? Is there a criminal? Is there a violent murder? Perhaps a psychologist would be better able to answer, but really, Stockton designed this frustrating masterpiece for the reader to decide. Owing to its immense success, not to mention the lamentations of curious and baffled readers, he was persuaded to write a sequel to settle the question once and for all, which he did (not) with "The Discourager of Hesitancy," a largely forgotten tale nowadays. In it, the narrator promises to reveal the solution — but only if another riddle can be solved first.

Born in Philadelphia, Stockton began writing at an early age, starting with children's stories and sketches, then continuing with popular stories and novels of humor, notably *The Rudder Grangers Abroad* (1891). His other contributions to the mystery genre include *The Stories of Three Burglars* (1890), *The Captain's Toll Gate* (1893), *The Adventures of Captain Horn* (1895), and several short stories.

"The Lady, or the Tiger?" was first published in the November 1892 issue of *Century Magazine;* it was first collected in *The Lady, or the Tiger? and Other Stories* (New York: Charles Scribner's Sons, 1894).

"The Discourager of Hesitancy" was first published in *Stockton's Stories: Sec-*

ond Series. The Christmas Wreck and Other Stories (New York: Charles Scribner's Sons, 1886).

• • •

THE LADY, OR THE TIGER?

IN THE VERY olden time there lived a semi-barbaric king, whose ideas, though somewhat polished and sharpened by the progressiveness of distant Latin neighbors, were still large, florid, and untrammeled, as became the half of him which was barbaric. He was a man of exuberant fancy, and, withal, of an authority so irresistible that, at his will, he turned his varied fancies into facts. He was greatly given to self-communing, and, when he and himself agreed upon anything, the thing was done. When every member of his domestic and political systems moved smoothly in its appointed course, his nature was bland and genial; but whenever there was a little hitch, and some of his orbs got out of their orbits, he was blander and more genial still, for nothing pleased him so much as to make the crooked straight and crush down uneven places.

Among the borrowed notions by which his barbarism had become semified was that of the public arena, in which, by exhibitions of manly and beastly valor, the minds of his subjects were refined and cultured.

But even here the exuberant and barbaric fancy asserted itself. The arena of the king was built, not to give the people an opportunity of hearing the rhapsodies of dying gladiators, nor to enable them to view the inevitable conclusion of a conflict between religious opinions and hungry jaws, but for purposes far better adapted to widen and develop the mental energies of the people. This vast amphitheater, with its encircling galleries, its mysterious vaults, and its unseen passages, was an agent of poetic justice, in which crime was punished, or virtue rewarded, by the decrees of an impartial and incorruptible chance.

When a subject was accused of a crime of sufficient importance to interest the king, public notice was given that on an appointed day the fate of the accused person would be decided in the king's arena, a structure which well deserved its name, for, although its form and plan were borrowed from afar, its purpose emanated solely from the brain of this man, who, every barleycorn a king, knew no tradition to which he owed more allegiance than pleased his fancy, and who ingrafted on every adopted form of human thought and action the rich growth of his barbaric idealism.

When all the people had assembled in the galleries, and the king, surrounded by his court, sat high up on his throne of royal state on one side of the arena, he gave a signal, a door beneath him opened, and the accused subject stepped out into the amphitheater. Directly opposite him, on the other side of the enclosed space, were two doors, exactly alike and side by side. It was the duty and the privilege of the person on trial to walk directly to these doors and open one of them. He could open either door he pleased; he was subject to no guidance or influence but that of the aforementioned impartial and incorruptible chance. If he opened the one, there came out of it a hungry tiger, the fiercest and most cruel that could be procured, which immediately sprang upon him and tore him to pieces as a punishment for his guilt. The moment that the case of the criminal was thus decided, doleful iron bells were clanged, great wails went up from the hired mourners posted on the outer rim of the arena, and the vast audience, with bowed heads and downcast hearts, wended slowly their homeward way, mourning greatly that one so young and fair, or so old and respected, should have merited so dire a fate.

But, if the accused person opened the other door, there came forth from it a lady, the most suitable to his years and station that his majesty could select among his fair subjects, and to this lady he was immediately married, as a reward of his innocence. It mattered not that he might already possess a wife and family, or that his affections might be engaged upon an object of his own selection; the king allowed no such subordinate arrangements to interfere with his great scheme of retribution and reward. The exercises, as in the other instance, took place immediately, and in the arena. Another door opened beneath the king, and a priest, followed by a band of choristers, and dancing maidens blowing joyous airs on golden horns and treading an epithalamic measure, advanced to where the pair stood, side by side, and the wedding was promptly and cheerily solemnized. Then the gay brass bells rang forth their merry peals, the people shouted glad hurrahs, and the innocent man, preceded by children strewing flowers on his path, led his bride to his home.

This was the king's semi-barbaric method of administering justice. Its perfect fairness is obvious. The criminal could not know out of which door would come the lady; he opened either he pleased, without having the slightest idea whether, in the next instant, he was to be devoured or married. On some occasions the tiger came out of one door, and on some out of the other. The decisions of this tribunal were not only fair, they were positively determinate: the accused person was instantly punished if he found himself guilty, and, if innocent, he was rewarded on the spot, whether he liked it or not. There was no escape from the judgments of the king's arena.

The institution was a very popular one. When the people gathered together on one of the great trial days, they never knew whether they were to witness a bloody slaughter or a hilarious wedding. This element of uncertainty lent an interest to the occasion which it could not otherwise have attained. Thus, the masses were entertained and pleased, and the thinking part of the community could bring no charge of unfairness against this plan, for did not the accused person have the whole matter in his own hands?

This semi-barbaric king had a daughter as blooming as his most florid fancies, and with a soul as fervent and imperious as his own. As is usual in such cases, she was the apple of his eye, and was loved by him above all humanity. Among his courtiers was a young man of that fineness of blood and lowness of station common to the conventional heroes of romance who love royal maidens. This royal maiden was well satisfied with her lover, for he was handsome and brave to a degree unsurpassed in all this kingdom, and she loved him with an ardor that had enough of barbarism in it to make it exceedingly warm and strong. This love affair moved on happily for many months, until one day the king happened to discover its existence. He did not hesitate nor waver in regard to his duty in the premises. The youth was immediately cast into prison, and a day was appointed for his trial in the king's arena. This, of course, was an especially important occasion, and his majesty, as well as all the people, was greatly interested in the workings and development of this trial. Never before had such a case occurred; never before had a subject dared to love the daughter of a king. In after-years such things became commonplace enough, but then they were, in no slight degree, novel and startling.

The tiger-cages of the kingdom were searched for the most savage and relentless beasts, from which the fiercest monster might be selected for the arena; and the ranks of maiden youth and beauty throughout the land were carefully surveyed by competent judges in order that the young man might have a fitting bride in case fate did not determine for him a different destiny. Of course, everybody knew that the deed with which the accused was charged had been done. He had loved the princess, and neither he, she, nor anyone else thought of denying the fact; but the king would not think of allowing any fact of this kind to interfere with the workings of the tribunal, in which he took such great delight and satisfaction. No matter how the affair turned out, the youth would be disposed of, and the king would take an aesthetic pleasure in watching the course of events, which would determine whether or not the young man had done wrong in allowing himself to love the princess.

The appointed day arrived. From far and near the people gathered, and thronged the great galleries of the arena, and crowds, unable to gain admittance, massed themselves against its outside walls. The king and his court were in their places, opposite the twin doors, those fateful portals, so terrible in their similarity.

All was ready. The signal was given. A door beneath the royal party opened, and the lover of the princess walked into the arena. Tall, beautiful, fair, his appearance was greeted with a low hum of admiration and anxiety. Half the audience had not known so grand a youth had lived among them. No wonder the princess loved him! What a terrible thing for him to be there!

As the youth advanced into the arena, he turned, as the custom was, to bow to the king, but he did not think at all of that royal personage. His eyes were fixed upon the princess, who sat to the right of her father. Had it not been for the moiety of barbarism in her nature, it is probable that lady would not have been there, but her intense and fervid soul would not allow her to be absent on an occasion in which she was so terribly interested. From the moment that the decree had gone forth that her lover should decide his fate in the king's arena, she had thought of nothing, night or day, but this great event and the various subjects connected with it. Possessed of more power, influence, and force of character than anyone who had ever before been interested in such a case, she had done what no other person had done — she had possessed herself of the secret of the doors. She knew in which of the two rooms that lay behind those doors stood the cage of the tiger, with its open front, and in which waited the lady. Through these thick doors, heavily curtained with skins on the inside, it was impossible that any noise or suggestion should come from within to the person who should approach to raise the latch of one of them. But gold, and the power of a woman's will, had brought the secret to the princess.

And not only did she know in which room stood the lady ready to emerge, all blushing and radiant, should her door be opened, but she knew who the lady was. It was one of the fairest and loveliest of the damsels of the court who had been selected as the reward of the accused youth, should he be proved innocent of the crime of aspiring to one so far above him; and the princess hated her. Often had she seen, or imagined that she had seen, this fair creature throwing glances of admiration upon the person of her lover, and sometimes she thought these glances were perceived and even returned. Now and then she had seen them talking together; it was but for a moment or two, but much can be said in a brief space; it may have been on most unimportant topics, but how could she know that? The girl was lovely, but she had dared to raise her eyes to the loved one of the princess; and, with all the intensity of the savage blood transmitted to her through long lines of wholly barbaric ancestors, she hated the woman who blushed and trembled behind that silent door.

When her lover turned and looked at her, and his eye met hers as she sat there, paler and whiter than anyone in the vast ocean of anxious faces about her, he saw, by that power of quick perception which is given to those whose souls are one, that she knew behind which door crouched the tiger, and behind which stood the lady. He had expected her to know it. He understood her nature, and his soul was assured that she would never rest until she had made plain to herself this thing, hidden to all other lookers-on, even to the king. The only hope for the youth in which there was any element of certainty was based upon the success of the princess in discovering this mystery; and the moment he looked upon her, he saw she had succeeded, as in his soul he knew she would succeed.

Then it was that his quick and anxious glance asked the question: "Which?" It was as plain to her as if he shouted it from where he stood. There was not an instant to be lost. The question was asked in a flash; it must be answered in another.

Her right arm lay on the cushioned parapet before her. She raised her hand, and made a slight, quick movement toward the right. No one but her lover saw her. Every eye but his was fixed on the man in the arena.

He turned, and with a firm and rapid step he walked across the empty space. Every heart stopped beating, every breath was held, every eye was fixed immovably upon that man. Without the slightest hesitation, he went to the door on the right, and opened it.

Now, the point of the story is this: Did the tiger come out of that door, or did the lady?

The more we reflect upon this question, the harder it is to answer. It involves a study of the human heart which leads us through devious mazes of passion, out of which it is difficult to find our way. Think of it, fair reader, not as if the decision of the question depended upon yourself, but upon that hot-blooded, semi-barbaric princess, her soul at a white heat beneath the combined fires of despair and jealousy. She had lost him, but who should have him?

How often, in her waking hours and in her dreams, had she started in wild horror, and covered her face with her hands as she thought of her lover opening the door on the other side of which waited the cruel fangs of the tiger!

But how much oftener had she seen him at the other door! How in her grievous reveries had she gnashed her teeth, and torn her hair, when she saw his start of rapturous delight as he opened the door of the lady! How her soul had burned in agony when she had seen him rush to meet that woman, with her flushing cheek and sparkling eye of triumph; when she had seen him lead her forth, his whole frame kindled with the joy of recovered life; when she had heard the glad shouts from the multitude, and the wild ringing of the happy bells; when she had seen the priest, with his joyous followers, advance to the couple, and make them man and wife before her very eyes; and when she had seen them walk away together upon their path of flowers, followed by the tremendous shouts of the hilarious multitude, in which her one despairing shriek was lost and drowned!

Would it not be better for him to die at once, and go to wait for her in the blessed regions of semi-barbaric futurity?

And yet, that awful tiger, those shrieks, that blood!

Her decision had been indicated in an instant, but it had been made after days and nights of anguished deliberation. She had known she would be asked, she had decided what she would answer, and, without the slightest hesitation, she had moved her hand to the right.

The question of her decision is one not to be lightly considered, and it is not for me to presume to set myself up as the one person able to answer it. And so I leave it with all of you: Which came out of the opened door — the lady, or the tiger?

THE DISCOURAGER OF HESITANCY

IT WAS NEARLY a year after the occurrence of that event in the arena of the semi-barbaric king known as the incident of the lady or the tiger, that there came to the palace of this monarch a deputation of five strangers from a far country. These men, of venerable and dignified aspect and demeanor, were received by a high officer of the court, and to him they made known their errand.

"Most noble officer," said the speaker of the deputation, "it so happened that one of our countrymen was present here, in your capital city, on that momentous occasion when a young man who had dared to aspire to the hand of your king's daughter had been placed in the arena, in the midst of the assembled multitude, and ordered to open one of two doors, not knowing whether a ferocious tiger would spring out upon him, or a beauteous lady would advance, ready to become his bride. Our fellow citizen who was then present was a man of super-sensitive feelings, and at the moment when the youth was about to open the door he was so fearful lest he should behold a horrible spectacle that his nerves failed him, and he fled precipitately from the arena, and, mounting his camel, rode homeward as fast as he could go.

"We were all very much interested in the story which our countryman told us, and we were extremely sorry that he did not wait to see the end of the affair. We hoped, however, that in a few weeks some traveler from your city would come among us and bring us further news, but up to that day when we left our country no such traveler had arrived. At last it was determined that the only thing to be done was to send a deputation to this country, and to ask the question: 'Which came out of the open door, the lady, or the tiger?'"

When the high officer had heard the mission of this most respectable deputation, he led the five strangers into an inner room, where they were seated upon soft cushions, and where he ordered coffee, pipes, sherbet, and other semi-barbaric refreshments to be served to them. Then, taking his seat before them, he thus addressed the visitors:

"Most noble strangers, before answering the question you have come so far to ask, I will relate to you an incident which occurred not very long after that to which you have referred. It is well known in all regions hereabout that our great king is very fond of the presence of beautiful women about his court. All the ladies-in-waiting upon the queen and royal family are most lovely maidens, brought here from every part of the kingdom. The fame of this concourse of beauty, unequaled in any other royal court, has spread far and wide, and had it not been for the equally wide-spread fame of the systems of impetuous justice adopted by our king, many foreigners would doubtless have visited our court.

"But not very long ago there arrived here from a distant land a prince of distinguished appearance and undoubted rank. To such a one, of course, a royal audience was granted, and our king met him very graciously, and begged him to make known the object of his visit. Thereupon the prince informed his Royal Highness that, having heard of the superior beauty of the ladies of his court, he had come to ask permission to make one of them his wife.

"When our king heard this bold announcement, his face reddened, he turned uneasily on his throne, and we were all in dread lest some quick words of furious condemnation should leap from out his quivering lips. But by a mighty effort he controlled himself, and after a moment's silence he turned to the prince and said: 'Your request is granted. Tomorrow at noon you shall wed one of the fairest damsels of our court.' Then turning to his officers, he said: 'Give orders that everything be prepared for a wedding in the palace at high noon tomorrow. Convey this royal prince to suitable apartments. Send to him tailors, bootmakers, hatters, jewelers, armorers, men of every craft whose services he may need. Whatever he asks, provide. And let all be ready for the ceremony tomorrow.'"

"'But, Your Majesty,' exclaimed the prince, 'before we make these preparations, I would like—'

"'Say no more!' roared the king. 'My royal orders have been given, and nothing more is needed to be said. You asked a boon. I granted it, and I will hear no more on the subject. Farewell, my prince, until tomorrow noon.'

"At this the king arose and left the audience chamber, while the prince was hurried away to the apartments selected for him. Here came to him tailors, hatters, jewelers, and everyone who was needed to fit him out in grand attire for the wedding. But the mind of the prince was much troubled and perplexed.

"'I do not understand,' he said to his attendants, 'this precipitancy of action. When am I to see the ladies, that I may choose among them? I wish opportunity, not only to gaze upon their forms and faces, but to become acquainted with their relative intellectual development.'

"'We can tell you nothing,' was the answer. 'What our king thinks right, that will he do. More than this we know not.'

"'His Majesty's notions seem to be very peculiar,' said the prince, 'and, so far as I can see, they do not at all agree with mine.'

"At that moment an attendant whom the prince had not noticed came and stood beside him. This was a broad-shouldered man of cheery aspect, who carried, its hilt in his right hand, and its broad back resting on his broad arm, an enormous scimitar, the upturned edge of which was keen and bright as any razor. Holding this formidable weapon as tenderly as though it had been a sleeping infant, this man drew closer to the prince and bowed.

"'Who are you?' exclaimed His Highness, starting back at the sight of the frightful weapon.

"'I,' said the other, with a courteous smile, 'am the Discourager of Hesitancy. When the king makes known his wishes to anyone, a subject or visitor, whose disposition in some little points may be supposed not wholly to coincide with that of His Majesty, I am appointed to attend him closely, that, should he think of pausing in the path of obedience to the royal will, he may look at me, and proceed.'

"The prince looked at him, and proceeded to be measured for a coat.

"The tailors and shoemakers and hatters worked all night, and the next morning, when everything was ready, and the hour of noon was drawing nigh, the prince again anxiously inquired of his attendants when he might expect to be introduced to the ladies.

"'The king will attend to that,' they said. 'We know nothing of the matter.'

"'Your Highness,' said the Discourager of Hesitancy, approaching with a courtly bow, 'will observe the excellent quality of this edge.' And drawing a hair from his head, he dropped it upon the upturned edge of his scimitar, upon which it was cut in two at the moment of touching.

"The prince glanced, and turned upon his heel.

"Now came officers to conduct him to the grand hall of the palace, in which the ceremony was to be performed. Here the prince found the king seated on the throne, with his nobles, his courtiers, and his officers standing about him in magnificent array. The prince was led to a position in front of the king, to whom he made obeisance, and then said:

"'Your Majesty, before I proceed further —'

"At this moment an attendant, who had approached with a long scarf of delicate silk, wound it about the lower part of the prince's face so quickly and adroitly that he was obliged to cease speaking. Then, with wonderful dexterity, the rest of the scarf was wound around the prince's head, so that he was completely blindfolded. Thereupon the attendant quickly made openings in the scarf over the mouth and ears, so that the prince might breathe and hear, and fastening the ends of the scarf securely, he retired.

"The first impulse of the prince was to snatch the silken folds from his head and face, but, as he raised his hands to do so, he heard beside him the voice of the Discourager of Hesitancy, who gently whispered: 'I am here, Your Highness.' And, with a shudder, the arms of the prince fell down by his side.

"Now before him he heard the voice of a priest, who had begun the marriage service in use in that semi-barbaric country. At his side he could hear a delicate rustle, which seemed to proceed from fabrics of soft silk. Gently putting forth his hand, he felt folds of such silk close behind him. Then came the voice of the priest requesting him to take the hand of the lady by his side; and reaching forth his right hand, the prince received within it another hand, so small, so soft, so delicately fashioned, and so delightful to the touch, that a thrill went through his being. Then, as was the custom of the country, the priest first asked the lady would she have this man to be her husband; to which the answer gently came, in the sweetest voice he had ever heard: 'I will.'

"Then ran raptures rampant through the prince's blood. The touch, the tone, enchanted him. All the ladies of that court were beautiful, the Discourager was behind him, and through his parted scarf he boldly answered: 'Yes, I will.'

"Whereupon the priest pronounced them man and wife.

"Now the prince heard a little bustle about him; the long scarf was rapidly unrolled from his head, and he turned, with a start, to gaze upon his bride. To his utter amazement, there was no one there. He stood alone. Unable on the instant to ask a question or say a word, he gazed blankly about him.

"Then the king arose from his throne, and came down, and took him by the hand."

" 'Where is my wife?' gasped the prince.

" 'She is here,' said the king, leading him to a curtained doorway at the side of the hall.

"The curtains were drawn aside, and the prince, entering, found himself in a long apartment, near the opposite wall of which stood a line of forty ladies, all dressed in rich attire, and each one apparently more beautiful than the rest.

"Waving his hand toward the line, the king said to the prince: 'There is your bride! Approach, and lead her forth! But remember this: that if you attempt to take away one of the unmarried damsels of our court, your execution will be instantaneous. Now, delay no longer. Step up and take your bride.'

"The prince, as in a dream, walked slowly along the line of ladies, and then walked slowly back again. Nothing could he see about any one of them to indicate that she was more of a bride than the others. Their dresses were all similar; they all blushed; they all looked up and then looked down. They all had charming little hands. Not one spoke a word.

Not one lifted a finger to make a sign. It was evident that the orders given them had been very strict.

"'Why this delay?' roared the king. 'If I had been married this day to one so fair as the lady who wedded you, I should not wait one second to claim her.'

"The bewildered prince walked again up and down the line. And this time there was a slight change in the countenances of two of the ladies. One of the fairest gently smiled as he passed her. Another, just as beautiful, slightly frowned.

"'Now,' said the prince to himself, 'I am sure that it is one of those two ladies whom I have married. But which? One smiled. And would not any woman smile when she saw, in such a case, her husband coming towards her? Then again, on the other hand, would not any woman frown when she saw her husband come towards her and fail to claim her? Would she not knit her lovely brows? And would she not inwardly say, "It is I! Don't you know it? Don't you feel it? Come!" But if this woman had not been married, would she not frown when she saw the man looking at her? Would she not say inwardly, "Don't stop at me! It is the next but one. It is two ladies above. Go on!" Then again, the one who married me did not see my face. Would she not smile if she thought me comely? While if I wedded the one who frowned, could she restrain her disapprobation if she did not like me? Smiles invite the approach of true love. A frown is a reproach to a tardy advance. A smile —'

"'Now, hear me!' loudly cried the king. 'In ten seconds, if you do not take the lady we have given you, she who has just been made your bride shall be made your widow.'

"And, as the last word was uttered, the Discourager of Hesitancy stepped close behind the prince and whispered: 'I am here!'

"Now the prince could not hesitate an instant; he stepped forward and took one of the two ladies by the hand.

"Loud rang the bells, loud cheered the people, and the king came forward to congratulate the prince. He had taken his lawful bride.

"'Now, then," said the high officer to the deputation of five strangers from a far country, "when you can decide among yourselves which lady the prince chose, the one who smiled or the one who frowned, then will I tell you which came out of the open door, the lady or the tiger!"

At the latest accounts the five strangers had not yet decided.

1883

MARK TWAIN

A THUMB-PRINT AND WHAT CAME OF IT

Generally regarded as America's greatest humorist, and possibly its greatest writer, SAMUEL LANGHORNE CLEMENS (1835–1910) took the pseudonym Mark Twain, a term used to describe the water's depth that he heard while working as a pilot on the Mississippi River. Although he described and commented on serious events of the day in his work, he generally employed humor to soften his often controversial positions.

It is seldom acknowledged, but Mark Twain played a major role in the development of detective fiction. His first published book, *The Celebrated Jumping Frog of Calaveras County and Other Sketches* (1867), tells the story of a slick stranger who filled Jim Smiley's frog with quail shot to win a bet—an early and outstanding tale of a confidence game. More important is Twain's *Life on the Mississippi* (1883), in which Chapter 31 is a complete, self-contained story, "A Thumb-print and What Came of It," which is the first time in fiction that fingerprints are used as a form of identification. Twain used the same device in *The Tragedy of Pudd'nhead Wilson* (1894), in which the entire plot revolves around Wilson's courtroom explanation of the uniqueness of a person's print.

Unlike the present story, which is extremely dark, most of Twain's contributions to the mystery genre are humorous. "The Stolen White Elephant, Etc." (1882) is an out-and-out parody, as is "A Double-Barrelled Detective Story" (1902), which has Sherlock Holmes in its crosshairs. "Tom Sawyer, Detective" (1896; also in this book) is a classic tale of the humorous consequences of leaping to conclusions. Less successful are *A Murder, a Mystery, and a Marriage* (1945), unpublished at the time of Twain's death and issued in an unauthorized sixteen-copy edition, and *Simon Wheeler, Detective* (1963), an unfinished novel published more than a half century after the author's death by the New York Public Library.

"A Thumb-print and What Came of It" was first published in *Life on the Mississippi* (Boston: James R. Osgood, 1883).

• • •

We were approaching Napoleon, Arkansas. So I began to think about my errand there. Time, noonday; and bright and sunny. This was bad — not best, anyway; for mine was not (preferably) a noonday kind of errand. The more I thought, the more that fact pushed itself upon me — now in one form, now in another. Finally, it took the form of a distinct question: is it good common sense to do the errand in daytime, when, by a little sacrifice of comfort and inclination, you can have night for it, and no inquisitive eyes around? This settled it. Plain question and plain answer make the shortest road out of most perplexities.

I got my friends into my stateroom, and said I was sorry to create annoyance and disappointment, but that upon reflection it really seemed best that we put our luggage ashore and stop over at Napoleon. Their disapproval was prompt and loud; their language mutinous. Their main argument was one which has always been the first to come to the surface, in such cases, since the beginning of time: "But you decided and *agreed* to stick to this boat," etc.; as if, having determined to do an unwise thing, one is thereby bound to go ahead and make *two* unwise things of it, by carrying out that determination.

I tried various mollifying tactics upon them, with reasonably good success: under which encouragement, I increased my efforts; and, to show them that *I* had not created this annoying errand, and was in no way to blame for it, I presently drifted into its history — substantially as follows:

Toward the end of last year, I spent a few months in Munich, Bavaria. In November I was living in Fräulein Dahlweiner's *pension,* 1a, Karlstrasse; but my working quarters were a mile from there, in the house of a widow who supported herself by taking lodgers. She and her two young children used to drop in every morning and talk German to me — by request. One day, during a ramble about the city, I visited one of the two establishments where the Government keeps and watches corpses until the doctors decide that they are permanently dead, and not in a trance state. It was a grisly place, that spacious room. There were thirty-six corpses of adults in sight, stretched on their backs on slightly slanted boards, in three long rows — all of them with wax-white, rigid faces, and all of them wrapped in white shrouds. Along the sides of the room were deep alcoves, like bay windows; and in each of these lay several marble-visaged babes, utterly hidden and buried under banks of fresh flowers, all but their faces and crossed hands. Around a finger of each of these fifty still forms, both great and small, was a ring; and from the ring a wire led to the ceiling, and thence to a bell in a watch-room yonder, where, day and night, a watchman sits always alert and ready to spring to the aid of any of that pallid company who, waking out of death, shall make a movement — for any, even the slightest, movement will twitch the wire and ring that fearful bell. I imagined myself a death-sentinel drowsing there alone, far in the dragging watches of some wailing, gusty night, and having in a twinkling all my body stricken to quivering jelly by the sudden clamor of that awful summons! So I inquired about this thing; asked what resulted usually? if the watchman died, and the restored corpse came and did what it could to make his last moments easy? But I was rebuked for trying to feed an idle and frivolous curiosity in so solemn and so mournful a place; and went my way with a humbled crest.

Next morning I was telling the widow my adventure when she exclaimed: "Come with me! I have a lodger who shall tell you all you want to know. He has been a night watchman there."

He was a living man, but he did not look it. He was abed, and had his head propped high on pillows; his face was wasted and colorless, his deep-sunken eyes were shut; his hand, lying on his breast, was talon-like, it was so bony and long-fingered. The widow began her introduction of me. The man's eyes opened slowly, and glittered wickedly out from the twilight of their caverns; he frowned a black frown; he lifted his lean hand and waved us peremptorily away. But the widow kept straight on, till she had got out the fact that I was a stranger and an American. The man's face changed at once, brightened, became even eager — and the next moment he and I were alone together.

I opened up in cast-iron German; he responded in quite flexible English; thereafter we gave the German language a permanent rest.

This consumptive and I became good friends. I visited him every day, and we talked about everything. At least, about everything but wives and children. Let anybody's wife or anybody's child be mentioned, and three things always followed: the most gracious and loving and tender light glimmered in the man's eyes for a moment; faded out the next, and in its place came that deadly look which had flamed there the first time I ever saw his lids unclose; thirdly, he ceased from speech, there and then for that day; lay silent, abstracted, and absorbed; apparently heard nothing that I said; took no notice of my good-byes, and plainly did not know, by either sight or hearing, when I left the room.

When I had been this Karl Ritter's daily and sole intimate during two months, he one day said abruptly: "I will tell you my story."

A DYING MAN'S CONFESSION

Then he went on as follows:

"I have never given up, until now. But now I have given up. I am going to die. I made up my mind last night that it must be, and very soon, too. You say you are going to revisit your river, by-and-by, when you find opportunity. Very well; that, together with a certain strange experience which fell to my lot last night, determines me to tell you my history — for you will see Napoleon, Arkansas; and for my sake you will stop there, and do a certain thing for me — a thing which you will willingly undertake after you shall have heard my narrative.

"Let us shorten the story wherever we can, for it will need it, being long. You already know how I came to go to America, and how I came to settle in that lonely region in the South. But you do not know that I had a wife. My wife was young, beautiful, loving, and oh, so divinely good and blameless and gentle! And our little girl was her mother in miniature. It was the happiest of happy households.

"One night — it was toward the close of the war — I woke up out of a sodden lethargy, and found myself bound and gagged, and the air tainted with chloroform! I saw two men in the room, and one was saying to the other, in a hoarse whisper, 'I *told* her I would, if she made a noise, and as for the child — '

"The other man interrupted in a low, half-crying voice: 'You said we'd only gag them and rob them, not hurt them; or I wouldn't have come.'

" 'Shut up your whining; *had* to change the plan when they waked up; you done all *you* could to protect them, now let that satisfy you. Come, help rummage.'

"Both men were masked, and wore coarse, ragged 'nigger' clothes; they had a bull's-eye lantern, and by its light I noticed that the gentler robber had no thumb on his right hand. They rummaged around my poor cabin for a moment; the head bandit then said, in his stage whisper: —

" 'It's a waste of time — *he* shall tell where it's hid. Undo his gag, and revive him up.'

"The other said: 'All right — provided no clubbing.'

" 'No clubbing it is, then — provided he keeps still.'

"They approached me. Just then there was a sound outside, a sound of voices and trampling hoofs; the robbers held their breath and listened; the sounds came slowly nearer and nearer; then came a shout:

"'*Hello,* the house! Show a light, we want water.'

"'The captain's voice, by G——!' said the stage-whispering ruffian, and both robbers fled by the way of the back door, shutting off their bull's-eye as they ran.

"The strangers shouted several times more, then rode by—there seemed to be a dozen of the horses—and I heard nothing more.

"I struggled, but could not free myself from my bonds. I tried to speak, but the gag was effective; I could not make a sound. I listened for my wife's voice and my child's—listened long and intently, but no sound came from the other end of the room where their bed was. This silence became more and more awful, more and more ominous, every moment. Could you have endured an hour of it, do you think? Pity me, then, who had to endure three. Three hours? it was three ages! Whenever the clock struck, it seemed as if years had gone by since I had heard it last. All this time I was struggling in my bonds; and at last, about dawn, I got myself free, and rose up and stretched my stiff limbs. I was able to distinguish details pretty well. The floor was littered with things thrown there by the robbers during their search for my savings. The first object that caught my particular attention was a document of mine which I had seen the rougher of the two ruffians glance at and then cast away. It had blood on it! I staggered to the other end of the room. Oh, poor unoffending, helpless ones, there they lay, their troubles ended, mine begun!

"Did I appeal to the law—I? Does it quench the pauper's thirst if the King drink for him? Oh, no, no, no—I wanted no impertinent interference of the law. Laws and the gallows could not pay the debt that was owing to me! Let the laws leave the matter in my hands, and have no fears: I would find the debtor and collect the debt. How accomplish this, do you say? How accomplish it, and feel so sure about it, when I had neither seen the robbers' faces, nor heard their natural voices, nor had any idea who they might be? Nevertheless, I *was* sure—quite sure, quite confident. I had a clue—a clue which you would not have valued—a clue which would not have greatly helped even a detective, since he would lack the secret of how to apply it. I shall come to that, presently—you shall see. Let us go on, now, taking things in their due order. There was one circumstance which gave me a slant in a definite direction to begin with: Those two robbers were manifestly soldiers in tramp disguise; and not new to military service, but old in it—regulars, perhaps; they did not acquire their soldierly attitude, gestures, carriage, in a day, nor a month, nor yet in a year. So I thought, but said nothing. And one of them had said, 'The captain's voice, by G——!'—the one whose life I would have. Two miles away, several regiments were in camp, and two companies of U.S. cavalry. When I learned that Captain Blakely, of Company C, had passed our way that night, with an escort, I said nothing, but in that company I resolved to seek my man. In conversation I studiously and persistently described the robbers as tramps, camp followers; and among this class the people made useless search, none suspecting the soldiers but me.

"Working patiently, by night, in my desolated home, I made a disguise for myself out of various odds and ends of clothing; in the nearest village I bought a pair of blue goggles. By-and-by, when the military camp broke up, and Company C was ordered a hundred miles north, to Napoleon, I secreted my small hoard of money in my belt, and took my departure in the night. When Company C arrived in Napoleon, I was already there. Yes, I was there, with a new trade—fortune-teller. Not to seem partial, I made friends and told fortunes among all the companies garrisoned there; but I gave Company C the great bulk of my attentions. I made myself limitlessly obliging to these particular men; they could ask me no favor, put upon me no risk, which I would decline. I became the willing butt of their jokes; this perfected my popularity; I became a favorite.

"I early found a private who lacked a thumb—what joy it was to me! And when I found that he alone, of all the company, had lost a thumb, my last misgiving vanished; I was *sure* I was on the right track. This man's name was Kruger, a German. There were nine Germans in the company. I watched, to see who might be his intimates; but he seemed to have no especial intimates. But *I* was his intimate; and I took care to make the intimacy grow. Sometimes I so hungered for my revenge that I could hardly restrain myself from going on my knees and begging him to point out the man who had murdered my wife and child; but I managed to bridle my tongue. I bided my time, and went on telling fortunes, as opportunity offered.

"My apparatus was simple: a little red paint and a bit of white paper. I painted the ball of the client's thumb, took a print of it on the paper, studied it that night, and revealed his fortune to him next day. What was my idea in this nonsense? It was this: When I was a youth, I knew an old Frenchman who had been a prison-keeper for thirty years, and he told me that there was one thing about a person which never changed, from the cradle to the grave—the lines in the ball of the thumb; and he said that these lines were never exactly alike in the thumbs of any two human beings. In these days, we photograph the new criminal, and hang his picture in the Rogues' Gallery for future reference; but that Frenchman, in his day, used to take a print of the ball of a new prisoner's thumb and put that away for future reference. He always said that pictures were no good—future disguises could make them useless. 'The thumb's the only sure thing,' said he; 'you can't disguise that.' And he used to prove his theory, too, on my friends and acquaintances; it always succeeded.

"I went on telling fortunes. Every night I shut myself in, all alone, and studied the day's thumb-prints with a magnifying-glass. Imagine the devouring eagerness with which I pored over those mazy red spirals, with that document by my side which bore the right-hand thumb- and finger-marks of that unknown murderer, printed with the dearest blood—to me—that was ever shed on this earth! And many and many a time I had to repeat the same old disappointed remark, 'Will they *never* correspond!'

"But my reward came at last. It was the print of the thumb of the forty-third man of Company C whom I had experimented on—Private Franz Adler. An hour before, I did not know the murderer's name, or voice, or figure, or face, or nationality; but now I knew all these things! I believed I might feel sure; the Frenchman's repeated demonstrations being so good a warranty. Still, there was a way to *make* sure. I had an impression of Kruger's left thumb. In the morning I took him aside when he was off duty; and when we were out of sight and hearing of witnesses, I said, impressively:

"'A part of your fortune is so grave, that I thought it would be better for you if I did not tell it in public. You and another man, whose fortune I was studying last night,—Private Adler—have been murdering a woman and a child! You are being dogged: within five days both of you will be assassinated.'

"He dropped on his knees, frightened out of his wits; and for five minutes he kept pouring out the same set of words, like a demented person, and in the same half-crying way which was one of my memories of that murderous night in my cabin—

"'I didn't do it; upon my soul I didn't do it; and I tried to keep *him* from doing it; I did, as God is my witness. He did it alone.'

"This was all I wanted. And I tried to get rid of the fool; but no, he clung to me, imploring me to save him from the assassin. He said:

"'I have money—ten thousand dollars—hid away, the fruit of loot and thievery; save me—tell me what to do, and you shall have it, every penny. Two-thirds of it is my cousin Adler's; but you can take it all. We hid it when we first came here. But I hid it in a new place yesterday, and have not told him — shall not tell him. I was going to desert, and get away with it all. It is gold, and too heavy to carry when one is running and dodging; but a woman who has been gone over the river two days to prepare my way for me is going to follow me with it; and if I got no chance to describe the hiding-place to her I was going to slip my silver watch into her hand, or send it to her, and she would understand. There's a piece of paper in the back of the case, which tells it all. Here, take the watch — tell me what to do!'

"He was trying to press his watch upon me, and was exposing the paper and explaining it to me, when Adler appeared on the scene, about a dozen yards away. I said to poor Kruger —

"'Put up your watch, I don't want it. You shan't come to any harm. Go, now; I must tell Adler his fortune. Presently I will tell you how to escape the assassin; meantime I shall have to examine your thumb-mark again. Say nothing to Adler about this thing — say nothing to anybody.'

"He went away filled with fright and gratitude, poor devil. I told Adler a long fortune — purposely so long that I could not finish it; promised to come to him on guard, that night, and tell him the really important part of it — the tragical part of it, I said — so must be out of reach of eavesdroppers. They always kept a picket-watch outside the town — mere discipline and ceremony — no occasion for it, no enemy around.

"Toward midnight I set out, equipped with the countersign, and picked my way toward the lonely region where Adler was to keep his watch. It was so dark that I stumbled right on a dim figure almost before I could get out a protecting word. The sentinel hailed and I answered, both at the same moment. I added, 'It's only me — the fortune-teller.' Then I slipped to the poor devil's side, and without a word I drove my dirk into his heart! *Ja wohl,* laughed I, it *was* the tragedy part of his fortune, indeed! As he fell from his horse, he clutched at me, and my blue goggles remained in his hand; and away plunged the beast, dragging him with his foot in the stirrup.

"I fled through the woods, and made good my escape, leaving the accusing goggles behind me in that dead man's hand.

"This was fifteen or sixteen years ago. Since then I have wandered aimlessly about the earth, sometimes at work, sometimes idle; sometimes with money, sometimes with none; but always tired of life, and wishing it was done, for my mission here was finished, with the act of that night; and the only pleasure, solace, satisfaction I had, in all those tedious years, was in the daily reflection, 'I have killed him!'

"Four years ago, my health began to fail. I had wandered into Munich, in my purposeless way. Being out of money, I sought work, and got it; did my duty faithfully about a year, and was then given the berth of night watchman yonder in that dead-house which you visited lately. The place suited my mood. I liked it. I liked being with the dead —liked being alone with them. I used to wander among those rigid corpses, and peer into their austere faces, by the hour. The later the time, the more impressive it was; I preferred the late time. Sometimes I turned the lights low: this gave perspective, you see; and the imagination could play; always, the dim receding ranks of the dead inspired one with weird and fascinating fancies. Two years ago—I had been there a year then—I was sitting all alone in the watch-room, one gusty winter's night, chilled, numb, comfortless; drowsing gradually into unconsciousness; the sobbing of the wind and the slamming of distant shutters falling fainter and fainter upon my dulling ear each moment, when sharp and suddenly that dead-bell rang out a blood-curdling alarum over my head! The shock of it nearly paralyzed me; for it was the first time I had ever heard it.

"I gathered myself together and flew to the corpse-room. About midway down the outside rank, a shrouded figure was sitting upright, wagging its head slowly from one side to the other—a grisly spectacle! Its side was toward me. I hurried to it and peered into its face. Heavens, it was Adler!

"Can you divine what my first thought was? Put into words, it was this: 'It seems, then, you escaped me once: there will be a different result this time!'

"Evidently this creature was suffering unimaginable terrors. Think what it must have been to wake up in the midst of that voiceless hush, and look out over that grim congregation of the dead! What gratitude shone in his skinny white face when he saw a living form before him! And how the fervency of this mute gratitude was augmented when his eyes fell upon the life-giving cordials which I carried in my hands! Then imagine the horror which came into this pinched face when I put the cordials behind me, and said mockingly:

"'Speak up, Franz Adler—call upon these dead. Doubtless they will listen and have pity; but here there is none else that will.'

"He tried to speak, but that part of the shroud which bound his jaws held firm and would not let him. He tried to lift imploring hands, but they were crossed upon his breast and tied. I said:

"'Shout, Franz Adler; make the sleepers in the distant streets hear you and bring help. Shout — and lose no time, for there is little to lose. What, you cannot? That is a pity; but it is no matter — it does not always bring help. When you and your cousin murdered a helpless woman and child in a cabin in Arkansas — my wife, it was, and my child! — they shrieked for help, you remember; but it did no good; you remember that it did no good, is it not so? Your teeth chatter — then why cannot you shout? Loosen the bandages with your hands — then you can. Ah, I see — your hands are tied, they cannot aid you. How strangely things repeat themselves, after long years; for *my* hands were tied, that night, you remember? Yes, tied much as yours are now — how odd that is. I could not pull free. It did not occur to you to untie me; it does not occur to me to untie you. Sh——! there's a late footstep. It is coming this way. Hark, how near it is! One can count the footfalls — one — two — three. There — it is just outside. Now is the time! Shout, man, shout! — it is the one sole chance between you and eternity! Ah, you see you have delayed too long — it is gone by. There — it is dying out. It is gone! Think of it — reflect upon it — you have heard a human footstep for the last time. How curious it must be, to listen to so common a sound as that, and know that one will never hear the fellow to it again.'

"Oh, my friend, the agony in that shrouded face was ecstasy to see! I thought of a new torture, and applied it — assisting myself with a trifle of lying invention:

"'That poor Kruger tried to save my wife and child, and I did him a grateful good turn for it when the time came. I persuaded him to rob you; and I and a woman helped him to desert, and got him away in safety.'

"A look as of surprise and triumph shone out dimly through the anguish in my victim's face. I was disturbed, disquieted. I said:

"'What, then — didn't he escape?'

"A negative shake of the head.

"'No? What happened, then?'

"The satisfaction in the shrouded face was still plainer. The man tried to mumble out some words — could not succeed; tried to express something with his obstructed hands — failed; paused a moment, then feebly tilted his head, in a meaning way, toward the corpse that lay nearest him.

"'Dead?' I asked. 'Failed to escape? — caught in the act and shot?'

"Negative shake of the head.

"'How, then?'

"Again the man tried to do something with his hands. I watched closely, but could not guess the intent. I bent over and watched still more intently. He had twisted a thumb around and was weakly punching at his breast with it.

"'Ah — stabbed, do you mean?'

"Affirmative nod, accompanied by a spectral smile of such peculiar devilishness, that it struck an awakening light through my dull brain, and I cried:

"'Did *I* stab him, mistaking him for you? — for that stroke was meant for none but you.'

"The affirmative nod of the re-dying rascal was as joyous as his failing strength was able to put into its expression.

"'O, miserable, miserable me, to slaughter the pitying soul that stood a friend to my darlings when they were helpless, and would have saved them if he could! miserable, oh, miserable, miserable me!'

"I fancied I heard the muffled gurgle of a mocking laugh. I took my face out of my hands, and saw my enemy sinking back upon his inclined board.

"He was a satisfactory long time dying. He had a wonderful vitality, an astonishing constitution. Yes, he was a pleasant long time at it. I got a chair and a newspaper, and sat down by him and read. Occasionally I took a sip of brandy. This was necessary, on account of the cold. But I did it partly because I saw that, along at first, whenever I reached for the bottle, he thought I was going to give him some. I read aloud: mainly imaginary accounts of people snatched from the grave's threshold and restored to life and vigor by a few spoonsful of liquor and a warm bath. Yes, he had a long, hard death of it — three hours and six minutes, from the time he rang his bell.

"It is believed that in all these eighteen years that have elapsed since the institution of the corpse-watch, no shrouded occupant of the Bavarian dead-houses has ever rung its bell. Well, it is a harmless belief. Let it stand at that.

"The chill of that death-room had penetrated my bones. It revived and fastened upon me the disease which had been afflicting me, but which, up to that night, had been steadily disappearing. That man murdered my wife and my child; and in three days hence he will have added me to his list. No matter — God! how delicious the memory of it! I caught him escaping from his grave, and thrust him back into it.

"After that night, I was confined to my bed for a week; but as soon as I could get about, I went to the dead-house books and got the number of the house which Adler had died in. A wretched lodging-house, it was. It was my idea that he would naturally have gotten hold of Kruger's effects, being his cousin; and I wanted to get Kruger's watch, if I could. But while I was sick, Adler's things had been sold and scattered, all except a few old letters, and some odds and ends of no value. However, through those letters, I traced out a son of Kruger's, the only relative left. He is a man of thirty now, a shoemaker by trade, and living at No. 14 Königstrasse, Mannheim — widower, with several small children. Without explaining to him why, I have furnished two-thirds of his support ever since.

"Now, as to that watch — see how strangely things happen! I traced it around and about Germany for more than a year, at considerable cost in money and vexation; and at last I got it. Got it, and was unspeakably glad; opened it, and found nothing in it! Why, I might have known that that bit of paper was not going to stay there all this time. Of course I gave up that ten thousand dollars then; gave it up, and dropped it out of my mind: and most sorrowfully, for I had wanted it for Kruger's son.

"Last night, when I consented at last that I must die, I began to make ready. I proceeded to burn all useless papers; and sure enough, from a batch of Adler's, not previously examined with thoroughness, out dropped that long-desired scrap! I recognized it in a moment. Here it is — I will translate it:

> Brick livery stable, stone foundation, middle of town, corner of Orleans and Market. Corner toward Court-house. Third stone, fourth row. Stick notice there, saying how many are to come.

"There — take it, and preserve it. Kruger explained that that stone was removable; and that it was in the north wall of the foundation, fourth row from the top, and third stone from the west. The money is secreted behind it. He said the closing sentence was a blind, to mislead in case the paper should fall into wrong hands. It probably performed that office for Adler.

"Now I want to beg that when you make your intended journey down the river, you will hunt out that hidden money, and send it to Adam Kruger, care of the Mannheim address which I have mentioned. It will make a rich man of him, and I shall sleep the sounder in my grave for knowing that I have done what I could for the son of the man who tried to save my wife and child—albeit my hand ignorantly struck him down, whereas the impulse of my heart would have been to shield and serve him."

1888

AMBROSE BIERCE

MY FAVORITE MURDER

Although AMBROSE (GWINNETT) BIERCE (1842–1914?) has been described as America's greatest writer of horror fiction between Edgar Allan Poe and H. P. Lovecraft, it seems that his entire life, and every word he wrote, was dark and cynical, earning him the sobriquet "Bitter Bierce." This story is a splendid example of how hilarious he could be, even as he was describing nothing less than a murder.

Born in Meigs County, Ohio, he grew up in Indiana with his mother and eccentric father as the tenth of thirteen children, all of whose names began with the letter *A*. When the Civil War broke out, he volunteered and was soon commissioned a first lieutenant in the Union Army, seeing action in the Battle of Shiloh.

Bierce became one of the most important and influential journalists in America, writing columns for William Randolph Hearst's *San Francisco Examiner.* His darkest book may be the devastating *Devil's Dictionary,* in which he defined a saint as "a sinner revised and edited," *befriend* as "to make an ingrate," and *birth* as "the first and direst of all tragedies." His most famous story is probably "An Occurrence at Owl Creek Bridge," in which a condemned prisoner believes he has been reprieved—just before the rope snaps his neck. It was filmed three times and was twice made for television, by Rod Serling for *The Twilight Zone* and by Alfred Hitchcock for *Alfred Hitchcock Presents.*

In 1913, during the Mexican Revolution, Bierce accompanied Pancho Villa's army as an observer. He wrote a letter to a friend dated December 26, 1913. He then vanished—one of the most famous disappearances in history, once as famous as those of Judge Crater and Amelia Earhart.

"My Favorite Murder" was first published in the September 16, 1888, edition of the *San Francisco Examiner;* it was first published in book form in *Can Such Things Be?* (New York: Cassell, 1893).

• • •

HAVING MURDERED MY mother under circumstances of singular atrocity, I was arrested and put upon my trial, which lasted seven years. In charging the jury, the judge of the Court of Acquittal remarked that it was one of the most ghastly crimes that he had ever been called upon to explain away.

At this, my attorney rose and said:

"May it please your Honor, crimes are ghastly or agreeable only by comparison. If you were familiar with the details of my client's previous murder of his uncle you would discern in his later offense (if offense it may be called) something in the nature of tender forbearance and filial consideration for the feelings of the victim. The appalling ferocity of the former assassination was indeed inconsistent with any hypothesis but that of guilt; and had it not been for the fact that the honorable judge before whom he was tried was the president of a life insurance company that took risks on hanging, and in which my client held a policy, it is hard to see how he could decently have been acquitted. If your Honor would like to hear about it for instruction and guidance of your Honor's mind, this unfortunate man, my client, will consent to give himself the pain of relating it under oath."

The district attorney said: "Your Honor, I object. Such a statement would be in the nature of evidence, and the testimony in this case is closed. The prisoner's statement should have been introduced three years ago, in the spring of 1881."

"In a statutory sense," said the judge, "you are right, and in the Court of Objections and Technicalities you would get a ruling in your favor. But not in a Court of Acquittal. The objection is overruled."

"I except," said the district attorney.

"You cannot do that," the judge said. "I must remind you that in order to take an exception you must first get this case transferred for a time to the Court of Exceptions on a formal motion duly supported by affidavits. A motion to that effect by your predecessor in office was denied by me during the first year of this trial. Mr. Clerk, swear the prisoner."

The customary oath having been administered, I made the following statement, which impressed the judge with so strong a sense of the comparative triviality of the offense for which I was on trial that he made no further search for mitigating circumstances, but simply instructed the jury to acquit, and I left the court, without a stain upon my reputation:

"I was born in 1856 in Kalamakee, Mich., of honest and reputable parents, one of whom Heaven has mercifully spared to comfort me in my later years. In 1867 the family came to California and settled near Nigger Head, where my father opened a road agency and prospered beyond the dreams of avarice. He was a reticent, saturnine man then, though his increasing years have now somewhat relaxed the austerity of his disposition, and I believe that nothing but his memory of the sad event for which I am now on trial prevents him from manifesting a genuine hilarity.

"Four years after we had set up the road agency an itinerant preacher came along, and having no other way to pay for the night's lodging that we gave him, favored us with an exhortation of such power that, praise God, we were all converted to religion. My father at once sent for his brother the Hon. William Ridley of Stockton, and on his arrival turned over the agency to him, charging him nothing for the franchise nor plant — the latter consisting of a Winchester rifle, a sawed-off shotgun, and an assortment of masks made out of flour sacks. The family then moved to Ghost Rock and opened a dance house. It was called 'The Saints' Rest Hurdy-Gurdy,' and the proceedings each night began with prayer. It was there that my now sainted mother, by her grace in the dance, acquired the *sobriquet* of 'The Bucking Walrus.'

"In the fall of '75 I had occasion to visit Coyote, on the road to Mahala, and took the stage at Ghost Rock. There were four other passengers. About three miles beyond Nigger Head, persons whom I identified as my Uncle William and his two sons held up the stage. Finding nothing in the express box, they went through the passengers. I acted a most honorable part in the affair, placing myself in line with the others, holding up my hands and permitting myself to be deprived of forty dollars and a gold watch. From my behavior no one could have suspected that I knew the gentlemen who gave the entertainment. A few days later, when I went to Nigger Head and asked for the return of my money and watch, my uncle and cousins swore they knew nothing of the matter, and they affected a belief that my father and I had done the job ourselves in dishonest violation of commercial good faith. Uncle William even threatened to retaliate by starting an opposition dance house at Ghost Rock. As 'The Saints' Rest' had become rather unpopular, I saw that this would assuredly ruin it and prove a paying enterprise, so I told my uncle that I was willing to overlook the past if he would take me into the scheme and keep the partnership a secret from my father. This fair offer he rejected, and I then perceived that it would be better and more satisfactory if he were dead.

"My plans to that end were soon perfected, and communicating them to my dear parents I had the gratification of receiving their approval. My father said he was proud of me, and my mother promised that although her religion forbade her to assist in taking human life I should have the advantage of her prayers for my success. As a preliminary measure looking to my security in case of detection I made an application for membership in that powerful order, the Knights of Murder, and in due course was received as a member of the Ghost Rock commandery. On the day that my probation ended I was for the first time permitted to inspect the records of the order and learn who belonged to it — all the rites of initiation having been conducted in masks. Fancy my delight when, in looking over the roll of membership, I found the third name to be that of my uncle, who indeed was junior vice-chancellor of the order! Here was an opportunity exceeding my wildest dreams — to murder I could add insubordination and treachery. It was what my good mother would have called 'a special Providence.'

"At about this time something occurred which caused my cup of joy, already full, to overflow on all sides, a circular cataract of bliss. Three men, strangers in that locality, were arrested for the stage robbery in which I had lost my money and watch. They were brought to trial and, despite my efforts to clear them and fasten the guilt upon three of the most respectable and worthy citizens of Ghost Rock, convicted on the clearest proof. The murder would now be as wanton and reasonless as I could wish.

"One morning I shouldered my Winchester rifle, and going over to my uncle's house, near Nigger Head, asked my Aunt Mary, his wife, if he were at home, adding that I had come to kill him. My aunt replied with her peculiar smile that so many gentlemen called on that errand and were afterward carried away without having performed it that I must excuse her for doubting my good faith in the matter. She said I did not look as if I would kill anybody, so, as a proof of good faith I leveled my rifle and wounded a Chinaman who happened to be passing the house. She said she knew whole families that could do a thing of that kind, but Bill Ridley was a horse of another color. She said, however, that I would find him over on the other side of the creek in the sheep lot; and she added that she hoped the best man would win.

"My Aunt Mary was one of the most fair-minded women that I have ever met.

"I found my uncle down on his knees engaged in skinning a sheep. Seeing that he had neither gun nor pistol handy I had not the heart to shoot him, so I approached him, greeted him pleasantly and struck him a powerful blow on the head with the butt of my rifle. I have a very good delivery and Uncle William lay down on his side, then rolled over on his back, spread out his fingers and shivered. Before he could recover the use of his limbs I seized the knife that he had been using and cut his hamstrings. You know, doubtless, that when you sever the *tendo Achillis* the patient has no further use of his leg; it is just the same as if he had no leg. Well, I parted them both, and when he revived he was at my service. As soon as he comprehended the situation, he said:

" 'Samuel, you have got the drop on me and can afford to be generous. I have only one thing to ask of you, and that is that you carry me to the house and finish me in the bosom of my family.'

"I told him I thought that a pretty reasonable request and I would do so if he would let me put him into a wheat sack; he would be easier to carry that way and if we were seen by the neighbors *en route* it would cause less remark. He agreed to that, and going to the barn I got a sack. This, however, did not fit him; it was too short and much wider than he; so I bent his legs, forced his knees up against his breast and got him into it that way, tying the sack above his head. He was a heavy man and I had all that I could do to get him on my back, but I staggered along for some distance until I came to a swing that some of the children had suspended to the branch of an oak. Here I laid him down and sat upon him to rest, and the sight of the rope gave me a happy inspiration. In twenty minutes my uncle, still in the sack, swung free to the sport of the wind.

"I had taken down the rope, tied one end tightly about the mouth of the bag, thrown the other across the limb and hauled him up about five feet from the ground. Fastening the other end of the rope also about the mouth of the sack, I had the satisfaction to see my uncle converted into a large, fine pendulum. I must add that he was not himself entirely aware of the nature of the change that he had undergone in his relation to the exterior world, though in justice to a good man's memory I ought to say that I do not think he would in any case have wasted much of my time in vain remonstrance.

"Uncle William had a ram that was famous in all that region as a fighter. It was in a state of chronic constitutional indignation. Some deep disappointment in early life had soured its disposition and it had declared war upon the whole world. To say that it would butt anything accessible is but faintly to express the nature and scope of its military activity: the universe was its antagonist; its methods that of a projectile. It fought like the angels and devils, in mid-air, cleaving the atmosphere like a bird, describing a parabolic curve and descending upon its victim at just the exact angle of incidence to make the most of its velocity and weight. Its momentum, calculated in foot-tons, was something incredible. It had been seen to destroy a four year old bull by a single impact upon that animal's gnarly forehead. No stone wall had ever been known to resist its downward swoop; there were no trees tough enough to stay it; it would splinter them into matchwood and defile their leafy honors in the dust. This irascible and implacable brute—this incarnate thunderbolt—this monster of the upper deep, I had seen reposing in the shade of an adjacent tree, dreaming dreams of conquest and glory. It was with a view to summoning it forth to the field of honor that I suspended its master in the manner described.

"Having completed my preparations, I imparted to the avuncular pendulum a gentle oscillation, and retiring to cover behind a contiguous rock, lifted up my voice in a long rasping cry whose diminishing final note was drowned in a noise like that of a swearing cat, which emanated from the sack. Instantly that formidable sheep was upon its feet and had taken in the military situation at a glance. In a few moments it had approached, stamping, to within fifty yards of the swinging foeman, who, now retreating and anon advancing, seemed to invite the fray. Suddenly I saw the beast's head drop earthward as if depressed by the weight of its enormous horns; then a dim, white, wavy streak of sheep prolonged itself from that spot in a generally horizontal direction to within about four yards of a point immediately beneath the enemy. There it struck sharply upward, and before it had faded from my gaze at the place whence it had set out I heard a horrid thump and a piercing scream, and my poor uncle shot forward, with a slack rope higher than the limb to which he was attached. Here the rope tautened with a jerk, arresting his flight, and back he swung in a breathless curve to the other end of his arc. The ram had fallen, a heap of indistinguishable legs, wool and horns, but pulling itself together and dodging as its antagonist swept downward it retired at random, alternately shaking its head and stamping its fore-feet. When it had backed about the same distance as that from which it had delivered the assault it paused again, bowed its head as if in prayer for victory and again shot forward, dimly visible as before—a prolonging white streak with monstrous undulations, ending with a sharp ascension. Its course this time was at a right angle to its former one, and its impatience so great that it struck the enemy before he had nearly reached the lowest point of his arc. In consequence he went flying round and round in a horizontal circle whose radius was about equal to half the length of the rope, which I forgot to say was nearly twenty feet long. His shrieks, *crescendo* in approach and *diminuendo* in recession, made the rapidity of his revolution more obvious to the ear than to the eye. He had evidently not yet been struck in a vital spot. His posture in the sack and the distance from the ground at which he hung compelled the ram to operate upon his lower extremities and the end of his back. Like a plant that has struck its root into some poisonous mineral, my poor uncle was dying slowly upward.

"After delivering its second blow the ram had not again retired. The fever of battle burned hot in its heart; its brain was intoxicated with the wine of strife. Like a pugilist who in his rage forgets his skill and fights ineffectively at half-arm's length, the angry beast endeavored to reach its fleeting foe by awkward vertical leaps as he passed overhead, sometimes, indeed, succeeding in striking him feebly, but more frequently overthrown by its own misguided eagerness. But as the impetus was exhausted and the man's circles narrowed in scope and diminished in speed, bringing him nearer to the ground, these tactics produced better results, eliciting a superior quality of screams, which I greatly enjoyed.

"Suddenly, as if the bugles had sung truce, the ram suspended hostilities and walked away, thoughtfully wrinkling and smoothing its great aquiline nose, and occasionally cropping a bunch of grass and slowly munching it. It seemed to have tired of war's alarms and resolved to beat the sword into a plowshare and cultivate the arts of peace. Steadily it held its course away from the field of fame until it had gained a distance of nearly a quarter of a mile. There it stopped and stood with its rear to the foe, chewing its cud and apparently half asleep. I observed, however, an occasional slight turn of its head, as if its apathy were more affected than real.

"Meantime Uncle William's shrieks had abated with his motion, and nothing was heard from him but long, low moans, and at long intervals my name, uttered in pleading tones exceedingly grateful to my ear. Evidently the man had not the faintest notion of what was being done to him, and was inexpressibly terrified. When Death comes cloaked in mystery he is terrible indeed. Little by little my uncle's oscillations diminished, and finally he hung motionless. I went to him and was about to give him the *coup de grâce,* when I heard and felt a succession of smart shocks which shook the ground like a series of light earthquakes, and turning in the direction of the ram, saw a long cloud of dust approaching me with inconceivable rapidity and alarming effect! At a distance of some thirty yards away it stopped short, and from the near end of it rose into the air what I at first thought a great white bird. Its ascent was so smooth and easy and regular that I could not realize its extraordinary celerity, and was lost in admiration of its grace. To this day the impression remains that it was a slow, deliberate movement, the ram

— for it was that animal — being upborne by some power other than its own impetus, and supported through the successive stages of its flight with infinite tenderness and care. My eyes followed its progress through the air with unspeakable pleasure, all the greater by contrast with my former terror of its approach by land. Onward and upward the noble animal sailed, its head bent down almost between its knees, its fore-feet thrown back, its hinder legs trailing to rear like the legs of a soaring heron.

"At a height of forty or fifty feet, as fond recollection presents it to view, it attained its zenith and appeared to remain an instant stationary; then, tilting suddenly forward without altering the relative position of its parts, it shot downward on a steeper and steeper course with augmenting velocity, passed immediately above me with a noise like the rush of a cannon shot and struck my poor uncle almost squarely on the top of the head! So frightful was the impact that not only the man's neck was broken, but the rope too; and the body of the deceased, forced against the earth, was crushed to pulp beneath the awful front of that meteoric sheep! The concussion stopped all the clocks between Lone Hand and Dutch Dan's, and Professor Davidson, a distinguished authority in matters seismic, who happened to be in the vicinity, promptly explained that the vibrations were from north to southwest.

"Altogether, I cannot help thinking that in point of artistic atrocity my murder of Uncle William has seldom been excelled."

1889

CHARLES W. CHESNUTT

THE SHERIFF'S CHILDREN

It was uncommon in nineteenth-century America for Negro writers to write and publish fiction successfully, but CHARLES W(ADDELL) CHESNUTT (1858–1932) overcame numerous obstacles to achieve his goal, producing stories that are still highly readable today. He was born in Cleveland, Ohio, the son of "free persons of color" who had moved north from Fayetteville, North Carolina. The family returned to Fayetteville after the Civil War, but Chesnutt and his new wife moved to New York City in 1878 in order for him to pursue a literary career; after six months, he moved back to Cleveland, where he passed the bar exam and established a successful legal stenography business.

He soon became a professional writer, his first short story, "The Goophered Grapevine," being published by *The Atlantic Monthly* in 1887, and he became a prolific producer of short fiction for numerous magazines and newspapers. His first published book was an important story collection, *The Conjure Woman* (1899), told in dialect in the vein of folktales by Uncle Julius, a freed slave, who entertained a white couple from the North with farfetched fantasies of ghosts, supernatural occurrences, and, of course, conjuring. It was quickly followed by *The Wife of His Youth and Other Stories of the Color Line* (1899). The same year saw the publication of a biography, *Frederick Douglass,* as well as the novel *The Passing of Grandison.* In 1900, the novel *The House Behind the Cedars* saw print, and *The Marrow of Tradition* came out the next year.

Poor sales of Chesnutt's books, in spite of the critical acclaim he received, eventually forced him to turn away from a literary life. The new, modern writers of the Harlem Renaissance regarded him as old-fashioned and his fiction as often illustrative of racial stereotypes, so he changed careers and in 1901 became a social and political activist, serving on the General Committee of the NAACP.

"The Sheriff's Children" was first published in the November 7, 1889, issue of the *New York Independent;* it was collected in *The Wife of His Youth and Other Stories of the Color Line* (Boston: Houghton Mifflin, 1899).

• • •

A MURDER WAS A rare event in Branson County. Every well-informed citizen could tell the number of homicides committed in the county for fifty years back, and whether the slayer, in any given instance, had escaped either by flight or acquittal, or had suffered the penalty of the law. So, when it became known in Troy early one Friday morning in summer, about ten years after the war, that old Captain Walker, who had served in Mexico under Scott, and had left an arm on the field of Gettysburg, had been foully murdered during the night, there was intense excitement in the village. Business was practically suspended, and the citizens gathered in little groups to discuss the murder, and speculate upon the identity of the murderer. It transpired from testimony at the coroner's inquest, held during the morning, that a strange mulatto had been seen going in the direction of Captain Walker's house the night before, and had been met going away from Troy early Friday morning, by a farmer on his way to town. Other circumstances seemed to connect the stranger with the crime. The sheriff organized a posse to search for him, and early in the evening, when most of the citizens of Troy were at supper, the suspected man was brought in and lodged in the county jail.

By the following morning the news of the capture had spread to the farthest limits of the county. A much larger number of people than usual came to town that Saturday — bearded men in straw hats and blue homespun shirts, and butternut trousers of great amplitude of material and vagueness of outline; women in homespun frocks and slat-bonnets, with faces as expressionless as the dreary sandhills which gave them a meager sustenance.

The murder was almost the sole topic of conversation. A steady stream of curious observers visited the house of mourning, and gazed upon the rugged face of the old veteran, now stiff and cold in death; and more than one eye dropped a tear at the remembrance of the cheery smile, and the joke — sometimes superannuated, generally feeble, but always good-natured — with which the captain had been wont to greet his acquaintances. There was a growing sentiment of anger among these stern men toward the murderer who had thus cut down their friend, and a strong feeling that ordinary justice was too slight a punishment for such a crime.

Toward noon there was an informal gathering of citizens in Dan Tyson's store.

"I hear it 'lowed that Square Kyahtah's too sick ter hol' co'te this evenin,'" said one, "an' that the purlim'nary hearin' 'll haf ter go over 'tel nex' week." A look of disappointment went round the crowd.

"Hit's the durndes', meanes' murder ever committed in this caounty," said another, with moody emphasis.

"I s'pose the nigger 'lowed the Cap'n had some greenbacks," observed a third speaker.

"The Cap'n," said another, with an air of superior information, "has left two bairls of Confedrit money, which he 'spected'd be good some day er nuther."

This statement gave rise to a discussion of the speculative value of Confederate money; but in a little while the conversation returned to the murder.

"Hangin' air too good fer the murderer," said one; "he oughter be burnt, stider bein' hung."

There was an impressive pause at this point, during which a jug of moonlight whiskey went the round of the crowd.

"Well," said a round-shouldered farmer, who, in spite of his peaceable expression and faded gray eye, was known to have been one of the most daring followers of a rebel guerrilla chieftain, "what air yer gwine ter do about it? Ef you fellers air gwine ter set down an' let a wuthless nigger kill the bes' white man in Branson, an' not say nuthin' ner do nuthin', *I'll* move outen the caounty."

This speech gave tone and direction to the rest of the conversation. Whether the fear of losing the round-shouldered farmer operated to bring about the result or not is immaterial to this narrative; but, at all events, the crowd decided to lynch the negro. They agreed that this was the least that could be done to avenge the death of their murdered friend, and that it was a becoming way in which to honor his memory. They had some vague notions of the majesty of the law and the rights of the citizen, but in the passion of the moment these sunk into oblivion; a white man had been killed by a negro.

"The Cap'n was an ole sodger," said one of his friends solemnly. "He'll sleep better when he knows that a co'te-martial has be'n hilt an' jestice done."

By agreement the lynchers were to meet at Tyson's store at five o'clock in the afternoon, and proceed thence to the jail, which was situated down the Lumberton Dirt Road (as the old turnpike antedating the plank-road was called), about half a mile south of the court-house. When the preliminaries of the lynching had been arranged, and a committee appointed to manage the affair, the crowd dispersed, some to go to their dinners, and some to secure recruits for the lynching party.

It was twenty minutes to five o'clock, when an excited negro, panting and perspiring, rushed up to the back door of Sheriff Campbell's dwelling, which stood at a little distance from the jail and somewhat farther than the latter building from the court-house. A turbaned colored woman came to the door in response to the negro's knock.

"Hoddy, Sis' Nance."

"Hoddy, Brer Sam."

"Is de shurff in?" inquired the negro.

"Yas, Brer Sam, he's eatin' his dinner," was the answer.

"Will yer ax 'im ter step ter de do' a minute, Sis' Nance?"

The woman went into the dining-room, and a moment later the sheriff came to the door. He was a tall, muscular man, of a ruddier complexion than is usual among Southerners. A pair of keen, deep-set gray eyes looked out from under bushy eyebrows, and about his mouth was a masterful expression, which a full beard, once sandy in color, but now profusely sprinkled with gray, could not entirely conceal. The day was hot; the sheriff had discarded his coat and vest, and had his white shirt open at the throat.

"What do you want, Sam?" he inquired of the negro, who stood hat in hand, wiping the moisture from his face with a ragged shirt-sleeve.

"Shurff, dey gwine ter hang de pris'ner w'at's lock' up in de jail. Dey're comin' dis a-way now. I wuz layin' down on a sack er corn down at de sto', behine a pile er flour-bairls, w'en I hearn Doc' Cain en Kunnel Wright talkin' erbout it. I slip' outen de back do', en run here as fas' as I could. I hearn you say down ter de sto' once't dat you wouldn't let nobody take a pris'ner 'way fum you widout walkin' over yo' dead body, en I thought I'd let you know 'fo' dey come, so yer could pertec' de pris'ner."

The sheriff listened calmly, but his face grew firmer, and a determined gleam lit up his gray eyes. His frame grew more erect, and he unconsciously assumed the attitude of a soldier who momentarily expects to meet the enemy face to face.

"Much obliged, Sam," he answered. "I'll protect the prisoner. Who's coming?"

"I dunno who-all *is* comin'," replied the negro. "Dere's Mistah McSwayne, en Doc' Cain, en Maje' McDonal', en Kunnel Wright, en a heap er yuthers. I wuz so skeered I done furgot mo' d'n half un em. I spec' dey mus' be mos' here by dis time, so I'll git outen de way, fer I don' want nobody fer ter think I wuz mix' up in dis business." The negro glanced nervously down the road toward the town, and made a movement as if to go away.

"Won't you have some dinner first?" asked the sheriff.

The negro looked longingly in at the open door, and sniffed the appetizing odor of boiled pork and collards.

"I ain't got no time fer ter tarry, Shurff," he said, "but Sis' Nance mought gin me sump'n I could kyar in my han' en eat on de way. "

A moment later Nancy brought him a huge sandwich of split cornpone, with a thick slice of fat bacon inserted between the halves, and a couple of baked yams. The negro hastily replaced his ragged hat on his head, dropped the yams in the pocket of his capacious trousers, and, taking the sandwich in his hand, hurried across the road and disappeared in the woods beyond.

The sheriff reentered the house, and put on his coat and hat. He then took down a double-barreled shotgun and loaded it with buckshot. Filling the chambers of a revolver with fresh cartridges, he slipped it into the pocket of the sack-coat which he wore.

A comely young woman in a calico dress watched these proceedings with anxious surprise.

"Where are you going, father?" she asked. She had not heard the conversation with the negro.

"I am goin' over to the jail," responded the sheriff. "There's a mob comin' this way to lynch the nigger we've got locked up. But they won't do it," he added, with emphasis.

"Oh, father! don't go!" pleaded the girl, clinging to his arm; "they'll shoot you if you don't give him up."

"You never mind me, Polly," said her father reassuringly, as he gently unclasped her hands from his arm. "I'll take care of myself and the prisoner, too. There ain't a man in Branson County that would shoot me. Besides, I have faced fire too often to be scared away from my duty. You keep close in the house," he continued, "and if any one disturbs you just use the old horse-pistol in the top bureau drawer. It's a little old-fashioned, but it did good work a few years ago."

The young girl shuddered at this sanguinary allusion, but made no further objection to her father's departure.

The sheriff of Branson was a man far above the average of the community in wealth, education, and social position. His had been one of the few families in the county that before the war had owned large estates and numerous slaves. He had graduated at the State University at Chapel Hill, and had kept up some acquaintance with current literature and advanced thought. He had traveled some in his youth, and was looked up to in the county as an authority on all subjects connected with the outer world. At first an ardent supporter of the Union, he had opposed the secession movement in his native state as long as opposition availed to stem the tide of public opinion. Yielding at last to the force of circumstances, he had entered the Confederate service rather late in the war, and served with distinction through several campaigns, rising in time to the rank of colonel. After the war he had taken the oath of allegiance, and had been chosen by the people as the most available candidate for the office of sheriff, to which he had been elected without opposition. He had filled the office for several terms, and was universally popular with his constituents.

Colonel or Sheriff Campbell, as he was indifferently called, as the military or civil title happened to be most important in the opinion of the person addressing him, had a high sense of the responsibility attaching to his office. He had sworn to do his duty faithfully, and he knew what his duty was as sheriff, perhaps more clearly than he had apprehended it in other passages of his life. It was, therefore, with no uncertainty in regard to his course that he prepared his weapons and went over to the jail. He had no fears for Polly's safety.

The sheriff had just locked the heavy front door of the jail behind him when a half dozen horsemen, followed by a crowd of men on foot, came round a bend in the road and drew near the jail. They halted in front of the picket fence that surrounded the building, while several of the committee of arrangements rode on a few rods farther to the sheriff's house. One of them dismounted and rapped on the door with his riding-whip.

"Is the sheriff at home?" he inquired.

"No, he has just gone out," replied Polly, who had come to the door.

"We want the jail keys," he continued.

"They are not here," said Polly. "The sheriff has them himself." Then she added, with assumed indifference, "He is at the jail now."

The man turned away, and Polly went into the front room, from which she peered anxiously between the slats of the green blinds of a window that looked toward the jail. Meanwhile the messenger returned to his companions and announced his discovery. It looked as though the sheriff had learned of their design and was preparing to resist it.

One of them stepped forward and rapped on the jail door.

"Well, what is it?" said the sheriff, from within.

"We want to talk to you, Sheriff," replied the spokesman.

There was a little wicket in the door; this the sheriff opened, and answered through it.

"All right, boys, talk away. You are all strangers to me, and I don't know what business you can have." The sheriff did not think it necessary to recognize anybody in particular on such an occasion; the question of identity sometimes comes up in the investigation of these extrajudicial executions.

"We're a committee of citizens and we want to get into the jail."

"What for? It ain't much trouble to get into jail. Most people want to keep out."

The mob was in no humor to appreciate a joke, and the sheriff's witticism fell dead upon an unresponsive audience.

"We want to have a talk with the nigger that killed Cap'n Walker."

"You can talk to that nigger in the courthouse, when he's brought out for trial. Court will be in session here next week. I know what you fellows want, but you can't get my prisoner today. Do you want to take the bread out of a poor man's mouth? I get seventy-five cents a day for keeping this prisoner, and he's the only one in jail. I can't have my family suffer just to please you fellows."

One or two young men in the crowd laughed at the idea of Sheriff Campbell's suffering for want of seventy-five cents a day; but they were frowned into silence by those who stood near them.

"Ef yer don't let us in," cried a voice, "we'll bus' the do' open."

"Bust away," answered the sheriff, raising his voice so that all could hear. "But I give you fair warning. The first man that tries it will be filled with buckshot. I'm sheriff of this county; I know my duty, and I mean to do it."

"What's the use of kicking, Sheriff?" argued one of the leaders of the mob. "The nigger is sure to hang anyhow; he richly deserves it; and we've got to do something to teach the niggers their places, or white people won't be able to live in the county."

"There's no use talking, boys," responded the sheriff. "I'm a white man outside, but in this jail I'm sheriff; and if this nigger's to be hung in this county, I propose to do the hanging. So you fellows might as well right-about-face, and march back to Troy. You've had a pleasant trip, and the exercise will be good for you. You know *me*. I've got powder and ball, and I've faced fire before now, with nothing between me and the enemy, and I don't mean to surrender this jail while I'm able to shoot." Having thus announced his determination, the sheriff closed and fastened the wicket, and looked around for the best position from which to defend the building.

The crowd drew off a little, and the leaders conversed together in low tones.

The Branson County jail was a small, two-story brick building, strongly constructed, with no attempt at architectural ornamentation. Each story was divided into two large cells by a passage running from front to rear. A grated iron door gave entrance from the passage to each of the four cells. The jail seldom had many prisoners in it, and the lower windows had been boarded up. When the sheriff had closed the wicket, he ascended the steep wooden stairs to the upper floor. There was no window at the front of the upper passage, and the most available position from which to watch the movements of the crowd below was the front window of the cell occupied by the solitary prisoner.

The sheriff unlocked the door and entered the cell. The prisoner was crouched in a corner, his yellow face, blanched with terror, looking ghastly in the semi-darkness of the room. A cold perspiration had gathered on his forehead, and his teeth were chattering with affright.

"For God's sake, Sheriff," he murmured hoarsely, "don't let 'em lynch me; I didn't kill the old man."

The sheriff glanced at the cowering wretch with a look of mingled contempt and loathing.

"Get up," he said sharply. "You will probably be hung sooner or later, but it shall not be today, if I can help it. I'll unlock your fetters, and if I can't hold the jail, you'll have to make the best fight you can. If I'm shot, I'll consider my responsibility at an end."

There were iron fetters on the prisoner's ankles, and handcuffs on his wrists. These the sheriff unlocked, and they fell clanking to the floor.

"Keep back from the window," said the sheriff. "They might shoot if they saw you."

The sheriff drew toward the window a pine bench which formed a part of the scanty furniture of the cell, and laid his revolver upon it. Then he took his gun in hand, and took his stand at the side of the window where he could with least exposure of himself watch the movements of the crowd below.

The lynchers had not anticipated any determined resistance. Of course they had looked for a formal protest, and perhaps a sufficient show of opposition to excuse the sheriff in the eye of any stickler for legal formalities. They had not however come prepared to fight a battle, and no one of them seemed willing to lead an attack upon the jail. The leaders of the party conferred together with a good deal of animated gesticulation, which was visible to the sheriff from his outlook, though the distance was too great for him to hear what was said. At length one of them broke away from the group, and rode back to the main body of the lynchers, who were restlessly awaiting orders.

"Well, boys," said the messenger, "we'll have to let it go for the present. The sheriff says he'll shoot, and he's got the drop on us this time. There ain't any of us that want to follow Cap'n Walker jest yet. Besides, the sheriff is a good fellow, and we don't want to hurt 'im. But," he added, as if to reassure the crowd, which began to show signs of disappointment, "the nigger might as well say his prayers, for he ain't got long to live."

There was a murmur of dissent from the mob, and several voices insisted that an attack be made on the jail. But pacific counsels finally prevailed, and the mob sullenly withdrew.

The sheriff stood at the window until they had disappeared around the bend in the road. He did not relax his watchfulness when the last one was out of sight. Their withdrawal might be a mere feint, to be followed by a further attempt. So closely, indeed, was his attention drawn to the outside, that he neither saw nor heard the prisoner creep stealthily across the floor, reach out his hand and secure the revolver which lay on the bench behind the sheriff, and creep as noiselessly back to his place in the corner of the room.

A moment after the last of the lynching party had disappeared there was a shot fired from the woods across the road; a bullet whistled by the window and buried itself in the wooden casing a few inches from where the sheriff was standing. Quick as thought, with the instinct born of a semi-guerrilla army experience, he raised his gun and fired twice at the point from which a faint puff of smoke showed the hostile bullet to have been sent. He stood a moment watching, and then rested his gun against the window, and reached behind him mechanically for the other weapon. It was not on the bench. As the sheriff realized this fact, he turned his head and looked into the muzzle of the revolver.

"Stay where you are, Sheriff," said the prisoner, his eyes glistening, his face almost ruddy with excitement.

The sheriff mentally cursed his own carelessness for allowing him to be caught in such a predicament. He had not expected anything of the kind. He had relied on the negro's cowardice and subordination in the presence of an armed white man as a matter of course. The sheriff was a brave man, but realized that the prisoner had him at an immense disadvantage. The two men stood thus for a moment, fighting a harmless duel with their eyes.

"Well, what do you mean to do?" asked the sheriff with apparent calmness.

"To get away, of course," said the prisoner, in a tone which caused the sheriff to look at him more closely, and with an involuntary feeling of apprehension; if the man was not mad, he was in a state of mind akin to madness, and quite as dangerous. The sheriff felt that he must speak to the prisoner fair, and watch for a chance to turn the tables on him. The keen-eyed, desperate man before him was a different being altogether from the groveling wretch who had begged so piteously for life a few minutes before.

At length the sheriff spoke: —

"Is this your gratitude to me for saving your life at the risk of my own? If I had not done so, you would now be swinging from the limb of some neighboring tree."

"True," said the prisoner, "you saved my life, but for how long? When you came in, you said court would sit next week. When the crowd went away they said I had not long to live. It is merely a choice of two ropes."

"While there's life there's hope," replied the sheriff. He uttered this commonplace mechanically, while his brain was busy in trying to think out some way of escape. "If you are innocent you can prove it."

The mulatto kept his eye upon the sheriff. "I didn't kill the old man," he replied; "but I shall never be able to clear myself. I was at his house at nine o'clock. I stole from it the coat that was on my back when I was taken. I would be convicted, even with a fair trial, unless the real murderer were discovered beforehand."

The sheriff knew this only too well. While he was thinking what argument next to use, the prisoner continued: —

"Throw me the keys — no, unlock the door."

The sheriff stood a moment irresolute. The mulatto's eye glittered ominously. The sheriff crossed the room and unlocked the door leading into the passage.

"Now go down and unlock the outside door."

The heart of the sheriff leaped within him. Perhaps he might make a dash for liberty, and gain the outside. He descended the narrow stairs, the prisoner keeping close behind him.

The sheriff inserted the huge iron key into the lock. The rusty bolt yielded slowly. It still remained for him to pull the door open.

"Stop!" thundered the mulatto, who seemed to divine the sheriff's purpose. "Move a muscle, and I'll blow your brains out."

The sheriff obeyed; he realized that his chance had not yet come.

"Now keep on that side of the passage, and go back upstairs."

Keeping the sheriff under cover of the revolver, the mulatto followed him up the stairs. The sheriff expected the prisoner to lock him into the cell and make his own escape. He had about come to the conclusion that the best thing he could do under the circumstances was to submit quietly, and take his chances of recapturing the prisoner after the alarm had been given. The sheriff had faced death more than once upon the battlefield. A few minutes before, well armed, and with a brick wall between him and them, he had dared a hundred men to fight; but he felt instinctively that the desperate man confronting him was not to be trifled with, and he was too prudent a man to risk his life against such heavy odds. He had Polly to look after, and there was a limit beyond which devotion to duty would be quixotic and even foolish.

"I want to get away," said the prisoner, "and I don't want to be captured; for if I am I know I will be hung on the spot. I am afraid," he added somewhat reflectively, "that in order to save myself I shall have to kill you."

"Good God!" exclaimed the sheriff in involuntary terror; "you would not kill the man to whom you owe your own life."

"You speak more truly than you know," replied the mulatto. "I indeed owe my life to you."

The sheriff started. He was capable of surprise, even in that moment of extreme peril. "Who are you?" he asked in amazement.

"Tom, Cicely's son," returned the other. He had closed the door and stood talking to the sheriff through the grated opening. "Don't you remember Cicely — Cicely whom you sold, with her child, to the speculator on his way to Alabama?"

The sheriff did remember. He had been sorry for it many a time since. It had been the old story of debts, mortgages, and bad crops. He had quarreled with the mother. The price offered for her and her child had been unusually large, and he had yielded to the combination of anger and pecuniary stress.

"Good God!" he gasped; "you would not murder your own father?"

"My father?" replied the mulatto. "It were well enough for me to claim the relationship, but it comes with poor grace from you to ask anything by reason of it. What father's duty have you ever performed for me? Did you give me your name, or even your protection? Other white men gave their colored sons freedom and money, and sent them to the free states. *You* sold *me* to the rice swamps."

"I at least gave you the life you cling to," murmured the sheriff.

"Life?" said the prisoner, with a sarcastic laugh. "What kind of a life? You gave me your own blood, your own features,—no man need look at us together twice to see that,—and you gave me a black mother. Poor wretch! She died under the lash, because she had enough womanhood to call her soul her own. You gave me a white man's spirit, and you made me a slave, and crushed it out."

"But you are free now," said the sheriff. He had not doubted, could not doubt, the mulatto's word. He knew whose passions coursed beneath that swarthy skin and burned in the black eyes opposite his own. He saw in this mulatto what he himself might have become had not the safeguards of parental restraint and public opinion been thrown around him.

"Free to do what?" replied the mulatto. "Free in name, but despised and scorned and set aside by the people to whose race I belong far more than to my mother's."

"There are schools," said the sheriff. "You have been to school." He had noticed that the mulatto spoke more eloquently and used better language than most Branson County people.

"I have been to school, and dreamed when I went that it would work some marvelous change in my condition. But what did I learn? I learned to feel that no degree of learning or wisdom will change the color of my skin and that I shall always wear what in my own country is a badge of degradation. When I think about it seriously I do not care particularly for such a life. It is the animal in me, not the man, that flees the gallows. I owe you nothing," he went on, "and expect nothing of you; and it would be no more than justice if I should avenge upon you my mother's wrongs and my own. But still I hate to shoot you; I have never yet taken human life—for I did *not* kill the old captain. Will you promise to give no alarm and make no attempt to capture me until morning, if I do not shoot?"

So absorbed were the two men in their colloquy and their own tumultuous thoughts that neither of them had heard the door below move upon its hinges. Neither of them had heard a light step come stealthily up the stairs, nor seen a slender form creep along the darkening passage toward the mulatto.

The sheriff hesitated. The struggle between his love of life and his sense of duty was a terrific one. It may seem strange that a man who could sell his own child into slavery should hesitate at such a moment, when his life was trembling in the balance. But the baleful influence of human slavery poisoned the very fountains of life, and created new standards of right. The sheriff was conscientious; his conscience had merely been warped by his environment. Let no one ask what his answer would have been; he was spared the necessity of a decision.

"Stop," said the mulatto, "you need not promise. I could not trust you if you did. It is your life for mine; there is but one safe way for me; you must die."

He raised his arm to fire, when there was a flash — a report from the passage behind him. His arm fell heavily at his side, and the pistol dropped at his feet.

The sheriff recovered first from his surprise, and throwing open the door secured the fallen weapon. Then seizing the prisoner he thrust him into the cell and locked the door upon him; after which he turned to Polly, who leaned half-fainting against the wall, her hands clasped over her heart.

"Oh, father, I was just in time!" she cried hysterically, and, wildly sobbing, threw herself into her father's arms.

"I watched until they all went away," she said. "I heard the shot from the woods and I saw you shoot. Then when you did not come out I feared something had happened, that perhaps you had been wounded. I got out the other pistol and ran over here. When I found the door open, I knew something was wrong, and when I heard voices I crept up stairs, and reached the top just in time to hear him say he would kill you. Oh, it was a narrow escape!"

When she had grown somewhat calmer, the sheriff left her standing there and went back into the cell. The prisoner's arm was bleeding from a flesh wound. His bravado had given place to a stony apathy. There was no sign in his face of fear or disappointment or feeling of any kind. The sheriff sent Polly to the house for cloth, and bound up the prisoner's wound with a rude skill acquired during his army life.

"I'll have a doctor come and dress the wound in the morning," he said to the prisoner. "It will do very well until then, if you will keep quiet. If the doctor asks you how the wound was caused, you can say that you were struck by the bullet fired from the woods. It would do you no good to have known that you were shot while attempting to escape."

The prisoner uttered no word of thanks or apology, but sat in sullen silence. When the wounded arm had been bandaged, Polly and her father returned to the house.

The sheriff was in an unusually thoughtful mood that evening. He put salt in his coffee at supper, and poured vinegar over his pancakes. To many of Polly's questions he returned random answers. When he had gone to bed he lay awake for several hours.

In the silent watches of the night, when he was alone with God, there came into his mind a flood of unaccustomed thoughts. An hour or two before, standing face to face with death, he had experienced a sensation similar to that which drowning men are said to feel — a kind of clarifying of the moral faculty, in which the veil of the flesh, with its obscuring passions and prejudices, is pushed aside for a moment, and all the acts of one's life stand out, in the clear light of truth, in their correct proportions and relations, — a state of mind in which one sees himself as God may be supposed to see him. In the reaction following his rescue, this feeling had given place for a time to far different emotions. But now, in the silence of midnight, something of this clearness of spirit returned to the sheriff. He saw that he had owed some duty to this son of his, — that neither law nor custom could destroy a responsibility inherent in the nature of mankind. He could not thus, in the eyes of God at least, shake off the consequences of his sin. Had he never sinned, this wayward spirit would never have come back from the vanished past to haunt him. As these thoughts came, his anger against the mulatto died away, and in its place there sprang up a great pity. The hand of parental authority might have restrained the passions he had seen burning in the prisoner's eyes when the desperate man spoke the words which had seemed to doom his father to death. The sheriff felt that he might have saved this fiery spirit from the slough of slavery; that he might have sent him to the free North, and given him there, or in some other land, an opportunity to turn to usefulness and honorable pursuits the talents that had run to crime, perhaps to madness; he might, still less, have given this son of his the poor simulacrum of liberty which men of his caste could possess in a slave-holding community; or least of all, but still something, he might have kept the boy on the plantation, where the burdens of slavery would have fallen lightly upon him.

The sheriff recalled his own youth. He had inherited an honored name to keep untarnished; he had had a future to make; the picture of a fair young bride had beckoned him on to happiness. The poor wretch now stretched upon a pallet of straw between the brick walls of the jail had had none of these things, — no name, no father, no mother — in the true meaning of motherhood, — and until the past few years no possible future, and then one vague and shadowy in its outline, and dependent for form and substance upon the slow solution of a problem in which there were many unknown quantities.

From what he might have done to what he might yet do was an easy transition for the awakened conscience of the sheriff. It occurred to him, purely as a hypothesis, that he might permit his prisoner to escape; but his oath of office, his duty as sheriff, stood in the way of such a course, and the sheriff dismissed the idea from his mind. He could, however, investigate the circumstances of the murder, and move Heaven and earth to discover the real criminal, for he no longer doubted the prisoner's innocence; he could employ counsel for the accused, and perhaps influence public opinion in his favor. An acquittal once secured, some plan could be devised by which the sheriff might in some degree atone for his crime against this son of his — against society — against God.

When the sheriff had reached this conclusion he fell into an unquiet slumber, from which he awoke late the next morning.

He went over to the jail before breakfast and found the prisoner lying on his pallet, his face turned to the wall; he did not move when the sheriff rattled the door.

"Good morning," said the latter, in a tone intended to waken the prisoner.

There was no response. The sheriff looked more keenly at the recumbent figure; there was an unnatural rigidity about its attitude.

He hastily unlocked the door and, entering the cell, bent over the prostrate form. There was no sound of breathing; he turned the body over — it was cold and stiff. The prisoner had torn the bandage from his wound and bled to death during the night. He had evidently been dead several hours.

1891

RICHARD HARDING DAVIS

GALLEGHER

A NEWSPAPER STORY

The fearless war correspondent par excellence Richard Harding Davis (1864–1916) was the most successful reporter of his time, working for the *New York Evening Sun, New York Times, New York Herald, Harper's Weekly,* and *Scribner's Magazine,* among others. He was the first journalist to cover the Spanish-American War and, as a close friend of Theodore Roosevelt, helped create the image and legend of the future president as the leading light of the Rough Riders. He was an adventurer as well as a journalist, often going to the front lines to cover stories while wearing pistols and wielding other weapons.

Very popular with other writers and journalists, the handsome, square-jawed Davis is reputed to have served as the model for the famous American illustrator Charles Dana Gibson's "Gibson Man," the male equivalent of the "Gibson Girl" as the personification of American beauty. He was the prime catalyst for American men to adopt the clean-shaven look at the turn of the twentieth century.

A prolific writer, Davis was the author of more than thirty-five books of fiction, biography, history, and memoir. His best-known book was probably *Soldier of Fortune* (1897), which he later turned into a successful play. In the mystery field, his most widely read book is the often-reprinted *In the Fog* (1901), comprising three connected short stories in the style of Robert Louis Stevenson's *New Arabian Nights* (1882); it contains two surprise endings.

"Gallegher" is as much a newspaper story as it is a mystery and has the charm of depicting life in journalism when it was a romantic and exciting profession, requiring a written story to be literally rushed to the office for it to be set in type and printed against stringent deadlines. It served as the basis for *Gallegher,* a television series on NBC's *Walt Disney's Wonderful World of Color* that starred Roger Mobley, Edmond O'Brien, and Harvey Korman, and ran as twelve one-hour episodes from January 1965 to March 1968.

"Gallegher" was first published in the August 1890 issue of *Scribner's Magazine;* it was first collected in *Gallegher and Other Stories* (New York: Charles Scribner's Sons, 1891).

• • •

WE HAD HAD so many office-boys before Gallegher came among us that they had begun to lose the characteristics of individuals, and became merged in a composite photograph of small boys, to whom we applied the generic title of "Here, you"; or "You, boy."

We had had sleepy boys, and lazy boys, and bright, "smart" boys, who became so familiar on so short an acquaintance that we were forced to part with them to save our own self-respect.

They generally graduated into district-messenger boys, and occasionally returned to us in blue coats with nickel-plated buttons, and patronized us.

But Gallegher was something different from anything we had experienced before. Gallegher was short and broad in build, with a solid, muscular broadness, and not a fat and dumpy shortness. He wore perpetually on his face a happy and knowing smile, as if you and the world in general were not impressing him as seriously as you thought you were, and his eyes, which were very black and very bright, snapped intelligently at you like those of a little black-and-tan terrier.

All Gallegher knew had been learnt on the streets; not a very good school in itself, but one that turns out very knowing scholars. And Gallegher had attended both morning and evening sessions. He could not tell you who the Pilgrim Fathers were, nor could he name the thirteen original states, but he knew all the officers of the twenty-second police district by name, and he could distinguish the clang of a fire-engine's gong from that of a patrol-wagon or an ambulance fully two blocks distant. It was Gallegher who rang the alarm when the Woolwich Mills caught fire, while the officer on the beat was asleep, and it was Gallegher who led the "Black Diamonds" against the "Wharf Rats," when they used to stone each other to their hearts' content on the coal-wharves of Richmond.

I am afraid, now that I see these facts written down, that Gallegher was not a reputable character; but he was so very young and so very old for his years that we all liked him very much nevertheless. He lived in the extreme northern part of Philadelphia, where the cotton and woolen mills run down to the river, and how he ever got home after leaving the

Press building at two in the morning, was one of the mysteries of the office. Sometimes he caught a night car, and sometimes he walked all the way, arriving at the little house, where his mother and himself lived alone, at four in the morning. Occasionally he was given a ride on an early milk-cart, or on one of the newspaper delivery wagons, with its high piles of papers still damp and sticky from the press. He knew several drivers of "night hawks" — those cabs that prowl the streets at night looking for belated passengers — and when it was a very cold morning he would not go home at all, but would crawl into one of these cabs and sleep, curled up on the cushions, until daylight.

Besides being quick and cheerful, Gallegher possessed a power of amusing the *Press*'s young men to a degree seldom attained by the ordinary mortal. His clog-dancing on the city editor's desk, when that gentleman was upstairs fighting for two more columns of space, was always a source of innocent joy to us, and his imitations of the comedians of the variety halls delighted even the dramatic critic, from whom the comedians themselves failed to force a smile.

But Gallegher's chief characteristic was his love for that element of news generically classed as "crime." Not that he ever did anything criminal himself. On the contrary, his was rather the work of the criminal specialist, and his morbid interest in the doings of all queer characters, his knowledge of their methods, their present whereabouts, and their past deeds of transgression often rendered him a valuable ally to our police reporter, whose daily feuilletons were the only portion of the paper Gallegher deigned to read.

In Gallegher the detective element was abnormally developed. He had shown this on several occasions, and to excellent purpose.

Once the paper had sent him into a Home for Destitute Orphans which was believed to be grievously mismanaged, and Gallegher, while playing the part of a destitute orphan, kept his eyes open to what was going on around him so faithfully that the story he told of the treatment meted out to the real orphans was sufficient to rescue the unhappy little wretches from the individual who had them in charge, and to have the individual himself sent to jail.

Gallegher's knowledge of the aliases, terms of imprisonment, and various misdoings of the leading criminals in Philadelphia was almost as thorough as that of the chief of police himself, and he could tell to an hour when "Dutchy Mack" was to be let out of prison, and could identify at a glance "Dick Oxford, confidence man," as "Gentleman Dan, petty thief."

There were, at this time, only two pieces of news in any of the papers. The least important of the two was the big fight between the Champion of the United States and the Would-be Champion, arranged to take place near Philadelphia; the second was the Burrbank murder, which was filling space in newspapers all over the world, from New York to Bombay.

Richard F. Burrbank was one of the most prominent of New York's railroad lawyers; he was also, as a matter of course, an owner of much railroad stock, and a very wealthy man. He had been spoken of as a political possibility for many high offices, and, as the counsel for a great railroad, was known even further than the great railroad itself had stretched its system.

At six o'clock one morning he was found by his butler lying at the foot of the hall stairs with two pistol wounds above his heart. He was quite dead. His safe, to which only he and his secretary had the keys, was found open, and $200,000 in bonds, stocks, and money, which had been placed there only the night before, was found missing. The secretary was missing also. His name was Stephen S. Hade, and his name and his description had been telegraphed and cabled to all parts of the world. There was enough circumstantial evidence to show, beyond any question or possibility of mistake, that he was the murderer.

It made an enormous amount of talk, and unhappy individuals were being arrested all over the country, and sent on to New York for identification. Three had been arrested at Liverpool, and one man just as he landed at Sydney, Australia. But so far the murderer had escaped.

We were all talking about it one night, as everybody else was all over the country, in the local room, and the city editor said it was worth a fortune to anyone who chanced to run across Hade and succeeded in handing him over to the police. Some of us thought Hade had taken passage from some one of the smaller seaports, and others were of the opinion that he had buried himself in some cheap lodging-house in New York, or in one of the smaller towns in New Jersey.

"I shouldn't be surprised to meet him out walking, right here in Philadelphia," said one of the staff. "He'll be disguised, of course, but you could always tell him by the absence of the trigger finger on his right hand. It's missing, you know; shot off when he was a boy."

"You want to look for a man dressed like a tough," said the city editor; "for as this fellow is to all appearances a gentleman, he will try to look as little like a gentleman as possible."

"No, he won't," said Gallegher, with that calm impertinence that made him dear to us. "He'll dress just like a gentleman. Toughs don't wear gloves, and you see he's got to wear 'em. The first thing he thought of after doing for Burrbank was of that gone finger, and how he was to hide it. He stuffed the finger of that glove with cotton so's to make it look like a whole finger, and the first time he takes off that glove they've got him — see, and he knows it. So what youse want to do is to look for a man with gloves on. I've been a-doing it for two weeks now, and I can tell you it's hard work, for everybody wears gloves this kind of weather. But if you look long enough you'll find him. And when you think it's him, go up to him and hold out your hand in a friendly way, like a bunco-steerer, and shake his hand; and if you feel that his forefinger ain't real flesh, but just wadded cotton, then grip to it with your right and grab his throat with your left, and holler for help."

There was an appreciative pause.

"I see, gentlemen," said the city editor, dryly, "that Gallegher's reasoning has impressed you; and I also see that before the week is out all of my young men will be under bonds for assaulting innocent pedestrians whose only offense is that they wear gloves in midwinter."

It was about a week after this that Detective Hefflefinger, of Inspector Byrnes's staff, came over to Philadelphia after a burglar, of whose whereabouts he had been misinformed by telegraph. He brought the warrant, requisition, and other necessary papers with him, but the burglar had flown. One of our reporters had worked on a New York paper and knew Hefflefinger, and the detective came to the office to see if he could help him in his so far unsuccessful search.

He gave Gallegher his card, and after Gallegher had read it, and had discovered who the visitor was, he became so demoralized that he was absolutely useless.

"One of Byrnes's men" was a much more awe-inspiring individual to Gallegher than a member of the Cabinet. He accordingly seized his hat and overcoat, and leaving his duties to be looked after by others, hastened out after the object of his admiration, who found his suggestions and knowledge of the city so valuable, and his company so entertaining, that they became very intimate, and spent the rest of the day together.

In the meanwhile the managing editor had instructed his subordinates to inform Gallegher, when he condescended to return, that his services were no longer needed. Gallegher had played truant once too often. Unconscious of this, he remained with his new friend until late the same evening, and started the next afternoon toward the *Press* office.

* * *

As I have said, Gallegher lived in the most distant part of the city, not many minutes' walk from the Kensington railroad station, where trains ran into the suburbs and on to New York.

It was in front of this station that a smoothly shaven, well-dressed man brushed past Gallegher and hurried up the steps to the ticket office.

He held a walking-stick in his right hand, and Gallegher, who now patiently scrutinized the hands of everyone who wore gloves, saw that while three fingers of the man's hand were closed around the cane, the fourth stood out in almost a straight line with his palm.

Gallegher stopped with a gasp and with a trembling all over his little body, and his brain asked with a throb if it could be possible. But possibilities and probabilities were to be discovered later. Now was the time for action.

He was after the man in a moment, hanging at his heels and his eyes moist with excitement. He heard the man ask for a ticket to Torresdale, a little station just outside of Philadelphia, and when he was out of hearing, but not out of sight, purchased one for the same place.

The stranger went into the smoking-car, and seated himself at one end toward the door. Gallegher took his place at the opposite end.

He was trembling all over, and suffered from a slight feeling of nausea. He guessed it came from fright, not of any bodily harm that might come to him, but at the probability of failure in his adventure and of its most momentous possibilities.

The stranger pulled his coat collar up around his ears, hiding the lower portion of his face, but not concealing the resemblance in his troubled eyes and close-shut lips to the likenesses of the murderer Hade.

They reached Torresdale in half an hour, and the stranger, alighting quickly, struck off at a rapid pace down the country road leading to the station.

Gallegher gave him a hundred yards' start, and then followed slowly after. The road ran between fields and past a few frame-houses set far from the road in kitchen gardens.

Once or twice the man looked back over his shoulder, but he saw only a dreary length of road with a small boy splashing through the slush in the midst of it and stopping every now and again to throw snowballs at belated sparrows.

After a ten minutes' walk the stranger turned into a side road which led to only one place, the Eagle Inn, an old roadside hostelry known now as the headquarters for pothunters from the Philadelphia game market and the battleground of many a cock fight.

Gallegher knew the place well. He and his young companions had often stopped there when out chestnutting on holidays in the autumn.

The son of the man who kept it had often accompanied them on their excursions, and though the boys of the city streets considered him a dumb lout, they respected him somewhat owing to his inside knowledge of dog and cock fights.

The stranger entered the inn at a side door, and Gallegher, reaching it a few minutes later, let him go for the time being, and set about finding his occasional playmate, young Keppler.

Keppler's offspring was found in the woodshed.

"'Tain't hard to guess what brings you out here," said the tavern-keeper's son, with a grin; "it's the fight."

"What fight?" asked Gallegher, unguardedly.

"What fight? Why, *the* fight," returned his companion, with the slow contempt of superior knowledge. "It's to come off here to-night. You knew that as well as me; anyway your sportin' editor knows it. He got the tip last night, but that won't help you any. You needn't think there's any chance of your getting a peep at it. Why, tickets is two hundred and fifty apiece!"

"Whew!" whistled Gallegher, "where's it to be?"

"In the barn," whispered Keppler. "I helped 'em fix the ropes this morning, I did."

"Gosh, but you're in luck," exclaimed Gallegher, with flattering envy. "Couldn't I jest get a peep at it?"

"Maybe," said the gratified Keppler. "There's a winder with a wooden shutter at the back of the barn. You can get in by it, if you have someone to boost you up to the sill."

"Sa-a-y," drawled Gallegher, as if something had but just that moment reminded him. "Who's that gent who come down the road just a bit ahead of me—him with the cape-coat! Has he got anything to do with the fight?"

"Him?" repeated Keppler in tones of sincere disgust. "No-oh, he ain't no sport. He's queer, Dad thinks. He come here one day last week about ten in the morning, said his doctor told him to go out 'en the country for his health. He's stuck up and citified, and wears gloves, and takes his meals private in his room, and all that sort of ruck. They was saying in the saloon last night that they thought he was hiding from something, and Dad, just to try him, asks him last night if he was coming to see the fight. He looked sort of scared, and said he didn't want to see no fight.

And then Dad says, 'I guess you mean you don't want no fighters to see you.' Dad didn't mean no harm by it, just passed it as a joke; but Mr. Carleton, as he calls himself, got white as a ghost an' says, 'I'll go to the fight willing enough,' and begins to laugh and joke. And this morning he went right into the bar-room, where all the sports were setting, and said he was going into town to see some friends; and as he starts off he laughs an' says, 'This don't look as if I was afraid of seeing people, does it?' but Dad says it was just bluff that made him do it, and Dad thinks that if he hadn't said what he did, this Mr. Carleton wouldn't have left his room at all."

Gallegher had got all he wanted, and much more than he had hoped for — so much more that his walk back to the station was in the nature of a triumphal march.

He had twenty minutes to wait for the next train, and it seemed an hour. While waiting he sent a telegram to Hefflefinger at his hotel. It read:

> Your man is near the Torresdale station, on Pennsylvania Railroad; take cab, and meet me at station. Wait until I come. GALLEGHER.

With the exception of one at midnight, no other train stopped at Torresdale that evening, hence the direction to take a cab.

The train to the city seemed to Gallegher to drag itself by inches. It stopped and backed at purposeless intervals, waited for an express to precede it, and dallied at stations, and when, at last, it reached the terminus, Gallegher was out before it had stopped and was in the cab and off on his way to the home of the sporting editor.

The sporting editor was at dinner and came out in the hall to see him, with his napkin in his hand. Gallegher explained breathlessly that he had located the murderer for whom the police of two continents were looking, and that he believed, in order to quiet the suspicions of the people with whom he was hiding, that he would be present at the fight that night.

The sporting editor led Gallegher into his library and shut the door. "Now," he said, "go over all that again."

Gallegher went over it again in detail, and added how he had sent for Hefflefinger to make the arrest in order that it might be kept from the knowledge of the local police and from the Philadelphia reporters.

"What I want Hefflefinger to do is to arrest Hade with the warrant he has for the burglar," explained Gallegher; "and to take him on to New

York on the owl train that passes Torresdale at one. It don't get to Jersey City until four o'clock, one hour after the morning papers go to press. Of course, we must fix Hefflefinger so's he'll keep quiet and not tell who his prisoner really is."

The sporting editor reached his hand out to pat Gallegher on the head, but changed his mind and shook hands with him instead.

"My boy," he said, "you are an infant phenomenon. If I can pull the rest of this thing off to-night it will mean the $5,000 reward and fame galore for you and the paper. Now, I'm going to write a note to the managing editor, and you can take it around to him and tell him what you've done and what I am going to do, and he'll take you back on the paper and raise your salary. Perhaps you didn't know you've been discharged?"

"Do you think you ain't a-going to take me with you?" demanded Gallegher.

"Why, certainly not. Why should I? It all lies with the detective and myself now. You've done your share, and done it well. If the man's caught, the reward's yours. But you'd only be in the way now. You'd better go to the office and make your peace with the chief."

"If the paper can get along without me, I can get along without the old paper," said Gallegher, hotly. "And if I ain't a-going with you, you ain't neither, for I know where Hefflefinger is to be, and you don't, and I won't tell you."

"Oh, very well, very well," replied the sporting editor, weakly capitulating. "I'll send the note by a messenger; only mind, if you lose your place, don't blame me."

Gallegher wondered how this man could value a week's salary against the excitement of seeing a noted criminal run down, and of getting the news to the paper, and to that one paper alone.

From that moment the sporting editor sank in Gallegher's estimation.

Mr. Dwyer sat down at his desk and scribbled off the following note:

> I have received reliable information that Hade, the Burrbank murderer, will be present at the fight to-night. We have arranged it so that he will be arrested quietly and in such a manner that the fact may be kept from all other papers. I need not point out to you that this will be the most important piece of news in the country to-morrow.
>
> Yours, etc.,
>
> MICHAEL E. DWYER.

The sporting editor stepped into the waiting cab, while Gallegher whispered the directions to the driver. He was told to go first to a district-messenger office, and from there up to the Ridge Avenue Road, out Broad Street, and on to the old Eagle Inn, near Torresdale.

It was a miserable night. The rain and snow were falling together, and freezing as they fell. The sporting editor got out to send his message to the *Press* office, and then lighting a cigar, and turning up the collar of his great-coat, curled up in the corner of the cab.

"Wake me when we get there, Gallegher," he said. He knew he had a long ride, and much rapid work before him, and he was preparing for the strain.

To Gallegher the idea of going to sleep seemed almost criminal. From the dark corner of the cab his eyes shone with excitement, and with the awful joy of anticipation. He glanced every now and then to where the sporting editor's cigar shone in the darkness, and watched it as it gradually burnt more dimly and went out. The lights in the shop windows threw a broad glare across the ice on the pavements, and the lights from the lamp-posts tossed the distorted shadow of the cab, and the horse, and the motionless driver, sometimes before and sometimes behind them.

After half an hour Gallegher slipped down to the bottom of the cab and dragged out a lap-robe, in which he wrapped himself. It was growing colder, and the damp, keen wind swept in through the cracks until the window-frames and woodwork were cold to the touch.

An hour passed, and the cab was still moving more slowly over the rough surface of partly paved streets, and by single rows of new houses standing at different angles to each other in fields covered with ash-heaps and brick-kilns. Here and there the gaudy lights of a drug-store, and the forerunner of suburban civilization, shone from the end of a new block of houses, and the rubber cape of an occasional policeman showed in the light of the lamp-post that he hugged for comfort.

Then even the houses disappeared, and the cab dragged its way between truck farms, with desolate-looking glass-covered beds, and pools of water, half-caked with ice, and bare trees, and interminable fences.

Once or twice the cab stopped altogether, and Gallegher could hear the driver swearing to himself, or at the horse, or the roads. At last they drew up before the station at Torresdale. It was quite deserted, and only a single light cut a swath in the darkness and showed a portion of the platform, the ties, and the rails glistening in the rain. They walked twice past the light before a figure stepped out of the shadow and greeted them cautiously.

"I am Mr. Dwyer, of the *Press*," said the sporting editor, briskly. "You've heard of me, perhaps. Well, there shouldn't be any difficulty in our making a deal, should there? This boy here has found Hade, and we have reason to believe he will be among the spectators at the fight to-night. We want you to arrest him quietly, and as secretly as possible. You can do it with your papers and your badge easily enough. We want you to pretend that you believe he is this burglar you came over after. If you will do this, and take him away without any one so much as suspecting who he really is, and on the train that passes here at 1.20 for New York, we will give you $500 out of the $5,000 reward. If, however, one other paper, either in New York or Philadelphia, or anywhere else, knows of the arrest, you won't get a cent. Now, what do you say?"

The detective had a great deal to say. He wasn't at all sure the man Gallegher suspected was Hade; he feared he might get himself into trouble by making a false arrest, and if it should be the man, he was afraid the local police would interfere.

"We've no time to argue or debate this matter," said Dwyer, warmly. "We agree to point Hade out to you in the crowd. After the fight is over you arrest him as we have directed, and you get the money and the credit of the arrest. If you don't like this, I will arrest the man myself, and have him driven to town, with a pistol for a warrant."

Hefflefinger considered in silence and then agreed unconditionally. "As you say, Mr. Dwyer," he returned. "I've heard of you for a thoroughbred sport. I know you'll do what you say you'll do; and as for me I'll do what you say and just as you say, and it's a very pretty piece of work as it stands."

They all stepped back into the cab, and then it was that they were met by a fresh difficulty, how to get the detective into the barn where the fight was to take place, for neither of the two men had $250 to pay for his admittance.

But this was overcome when Gallegher remembered the window of which young Keppler had told him.

In the event of Hade's losing courage and not daring to show himself in the crowd around the ring, it was agreed that Dwyer should come to the barn and warn Hefflefinger; but if he should come, Dwyer was merely to keep near him and to signify by a prearranged gesture which one of the crowd he was.

They drew up before a great black shadow of a house, dark, forbidding, and apparently deserted. But at the sound of the wheels on the gravel the door opened, letting out a stream of warm, cheerful light, and a man's voice said, "Put out those lights. Don't youse know no better than that?" This was Keppler, and he welcomed Mr. Dwyer with effusive courtesy.

The two men showed in the stream of light, and the door closed on them, leaving the house as it was at first, black and silent, save for the dripping of the rain and snow from the eaves.

The detective and Gallegher put out the cab's lamps and led the horse toward a long, low shed in the rear of the yard, which they now noticed was almost filled with teams of many different makes, from the Hobson's choice of a livery stable to the brougham of the man about town.

"No," said Gallegher, as the cabman stopped to hitch the horse beside the others, "we want it nearest that lower gate. When we newspaper men leave this place we'll leave it in a hurry, and the man who is nearest town is likely to get there first. You won't be a-following of no hearse when you make your return trip."

Gallegher tied the horse to the very gate-post itself, leaving the gate open and allowing a clear road and a flying start for the prospective race to Newspaper Row.

The driver disappeared under the shelter of the porch, and Gallegher and the detective moved off cautiously to the rear of the barn. "This must be the window," said Hefflefinger, pointing to a broad wooden shutter some feet from the ground.

"Just you give me a boost once, and I'll get that open in a jiffy," said Gallegher.

The detective placed his hands on his knees, and Gallegher stood upon his shoulders, and with the blade of his knife lifted the wooden button that fastened the window on the inside, and pulled the shutter open.

Then he put one leg inside over the sill, and leaning down helped to draw his fellow-conspirator up to a level with the window. "I feel just like I was burglarizing a house," chuckled Gallegher, as he dropped noiselessly to the floor below and refastened the shutter. The barn was a large one, with a row of stalls on either side in which horses and cows were dozing. There was a hay-mow over each row of stalls, and at one end of the barn a number of fence-rails had been thrown across from one mow to the other. These rails were covered with hay.

In the middle of the floor was the ring. It was not really a ring, but a square, with wooden posts at its four corners through which ran a heavy rope. The space enclosed by the rope was covered with sawdust.

Gallegher could not resist stepping into the ring, and after stamping the sawdust once or twice, as if to assure himself that he was really there, began dancing around it, and indulging in such a remarkable series of fistic maneuvers with an imaginary adversary that the unimaginative detective precipitately backed into a corner of the barn.

"Now, then," said Gallegher, having apparently vanquished his foe, "you come with me." His companion followed quickly as Gallegher climbed to one of the hay-mows, and crawling carefully out on the fence-rail, stretched himself at full length, face downward. In this position, by moving the straw a little, he could look down, without being himself seen, upon the heads of whomsoever stood below. "This is better'n a private box, ain't it?" said Gallegher.

The boy from the newspaper office and the detective lay there in silence, biting at straws and tossing anxiously on their comfortable bed.

It seemed fully two hours before they came. Gallegher had listened without breathing, and with every muscle on a strain, at least a dozen times, when some movement in the yard had led him to believe that they were at the door. And he had numerous doubts and fears. Sometimes it was that the police had learnt of the fight, and had raided Keppler's in his absence, and again it was that the fight had been postponed, or, worst of all, that it would be put off until so late that Mr. Dwyer could not get back in time for the last edition of the paper. Their coming, when at last they came, was heralded by an advance-guard of two sporting men, who stationed themselves at either side of the big door.

"Hurry up, now, gents," one of the men said with a shiver, "don't keep this door open no longer'n is needful."

It was not a very large crowd, but it was wonderfully well selected. It ran, in the majority of its component parts, to heavy white coats with pearl buttons. The white coats were shouldered by long blue coats with astrakhan fur trimmings, the wearers of which preserved a cliqueness not remarkable when one considers that they believed everyone else present to be either a crook or a prize-fighter.

There were well-fed, well-groomed club-men and brokers in the crowd, a politician or two, a popular comedian with his manager, amateur boxers from the athletic clubs, and quiet, close-mouthed sporting men from every city in the country. Their names if printed in the papers would have been as familiar as the types of the papers themselves.

And among these men, whose only thought was of the brutal sport to come, was Hade, with Dwyer standing at ease at his shoulder — Hade, white, and visibly in deep anxiety, hiding his pale face beneath a cloth travelling-cap, and with his chin muffled in a woolen scarf. He had dared to come because he feared his danger from the already suspicious Keppler was less than if he stayed away. And so he was there, hovering restlessly on the border of the crowd, feeling his danger and sick with fear.

When Hefflefinger first saw him he started up on his hands and elbows and made a movement forward as if he would leap down then and there and carry off his prisoner single-handed.

"Lie down," growled Gallegher; "an officer of any sort wouldn't live three minutes in that crowd."

The detective drew back slowly and buried himself again in the straw, but never once through the long fight which followed did his eyes leave the person of the murderer. The newspaper men took their places in the foremost row close around the ring, and kept looking at their watches and begging the master of ceremonies to "shake it up, do."

There was a great deal of betting, and all of the men handled the great rolls of bills they wagered with a flippant recklessness which could only be accounted for in Gallegher's mind by temporary mental derangement. Someone pulled a box out into the ring and the master of ceremonies mounted it, and pointed out in forcible language that as they were almost all already under bonds to keep the peace, it behooved all to curb their excitement and to maintain a severe silence, unless they wanted to bring the police upon them and have themselves "sent down" for a year or two.

Then two very disreputable-looking persons tossed their respective principals' high hats into the ring, and the crowd, recognizing in this relic of the days when brave knights threw down their gauntlets in the lists as only a sign that the fight was about to begin, cheered tumultuously.

This was followed by a sudden surging forward, and a mutter of admiration much more flattering than the cheers had been, when the principals followed their hats and, slipping out of their great-coats, stood forth in all the physical beauty of the perfect brute.

Their pink skin was as soft and healthy-looking as a baby's, and glowed in the lights of the lanterns like tinted ivory, and underneath this silken covering the great biceps and muscles moved in and out and looked like the coils of a snake around the branch of a tree.

Gentleman and blackguard shouldered each other for a nearer view; the coachmen, whose metal buttons were unpleasantly suggestive of police, put their hands, in the excitement of the moment, on the shoulders of their masters; the perspiration stood out in great drops on the foreheads of the backers, and the newspaper men bit somewhat nervously at the ends of their pencils.

And in the stalls the cows munched contentedly at their cuds and gazed with gentle curiosity at their two fellow-brutes, who stood waiting the signal to fall upon and kill each other, if need be, for the delectation of their brothers.

"Take your places," commanded the master of ceremonies.

In the moment in which the two men faced each other the crowd became so still that, save for the beating of the rain upon the shingled roof and the stamping of a horse in one of the stalls, the place was as silent as a church.

"Time," shouted the master of ceremonies.

The two men sprang into a posture of defense, which was lost as quickly as it was taken, one great arm shot out like a piston-rod; there was the sound of bare fists beating on naked flesh; there was an exultant indrawn gasp of savage pleasure and relief from the crowd, and the great fight had begun.

How the fortunes of war rose and fell, and changed and rechanged that night, is an old story to those who listen to such stories; and those who do not will be glad to be spared the telling of it. It was, they say, one of the bitterest fights between two men that this country has ever known.

But all that is of interest here is that after an hour of this desperate, brutal business the champion ceased to be the favorite; the man whom he had taunted and bullied, and for whom the public had but little sympathy, was proving himself a likely winner, and under his cruel blows, as sharp and clean as those from a cutlass, his opponent was rapidly giving way.

The men about the ropes were past all control now; they drowned Keppler's petitions for silence with oaths and in inarticulate shouts of anger, as if the blows had fallen upon them, and in mad rejoicings. They swept from one end of the ring to the other, with every muscle leaping in unison with those of the man they favored, and when a New York correspondent muttered over his shoulder that this would be the biggest sporting surprise since the Heenan-Sayers fight, Mr. Dwyer nodded his head sympathetically in assent.

In the excitement and tumult it is doubtful if any heard the three quickly repeated blows that fell heavily from the outside upon the big doors of the barn. If they did, it was already too late to mend matters, for the door fell, torn from its hinges, and as it fell a captain of police sprang into the light from out of the storm, with his lieutenants and their men crowding close at his shoulder.

In the panic and stampede that followed, several of the men stood as helplessly immovable as though they had seen a ghost; others made a mad rush into the arms of the officers and were beaten back against the ropes of the ring; others dived headlong into the stalls, among the horses and cattle, and still others shoved the rolls of money they held into the hands of the police and begged like children to be allowed to escape.

The instant the door fell and the raid was declared Hefflefinger slipped over the cross rails on which he had been lying, hung for an instant by his hands, and then dropped into the center of the fighting mob on the floor. He was out of it in an instant with the agility of a pickpocket, was across the room and at Hade's throat like a dog. The murderer, for the moment, was the calmer man of the two.

"Here," he panted, "hands off, now. There's no need for all this violence. There's no great harm in looking at a fight, is there? There's a hundred-dollar bill in my right hand; take it and let me slip out of this. No one is looking. Here."

But the detective only held him the closer.

"I want you for burglary," he whispered under his breath. "You've got to come with me now, and quick. The less fuss you make, the better for both of us. If you don't know who I am, you can feel my badge under my coat there. I've got the authority. It's all regular, and when we're out of this d—d row I'll show you the papers."

He took one hand from Hade's throat and pulled a pair of handcuffs from his pocket.

"It's a mistake. This is an outrage," gasped the murderer, white and trembling, but dreadfully alive and desperate for his liberty. "Let me go, I tell you! Take your hands off of me! Do I look like a burglar, you fool?"

"I know who you look like," whispered the detective, with his face close to the face of his prisoner. "Now, will you go easy as a burglar, or shall I tell these men who you are and what I *do* want you for? Shall I call out your real name or not? Shall I tell them? Quick, speak up; shall I?"

There was something so exultant—something so unnecessarily savage in the officer's face that the man he held saw that the detective knew him for what he really was, and the hands that had held his throat slipped down around his shoulders, or he would have fallen. The man's eyes opened and closed again, and he swayed weakly backward and forward, and choked as if his throat were dry and burning. Even to such a hardened connoisseur in crime as Gallegher, who stood closely by, drinking it in, there was something so abject in the man's terror that he regarded him with what was almost a touch of pity.

"For God's sake," Hade begged, "let me go. Come with me to my room and I'll give you half the money. I'll divide with you fairly. We can both get away. There's a fortune for both of us there. We both can get away. You'll be rich for life. Do you understand — for life!"

But the detective, to his credit, only shut his lips the tighter.

"That's enough," he whispered, in return. "That's more than I expected. You've sentenced yourself already. Come!"

Two officers in uniform barred their exit at the door, but Hefflefinger smiled easily and showed his badge.

"One of Byrnes's men," he said, in explanation; "came over expressly to take this chap. He's a burglar; 'Arlie' Lane, *alias* Carleton. I've shown the papers to the captain. It's all regular. I'm just going to get his traps at the hotel and walk him over to the station. I guess we'll push right on to New York tonight."

The officers nodded and smiled their admiration for the representative of what is, perhaps, the best detective force in the world, and let him pass.

Then Hefflefinger turned and spoke to Gallegher, who still stood as watchful as a dog at his side. "I'm going to his room to get the bonds and stuff," he whispered; "then I'll march him to the station and take that train. I've done my share; don't forget yours!"

"Oh, you'll get your money right enough," said Gallegher. "And, say," he added, with the appreciative nod of an expert, "do you know, you did it rather well."

Mr. Dwyer had been writing while the raid was settling down, as he had been writing while waiting for the fight to begin. Now he walked over to where the other correspondents stood in angry conclave.

The newspaper men had informed the officers who hemmed them in that they represented the principal papers of the country, and were expostulating vigorously with the captain, who had planned the raid, and who declared they were under arrest.

"Don't be an ass, Scott," said Mr. Dwyer, who was too excited to be polite or politic. "You know our being here isn't a matter of choice. We came here on business, as you did, and you've no right to hold us."

"If we don't get our stuff on the wire at once," protested a New York man, "we'll be too late for tomorrow's paper, and—"

Captain Scott said he did not care a profanely small amount for tomorrow's paper, and that all he knew was that to the station-house the newspaper men would go. There they would have a hearing, and if the magistrate chose to let them off, that was the magistrate's business, but that his duty was to take them into custody.

"But then it will be too late, don't you understand?" shouted Mr. Dwyer. "You've got to let us go *now,* at once."

"I can't do it, Mr. Dwyer," said the captain, "and that's all there is to it. Why, haven't I just sent the president of the Junior Republican Club to the patrol-wagon, the man that put this coat on me, and do you think I can let you fellows go after that? You were all put under bonds to keep the peace not three days ago, and here you're at it—fighting like badgers. It's worth my place to let one of you off."

What Mr. Dwyer said next was so uncomplimentary to the gallant Captain Scott that that overwrought individual seized the sporting editor by the shoulder, and shoved him into the hands of two of his men.

This was more than the distinguished Mr. Dwyer could brook, and he excitedly raised his hand in resistance. But before he had time to do anything foolish his wrist was gripped by one strong little hand, and he was conscious that another was picking the pocket of his great-coat.

He slapped his hands to his sides, and looking down, saw Gallegher standing close behind him and holding him by the wrist. Mr. Dwyer had forgotten the boy's existence, and would have spoken sharply if something in Gallegher's innocent eyes had not stopped him.

Gallegher's hand was still in that pocket, in which Mr. Dwyer had shoved his note-book filled with what he had written of Gallegher's work and Hade's final capture, and with a running descriptive account of the fight. With his eyes fixed on Mr. Dwyer, Gallegher drew it out, and with a quick movement shoved it inside his waistcoat. Mr. Dwyer gave a nod of comprehension. Then glancing at his two guardsmen, and finding that they were still interested in the wordy battle of the correspondents with their chief, and had seen nothing, he stooped and whispered to Gallegher: "The forms are locked at twenty minutes to three. If you don't get there by that time it will be of no use, but if you're on time you'll beat the town—and the country too."

Gallegher's eyes flashed significantly, and nodding his head to show he understood, started boldly on a run toward the door. But the officers who guarded it brought him to an abrupt halt, and, much to Mr. Dwyer's astonishment, drew from him what was apparently a torrent of tears.

"Let me go to me father. I want me father," the boy shrieked, hysterically. "They've 'rested father. Oh, daddy, daddy. They're a-goin' to take you to prison."

"Who is your father, sonny?" asked one of the guardians of the gate.

"Keppler's me father," sobbed Gallegher. "They're a-goin' to lock him up, and I'll never see him no more."

"Oh, yes, you will," said the officer, good-naturedly; "he's there in that first patrol-wagon. You can run over and say good-night to him, and then you'd better get to bed. This ain't no place for kids of your age."

"Thank you, sir," sniffed Gallegher, tearfully, as the two officers raised their clubs, and let him pass out into the darkness.

The yard outside was in a tumult, horses were stamping, and plunging, and backing the carriages into one another; lights were flashing from every window of what had been apparently an uninhabited house, and the voices of the prisoners were still raised in angry expostulation.

Three police patrol-wagons were moving about the yard, filled with unwilling passengers, who sat or stood, packed together like sheep, and with no protection from the sleet and rain.

Gallegher stole off into a dark corner, and watched the scene until his eyesight became familiar with the position of the land.

Then with his eyes fixed fearfully on the swinging light of a lantern with which an officer was searching among the carriages, he groped his way between horses' hoofs and behind the wheels of carriages to the cab which he had himself placed at the furthermost gate. It was still there, and the horse, as he had left it, with its head turned toward the city. Gallegher opened the big gate noiselessly, and worked nervously at the hitching strap. The knot was covered with a thin coating of ice, and it was several minutes before he could loosen it. But his teeth finally pulled it apart, and with the reins in his hands he sprang upon the wheel. And as he stood so, a shock of fear ran down his back like an electric current, his breath left him, and he stood immovable, gazing with wide eyes into the darkness.

The officer with the lantern had suddenly loomed up from behind a carriage not fifty feet distant, and was standing perfectly still, with his lantern held over his head, peering so directly toward Gallegher that the boy felt that he must see him. Gallegher stood with one foot on the hub of the wheel and with the other on the box waiting to spring. It seemed a minute before either of them moved, and then the officer took a step forward, and demanded sternly, "Who is that? What are you doing there?"

There was no time for parley then. Gallegher felt that he had been taken in the act, and that his only chance lay in open flight. He leaped up on the box, pulling out the whip as he did so, and with a quick sweep lashed the horse across the head and back. The animal sprang forward with a snort, narrowly clearing the gate-post, and plunged off into the darkness.

"Stop!" cried the officer.

So many of Gallegher's acquaintances among the 'longshoremen and mill hands had been challenged in so much the same manner that Gallegher knew what would probably follow if the challenge was disregarded. So he slipped from his seat to the footboard below, and ducked his head.

The three reports of a pistol, which rang out briskly from behind him, proved that his early training had given him a valuable fund of useful miscellaneous knowledge.

"Don't you be scared," he said, reassuringly, to the horse; "he's firing in the air."

The pistol-shots were answered by the impatient clangor of a patrol-wagon's gong, and glancing over his shoulder Gallegher saw its red and green lanterns tossing from side to side and looking in the darkness like the side-lights of a yacht plunging forward in a storm.

"I hadn't bargained to race you against no patrol-wagons," said Gallegher to his animal; "but if they want a race, we'll give them a tough tussle for it, won't we?"

Philadelphia, lying four miles to the south, sent up a faint yellow glow to the sky. It seemed very far away, and Gallegher's braggadocio grew cold within him at the loneliness of his adventure and the thought of the long ride before him.

It was still bitterly cold.

The rain and sleet beat through his clothes, and struck his skin with a sharp chilling touch that set him trembling.

Even the thought of the over-weighted patrol-wagon probably sticking in the mud some safe distance in the rear, failed to cheer him, and the excitement that had so far made him callous to the cold died out and left him weaker and nervous. But his horse was chilled with the long standing, and now leaped eagerly forward, only too willing to warm the half-frozen blood in its veins.

"You're a good beast," said Gallegher, plaintively. "You've got more nerve than me. Don't you go back on me now. Mr. Dwyer says we've got to beat the town." Gallegher had no idea what time it was as he rode through the night, but he knew he would be able to find out from a big clock over a manufactory at a point nearly three-quarters of the distance from Keppler's to the goal.

He was still in the open country and driving recklessly, for he knew the best part of his ride must be made outside the city limits.

He raced between desolate-looking corn-fields with bare stalks and patches of muddy earth rising above the thin covering of snow; truck farms and brick-yards fell behind him on either side. It was very lonely work, and once or twice the dogs ran yelping to the gates and barked after him.

Part of his way lay parallel with the railroad tracks, and he drove for some time beside long lines of freight and coal cars as they stood resting for the night. The fantastic Queen Anne suburban stations were dark and deserted, but in one or two of the block-towers he could see the operators writing at their desks, and the sight in some way comforted him.

Once he thought of stopping to get out the blanket in which he had wrapped himself on the first trip, but he feared to spare the time, and drove on with his teeth chattering and his shoulders shaking with the cold.

He welcomed the first solitary row of darkened houses with a faint cheer of recognition. The scattered lamp-posts lightened his spirits, and even the badly paved streets rang under the beats of his horse's feet like music. Great mills and manufactories, with only a night-watchman's light in the lowest of their many stories, began to take the place of the gloomy farm-houses and gaunt trees that had startled him with their grotesque shapes. He had been driving nearly an hour, he calculated, and in that time the rain had changed to a wet snow, that fell heavily and clung to whatever it touched. He passed block after block of trim workmen's houses, as still and silent as the sleepers within them, and at last he turned the horse's head into Broad Street, the city's great thoroughfare, that stretches from its one end to the other and cuts it evenly in two.

He was driving noiselessly over the snow and slush in the street, with his thoughts bent only on the clock-face he wished so much to see, when a hoarse voice challenged him from the sidewalk. "Hey, you, stop there, hold up!" said the voice.

Gallegher turned his head, and though he saw that the voice came from under a policeman's helmet, his only answer was to hit his horse sharply over the head with his whip and to urge it into a gallop.

This, on his part, was followed by a sharp, shrill whistle from the policeman. Another whistle answered it from a street-corner one block ahead of him. "Whoa," said Gallegher, pulling on the reins. "There's one too many of them," he added, in apologetic explanation. The horse stopped, and stood, breathing heavily, with great clouds of steam rising from its flanks.

"Why in hell didn't you stop when I told you to?" demanded the voice, now close at the cab's side.

"I didn't hear you," returned Gallegher, sweetly. "But I heard you whistle, and I heard your partner whistle, and I thought maybe it was me you wanted to speak to, so I just stopped."

"You heard me well enough. Why aren't your lights lit?" demanded the voice.

"Should I have 'em lit?" asked Gallegher, bending over and regarding them with sudden interest.

"You know you should, and if you don't, you've no right to be driving that cab. I don't believe you're the regular driver, anyway. Where'd you get it?"

"It ain't my cab, of course," said Gallegher, with an easy laugh. "It's Luke McGovern's. He left it outside Cronin's while he went in to get a drink, and he took too much, and me father told me to drive it round to the stable for him. I'm Cronin's son. McGovern ain't in no condition to drive. You can see yourself how he's been misusing the horse. He puts it up at Bachman's livery stable, and I was just going around there now."

Gallegher's knowledge of the local celebrities of the district confused the zealous officer of the peace. He surveyed the boy with a steady stare that would have distressed a less skillful liar, but Gallegher only shrugged his shoulders slightly, as if from the cold, and waited with apparent indifference to what the officer would say next.

In reality his heart was beating heavily against his side, and he felt that if he was kept on a strain much longer he would give way and break down. A second snow-covered form emerged suddenly from the shadow of the houses.

"What is it, Reeder?" it asked.

"Oh, nothing much," replied the first officer. "This kid hadn't any lamps lit, so I called to him to stop and he didn't do it, so I whistled to you. It's all right, though. He's just taking it round to Bachman's. Go ahead," he added, sulkily.

"Get up!" chirped Gallegher. "Good night," he added, over his shoulder.

Gallegher gave a hysterical little gasp of relief as he trotted away from the two policemen, and poured bitter maledictions on their heads for two meddling fools as he went.

"They might as well kill a man as scare him to death," he said, with an attempt to get back to his customary flippancy. But the effort was somewhat pitiful, and he felt guiltily conscious that a salt, warm tear was creeping slowly down his face, and that a lump that would not keep down was rising in his throat.

"'Tain't no fair thing for the whole police force to keep worrying at a little boy like me," he said, in shame-faced apology. "I'm not doing nothing wrong, and I'm half froze to death, and yet they keep a-nagging at me."

It was so cold that when the boy stamped his feet against the footboard to keep them warm, sharp pains shot up through his body, and when he beat his arms about his shoulders, as he had seen real cabmen do, the blood in his finger-tips tingled so acutely that he cried aloud with the pain.

He had often been up that late before, but he had never felt so sleepy. It was as if someone was pressing a sponge heavy with chloroform near his face, and he could not fight off the drowsiness that lay hold of him.

He saw, dimly hanging above his head, a round disk of light that seemed like a great moon, and which he finally guessed to be the clock-face for which he had been on the lookout. He had passed it before he realized this; but the fact stirred him into wakefulness again, and when his cab's wheels slipped around the City Hall corner, he remembered to look up at the other big clock-face that keeps awake over the railroad station and measures out the night.

He gave a gasp of consternation when he saw that it was half-past two, and that there was but ten minutes left to him. This, and the many electric lights and the sight of the familiar pile of buildings, startled him into a semi-consciousness of where he was and how great was the necessity for haste.

He rose in his seat and called on the horse, and urged it into a reckless gallop over the slippery asphalt. He considered nothing else but speed, and looking neither to the left nor right dashed off down Broad Street into Chestnut, where his course lay straight away to the office, now only seven blocks distant.

Gallegher never knew how it began, but he was suddenly assaulted by shouts on either side, his horse was thrown back on its haunches, and he found two men in cabmen's livery hanging at its head, and patting its sides, and calling it by name. And the other cabmen who have their stand at the corner were swarming about the carriage, all of them talking and swearing at once, and gesticulating wildly with their whips.

They said they knew the cab was McGovern's, and they wanted to know where he was, and why he wasn't on it; they wanted to know where Gallegher had stolen it, and why he had been such a fool as to drive it into the arms of its owner's friends; they said that it was about time that a cab-driver could get off his box to take a drink without having his cab run away with, and some of them called loudly for a policeman to take the young thief in charge.

Gallegher felt as if he had been suddenly dragged into consciousness out of a bad dream, and stood for a second like a half-awakened somnambulist.

They had stopped the cab under an electric light, and its glare shone coldly down upon the trampled snow and the faces of the men around him.

Gallegher bent forward, and lashed savagely at the horse with his whip.

"Let me go," he shouted, as he tugged impotently at the reins. "Let me go, I tell you. I haven't stole no cab, and you've got no right to stop me. I only want to take it to the *Press* office," he begged. "They'll send it back to you all right. They'll pay you for the trip. I'm not running away with it. The driver's got the collar — he's 'rested — and I'm only a-going to the *Press* office. Do you hear me?" he cried, his voice rising and breaking in a shriek of passion and disappointment. "I tell you to let go those reins. Let me go, or I'll kill you. Do you hear me? I'll kill you." And leaning forward, the boy struck savagely with his long whip at the faces of the men about the horse's head.

Someone in the crowd reached up and caught him by the ankles, and with a quick jerk pulled him off the box, and threw him on to the street. But he was up on his knees in a moment, and caught at the man's hand.

"Don't let them stop me, mister," he cried, "please let me go. I didn't steal the cab, sir. S'help me, I didn't. I'm telling you the truth. Take me to the *Press* office, and they'll prove it to you. They'll pay you anything you ask 'em. It's only such a little ways now, and I've come so far, sir. Please don't let them stop me," he sobbed, clasping the man about the knees. "For Heaven's sake, mister, let me go!"

* * *

The managing editor of the *Press* took up the india-rubber speaking-tube at his side, and answered, "Not yet" to an inquiry the night editor had already put to him five times within the last twenty minutes.

Then he snapped the metal top of the tube impatiently, and went upstairs. As he passed the door of the local room, he noticed that the reporters had not gone home, but were sitting about on the tables and chairs, waiting. They looked up inquiringly as he passed, and the city editor asked, "Any news yet?" and the managing editor shook his head.

The compositors were standing idle in the composing-room, and their foreman was talking with the night editor.

"Well," said that gentleman, tentatively.

"Well," returned the managing editor, "I don't think we can wait; do you?"

"It's a half-hour after time now," said the night editor, "and we'll miss the suburban trains if we hold the paper back any longer. We can't afford to wait for a purely hypothetical story. The chances are all against the fight's having taken place or this Hade's having been arrested."

"But if we're beaten on it—" suggested the chief. "But I don't think that is possible. If there were any story to print, Dwyer would have had it here before now."

The managing editor looked steadily down at the floor.

"Very well," he said, slowly, "we won't wait any longer. Go ahead," he added, turning to the foreman with a sigh of reluctance. The foreman whirled himself about, and began to give his orders; but the two editors still looked at each other doubtfully.

As they stood so, there came a sudden shout and the sound of people running to and fro in the reportorial rooms below. There was the tramp of many footsteps on the stairs, and above the confusion they heard the voice of the city editor telling someone to "run to Madden's and get some brandy, quick."

No one in the composing-room said anything; but those compositors who had started to go home began slipping off their overcoats, and every one stood with his eyes fixed on the door.

It was kicked open from the outside, and in the doorway stood a cab-driver and the city editor, supporting between them a pitiful little figure of a boy, wet and miserable, and with the snow melting on his clothes and running in little pools to the floor. "Why, it's Gallegher," said the night editor, in a tone of the keenest disappointment.

Gallegher shook himself free from his supporters, and took an unsteady step forward, his fingers fumbling stiffly with the buttons of his waistcoat.

"Mr. Dwyer, sir," he began faintly, with his eyes fixed fearfully on the managing editor, "he got arrested — and I couldn't get here no sooner, 'cause they kept a-stopping me, and they took me cab from under me — but —" he pulled the notebook from his breast and held it out with its covers damp and limp from the rain — "but we got Hade, and here's Mr. Dwyer's copy."

And then he asked, with a queer note in his voice, partly of dread and partly of hope, "Am I in time, sir?"

The managing editor took the book, and tossed it to the foreman, who ripped out its leaves and dealt them out to his men as rapidly as a gambler deals out cards.

Then the managing editor stooped and picked Gallegher up in his arms, and, sitting down, began to unlace his wet and muddy shoes.

Gallegher made a faint effort to resist this degradation of the managerial dignity; but his protest was a very feeble one, and his head fell back heavily on the managing editor's shoulder.

To Gallegher the incandescent lights began to whirl about in circles, and to burn in different colors; the faces of the reporters kneeling before him and chafing his hands and feet grew dim and unfamiliar, and the roar and rumble of the great presses in the basement sounded far away, like the murmur of the sea.

And then the place and the circumstances of it came back to him again sharply and with sudden vividness.

Gallegher looked up, with a faint smile, into the managing editor's face. "You won't turn me off for running away, will you?" he whispered.

The managing editor did not answer immediately. His head was bent, and he was thinking, for some reason or other, of a little boy of his own, at home in bed. Then he said, quietly, "Not this time, Gallegher."

Gallegher's head sank back comfortably on the older man's shoulder, and he smiled comprehensively at the faces of the young men crowded around him. "You hadn't ought to," he said, with a touch of his old impudence, "'cause — I beat the town."

1892

WILLIAM NORR

'ROUND THE OPIUM LAMP

Working as a newspaperman in New York, WILLIAM NORR made the Chinatown neighborhood his special area of expertise. He wrote true stories of life in what was then a small part of Manhattan (mainly centered on Mott Street, as it still is today in its vastly expanded section of lower Manhattan). He also tried his hand at fiction, but his sketches were filled with real-life characters whose stories were largely based on true incidents.

To most Americans, the Chinese were so alien that they might as well have come from outer space. The tales in the little-known Norr's only published book (and self-published, at that), the very rare *Stories of Chinatown* (1892), are typical of several other collections of stories about the Chinese living in pre–World War I America, mostly in New York's and San Francisco's Chinatowns. That they are racist may be taken for granted, even if there may be no particular malevolence of spirit. The story collected here is included in this volume more as a representative of a type of fiction than for any exceptional literary qualities, though it moves along nicely without wasted words or pretension.

Similar collections, such as Chester B. Fernald's *The Cat and the Cherub and Other Stories* (1896), Helen F. Clark's *The Lady of the Lily Feet; and Other Tales of Chinatown* (1900), and Dr. C. W. Doyle's *The Shadow of Quong Lung* (1900), mainly feature portraits of sneaky and ignorant yellow-skinned male criminals and subjugated lotus-blossom-like girls. Perhaps because of Norr's own frequenting of opium dens, as he writes in his introduction, his tales feature as many white people as they do Chinese, though they all tend to be treated as equals once they are "on the pipe."

"'Round the Opium Lamp" was first published in *Stories of Chinatown: Sketches from Life in the Chinese Colony* (New York: William Norr, 1892).

• • •

YOU HAVEN'T FORGOTTEN how to handle the yen-hok, Jim," said Frank the Kid, as he watched the cook deftly "chy" the pill above the tiny flame of the opium lamp. "By the way, how did they ever nail you? I never got the rights of that story. I was out in Denver and nearly dropped dead when Jimmy Hannon wrote me you'd gone away for fourteen years. There was some woman in it, wasn't there?"

"Yes," said Jim, slowly, as he passed over the pipe, "there was a woman in it. But she wasn't as much to blame as my own pigheadedness. If I'd treated her right I'd never done that long bit."

"That's right," said Jennie, as she playfully pulled the Kid's ear. "Some people want to put the blame of everything on the women."

"And they call the turn nine times out of ten," retorted the Kid. "But let's hear the story, Jim. Nobody seems to have it quite straight. I know you went away wrong on some job of Pete Reagan's, but where did the woman come in on the game?"

"Well," said Jim, "it's all of ten years ago now. I was working for Barney Maguire at the time, and I tell you they were great old times. There's as much difference between the sawdust business then and the game going on now as there is between night and day. We were in a basement on Sixth street, near Second avenue, and we'd run as high as ten suckers a day. It was great grafting, and the gang was in clover. Maguire was making so much money he didn't know what to do with it. We were all up against the dope, and it was a great crowd that smoked at 4, 11 and 17 Mott street in those days. Almost any night you'd see Barney Maguire, Frank Maguire, his cousin; big George Butler, Tony Martin, Georgie Morton, Jimmie Hannon, Tommy Wilson, California Frank, California Jack, Dick Cronin, Billy Ferguson, Fitz the Kid, 'Pretty Pinkie' and lots of other good people.

"Actors and actresses came down to Mott street then to go against the pipe, for there were no uptown joints. One night a young girl who played a small part in Stevens's 'Unknown' came down. She was a nice little thing, white skin, reddish hair and big blue eyes. We cottoned to each other at once, and when the company went out on the road she wasn't with it. We got along splendidly for a while. She got hitting the pipe heavily—I never see a woman, or man either, for that matter, take to the dope the way she did. She was at it day and night. She'd be down in Sing's at 17 Mott street every afternoon. I'd meet her there at night and we'd never go home till daylight.

"After some time I noticed that whenever I'd get to Sing's I'd find Ida—that was her name—smoking with Georgie Appo. You know him, don't you, a Chinese half-breed, son of Quimbo Appo, the Chinese murderer there was so much fuss over some fifteen years ago? Well, Georgie was a petty-larceny grafter and I had no use for him. I didn't like him to be smoking with Ida, but didn't think he was enough account to fuss about. But pretty soon the gang got kidding me on the steady company Ida was keeping. I didn't believe Ida would do me dirt, especially with a Chink, but the jollying got me off and one morning when we got home I said to Ida:

"'Georgie Appo is no friend of mine, Ida, and I'd sooner you'd smoke with any of the other boys when I'm not around.'

"Well, like all red-headed girls, she had a devil of a temper, and she just ripped out:

"'But I prefer to smoke with him.'

"I was only a kid in those days and knew nothing about women or handling them, and her answer just set me wild. So I said:

"'Let me catch you smoking with that Chink again and I'll smash that baby-face of yours and have nothing more to do with you.'

"She turned around with a proud look she could always put on, and said: 'You may do as you please about having anything to do with me, but don't ever lay a hand on me or you'll regret it.'

"'Just let me see you laying on the same bunk with him again,' was all I answered.

"George Butler and I had to meet a sucker in Philadelphia that day and it was late the following morning when I got to the joint. Ida had gone home. I smoked a few pills and then asked Tommy Wilson:

"'Who was Ida smoking with last night?'

"'She and Georgie Appo had a lay-out between them,' he answered.

"'The gang kept kidding her that you were pinched and she went home early.'

"I never said a word, but got my fill of dope and then went to the flat. Ida had just undressed and as she opened the door for me she threw her arms around me and said:

"'Oh, Jim, where have you been? The boys wouldn't tell me and I've been awful anxious.'

"I pushed her away and asked: 'What did I tell you about smoking with that Chink?'

"She put on that proud look of hers again, and said something about her right to smoke with anybody she liked as long as they treated her right. Well, it was the first time I ever struck a woman, but she set me crazy, and, getting hold of her long hair, I pounded her face until she was a sight. Then I let her sink to the floor, gave her a few kicks for good measure, and said: 'Get your traps out of here, you Chinese ——. I'm done with you.'

"She just lay on the floor with the blood flowing over her nightgown and the carpet, and kept moaning: 'Oh, Jim! and I loved you so much. Oh, Jim!'

"I left her laying there and went to bed. When I got up in the afternoon she was gone. I went to the damper to see if she had taken the roll, but there wasn't a cent gone. I felt sorry for what I'd done and would have given a good many dollars to undo it. I had just got dressed when there came a knock at the door. 'There she is now,' I said to myself. I opened the door and my lady, with three Central Office people, came in. She raised her veil — you should have seen how her pretty face was banged up — and said: 'You'll find what you want in the fireplace there.'

"Well, I tell you, I was paralyzed, for I knew I was done. Pete Reagan and Kid Carroll had turned off some big nabob, and, getting leery, had given me the stuff to keep until the thing blew over. There was a lot of diamonds and jewelry, and Ida, seeing me bury the stuff, thought it was my job. She had hurried off to headquarters while I was asleep to get square for the punching.

"'I told you I'd make you regret it if you laid your hand on me,' she said, as the flatties closed in on me to put on the nippers before looking up the stuff. I managed to let a vase fly at her before they got me, just missing her nut by an inch. Well, they found the stuff all right, and were taking me out, when suddenly my lady went down on her knees, begging them to take the stuff and let me go. And, by ——! they had to fight her to get me away.

"Well, to cut the story short, the gang spent a barrel, but it was money thrown away. The sucker and his wife had been chloroformed and one of the servants knocked over the head, and the thing couldn't be fixed. I was game and didn't open my mouth on Reagan and the Kid. Ida couldn't be found by the flatties when they went to get her as a witness, but it didn't make any difference. The fellow who had his nut opened swore positively I was the man he met in the hall, and who had hit him with a billy. It was a clear case against me, and I got soaked for fourteen years and two months. I was just getting into the hearse after being sentenced when Ida ran up, and, before I knew what was what, had her arms around me, and was kissing me with a 'Good-by, dear Jim! God forgive me.' Well, if she'd got the kick I made at her, she might have been done for then and there.

"I had been up about a year when Georgie Appo was brought along for snatching a 'yellow bird' on Park Row. I wouldn't have anything to do with him, for, although nobody knew anything about it, I blamed him for the trouble I was in. However, I was anxious to hear something about the boys, for nobody had come to see me. It's queer how soon you're forgot when you're put away. I'd got so that I might have forgiven Ida if she'd come or written to me, but I never heard of her, and I supposed she was with somebody else, which didn't make me feel any too good towards Appo. But I wanted news, and one day I spoke to him. One thing led to another, and it wasn't long before I learned that Ida had been all straight with Appo; that she had smoked with Appo because the boys were constantly making play for her, and she wouldn't listen to them. On the last night she had smoked with Appo she had told him that I didn't like her to smoke with him, and that she was not coming down to the joint any more. She would smoke at home alone, and try and give up the habit altogether.

"So you see," concluded Jim, "that while there was a woman in my going away, she wasn't so very much to blame, although her pride had something to do with it. But I blame myself only for the nine years I done."

"But," asked Jennie, "didn't she ever write or care to see you in all that time?"

Jim was slowly kneading a pill with a faraway look in his eyes, and simply shook his head.

"That's just like a woman," said the Kid, warmly.

"No, it isn't," flashed Jennie, with tears in her eyes. "I think it's very cruel of her. Of course, Jim treated her dreadfully, but if she loved him she'd have forgotten all when he was in prison. I can overlook her rushing to the police in a passion. But not the other. I'm sure she never really loved you, Jim."

"I think she did, Jen," said Jim in a low tone, "for the morning after I was sentenced they found her dead in bed, with the gas turned on."

1894

PERCIVAL POLLARD

LINGO DAN

One of the rarest books in the world of crime fiction (no copy has been known to be offered for sale in more than fifty years), *Lingo Dan* is a collection of stories about an extremely unusual fictional character. Receiving his sobriquet because of the flowery language he uses, he is a hobo, thief, con man, and shockingly cold-blooded murderer — extremely unusual for the nineteenth century. Although Lingo Dan also proves himself to be a patriotic American with a deep streak of sentimentality, he remains an unpleasant fellow who nonetheless has a significant position in the history of the mystery story: the year of the first story and the subsequent book make him the first serial criminal in American literature.

(Joseph) Percival Pollard (1869–1911) was an important literary critic in his day, befriended by both Ambrose Bierce and H. L. Mencken. He wrote twelve books before his early death at the age of forty-two, but *Lingo Dan* was his only mystery. He was best known for his works of literary criticism, most successfully *Their Day in Court* (1909).

In his scholarly work *The Detective Short Story: A Bibliography,* Ellery Queen (a collector and scholar of mystery fiction as well as a best-selling novelist), quotes from an inscribed copy of the book in which Pollard wrote: "I expect for [*Lingo Dan*] neither the success of Sherlock Holmes, Raffles, etc., nor yet the immunity from comparison with those gentlemen. Yet it is at least one thing the others are not: American." Today no one compares his character to those he cites, as Lingo Dan is one of the forgotten figures in the literature of roguery.

"Lingo Dan" was first published in the *San Francisco Argonaut* in 1894. It was first published in book form in *Lingo Dan* (Washington, D.C.: Neale Publishing Co., 1903).

• • •

The snow that lined the sides of what the railroad men of that section called the "Brighton Cut" was, fortunately for two persons who suddenly found themselves transported from the cold hospitality of a freight-car to the colder embraces of the wide, white world that encompassed the track, very deep. After a moment or two of partial insensibility, more the result of bewilderment than of actual physical hurt, these two lifted their heads up out of the white counterpane that clung to them like some active envelope, and looked after the train that was now merely a mist of smoke and an echo faint beyond the curves of the forest.

"H'm," said the first one of the two derelicts to rise and shake the snow off his thin form, "that was a fearful breach of hospitality. We invest a common carrier, so termed in law, with the dignity of carrying such uncommon personages as ourselves, and this—this is the treatment we receive! Billy, this is a heathen country!" He took off his cap and passed eight long and bony fingers through his snow-invested hair.

"Damn his eyes!" said Billy. He was a person of few words, and fewer attractions. He was short, and his general effect was toward the loutish.

"Yes," the other replied, looking about him, "I have no doubt you are right. Billy, your explanation is a most agreeable one. It was owing to some curious defect in that brakeman's eyes, doubtless, that he failed to notice our high estate; if any part of him is to suffer condemnation, it is his eyes. Billy, I agree with you; say it again!"

Billy, for a brief minute, looked as if he would like to include other and nearer eyes in his anathema. He contented himself, however, with a muttered "Argh!" a circular look at the prospect of sloping meadowland, and a "What next, cully?"

"Stranded as we are upon an apparently shoreless sea of snow," responded the gentleman addressed, "our next move should be toward shelter." He paused to kick some snow out of a boot that was, as to the toes, over-hospitable to the elements. "This is a dismal spot!"

To tell the truth, the "Brighton Cut" is one of the bleakest places in the State. The railway track comes winding down a steep grade until it reaches this cut; the soil thereabouts is not tillable, and there are no fences for over half a mile. A thin strip of forest shuts out the western view. On a gray afternoon in midwinter it looks very lonely, and there is something in the silence of it, after the rattle of a freight-train has echoed away, that strikes a chill even when the sun is shining. It was no wonder, then, that to these two, just stranded there, from the comparatively warm recesses of a lumber-car, the place should seem decidedly dismal. They were used to dismal things, to be sure; but that ever-present yearning for luxury and its attendant inexertion—a yearning that had made them what they were—rebelled at every repetition of the unwelcome reality. It is not necessary to state very particularly who these two were. The one with the tall frame and the taller language might have been a great many things, some of them great; the fact that he was none of these is explanation enough for his title as a tramp. As for the other one, it is doubtful whether he had ever had even possibilities; he was, by lapse of all other capabilities, a tramp for sure. Just as it is sufficient of a man to say that he is a king, so it is enough introduction to make certain that he is a tramp. These two were indubitably tramps. It was evident in the consummate grace with which they wore their curiously allotted clothes. It was patent in the air of nobility that stamped them as true lords of the air. It was on their breath.

"I may say, without exaggeration," continued the taller of the two, "that this is a place unfit for such as we are to rest in. Wherefore, let us reconnoiter."

As they passed up the slope toward the north it began to snow steadily. Over in the west, the faint, gray light of day was dimming to the almost colorless shade of white upon white. It was an arduous task, stamping through the drifting snow. From time to time one might have heard, had one been within earshot, the voice of Billy, cursing as he walked.

On what is known in that county as the Brighton Mill Road, there is, for the most part, a sprinkling of as fine farms as there are anywhere in the West. The farm-houses are well-painted, and the barns are roomy and new enough to be the envy of many a man who has gone further toward the plains and rented a log cabin. For a distance of about a mile, east and west, however, this highway passes through a barren district that is marked by nothing save a tumble-down shanty, with a roof the bricks of which have fallen eastward. This shanty stands at a point where the highway is nearest to that point on the railway known as the "Brighton Cut," on the summit of the arid slope leading down to the rails. For a good many years this shanty had been the home, if one may use the word so lightly, of a certain Doc Middals, concerning whom but little seemed to be known, save that he was "baching it." Just what presumption of ownership or interest in the shanty or its surroundings went with Middals's system of occupation there seemed to be no one willing to testify. This Doc Middals was a queer fellow who rarely spent more than a month or two at a time in the shanty, and his goings and comings were so erratic, his place so remote from the view of other habitations, that the question of his presence or absence was always an open one. The farmers who passed on the highway had long since given up speculating on the subject; Middals frequently denied himself a fire even in midwinter, so not even the absence of smoke about the shattered chimney was proof positive of the man's presence elsewhere.

It was in this cottage that Lingo Dan—by this *sobriquet* was the taller of the two tramps, who had been lately deposited in the "Brighton Cut" by an inhospitable brakeman, known in such circles as knew him at all intimately—and his partner Billy were housed about a week after their advent in that part of the country. By a marvelous, instinctive faculty of penetration, of stilling his own curiosity, Lingo Dan had fully possessed himself of all the facts in connection with that shanty before he entered it.

Covered by the drifting of the snow, the presence of these two was absolutely unknown to a soul. In the driving storm that followed their arrival like a wail of omen, all their tracks through the snow had been obliterated.

Looking out of the eastern window of the Middals shanty, Lingo Dan gave a sigh of admiration. The sun was making a million diamonds dance about the crust of snow that stretched away over the fields and on the highway; it was like a rollicking cowboy shooting until his victims dance for dear life. Clear as crystal, the air was intensely sensitive to tone; a far-off ringing of sleigh-bells sounded with a distinctness that belied distance. Out of the blue of the sky, the glitter of the sun, and the fierce purity of the snow, there arose a splendid dazzlement that blinded unaccustomed eyes.

"It would be pathetic," mused Lingo Dan aloud, after passing his hand over his eyes to shut out the glare that began to hurt him, "if we should find our opportunity on such a day. Look, Billy, what a day it is! H'm, I had not thought this country capable of so magnificent an effect. And yet, do you know, I think it is going to snow again before night."

Billy offered no reply. He was engaged in cleaning out a rifle, and at intervals he contorted his face into a squint so that he might gauge the nicety of the barrel's internal polish.

"When I come to consider the matter," Lingo Dan went on, "I begin to regret my harsh words anent that brakeman. He was, as I now see it, an instrument of a benign providence. Providence is, indeed, singularly benign. What could be handier to our purpose than this cottage and its associations? Occupied by a harmless hermit, it takes on all the innocuousness possible. Benign providence! This man Middals is absent, leaving us his shanty and his shooting irons. Benign providence! I feel it in my veins, now tingling with the excitation so beautiful a day has put me in, that there will presently come some one whose necessity is not so great as ours. In the interests of liberty and equality, we must relieve his person of its valuables ere we release him. I trust he will not resist. I sincerely trust so. But if he does —" He looked at Billy's employment. "Is it clean?"

"Slick as grease," was Billy's answer.

"Benign providence!"

It was as if in response to Lingo Dan's devout utterance that the eastern hilltop became at this moment slightly clouded with a fine powdery mist. Then the forms of two persons on horseback appeared upon the slope; it was evident that their ascent of the farther side had been accomplished at a canter. Even at that distance, so clear was the day, the breath of the horses' nostrils could be seen rising about them like a halo. At the first sight of them, Lingo Dan, smiling unctuously, said: "Ah, Billy, our prey approaches."

"One?"

"No; there are two of them. They are riding. One is a man; the other, a woman. They are young. Judging by their present loitering and the interest each exhibits in the other, I should say they were lovers."

"No good — they ain't!" Billy gave the rifle a last vicious wipe, and laid it upon a shelf.

"Haste, my boy, is a dangerous indulgence. I beg to differ; I think we are in particularly good luck. Such slight observance of the ways of my kind as I have been able to take has taught me that in certain walks of life a young man never permits himself the company of a young lady without being sure that he has money in his pocket. Yonder young man is of that walk in life. There are, you see, so many possibilities, such contingencies, that to provide one's self with money before providing one's self with a companion is merely to prove one's appreciation of the world we live in; this applies to a ride of an hour as well as to a marriage for life."

Billy was apparently used to such lengthy philosophics, for he replied, as if unconscious of the other's wordy efforts: "Say! How about getting away?"

"Easy — ridiculously easy. After obtaining the reward of our exertions, we drift gently down the slope to the railway, and presently, boarding a freight, turn our faces to the Golden West. I have observed a ledge of rock from which we can easily propel ourselves on to the moving cars while the train is toiling up the steep grade of the cut. We will not be found—if we ever are—until many miles have been traversed; an *alibi* will be complete."

"But our tracks from here to the cut?"

"Billy, you are singularly slow. Do you see that cloud on the horizon? Before night it will snow; our foot-marks will be utterly wiped out."

Billy considered a moment. Then he said, triumphantly: "But the impressions will harden this surface; they'll get on to us if ever they sweep away the new fall of snow."

Lingo Dan shrugged his shoulders. "Whence the inspiration of that remark, I know not. I think you must have been reading Conan Doyle. Well, you can be quite sure that there is no Sherlock Holmes in this part of the country. Dear me!"

At this last exclamation Billy looked curious. "What's up?" he asked.

For an instant or two Lingo Dan made no reply. He was looking intently at the highway on which the two riders were approaching. In point of fact, the occurrence that attracted his attention was singular enough. As they rode slowly, side by side, down the slope of the road that came to the shanty from the east, the young man's left arm slowly disengaged itself from the reins of his horse and passed behind the waist of his human companion; their bodies and their heads came gently, carefully together; the girl's hand went up to her chin, detaching the veil and relegating it to her forehead, and then her arm encircled the young man; their faces met in a kiss. The horses' heads hung down and their feet ambled leisurely; tired after their hill-climbing canter, they took this respite thankfully enough. It was a kiss that lasted longer than do most kisses; the adventurous circumstances and the perilous nature of their position tended to fill both these riders with the advisability of making the most of bliss; to them, the kiss was but an infinitesimal instant of happiness; to any one not concerned in it, its length would have seemed an eternity. All these things the watcher in the cottage observed.

"It is evident," he said, presently, "that this is no ordinary case. They are lovers, but they are also more: they are eloping. This complicates matters. It makes our booty greater, but it increases the—h'm—the difficulty. Yes, I am afraid this will be a—what did we say in the Quadrangle?—*a mauvais quart d'heure.*"

"What're you drivin' at?" Billy glowered at his companion in evident disgust at his high-flown phrases.

"My dear Billy, here are the facts: Two persons, when they elope, are preparing for a future; hence, the young man lines his pockets before he starts. He lines his pockets, however, both from without and within. Realizing the risk he is running, he puts pistols in his hip-pockets, as well as a purse over his breast."

"I reckon that's likely."

"Thank you. Your acquiescence, Billy, soothes a spirit slightly ruffled by the prospect of discourtesy. For, to tell the truth, I fear we shall have to — h'm — silence these two first, and inquire afterward. It would be so infernally unpleasant, you see, if he got the drop on us. Understand, then, that we are not to take risks. You, Billy, will sight for the girl; I'll take the man."

There was a click as Billy sent the hammer of his rifle to the full-cock. Lingo Dan stretched out his long arm, picked up the other weapon and rested the barrel carefully on the window-sill.

The riders were quite close to the house, and the love in the eyes of each shone out with a sort of spiritual brilliance. They leaned together again and joined lips in a long, delicious kiss.

And while they kissed, two shots rang out on the crystal air.

An old woman living on the outskirts of Libertytown rejoices in the peculiar *sobriquet* of Mrs. Early Worm. This is, one can only suppose, due to her habit of rising at a most infinitesimal hour, in midwinter as well as in midsummer. As to her reasons for this singular course, there is nothing but conjecture. She is said to have driven her husband to an early grave, and then, overcome by remorse, to have sworn to seek none but an early grave herself. However that may be, the things that Mrs. Early Worm saw on the morning of the twentieth of February, 189–, are facts, and have nothing to do with the realm of conjecture.

When she arose, the world was still, in spite of its coating of snow, very dark. There was light, to be sure, of that curious, indefinite gray that distinguishes the birth of a day in winter time. She was proceeding to the woodshed to pick up the usual armful of kindling-wood for the kitchen stove, when suddenly she said, "Land sakes, what is that?" and stood stock-still in the middle of the yard.

What she saw was this: Through the gray dawn light that hung between the earth's white coverlet and the night's flying wings of sable, there approached the apparition of two horses and two riders. In the gray haze they shone like angels of whiteness; that was the awful part of it — they were all white! Against the horizon, where night still held sway, their forms were cut as clearly as in ivory. As they came nearer, the old woman, shivering now with cold and fear, observed that one rider was a man, the other, a girl. They sat motionless, rigid, as if carved of marble. They were covered with frost from head to foot; they were white with the hue of cold. The horses, as they stepped rhythmically forward, blew out mists of steam that came back to them frozen coatings of ice.

The old woman, with an effort, found energy enough to wrench herself out of the strange, lethargic fascination she had been in. She began to run, as fast as her old legs could carry her, toward the nearest house, about a hundred yards away.

Presently the entire village was aroused to the presence of this ghastly phenomenon.

Heedless of the terror they occasioned, the horses stepped on with a tired and even gait.

And now it was observed that the riders were linked together, that the two were one, that here was some awful unity of horror. Their arms were intertwined, their faces touching. The man's right hand held his horse's reins and a hunting-crop, while his left was about the girl's waist; her right was about his shoulders, and her left held the reins. Their shoulders touched; it was as if they were hewn out of one stone.

But there was no breath from their nostrils. White as ghosts, still as eternity, they rode on into the heart of the village.

Numb with dread, no one dared approach them. All knew their faces well; no one spoke their names; even curiosity was stifled in the greatness of their terror.

With the resonant clamor of iron shoes upon wood, both horses ascended the slight sloping entrance to the livery barn. Roused by the sound, the livery man came out of his office. He looked, in dazed astonishment, at these colorless, silent, motionless riders, he noticed what no one had yet seen: upon the breast of each a crimson stain, not quite hidden by the coating of frost.

"Great God!" he said; "they're stone dead!"

The sun, shimmering through the planks of a lumber-car, part of a freight-train traveling through the farther West, rested for an instant on the eyes of Lingo Dan as he slept the sleep of the careless. Its radiance woke him; he rubbed his eyes, gave Billy a nudge with his elbow, and said: "Hello, Billy; here we are again!"

"Oh," grunted Billy, viciously, "you be d——d!"

"I admit it, Billy; I probably shall be. What for? For gross incompetence in judging the idiocy of a man in love. For, I leave it to any one, is it conceivable that any one but a lunatic would start upon a voyage for life, with a life-companion, without a *sou* in his pocket? A lunatic, Billy, is, as I now see, a simile for a man in love. Billy, when I was at college I played tennis; in tennis, love means nothing. It is the same here. Let us go to sleep again. Great Greeley! — without a *sou* — without a *sou!*"

Turning over, they went to sleep again.

1895

RODRIGUES OTTOLENGUI

THE NAMELESS MAN and THE MONTEZUMA EMERALD

Strangely unread and forgotten in the mystery world, (BENJAMIN ADOLPH) RODRIGUES OTTOLENGUI (known as "Rod" to family and friends) (1861–1937) remains a familiar name in the field of dentistry, as he pioneered such significant advances as the early use of X-rays, created several methods of filling teeth, especially root canals, and developed methods to restore cleft palates. His book *Methods of Filling Teeth* (1892) was a standard textbook for several decades, and for nearly forty years he edited and wrote for a journal, *Items of Interest,* later retitled *Dental Items of Interest,* resulting in a book, *Table Talks on Dentistry* (1928). He also was one of the first writers of fiction to use the patterns of dental fillings as a way to identify a corpse.

Ottolengui wrote four novels and a short story collection featuring a professional private detective, John Barnes, and all but one also included Robert Leroy Mitchel, a wealthy amateur detective who often challenged his friend to solve crimes, most of which were of a humorous nature. The author largely "gave up the sleuth for the tooth," as the noted mystery critic Anthony Boucher once said, after his collection, *Final Proof,* was published in 1898, with only a half-dozen later stories appearing in magazines.

His first book, *An Artist in Crime* (1892), saw the two sleuths sometimes cooperating, sometimes competing, and was followed by *A Conflict of Evidence* (1893), *A Modern Wizard* (1894), and *The Crime of the Century* (1896), all of which included various forms of 1890s sensationalism and a dose of fantasy and science fiction. Ellery Queen described Ottolengui as "one of the most neglected authors in the entire history of the detective story" in *Queen's Quorum,* his important book detailing the 106 most important short story collections in the history of detective fiction, and included *Final Proof* in that list. Two stories are included in this anthology to establish the interesting and unusual relationship between the two sleuths.

"The Nameless Man" was first published in England in the January 1895 issue of *The Idler.* "The Montezuma Emerald" was first published in the February

1895 issue of *The Idler.* Both stories were first collected in *Final Proof* (New York: G. P. Putnam's Sons, 1898).

• • •

THE NAMELESS MAN

Mr. Barnes was sitting in his private room, with nothing of special importance to occupy his thoughts, when his office boy announced a visitor.

"What name?" asked Mr. Barnes.

"None!" was the reply.

"You mean," said the detective, "that the man did not give you his name. He must have one, of course. Show him in."

A minute later the stranger entered, and, bowing courteously, began the conversation at once.

"Mr. Barnes, the famous detective, I believe?" said he.

"My name is Barnes," replied the detective. "May I have the pleasure of knowing yours?"

"I sincerely hope so," continued the stranger. "The fact is, I suppose I have forgotten it."

"Forgotten your name?" Mr. Barnes scented an interesting case, and became doubly attentive.

"Yes!" said the visitor. "That is precisely my singular predicament. I seem to have lost my identity. That is the object of my call. I wish you to discover who I am. As I am evidently a full-grown man, I can certainly claim that I have a past history, but to me that past is entirely blank. I awoke this morning in this condition, yet apparently in possession of all my faculties, so much so that I at once saw the advisability of consulting a first-class detective, and, upon inquiry, I was directed to you."

"Your case is most interesting—from my point of view, I mean. To you, of course, it must seem unfortunate. Yet it is not unparalleled. There have been many such cases recorded, and, for your temporary relief, I may say that sooner or later, complete restoration of memory usually occurs. But now, let us try to unravel your mystery as soon as possible, that you may suffer as little inconvenience as there need be. I would like to ask you a few questions."

"As many as you like, and I will do my best to answer."

"Do you think that you are a New Yorker?"

"I have not the least idea whether I am or not."

"You say you were advised to consult me. By whom?"

"The clerk at the Waldorf Hotel, where I slept last night."

"Then, of course, he gave you my address. Did you find it necessary to ask him how to find my offices?"

"Well, no, I did not. That seems strange, does it not? I certainly had no difficulty in coming here. I suppose that must be a significant fact, Mr. Barnes?"

"It tends to show that you have been familiar with New York, but we must still find out whether you live here or not. How did you register at the hotel?"

"M.J.G. Remington, City."

"You are quite sure that Remington is not your name?"

"Quite sure. After breakfast this morning I was passing through the lobby when the clerk called me twice by that name. Finally, one of the hall-boys touched me on the shoulder and explained that I was wanted at the desk. I was very much confused to find myself called 'Mr. Remington,' a name which certainly is not my own. Before I fully realized my position, I said to the clerk, 'Why do you call me Remington?' and he replied, 'Because you registered under that name.' I tried to pass it off, but I am sure that the clerk looks upon me as a suspicious character."

"What baggage have you with you at the hotel?"

"None. Not even a satchel."

"May there not be something in your pockets that would help us; letters, for example?"

"I am sorry to say that I have made a search in that direction, but found nothing. Luckily I did have a pocketbook, though."

"Much money in it?"

"In the neighborhood of five hundred dollars."

Mr. Barnes turned to his table and made a few notes on a pad of paper. While he was so engaged his visitor took out a fine gold watch, and, after a glance at the face, was about to return it to his pocket when Mr. Barnes wheeled around in his chair, and said:

"That is a handsome watch you have there. Of a curious pattern too. I am rather interested in old watches."

The stranger seemed confused for an instant, and quickly put up his watch, saying:

"There is nothing remarkable about it. Merely an old family relic. I value it more for that than anything else. But about my case, Mr. Barnes; how long do you think it will take to restore my identity to me? It is rather awkward to go about under a false name."

"I should think so," said the detective. "I will do my best for you, but you have given me absolutely no clue to work upon, so that it is impossible to say what my success will be. Still I think forty-eight hours should suffice. At least in that time I ought to make some discoveries for you. Suppose you call again on the day after to-morrow, at noon precisely. Will that suit you?"

"Very well, indeed. If you can tell me who I am at that time I shall be more than convinced that you are a great detective, as I have been told."

He arose and prepared to go, and upon the instant Mr. Barnes touched a button under his table with his foot, which caused a bell to ring in a distant part of the building, no sound of which penetrated the private office. Thus anyone could visit Mr. Barnes in his den, and might leave unsuspicious of the fact that a spy would be awaiting him out in the street who would shadow him persistently day and night until recalled by his chief. After giving the signal, Mr. Barnes held his strange visitor in conversation a few moments longer to allow his spy opportunity to get to his post.

"How will you pass the time away, Mr. Remington?" said he. "We may as well call you by that name, until I find your true one."

"Yes, I suppose so. As to what I shall do during the next forty-eight hours, why, I think I may as well devote myself to seeing the sights. It is a remarkably pleasant day for a stroll, and I think I will visit your beautiful Central Park."

"A capital idea. By all means, I would advise occupation of that kind. It would be best not to do any business until your memory is restored to you."

"Business. Why, of course, I can do no business."

"No. If you were to order any goods, for example, under the name of Remington, later on when you resume your proper identity, you might be arrested as an impostor."

"By George! I had not thought of that. My position is more serious than I had realized. I thank you for the warning. Sight-seeing will assuredly be my safest plan for the next two days."

"I think so. Call at the time agreed upon, and hope for the best. If I should need you before then, I will send to your hotel."

Then, saying "Good morning," Mr. Barnes turned to his desk again, and, as the stranger looked at him before stepping out of the room, the detective seemed engrossed with some papers before him. Yet scarcely had the door closed upon the retreating form of his recent visitor, when Mr. Barnes looked up, with an air of expectancy. A moment later a very tiny bell in a drawer of his desk rang, indicating that the man had left the building, the signal having been sent to him by one of his employees, whose business it was to watch all departures, and notify his chief. A few moments later Mr. Barnes himself emerged, clad in an entirely different suit of clothing, and with such an alteration in the color of his hair that more than a casual glance would have been required to recognize him.

When he reached the street the stranger was nowhere in sight, but Mr. Barnes went to a doorway opposite, and there he found, written in blue pencil, the word "up", whereupon he walked rapidly uptown as far as the next corner, where once more he examined a door-post, upon which he found the word "right," which indicated the way the men ahead of him had turned. Beyond this he could expect no signals, for the spy shadowing the stranger did not know positively that his chief would take part in the game. The two signals which he had written on the doors were merely a part of a routine, and intended to aid Mr. Barnes should he follow; but if he did so, he would be expected to be in sight of the spy by the time the second signal was reached. And so it proved in this instance, for as Mr. Barnes turned the corner to the right, he easily discerned his man about two blocks ahead, and presently was near enough to see "Remington" also.

The pursuit continued until Mr. Barnes was surprised to see him enter the Park, thus carrying out his intention as stated in his interview with the detective. Entering at the Fifth Avenue gate he made his way towards the menagerie, and here a curious incident occurred. The stranger had mingled with the crowd in the monkey-house, and was enjoying the antics of the mischievous little animals, when Mr. Barnes, getting close behind him, deftly removed a pocket-handkerchief from the tail of his coat and swiftly transferred it to his own.

On the day following, shortly before noon, Mr. Barnes walked quickly into the reading-room of the Fifth Avenue Hotel. In one corner there is a handsome mahogany cabinet, containing three compartments, each of which is entered through double doors, having glass panels in the upper half. About these panels are draped yellow silk curtains, and in the center of each appears a white porcelain numeral. These compartments are used as public telephone stations, the applicant being shut in, so as to be free from the noise of the outer room.

Mr. Barnes spoke to the girl in charge, and then passed into the compartment numbered "2." Less than five minutes later Mr. Leroy Mitchel came into the reading-room. His keen eyes peered about him, scanning the countenances of those busy with the papers or writing, and then he gave the telephone girl a number, and went into the compartment numbered "1." About ten minutes elapsed before Mr. Mitchel came out again, and, having paid the toll, he left the hotel. When Mr. Barnes emerged, there was an expression of extreme satisfaction upon his face. Without lingering, he also went out. But instead of following Mr. Mitchel through the main lobby to Broadway, he crossed the reading-room and reached Twenty-third Street through the side door. Thence he proceeded to the station of the elevated railroad, and went uptown. Twenty minutes later he was ringing the bell of Mr. Mitchel's residence. The "buttons" who answered his summons informed him that his master was not at home.

"He usually comes in to luncheon, however, does he not?" asked the detective.

"Yes, sir," responded the boy.

"Is Mrs. Mitchel at home?"

"No, sir."

"Miss Rose?"

"Yes, sir."

"Ah; then I'll wait. Take my card to her."

Mr. Barnes passed into the luxurious drawing-room, and was soon joined by Rose, Mr. Mitchel's adopted daughter.

"I am sorry papa is not at home, Mr. Barnes," said the little lady, "but he will surely be in to luncheon, if you will wait."

"Yes, thank you, I think I will. It is quite a trip up, and, being here, I may as well wait a while and see your father, though the matter is not of any great importance."

"Some interesting case, Mr. Barnes? If so, do tell me about it. You know I am almost as much interested in your cases as papa is."

"Yes, I know you are, and my vanity is flattered. But I am sorry to say I have nothing on hand at present worth relating. My errand is a very simple one. Your father was saying, a few days ago, that he was thinking of buying a bicycle, and yesterday, by accident, I came across a machine of an entirely new make, which seems to me superior to anything yet produced. I thought he might be interested to see it, before deciding what kind to buy."

"I am afraid you are too late, Mr. Barnes. Papa has bought a bicycle already."

"Indeed! What style did he choose?"

"I really do not know, but it is down in the lower hall, if you care to look at it."

"It is hardly worth while, Miss Rose. After all, I have no interest in the new model, and if your father has found something that he likes, I won't even mention the other to him. It might only make him regret his bargain. Still, on second thoughts, I will go down with you, if you will take me into the dining-room and show me the head of that moose which your father has been bragging about killing. I believe it has come back from the taxidermist's?"

"Oh, yes! He is just a monster. Come on!"

They went down to the dining-room, and Mr. Barnes expressed great admiration for the moose's head, and praised Mr. Mitchel's skill as a marksman. But he had taken a moment to scrutinize the bicycle which stood in the hallway, while Rose was opening the blinds in the dining-room. Then they returned to the drawing-room, and after a little more conversation Mr. Barnes departed, saying that he could not wait any longer, but he charged Rose to tell her father that he particularly desired him to call at noon on the following day.

Promptly at the time appointed, "Remington" walked into the office of Mr. Barnes, and was announced. The detective was in his private room. Mr. Leroy Mitchel had been admitted but a few moments before.

"Ask Mr. Remington in," said Mr. Barnes to his boy, and when that gentleman entered, before he could show surprise to find a third party present, the detective said:

"Mr. Mitchel, this is the gentleman whom I wish you to meet. Permit me to introduce to you Mr. Mortimer J. Goldie, better known to the sporting fraternity as G. J. Mortimer, the champion short-distance bicycle rider, who recently rode a mile in the phenomenal time of 1.56, on a three-lap track."

As Mr. Barnes spoke, he gazed from one to the other of his companions, with a half-quizzical, and wholly pleased expression on his face. Mr. Mitchel appeared much interested, but the newcomer was evidently greatly astonished. He looked blankly at Mr. Barnes a moment, then dropped into a chair with the query:

"How in the name of conscience did you find that out?"

"That much was not very difficult," replied the detective. "I can tell you much more; indeed, I can supply your whole past history, provided your memory has been sufficiently restored for you to recognize my facts as true."

Mr. Barnes looked at Mr. Mitchel, and winked one eye in a most suggestive manner, at which that gentleman burst out into hearty laughter, finally saying:

"We may as well admit that we are beaten, Goldie. Mr. Barnes has been too much for us."

"But I want to know how he has done it," persisted Mr. Goldie.

"I have no doubt that Mr. Barnes will gratify you. Indeed, I am as curious as you are to know by what means he has arrived at his quick solution of the problem which we set for him."

"I will enlighten you as to detective methods with pleasure," said Mr. Barnes. "Let me begin with the visit made to me by this gentleman two days ago. At the very outset his statement aroused my suspicion, though I did my best not to let him think so. He announced to me that he had lost his identity, and I promptly told him that his case was not uncommon. I said that in order that he might feel sure that I did not doubt his tale. But truly, his case, if he was telling the truth, was absolutely unique. Men have lost recollection of their past, and even have forgotten their names. But I have never before heard of a man who had forgotten his name, *and at the same time knew that he had done so.*"

"A capital point, Mr. Barnes," said Mr. Mitchel. "You were certainly shrewd to suspect fraud so early."

"Well, I cannot say that I suspected fraud so soon, but the story was so improbable that I could not believe it immediately. I therefore was what I might call 'analytically attentive' during the rest of the interview. The next point worth noting which came out was that, although he had forgotten himself, he had not forgotten New York, for he admitted having come to me without special guidance."

"I remember that," interrupted Mr. Goldie, "and I think I even said to you at the time that it was significant."

"And I told you that it at least showed that you had been familiar with New York. This was better proven when you said that you would spend the day at Central Park, and when, after leaving here, you had no difficulty in finding your way thither."

"Do you mean to say that you had me followed? I made sure that no one was after me."

"Well, yes, you were followed," said Mr. Barnes, with a smile. "I had a spy after you, and I followed you as far as the Park myself. But let me come to the other points in your interview and my deductions. You told me that you had registered as 'M.J.G. Remington.' This helped me considerably, as we shall see presently. A few minutes later you took out your watch, and in that little mirror over my desk, which I use occasionally when I turn my back upon a visitor, I noted that there was an inscription on the outside of the case. I turned and asked you something about the watch, when you hastily returned it to your pocket, with the remark that it was 'an old family relic.' Now can you explain how you could have known that, supposing that you had forgotten who you were?"

"Neatly caught, Goldie," laughed Mr. Mitchel. "You certainly made a mess of it there."

"It was an asinine slip," said Mr. Goldie, laughing also.

"Now then," continued Mr. Barnes, "you readily see that I had good reason for believing that you had not forgotten your name. On the contrary, I was positive that your name was a part of the inscription on the watch. What, then, could be your purpose in pretending otherwise? I did not discover that for some time. However, I decided to go ahead, and find you out if I could. Next I noted two things. Your coat opened once, so that I saw, pinned to your vest, a bicycle badge, which I recognized as the emblem of the League of American Wheelmen."

"Oh! Oh!" cried Mr. Mitchel. "Shame on you, Goldie, for a blunderer."

"I had entirely forgotten the badge," said Mr. Goldie.

"I also observed," the detective went on, "little indentations on the sole of your shoe, as you had your legs crossed, which satisfied me that you were a rider even before I observed the badge. Now, then, we come to the name, and the significance thereof. Had you really lost your memory, the choosing of a name when you registered at a hotel would have been a haphazard matter of no importance to me. But as soon as I decided that you were imposing upon me, I knew that your choice of a name had been a deliberate act of the mind; one from which deductions could be drawn."

"Ah! Now we come to the interesting part," said Mr. Mitchel. "I love to follow a detective when he uses his brains."

"The name as registered, and I examined the registry to make sure, was odd. Three initials are unusual. A man without memory, and therefore not quite sound mentally, would hardly have chosen so many. Then why had it been done in this instance? What more natural than that these initials represented the true name? In assuming an alias, it is the most common method to transpose the real name in some way. At least it was a working hypothesis. Then the last name might be very significant. 'Remington.' The Remingtons make guns, sewing-machines, typewriters, and bicycles. Now, this man was a bicycle rider, I was sure. If he chose his own initials as a part of the alias, it was possible that he selected 'Remington' because it was familiar to him. I even imagined that he might be an agent for Remington bicycles, and I had arrived at that point during our interview, when I advised him not to buy anything until his identity was restored. But I was sure of my quarry when I stole a handkerchief from him at the park, and found the initials 'M.J.G.' upon the same."

"Marked linen on your person!" exclaimed Mr. Mitchel. "Worse and worse! We'll never make a successful criminal of you, Goldie."

"Perhaps not! I shan't cry over it."

"I felt sure of my success by this time," continued Mr. Barnes, "yet at the very next step I was balked. I looked over a list of L.A.W. members and could not find a name to fit my initials, which shows, as you will see presently, that, as I may say, 'too many clues spoil the broth.' Without the handkerchief I would have done better. Next I secured a catalogue of the Remingtons, which gave a list of their authorized agents, and again I failed. Returning to my office I received information from my spy, sent in by messenger, which promised to open a way for me. He had followed you about, Mr. Goldie, and I must say you played your part very well, so far as avoiding acquaintances is concerned. But at last you went to a public telephone, and called up someone. My man saw the importance of discovering to whom you had spoken, and bribed the telephone attendant to give him the information. All that he learned, however, was that you had spoken to the public station at the Fifth Avenue Hotel. My spy thought that this was inconsequent, but it proved to me at once that there was collusion, and that your man must have been at the other station by previous appointment. As that was at noon, a few minutes before the same hour on the following day, that is to say, yesterday, I went to the Fifth Avenue Hotel telephone and secreted myself in the middle compartment, hoping to hear what your partner might say to you. I failed in this, as the boxes are too well made to permit sound to pass from one to the other; but imagine my gratification to see Mr. Mitchel himself go into the box."

"And why?" asked Mr. Mitchel.

"Why, as soon as I saw you, I comprehended the whole scheme. It was you who had concocted the little diversion to test my ability. Thus, at last, I understood the reason for the pretended loss of identity. With the knowledge that you were in it, I was more than ever determined to get at the facts. Knowing that you were out, I hastened to your house, hoping for a chat with little Miss Rose, as the most likely member of your family to get information from."

"Oh, fie! Mr. Barnes," said Mr. Mitchel, "to play upon the innocence of childhood! I am ashamed of you!"

" 'All's fair,' etc. Well, I succeeded. I found Mr. Goldie's bicycle in your hallway, and, as I suspected, it was a Remington. I took the number and hurried down to the agency, where I readily discovered that wheel no. 5086 is ridden by G. J. Mortimer, one of their regular racing team. I also learned that Mortimer's private name is Mortimer J. Goldie. I was much pleased at this, because it showed how good my reasoning had been about the alias, for you observe that the racing name is merely a transposition of the family name. The watch, of course, is a prize, and the inscription would have proved that you were imposing upon me, Mr. Goldie, had you permitted me to see it."

"Of course; that was why I put it back in my pocket."

"I said just now," said Mr. Barnes, "that without the stolen handkerchief I would have done better. Having it, when I looked over the L.A.W. list I went through the 'G's' only. Without it, I should have looked through the 'G's,' 'J's,' and 'M's,' not knowing how the letters may have been transposed. In that case I should have found 'G. J. Mortimer,' and the initials would have proved that I was on the right track."

"You have done well, Mr. Barnes," said Mr. Mitchel. "I asked Goldie to play the part of a nameless man for a few days, to have some fun with you. But you have had fun with us, it seems. Though, I am conceited enough to say, that had it been possible for me to play the principal part, you would not have pierced my identity so soon."

"Oh, I don't know," said Mr. Barnes. "We are both of us a little egotistical, I fear."

"Undoubtedly. Still, if I ever set another trap for you, I will assign myself the chief *rôle.*"

"Nothing would please me better," said Mr. Barnes. "But, gentlemen, as you have lost in this little game, it seems to me that someone owes me a dinner, at least."

"I'll stand the expense with pleasure," said Mr. Mitchel.

"Not at all," interrupted Mr. Goldie. "It was through my blundering that we lost, and I'll pay the piper."

"Settle it between you," cried Mr. Barnes. "But let us walk on. I am getting hungry."

Whereupon they adjourned to Delmonico's.

THE MONTEZUMA EMERALD

"IS THE INSPECTOR IN?"

Mr. Barnes immediately recognized the voice, and turned to greet the speaker. The man was Mr. Leroy Mitchel's English valet. Contrary to all precedent and tradition, he did not speak in cockney dialect, not even stumbling over the proper distribution of the letter "h" throughout his vocabulary. That he was English, however, was apparent to the ear, because of a certain rather attractive accent, peculiar to his native island, and to the eye because of a deferential politeness of manner, too seldom observed in American servants. He also always called Mr. Barnes "Inspector," oblivious of the fact that he was not a member of the regular police, and mindful only of the English application of the word to detectives.

"Step right in, Williams," said Mr. Barnes. "What is the trouble?"

"I don't rightly know, Inspector," said Williams. "Won't you let me speak to you alone? It's about the master."

"Certainly. Come into my private room." He led the way and Williams followed, remaining standing, although Mr. Barnes waved his hand towards a chair as he seated himself in his usual place at his desk. "Now then," continued the detective, "what's wrong? Nothing serious, I hope?"

"I hope not, sir, indeed! But the master's disappeared."

"Disappeared, has he!" Mr. Barnes smiled slightly. "Now, Williams, what do you mean by that? You did not see him vanish, eh?"

"No, sir, of course not. If you'll excuse my presumption, Inspector, I don't think this is a joke, sir, and you're laughing."

"All right, Williams," answered Mr. Barnes, assuming a more serious tone. "I will give your tale my sober consideration. Proceed!"

"Well, I hardly know where to begin, Inspector. But I'll just give you the facts, without any unnecessary opinions of my own."

Williams rather prided himself upon his ability to tell what he called "a straight story". He placed his hat on a chair, and, standing behind it, with one foot resting on a rung, checked off the points of his narrative, as he made them, by tapping the palm of one hand with the index finger of the other.

"To begin then," said he. "Mrs. Mitchel and Miss Rose sailed for England, Wednesday morning of last week. That same night, quite unexpected, the master says to me, says he, 'Williams, I think you have a young woman you're sweet on down at Newport?' 'Well, sir,' says I, 'I do know a person as answers that description,' though I must say to you, Inspector, that how he ever came to know it beats me. But that's aside, and digression is not my habit. 'Well, Williams,' the master went on, 'I shan't need you for the rest of this week, and if you'd like to take a trip to the seashore, I shan't mind standing the expense, and letting you go.' Of course, I thanked him very much, and I went, promising to be back on Monday morning as directed. And I kept my word, Inspector; though it was a hard wrench to leave the young person last Sunday in time to catch the boat; the moon being bright and everything most propitious for a stroll, it being her Sunday off and all that. But as I said, I kept my word, and was up to the house Monday morning only a little after seven, the boat having got in at six. I was a little surprised to find the master was not at home, but then it struck me as how he must have gone out of town over Sunday, and I looked for him to be in for dinner. But he did not come to dinner, nor at all that night. Still, I did not worry about it. It was the master's privilege to stay away as long as he liked. Only I could not help thinking I might just as well have had that stroll in the moonlight, Sunday night. But when all Tuesday and Tuesday night went by, and no word from the master, I must confess that I got uneasy; and now here's Wednesday noon, and no news; so I just took the liberty to come down and ask your opinion in the matter, seeing as how you are a particular friend of the family, and an Inspector to boot."

"Really, Williams," said Mr. Barnes, "all I see in your story is that Mr. Mitchel, contemplating a little trip off somewhere with friends, let you go away. He expected to be back by Monday, but, enjoying himself, has remained longer."

"I hope that's all, sir, and I've tried to think so. But this morning I made a few investigations of my own, and I'm bound to say what I found don't fit that theory."

"Ah, you have some more facts. What are they?"

"One of them is this cablegram that I found only this morning under a book on the table in the library." He handed a blue paper to Mr. Barnes, who took it and read the following, on a cable blank:

> Emerald. Danger. Await letter.

For the first time during the interview, Mr. Barnes's face assumed a really serious expression. He studied the dispatch silently for a full minute, and then, without raising his eyes, said:

"What else?"

"Well, Inspector, I don't know that this has anything to do with the affair, but the master had a curious sort of jacket, made of steel links, so tight and so closely put together, that I've often wondered what it was for. Once I made so bold as to ask him, and he said, said he, 'Williams, if I had an enemy, it would be a good idea to wear that, because it would stop a bullet or a knife.' Then he laughed, and went on, 'Of course, I shan't need it for myself. I bought it when I was abroad once, merely as a curiosity.' Now, Inspector, that jacket's disappeared also."

"Are you quite sure?"

"I've looked from dining-room to garret for it. The master's derringer is missing, too. It's a mighty small affair. Could be held in the hand without being noticed, but it carries a nasty-looking ball."

"Very well, Williams, there may be something in your story. I'll look into the matter at once. Meanwhile, go home, and stay there so that I may find you if I want you."

"Yes, sir; I thank you for taking it up. It takes a load off my mind to know you're in charge, Inspector. If there's harm come to the master, I'm sure you'll track the party down. Good morning, sir!"

"Good morning, Williams."

After the departure of Williams, the detective sat still for several minutes, lost in thought. He was weighing two ideas. He seemed still to hear the words which Mr. Mitchel had uttered after his success in unraveling the mystery of Mr. Goldie's lost identity. "Next time I will assign myself the chief *rôle,*" or words to that effect, Mr. Mitchel had said. Was this disappearance a new riddle for Mr. Barnes to solve? If so, of course, he would undertake it, as a sort of challenge which his professional pride could not reject. On the other hand, the cable dispatch and the missing coat of mail might portend ominously. The detective felt that Mr. Mitchel was somewhat in the position of the fabled boy who cried "Wolf!" so often that, when at last the wolf really appeared, no assistance was sent to him. Only Mr. Barnes decided that he must chase the "wolf," whether it be real or imaginary. He wished, though, that he knew which.

Ten minutes later he decided upon a course of action, and proceeded to a telegraph office, where he found that, as he had supposed, the dispatch had come from the Paris firm of jewelers from which Mr. Mitchel had frequently bought gems. He sent a lengthy message to them, asking for an immediate reply.

While waiting for the answer, the detective was not inactive. He went direct to Mr. Mitchel's house, and once more questioned the valet, from whom he obtained an accurate description of the clothes which his master must have worn, only one suit being absent. This fact alone seemed significantly against the theory of a visit to friends out of town. Next, Mr. Barnes interviewed the neighbors, none of whom remembered to have seen Mr. Mitchel during the week. At the sixth house below, however, he learned something definite. Here he found Mr. Mordaunt, a personal acquaintance, and member of one of Mr. Mitchel's clubs. This gentleman stated that he had dined at the club with Mr. Mitchel on the previous Thursday, and had accompanied him home, in the neighborhood of eleven o'clock, parting with him at the door of his own residence. Since then he had neither seen nor heard from him. This proved that Mr. Mitchel was at home one day after Williams went to Newport.

Leaving the house, Mr. Barnes called at the nearest telegraph office and asked whether a messenger summons had reached them during the week, from Mr. Mitchel's house. The record slips showed that the last call had been received at 12.30 A.M. on Friday. A cab had been demanded, and was sent, reaching the house at one o'clock. At the stables, Mr. Barnes questioned the cab-driver, and learned that Mr. Mitchel had alighted at Madison Square.

"But he got right into another cab," added the driver. "It was just a chance I seen him, 'cause he made as if he was goin' into the Fifth Avenoo; but luck was agin' him, for I'd scarcely gone two blocks back, when I had to get down to fix my harness, and while I was doin' that, who should I see but my fare go by in another cab."

"You did not happen to know the driver of that vehicle?" suggested Mr. Barnes.

"That's just what I did happen to know. He's always by the Square, along the curb by the Park. His name's Jerry. You'll find him easy enough, and he'll tell you where he took that fly bird."

Mr. Barnes went downtown again, and did find Jerry, who remembered driving a man at the stated time, as far as the Imperial Hotel; but beyond that the detective learned nothing, for at the hotel no one knew Mr. Mitchel, and none recollected his arrival early Friday morning.

From the fact that Mr. Mitchel had changed cabs, and doubled on his track, Mr. Barnes concluded that he was after all merely hiding away for the pleasure of baffling him, and he felt much relieved to divest the case of its alarming aspect. However, he was not long permitted to hold this opinion. At the telegraph office he found a cable dispatch awaiting him, which read as follows:

> Montezuma Emerald forwarded Mitchel tenth. Previous owner murdered London eleventh. Mexican suspected. Warned Mitchel.

This assuredly looked very serious. Casting aside all thought of a practical joke, Mr. Barnes now threw himself heart and soul into the task of finding Mitchel, dead or alive. From the telegraph office he hastened to the Custom House, where he learned that an emerald, the invoiced value of which was no less than twenty thousand dollars, had been delivered to Mr. Mitchel in person, upon payment of the custom duties, at noon of the previous Thursday. Mr. Barnes, with this knowledge, thought he knew why Mr. Mitchel had been careful to have a friend accompany him to his home on that night. But why had he gone out again? Perhaps he felt safer at a hotel than at home, and, having reached the Imperial, taking two cabs to mystify the villain who might be tracking him, he might have registered under an alias. What a fool he had been not to examine the registry, as he could certainly recognize Mr. Mitchel's handwriting, though the name signed would of course be a false one.

Back, therefore, he hastened to the Imperial, where, however, his search for familiar chirography was fruitless. Then an idea occurred to him. Mr. Mitchel was so shrewd that it would not be unlikely that, meditating a disappearance to baffle the men on his track, he had registered at the hotel several days prior to his permanently stopping there. Turning the page over, Mr. Barnes still failed to find what he sought, but a curious name caught his eye.

Miguel Palma — City of Mexico.

Could this be the London murderer? Was this the suspected Mexican? If so, here was a bold and therefore dangerous criminal who openly put up at one of the most prominent hostelries. Mr. Barnes was turning this over in his mind, when a diminutive newsboy rushed into the corridor, shouting:

"Extra *Sun!* Extra *Sun!* All about the horrible murder. Extra!"

Mr. Barnes purchased a paper and was stupefied at the headlines.

ROBERT LEROY MITCHEL DROWNED!
His Body Found Floating in the East River.
A DAGGER IN HIS BACK
Indicates Murder.

Mr. Barnes rushed out of the hotel, and, quickly finding a cab, instructed the man to drive rapidly to the Morgue. On the way, he read the details of the crime as recounted in the newspaper. From this he gathered that the body had been discovered early that morning by two boatmen, who towed it to shore and handed it over to the police. An examination at the Morgue had established the identity by letters found on the corpse and the initials marked on the clothing. Mr. Barnes was sad at heart, and inwardly fretted because his friend had not asked his aid when in danger.

Jumping from the cab almost before it had fully stopped in front of the Morgue, he stumbled and nearly fell over a decrepit-looking beggar, upon whose breast was a printed card soliciting alms for the blind. Mr. Barnes dropped a coin, a silver quarter, into his outstretched palm, and hurried into the building. As he did so he was jostled by a tall man who was coming out, and who seemed to have lost his temper, as he muttered an imprecation under his breath in Spanish. As the detective's keen ear noted the foreign tongue an idea occurred to him which made him turn and follow the stranger. When he reached the street again he received a double surprise. The stranger had already signaled the cab which Mr. Barnes had but just left, and was entering it, so that he had only a moment in which to observe him. Then the door was slammed, and the driver whipped up his horses and drove rapidly away. At the same moment the blind beggar jumped up, and ran in the direction taken by the cab. Mr. Barnes watched them till both cab and beggar disappeared around the next corner, and then he went into the building again, deeply thinking over the episode.

He found the Morgue-keeper, and was taken to the corpse. He recognized the clothing at once, both from the description given by Williams, and because he now remembered to have seen Mr. Mitchel so dressed. It was evident that the body had been in the water for several days, and the marks of violence plainly pointed to murder. Still sticking in the back was a curious dagger of foreign make, the handle projecting between the shoulders. The blow must have been a powerful stroke, for the blade was so tightly wedged in the bones of the spine that it resisted ordinary efforts to withdraw it. Moreover, the condition of the head showed that a crime had been committed, for the skull and face had been beaten into a pulpy mass with some heavy instrument. Mr. Barnes turned away from the sickening sight to examine the letters found upon the corpse. One of these bore the Paris postmark, and he was allowed to read it. It was from the jewelers, and was the letter alluded to in the warning cable. Its contents were:

Dear Sir—

As we have previously advised you, the Montezuma Emerald was shipped to you on the tenth instant. On the following day the man from whom we had bought it was found dead in Dover Street, London, killed by a dagger-thrust between the shoulders. The meagre accounts telegraphed to the papers here, state that there is no clue to the assassin. We were struck by the name, and remembered that the deceased had urged us to buy the emerald, because, as he declared, he feared that a man had followed him from Mexico, intending to murder him to get possession of it. Within an hour of reading the newspaper story, a gentlemanly-looking man, giving the name of Miguel Palma, entered our store, and asked if we had purchased the Montezuma Emerald. We replied negatively, and he smiled and left. We notified the police, but they have not yet been able to find this man. We deemed it our duty to warn you, and did so by cable.

The signature was that of the firm from which Mr. Barnes had received the cable in the morning. The plot seemed plain enough now. After the fruitless murder of the man in London, the Mexican had traced the emerald to Mr. Mitchel, and had followed it across the water. Had he succeeded in obtaining it? Among the things found on the corpse was an empty jewel-case, bearing the name of the Paris firm. It seemed from this that the gem had been stolen. But if so, this man, Miguel Palma, must be made to explain his knowledge of the affair.

Once more visiting the Imperial, Mr. Barnes made inquiry, and was told that Mr. Palma had left the hotel on the night of the previous Thursday, which was just a few hours before Mr. Mitchel had undoubtedly reached there alive. Could it be that the man at the Morgue had been he? If so, why was he visiting that place to view the body of his victim? This was a problem over which Mr. Barnes puzzled, as he was driven up to the residence of Mr. Mitchel. Here he found Williams, and imparted to that faithful servant the news of his master's death, and then inquired for the address of the family abroad, that he might notify them by cable, before they could read the bald statement in a newspaper.

"As they only sailed a week ago to-day," said Williams, "they're hardly more than due in London. I'll go up to the master's desk and get the address of his London bankers."

As Williams turned to leave the room, he started back amazed at the sound of a bell.

"That's the master's bell, Inspector! Someone is in his room! Come with me!"

The two men bounded upstairs, two steps at a time, and Williams threw open the door of Mr. Mitchel's boudoir, and then fell back against Mr. Barnes, crying:

"The master himself!"

Mr. Barnes looked over the man's shoulder, and could scarcely believe his eyes when he observed Mr. Mitchel, alive and well, brushing his hair before a mirror.

"I've rung for you twice, Williams," said Mr. Mitchel, and then, seeing Mr. Barnes, he added, "Ah, Mr. Barnes! You are very welcome. Come in. Why, what is the matter, man? You are as white as though you had seen a ghost."

"Thank God you are safe!" fervently ejaculated the detective, going forward and grasping Mr. Mitchel's hand. "Here, read this, and you will understand." He drew out the afternoon paper and handed it to him.

"Oh, that," said Mr. Mitchel, carelessly. "I've read that. Merely a sensational lie, worked off upon a guileless public. Not a word of truth in it, I assure you."

"Of course not, since you are alive; but there is a mystery about this which is yet to be explained."

"What? A mystery, and the great Mr. Barnes has not solved it? I am surprised. I am, indeed. But then, you know, I told you after Goldie made a fizzle of our little joke that if I should choose to play the principal part you would not catch me. You see, I have beaten you this time. Confess. You thought that was my corpse which you gazed upon at the Morgue?"

"Well," said Mr. Barnes reluctantly, "the identification certainly seemed complete, in spite of the condition of the face, which made recognition impossible."

"Yes; I flatter myself the whole affair was artistic."

"Do you mean that this whole thing is nothing but a joke? That you went so far as to invent cables and letters from Paris just for the trifling amusement of making a fool of me?"

Mr. Barnes was evidently slightly angry, and Mr. Mitchel, noting this fact, hastened to mollify him.

"No! No! It is not quite so bad as that," he said. "I must tell you the whole story, for there is yet important work to do, and you must help me. No, Williams, you need not go out. Your anxiety over my absence entitles you to a knowledge of the truth. A short time ago I heard that a very rare gem was in the market, no less a stone than the original emerald which Cortez stole from the crown of Montezuma. The emerald was offered in Paris, and I was notified at once by the dealer, and authorized the purchase by cable. A few days later I received a dispatch warning me that there was danger. I understood at once, for similar danger has lurked about other large stones which are now in my collection. The warning meant that I should not attempt to get the emerald from the Custom House until further advices reached me, which would indicate the exact nature of the danger. Later, I received the letter which was found on the body now at the Morgue, and which I suppose you have read?"

Mr. Barnes nodded assent.

"I readily located the man Palma at the Imperial, and from his openly using his name I knew that I had a dangerous adversary. Criminals who disdain aliases have brains, and use them. I kept away from the Custom House until I had satisfied myself that I was being dogged by a veritable cutthroat, who, of course, was the tool hired by Palma to rob, perhaps to kill me. Thus acquainted with my adversaries, I was ready for the enterprise."

"Why did you not solicit my assistance?" asked Mr. Barnes.

"Partly because I wanted all the glory, and partly because I saw a chance to make you admit that I am still the champion detective-baffler. I sent my wife and daughter to Europe that I might have time for my scheme. On the day after their departure I boldly went to the Custom House and obtained the emerald. Of course I was dogged by the hireling, but I had arranged a plan which gave him no advantage over me. I had constructed a pair of goggles which looked like simple smoked glasses, but in one of these I had a little mirror so arranged that I could easily watch the man behind me, should he approach too near. However, I was sure that he would not attack me in a crowded thoroughfare, and I kept in crowds until time for dinner, when, by appointment, I met my neighbor Mordaunt, and remained in his company until I reached my own doorway late at night. Here he left me, and I stood on the stoop until he disappeared into his own house. Then I turned, and apparently had much trouble to place my latch-key in the lock. This offered the assassin the chance he had hoped for, and, gliding stealthily forward, he made a vicious stab at me. But, in the first place, I had put on a chain-armor vest, and, in the second, expecting the attack to occur just as it did, I turned swiftly and with one blow with a club I knocked the weapon from the fellow's hand, and with another I struck him over the head so that he fell senseless at my feet."

"Bravo!" cried Mr. Barnes. "You have a cool nerve."

"I don't know. I think I was very much excited at the crucial moment, but with my chain armor, a stout loaded club in one hand and a derringer in the other, I never was in any real danger. I took the man down to the wine cellar and locked him in one of the vaults. Then I called a cab, and went down to the Imperial, in search of Palma; but I was too late. He had vanished."

"So I discovered," interjected Mr. Barnes.

"I could get nothing out of the fellow in the cellar. Either he cannot or he will not speak English. So I have merely kept him a prisoner, visiting him at midnight only, to avoid Williams, and giving him rations for another day. Meanwhile, I disguised myself and looked for Palma. I could not find him. I had another card, however, and the time came at last to play it. I deduced from Palma's leaving the hotel on the very day when I took the emerald from the Custom House, that it was prearranged that his hireling should stick to me until he obtained the gem, and then meet him at some rendezvous, previously appointed. Hearing nothing during the past few days, he has perhaps thought that I had left the city, and that his man was still upon my track. Meanwhile I was perfecting my grand *coup*. With the aid of a physician, who is a confidential friend, I obtained a corpse from one of the hospitals, a man about my size, whose face we battered beyond description. We dressed him in my clothing, and fixed the dagger which I had taken from my would-be assassin so tightly in the backbone that it would not drop out. Then one night we took our dummy to the river and securely anchored it in the water. Last night I simply cut it loose and let it drift down the river."

"You knew of course that it would be taken to the Morgue," said Mr. Barnes.

"Precisely. Then I dressed myself as a blind beggar, posted myself in front of the Morgue, and waited."

"You were the beggar?" ejaculated the detective.

"Yes. I have your quarter, and shall prize it as a souvenir. Indeed, I made nearly four dollars during the day. Begging seems to be lucrative. After the newspapers got on the street with the account of my death, I looked for developments. Palma came in due time, and went in. I presume that he saw the dagger, which was placed there for his special benefit, as well as the empty jewel-case, and at once concluded that his man had stolen the gem, and meant to keep it for himself. Under these circumstances he would naturally be angry, and therefore less cautious, and more easily shadowed. Before he came out, you turned up and stupidly brought a cab, which allowed my man to get a start of me. However, I am a good runner, and as he only rode as far as Third Avenue, and then took the elevated railroad, I easily followed him to his lair. Now I will explain to you what I wish you to do, if I may count on you?"

"Assuredly."

"You must go into the street, and when I release the man in the cellar, you must track him. I will go to the other place, and we will see what happens when the men meet. We will both be there to see the fun."

An hour later, Mr. Barnes was skillfully dogging a sneaking Mexican, who walked rapidly through one of the lowest streets on the East Side, until finally he dodged into a blind alley, and before the detective could make sure which of the many doors had allowed him ingress, he had disappeared. A moment later a low whistle attracted his attention, and across in a doorway he saw a figure which beckoned to him. He went over and found Mr. Mitchel.

"Palma is here. I have seen him. You see I was right. This is the place of appointment, and the cutthroat has come here straight. Hush! What was that?"

There was a shriek, followed by another, and then silence.

"Let us go up," said Mr. Barnes. "Do you know which door?"

"Yes; follow me."

Mr. Mitchel started across, but just as they reached the door, footsteps were heard rapidly descending the stairs. Both men stood aside and waited. A minute later a cloaked figure bounded out, only to be gripped instantly by those in hiding. It was Palma, and he fought like a demon, but the long, powerful arms of Mr. Barnes encircled him, and, with a hug that would have made a bear envious, the scoundrel was soon subdued. Mr. Barnes then manacled him, while Mr. Mitchel ascended the stairs to see about the other man. He lay sprawling on the floor, face downward, stabbed in the heart.

1895

ANNA KATHARINE GREEN

THE DOCTOR, HIS WIFE, AND THE CLOCK

Known variously as the mother, grandmother, and godmother of the American detective story, ANNA KATHARINE GREEN (ROHLFS) (1846–1935) has popularly and famously been credited with writing the first American detective novel by a woman, *The Leavenworth Case* (1878). The fact that her novel was preceded by *The Dead Letter* in 1866, written by Seeley Register (the nom de plume of Mrs. Metta Victoria Fuller Victor), is significant only to historians and pedants, as *The Dead Letter* sank without a trace, while *The Leavenworth Case* became one of the best-selling detective novels of the nineteenth century.

That landmark novel introduced Ebenezer Gryce, a stolid, competent, and colorless policeman who bears many of the characteristics of Charles Dickens's Inspector Bucket (from *Bleak House,* 1852–1853) and Wilkie Collins's Sergeant Cuff (from *The Moonstone,* 1868). Gryce, dignified and gentle, inspires confidence even in those he interrogates. Unlike many of the detectives who appeared in later works, such as Sherlock Holmes, Hercule Poirot, and, well, most every other literary crime fighter who followed in his footsteps, he appears to have no idiosyncrasies.

The enormous success of Gryce and *The Leavenworth Case* induced Green to invent many more mysteries for him to solve, including *A Strange Disappearance* (1880), *Hand and Glove* (1883), and others; the last, *The Mystery of the Hasty Arrow* (1917), was published nearly forty years after the first.

Green was also one of the first authors to produce female detective protagonists, notably Violet Strange (in *The Golden Slipper and Other Problems for Violet Strange,* 1915) and Amelia Butterworth, who often worked with Gryce. She was of a higher social standing than the policeman, thereby giving him access to a level of society that otherwise might have presented difficulties.

The following story, related by Gryce, was selected for publication in the prestigious *The World's Great Detective Stories* (1928), selected by S. S. Van Dine, at the time the best-selling mystery writer in America.

"The Doctor, His Wife, and the Clock" was first published as a slim volume with no other stories in a short-lived series called the Autonym Library (New York: G. P. Putnam's Sons, 1895).

• • •

I.

On the 17th of July, 1851, a tragedy of no little interest occurred in one of the residences of the Colonnade in Lafayette Place.

Mr. Hasbrouck, a well-known and highly respected citizen, was attacked in his room by an unknown assailant, and shot dead before assistance could reach him. His murderer escaped, and the problem offered to the police was, how to identify this person who, by some happy chance or by the exercise of the most remarkable forethought, had left no traces behind him, or any clue by which he could be followed.

The affair was given to a young man, named Ebenezer Gryce, to investigate, and the story, as he tells it, is this:

When, sometime after midnight, I reached Lafayette Place, I found the block lighted from end to end. Groups of excited men and women peered from the open doorways, and mingled their shadows with those of the huge pillars which adorn the front of this picturesque block of dwellings.

The house in which the crime had been committed was near the center of the row, and, long before I reached it, I had learned from more than one source that the alarm was first given to the street by a woman's shriek, and secondly by the shouts of an old man-servant who had appeared, in a half-dressed condition, at the window of Mr. Hasbrouck's room, crying "Murder! murder!"

But when I had crossed the threshold, I was astonished at the paucity of the facts to be gleaned from the inmates themselves. The old servitor, who was the first to talk, had only this account of the crime to give.

The family, which consisted of Mr. Hasbrouck, his wife, and three servants, had retired for the night at the usual hour and under the usual auspices. At eleven o'clock the lights were all extinguished, and the whole household asleep, with the possible exception of Mr. Hasbrouck himself, who, being a man of large business responsibilities, was frequently troubled with insomnia.

Suddenly Mrs. Hasbrouck woke with a start. Had she dreamed the words that were ringing in her ears, or had they been actually uttered in her hearing? They were short, sharp words, full of terror and menace, and she had nearly satisfied herself that she had imagined them, when there came, from somewhere near the door, a sound she neither understood nor could interpret, but which filled her with inexplicable terror, and made her afraid to breathe, or even to stretch forth her hand towards her husband, whom she supposed to be sleeping at her side. At length another strange sound, which she was sure was not due to her imagination, drove her to make an attempt to rouse him, when she was horrified to find that she was alone in the bed, and her husband nowhere within reach.

Filled now with something more than nervous apprehension, she flung herself to the floor, and tried to penetrate, with frenzied glances, the surrounding darkness. But the blinds and shutters both having been carefully closed by Mr. Hasbrouck before retiring, she found this impossible, and she was about to sink in terror to the floor, when she heard a low gasp on the other side of the room, followed by the suppressed cry:

"God! what have I done!"

The voice was a strange one, but before the fear aroused by this fact could culminate in a shriek of dismay, she caught the sound of retreating footsteps, and, eagerly listening, she heard them descend the stairs and depart by the front door.

Had she known what had occurred — had there been no doubt in her mind as to what lay in the darkness on the other side of the room — it is likely that, at the noise caused by the closing front door, she would have made at once for the balcony that opened out from the window before which she was standing, and taken one look at the flying figure below. But her uncertainty as to what lay hidden from her by the darkness chained her feet to the floor, and there is no knowing when she would have moved, if a carriage had not at that moment passed down Astor Place, bringing with it a sense of companionship which broke the spell that held her, and gave her strength to light the gas, which was in ready reach of her hand.

As the sudden blaze illuminated the room, revealing in a burst the old familiar walls and well-known pieces of furniture, she felt for a moment as if released from some heavy nightmare and restored to the common experiences of life. But in another instant her former dread returned, and she found herself quaking at the prospect of passing around the foot of the bed into that part of the room which was as yet hidden from her eyes.

But the desperation which comes with great crises finally drove her from her retreat; and, creeping slowly forward, she cast one glance at the floor before her, when she found her worst fears realized by the sight of the dead body of her husband lying prone before the open doorway, with a bullet-hole in his forehead.

Her first impulse was to shriek, but, by a powerful exercise of will, she checked herself, and, ringing frantically for the servants who slept on the top-floor of the house, flew to the nearest window and endeavored to open it. But the shutters had been bolted so securely by Mr. Hasbrouck, in his endeavor to shut out light and sound, that by the time she had succeeded in unfastening them, all trace of the flying murderer had vanished from the street.

Sick with grief and terror, she stepped back into the room just as the three frightened servants descended the stairs. As they appeared in the open doorway, she pointed at her husband's inanimate form, and then, as if suddenly realizing in its full force the calamity which had befallen her, she threw up her arms, and sank forward to the floor in a dead faint.

The two women rushed to her assistance, but the old butler, bounding over the bed, sprang to the window, and shrieked his alarm to the street.

In the interim that followed, Mrs. Hasbrouck was revived, and the master's body laid decently on the bed; but no pursuit was made, nor any inquiries started likely to assist me in establishing the identity of the assailant.

Indeed, every one, both in the house and out, seemed dazed by the unexpected catastrophe, and as no one had any suspicions to offer as to the probable murderer, I had a difficult task before me.

I began, in the usual way, by inspecting the scene of the murder. I found nothing in the room, or in the condition of the body itself, which added an iota to the knowledge already obtained. That Mr. Hasbrouck had been in bed; that he had risen upon hearing a noise; and that he had been shot before reaching the door, were self-evident facts. But there was nothing to guide me further. The very simplicity of the circumstances caused a dearth of clues, which made the difficulty of procedure as great as any I ever encountered.

My search through the hall and down the stairs elicited nothing; and an investigation of the bolts and bars by which the house was secured, assured me that the assassin had either entered by the front door, or had already been secreted in the house when it was locked up for the night.

"I shall have to trouble Mrs. Hasbrouck for a short interview," I hereupon announced to the trembling old servitor, who had followed me like a dog about the house.

He made no demur, and in a few minutes I was ushered into the presence of the newly made widow, who sat quite alone, in a large chamber in the rear. As I crossed the threshold she looked up, and I encountered a good plain face, without the shadow of guile in it.

"Madam," said I, "I have not come to disturb you. I will ask two or three questions only, and then leave you to your grief. I am told that some words came from the assassin before he delivered his fatal shot. Did you hear these distinctly enough to tell me what they were?"

"I was sound asleep," said she, "and dreamt, as I thought, that a fierce, strange voice cried somewhere to some one: 'Ah! you did not expect *me!*' But I dare not say that these words were really uttered to my husband, for he was not the man to call forth hate, and only a man in the extremity of passion could address such an exclamation in such a tone as rings in my memory in connection with the fatal shot which woke me."

"But that shot was not the work of a friend," I argued. "If, as these words seem to prove, the assassin had some other motive than gain in his assault, then your husband had an enemy, though you never suspected it."

"Impossible!" was her steady reply, uttered in the most convincing tone. "The man who shot him was a common burglar, and, frightened at having been betrayed into murder, fled without looking for booty. I am sure I heard him cry out in terror and remorse: 'God! what have I done!' "

"Was that before you left the side of the bed?"

"Yes; I did not move from my place till I heard the front door close. I was paralyzed by my fear and dread."

"Are you in the habit of trusting to the security of a latch-lock only in the fastening of your front door at night? I am told that the big key was not in the lock, and that the bolt at the bottom of the door was not drawn."

"The bolt at the bottom of the door is never drawn. Mr. Hasbrouck was so good a man he never mistrusted any one. That is why the big lock was not fastened. The key, not working well, he took it some days ago to the locksmith, and when the latter failed to return it, he laughed, and said he thought no one would ever think of meddling with his front door."

"Is there more than one night-key to your house?" I now asked.

She shook her head.

"And when did Mr. Hasbrouck last use his?"

"To-night, when he came home from prayer-meeting," she answered, and burst into tears.

Her grief was so real and her loss so recent that I hesitated to afflict her by further questions. So returning to the scene of the tragedy, I stepped out upon the balcony which ran in front. Soft voices instantly struck my ears. The neighbors on either side were grouped in front of their own windows, and were exchanging the remarks natural under the circumstances. I paused, as in duty bound, and listened. But I heard nothing worth recording, and would have instantly re-entered the house, if I had not been impressed by the appearance of a very graceful woman who stood at my right. She was clinging to her husband, who was gazing at one of the pillars before him in a strange, fixed way which astonished me till he attempted to move, and then I saw that he was blind. Instantly I remembered that there lived in this row a blind doctor, equally celebrated for his skill and for his uncommon personal attractions, and, greatly interested not only in his affliction, but in the sympathy evinced for him by his young and affectionate wife, I stood still till I heard her say in the soft and appealing tones of love:

"Come in, Constant; you have heavy duties for to-morrow, and you should get a few hours' rest, if possible."

He came from the shadow of the pillar, and for one minute I saw his face with the lamplight shining full upon it. It was as regular of feature as a sculptured Adonis, and it was as white.

"Sleep!" he repeated, in the measured tones of deep but suppressed feeling. "Sleep! with murder on the other side of the wall!" And he stretched out his arms in a dazed way that insensibly accentuated the horror I myself felt of the crime which had so lately taken place in the room behind me.

She, noting the movement, took one of the groping hands in her own and drew him gently towards her.

"This way," she urged; and, guiding him into the house, she closed the window and drew down the shades, making the street seem darker by the loss of her exquisite presence.

This may seem a digression, but I was at the time a young man of thirty, and much under the dominion of woman's beauty. I was therefore slow in leaving the balcony, and persistent in my wish to learn something of this remarkable couple before leaving Mr. Hasbrouck's house.

The story told me was very simple. Dr. Zabriskie had not been born blind, but had become so after a grievous illness which had stricken him down soon after he received his diploma. Instead of succumbing to an affliction which would have daunted most men, he expressed his intention of practicing his profession, and soon became so successful in it that he found no difficulty in establishing himself in one of the best-paying quarters of the city. Indeed, his intuition seemed to have developed in a remarkable degree after his loss of sight, and he seldom, if ever, made a mistake in diagnosis. Considering this fact, and the personal attractions which gave him distinction, it was no wonder that he soon became a popular physician whose presence was a benefaction and whose word a law.

He had been engaged to be married at the time of his illness, and, when he learned what was likely to be its results, had offered to release the young lady from all obligation to him. But she would not be released, and they were married. This had taken place some five years previous to Mr. Hasbrouck's death, three of which had been spent by them in Lafayette Place.

So much for the beautiful woman next door.

There being absolutely no clue to the assailant of Mr. Hasbrouck, I naturally looked forward to the inquest for some evidence upon which to work. But there seemed to be no underlying facts to this tragedy. The most careful study into the habits and conduct of the deceased brought nothing to light save his general beneficence and rectitude, nor was there in his history or in that of his wife any secret or hidden obligation calculated to provoke any such act of revenge as murder. Mrs. Hasbrouck's surmise that the intruder was simply a burglar, and that she had rather imagined than heard the words that pointed to the shooting as a deed of vengeance, soon gained general credence. But, though the police worked long and arduously in this new direction, their efforts were without fruit, and the case bade fair to remain an unsolvable mystery.

But the deeper the mystery the more persistently does my mind cling to it, and some five months after the matter had been delegated to oblivion, I found myself starting suddenly from sleep, with these words ringing in my ears:

"*Who uttered the scream that gave the first alarm of Mr. Hasbrouck's violent death?*"

I was in such a state of excitement that the perspiration stood out on my forehead. Mrs. Hasbrouck's story of the occurrence returned to me, and I remembered as distinctly as if she were then speaking, that she had expressly stated that she did not scream when confronted by the sight of her husband's dead body. But someone had screamed, and that very loudly. Who was it, then? One of the maids, startled by the sudden summons from below, or someone else — some involuntary witness of the crime, whose testimony had been suppressed at the inquest, by fear or influence?

The possibility of having come upon a clue even at this late day, so fired my ambition, that I took the first opportunity of revisiting Lafayette Place. Choosing such persons as I thought most open to my questions, I learned that there were many who could testify to having heard a woman's shrill scream on that memorable night just prior to the alarm given by old Cyrus, but no one who could tell from whose lips it had come. One fact, however, was immediately settled. It had not been the result of the servant-women's fears. Both of the girls were positive that they had uttered no sound, nor had they themselves heard any, till Cyrus rushed to the window with his wild cries. As the scream, by whomever given, was uttered before they descended the stairs, I was convinced by these assurances that it had issued from one of the front windows, and not from the rear of the house, where their own rooms lay. Could it be that it had sprung from the adjoining dwelling, and that — My thoughts went no further, but I made up my mind to visit the Doctor's house at once.

It took some courage to do this, for the Doctor's wife had attended the inquest, and her beauty, seen in broad daylight, had worn such an aspect of mingled sweetness and dignity, that I hesitated to encounter it under any circumstances likely to disturb its pure serenity. But a clue, once grasped, cannot be lightly set aside by a true detective, and it would have taken more than a woman's frown to stop me at this point. So I rang Dr. Zabriskie's bell.

I am seventy years old now and am no longer daunted by the charms of a beautiful woman, but I confess that when I found myself in the fine reception parlor on the first floor, I experienced no little trepidation at the prospect of the interview which awaited me.

But as soon as the fine commanding form of the Doctor's wife crossed the threshold, I recovered my senses and surveyed her with as direct a gaze as my position allowed. For her aspect bespoke a degree of emotion that astonished me; and even before I spoke I perceived her to be trembling, though she was a woman of no little natural dignity and self-possession.

"I seem to know your face," she said, advancing courteously towards me, "but your name" — and here she glanced at the card she held in her hand — "is totally unfamiliar to me."

"I think you saw me some eighteen months ago," said I. "I am the detective who gave testimony at the inquest which was held over the remains of Mr. Hasbrouck."

I had not meant to startle her, but at this introduction of myself I saw her naturally pale cheek turn paler, and her fine eyes, which had been fixed curiously upon me, gradually sink to the floor.

"Great heaven!" thought I, "what is this I have stumbled upon!"

"I do not understand what business you can have with me," she presently remarked, with a show of gentle indifference that did not in the least deceive me.

"I do not wonder," I rejoined. "The crime which took place next door is almost forgotten by the community, and even if it were not, I am sure you would find it difficult to conjecture the nature of the question I have to put to you."

"I am surprised," she began, rising in her involuntary emotion and thereby compelling me to rise also. "How can you have any question to ask me on this subject? Yet if you have," she continued, with a rapid change of manner that touched my heart in spite of myself, "I shall, of course, do my best to answer you."

There are women whose sweetest tones and most charming smiles only serve to awaken distrust in men of my calling; but Mrs. Zabriskie was not of this number. Her face was beautiful, but it was also candid in its expression, and beneath the agitation which palpably disturbed her, I was sure there lurked nothing either wicked or false. Yet I held fast by the clue which I had grasped, as it were, in the dark, and without knowing whither I was tending, much less whither I was leading her, I proceeded to say:

"The question which I presume to put to you as the next-door neighbor of Mr. Hasbrouck, is this: Who was the woman who screamed out so loudly that the whole neighborhood heard her on the night of that gentleman's assassination?"

The gasp she gave answered my question in a way she little realized, and, struck as I was by the impalpable links that had led me to the threshold of this hitherto unsolvable mystery, I was about to press my advantage and ask another question, when she quickly started forward and laid her hand on my lips.

Astonished, I looked at her inquiringly, but her head was turned aside, and her eyes, fixed upon the door, showed the greatest anxiety. Instantly I realized what she feared. Her husband was entering the house, and she dreaded lest his ears should catch a word of our conversation.

Not knowing what was in her mind, and unable to realize the importance of the moment to her, I yet listened to the advance of her blind husband with an almost painful interest. Would he enter the room where we were, or would he pass immediately to his office in the rear? She seemed to wonder too, and almost held her breath as he neared the door, paused, and stood in the open doorway, with his ear turned towards us.

As for myself, I remained perfectly still, gazing at his face in mingled surprise and apprehension. For besides its beauty, which was of a marked order, as I have already observed, it had a touching expression which irresistibly aroused both pity and interest in the spectator. This may have been the result of his affliction, or it may have sprung from some deeper cause; but, whatever its source, this look in his face produced a strong impression upon me and interested me at once in his personality. Would he enter? Or would he pass on? Her look of silent appeal showed me in which direction her wishes lay, but while I answered her glance by complete silence, I was conscious in some indistinct way that the business I had undertaken would be better furthered by his entrance.

The blind have been often said to possess a sixth sense in place of the one they have lost. Though I am sure we made no noise, I soon perceived that he was aware of our presence. Stepping hastily forward he said, in the high and vibrating tone of restrained passion:

"Helen, are you here?"

For a moment I thought she did not mean to answer, but knowing doubtless from experience the impossibility of deceiving him, she answered with a cheerful assent, dropping her hand as she did so from before my lips.

He heard the slight rustle which accompanied the movement, and a look I found it hard to comprehend flashed over his features, altering his expression so completely that he seemed another man.

"You have someone with you," he declared, advancing another step but with none of the uncertainty which usually accompanies the movements of the blind. "Some dear friend," he went on, with an almost sarcastic emphasis and a forced smile that had little of gaiety in it.

The agitated and distressed blush which answered him could have but one interpretation. He suspected that her hand had been clasped in mine, and she perceived his thought and knew that I perceived it also.

Drawing herself up, she moved towards him, saying in a sweet womanly tone that to me spoke volumes:

"It is no friend, Constant, not even an acquaintance. The person whom I now present to you is an agent from the police. He is here upon a trivial errand which will be soon finished, when I will join you in your office."

I knew she was but taking a choice between two evils. That she would have saved her husband the knowledge of a detective's presence in the house, if her self-respect would have allowed it, but neither she nor I anticipated the effect which this presentation produced upon him.

"A police officer," he repeated, staring with his sightless eyes, as if, in his eagerness to see, he half hoped his lost sense would return. "He can have no trivial errand here; he has been sent by God Himself to—"

"Let me speak for you," hastily interposed his wife, springing to his side and clasping his arm with a fervor that was equally expressive of appeal and command. Then turning to me, she explained: "Since Mr. Hasbrouck's unaccountable death, my husband has been laboring under an hallucination which I have only to mention for you to recognize its perfect absurdity. He thinks—oh! do not look like that, Constant; you know it is an hallucination which must vanish the moment we drag it into broad daylight—that he—*he,* the best man in all the world, was himself the assailant of Mr. Hasbrouck."

Good God!

"I say nothing of the impossibility of this being so," she went on in a fever of expostulation. "He is blind, and could not have delivered such a shot even if he had desired to; besides, he had no weapon. But the inconsistency of the thing speaks for itself, and should assure him that his mind is unbalanced and that he is merely suffering from a shock that was greater than we realized. He is a physician and has had many such instances in his own practice. Why, he was very much attached to Mr. Hasbrouck! They were the best of friends, and though he insists that he killed him, he cannot give any reason for the deed."

At these words the Doctor's face grew stern, and he spoke like an automaton repeating some fearful lesson.

"I killed him. I went to his room and deliberately shot him. I had nothing against him, and my remorse is extreme. Arrest me, and let me pay the penalty of my crime. It is the only way in which I can obtain peace."

Shocked beyond all power of self-control by this repetition of what she evidently considered the unhappy ravings of a madman, she let go his arm and turned upon me in frenzy.

"Convince him!" she cried. "Convince him by your questions that he never could have done this fearful thing."

I was laboring under great excitement myself, for I felt my youth against me in a matter of such tragic consequence. Besides, I agreed with her that he was in a distempered state of mind, and I hardly knew how to deal with one so fixed in his hallucination and with so much intelligence to support it. But the emergency was great, for he was holding out his wrists in the evident expectation of my taking him into instant custody; and the sight was killing his wife, who had sunk on the floor between us, in terror and anguish.

"You say you killed Mr. Hasbrouck," I began. "Where did you get your pistol, and what did you do with it after you left his house?"

"My husband had no pistol; never had any pistol," put in Mrs. Zabriskie, with vehement assertion. "If I had seen him with such a weapon —"

"I threw it away. When I left the house, I cast it as far from me as possible, for I was frightened at what I had done, horribly frightened."

"No pistol was ever found," I answered, with a smile, forgetting for the moment that he could not see. "If such an instrument had been found in the street after a murder of such consequence it certainly would have been brought to the police."

"You forget that a good pistol is valuable property," he went on stolidly. "Someone came along before the general alarm was given; and seeing such a treasure lying on the sidewalk, picked it up and carried it off. Not being an honest man, he preferred to keep it to drawing the attention of the police upon himself."

"Hum, perhaps," said I; "but where did *you* get it? Surely you can tell where you procured such a weapon, if, as your wife intimates, you did not own one."

"I bought it that self-same night of a friend; a friend whom I will not name, since he resides no longer in this country. I —" He paused; intense passion was in his face; he turned towards his wife, and a low cry escaped him, which made her look up in fear.

"I do not wish to go into any particulars," said he. "God forsook me and I committed a horrible crime. When I am punished, perhaps peace will return to me and happiness to her. I would not wish her to suffer too long or too bitterly for my sin."

"Constant!" What love was in the cry! and what despair! It seemed to move him and turn his thoughts for a moment into a different channel.

"Poor child!" he murmured, stretching out his hands by an irresistible impulse towards her. But the change was but momentary, and he was soon again the stern and determined self-accuser. "Are you going to take me before a magistrate?" he asked. "If so, I have a few duties to perform which you are welcome to witness."

"I have no warrant," I said; "besides, I am scarcely the one to take such a responsibility upon myself. If, however, you persist in your declaration, I will communicate with my superiors, who will take such action as they think best."

"That will be still more satisfactory to me," said he; "for though I have many times contemplated giving myself up to the authorities, I have still much to do before I can leave my home and practice without injury to others. Good-day; when you want me, you will find me here."

He was gone, and the poor young wife was left crouching on the floor alone. Pitying her shame and terror, I ventured to remark that it was not an uncommon thing for a man to confess to a crime he had never committed, and assured her that the matter would be inquired into very carefully before any attempt was made upon his liberty.

She thanked me, and, slowly rising, tried to regain her equanimity; but the manner as well as the matter of her husband's self-condemnation was too overwhelming in its nature for her to recover readily from her emotions.

"I have long dreaded this," she acknowledged. "For months I have foreseen that he would make some rash communication or insane avowal. If I had dared, I would have consulted some physician about this hallucination of his; but he was so sane on other points that I hesitated to give my dreadful secret to the world. I kept hoping that time and his daily pursuits would have their effect and restore him to himself. But his illusion grows, and now I fear that nothing will ever convince him that he did not commit the deed of which he accuses himself. If he were not blind I would have more hope, but the blind have so much time for brooding."

"I think he had better be indulged in his fancies for the present," I ventured. "If he is laboring under an illusion it might be dangerous to cross him."

"*If?*" she echoed in an indescribable tone of amazement and dread. "Can you for a moment harbor the idea that he has spoken the truth?"

"Madam," I returned, with something of the cynicism of my later years, "what caused you to give such an unearthly scream just before this murder was made known to the neighborhood?"

She stared, paled, and finally began to tremble, not, as I now believe, at the insinuation latent in my words, but at the doubts which my question aroused in her own breast.

"Did I?" she asked; then with a great burst of candor, which seemed inseparable from her nature, she continued: "Why do I try to mislead you or deceive myself? I did give a shriek just before the alarm was raised next door; but it was not from any knowledge I had of a crime having been committed, but because I unexpectedly saw before me my husband whom I supposed to be on his way to Poughkeepsie. He was looking very pale and strange, and for a moment I thought I was beholding his ghost. But he soon explained his appearance by saying that he had fallen from the train and had been only saved by a miracle from being dismembered; and I was just bemoaning his mishap and trying to calm him and myself, when that terrible shout was heard next door of 'Murder! murder!' Coming so soon after the shock he had himself experienced, it quite unnerved him, and I think we can date his mental disturbance from that moment. For he began almost immediately to take a morbid interest in the affair next door, though it was weeks, if not months, before he let a word fall of the nature of those you have just heard. Indeed it was not till I repeated to him some of the expressions he was continually letting fall in his sleep, that he commenced to accuse himself of crime and talk of retribution."

"You say that your husband frightened you on that night by appearing suddenly at the door when you thought him on his way to Poughkeepsie. Is Dr. Zabriskie in the habit of thus going and coming alone at an hour so late as this must have been?"

"You forget that to the blind, night is less full of perils than the day. Often and often has my husband found his way to his patients' houses alone after midnight; but on this especial evening he had Harry with him. Harry was his driver, and always accompanied him when he went any distance."

"Well, then," said I, "all we have to do is to summon Harry and hear what he has to say concerning this affair. He surely will know whether or not his master went into the house next door."

"Harry has left us," she said. "Dr. Zabriskie has another driver now. Besides — (I have nothing to conceal from you) — Harry was not with him when he returned to the house that evening, or the Doctor would not have been without his portmanteau till the next day. Something — I have never known what—caused them to separate, and that is why I have no answer to give the Doctor when he accuses himself of committing a deed on that night which is wholly out of keeping with every other act of his life."

"And have you never questioned Harry why they separated and why he allowed his master to come home alone after the shock he had received at the station?"

"I did not know there was any reason for doing so till long after he left us."

"And when did he leave?"

"That I do not remember. A few weeks or possibly a few days after that dreadful night."

"And where is he now?"

"Ah, that I have not the least means of knowing. But," she suddenly cried, "what do you want of Harry? If he did not follow Dr. Zabriskie to his own door, he could tell us nothing that would convince my husband that he is laboring under an illusion."

"But he might tell us something which would convince us that Dr. Zabriskie was not himself after the accident, that he—"

"Hush!" came from her lips in imperious tones. "I will not believe that he shot Mr. Hasbrouck even if you prove him to have been insane at the time. How could he? My husband is blind. It would take a man of very keen sight to force himself into a house that was closed for the night, and kill a man in the dark at one shot."

"Rather," cried a voice from the doorway, "it is only a blind man who could do this. Those who trust to eyesight must be able to catch some glimpse of the mark they aim at, and this room, as I have been told, was without a glimmer of light. But the blind trust to sound, and as Mr. Hasbrouck spoke—"

"Oh!" burst from the horrified wife, "is there no one to stop him when he speaks like that?"

II.

When I related to my superiors the details of the foregoing interview, two of them coincided with the wife in thinking that Dr. Zabriskie was in an irresponsible condition of mind which made any statement of his questionable. But the third seemed disposed to argue the matter, and, casting me an inquiring look, seemed to ask what my opinion was on the subject. Answering him as if he had spoken, I gave my conclusion as follows: That whether insane or not, Dr. Zabriskie had fired the shot which terminated Mr. Hasbrouck's life.

It was the Inspector's own idea, but it was not shared in by the others, one of whom had known the Doctor for years. Accordingly they compromised by postponing all opinion till they had themselves interrogated the Doctor, and I was detailed to bring him before them the next afternoon.

He came without reluctance, his wife accompanying him. In the short time which elapsed between their leaving Lafayette Place and entering Headquarters, I embraced the opportunity of observing them, and I found the study equally exciting and interesting. His face was calm but hopeless, and his eye, which should have shown a wild glimmer if there was truth in his wife's hypothesis, was dark and unfathomable, but neither frenzied nor uncertain. He spoke but once and listened to nothing, though now and then his wife moved as if to attract his attention, and once even stole her hand toward his, in the tender hope that he would feel its approach and accept her sympathy. But he was deaf as well as blind; and sat wrapped up in thoughts which she, I know, would have given worlds to penetrate.

Her countenance was not without its mystery also. She showed in every lineament passionate concern and misery, and a deep tenderness from which the element of fear was not absent. But she, as well as he, betrayed that some misunderstanding, deeper than any I had previously suspected, drew its intangible veil between them and made the near proximity in which they sat, at once a heart-piercing delight and an unspeakable pain. What was this misunderstanding? And what was the character of the fear that modified her every look of love in his direction? Her perfect indifference to my presence proved that it was not connected with the position in which he had put himself towards the police by his voluntary confession of crime, nor could I thus interpret the expression of frantic question which now and then contracted her features, as she raised her eyes towards his sightless orbs, and strove to read, in his firm-set lips, the meaning of those assertions she could only ascribe to a loss of reason.

The stopping of the carriage seemed to awaken both from thoughts that separated rather than united them. He turned his face in her direction, and she, stretching forth her hand, prepared to lead him from the carriage, without any of that display of timidity which had been previously evident in her manner.

As his guide she seemed to fear nothing; as his lover, everything.

"There is another and a deeper tragedy underlying the outward and obvious one," was my inward conclusion, as I followed them into the presence of the gentlemen awaiting them.

Dr. Zabriskie's appearance was a shock to those who knew him; so was his manner, which was calm, straightforward, and quietly determined.

"I shot Mr. Hasbrouck," was his steady affirmation, given without any show of frenzy or desperation. "If you ask me why I did it, I cannot answer; if you ask me how, I am ready to state all that I know concerning the matter."

"But, Dr. Zabriskie," interposed his friend, "the why is the most important thing for us to consider just now. If you really desire to convince us that you committed the dreadful crime of killing a totally inoffensive man, you should give us some reason for an act so opposed to all your instincts and general conduct."

But the Doctor continued unmoved:

"I had no reason for murdering Mr. Hasbrouck. A hundred questions can elicit no other reply; you had better keep to the how."

A deep-drawn breath from the wife answered the looks of the three gentlemen to whom this suggestion was offered. "You see," that breath seemed to protest, "that he is not in his right mind."

I began to waver in my own opinion, and yet the intuition which has served me in cases as seemingly impenetrable as this, bade me beware of following the general judgment.

"Ask him to inform you how he got into the house," I whispered to Inspector D——, who sat nearest me.

Immediately the Inspector put the question I had suggested:

"By what means did you enter Mr. Hasbrouck's house at so late an hour as this murder occurred?"

The blind doctor's head fell forward on his breast, and he hesitated for the first and only time.

"You will not believe me," said he; "but the door was ajar when I came to it. Such things make crime easy; it is the only excuse I have to offer for this dreadful deed."

The front door of a respectable citizen's house ajar at half-past eleven at night. It was a statement that fixed in all minds the conviction of the speaker's irresponsibility. Mrs. Zabriskie's brow cleared, and her beauty became for a moment dazzling as she held out her hands in irrepressible relief towards those who were interrogating her husband. I alone kept my impassibility. A possible explanation of this crime had flashed like lightning across my mind; an explanation from which I inwardly recoiled, even while I was forced to consider it.

"Dr. Zabriskie," remarked the Inspector who was most friendly to him, "such old servants as those kept by Mr. Hasbrouck do not leave the front door ajar at twelve o'clock at night."

"Yet ajar it was," repeated the blind doctor, with quiet emphasis; "and finding it so, I went in. When I came out again, I closed it. Do you wish me to swear to what I say? If so, I am ready."

What could we reply? To see this splendid-looking man, hallowed by an affliction so great that in itself it called forth the compassion of the most indifferent, accusing himself of a cold-blooded crime, in tones that sounded dispassionate because of the will that forced their utterance, was too painful in itself for us to indulge in any unnecessary words. Compassion took the place of curiosity, and each and all of us turned involuntary looks of pity upon the young wife pressing so eagerly to his side.

"For a blind man," ventured one, "the assault was both deft and certain. Are you accustomed to Mr. Hasbrouck's house, that you found your way with so little difficulty to his bedroom?"

"I am accustomed —" he began.

But here his wife broke in with irrepressible passion:

"He is not accustomed to that house. He has never been beyond the first floor. Why, why do you question him? Do you not see —"

His hand was on her lips.

"Hush!" he commanded. "You know my skill in moving about a house; how I sometimes deceive those who do not know me into believing that I can see, by the readiness with which I avoid obstacles and find my way even in strange and untried scenes. Do not try to make them think I am not in my right mind, or you will drive me into the very condition you deprecate."

His face, rigid, cold, and set, looked like that of a mask. Hers, drawn with horror and filled with question that was fast taking the form of doubt, bespoke an awful tragedy from which more than one of us recoiled.

"Can you shoot a man dead without seeing him?" asked the Superintendent, with painful effort.

"Give me a pistol and I will show you," was the quick reply.

A low cry came from the wife. In a drawer near to every one of us there lay a pistol, but no one moved to take it out. There was a look in the Doctor's eye which made us fear to trust him with a pistol just then.

"We will accept your assurance that you possess a skill beyond that of most men," returned the Superintendent. And beckoning me forward, he whispered: "This is a case for the doctors and not for the police. Remove him quietly, and notify Dr. Southyard of what I say."

But Dr. Zabriskie, who seemed to have an almost supernatural acuteness of hearing, gave a violent start at this and spoke up for the first time with real passion in his voice:

"No, no, I pray you. I can bear anything but that. Remember, gentlemen, that I am blind; that I cannot see who is about me; that my life would be a torture if I felt myself surrounded by spies watching to catch some evidence of madness in me. Rather conviction at once, death, dishonor, and obloquy. These I have incurred. These I have brought upon myself by crime, but not this worse fate — oh! not this worse fate."

His passion was so intense and yet so confined within the bounds of decorum, that we felt strangely impressed by it. Only the wife stood transfixed, with the dread growing in her heart, till her white, waxen visage seemed even more terrible to contemplate than his passion-distorted one.

"It is not strange that my wife thinks me demented," the Doctor continued, as if afraid of the silence that answered him. "But it is your business to discriminate, and you should know a sane man when you see him."

Inspector D—— no longer hesitated.

"Very well," said he, "give us the least proof that your assertions are true, and we will lay your case before the prosecuting attorney."

"Proof? Is not a man's word —"

"No man's confession is worth much without some evidence to support it. In your case there is none. You cannot even produce the pistol with which you assert yourself to have committed the deed."

"True, true. I was frightened by what I had done, and the instinct of self-preservation led me to rid myself of the weapon in any way I could. But someone found this pistol; someone picked it up from the sidewalk of Lafayette Place on that fatal night. Advertise for it. Offer a reward. I will give you the money." Suddenly he appeared to realize how all this sounded. "Alas!" cried he, "I know the story seems improbable; all I say seems improbable; but it is not the probable things that happen in this life, but the improbable, as you should know, who every day dig deep into the heart of human affairs."

Were these the ravings of insanity? I began to understand the wife's terror.

"I bought the pistol," he went on, "of—alas! I cannot tell you his name. Everything is against me. I cannot adduce one proof; yet she, even she, is beginning to fear that my story is true. I know it by her silence, a silence that yawns between us like a deep and unfathomable gulf."

But at these words her voice rang out with passionate vehemence.

"No, no, it is false! I will never believe that your hands have been plunged in blood. You are my own pure-hearted Constant, cold, perhaps, and stern, but with no guilt upon your conscience, save in your own wild imagination."

"Helen, you are no friend to me," he declared, pushing her gently aside. "Believe me innocent, but say nothing to lead these others to doubt my word."

And she said no more, but her looks spoke volumes.

The result was that he was not detained, though he prayed for instant commitment. He seemed to dread his own home, and the surveillance to which he instinctively knew he would henceforth be subjected. To see him shrink from his wife's hand as she strove to lead him from the room was sufficiently painful; but the feeling thus aroused was nothing to that with which we observed the keen and agonized expectancy of his look as he turned and listened for the steps of the officer who followed him.

"I shall never again know whether or not I am alone," was his final observation as he left our presence.

I said nothing to my superiors of the thoughts I had had while listening to the above interrogatories. A theory had presented itself to my mind which explained in some measure the mysteries of the Doctor's conduct, but I wished for time and opportunity to test its reasonableness before submitting it to their higher judgment. And these seemed likely to be given me, for the Inspectors continued divided in their opinion of the blind physician's guilt, and the District-Attorney, when told of the affair, pooh-poohed it without mercy, and declined to stir in the matter unless some tangible evidence were forthcoming to substantiate the poor Doctor's self-accusations.

"If guilty, why does he shrink from giving his motives," said he, "and if so anxious to go to the gallows, why does he suppress the very facts calculated to send him there? He is as mad as a March hare, and it is to an asylum he should go and not to a jail."

In this conclusion I failed to agree with him, and as time wore on my suspicions took shape and finally ended in a fixed conviction. Dr.

Zabriskie had committed the crime he avowed, but—let me proceed a little further with my story before I reveal what lies beyond that "but."

Notwithstanding Dr. Zabriskie's almost frenzied appeal for solitude, a man had been placed in surveillance over him in the shape of a young doctor skilled in diseases of the brain. This man communicated more or less with the police, and one morning I received from him the following extracts from the diary he had been ordered to keep.

"The Doctor is settling into a deep melancholy from which he tries to rise at times, but with only indifferent success. Yesterday he rode around to all his patients for the purpose of withdrawing his services on the plea of illness. But he still keeps his office open, and to-day I had the opportunity of witnessing his reception and treatment of the many sufferers who came to him for aid. I think he was conscious of my presence, though an attempt had been made to conceal it. For the listening look never left his face from the moment he entered the room, and once he rose and passed quickly from wall to wall, groping with outstretched hands into every nook and corner, and barely escaping contact with the curtain behind which I was hidden. But if he suspected my presence, he showed no displeasure at it, wishing perhaps for a witness to his skill in the treatment of disease.

"And truly I never beheld a finer manifestation of practical insight in cases of a more or less baffling nature than I beheld in him to-day. He is certainly a most wonderful physician, and I feel bound to record that his mind is as clear for business as if no shadow had fallen upon it.

"Dr. Zabriskie loves his wife, but in a way that tortures both himself and her. If she is gone from the house he is wretched and yet when she returns he often forbears to speak to her, or if he does speak, it is with a constraint that hurts her more than his silence. I was present when she came in to-day. Her step, which had been eager on the stairway, flagged as she approached the room, and he naturally noted the change and gave his own interpretation to it. His face, which had been very pale, flushed suddenly, and a nervous trembling seized him which he sought in vain to hide. But by the time her tall and beautiful figure stood in the doorway he was his usual self again in all but the expression of his eyes, which stared straight before him in an agony of longing only to be observed in those who have once seen.

"'Where have you been, Helen?' he asked, as, contrary to his wont, he moved to meet her.

"'To my mother's, to Arnold & Constable's, and to the hospital, as you requested,' was her quick answer, made without faltering or embarrassment.

"He stepped still nearer and took her hand, and as he did so my physician's eye noted how his finger lay over her pulse in seeming unconsciousness.

"'Nowhere else?' he queried.

"She smiled the saddest kind of smile and shook her head; then, remembering that he could not see this movement, she cried in a wistful tone:

"'Nowhere else, Constant; I was too anxious to get back.'

"I expected him to drop her hand at this, but he did not; and his finger still rested on her pulse.

"'And whom did you see while you were gone?' he continued.

"She told him, naming over several names.

"'You must have enjoyed yourself,' was his cold comment, as he let go her hand and turned away. But his manner showed relief, and I could not but sympathize with the pitiable situation of a man who found himself forced to means like these for probing the heart of his young wife.

"Yet when I turned towards her I realized that her position was but little happier than his. Tears are no strangers to her eyes, but those that welled up at this moment seemed to possess a bitterness that promised but little peace for her future. Yet she quickly dried them and busied herself with ministrations for his comfort.

"If I am any judge of woman, Helen Zabriskie is superior to most of her sex. That her husband mistrusts her is evident, but whether this is the result of the stand she has taken in his regard, or only a manifestation of dementia, I have as yet been unable to determine. I dread to leave them alone together, and yet when I presume to suggest that she should be on her guard in her interviews with him, she smiles very placidly and tells me that nothing would give her greater joy than to see him lift his hand against her, for that would argue that he is not accountable for his deeds or for his assertions.

"Yet it would be a grief to see her injured by this passionate and unhappy man.

"You have said that you wanted all details I could give; so I feel bound to say, that Dr. Zabriskie tries to be considerate of his wife, though he often fails in the attempt. When she offers herself as his guide, or assists him with his mail, or performs any of the many acts of kindness by which she continually manifests her sense of his affliction, he thanks her with courtesy and often with kindness, yet I know she would willingly exchange all his set phrases for one fond embrace or impulsive smile of affection. That he is not in the full possession of his faculties would be too much to say, and yet upon what other hypothesis can we account for the inconsistencies of his conduct.

"I have before me two visions of mental suffering. At noon I passed the office door, and looking within, saw the figure of Dr. Zabriskie seated in his great chair, lost in thought or deep in those memories which make an abyss in one's consciousness. His hands, which were clenched, rested upon the arms of his chair, and in one of them I detected a woman's glove, which I had no difficulty in recognizing as one of the pair worn by his wife this morning. He held it as a tiger might hold his prey or a miser his gold, but his set features and sightless eyes betrayed that a conflict of emotions was waging within him, among which tenderness had but little share.

"Though alive, as he usually is, to every sound, he was too absorbed at this moment to notice my presence though I had taken no pains to approach quietly. I therefore stood for a full minute watching him, till an irresistible sense of the shame of thus spying upon a blind man in his moments of secret anguish seized upon me and I turned away. But not before I saw his features relax in a storm of passionate feeling, as he rained kisses after kisses on the senseless kid he had so long held in his motionless grasp. Yet when an hour later he entered the dining-room on his wife's arm, there was nothing in his manner to show that he had in any way changed in his attitude towards her.

"The other picture was more tragic still. I have no business with Mrs. Zabriskie's affairs; but as I passed upstairs to my room an hour ago, I caught a fleeting vision of her tall form, with the arms thrown up over her head in a paroxysm of feeling which made her as oblivious to my presence as her husband had been several hours before. Were the words that escaped her lips 'Thank God we have no children!' or was this exclamation suggested to me by the passion and unrestrained impulse of her action?"

Side by side with these lines, I, Ebenezer Gryce, placed the following extracts from my own diary:

"Watched the Zabriskie mansion for five hours this morning, from the second story window of an adjoining hotel. Saw the Doctor when he drove away on his round of visits, and saw him when he returned. A colored man accompanied him.

"To-day I followed Mrs. Zabriskie. I had a motive for this, the nature of which I think it wisest not to divulge. She went first to a house in Washington Place where I am told her mother lives. Here she stayed some time, after which she drove down to Canal Street, where she did some shopping, and later stopped at the hospital, into which I took the liberty of following her. She seemed to know many there, and passed from cot to cot with a smile in which I alone discerned the sadness of a broken heart. When she left, I left also, without having learned anything beyond the fact that Mrs. Zabriskie is one who does her duty in sorrow as in happiness. A rare and trustworthy woman I should say, and yet her husband does not trust her. Why?

"I have spent this day in accumulating details in regard to Dr. and Mrs. Zabriskie's life previous to the death of Mr. Hasbrouck. I learned from sources it would be unwise to quote just here, that Mrs. Zabriskie had not lacked enemies ready to charge her with coquetry; that while she had never sacrificed her dignity in public, more than one person had been heard to declare, that Dr. Zabriskie was fortunate in being blind, since the sight of his wife's beauty would have but poorly compensated him for the pain he would have suffered in seeing how that beauty was admired.

"That all gossip is more or less tinged with exaggeration I have no doubt, yet when a name is mentioned in connection with such stories, there is usually some truth at the bottom of them. And a name is mentioned in this case, though I do not think it worth my while to repeat it here; and loath as I am to recognize the fact, it is a name that carries with it doubts that might easily account for the husband's jealousy. True, I have found no one who dares to hint that she still continues to attract attention or to bestow smiles in any direction save where they legally belong. For since a certain memorable night which we all know, neither Dr. Zabriskie nor his wife have been seen save in their own domestic circle, and it is not into such scenes that this serpent, of which I have spoken, ever intrudes, nor is it in places of sorrow or suffering that his smile shines, or his fascinations flourish.

"And so one portion of my theory is proved to be sound. Dr. Zabriskie is jealous of his wife: whether with good cause or bad I am not prepared to decide; for her present attitude, clouded as it is by the tragedy in which she and her husband are both involved, must differ very much from that which she held when her life was unshadowed by doubt, and her admirers could be counted by the score.

"I have just found out where Harry is. As he is in service some miles up the river, I shall have to be absent from my post for several hours, but I consider the game well worth the candle.

"Light at last. I have seen Harry, and, by means known only to the police, have succeeded in making him talk. His story is substantially this: That on the night so often mentioned, he packed his master's portmanteau at eight o'clock and at ten called a carriage and rode with the Doctor to the Twenty-ninth Street station. He was told to buy tickets for Poughkeepsie where his master had been called in consultation, and having done this, hurried back to join his master on the platform. They had walked together as far as the cars, and Dr. Zabriskie was just stepping on to the train when a man pushed himself hurriedly between them and whispered something into his master's ear, which caused him to fall back and lose his footing. Dr. Zabriskie's body slid half under the car, but he was withdrawn before any harm was done, though the cars gave a lurch at that moment which must have frightened him exceedingly, for his face was white when he rose to his feet, and when Harry offered to assist him again on to the train, he refused to go and said he would return home and not attempt to ride to Poughkeepsie that night.

"The gentleman, whom Harry now saw to be Mr. Stanton, an intimate friend of Dr. Zabriskie, smiled very queerly at this and taking the Doctor's arm led him away to a carriage. Harry naturally followed them, but the Doctor, hearing his steps, turned and bade him, in a very peremptory tone, to take the omnibus home, and then, as if on second thought, told him to go to Poughkeepsie in his stead and explain to the people there that he was too shaken up by his misstep to do his duty, and that he would be with them next morning. This seemed strange to Harry, but he had no reasons for disobeying his master's orders, and so rode to Poughkeepsie. But the Doctor did not follow him the next day; on the contrary he telegraphed for him to return, and when he got back dismissed him with a month's wages. This ended Harry's connection with the Zabriskie family.

"A simple story bearing out what the wife has already told us; but it furnishes a link which may prove invaluable. Mr. Stanton, whose first name is Theodore, knows the real reason why Dr. Zabriskie returned home on the night of the seventeenth of July, 1851. Mr. Stanton, consequently, I must see, and this shall be my business to-morrow.

"Checkmate! Theodore Stanton is not in this country. Though this points him out as the man from whom Dr. Zabriskie bought the pistol, it does not facilitate my work, which is becoming more and more difficult.

"Mr. Stanton's whereabouts are not even known to his most intimate friends. He sailed from this country most unexpectedly on the eighteenth of July a year ago, which was *the day after the murder of Mr. Hasbrouck.* It looks like a flight, especially as he has failed to maintain open communication even with his relatives. Was he the man who shot Mr. Hasbrouck? No; but he was the man who put the pistol in Dr. Zabriskie's hand that night, and, whether he did this with purpose or not, was evidently so alarmed at the catastrophe which followed that he took the first outgoing steamer to Europe. So far, all is clear, but there are mysteries yet to be solved, which will require my utmost tact. What if I should seek out the gentleman with whose name that of Mrs. Zabriskie has been linked, and see if I can in any way connect him with Mr. Stanton or the events of that night?

"Eureka! I have discovered that Mr. Stanton cherished a mortal hatred for the gentleman above mentioned. It was a covert feeling, but no less deadly on that account; and while it never led him into any extravagances, it was of force sufficient to account for many a secret misfortune which happened to that gentleman. Now, if I can prove he was the Mephistopheles who whispered insinuations into the ear of our blind Faust, I may strike a fact that will lead me out of this maze.

"But how can I approach secrets so delicate without compromising the woman I feel bound to respect, if only for the devoted love she manifests for her unhappy husband!

"I shall have to appeal to Joe Smithers. This is something which I always hate to do, but as long as he will take money, and as long as he is fertile in resources for obtaining the truth from people I am myself unable to reach, so long must I make use of his cupidity and his genius. He is an honorable fellow in one way, and never retails as gossip what he acquires for our use. How will he proceed in this case, and by what tactics will he gain the very delicate information which we need? I own that I am curious to see.

"I shall really have to put down at length the incidents of this night. I always knew that Joe Smithers was invaluable to the police, but I really did not know he possessed talents of so high an order. He wrote me this morning that he had succeeded in getting Mr. T——'s promise to spend the evening with him, and advised me that if I desired to be present also, his own servant would not be at home, and that an opener of bottles would be required.

"As I was very anxious to see Mr. T—— with my own eyes, I accepted the invitation to play the spy upon a spy, and went at the proper hour to Mr. Smithers's rooms, which are in the University Building. I found them picturesque in the extreme. Piles of books stacked here and there to the ceiling made nooks and corners which could be quite shut off by a couple of old pictures that were set into movable frames that swung out or in at the whim or convenience of the owner.

"As I liked the dark shadows cast by these pictures, I pulled them both out, and made such other arrangements as appeared likely to facilitate the purpose I had in view, then I sat down and waited for the two gentlemen who were expected to come in together.

"They arrived almost immediately, whereupon I rose and played my part with all necessary discretion. While ridding Mr. T—— of his overcoat, I stole a look at his face. It is not a handsome one, but it boasts of a gay, devil-may-care expression which doubtless makes it dangerous to many women, while his manners are especially attractive, and his voice the richest and most persuasive that I ever heard. I contrasted him, almost against my will, with Dr. Zabriskie, and decided that with most women the former's undoubted fascinations of speech and bearing would outweigh the latter's great beauty and mental endowments; but I doubted if they would with her.

"The conversation which immediately began was brilliant but desultory, for Mr. Smithers, with an airy lightness for which he is remarkable, introduced topic after topic, perhaps for the purpose of showing off Mr. T——'s versatility, and perhaps for the deeper and more sinister purpose of shaking the kaleidoscope of talk so thoroughly, that the real topic which we were met to discuss should not make an undue impression on the mind of his guest.

"Meanwhile one, two, three bottles passed, and I saw Joe Smithers's eye grow calmer and that of Mr. T—— more brilliant and more uncertain. As the last bottle showed signs of failing, Joe cast me a meaning glance, and the real business of the evening began.

"I shall not attempt to relate the half-dozen failures which Joe made in endeavoring to elicit the facts we were in search of, without arousing the suspicion of his visitor. I am only going to relate the successful attempt. They had been talking now for some hours, and I, who had long before been waved from their immediate presence, was hiding my curiosity and growing excitement behind one of the pictures, when suddenly I heard Joe say:

" 'He has the most remarkable memory I ever met. He can tell to a day when any notable event occurred.'

" 'Pshaw!' answered his companion, who, by the by, was known to pride himself upon his own memory for dates, 'I can state where I went and what I did on every day in the year. That may not embrace what you call 'notable events,' but the memory required is all the more remarkable, is it not?'

" 'Pooh!' was his friend's provoking reply, 'you are bluffing, Ben; I will never believe that.'

"Mr. T——, who had passed by this time into that state of intoxication which makes persistence in an assertion a duty as well as a pleasure, threw back his head, and as the wreaths of smoke rose in airy spirals from his lips, reiterated his statement, and offered to submit to any test of his vaunted powers which the other might dictate.

" 'You have a diary—' began Joe.

" 'Which is at home,' completed the other.

" 'Will you allow me to refer to it to-morrow, if I am suspicious of the accuracy of your recollections?'

" 'Undoubtedly,' returned the other.

" 'Very well, then, I will wager you a cool fifty, that you cannot tell where you were between the hours of ten and eleven on a certain night which I will name.'

" 'Done!' cried the other, bringing out his pocket-book and laying it on the table before him.

"Joe followed his example and then summoned me.

" 'Write a date down here,' he commanded, pushing a piece of paper towards me, with a look keen as the flash of a blade. 'Any date, man,' he added, as I appeared to hesitate in the embarrassment I thought natural under the circumstances. 'Put down day, month, and year, only don't go too far back; not farther than two years.'

"Smiling with the air of a flunkey admitted to the sports of his superiors, I wrote a line and laid it before Mr. Smithers, who at once pushed it with a careless gesture towards his companion. You can of course guess the date I made use of: July 17, 1851. Mr. T——, who had evidently looked upon this matter as mere play, flushed scarlet as he read these words, and for one instant looked as if he had rather flee our presence than answer Joe Smithers's nonchalant glance of inquiry.

" 'I have given my word and will keep it,' he said at last, but with a look in my direction that sent me reluctantly back to my retreat. 'I don't suppose you want names,' he went on, 'that is, if anything I have to tell is of a delicate nature?'

" 'O no,' answered the other, 'only facts and places.'

" 'I don't think places are necessary either,' he returned. 'I will tell you what I did and that must serve you. I did not promise to give number and street.'

" 'Well, well,' Joe exclaimed; 'earn your fifty, that is all. Show that you remember where you were on the night of'—and with an admirable show of indifference he pretended to consult the paper between them —'the seventeenth of July, 1851, and I shall be satisfied.'

" 'I was at the club for one thing,' said Mr. T——; 'then I went to see a lady friend, where I stayed till eleven. She wore a blue muslin— What is that?'

"I had betrayed myself by a quick movement which sent a glass tumbler crashing to the floor. Helen Zabriskie had worn a blue muslin on that same night. I had noted it when I stood on the balcony watching her and her husband.

" 'That noise?' It was Joe who was speaking. 'You don't know Reuben as well as I do or you wouldn't ask. It is his practice, I am sorry to say, to accentuate his pleasure in draining my bottles, by dropping a glass at every third one.'

"Mr. T—— went on.

" 'She was a married woman and I thought she loved me; but—and this is the greatest proof I can offer you that I am giving you a true account of that night—she had not had the slightest idea of the extent of my passion, and only consented to see me at all because she thought, poor thing, that a word from her would set me straight, and rid her of attentions that were fast becoming obnoxious. A sorry figure for a fellow to cut who has not been without his triumphs; but you caught me on the most detestable date in my calendar, and—'

"There is where he stopped being interesting, so I will not waste time by quoting further. And now what reply shall I make when Joe Smithers asks me double his usual price, as he will be sure to do, next time? Has he not earned an advance? I really think so.

"I have spent the whole day in weaving together the facts I have gleaned, and the suspicions I have formed, into a consecutive whole likely to present my theory in a favorable light to my superiors. But just as I thought myself in shape to meet their inquiries, I received an immediate summons into their presence, where I was given a duty to perform of so extraordinary and unexpected a nature, that it effectually drove from my mind all my own plans for the elucidation of the Zabriskie mystery.

"This was nothing more nor less than to take charge of a party of people who were going to the Jersey heights for the purpose of testing Dr. Zabriskie's skill with a pistol."

III.

THE CAUSE OF this sudden move was soon explained to me. Mrs. Zabriskie, anxious to have an end put to the present condition of affairs, had begged for a more rigid examination into her husband's state. This being accorded, a strict and impartial inquiry had taken place, with a result not unlike that which followed the first one. Three out of his four interrogators judged him insane, and could not be moved from their opinion though opposed by the verdict of the young expert who had been living in the house with him. Dr. Zabriskie seemed to read their thoughts, and, showing extreme agitation, begged as before for an opportunity to prove his sanity by showing his skill in shooting. This time a disposition was evinced to grant his request, which Mrs. Zabriskie no sooner perceived than she added her supplications to his that the question might be thus settled.

A pistol was accordingly brought; but at sight of it her courage failed, and she changed her prayer to an entreaty that the experiment should be postponed till the next day, and should then take place in the woods away from the sight and hearing of needless spectators.

Though it would have been much wiser to have ended the matter there and then, the Superintendent was prevailed upon to listen to her entreaties, and thus it was that I came to be a spectator, if not a participator, in the final scene of this most somber drama.

There are some events which impress the human mind so deeply that their memory mingles with all after-experiences. Though I have made it a rule to forget as soon as possible the tragic episodes into which I am constantly plunged, there is one scene in my life which will not depart at my will; and that is the sight which met my eyes from the bow of the small boat in which Dr. Zabriskie and his wife were rowed over to Jersey on that memorable afternoon.

Though it was by no means late in the day, the sun was already sinking, and the bright red glare which filled the heavens and shone full upon the faces of the half-dozen persons before me added much to the tragic nature of the scene, though we were far from comprehending its full significance.

The Doctor sat with his wife in the stern, and it was upon their faces my glance was fixed. The glare shone luridly on his sightless eyeballs, and as I noticed his unwinking lids I realized as never before what it was to be blind in the midst of sunshine. Her eyes, on the contrary, were lowered, but there was a look of hopeless misery in her colorless face which made her appearance infinitely pathetic, and I felt confident that if he could only have seen her, he would not have maintained the cold and unresponsive manner which chilled the words on her lips and made all advance on her part impossible.

On the seat in front of them sat the Inspector and a doctor, and from some quarter, possibly from under the Inspector's coat, there came the monotonous ticking of a small clock, which, I had been told, was to serve as a target for the blind man's aim.

This ticking was all I heard, though the noise and bustle of a great traffic was pressing upon us on every side. And I am sure it was all that she heard, as, with hand pressed to her heart and eyes fixed on the opposite shore, she waited for the event which was to determine whether the man she loved was a criminal or only a being afflicted of God, and worthy of her unceasing care and devotion.

As the sun cast its last scarlet gleam over the water, the boat grounded, and it fell to my lot to assist Mrs. Zabriskie up the bank. As I did so, I allowed myself to say: "I am your friend, Mrs. Zabriskie," and was astonished to see her tremble, and turn toward me with a look like that of a frightened child.

But there was always this characteristic blending in her countenance of the childlike and the severe, such as may so often be seen in the faces of nuns, and beyond an added pang of pity for this beautiful but afflicted woman, I let the moment pass without giving it the weight it perhaps demanded.

"The Doctor and his wife had a long talk last night," was whispered in my ear as we wound our way along into the woods. I turned and perceived at my side the expert physician, portions of whose diary I have already quoted. He had come by another boat.

"But it did not seem to heal whatever breach lies between them," he proceeded. Then in a quick, curious tone, he asked: "Do you believe this attempt on his part is likely to prove anything but a farce?"

"I believe he will shatter the clock to pieces with his first shot," I answered, and could say no more, for we had already reached the ground which had been selected for this trial at arms, and the various members of the party were being placed in their several positions.

The Doctor, to whom light and darkness were alike, stood with his face towards the western glow, and at his side were grouped the Inspector and the two physicians. On the arm of one of the latter hung Dr. Zabriskie's overcoat, which he had taken off as soon as he reached the field.

Mrs. Zabriskie stood at the other end of the opening, near a tall stump, upon which it had been decided that the clock should be placed when the moment came for the Doctor to show his skill. She had been accorded the privilege of setting the clock on this stump, and I saw it shining in her hand as she paused for a moment to glance back at the circle of gentlemen who were awaiting her movements. The hands of the clock stood at five minutes to five, though I scarcely noted the fact at the time, for her eyes were on mine, and as she passed me she spoke:

"If he is not himself, he cannot be trusted. Watch him carefully, and see that he does no mischief to himself or others. Be at his right hand, and stop him if he does not handle his pistol properly."

I promised, and she passed on, setting the clock upon the stump and immediately drawing back to a suitable distance at the right, where she stood, wrapped in her long dark cloak, quite alone. Her face shone ghastly white, even in its environment of snow-covered boughs which surrounded her, and, noting this, I wished the minutes fewer between the present moment and the hour of five, at which he was to draw the trigger.

"Dr. Zabriskie," quoth the Inspector, "we have endeavored to make this trial a perfectly fair one. You are to have one shot at a small clock which has been placed within a suitable distance, and which you are expected to hit, guided only by the sound which it will make in striking the hour of five. Are you satisfied with the arrangement?"

"Perfectly. Where is my wife?"

"On the other side of the field, some ten paces from the stump upon which the clock is fixed."

He bowed, and his face showed satisfaction.

"May I expect the clock to strike soon?"

"In less than five minutes," was the answer.

"Then let me have the pistol; I wish to become acquainted with its size and weight."

We glanced at each other, then across at her.

She made a gesture; it was one of acquiescence.

Immediately the Inspector placed the weapon in the blind man's hand. It was at once apparent that the Doctor understood the instrument, and my last doubt vanished as to the truth of all he had told us.

"Thank God I am blind this hour and cannot see *her,*" fell unconsciously from his lips; then, before the echo of these words had left my ears, he raised his voice and observed calmly enough, considering that he was about to prove himself a criminal in order to save himself from being thought a madman,

"Let no one move. I must have my ears free for catching the first stroke of the clock." And he raised the pistol before him.

There was a moment of torturing suspense and deep, unbroken silence. My eyes were on him, and so I did not watch the clock, but suddenly I was moved by some irresistible impulse to note how Mrs. Zabriskie was bearing herself at this critical moment, and, casting a hurried glance in her direction, I perceived her tall figure swaying from side to side, as if under an intolerable strain of feeling. Her eyes were on the clock, the hands of which seemed to creep with snail-like pace along the dial, when unexpectedly, and a full minute before the minute hand had reached the stroke of five, I caught a movement on her part, saw the flash of something round and white show for an instant against the darkness of her cloak, and was about to shriek warning to the Doctor, when the shrill, quick stroke of a clock rung out on the frosty air, followed by the ping and flash of a pistol.

A sound of shattered glass, followed by a suppressed cry, told us that the bullet had struck the mark, but before we could move, or rid our eyes of the smoke which the wind had blown into our faces, there came another sound which made our hair stand on end and sent the blood back in terror to our hearts. Another clock was striking, the clock which we now perceived was still standing upright on the stump where Mrs. Zabriskie had placed it.

Whence came the clock, then, which had struck before the time and been shattered for its pains? One quick look told us. On the ground, ten paces at the right, lay Helen Zabriskie, a broken clock at her side, and in her breast a bullet which was fast sapping the life from her sweet eyes.

We had to tell him, there was such pleading in her looks; and never shall I forget the scream that rang from his lips as he realized the truth. Breaking from our midst, he rushed forward, and fell at her feet as if guided by some supernatural instinct.

"Helen," he shrieked, "what is this? Were not my hands dyed deep enough in blood that you should make me answerable for your life also?"

Her eyes were closed, but she opened them. Looking long and steadily at his agonized face, she faltered forth:

"It is not you who have killed me; it is your crime. Had you been innocent of Mr. Hasbrouck's death, your bullet would never have found my heart. Did you think I could survive the proof that you had killed that good man?"

"I—I did it unwittingly. I—"

"Hush!" she commanded, with an awful look, which, happily, he could not see. "I had another motive. I wished to prove to you, even at the cost of my life, that I loved you, had always loved you, and not—"

It was now his turn to silence her. His hand crept over her lips, and his despairing face turned itself blindly towards us.

"Go," he cried; "leave us! Let me take a last farewell of my dying wife, without listeners or spectators."

Consulting the eye of the physician who stood beside me, and seeing no hope in it, I fell slowly back. The others followed, and the Doctor was left alone with his wife. From the distant position we took, we saw her arms creep round his neck, saw her head fall confidingly on his breast, then silence settled upon them and upon all nature, the gathering twilight deepening, till the last glow disappeared from the heavens above and from the circle of leafless trees which enclosed this tragedy from the outside world.

But at last there came a stir, and Dr. Zabriskie, rising up before us, with the dead body of his wife held closely to his breast, confronted us with a countenance so rapturous that he looked like a man transfigured.

"I will carry her to the boat," said he. "Not another hand shall touch her. She was my true wife, my true wife!" And he towered into an attitude of such dignity and passion, that for a moment he took on heroic proportions and we forgot that he had just proved himself to have committed a cold-blooded and ghastly crime.

The stars were shining when we again took our seats in the boat; and if the scene of our crossing to Jersey was impressive, what shall be said of that of our return.

The Doctor, as before, sat in the stern, an awesome figure, upon which the moon shone with a white radiance that seemed to lift his face out of the surrounding darkness and set it, like an image of frozen horror, before our eyes. Against his breast he held the form of his dead wife, and now and then I saw him stoop as if he were listening for some tokens of life at her set lips. Then he would lift himself again, with hopelessness stamped upon his features, only to lean forward in renewed hope that was again destined to disappointment.

The Inspector and the accompanying physician had taken seats in the bow, and unto me had been assigned the special duty of watching over the Doctor. This I did from a low seat in front of him. I was therefore so close that I heard his laboring breath, and though my heart was full of awe and compassion, I could not prevent myself from bending towards him and saying these words:

"Dr. Zabriskie, the mystery of your crime is no longer a mystery to me. Listen and see if I do not understand your temptation, and how you, a conscientious and God-fearing man, came to slay your innocent neighbor.

"A friend of yours, or so he called himself, had for a long time filled your ears with tales tending to make you suspicious of your wife and jealous of a certain man whom I will not name. You knew that your friend had a grudge against this man, and so for many months turned a deaf ear to his insinuations. But finally some change which you detected in your wife's bearing or conversation roused your own suspicions, and you began to doubt if all was false that came to your ears, and to curse your blindness, which in a measure rendered you helpless. The jealous fever grew and had risen to a high point, when one night — a memorable night — this friend met you just as you were leaving town, and with cruel craft whispered in your ear that the man you hated was even then with your wife, and that if you would return at once to your home you would find him in her company.

"The demon that lurks at the heart of all men, good or bad, thereupon took complete possession of you, and you answered this false friend by saying that you would not return without a pistol. Whereupon he offered to take you to his house and give you his. You consented, and getting rid of your servant by sending him to Poughkeepsie with your excuses, you entered a coach with your friend.

"You say you bought the pistol, and perhaps you did, but, however that may be, you left his house with it in your pocket and, declining companionship, walked home, arriving at the Colonnade a little before midnight.

"Ordinarily you have no difficulty in recognizing your own doorstep. But, being in a heated frame of mind, you walked faster than usual and so passed your own house and stopped at that of Mr. Hasbrouck's, one door beyond. As the entrances of these houses are all alike, there was but one way by which you could have made yourself sure that you had reached your own dwelling, and that was by feeling for the doctor's sign at the side of the door. But you never thought of that. Absorbed in dreams of vengeance, your sole impulse was to enter by the quickest means possible. Taking out your night-key, you thrust it into the lock. It fitted, but it took strength to turn it, so much strength that the key was twisted and bent by the effort. But this incident, which would have attracted your attention at another time, was lost upon you at this moment. An entrance had been effected, and you were in too excited a frame of mind to notice at what cost, or to detect the small differences apparent in the atmosphere and furnishings of the two houses — trifles which would have arrested your attention under other circumstances, and made you pause before the upper floor had been reached.

"It was while going up the stairs that you took out your pistol, so that by the time you arrived at the front-room door you held it ready cocked and drawn in your hand. For, being blind, you feared escape on the part of your victim, and so waited for nothing but the sound of a man's voice before firing. When, therefore, the unfortunate Mr. Hasbrouck, roused by this sudden intrusion, advanced with an exclamation of astonishment, you pulled the trigger, killing him on the spot. It must have been immediately upon his fall that you recognized from some word he uttered, or from some contact you may have had with your surroundings, that you were in the wrong house and had killed the wrong man; for you cried out, in evident remorse, 'God! what have I done!' and fled without approaching your victim.

"Descending the stairs, you rushed from the house, closing the front door behind you and regaining your own without being seen. But here you found yourself baffled in your attempted escape, by two things.

First, by the pistol you still held in your hand, and secondly, by the fact that the key upon which you depended for entering your own door was so twisted out of shape that you knew it would be useless for you to attempt to use it. What did you do in this emergency? You have already told us, though the story seemed so improbable at the time, you found nobody to believe it but myself. The pistol you flung far away from you down the pavement, from which, by one of those rare chances which sometimes happen in this world, it was presently picked up by some late passer-by of more or less doubtful character. The door offered less of an obstacle than you anticipated; for when you turned to it again you found it, if I am not greatly mistaken, ajar, left so, as we have reason to believe, by one who had gone out of it but a few minutes before in a state which left him but little master of his actions. It was this fact which provided you with an answer when you were asked how you succeeded in getting into Mr. Hasbrouck's house after the family had retired for the night.

"Astonished at the coincidence, but hailing with gladness the deliverance which it offered, you went in and ascended at once into your wife's presence; and it was from her lips, and not from those of Mrs. Hasbrouck, that the cry arose which startled the neighborhood and prepared men's minds for the tragic words which were shouted a moment later from the next house.

"But she who uttered the scream knew of no tragedy save that which was taking place in her own breast. She had just repulsed a dastardly suitor, and, seeing you enter so unexpectedly in a state of unaccountable horror and agitation, was naturally stricken with dismay, and thought she saw your ghost, or, what was worse, a possible avenger; while you, having failed to kill the man you sought, and having killed a man you esteemed, let no surprise on her part lure you into any dangerous self-betrayal. You strove instead to soothe her, and even attempted to explain the excitement under which you labored, by an account of your narrow escape at the station, till the sudden alarm from next door distracted her attention, and sent both your thoughts and hers in a different direction. Not till conscience had fully awakened and the horror of your act had had time to tell upon your sensitive nature, did you breathe forth those vague confessions, which, not being supported by the only explanations which would have made them credible, led her, as well as the police, to consider you affected in your mind. Your pride as a man, and your consideration for her as a woman, kept you silent, but did not keep the worm from preying upon your heart.

"Am I not correct in my surmises, Dr. Zabriskie, and is not this the true explanation of your crime?"

With a strange look, he lifted up his face.

"Hush!" said he; "you will awaken her. See how peacefully she sleeps! I should not like to have her awakened now, she is so tired, and I—I have not watched over her as I should."

Appalled at his gesture, his look, his tone, I drew back, and for a few minutes no sound was to be heard but the steady dip-dip of the oars and the lap-lap of the waters against the boat. Then there came a quick uprising, the swaying before me of something dark and tall and threatening, and before I could speak or move, or even stretch forth my hands to stay him, the seat before me was empty and darkness had filled the place where but an instant previous he had sat, a fearsome figure, erect and rigid as a sphinx.

What little moonlight there was only served to show us a few rising bubbles, marking the spot where the unfortunate man had sunk with his much-loved burden. We could not save him. As the widening circles fled farther and farther out, the tide drifted us away, and we lost the spot which had seen the termination of one of earth's saddest tragedies.

The bodies were never recovered. The police reserved to themselves the right of withholding from the public the real facts which made this catastrophe an awful remembrance to those who witnessed it. A verdict of accidental death by drowning answered all purposes, and saved the memory of the unfortunate pair from such calumny as might have otherwise assailed it. It was the least we could do for two beings whom circumstances had so greatly afflicted.

1895

WILLIAM M. HINKLEY

A VERY STRANGE CASE

Virtually nothing is known of WILLIAM M. HINKLEY, the accomplished author of this historically significant short story. Throughout most of world literature, criminals were almost always portrayed as one of two types. The first was in the Robin Hood school and thought it perfectly legitimate to steal, so long as it was from the rich and the proceeds were then distributed to the poor (generally with a tidy sum retained by the crook). The second was a man (usually) so desperate, such a hopeless victim of society and its inequities, that there was no alternative but to steal in order to live.

"A Very Strange Case" is a macabre tale of a different kind of criminal, a wealthy young aristocrat who commits heinous crimes out of sheer boredom. The story is told as a diary entry by Marden in a breezy, cynical tone which somewhat mitigates the darkness of his adventures.

Outing, the magazine in which the story was first published, was widely circulated, billing itself as the premier magazine of "Amateur Sports and Outdoor Amusements" at the turn of the last century. It ran monthly for more than forty years, beginning in 1882 as *Wheelman,* devoted to cycling, and undergoing three more title changes until it ceased publication in 1923. Its great moment may have occurred when it published the Jack London classic *White Fang* in serial form in 1905, though it is noted for also publishing the first Hopalong Cassidy story, by Clarence E. Mumford, and numerous western illustrations by Frederic Remington.

"A Very Strange Case" was first collected in the anonymously edited *Short Stories from Outing* (New York: The Outing Publishing Company, 1895). It has never been reprinted until this collection.

• • •

MANY SINGULAR THINGS have come under my notice during an experience of thirty years in the tracing of criminals and the punishment of their misdeeds, but I think the case of the unfortunate young fellow whose photograph you see there is the most remarkable."

The speaker, a grizzled inspector of police of the city of N——, tapped the glass covering the likeness of a handsome man of not more than thirty. The face was that of a person of refinement and intelligence, and I was prepared for the next words which fell from my companion's lips.

"It is seldom that a man is led to do wrong, when apparently he has no reason for it, as was the case with young Marden, whose picture that is. We are not surprised when a man steals because fortune has not given him enough to live on, or when he feels that society 'owes him a living,' as the saying is; but this young fellow came of one of the best families in the State, and never wanted for a thing that money could buy, yet for him the life of a criminal possessed a fatal attraction."

We were interrupted by the entrance of a subordinate, who saluted and presented a note. Hastily tearing it open, the inspector read it, and turning to me said: "An appointment down town at four. I have just time to make it; I'll be back in the course of an hour. In the meantime make yourself at home. You'll find a box of Havanas in the top drawer — matches there; and here, read this — it's a sort of diary that we found at the Marden house when the end of the young fellow's career came"; and, thrusting into my hand a dozen or fifteen loose sheets of foolscap, the veteran hastily quitted the room.

I had plenty of leisure, and the cozy little office at headquarters was not at all an unpleasant place in which to pass time, so, taking the manuscript, I lighted one of my friend's cigars and seated myself in his revolving chair, prepared to learn the history of the young fellow of whom we had been speaking. I could not, however, put his face from my mind, and, rising, I strode across the room to where the photograph hung in its small oak frame. "Surely," thought I, "his was never intended for the life of a criminal! Men of that class show evidences of their evil lives in their countenances, but here is one whom I could not think to find in a place of this sort." I gazed at it long and earnestly, before resuming my chair, and then took up the manuscript, strongly predisposed toward the writer.

The characters were firm and regular, and the closely-written sheets were as legible as type. They bore no title, and, judging from their general appearance, were evidently not intended to become public property. They read as follows:

"To-day there comes over me a presentiment I cannot throw off, and something beyond my power to resist bids me set down here the history of my wasted life.

"I am young — not yet thirty, wealthy and — yes — and handsome, so my friends tell me, though perhaps their judgment is at fault. I was born in this old place, and have lived here most of my life, since my father's death with no other companion than my Scotch collie 'Mac.' Two old and tried servants of my family, Elias the butler and his wife Emily, manage to keep things in order about the house for me, and yield unquestioning obedience to their master's somewhat capricious wishes. My numerous friends often wonder that I have never married, but not having met my ideal in the other sex, I am satisfied to wait, and, indeed, if the truth were told, well contented to enjoy so-called single blessedness for some years to come.

"I fear I am a good deal of a hermit in my inclinations, and could wish that I was beyond the reach of boredom, in which dwell so many of those who style themselves my friends. As it is, I doubt not that they think me a crank, but I regard their opinion on this point rather lightly. I find entertainment in the companionship of Mac, and together we spend many hours roaming about the estate in fine weather, or remaining in my old-fashioned library when the elements combine to make outdoor life disagreeable. At such seasons it is my pleasure to take down from the shelves such of the old volumes as appeal to my love of the mysterious and the romantic, while old Mac lies stretched at my feet with a satisfied look in his brown eyes, as though that was the one spot in the world in which he wished to be at that particular moment. Sometimes I find my thoughts wandering into the land of reverie and speculation, and Mac seems to know just what I'm scheming about, for he appears to give a knowing wink, as though congratulating himself upon being his master's only *confidant*.

"I have said I loved mystery. Ever since childhood, when my old nurse poured into my listening ear strange stories of brownies, kelpies, hobgoblins, elves and such folk, I have been keenly alive to things supernatural, and, as I grew to the impressionable age of boyhood, my taste for literature naturally fell into the channels one might expect from such antecedents. Doubtless my good old father would have been in despair had he been told of this phase of his hopeful son's character, but he did not know. My mother died when I was a small child, and he relied implicitly upon the judgment and good sense of old nurse to look after my mental and physical development, merely inquiring into the plans and projects affecting my welfare. My voracious appetite for reading, therefore, satiated itself with stories of brigands and highwaymen, freebooters and plunder, detectives and crime, to an alarming extent. Poor old nurse was but a sorry scholar, and knew little or nothing about books, so, when she saw me leave the house with a volume under my arm, and knew that I could be found at any hour thereafter lying under the outspreading branches of the majestic trees at the edge of the grove near the house, she was satisfied, and went about her other duties, undoubtedly feeling that her charge was fast growing to be an adornment to the world of literature and wisdom generally.

"As years passed, it became necessary for me to fit myself for the position in society which the wealth and standing of my father assured me, and I was accordingly sent to a university, where I made rapid progress, and from which I was graduated at the age of twenty with fair groundwork on which to lay my future career. Then followed several years spent in traveling, in company with my parent, who dearly loved to go about, and we visited nearly every country on the globe, passing our time judiciously in such places as took our fancy, and naturally I saw many things that fed the flame of my earlier thoughts, modified but not eradicated by a broader experience.

"At the time of life when young men most need the counsel of their parents I was left an orphan and sole heir to this estate and the immense wealth of my father.

"Early in the morning of an oppressive day in July, several years ago, I was seated in my customary easy chair reading the daily paper, old Mac, as usual, at my feet, when my eye fell upon an account of a burglary committed in a neighboring city. The burglar was evidently a blunderer, at least so I thought, for he had been taken almost in the act, and I fell to mentally criticizing his mistakes. With the aid of the newspaper description, I was able to arrange the crime for him as it should have been carried out, and so sure was I of the success of my method that I conceived the ridiculous idea of putting it into execution, 'just to prove the correctness of my theory,' I said to myself. I laughed aloud at the utter absurdity of a wealthy and independent man like me becoming a housebreaker, and, strange to relate, the ethical side of the matter did not then present itself to my mind, or, if so, with little emphasis, and I looked upon the thing as a monstrously good joke.

"As I pondered over it, the scheme seemed more and more feasible, and presently I had evolved a plan of campaign which promised much diversion. To be sure there was an element of danger in it, but I liked it rather better on that account.

"With men of my temperament, action follows promptly upon the conception of an idea, and I at once wrote to a firm of safe-makers in a distant city, who were familiar to me, asking them to send a representative to N—— for consultation. It was my intention, as part of my scheme, to have an iron vault constructed below ground, and in due time I arranged the preliminaries to my entire satisfaction.

"To the vault builders I was simply a man of evident wealth, requiring a place of security in which to keep valuables, and my request that the matter be kept a profound secret was to them a most natural one. I did not wish even my good servants to be informed of the proposed extension to the house, and to insure their ignorance on this point I gave them permission to pay a visit of a few weeks to a relative living at some distance. I told them I expected to have some slight improvements made, and until these were completed would take up my residence at one of the hotels in the city. The simple-hearted old people were delighted at the opportunity given them for an outing, and were soon on their way.

"To keep the existence of the vault from the knowledge of my somewhat inquisitive neighbors was a matter of more difficulty, but this, too, was accomplished by having the metal plates brought to the house in boxes, while the bricks and other material would as well have suggested any ordinary mason work and excited little comment.

"So quickly and well did the builders perform their work that my vault was completed and ready for inspection within a little more than ten days. The interior is provided with several tiers of strong boxes, each in itself as secure as it could be made, while the vault is a model of its kind and thoroughly *burglar proof*, as I spared no expense to have it made so. Its dimensions inside are about six feet each way, which gives ample space for a person to stand within it comfortably. The room in which it is built is just enough larger than the vault to admit of the door of the latter opening freely, while it is in turn closed by a door, somewhat less secure than that of the vault, but calculated to act as a safeguard in case of necessity. To conceal the approach to the vault, the bookcase on the north side of the room has been arranged to swing on invisible hinges, and is fastened by a spring-lock from behind, which is released by a wire conducted to another part of the library. Leading from the entrance thus provided is a flight of stone steps, which ends abruptly at the door of the vault-room. As I look back upon this stage of my new career, I remember the feeling of intense satisfaction which I had at the successful issue of this step — there were the burglar and his hiding-place and it only remained to provide something to hide.

"With the return of Elias and Emily our little household resumed its former quiet routine, as far as *they* were concerned, but not so with their master; having taken the first step on his downward career, he was impatient to take the next, and to that end it was necessary to provide some kind of a disguise. A rusty old suit of my father's (wicked perversion of its former character), together with an old slouch hat, served very well for this purpose, but to obtain the needed tools with which to ply my nefarious craft, without attracting attention, was a source of considerable anxiety to me, and, indeed, the danger of discovery seemed so great that I finally determined to make them myself. A taste for mechanics when I was a lad had resulted in a workshop being fitted up on the place, and this still remained as I left it years ago. To convert an old crow-bar into a very respectable 'jimmy' (if such an instrument is ever respectable), was an easy matter, and as I had not contemplated attacking safes, I did not provide a very extensive outfit beyond this. As I write, the incongruity of my position comes to me, and I see myself as I would appear to the world at large, were they aware that the talented man of wealth, Ernest Marden, was a common, or rather an uncommon, housebreaker.

"Having settled upon the country which I deemed most promising as a field of operations, I informed my servants of my intention to be absent for a week or so, which was nothing unusual, as it is my habit to come and go as my somewhat eccentric fancy prompts, and, with grip in hand I found myself toward dusk in a town of considerable size, about fifty miles east of here, where I obtained lodgings at an inn of moderate charges. As the time approached for my first attempt at burglary, I felt my courage oozing through my fingertips, and realized that my whole scheme would be a fiasco unless I summoned my former confidence; but with the coming of darkness all my old spirit of recklessness and bravado returned, and, having dropped my valise from my window, I silently quitted my room, fully equipped for the work before me.

"I directed my steps through unfrequented streets to a handsome residence on the outskirts of the town, which I had been told by one of the townspeople, in reply to an off-hand question, was the property of a wealthy family who were then absent for the summer season. I was also told that the only persons in charge of the place, in the absence of the owner, were two or three female servants and an old butler.

"A brisk walk brought me to the hedge surrounding the grounds, which I readily recognized from my informant's description, and, peering over, I could see the house—a fine old place surrounded by stately elms, as near as I could judge in the darkness. An oil lamp at the carriage entrance threw out the only light visible in the immediate neighborhood, and, as if to further aid me, the dark wind-clouds scurrying across the sky made the blackness more profound, while the muttering thunder in the distance gave promise of a storm. Every condition seemed favorable to a successful termination of my venture.

"'Just such a night as I could have wished,' I murmured to myself, and, pulling my hat down so as to somewhat disguise my features, I grasped my valise firmly, and, leaping lightly over the hedge, paused for a further inspection of the place, which showed me that the house was about fifty yards back from the road, and was surrounded by many shrubs and plants.

"I carefully began a circuit of inspection to make sure of leaving no source of danger between me and my base of operations, and it was well I did so, for at the rear I came upon a large dog asleep in front of his kennel. So still did he lie that he might have been taken for a stone image, but his presence was most unwelcome at that particular time and place. He seemed a fine fellow, and I was loath to do so, but I knew it was necessary to deprive him of the means of giving an alarm, so I grasped my jimmy and approached him as noiselessly as a panther. To raise the terrible weapon with both hands and bring it down on his head was the work of an instant. I don't believe he ever knew what killed him, for the blow caused the heavy bar to crush through his skull, and he uttered not a sound, a convulsive quivering of his body being all that denoted it to have possessed life a moment before.

"Quickly recovering my balance, for I had been well-nigh overthrown by the sudden termination of the stroke, I hastily withdrew to the protection of a large bush and awaited developments. The wind moaning in the trees about the mansion, coupled with a feeling of repulsion at the deed I had just committed, gave me the 'creevils' (as old nurse was wont to term the uncanny feeling produced on her nerves by anything unnatural in her vicinity), but the fast flying moments warned me to proceed.

"Banishing the uneasiness which had begun to steal into my mind, I crept to the nearest window and peeped in. A chance flash of lightning illuminated the interior, and showed me that I was at a favorable point for entrance, so I inserted the jaw of my jimmy under the sash, the blinds being open, and cautiously forced it upward. Slowly it rose, with a crunching sound, the screws of the old-fashioned catch giving way under the strain, and presently I had an opening wide enough to put my arm through. I waited a few minutes to see if the slight noise had aroused any of the inmates, but, all remaining as silent as before, I raised the window and stealthily entered. My heart thrilled with a new and strange emotion as I realized that I was actually committing an unlawful act, and, feeling the danger of my position if discovered, I panted with excitement till it seemed to my sensitive nerves that I would surely betray my presence. But I grew calmer, and with careful tread began an inspection of the rooms. That in which I stood seemed to be the library, while beyond was the dining-room, the drawing-room being located on the opposite side of the wide hall, the linen-covered furniture within it standing out in ghostly prominence as the constantly recurring flashes of lightning chased the darkness from the rooms for an instant. Without, the storm was now at its height, and the thunder crashed and rumbled so incessantly that I doubt not I could have upset a table with very little danger of the sound reaching the dull ears of the persons sleeping above. A strong odor of wine pervaded the dining-room, and I saw by the remains of a feast that the servants must have been carousing earlier in the night, and the empty bottles and glasses, soiled table, and generally untidy appearance of everything encouraged me to look for little interruption in my work, as far as the revelers were concerned, and so it proved; for although I spent an hour or more rummaging the rooms for booty, nothing occurred to cause me any alarm, and I left by the open window, having secured a French clock, several fine bisque pieces, which I wrapped in heavy linen napkins from the buffet, some small articles of table silver, and such other things of value as I could stow into my valise without arousing suspicion, and was altogether quite satisfied with the results of my maiden effort.

"I reached my lodgings without attracting attention, though feeling wet and uncomfortable from the still falling rain, and the next day left town at an early hour, once more attired in my expensive clothes, and not at all a suspicious-looking individual. Arrived at home, and having bathed and attired myself in a lounging suit, I called Elias and instructed him not to permit any one to disturb me, and entered my library, to all intents and purposes with the idea of spending an afternoon with my books.

"I was highly elated at the unbounded success which attended my first adventure, and truly a burglar could not have been more favored had his patron saint arranged his affairs for him. I swung the book-case concealing the secret stairway, and, drawing it into place behind me, descended to the vault. Here I opened one of the small strong boxes and deposited my ill-gotten property, pasting upon the outside of the door a paper bearing the date of the burglary, name of the place, and a brief list of my trophies.

"When I returned to my easy chair, with all traces of my late expedition removed from sight, I gave myself up to keen enjoyment. That I had proved my theory to be correct, and given an exhibition of my skill (perhaps I should say my good fortune), was patent, and I resolved to try again.

"The newspapers of the following morning contained a graphic account of the crime, and announced that a tramp, who had been seen about the place the previous day and could give no satisfactory explanation of his presence, was in custody on suspicion of having committed it. I could not restrain a feeling of fraternal sympathy for the poor wretch, but eased my conscience (for I still had one), with the thought that he was probably where he belonged. One thing that caused me huge delight was the fact that the owner of the house was reported to be a Mr. Scarborough, who I remembered, with a start, was my father's former law partner! The idea was so inexpressibly funny that I was strongly tempted to drop him a line stating that I had knowledge of the thief, who could be persuaded to return the stolen property if assured of immunity from prosecution, but a realization of the embarrassing position in which I should place myself warned me not to attempt it. Dignified old Judge Scarborough! How amazed he would have been to have learned that the son of his old friend had called to see him in his absence, and feloniously abstracted some of his goods and chattels!

"As time passed I added to the property in my vault, choosing as the scenes of my exploits the houses of wealthy persons who were away from home, until six of the boxes were filled and labeled, and the newspapers teemed with reports of mysterious burglaries, no clue to the perpetrators being discovered. I remember the sense of humiliation which weighed down my soul upon reading in one of these accounts: 'The burglar is evidently a novice, as he took articles of small value, passing over property worth ten times as much as he secured.' I allowed sufficient time to elapse for the occupants of that house to be lulled into a sense of security, then I went and removed the more valuable property that I had overlooked on my first visit. I think those people will be more reticent when talking to press reporters in future.

"Flushed with success, in an evil moment I attempted an entrance into a house in this city and made a signal failure of it. Indeed, I nearly met my Waterloo there, though I managed to escape detection by a fortunate train of circumstances. This led to unusual activity among the local police, and an abandonment of any more attempts in my immediate neighborhood; but to make sure that no suspicion could rest upon me, I thought it necessary to commit a cautious robbery of my own house, by which I *lost* considerable property, the difference between me and my other victims being that *I* knew where to find mine. As a further precaution, I employed a detective to trace the perpetrator of this last impudent theft, but so well had I managed that he was finally compelled to admit himself baffled, though he said he strongly suspected my butler. I could hardly maintain a straight face at this remarkable conclusion of my efforts to hide my tracks, but I managed to conceal my amusement and, with an affected sigh of disappointment, paid the detective's fee, and he retired, rather crestfallen at his failure.

After his departure I did not make another attempt for several weeks, and, indeed, it was not until ten days ago that I renewed my ill-favored pastime. This last burglary has been the most profitable of all, and box number seven contains property of great value. Among other things, there reposes within it a masterpiece of the jeweler's art in the form of a Swiss watch of priceless worth. I rather pitied the owner for its loss but kept it with the idea that I might be encouraging the jeweler's trade by so doing.

"One by one my—"

Here the strange narrative of young Marden abruptly terminated, and though I searched for further documents bearing upon his case, I could find no more, so there was nothing to be done but to wait for the return of the inspector, who I thought could probably throw more light on his subsequent history. In the mean time I read the story again and again, with added interest, and found myself hesitating between amazement at the direction taken by the genius of the young fellow and admiration at the skillful way in which he had escaped detection. One thing which puzzled me a good deal was the fact that the inspector had spoken of him as being "unfortunate," whereas, according to his own account, he appeared to have been anything but that. But my musings were brought to an end by the arrival of the old man, who, seeing me still occupied with the manuscript, surmised what I had in mind.

"Well, sir," said he, "what do you think of him?"

"I hardly know," I answered. "It is most disappointing to find the manuscript incomplete. I wish he had finished it instead of stopping so abruptly. Can you tell me anything more about him? You spoke of him as being 'unfortunate'—what did you mean?"

"Certainly, I can tell you what our investigation disclosed, though it was by the merest accident. You will observe that Marden speaks of his dog Mac. Well, the brute was the unwitting cause of his unhappy master's death, and the way it happened was this: those papers which you have in your hand I found scattered about the floor of the vault-room. His statement that the police could find no trace of the person who committed the robberies is quite true, for I was captain of this precinct then, and confess I was never more puzzled and chagrined in my life. One day, when the mysterious crimes were still fresh in the public mind, I was seated at my desk writing, when a note was brought to me by the sergeant on duty. It was evidently written by an illiterate person, or one unaccustomed to handling a pen, and stated that Mr. Ernest Marden had been absent from home for such a long time that it was feared something had happened to him. The note was signed by 'Elias Comerford,' who proved to be the butler of whom the manuscript speaks. I thought little of the matter then, as mysterious disappearances are quite common occurrences, the missing persons generally turning up all right, and I made up my mind that the same thing was true in this case, especially as I knew young Marden was somewhat eccentric about his traveling. But nothing was heard of him, and at the earnest entreaty of the family servants up at the homestead I sent an agent there to look into the matter. He returned after an absence of two or three hours, wearing a most perplexed look on his face, and asked me to go back with him, as he could not account for the queer actions of young Marden's dog.

"I found Mac stretched out at full length in front of a book-case in the library, growling savagely. At first I supposed him mad, and ordered my assistant to shoot him where he lay, but the old butler pleaded so hard, and seemed so confident that that was not the trouble, that I countermanded the order and tried to coax the dog from his position. I used every means known to me, but without success, and then I noticed that once in a while he would stop growling and sniff under the case, the bottom of which he had gnawed in a dozen places. Now, I knew very well that an intelligent dog would not act that way without cause, assuming that he was not mad, so I fearlessly crossed the room and made a hasty examination. At this the dog showed every sign of delight, running about me and sniffing in a state of great excitement. I called John, my man, to my assistance, and we exerted our united efforts to move the case, but it would not budge. Then I told him to get something with which to pry it out, and he presently returned with an iron bar, which we inserted in the narrow opening behind it. In response to the pull which we gave, it swung outwardly with a crash, accompanied by the sound of the snapping of the lock, and, to our surprise, moved off to one side without upsetting. Then we saw the stone steps leading to the vault, down which the dog bounded like a flash, I followed him as fast as possible, but quickly repented my rashness, for I came into collision with the door at the foot of the steps. I opened this, but could see nothing in the pitchy darkness of the vault. Calling to John to procure a candle, I retreated to the steps and waited for the light. Meanwhile the dog had entered the vault-room and presently there came from him a howl that made my hair rise on my head in spite of myself. I was mighty glad to get the light which John held, and drawing my revolver, cautiously entered the mysterious chamber. The dog was crouched in front of the vault-door, with his muzzle raised, emitting the most blood-curdling howls.

"I finally succeeded in dislodging him, and opening the door carefully, by means of the combination knob, I beheld a startling sight. Crouched in a corner, his form almost reduced to a skeleton, was all that remained of Ernest Marden. The knees drawn up to the chin, the clenched hands and terrible appearance of the face, told me the story as plainly as though the dead man was speaking to me in life. By his side we found this"; and going to a cabinet containing various articles collected in the course of his professional life, the inspector brought me an ordinary linen cuff, on which were still discernible the straggled lines made in the dark by a lead-pencil. They were in the same hand as the manuscript I had just read, and were in truth a message from the dead. With straining sight I read:

August 14th, 1887. When this is found I shall be beyond hope of life. While standing before the boxes above me, I heard Mac coming down the steps, and too late it flashed through my mind that I had not drawn the bookcase into place, intending to return at once. The poor fellow could see nothing in the darkness, and before I could prevent it he struck the door of the vault, which was closed behind me. To my horror I find that the jar has thrown the bolts just enough to cause them to catch in the sockets, and I am caught as a rat in a trap. Bitterly do I regret the folly of the past few years of my life, and yet I cannot but acknowledge the justice of my punishment. I desire that if my body is found it shall be buried beside those of my parents; my attorney has instructions as to my estate.

I am calm now, but it is the calmness of utter despair, for I do not hope for rescue from my strange tomb. I can live but another day in this confined space, and already the weakness of dissolution is stealing upon me. Farewell.

Ernest Marden.

The terrible document fell from my nerveless hand, and I stared at the inspector in speechless horror. When I recovered myself I managed to gasp: "For Heaven's sake, tell me the end of this fearful tale!"

"There is nothing more to tell beyond the fact that the stolen property was all sent back to the rightful owners by the help of the labels on the boxes. I have always thought poor Marden intended to return it at some time. Certainly he did not need more wealth who was so rich himself."

1895

MARY E. WILKINS

THE LONG ARM

Recognized today as a first-rate author of ghost stories and supernatural fiction, MARY E(LEANOR) WILKINS (FREEMAN) (1852–1930) began writing while still a teenager, producing short stories and poetry for children before turning to adult novels and stories. She worked for a time as the secretary of Oliver Wendell Holmes, the noted author and poet and father of the distinguished Supreme Court justice.

Writing prolifically, with nearly thirty books published between 1883 and 1914, Wilkins created a vivid picture of New England in many of her books, combining the natural realism of normal, everyday life with chilling supernatural overtones. While somewhat reclusive and not a significant member of the flourishing literary circles of New England, she was awarded the very first William Dean Howells Medal for distinction in fiction by the American Academy of Arts and Letters, in 1926, and in the same year she and Edith Wharton became the first women inducted into the National Institute of Arts and Letters. When informed that the institute might be divided on the question of admitting women, Wilkins wrote with characteristic wryness that she could "very readily see that many would object."

Although it is her tales of the occult that remain read today (the prestigious publisher of horror fiction Arkham House released her *Collected Ghost Stories* in 1974), she also played a significant role in the history of detective fiction. *The Long Arm and Other Detective Stories,* issued in 1895 in London, is the first anthology of detective fiction ever published. Ironically, as Wilkins was far more successful in her own country than in England, it never found an American publisher.

"The Long Arm" was first published in the December 1895 issue of *The Pocket Magazine;* it was first published in book form in *The Long Arm and Other Detective Stories (Tales);* the word *stories* appears on the title page, while the word *tales* appears on the spine (London: Chapman & Hall, 1895).

• • •

CHAPTER I: THE TRAGEDY

(From notes written by Miss Sarah Fairbanks immediately after the report of the Grand Jury.)

As I TAKE my pen to write this, I have a feeling that I am on the witness stand — for or against myself, which? The place of the criminal in the dock I will not voluntarily take. I will affirm neither my innocence nor my guilt. I will present the facts of the case as impartially and as coolly as if I had nothing at stake. I will let all who may read this judge me as they will.

This I am bound to do, since I am condemned to something infinitely worse than the life-cell or the gallows. I will try my own self in lieu of judge and jury; my guilt or my innocence I will prove to you all, if it be in mortal power. In my despair I am tempted to say I care not which it may be, so something be proved. Open condemnation could not overwhelm me like universal suspicion.

Now, first, as I have heard is the custom in courts of law, I will present the case. I am Sarah Fairbanks, a country schoolteacher, twenty-nine years of age. My mother died when I was twenty-three. Since then, while I have been away teaching at Digby, a cousin of my father's, Rufus Bennett, and his wife have lived with my father. During the long summer vacations they returned to their little farm in Vermont, and I kept house for my father.

For five years I have been engaged to be married to Henry Ellis, a young man whom I met in Digby. My father was very much opposed to the match, and has told me repeatedly that if I insisted upon marrying him in his lifetime he would disinherit me. On this account Henry has never visited me at my own home. While I could not bring myself to break off my engagement, I wished to avoid an open rupture with my father. He was quite an old man, and I was the only one he had left of a large family.

I believe that parents should honor their children, as well as children their parents, but I had arrived at this conclusion: In nine-tenths of the cases wherein children marry against their parents' wishes, even when the parents have no just grounds for opposition, the marriages are unhappy.

I sometimes felt that I was unjust to Henry, and resolved that if ever I suspected that his fancy turned toward any other girl I would not hinder it, especially as I was getting older, and, I thought, losing my good looks.

A little while ago, a young and pretty girl came to Digby to teach the school in the south district. She boarded in the same house with Henry. I heard that he was somewhat attentive to her, and I made up my mind I would not interfere. At the same time it seemed to me my heart was breaking. I heard her people had money, too, and she was an only child. I had always felt that Henry ought to marry a wife with money, because he had nothing himself, and was not very strong.

School closed five weeks ago, and I came home for the summer vacation. The night before I left Henry came to see me, and urged me to marry him. I refused again; but I never before had felt that my father was so hard and cruel as I did that night. Henry said that he should certainly see me during the vacation, and when I replied that he must not come, he was angry, and said — but such foolish things are not worth repeating. Henry has really a very sweet temper, and would not hurt a fly.

The very night of my return home Rufus Bennett and my father had words about some maple sugar which Rufus made on his Vermont farm and sold to my father, who made a good trade for it to some people in Boston. That was father's business. He had once kept a store, but had given it up, and sold a few articles that he could make a large profit on here and there at wholesale. He used to send to New Hampshire and Vermont for butter, eggs, and cheese. Cousin Rufus thought father did not allow him enough of his profit on the maple sugar, and in the dispute father lost his temper and said that Rufus had given him under weight. At that, Rufus swore an oath and seized father by the throat. Rufus's wife screamed, "Oh, don't! don't! Oh, he'll kill him!"

I went up to Rufus and took hold of his arm.

"Rufus Bennett," said I, "you let my father go!"

But Rufus's eyes glared like a madman's, and he would not let go. Then I went to the desk-drawer where father had kept a pistol since some houses in the village were broken into. I got out the pistol, laid hold of Rufus again, and held the muzzle against his forehead.

"You let go my father," said I, "or I'll fire!"

Then Rufus let go, and father dropped like a log. He was purple in the face. Rufus's wife and I worked a long time over him to bring him to.

"Rufus Bennett," said I, "go to the well and get a pitcher of water." He went, but when father had revived and got up, Rufus gave him a look that showed he was not over his rage.

"I'll get even with you yet, Martin Fairbanks, old man as you are!" he shouted out, and went into the other room.

We got father to bed soon. He slept in the bedroom downstairs, out of the sitting room. Rufus and his wife had the north chamber, and I had the south one. I left my door open that night, and did not sleep any. I listened; no one stirred in the night. Rufus and his wife were up very early in the morning, and before nine o'clock left for Vermont. They had a day's journey and would reach home about nine in the evening. Rufus's wife bade father good-bye, crying, while Rufus was getting their trunks downstairs, but Rufus did not go near father nor me. He ate no breakfast; his very back looked ugly when he went out of the yard.

That very day, about seven o'clock in the evening, after tea, I had just washed the dishes and put them away and went out on the north doorstep, where father was sitting, and sat down on the lowest step. There was a cool breeze there; it had been a very hot day.

"I want to know if that Ellis fellow has been to see you any lately?" said father all at once.

"Not a great deal," I answered.

"Did he come to see you the last night you were there?" said father.

"Yes, sir," said I, "he did come."

"If you ever have another word to say to that fellow while I live, I'll kick you out of this house like a dog, daughter of mine though you be!" said he. Then he swore a great oath and called God to witness. "Speak to that fellow again, if you dare, while I live!" said he.

I did not say a word; I just looked up at him as I sat there. Father turned pale, and shrank back, and put his hand to his throat, where Rufus had clutched him. There were some purple finger-prints there.

"I suppose you would have been glad if he'd killed me," father cried out.

"I saved your life," said I.

"What did you do with that pistol?" he asked.

"I put it back in the desk-drawer."

I got up and went around and sat on the west doorstep, which is the front one. As I sat there the bell rang for the Tuesday evening meeting, and Phoebe Dole and Maria Woods, two old maiden ladies, dressmakers, our next-door neighbors, went past on their way to the meeting. Phoebe stopped and asked if Rufus and his wife had gone. Maria went around the house. Very soon they went on, and several other people passed. When they had all gone it was as still as death.

I sat alone a long time, until I could see by the shadows that the full moon had risen. Then I went up to my room and went to bed.

I lay awake a long time, crying. It seemed to me that all hope of marriage between Henry and me was over. I could not expect him to wait for me. I thought of that other girl; I could see her pretty face wherever I looked. But at last I cried myself to sleep.

At about five o'clock I woke and got up. Father always wanted his breakfast at six o'clock, and I had to prepare it now.

When father and I were alone, he always built the fire in the kitchen stove. But that morning I did not hear him stirring as usual, and I fancied that he must be so out of temper with me that he would not build the fire.

I went to my closet for a dark-blue calico dress which I wore to do housework in. It had hung there during all the school term. As I took it off the hook, my attention was caught by something strange about the dress I had worn the night before. This dress was made of thin summer silk; it was green in color, sprinkled over with white rings. It had been my best dress for two summers, but now I was wearing it on hot afternoons at home, for it is the coolest dress I have. The night before, too, I had thought of the possibility of Henry's driving over from Digby and passing the house. He had done this sometimes during the last summer vacation, and I wished to look my best if he did.

As I took down the calico dress I saw what seemed to be a stain on the green silk. I threw on the calico hastily and then took the green silk and carried it over to the window. It was covered with spots — horrible great splashes and streaks down the front. The right sleeve, too, was stained, and all the stains were wet.

"What have I got on my dress?" said I.

It looked like blood. Then I smelled of it, and it was sickening in my nostrils, but I was not sure what the smell of blood was like. I thought I must have got the stains by some accident the night before.

"If that is blood on my dress," I said, "I must do something to get it off at once, or the dress will be ruined."

It came to my mind that I had been told that blood-stains had been removed from cloth by an application of flour paste on the wrong side. I took my green silk and ran down the back stairs, which lead, having a door at the foot, directly into the kitchen.

There was no fire in the kitchen stove, as I had thought. Everything was very solitary and still, except for the ticking of the clock on the shelf.

When I crossed the kitchen to the pantry, however, the cat mewed to be let in from the shed. She had a little door of her own by which she could enter or leave the shed at will—an aperture just large enough for her Maltese body to pass at ease beside the shed door. It had a little lid, too, hung upon a leather hinge. On my way I let in the cat; then I went to the pantry and got a bowl of flour. This I mixed with water into a stiff paste and applied to the under surface of the stains on my dress. I then hung the dress up to dry in the dark end of a closet leading out of the kitchen, which contained some old clothes of father's.

Then I made up the fire in the kitchen stove; I made coffee, baked biscuits, and poached some eggs for breakfast.

Then I opened the door into the sitting room and called, "Father, breakfast is ready." Suddenly I started. There was a red stain on the inside of the sitting-room door. My heart began to beat in my ears.

"Father!" I called out; "father!"

There was no answer.

"Father!" I again called, as loud as I could scream. "Why don't you speak? What is the matter?"

The door of his bedroom stood open. I had a feeling that I saw a red reflection in there. I gathered myself together and went across the sitting room to father's bedroom door. His little looking-glass hung over his bureau directly opposite his bed, which was reflected in it.

That was the first thing I saw when I reached the door. I could see father in the looking-glass, and the bed. Father was dead there; he had been murdered in the night.

CHAPTER II: THE KNOT OF RIBBON

I THINK I MUST have fainted away; for presently I found myself upon the floor, and for a minute I could not remember what had happened. Then I remembered; and an awful, unreasoning terror seized me. "I must lock all the doors quick," I thought, "quick, or the murderer will come back!" I tried to get up, but I could not stand. I sank down again. I had to crawl out of the room on my hands and knees.

I went first to the front door. It was locked with a key and a bolt. I went next to the north door, and that was locked with a key and a bolt. I went to the north shed door, and that was bolted. Then I went to the little-used east door in the shed, beside which the cat has her little passageway, and that was fastened with an iron hook. It has no latch.

The whole house was fastened on the inside. The thought struck me like an icy hand. "The murderer is in this house!" I rose to my feet then; I unhooked that door and ran out of the house and out of the yard, as for my life.

I took the road to the village. The first house, where Phoebe Dole and Maria Woods live, is across a wide field from ours. I did not intend to stop there, for they were only women and could do nothing; but seeing Phoebe looking out of the window, I ran into the yard. She opened the window.

"What is it?" said she. "What is the matter, Sarah Fairbanks?"

Maria Woods came and leaned over her shoulder. Her face looked almost as white as her white hair, and her blue eyes were dilated. My face must have frightened her.

"Father — father is murdered in his bed!" I said.

There was a scream, and Maria Woods's face disappeared from over Phoebe Dole's shoulder — she had fainted. I don't know whether Phoebe looked paler — she is always very pale — but I saw in her black eyes a look I shall never forget. I think she began to suspect me at that moment.

Phoebe glanced back at Maria, but she asked me another question. "Has he had words with anybody?" said she.

"Only with Rufus," I said; "but Rufus is gone."

Phoebe turned away from the window to attend to Maria, and I ran on to the village.

A hundred people can testify what I did next — can tell how I called for the doctor and the deputy sheriff; how I went back to my own home with the horror-stricken crowd; how they flocked in and looked at poor father — but only the doctor touched him, very carefully, to see if he were quite dead; how the coroner came, and all the rest.

The pistol was in the bed beside father, but it had not been fired; the charge was still in the barrel. It was blood-stained, and there was one bruise on father's head which might have been inflicted by the pistol, used as a club. But the wound which caused his death was in his breast, and made evidently by some cutting instrument, though the cut was not a clean one; the weapon must have been dull.

They searched the house, lest the murderer should be hidden away. I heard Rufus Bennett's name whispered by one and another. Everybody seemed to know that he and father had had words the night before; I could not understand how, because I had told nobody except Phoebe Dole, who had had no time to spread the news, and I was sure that no one else had spoken of it.

They looked in the closet where my green silk dress hung, and pushed it aside, to be sure nobody was concealed behind it, but they did not notice anything wrong about it. It was dark in the closet, and besides, they did not look for anything like that until later.

All these people — the deputy sheriff, and afterward the high sheriff and other out-of-town officers for whom they had telegraphed, and the neighbors — all hunted their own suspicion, and that was Rufus Bennett. All believed that he had come back and killed my father. They fitted all the facts to that belief. They made him do the deed with a long, slender screwdriver which he had recently borrowed from one of the neighbors and had not returned. They made his finger-marks, which were still on my father's throat, fit the red prints on the sitting-room door. They made sure that he had returned and stolen into the house by the east shed door, while father and I sat on the doorsteps the evening before; that he had hidden himself away, perhaps in that very closet where my dress hung, and afterward stolen out and killed my father and then escaped.

They were not shaken when I told them that every door was bolted and barred that morning. They themselves found all the windows fastened down, except a few which were open on account of the heat, and even these last were raised only the width of a sash, and fastened with sticks so that they could be raised no higher. Father was very cautious about fastening the house, for he sometimes had considerable sums of money by him. The officers saw all these difficulties in the way, but they fitted them somehow to their theory, and two deputy sheriffs were at once sent to apprehend Rufus.

They had not begun to suspect me then, and not the slightest watch was kept on my movements. The neighbors were very kind, and did everything to help me, relieving me altogether of all those last offices — in this case much sadder than usual.

An inquest was held, and I told freely all I knew, except about the blood-stains on my dress. I hardly knew why I kept that back. I had no feeling then that I might have done the deed myself, and I could not bear to convict myself, if I was innocent.

Two of the neighbors, Mrs. Holmes and Mrs. Adams, remained with me all that day. Toward evening, when there were very few in the house, they went into the parlor to put it in order for the funeral, and I sat down alone in the kitchen. As I sat there by the window I thought of my green silk dress, and wondered if the stains were out. I went to the closet and brought the dress out to the light. The spots and streaks had almost disappeared. I took the dress out in the shed and scraped off the flour paste, which was quite dry; I swept up the paste, burned it in the stove, took the dress upstairs to my own closet, and hung it in its old place. Neighbors remained with me all night.

At three o'clock in the afternoon of the next day, which was Thursday, I went over to Phoebe Dole's to see about a black dress to wear to the funeral. The neighbors had urged me to have my black silk dress altered a little and trimmed with crape.

I found only Maria Woods at home. When she saw me she gave a little scream and began to cry. She looked as if she had already been weeping for hours. Her blue eyes were bloodshot.

"Phoebe's gone over to — Mrs. Whitney's to — try on her dress," she sobbed.

"I want to get my black silk dress fixed a little," said I.

"She'll be home — pretty soon," said Maria.

I laid my dress on the sofa and sat down. Nobody ever consults Maria about a dress. She sews well, but Phoebe does all the planning.

Maria Woods continued to sob like a child, holding her little soaked handkerchief over her face. Her shoulders heaved. As for me, I felt like a stone; I could not weep.

"Oh," she gasped out finally, "I knew, I knew! I told Phoebe — I knew just how it would be. I — knew!"

I roused myself at that. "What do you mean?" said I.

"When Phoebe came home Tuesday night and said she heard your father and Rufus Bennett having words, I knew how it would be," she choked out. "I knew he had a dreadful temper."

"Did Phoebe Dole know Tuesday night that father and Rufus Bennett had words?" said I.

"Yes," said Maria Woods.

"How did she know?"

"She was going through your yard, the short cut to Mrs. Ormsby's, to carry her brown alpaca dress home. She came right home and told me; and she overheard them."

"Have you spoken of it to anybody but me?" said I.

Maria said she didn't know; she might have done so. Then she remembered Phoebe herself speaking of it to Harriet Sargent when she came in to try on her dress. It was easy to see how people knew about it.

I did not say any more, but I thought it was strange that Phoebe Dole had asked me if father had had words with anybody when she knew it all the time.

Phoebe came in before long. I tried on my dress, and she made her plan about the alterations and the trimming. I made no suggestions. I did not care how it was done, but if I had cared, it would have made no difference. Phoebe always does things her own way. All the women in this village are in a manner under Phoebe Dole's thumb. Their garments are visible proofs of her force of will.

While she was taking up my black silk on the shoulder seams, Phoebe Dole said: "Let me see — you had a green silk dress made at Digby three summers ago, didn't you?"

"Yes," I said.

"Well," said she, "why don't you have it dyed black? those thin silks dye real nice. It would make you a good dress."

I scarcely replied, and then she offered to dye it for me herself. She had a recipe, which she had used with great success. I thought it very kind of her, but did not say whether I would accept her offer or not. I could not fix my mind upon anything but the awful trouble I was in.

"I'll come over and get it to-morrow morning," said Phoebe.

I thanked her. I thought of the stains, and then my mind seemed to wander away again to the one subject.

All the time Maria Woods sat weeping. Finally Phoebe turned to her with impatience. "If you can't keep calmer, you'd better go upstairs, Maria," said she. "You'll make Sarah sick. Look at her! She doesn't give way — and think of the reason she's got."

"I've got reason, too," Maria broke out; then, with a piteous shriek: "Oh, I've got reason!"

"Maria Woods, go out of the room!" said Phoebe. Her sharpness made me jump, half dazed as I was.

Maria got up without a word and went out of the room, bending almost double with convulsive sobs.

"She's been dreadful worked up over your father's death," said Phoebe calmly, going on with the fitting. "She's terribly nervous. Sometimes I have to be real sharp with her, for her own good."

I nodded. Maria Woods has always been considered a sweet, weakly, dependent woman, and Phoebe Dole is undoubtedly very fond of her. She has seemed to shield her and take care of her nearly all her life. The two have lived together since they were young girls.

Phoebe is tall and very pale and thin; but she never had a day's illness. She is plain, yet there is a kind of severe goodness and faithfulness about her colorless face, with the smooth bands of white hair over her ears.

I went home as soon as my dress was fitted. That evening Henry Ellis came over to see me. I do not need to go into details concerning that visit. It is enough to say that he tendered the fullest sympathy and protection, and I accepted them. I cried a little, for the first time, and he soothed and comforted me.

Henry had driven over from Digby and tied his horse in the yard. At ten o'clock he bade me good-night on the doorstep, and was just turning his buggy around when Mrs. Adams came running to the door.

"Is this yours?" said she, and she held out a knot of yellow ribbon.

"Why, that's the ribbon you have around your whip, Henry," said I.

He looked at it. "So it is," he said. "I must have dropped it." He put it into his pocket and drove away.

"He didn't drop that ribbon to-night!" said Mrs. Adams. "I found it Wednesday morning, out in the yard. I thought I remembered seeing him have a yellow ribbon on his whip."

CHAPTER III: SUSPICION IS NOT PROOF

When Mrs. Adams told me that she had picked up Henry's whip ribbon Wednesday morning, I said nothing, but thought that Henry must have driven over Tuesday evening after all, and even come up into the yard, although the house was shut up and I in bed, to get a little nearer to me. I felt conscience-stricken because I could not help a thrill of happiness, when my father lay dead in the house.

My father was buried as privately and quietly as we could bring it about. But it was a terrible ordeal. Meantime word came from Vermont that Rufus Bennett had been arrested on his farm. He was perfectly willing to come back with the officers, and, indeed, had not the slightest trouble in proving that he was at his home in Vermont when the murder took place. He proved by several witnesses that he was out of the state long before my father and I sat on the step together that evening, and that he proceeded directly to his home as fast as the train and stage-coach could carry him.

The screwdriver with which the deed was supposed to have been committed was found, by the neighbor from whom it had been borrowed, in his wife's bureau drawer. It had been returned, and she had used it to put up a picture-hook in her chamber. Bennett was discharged, and returned to Vermont.

Then Mrs. Adams told of her finding the yellow ribbon from Henry Ellis's whip, and he was arrested, since he was held to have a motive for putting my father out of the world. Father's opposition to our marriage was well known, and Henry was suspected also of having had an eye to his money. It was found, indeed, that my father had more money than I had known myself.

Henry owned to having driven into our yard that night, and to having missed the ribbon from his whip on his return; but one of the hostlers in the livery stable in Digby, where he kept his horse and buggy, came forward and testified to finding the yellow ribbon in the carriage-room that Tuesday night before Henry returned from his drive. There were two yellow ribbons in evidence, therefore, and the one produced by the hostler seemed to fit Henry's whipstock the more exactly.

Moreover, nearly the exact minute of the murder was claimed to be proved by the post-mortem examination; and by the testimony of the stableman as to the hour of Henry's return and the speed of his horse he was further cleared of suspicion; for, if the opinion of the medical experts was correct, Henry must have returned to the livery stable too soon to have committed the murder.

He was discharged, at any rate, although suspicion still clung to him. Many people believe now in his guilt — those who do not, believe in mine; and some believe we were accomplices.

After Henry's discharge I was arrested. There was no one else left to accuse. There must be a motive for the murder; I was the only person left with a motive. Unlike the others, who were discharged after a preliminary examination, I was held to the grand jury and taken to Dedham, where I spent four weeks in jail, awaiting the meeting of the grand jury.

Neither at the preliminary examination nor before the grand jury was I allowed to make the full and frank statement that I am making here. I was told simply to answer the questions that were put to me, and to volunteer nothing, and I obeyed.

I know nothing about law. I wished to do the best I could — to act in the wisest manner, for Henry's sake and my own. I said nothing about the green silk dress. They searched the house for all manner of things, at the time of my arrest, but the dress was not there — it was in Phoebe Dole's dye-kettle. She had come over after it herself one day when I was picking beans in the garden, and had taken it out of the closet. She brought it back herself and told me this, after I had returned from Dedham.

"I thought I'd get it and surprise you," said she. "It's taken a beautiful black."

She gave me a strange look: half as if she would see into my very soul, in spite of me, half as if she were in terror of what she would see there, as she spoke. I do not know just what Phoebe Dole's look meant. There may have been a stain left on that dress after all, and she may have seen it.

I suppose if it had not been for that flour paste which I had learned to make, I should have been hung for the murder of my father. As it was, the grand jury found no bill against me, because there was absolutely no evidence to convict me; and I came home a free woman. And if people were condemned for their motives, would there be enough hangmen in the world?

They found no weapon with which I could have done the deed. They found no blood-stains on my clothes. The one thing which told against me, aside from my ever-present motive, was the fact that on that morning after the murder the doors and windows were fastened. My volunteering that information had, of course, weakened its force as against myself.

Then, too, some held that I might have been mistaken in my terror and excitement, and there was a theory, advanced by a few, that the murderer had meditated making me also a victim, and had locked the doors that he might not be frustrated in his designs, but had lost heart at the last and allowed me to escape, and then fled himself. Some held that he had intended to force me to reveal the whereabouts of father's money, but his courage had failed him.

Father had quite a sum in a hiding place which only he and I knew. But no search for money had been made, so far as anyone could see — not a bureau drawer had been disturbed, and father's gold watch was ticking peacefully under his pillow; even his wallet in his vest pocket had not been opened. There was a small roll of banknotes in it, and some change; father never carried much money. I suppose if father's wallet and watch had been taken, I should not have been suspected at all.

I was discharged, as I have said, from lack of evidence, and have returned to my home, free, indeed, but with this awful burden of suspicion upon my shoulders. That brings me up to the present day. I returned yesterday evening. This evening Henry Ellis has been over to see me; he will not come again, for I have forbidden him to do so. This is what I said to him:

"I know you are innocent, you know I am innocent. To all the world we are under suspicion — I more than you, but we are both under suspicion. If we are known to be together, that suspicion is increased for both of us. I do not care for myself, but I do care for you. Separated from me, the stigma attached to you will soon fade away, especially if you should marry elsewhere."

Then Henry interrupted me. "I will never marry elsewhere!" said he.

I could not help being glad that he said it, but I was firm.

"If you should see some good woman whom you can love, it will be better for you to marry elsewhere," said I.

"I never will!" he said again. He put his arms around me, but I had strength to push him away.

"You never need, if I succeed in what I undertake before you meet the other," said I. I began to think he had not cared for that pretty girl who boarded in the same house after all.

"What is that?" he said. "What are you going to undertake?"

"To find my father's murderer," said I.

Henry gave me a strange look; then, before I could stop him, he took me fast in his arms and kissed my forehead.

"As God is my witness, Sarah, I believe in your innocence," he said. And from that minute I have felt sustained and fully confident of my power to do what I have undertaken.

My father's murderer I will find. To-morrow I begin my search. I shall first make an exhaustive examination of the house, such as no officer in the case has yet made, in the hope of finding a clue. Every room I propose to divide into square yards, by line and measure, and every one of those square yards I will study as if it were a problem in algebra.

I have a theory that it is impossible for any human being to enter any house and commit in it a deed of this kind and not leave behind traces which are the known quantities in an algebraic equation to those who can use them.

There is a chance that I shall not be quite unaided. Henry has promised not to come again until I bid him, but he is to send a detective here from Boston—one whom he knows. In fact, the man is a cousin of his, or else there would be small hope of our securing him, even if I were to offer him a large price.

The man has been remarkably successful in several cases, but his health is not good; the work is a severe strain upon his nerves, and he is not driven to it by any lack of money. The physicians had forbidden him to undertake any new case, for a year at least, but Henry is confident that we may rely upon him for this.

I will now lay this aside and go to bed. To-morrow is Wednesday; my father will have been dead seven weeks. To-morrow morning I commence the work, in which, if it be in human power, aided by a higher wisdom, I shall succeed.

CHAPTER IV: THE BOX OF CLUES

(The pages which follow are from Miss Fairbanks's journal, begun after the conclusion of the notes already given to the reader.)

WEDNESDAY NIGHT. — I have resolved to record carefully each day the progress I make in my examination of the house. I began to-day at the bottom — that is, with the room least likely to contain any clue, the parlor. I took a chalk line and a yard stick, and divided the floor into square yards, and every one of these squares I examined on my hands and knees. I found in this way literally nothing on the carpet but dust, lint, two common white pins, and three inches of blue sewing silk.

At last I got the dust-pan and brush, and yard by yard swept the floor. I took the sweepings in a white pasteboard box out into the yard in the strong sunlight, and examined them. There was nothing but dust and lint and five inches of brown woolen thread — evidently a raveling from some dress material. The blue silk and the brown thread are the only possible clues which I have found to-day, and they are hardly possible. Rufus's wife can probably account for them. I have written to her about them.

Nobody has come to the house all day. I went down to the store this afternoon to get some necessary provisions, and people stopped talking when I came in. The clerk took my money as if it were poison.

Thursday night. — To-day I have searched the sitting room, out of which my father's bedroom opens. I found two bloody footprints on the carpet which no one had noticed before — perhaps because the carpet itself is red and white. I used a microscope which I had in my school work. The footprints, which are close to the bedroom door, pointing out into the sitting room, are both from the right foot; one is brighter than the other, but both are faint. The foot was evidently either bare or clad only in a stocking — the prints are so widely spread. They are wider than my father's shoes. I tried one in the brightest print.

I found nothing else new in the sitting room. The blood-stains on the doors, which have been already noted, are still there. They had not been washed away, first by order of the sheriff, and next by mine. These stains are of two kinds; one looks as if made by a bloody garment brushing against it; the other, I should say, was made in the first place by the grasp of a bloody hand, and then brushed over with a cloth. There are none of these marks upon the door leading into the front entry and the china closet. The china closet is really a pantry, although I use it only for my best dishes and preserves.

Friday night.—To-day I searched the closet. One of the shelves, which is about as high as my shoulders, was blood-stained. It looked to me as if the murderer might have caught hold of it to steady himself. Did he turn faint, after his dreadful deed? Some tumblers of jelly were ranged on that shelf and they had not been disturbed. There was only that bloody clutch on the edge.

I found on this closet floor, under the shelves, as if it had been rolled there by a careless foot, a button, evidently from a man's clothing. It is an ordinary black enameled metal trousers button; it had evidently been worn off and clumsily sewn on again, for a quantity of stout white thread is still clinging to it. This button must have belonged either to a single man or to one with an idle wife.

If one black button has been sewn on with white thread, another is likely to be. I may be wrong, but I regard this button as a clue.

The pantry was thoroughly swept—cleaned, indeed, by Rufus's wife the day before she left. Neither my father nor Rufus could have dropped it there, and they never had occasion to go to the closet. The murderer dropped the button.

I have a white pasteboard box which I have marked, "Clues." In it I have put the button.

This afternoon Phoebe Dole came in. She is very kind. She has re-cut the dyed silk, and she fitted it to me. Her great shears, clicking in my ears, made me nervous. I did not feel like stopping to think about clothes. I hope I did not appear ungrateful, for she is the only soul besides Henry who has treated me as before this happened.

Phoebe asked me what I found to busy myself about, and I replied, "I am searching for my father's murderer." She asked me if I thought I should find a clue, and I replied, "I think so." I had found the button then, but I did not speak of it. She said Maria was not very well.

I saw her eyeing the stains on the doors, and I said I had not washed them off, for I thought they might yet serve a purpose in detecting the murderer. She looked at those on the entry door—the brightest ones—and said she did not see how they could help, for there were no plain finger-marks there, and she should think they would make me nervous.

"I'm beyond being nervous," said I.

Saturday.—To-day I have found something which I cannot understand. I have been at work in the room where my father came to his dreadful end. Of course some of the most startling evidences have been removed. The bed is clean, and the carpet washed, but the worst horror of it all clings to that room. The spirit of murder seems to haunt it. It seemed to me at first that I could not enter that room, but in it I made a strange discovery.

My father, while he carried little money about his person, was in the habit of keeping considerable sums in the house; there is no bank within ten miles. However, he was wary; he had a hiding place which he had revealed to no one but myself. He had a small stand in his room near the head of his bed. Under this stand, or rather under the top of it, he had tacked a large leather wallet. In this he kept all his spare money. I remember how his eyes twinkled when he showed it to me.

"The average mind thinks things have either got to be in or on," said my father. "They don't consider there's ways of getting around gravitation and calculation."

In searching my father's room I called to mind that saying of his, and his peculiar system of concealing, and then I made my discovery. I have argued that in a search of this kind I ought not only to search for hidden traces of the criminal, but for everything which had been for any reason concealed. Something which my father himself had hidden, something from his past history, may furnish a motive for someone else.

The money in the wallet under the table, some five hundred dollars, had been removed and deposited in the bank. Nothing more was to be found there. I examined the bottom of the bureau, and the undersides of the chair seats. There are two chairs in the room, besides the cushioned rocker—green-painted wooden chairs, with flag seats. I found nothing under the seats.

Then I turned each of the green chairs completely over, and examined the bottoms of the legs. My heart leaped when I found a bit of leather nicely tacked over one. I got the tack hammer and drew the tacks. The chair leg had been hollowed out, and for an inch the hole was packed tight with cotton. I began picking out the cotton, and soon I felt something hard. It proved to be an old-fashioned gold band, quite wide and heavy, like a wedding ring.

I took it over to the window and found this inscription on the inside: "Let love abide forever." There were two dates—one in August, forty years ago, and the other in August of this present year.

I think the ring has never been worn; while the first part of the inscription is perfectly clear, it looks old, and the last is evidently freshly cut.

This could not have been my mother's ring. She had only her wedding ring, and that was buried with her. I think my father must have treasured up this ring for years; but why? What does it mean? This can hardly be a clue; this can hardly lead to the discovery of a motive, but I will put it in the box with the rest.

Sunday night. — To-day, of course, I did not pursue my search. I did not go to church. I could not face old friends that could not face me. Sometimes I think that everybody in my native village believes in my guilt. What must I have been in my general appearance and demeanor all my life? I have studied myself in the glass, and tried to discover the possibilities of evil that they must see in my face.

This afternoon, about three o'clock, the hour when people here have just finished their Sunday dinner, there was a knock on the north door. I answered it, and a strange young man stood there with a large book under his arm. He was thin and cleanly shaved, with a clerical air.

"I have a work here to which I would like to call your attention," he began; and I stared at him in astonishment, for why should a book agent be peddling his wares upon the Sabbath?

His mouth twitched a little. "It's a Biblical Cyclopedia," said he.

"I don't think I care to take it," said I.

"You are Miss Sarah Fairbanks, I believe?"

"That is my name," I replied stiffly.

"Mr. Henry Ellis of Digby sent me here," he said next. "My name is Dix — Francis Dix."

Then I knew that he was Henry's cousin from Boston — the detective who had come to help me. I felt tears coming to my eyes. "You are very kind to come," I managed to say.

"I am very selfish, not kind," he returned, "but you had better let me come in, or my chance of success in my book agency is lost, if the neighbors see me trying to sell it on a Sunday. And, Miss Fairbanks, this is a *bona fide* agency. I shall canvass the town."

He came in. I showed him all this that I have written, and he read it carefully. When he had finished he sat still for a long time, with his face screwed up in a peculiar, meditative fashion.

"We'll ferret this out in three days at the most," said he finally, with a sudden clearing of his face and a flash of his eyes at me.

"I had planned for three years, perhaps," said I.

"I tell you, we'll do it in three days," he repeated. "Where can I get board while I canvass for this remarkable and interesting book under my arm? I can't stay here, of course, and there is no hotel. Do you think the two dressmakers next door, Phoebe Dole and the other one, would take me in?"

I said they had never taken boarders.

"Well, I'll go over and inquire," said Mr. Dix; and he had gone, with his book under his arm, almost before I knew it.

Never have I seen anyone act with the strange, noiseless, soft speed that this man does. Can he prove me innocent in three days? He must have succeeded in getting board at Phoebe Dole's, for I saw him go past to meeting with her this evening. I feel sure he will be over very early to-morrow morning.

CHAPTER V: THE EVIDENCE POINTS TO ONE

MONDAY NIGHT. — The detective came as I expected. I was up as soon as it was light, and he came across the dewy fields with his cyclopedia under his arm. He had stolen out of Phoebe Dole's back door.

He had me bring my father's pistol; then he bade me come with him out into the back yard. "Now fire it," he said, thrusting the pistol into my hands. As I have said before, the charge was still in the barrel.

"I shall arouse the neighborhood," I said.

"Fire it!" he ordered.

I tried; I pulled the trigger as hard as I could.

"I can't do it," I said.

"And you are a reasonably strong woman, too, aren't you?"

I said I had been considered so. Oh, how much I have heard about the strength of my poor woman's arms, and their ability to strike that murderous weapon home!

Mr. Dix took the pistol himself, and drew a little at the trigger. "I could do it," he said, "but I won't. It would arouse the neighborhood."

"This is more evidence against me," I said despairingly. "The murderer had tried to fire the pistol and failed."

"It is more evidence against the murderer," said Mr. Dix.

We went into the house, where he examined my box of clues long and carefully. Looking at the ring, he asked whether there was a jeweler in this village, and I said there was not. I told him that my father oftener went on business to Acton, ten miles away, than elsewhere.

He examined very carefully the button which I found in the closet, and then asked to see my father's wardrobe. That was soon done. Besides the suit in which father was laid away, there was one other complete one in the closet in his room. Besides that, there were in this closet two overcoats, an old black frock coat, a pair of pepper-and-salt trousers, and two black vests. Mr. Dix examined all the buttons; not one was missing.

There was still another old suit in the closet off the kitchen. This was examined, and no button found wanting.

"What did your father do for work the day before he died?" he asked then. I reflected, and said that he had unpacked some stores which had come down from Vermont, and done some work out in the garden.

"What did he wear?"

"I think he wore the pepper-and-salt trousers and the black vest. He wore no coat while at work."

Mr. Dix went quickly back to father's room and his closet, I following. He took out the gray trousers and the black vest, and examined them closely.

"What did he wear to protect these?" he asked.

"Why, he wore overalls!" I said at once. As I spoke I remembered seeing father go around the path to the yard, with those blue overalls drawn up high under the arms.

"Where are they?"

"Weren't they in the kitchen closet?"

"No."

We looked again, however, in the kitchen closet; we searched the shed thoroughly. The cat came in through her little door, as we stood there, and brushed around our feet. Mr. Dix stooped and stroked her. Then he went quickly to the door, beside which her little entrance was arranged, unhooked it and stepped out. I was following him, but he motioned me back.

"None of my boarding mistress's windows command us," he said, "but she might come to her back door."

I watched him. He passed slowly along the little winding footpath which skirted the rear of our house and extended faintly through the grassy field to the rear of Phoebe Dole's. He stopped, searched a clump of sweetbriar, went on to an old well, and stopped there. The well has been dry many a year, and was choked up with stones and rubbish. Some boards are laid over it, and a big stone or two, to keep them in place.

Mr. Dix, glancing across at Phoebe Dole's back door, went down on his knees, rolled the stones away, then removed the boards, and peered down the well. He stretched far over the brink and reached down. He made many efforts; then he got up and came to me, and asked me to get for him an umbrella with a crooked handle, or something that he could hook into clothing.

I brought my own umbrella, the silver handle of which formed an exact hook. He went back to the well, knelt again, thrust in the umbrella and drew up, easily enough, what he had been fishing for. Then he came, bringing it to me.

"Don't faint!" he said, and took hold of my arm. I gasped when I saw what he had — my father's blue overalls, all stained and splotched with blood!

I looked at them, then at him.

"Don't faint!" he said again. "We're on the right track. This is where the button came from. See?" He pointed to one of the straps of the overalls, and the button was gone. Some white thread clung to it. Another black metal button was sewed on roughly with the same white thread I had found on the button in my box of clues.

"What does it mean?" I gasped out. My brain reeled.

"You shall know soon," he said. He looked at his watch. Then he laid down the ghastly bundle he carried. "It has puzzled you to know how the murderer went in and out, and yet kept the doors locked, has it not?" he said.

"Yes."

"Well, I am going out now. Hook that door after me."

He went out, still carrying my umbrella. I hooked the door. Presently I saw the lid of the cat's door lifted, and his hand and arm thrust through. He curved his arm up toward the hook, but it came short by a half-foot. Then he withdrew his arm, and thrust in my silver-handled umbrella. He reached the door-hook easily enough with that.

Then he hooked it again. That was not so easy — he had to work a long time. Finally he accomplished it, unhooked the door again, and came in.

"That was how?" I said.

"No, it was not," he returned. "No human being, fresh from such a deed, could have used such patience as that to fasten the door after him. Please hang your arm down by your side."

I obeyed. He looked at my arm, then at his own.

"Have you a tape measure?" he asked.

I brought one out of my work basket. He measured his arm, then mine, and then the distance from the cat-door to the hook.

"I have two tasks for you to-day and to-morrow," he said. "I shall come here very little. Find all your father's old letters and read them. Find a man or woman in this town whose arm is six inches longer than yours. Now I must go home, or my boarding mistress will get curious."

He went through the house to the front door, looked all ways to be sure no eyes were upon him, made three strides down the yard, and was pacing soberly up the street with his cyclopedia under his arm.

I made myself a cup of coffee; then I went about obeying his instructions. I read old letters all the forenoon; I found packages in trunks in the garret — there were quantities in father's desk. I have selected several to submit to Mr. Dix. One of them treats of an old episode in father's youth, which must have years since ceased to interest him. It was concealed after his favorite fashion — tacked under the bottom of his desk. It was written forty years ago, by Maria Woods — two years before my father's marriage — and it was a refusal of an offer of his hand. It was written in the stilted fashion of that day; it might have been copied from a "Complete Letter-writer."

My father must have loved Maria Woods as dearly as I love Henry, to keep that letter so carefully all these years. I thought he cared for my mother. He seemed as fond of her as other men of their wives, although I did use to wonder if Henry and I would ever get to be quite so much accustomed to each other.

Maria Woods must have been as beautiful as an angel when she was a girl. Mother was not pretty — she was stout, too, and awkward, and I suppose people would have called her rather slow and dull. But she was a good woman and tried to do her duty.

Tuesday evening. — This evening was my first opportunity to obey the second of Mr. Dix's orders. It seemed to me the best way to compare the average length of arms was to go to the prayer meeting. I could not go about the town with my tape measure and demand of people that they should hold out their arms. Nobody knows how I dreaded to go to that meeting, but I went, and I looked not at my neighbor's cold, altered faces, but at their arms.

I discovered what Mr. Dix wished me to, but the discovery can avail nothing, and it is one he could have made himself. Phoebe Dole's arm is fully seven inches longer than mine. I never noticed it before, but she has an almost abnormally long arm. But why should Phoebe Dole have unhooked that door?

She made a prayer — a beautiful prayer; it comforted even me a little. She spoke of the tenderness of God in all the troubles of life, and how it never failed us.

When we were all going out I heard several persons speak of Mr. Dix and his Biblical Cyclopedia. They decided that he was a theological student, book canvassing to defray the expenses of his education.

Maria Woods was not at the meeting. Several asked Phoebe how she was, and she replied, "Not very well."

It was very late. I thought Mr. Dix might be over to-night, but he has not been here.

Wednesday. — I can scarcely believe what I am about to write. Our investigations seem all to point to one person, and that person — it is incredible! I will not believe it. Mr. Dix came as before, at dawn. He reported, and I reported. I showed Maria Woods's letter. He said he had driven to Acton and found that the jeweler there had engraved the last date in the ring about six weeks ago.

"I don't want to seem rough, but your father was going to get married again," said Mr. Dix.

"I never knew him to go near any woman since mother died," I protested.

"Nevertheless he had made arrangements to be married," persisted Mr. Dix.

"Who was the woman?"

He pointed at the letter in my hand.

"Maria Woods?"

He nodded.

I stood looking at him — dazed. Such a possibility had never entered my head.

He produced an envelope from his pocket, and took out a little card with blue and brown threads neatly wound upon it. "Let me see those threads you found," he said.

I got the box, and we compared them. He had a number of pieces of blue sewing silk and brown woolen ravelings, and they matched mine exactly.

"Where did you find them?" I asked.

"In my boarding mistress's piece-bag."

I stared at him. "What does it mean?" I gasped out.

"What do you think?"

"It is impossible!"

CHAPTER VI: THE REVELATION

WEDNESDAY (CONTINUED). — When Mr. Dix thus suggested to me the absurd possibility that Phoebe Dole had committed the murder, he and I were sitting in the kitchen. He was near the table; he laid a sheet of paper upon it and began to write. The paper is before me.

"First," said Mr. Dix, and he wrote as he talked, "whose arm is of such length that it might unlock and lock a certain door of this house from the outside? Phoebe Dole's.

"Second, who had in her piece-bag bits of the same threads and ravelings found upon your parlor floor, where she had not by your knowledge entered? Phoebe Dole.

"Third, who interested herself most strangely in your blood-stained green silk dress, even to dyeing it? Phoebe Dole.

"Fourth, who was caught in a lie, while trying to force the guilt of the murder upon an innocent man? Phoebe Dole."

Mr. Dix looked at me. I had gathered myself together.

"That proves nothing," I said. "There is no motive in her case."

"There is a motive."

"What is it?"

"Maria Woods shall tell you this afternoon."

He then wrote:

"Fifth, who was seen to throw a bundle down the old well, in the rear of Martin Fairbanks's house, at one o'clock in the morning? Phoebe Dole."

"Was she — seen?" I gasped.

Mr. Dix nodded. Then he wrote:

"Sixth, who had a strong motive, which had been in existence many years ago? Phoebe Dole."

Mr. Dix laid down his pen and looked at me again. "Well, what have you to say?" he asked.

"It is impossible!"

"Why?"

"She is a woman."

"A man could have fired that pistol, as she tried to do."

"It would have taken a man's strength to kill with the kind of weapon that was used," I said.

"No, it would not. No great strength is required for such a blow."

"But she is a woman!"

"Crime has no sex."

"But she is a good woman, a church member. I heard her pray yesterday afternoon. It is not in character."

"It is not for you, nor for me, nor for any mortal intelligence to know what is or is not in character," said Mr. Dix.

He arose and went away. I could only stare at him in a half-dazed manner.

Maria Woods came this afternoon, taking advantage of Phoebe's absence on a dressmaking errand. Maria has aged ten years in the last few weeks. Her hair is white, her cheeks are fallen in, her pretty color is gone.

"May I have the ring — he gave me — forty years ago?" she faltered.

I gave it to her; she kissed it and sobbed like a child. "Phoebe took it away from me before," she said, "but she shan't this time."

Maria related, with piteous little sobs, the story of her long subordination to Phoebe Dole. This sweet, child-like woman had always been completely under the sway of the other's stronger nature. The subordination went back beyond my father's original proposal to her; she had, before he made love to her as a girl, promised Phoebe she would not marry, and it was Phoebe who had, by representing to her that she was bound by this solemn promise, led her to write the letter to my father declining his offer, and sending back the ring.

"And after all, we were going to get married, if he had not — died," she said. "He was going to give me this ring again, and he had had the other date put in. I should have been so happy!"

She stopped, and stared at me with horror-stricken inquiry.

"What was Phoebe doing out in your back yard at one o'clock that night?" she cried.

"What do you mean?" I returned.

"I saw Phoebe come out of your back shed door at one o'clock that very night. She had a bundle in her arms. She went along the path about as far as the old well; then she stooped down, and seemed to be working at something. When she got up, she didn't have the bundle. I was watching at our back door. I thought I heard her go out a little while before, and went downstairs, and found that door unlocked. I went in quick, and up to my chamber, and into my bed, when she started home across the field. Pretty soon I heard her come in; then I heard the pump going. She slept downstairs; she went on to her bedroom. What was she doing in your back yard that night?"

"You must ask her," said I. I felt my blood running cold.

"I've been afraid to," moaned Maria Woods. "She's been dreadful strange lately. I wish that book agent was going to stay at our house."

Maria Woods went home in about an hour. I got a ribbon for her, and she has my poor father's ring concealed in her withered bosom. Again, I cannot believe this.

Thursday.—It is all over; Phoebe Dole has confessed! I do not know now in exactly what way Mr. Dix brought it about—how he accused her of her crime. After breakfast I saw them coming across the field. Phoebe came first, advancing with rapid strides like a man; Mr. Dix followed, and my father's poor old sweetheart tottered behind, with her handkerchief at her eyes. Just as I noticed them the front door bell rang; I found several people there, headed by the high sheriff. They crowded into the sitting room, just as Phoebe Dole came rushing in, with Mr. Dix and Maria Woods.

"I did it!" Phoebe cried out to me. "I am found out, and I have made up my mind to confess. She was going to marry your father—I found it out. I stopped it once before. This time I knew I couldn't, unless I killed him. She's lived with me in that house for over forty years. There are other ties as strong as the marriage one that are just as sacred! What right had he to take her away from me and break up my home?

"I overheard your father and Rufus Bennett having words. I thought folks would think he did it. I reasoned it all out. I had watched your cat go in that little door. I knew the shed door unhooked; I knew how long my arm was; I thought I could undo it. I stole over here a little after midnight. I went all round the house to be sure nobody was awake. Out in the front yard I happened to think my shears were tied on my belt with a ribbon, and I untied them. I thought I put the ribbon in my pocket—it was a piece of yellow ribbon—but I suppose I didn't, because they found it afterward, and thought it came off your young man's whip.

"I went round to the shed door, unhooked it, and went in. The moon gave light enough. I got out your father's overalls from the kitchen closet; I knew where they were. I went through the sitting room to the parlor. In there I slipped off my dress and my skirts and put on the overalls. I put a handkerchief over my face, leaving only my eyes exposed. I crept out then into the sitting room; there I pulled off my shoes and went into the bedroom.

"Your father was fast asleep; it was such a hot night the clothes were thrown back and his chest was bare. The first thing I saw was that pistol on the stand beside his bed. I suppose he had had some fear of Rufus Bennett coming back after all. Suddenly I thought I'd better shoot him. It would be surer and quicker; and, if you were aroused, I knew that I could get away and everybody would suppose he had shot himself.

"I took up the pistol and held it close to his head. I had never fired a pistol, but I knew how it was done. I pulled, but it would not go off. Your father stirred a little — I was mad with terror — I struck at his head with the pistol. He opened his eyes and cried out; then I dropped the pistol and took these" — Phoebe Dole pointed to the great shining shears hanging at her waist — "for I am strong in my wrists. I only struck twice, over his heart.

"Then I went back into the sitting room. I thought I heard a noise in the kitchen — I was full of terror then — and slipped into the sitting-room closet. I felt as if I were fainting, and clutched the shelf to keep from falling.

"I felt that I must go up stairs to see if you were asleep — to be sure you had not waked up when your father cried out. I thought if you had, I should have to do the same by you. I crept upstairs to your chamber. You seemed asleep, but, as I watched, you stirred a little. But instead of striking at you I slipped into your closet. I heard nothing more from you. I felt myself wet with blood. I caught hold of something hanging in your closet, and wiped myself off with it. I knew by the feeling it was your green silk. You kept quiet and I saw you were asleep, so I crept out of the closet and down the stairs, got my clothes and shoes, and, out in the shed, took off the overalls and dressed myself. I rolled up the overalls and took a board away from the old well and threw them in as I went home. I thought if they were found, it would be no clue to me. The handkerchief, which was not much stained, I put to soak that night and washed out next morning before Maria was up. I washed my hands and arms carefully that night, and also my shears.

"I expected Rufus Bennett would be accused of the murder, and maybe hung. I was prepared for that, but I did not like to think I had thrown suspicion upon you by staining your dress. I had nothing against you. I made up my mind I'd get hold of that dress, before anybody suspected you, and dye it black. I came in and got it, as you know. I was astonished not to see any more stains on it. I only found two or three little streaks that scarcely anybody would have noticed. I didn't know what to think. I suspected, of course, that you had found the stains and got them off, thinking they might bring suspicion upon you.

"I did not see how you could possibly suspect me, in any case. I was glad when your young man was cleared. I had nothing against him. That is all I have to say."

I think I must have fainted away then. I cannot describe the dreadful calmness with which that woman told this — that woman with the good face, whom I had last heard praying like a saint, in meeting. I believe in demoniacal possession after this.

When I came to, the neighbors were around me, putting camphor on my head, and saying soothing things to me, and the old friendly faces had returned. But I wish I could forget!

They have taken Phoebe Dole away — I only know that. I cannot bear to talk any more about it. When I think there must be a trial, and I must go!

Henry has been over this evening. I suppose we shall be happy after all, when I have had a little time to get over this. He says I have nothing to worry about. Mr. Dix has gone home. I hope Henry and I may be able to repay his kindness some day.

A month later. I have just heard that Phoebe Dole has died in prison! This is my last entry. May God help all other innocent women in hard straits as He has helped me!

1896

CLEVELAND MOFFETT

THE MYSTERIOUS CARD and THE MYSTERIOUS CARD UNVEILED

The most famous story written by CLEVELAND MOFFETT (1863–1926), and one of the two most famous riddle stories of all time (along with Frank Stockton's "The Lady, or the Tiger?"), is "The Mysterious Card." First published in 1895 (though the magazine was dated 1896), it is the story of an American in Paris who is given a card bearing some words that he cannot translate and that causes everyone to whom he appeals for a translation to turn from him in violent loathing and disgust. The story caused such an uproar that the author was all but forced to produce a sequel the following year, "The Mysterious Card Unveiled." An enterprising publisher then put both stories together in book form with a gimmick: the second part was sealed, and the purchaser was promised a refund if the book was returned to the bookseller with its seal unbroken.

An American dramatist, journalist, novelist, and short story writer, Moffett spent many years in Europe as a correspondent for several newspapers, and even after he returned to live permanently in the United States, he set many of his stories abroad, mostly in France. He lived his last years in Paris.

Moffett made several major contributions to the mystery genre, notably the novel *Through the Wall* (1909), which is a Haycraft-Queen Cornerstone; *True Tales from the Archives of the Pinkertons* (1897), accounts that are almost as fictionalized as those written by Allan, Frank, and Myron Pinkerton years earlier; *The Bishop's Purse* (1913), coauthored with Oliver Herford, a humorous tale of robbery and impersonation set in England; and *The Seine Mystery* (1925), about an American journalist in Paris who does amateur sleuthing.

"The Mysterious Card" was first published in the February 1896 issue of *The Black Cat;* "The Mysterious Card Unveiled" was first published in the August 1896 issue of *The Black Cat.* Both stories were collected in *The Mysterious Card and The Mysterious Card Unveiled* (Boston: Small, Maynard, 1912).

• • •

THE MYSTERIOUS CARD

RICHARD BURWELL, OF New York, will never cease to regret that the French language was not made a part of his education.

This is why:

On the second evening after Burwell arrived in Paris, feeling lonely without his wife and daughter, who were still visiting a friend in London, his mind naturally turned to the theater. So, after consulting the daily amusement calendar, he decided to visit the *Folies Bergère,* which he had heard of as one of the notable sights. During an intermission he went into the beautiful garden, where gay crowds were strolling among the flowers, and lights, and fountains. He had just seated himself at a little three-legged table, with a view to enjoying the novel scene, when his attention was attracted by a lovely woman, gowned strikingly, though in perfect taste, who passed near him, leaning on the arm of a gentleman. The only thing that he noticed about this gentleman was that he wore eye-glasses.

Now Burwell had never posed as a captivator of the fair sex, and could scarcely credit his eyes when the lady left the side of her escort and, turning back as if she had forgotten something, passed close by him, and deftly placed a card on his table. The card bore some French words written in purple ink, but, not knowing that language, he was unable to make out their meaning. The lady paid no further heed to him, but, rejoining the gentleman with the eye-glasses, swept out of the place with the grace and dignity of a princess. Burwell remained staring at the card.

Needless to say, he thought no more of the performance or of the other attractions about him. Everything seemed flat and tawdry compared with the radiant vision that had appeared and disappeared so mysteriously. His one desire now was to discover the meaning of the words written on the card.

Calling a fiacre, he drove to the Hôtel Continental, where he was staying. Proceeding directly to the office and taking the manager aside, Burwell asked if he would be kind enough to translate a few words of French into English. There were no more than twenty words in all.

"Why, certainly," said the manager, with French politeness, and cast his eyes over the card. As he read, his face grew rigid with astonishment, and, looking at his questioner sharply, he exclaimed: "Where did you get this, monsieur?"

Burwell started to explain, but was interrupted by: "That will do, that will do. You must leave the hotel."

"What do you mean?" asked the man from New York, in amazement.

"You must leave the hotel now — tonight — without fail," commanded the manager excitedly.

Now it was Burwell's turn to grow angry, and he declared heatedly that if he wasn't wanted in this hotel there were plenty of others in Paris where he would be welcome. And, with an assumption of dignity, but piqued at heart, he settled his bill, sent for his belongings, and drove up the Rue de la Paix to the Hôtel Bellevue, where he spent the night.

The next morning he met the proprietor, who seemed to be a good fellow, and, being inclined now to view the incident of the previous evening from its ridiculous side, Burwell explained what had befallen him, and was pleased to find a sympathetic listener.

"Why, the man was a fool," declared the proprietor. "Let me see the card; I will tell you what it means." But as he read, his face and manner changed instantly.

"This is a serious matter," he said sternly. "Now I understand why my confrère refused to entertain you. I regret, monsieur, but I shall be obliged to do as he did."

"What do you mean?"

"Simply that you cannot remain here."

With that he turned on his heel, and the indignant guest could not prevail upon him to give any explanation.

"We'll see about this," said Burwell, thoroughly angered.

It was now nearly noon, and the New Yorker remembered an engagement to lunch with a friend from Boston, who with his family, was stopping at the Hôtel de l'Alma. With his luggage on the carriage, he ordered the *cocher* to drive directly there, determined to take counsel with his countryman before selecting new quarters. His friend was highly indignant when he heard the story — a fact that gave Burwell no little comfort, knowing, as he did, that the man was accustomed to foreign ways from long residence abroad.

"It is some silly mistake, my dear fellow; I wouldn't pay any attention to it. Just have your luggage taken down and stay here. It is a nice, homelike place, and it will be very jolly, all being together. But, first, let me prepare a little 'nerve settler' for you."

After the two had lingered a moment over their Manhattan cocktails, Burwell's friend excused himself to call the ladies. He had proceeded only two or three steps when he turned, and said: "Let's see that mysterious card that has raised all this row."

He had scarcely withdrawn it from Burwell's hand when he started back, and exclaimed: —

"Great God, man! Do you mean to say — this is simply —"

Then, with a sudden movement of his hand to his head, he left the room.

He was gone perhaps five minutes, and when he returned his face was white.

"I am awfully sorry," he said nervously; "but the ladies tell me they — that is, my wife — she has a frightful headache. You will have to excuse us from the lunch."

Instantly realizing that this was only a flimsy pretense, and deeply hurt by his friend's behavior, the mystified man arose at once and left without another word. He was now determined to solve this mystery at any cost. What could be the meaning of the words on that infernal piece of pasteboard?

Profiting by his humiliating experiences, he took good care not to show the card to any one at the hotel where he now established himself, — a comfortable little place near the Grand Opera House.

All through the afternoon he thought of nothing but the card, and turned over in his mind various ways of learning its meaning without getting himself into further trouble. That evening he went again to the *Folies Bergère* in hope of finding the mysterious woman, for he was now more than ever anxious to discover who she was. It even occurred to him that she might be one of those beautiful Nihilist conspirators, or, perhaps, a Russian spy, such as he had read of in novels. But he failed to find her, either then or on the three subsequent evenings which he passed in the same place. Meanwhile the card was burning in his pocket like a hot coal. He dreaded the thought of meeting anyone that he knew, while this horrible cloud hung over him. He bought a French-English dictionary and tried to pick out the meaning word by word, but failed. It was all Greek to him. For the first time in his life, Burwell regretted that he had not studied French at college.

After various vain attempts to either solve or forget the torturing riddle, he saw no other course than to lay the problem before a detective agency. He accordingly put his case in the hands of an *agent de la sûreté* who was recommended as a competent and trustworthy man. They had a talk together in a private room, and, of course, Burwell showed the card. To his relief, his adviser at least showed no sign of taking offense. Only he did not and would not explain what the words meant.

"It is better," he said, "that monsieur should not know the nature of this document for the present. I will do myself the honor to call upon monsieur tomorrow at his hotel, and then monsieur shall know everything."

"Then it is really serious?" asked the unfortunate man.

"Very serious," was the answer.

The next twenty-four hours Burwell passed in a fever of anxiety. As his mind conjured up one fearful possibility after another he deeply regretted that he had not torn up the miserable card at the start. He even seized it,—prepared to strip it into fragments, and so end the whole affair. And then his Yankee stubbornness again asserted itself, and he determined to see the thing out, come what might.

"After all," he reasoned, "it is no crime for a man to pick up a card that a lady drops on his table."

Crime or no crime, however, it looked very much as if he had committed some grave offense when, the next day, his detective drove up in a carriage, accompanied by a uniformed official, and requested the astounded American to accompany them to the police headquarters.

"What for?" he asked.

"It is only a formality," said the detective; and when Burwell still protested the man in uniform remarked: "You'd better come quietly, monsieur; you will have to come, anyway."

An hour later, after severe cross-examination by another official, who demanded many facts about the New Yorker's age, place of birth, residence, occupation, etc., the bewildered man found himself in the Conciergerie prison. Why he was there or what was about to befall him Burwell had no means of knowing; but before the day was over he succeeded in having a message sent to the American Legation, where he demanded immediate protection as a citizen of the United States. It was not until evening, however, that the Secretary of Legation, a consequential person, called at the prison. There followed a stormy interview, in which the prisoner used some strong language, the French officers gesticulated violently and talked very fast, and the Secretary calmly listened to both sides, said little, and smoked a good cigar.

"I will lay your case before the American minister," he said as he rose to go, "and let you know the result tomorrow."

"But this is an outrage. Do you mean to say—"

Before he could finish, however, the Secretary, with a strangely suspicious glance, turned and left the room.

That night Burwell slept in a cell.

The next morning he received another visit from the non-committal

Secretary, who informed him that matters had been arranged, and that he would be set at liberty forthwith.

"I must tell you, though," he said, "that I have had great difficulty in accomplishing this, and your liberty is granted only on condition that you leave the country within twenty-four hours, and never under any conditions return."

Burwell stormed, raged, and pleaded; but it availed nothing. The Secretary was inexorable, and yet he positively refused to throw any light upon the causes of this monstrous injustice.

"Here is your card," he said, handing him a large envelope closed with the seal of Legation. "I advise you to burn it and never refer to the matter again."

That night the ill-fated man took the train for London, his heart consumed by hatred for the whole French nation, together with a burning desire for vengeance. He wired his wife to meet him at the station, and for a long time debated with himself whether he should at once tell her the sickening truth. In the end he decided that it was better to keep silent. No sooner, however, had she seen him than her woman's instinct told her that he was laboring under some mental strain. And he saw in a moment that to withhold from her his burning secret was impossible, especially when she began to talk of the trip they had planned through France. Of course no trivial reason would satisfy her for his refusal to make this trip, since they had been looking forward to it for years; and yet it was impossible now for him to set foot on French soil.

So he finally told her the whole story, she laughing and weeping in turn. To her, as to him, it seemed incredible that such overwhelming disasters could have grown out of so small a cause, and, being a fluent French scholar, she demanded a sight of the fatal piece of pasteboard. In vain her husband tried to divert her by proposing a trip through Italy. She would consent to nothing until she had seen the mysterious card which Burwell was now convinced he ought long ago to have destroyed. After refusing for a while to let her see it, he finally yielded. But, although he had learned to dread the consequences of showing that cursed card, he was little prepared for what followed. She read it, turned pale, gasped for breath, and nearly fell to the floor.

"I told you not to read it," he said; and then, growing tender at the sight of her distress, he took her hand in his and begged her to be calm. "At least tell me what the thing means," he said. "We can bear it together; you surely can trust me."

But she, as if stung by rage, pushed him from her and declared, in a tone such as he had never heard from her before, that never, never again would she live with him. "You are a monster!" she exclaimed. And those were the last words he heard from her lips.

Failing utterly in all efforts at reconciliation, the half-crazed man took the first steamer for New York, having suffered in scarcely a fortnight more than in all his previous life. His whole pleasure trip had been ruined, he had failed to consummate important business arrangements, and now he saw his home broken up and his happiness ruined. During the voyage he scarcely left his stateroom, but lay there prostrated with agony. In this black despondency the one thing that sustained him was the thought of meeting his partner, Jack Evelyth, the friend of his boyhood, the sharer of his success, the bravest, most loyal fellow in the world. In the face of even the most damning circumstances, he felt that Evelyth's rugged common sense would evolve some way of escape from this hideous nightmare. Upon landing at New York he hardly waited for the gang-plank to be lowered before he rushed on shore and grasped the hand of his partner, who was waiting on the wharf.

"Jack," was his first word, "I am in dreadful trouble, and you are the only man in the world who can help me."

An hour later Burwell sat at his friend's dinner table, talking over the situation. Evelyth was all kindness, and several times as he listened to Burwell's story his eyes filled with tears.

"It does not seem possible, Richard," he said, "that such things can be; but I will stand by you; we will fight it out together. But we cannot strike in the dark. Let me see this card."

"There is the damned thing," Burwell said, throwing it on the table.

Evelyth opened the envelope, took out the card, and fixed his eyes on the sprawling purple characters.

"Can you read it?" Burwell asked excitedly.

"Perfectly," his partner said. The next moment he turned pale, and his voice broke. Then he clasped the tortured man's hand in his with a strong grip. "Richard," he said slowly, "if my only child had been brought here dead it would not have caused me more sorrow than this does. You have brought me the worst news one man could bring another."

His agitation and genuine suffering affected Burwell like a death sentence.

"Speak, man," he cried; "do not spare me. I can bear anything rather than this awful uncertainty. Tell me what the card means."

Evelyth took a swallow of brandy and sat with head bent on his clasped hands.

"No, I can't do it; there are some things a man must not do."

Then he was silent again, his brows knitted. Finally he said solemnly: —

"No, I can't see any other way out of it. We have been true to each other all our lives; we have worked together and looked forward to never separating. I would rather fail and die than see this happen. But we have got to separate, old friend; we have got to separate."

They sat there talking until late into the night. But nothing that Burwell could do or say availed against his friend's decision. There was nothing for it but that Evelyth should buy his partner's share of the business or that Burwell buy out the other. The man was more than fair in the financial proposition he made; he was generous, as he always had been, but his determination was inflexible; the two must separate. And they did.

With his old partner's desertion, it seemed to Burwell that the world was leagued against him. It was only three weeks from the day on which he had received the mysterious card; yet in that time he had lost all that he valued in the world, — wife, friends, and business. What next to do with the fatal card was the sickening problem that now possessed him.

He dared not show it; yet he dared not destroy it. He loathed it; yet he could not let it go from his possession. Upon returning to his house he locked the accursed thing away in his safe as if it had been a package of dynamite or a bottle of deadly poison. Yet not a day passed that he did not open the drawer where the thing was kept and scan with loathing the mysterious purple scrawl.

In desperation he finally made up his mind to take up the study of the language in which the hateful thing was written. And still he dreaded the approach of the day when he should decipher its awful meaning.

One afternoon, less than a week after his arrival in New York, as he was crossing Twenty-third Street on the way to his French teacher, he saw a carriage rolling up Broadway. In the carriage was a face that caught his attention like a flash. As he looked again he recognized the woman who had been the cause of his undoing. Instantly he sprang into another cab and ordered the driver to follow after. He found the house where she was living. He called there several times; but always received the same reply, that she was too much engaged to see anyone. Next he was told that she was ill, and on the following day the servant said she was much worse. Three physicians had been summoned in consultation. He sought out one of these and told him it was a matter of life or death that he see this woman. The doctor was a kindly man and promised to assist him. Through his influence, it came about that on that very night Burwell stood by the bedside of this mysterious woman. She was beautiful still, though her face was worn with illness.

"Do you recognize me?" he asked tremblingly, as he leaned over the bed, clutching in one hand an envelope containing the mysterious card. "Do you remember seeing me at the *Folies Bergère* a month ago?"

"Yes," she murmured, after a moment's study of his face; and he noted with relief that she spoke English.

"Then, for God's sake, tell me, what does it all mean?" he gasped, quivering with excitement.

"I gave you the card because I wanted you to — to —"

Here a terrible spasm of coughing shook her whole body, and she fell back exhausted.

An agonizing despair tugged at Burwell's heart. Frantically snatching the card from its envelope, he held it close to the woman's face.

"Tell me! Tell me!"

With a supreme effort, the pale figure slowly raised itself on the pillow, its fingers clutching at the counterpane.

Then the sunken eyes fluttered — forced themselves open — and stared in stony amazement upon the fatal card, while the trembling lips moved noiselessly, as if in an attempt to speak. As Burwell, choking with eagerness, bent his head slowly to hers, a suggestion of a smile flickered across the woman's face. Again the mouth quivered, the man's head bent nearer and nearer to hers, his eyes riveted upon the lips. Then, as if to aid her in deciphering the mystery, he turned his eyes to the card.

With a cry of horror he sprang to his feet, his eyeballs starting from their sockets. Almost at the same moment the woman fell heavily upon the pillow.

Every vestige of the writing had faded! The card was blank!

The woman lay there dead.

THE MYSTERIOUS CARD UNVEILED

NO PHYSICIAN WAS ever more scrupulous than I have been, during my thirty years of practice, in observing the code of professional secrecy; and it is only for grave reasons, partly in the interests of medical science, largely as a warning to intelligent people, that I place upon record the following statements.

One morning a gentleman called at my offices to consult me about some nervous trouble. From the moment I saw him, the man made a deep impression on me, not so much by the pallor and worn look of his face as by a certain intense sadness in his eyes, as if all hope had gone out of his life. I wrote a prescription for him, and advised him to try the benefits of an ocean voyage. He seemed to shiver at the idea, and said that he had been abroad too much, already.

As he handed me my fee, my eye fell upon the palm of his hand, and I saw there, plainly marked on the Mount of Saturn, a cross surrounded by two circles. I should explain that for the greater part of my life I have been a constant and enthusiastic student of palmistry. During my travels in the Orient, after taking my degree, I spent months studying this fascinating art at the best sources of information in the world. I have read everything published on palmistry in every known language, and my library on the subject is perhaps the most complete in existence. In my time I have examined at least fourteen thousand palms, and taken casts of many of the more interesting of them. But I had never seen such a palm as this; at least, never but once, and the horror of the case was so great that I shudder even now when I call it to mind.

"Pardon me," I said, keeping the patient's hand in mine, "would you let me look at your palm?"

I tried to speak indifferently, as if the matter were of small consequence, and for some moments I bent over the hand in silence. Then, taking a magnifying glass from my desk, I looked at it still more closely. I was not mistaken; here was indeed the sinister double circle on Saturn's mount, with the cross inside,—a marking so rare as to portend some stupendous destiny of good or evil, more probably the latter.

I saw that the man was uneasy under my scrutiny, and, presently, with some hesitation, as if mustering courage, he asked: "Is there anything remarkable about my hand?"

"Yes," I said, "there is. Tell me, did not something very unusual, something very horrible, happen to you about ten or eleven years ago?"

I saw by the way the man started that I had struck near the mark, and, studying the stream of fine lines that crossed his lifeline from the Mount of Venus, I added: "Were you not in some foreign country at that time?"

The man's face blanched, but he only looked at me steadily out of those mournful eyes. Now I took his other hand, and compared the two, line by line, mount by mount, noting the short square fingers, the heavy thumb, with amazing willpower in its upper joint, and gazing again and again at that ominous sign on Saturn.

"Your life has been strangely unhappy, your years have been clouded by some evil influence."

"My God," he said weakly, sinking into a chair, "how can you know these things?"

"It is easy to know what one sees," I said, and tried to draw him out about his past, but the words seemed to stick in his throat.

"I will come back and talk to you again," he said, and he went away without giving me his name or any revelation of his life.

Several times he called during subsequent weeks, and gradually seemed to take on a measure of confidence in my presence. He would talk freely of his physical condition, which seemed to cause him much anxiety. He even insisted upon my making the most careful examination of all his organs, especially of his eyes, which, he said, had troubled him at various times. Upon making the usual tests, I found that he was suffering from a most uncommon form of color blindness, that seemed to vary in its manifestations, and to be connected with certain hallucinations or abnormal mental states which recurred periodically, and about which I had great difficulty in persuading him to speak. At each visit I took occasion to study his hand anew, and each reading of the palm gave me stronger conviction that here was a life mystery that would abundantly repay any pains taken in unraveling it.

While I was in this state of mind, consumed with a desire to know more of my unhappy acquaintance and yet not daring to press him with questions, there came a tragic happening that revealed to me with startling suddenness the secret I was bent on knowing. One night, very late, —in fact it was about four o'clock in the morning,—I received an urgent summons to the bedside of a man who had been shot. As I bent over him I saw that it was my friend, and for the first time I realized that he was a man of wealth and position, for he lived in a beautifully furnished house filled with art treasures and looked after by a retinue of servants. From one of these I learned that he was Richard Burwell, one of New York's most respected citizens—in fact, one of her best-known philanthropists, a man who for years had devoted his life and fortune to good works among the poor.

But what most excited my surprise was the presence in the house of two officers, who informed me that Mr. Burwell was under arrest, charged with murder. The officers assured me that it was only out of deference to his well-known standing in the community that the prisoner had been allowed the privilege of receiving medical treatment in his own home; their orders were peremptory to keep him under close surveillance.

Giving no time to further questionings, I at once proceeded to examine the injured man, and found that he was suffering from a bullet wound in the back at about the height of the fifth rib. On probing for the bullet, I found that it had lodged near the heart, and decided that it would be exceedingly dangerous to try to remove it immediately. So I contented myself with administering a sleeping potion.

As soon as I was free to leave Burwell's bedside I returned to the officers and obtained from them details of what had happened. A woman's body had been found a few hours before, shockingly mutilated, on Water Street, one of the dark ways in the swarming region along the river front. It had been found at about two o'clock in the morning by some printers from the office of the *Courier des Etats Unis,* who, in coming from their work, had heard cries of distress and hurried to the rescue. As they drew near they saw a man spring away from something huddled on the sidewalk, and plunge into the shadows of the night, running from them at full speed.

Suspecting at once that here was the mysterious assassin so long vainly sought for many similar crimes, they dashed after the fleeing man, who darted right and left through the maze of dark streets, giving out little cries like a squirrel as he ran. Seeing that they were losing ground, one of the printers fired at the fleeing shadow, his shot being followed by a scream of pain, and hurrying up they found a man writhing on the ground. The man was Richard Burwell.

The news that my sad-faced friend had been implicated in such a revolting occurrence shocked me inexpressibly, and I was greatly relieved the next day to learn from the papers that a most unfortunate mistake had been made. The evidence given before the coroner's jury was such as to abundantly exonerate Burwell from all shadow of guilt. The man's own testimony, taken at his bedside, was in itself almost conclusive in his favor. When asked to explain his presence so late at night in such a part of the city, Burwell stated that he had spent the evening at the Florence Mission, where he had made an address to some unfortunates gathered there, and that later he had gone with a young missionary worker to visit a woman living on Frankfort Street, who was dying of consumption. This statement was borne out by the missionary worker himself, who testified that Burwell had been most tender in his ministrations to the poor woman and had not left her until death had relieved her sufferings.

Another point which made it plain that the printers had mistaken their man in the darkness, was the statement made by all of them that, as they came running up, they had overheard some words spoken by the murderer, and that these words were in their own language, French. Now it was shown conclusively that Burwell did not know the French language, that indeed he had not even an elementary knowledge of it.

Another point in his favor was a discovery made at the spot where the body was found. Some profane and ribald words, also in French, had been scrawled in chalk on the door and doorsill, being in the nature of a coarse defiance to the police to find the assassin, and experts in handwriting who were called testified unanimously that Burwell, who wrote a refined, scholarly hand, could never have formed those misshapen words.

Furthermore, at the time of his arrest no evidence was found on the clothes or person of Burwell, nothing in the nature of bruises or bloodstains that would tend to implicate him in the crime. The outcome of the matter was that he was honorably discharged by the coroner's jury, who were unanimous in declaring him innocent, and who brought in a verdict that the unfortunate woman had come to her death at the hand of some person or persons unknown.

On visiting my patient late on the afternoon of the second day I saw that his case was very grave, and I at once instructed the nurses and attendants to prepare for an operation. The man's life depended upon my being able to extract the bullet, and the chance of doing this was very small. Mr. Burwell realized that his condition was critical, and, beckoning me to him, told me that he wished to make a statement he felt might be his last. He spoke with agitation which was increased by an unforeseen happening. For just then a servant entered the room and whispered to me that there was a gentleman downstairs who insisted upon seeing me, and who urged business of great importance. This message the sick man overheard, and lifting himself with an effort, he said excitedly: "Tell me, is he a tall man with glasses?"

The servant hesitated.

"I knew it; you cannot deceive me; that man will haunt me to my grave. Send him away, doctor; I beg of you not to see him."

Humoring my patient, I sent word to the stranger that I could not see him, but, in an undertone, instructed the servant to say that the man might call at my office the next morning. Then, turning to Burwell, I begged him to compose himself and save his strength for the ordeal awaiting him.

"No, no," he said, "I need my strength now to tell you what you must know to find the truth. You are the only man who has understood that there has been some terrible influence at work in my life. You are the only man competent to study out what that influence is, and I have made provision in my will that you shall do so after I am gone. I know that you will heed my wishes?"

The intense sadness of his eyes made my heart sink; I could only grip his hand and remain silent.

"Thank you; I was sure I might count on your devotion. Now, tell me, doctor, you have examined me carefully, have you not?"

I nodded.

"In every way known to medical science?"

I nodded again.

"And have you found anything wrong with me, — I mean, besides this bullet, anything abnormal?"

"As I have told you, your eyesight is defective; I should like to examine your eyes more thoroughly when you are better."

"I shall never be better; besides it isn't my eyes; I mean myself, my soul, — you haven't found anything wrong there?"

"Certainly not; the whole city knows the beauty of your character and your life."

"Tut, tut; the city knows nothing. For ten years I have lived so much with the poor that people have almost forgotten my previous active life when I was busy with money-making and happy in my home. But there is a man out West, whose head is white and whose heart is heavy, who has not forgotten, and there is a woman in London, a silent, lonely woman, who has not forgotten. The man was my partner, poor Jack Evelyth; the woman was my wife. How can a man be so cursed, doctor, that his love and friendship bring only misery to those who share it? How can it be that one who has in his heart only good thoughts can be constantly under the shadow of evil? This charge of murder is only one of several cases in my life where, through no fault of mine, the shadow of guilt has been cast upon me.

"Years ago, when my wife and I were perfectly happy, a child was born to us, and a few months later, when it was only a tender, helpless little thing that its mother loved with all her heart, it was strangled in its cradle, and we never knew who strangled it, for the deed was done one night when there was absolutely no one in the house but my wife and myself. There was no doubt about the crime, for there on the tiny neck were the finger marks where some cruel hand had closed until life went.

"Then a few years later, when my partner and I were on the eve of fortune, our advance was set back by the robbery of our safe. Someone opened it in the night, someone who knew the combination, for it was the work of no burglar, and yet there were only two persons in the world who knew that combination, my partner and myself. I tried to be brave when these things happened, but as my life went on it seemed more and more as if some curse were on me.

"Eleven years ago I went abroad with my wife and daughter. Business took me to Paris, and I left the ladies in London, expecting to have them join me in a few days. But they never did join me, for the curse was on me still, and before I had been forty-eight hours in the French capital something happened that completed the wreck of my life. It doesn't seem possible, does it, that a simple white card with some words scrawled on it in purple ink could effect a man's undoing? And yet that was my fate. The card was given me by a beautiful woman with eyes like stars. She is dead long ago, and why she wished to harm me I never knew. You must find that out.

"You see, I did not know the language of the country, and, wishing to have the words translated, — surely that was natural enough, — I showed the card to others. But no one would tell me what it meant. And, worse than that, wherever I showed it, and to whatever person, there evil came upon me quickly. I was driven from one hotel after another; an old acquaintance turned his back on me; I was arrested and thrown into prison; I was ordered to leave the country."

The sick man paused for a moment in his weakness, but with an effort forced himself to continue: —

"When I went back to London, sure of comfort in the love of my wife, she too, on seeing the card, drove me from her with cruel words. And when finally, in deepest despair, I returned to New York, dear old Jack, the friend of a lifetime, broke with me when I showed him what was written. What the words were I do not know, and suppose no one will ever know, for the ink has faded these many years. You will find the card in my safe with other papers. But I want you, when I am gone, to find out the mystery of my life; and — and — about my fortune, that must be held until you have decided. There is no one who needs my money as much as the poor in this city, and I have bequeathed it to them unless — "

In an agony of mind, Mr. Burwell struggled to go on, I soothing and encouraging him.

"Unless you find what I am afraid to think, but — but — yes, I must say it, — that I have not been a good man, as the world thinks, but have — O doctor, if you find that I have unknowingly harmed any human being, I want that person, or these persons, to have my fortune. Promise that."

Seeing the wild light in Burwell's eyes, and the fever that was burning him, I gave the promise asked of me, and the sick man sank back calmer.

A little later, the nurse and attendants came for the operation. As they were about to administer the ether, Burwell pushed them from him, and insisted on having brought to his bedside an iron box from the safe.

"The card is here," he said, laying his trembling hand upon the box, "you will remember your promise!"

Those were his last words, for he did not survive the operation.

Early the next morning I received this message: "The stranger of yesterday begs to see you"; and presently a gentleman of fine presence and strength of face, a tall, dark-complexioned man wearing glasses, was shown into the room.

"Mr. Burwell is dead, is he not?" were his first words.

"Who told you?"

"No one told me, but I know it, and I thank God for it."

There was something in the stranger's intense earnestness that convinced me of his right to speak thus, and I listened attentively.

"That you may have confidence in the statement I am about to make, I will first tell you who I am"; and he handed me a card that caused me to lift my eyes in wonder, for it bore a very great name, that of one of Europe's most famous savants.

"You have done me much honor, sir," I said with respectful inclination.

"On the contrary, you will oblige me by considering me in your debt, and by never revealing my connection with this wretched man. I am moved to speak partly from considerations of human justice, largely in the interest of medical science. It is right for me to tell you, doctor, that your patient was beyond question the Water Street assassin."

"Impossible!" I cried.

"You will not say so when I have finished my story, which takes me back to Paris, to the time, eleven years ago, when this man was making his first visit to the French capital."

"The mysterious card!" I exclaimed.

"Ah, he has told you of his experience, but not of what befell the night before, when he first met my sister."

"Your sister?"

"Yes, it was she who gave him the card, and, in trying to befriend him, made him suffer. She was in ill health at the time, so much so that we had left our native India for extended journeyings. Alas! we delayed too long, for my sister died in New York, only a few weeks later, and I honestly believe her taking off was hastened by anxiety inspired by this man."

"Strange," I murmured, "how the life of a simple New York merchant could become entangled with that of a great lady of the East."

"Yet so it was. You must know that my sister's condition was due mainly to an over fondness for certain occult investigations, from which I had vainly tried to dissuade her. She had once befriended some adepts, who, in return, had taught her things about the soul she had better have left unlearned. At various times while with her I had seen strange things happen, but I never realized what unearthly powers were in her until that night in Paris. We were returning from a drive in the Bois; it was about ten o'clock, and the city lay beautiful around us as Paris looks on a perfect summer's night. Suddenly my sister gave a cry of pain and put her hand to her heart. Then, changing from French to the language of our country, she explained to me quickly that something frightful was taking place there, where she pointed her finger across the river, that we must go to the place at once — the driver must lash his horses — every second was precious.

"So affected was I by her intense conviction, and such confidence had I in my sister's wisdom, that I did not oppose her, but told the man to drive as she directed. The carriage fairly flew across the bridge, down the Boulevard St. Germain, then to the left, threading its way through the narrow streets that lie along the Seine. This way and that, straight ahead here, a turn there, she directing our course, never hesitating, as if drawn by some unseen power, and always urging the driver on to greater speed. Finally, we came to a black-mouthed, evil-looking alley, so narrow and roughly paved that the carriage could scarcely advance.

" 'Come on!' my sister cried, springing to the ground; 'we will go on foot, we are nearly there. Thank God, we may yet be in time.'

"No one was in sight as we hurried along the dark alley, and scarcely a light was visible, but presently a smothered scream broke the silence, and, touching my arm, my sister exclaimed: —

" 'There, draw your weapon, quick, and take the man at any cost!'

"So swiftly did everything happen after that that I hardly know my actions, but a few minutes later I held pinioned in my arms a man whose blows and writhings had been all in vain; for you must know that much exercise in the jungle had made me strong of limb. As soon as I had made the fellow fast I looked down and found moaning on the ground a poor woman, who explained with tears and broken words that the man had been in the very act of strangling her. Searching him, I found a long-bladed knife of curious shape, and keen as a razor, which had been brought for what horrible purpose you may perhaps divine.

"Imagine my surprise, on dragging the man back to the carriage, to find, instead of the ruffianly assassin I expected, a gentleman as far as could be judged from face and manner. Fine eyes, white hands, careful speech, all the signs of refinement and the dress of a man of means.

" 'How can this be?' I said to my sister in our own tongue as we drove away, I holding my prisoner on the opposite seat where he sat silent.

" 'It is a *kulos*-man,' she said, shivering, 'it is a fiend-soul. There are a few such in the whole world, perhaps two or three in all.'

" 'But he has a good face.'

" 'You have not seen his real face yet; I will show it to you, presently.'

"In the strangeness of these happenings and the still greater strangeness of my sister's words, I had all but lost the power of wonder. So we sat without further word until the carriage stopped at the little chateau we had taken near the Parc Monteau.

"I could never properly describe what happened that night; my knowledge of these things is too limited. I simply obeyed my sister in all that she directed, and kept my eyes on this man as no hawk ever watched its prey. She began by questioning him, speaking in a kindly tone which I could ill understand. He seemed embarrassed, dazed, and professed to have no knowledge of what had occurred, or how he had come where we found him. To all my inquiries as to the woman or the crime he shook his head blankly, and thus aroused my wrath.

" 'Be not angry with him, brother; he is not lying, it is the other soul.'

"She asked him about his name and country, and he replied without hesitation that he was Richard Burwell, a merchant from New York, just arrived in Paris, traveling for pleasure in Europe with his wife and daughter. This seemed reasonable, for the man spoke English, and, strangely enough, seemed to have no knowledge of French, although we both remember hearing him speak French to the woman.

" 'There is no doubt,' my sister said. 'It is indeed a *kulos*-man; It knows that I am here, that I am Its master. Look, look!' she cried sharply, at the same time putting her eyes so close to the man's face that their fierce light seemed to burn into him. What power she exercised I do not know, nor whether some words she spoke, unintelligible to me, had to do with what followed, but instantly there came over this man, this pleasant-looking, respectable American citizen, such a change as is not made by death worms gnawing in a grave. Now there was a fiend groveling at her feet, a foul, sin-stained fiend.

"'Now you see the demon-soul,' said my sister. 'Watch It writhe and struggle; it has served me well, brother, sayest thou not so, the lore I gained from our wise men?'

"The horror of what followed chilled my blood; nor would I trust my memory were it not that there remained and still remains plain proof of all that I affirm. This hideous creature, dwarfed, crouching, devoid of all resemblance to the man we had but now beheld, chattering to us in curious old-time French, poured out such horrid blasphemy as would have blanched the cheek of Satan, and made recital of such evil deeds as never mortal ear gave heed to. And as she willed my sister checked It or allowed It to go on. What it all meant was more than I could tell. To me it seemed as if these tales of wickedness had no connection with our modern life, or with the world around us, and so I judged presently from what my sister said.

"'Speak of the later time, since thou wast in this clay.'

"Then I perceived that the creature came to things of which I knew: It spoke of New York, of a wife, a child, a friend. It told of strangling the child, of robbing the friend; and was going on to tell God knows what other horrid deeds when my sister stopped It.

"'Stand as thou didst in killing the little babe, stand, stand!' and once more she spoke some words unknown to me. Instantly the demon sprang forward, and, bending Its clawlike hands, clutched them around some little throat that was not there,—but I could see it in my mind. And the look on its face was a blackest glimpse of hell.

"'And now stand as thou didst in robbing the friend, stand, stand'; and again came the unknown words, and again the fiend obeyed.

"'These we will take for future use,' said my sister. And bidding me watch the creature carefully until she should return, she left the room, and, after none too short an absence, returned bearing a black box that was an apparatus for photography, and something more besides,—some newer, stranger kind of photography that she had learned. Then, on a strangely fashioned card, a transparent white card, composed of many layers of finest Oriental paper, she took the pictures of the creature in those two creeping poses. And when it all was done, the card seemed as white as before, and empty of all meaning until one held it up and examined it intently. Then the pictures showed. And between the two there was a third picture, which somehow seemed to show, at the same time, two faces in one, two souls, my sister said, the kindly visaged man we first had seen, and then the fiend.

"Now my sister asked for pen and ink and I gave her my pocket pen, which was filled with purple ink. Handing this to the *kulos*-man, she bade him write under the first picture: 'Thus I killed my babe.' And under the second picture: 'Thus I robbed my friend.' And under the third, the one that was between the other two: 'This is the soul of Richard Burwell.' An odd thing about this writing was that it was in the same old French the creature had used in speech, and yet Burwell knew no French.

"My sister was about to finish with the creature when a new idea took her, and she said, looking at It as before: — 'Of all thy crimes, which one is the worst? Speak, I command thee!'

"Then the fiend told how once It had killed every soul in a house of holy women and buried the bodies in a cellar under a heavy door.

" 'Where was the house?'

" 'At No. 19 Rue Picpus, next to the old graveyard.'

" 'And when was this?'

"Here the fiend seemed to break into fierce rebellion, writhing on the floor with hideous contortions, and pouring forth words that meant nothing to me, but seemed to reach my sister's understanding, for she interrupted from time to time, with quick, stern words that finally brought It to subjection.

" 'Enough,' she said, 'I know all,' and then she spoke some words again, her eyes fixed as before, and the reverse change came. Before us stood once more the honest-looking, fine-appearing gentleman, Richard Burwell, of New York.

" 'Excuse me, madame,' he said, awkwardly, but with deference; 'I must have dozed a little. I am not myself to-night.'

" 'No,' said my sister, 'you have not been yourself to-night.'

"A little later I accompanied the man to the Continental Hotel, where he was stopping, and, returning to my sister, I talked with her until late into the night. I was alarmed to see that she was wrought to a nervous tension that augured ill for her health. I urged her to sleep, but she would not.

" 'No,' she said, 'think of the awful responsibility that rests upon me.' And then she went on with her strange theories and explanations, of which I understood only that here was a power for evil more terrible than a pestilence, menacing all humanity.

" 'Once in many cycles it happens,' she said, 'that a *kulos*-soul pushes itself within the body of a new-born child, when the pure soul waiting to enter is delayed. Then the two live together through that life, and this hideous principle of evil has a chance upon the earth. It is my will, as I feel it my duty, to see this poor man again. The chances are that he will never know us, for the shock of this night to his normal soul is so great as to wipe out memory.'

"The next evening, about the same hour, my sister insisted that I should go with her to the *Folies Bergère,* a concert garden, none too well frequented, and when I remonstrated, she said: 'I must go, — It is there,' and the words sent a shiver through me.

"We drove to this place, and passing into the garden, presently discovered Richard Burwell seated at a little table, enjoying the scene of pleasure, which was plainly new to him. My sister hesitated a moment what to do, and then, leaving my arm, she advanced to the table and dropped before Burwell's eyes the card she had prepared. A moment later, with a look of pity on her beautiful face, she rejoined me and we went away. It was plain he did not know us."

To so much of the savant's strange recital I had listened with absorbed interest, though without a word, but now I burst in with questions.

"What was your sister's idea in giving Burwell the card?" I asked.

"It was in the hope that she might make the man understand his terrible condition, that is, teach the pure soul to know its loathsome companion."

"And did her effort succeed?"

"Alas! it did not; my sister's purpose was defeated by the man's inability to see the pictures that were plain to every other eye. It is impossible for the *kulos*-man to know his own degradation."

"And yet this man has for years been leading a most exemplary life?"

My visitor shook his head. "I grant you there has been improvement, due largely to experiments I have conducted upon him according to my sister's wishes. But the fiend soul was never driven out. It grieves me to tell you, doctor, that not only was this man the Water Street assassin, but he was the mysterious murderer, the long-sought-for mutilator of women, whose red crimes have baffled the police of Europe and America for the past ten years."

"You know this," said I, starting up, "and yet did not denounce him?"

"It would have been impossible to prove such a charge, and besides, I had made oath to my sister that I would use the man only for these soul-experiments. What are his crimes compared with the great secret of knowledge I am now able to give the world?"

"A secret of knowledge?"

"Yes," said the savant, with intense earnestness, "I may tell you now, doctor, what the whole world will know, ere long, that it is possible to compel every living person to reveal the innermost secrets of his or her life, so long as memory remains, for memory is only the power of producing in the brain material pictures that may be projected externally by the thought rays and made to impress themselves upon the photographic plate, precisely as ordinary pictures do."

"You mean," I exclaimed, "that you can photograph the two principles of good and evil that exist in us?"

"Exactly that. The great truth of a dual soul existence, that was dimly apprehended by one of your Western novelists, has been demonstrated by me in the laboratory with my camera. It is my purpose, at the proper time, to entrust this precious knowledge to a chosen few who will perpetuate it and use it worthily."

"Wonderful, wonderful!" I cried, "and now tell me, if you will, about the house on the Rue Picpus. Did you ever visit the place?"

"We did, and found that no buildings had stood there for fifty years, so we did not pursue the search."*

"And the writing on the card, have you any memory of it, for Burwell told me that the words have faded?"

"I have something better than that; I have a photograph of both card and writing, which my sister was careful to take. I had a notion that the ink in my pocket pen would fade, for it was a poor affair. This photograph I will bring you tomorrow."

"Bring it to Burwell's house," I said.

* * *

The next morning the stranger called as agreed upon.

"Here is the photograph of the card," he said.

"And here is the original card," I answered, breaking the seal of the envelope I had taken from Burwell's iron box. "I have waited for your

---

* Years later, some workmen in Paris, making excavations in the Rue Picpus, came upon a heavy door buried under a mass of debris, under an old cemetery. On lifting the door they found a vault-like chamber in which were a number of female skeletons, and graven on the walls were blasphemous words written in French, which experts declared dated from fully two hundred years before. They also declared this handwriting identical with that found on the door at the Water Street murder in New York. Thus we may deduce a theory of fiend reincarnation; for it would seem clear, almost to the point of demonstration, that this murder of the seventeenth century was the work of the same evil soul that killed the poor woman on Water Street towards the end of the nineteenth century.

arrival to look at it. Yes, the writing has indeed vanished; the card seems quite blank."

"Not when you hold it this way," said the stranger, and as he tipped the card I saw such a horrid revelation as I can never forget. In an instant I realized how the shock of seeing that card had been too great for the soul of wife or friend to bear. In these pictures was the secret of a cursed life. The resemblance to Burwell was unmistakable, the proof against him was overwhelming. In looking upon that piece of pasteboard the wife had seen a crime which the mother could never forgive, the partner had seen a crime which the friend could never forgive. Think of a loved face suddenly melting before your eyes into a grinning skull, then into a mass of putrefaction, then into the ugliest fiend of hell, leering at you, distorted with all the marks of vice and shame. That is what I saw, that is what they had seen!

"Let us lay these two cards in the coffin," said my companion impressively, "we have done what we could."

Eager to be rid of the hateful piece of pasteboard (for who could say that the curse was not still clinging about it?), I took the strange man's arm, and together we advanced into the adjoining room where the body lay. I had seen Burwell as he breathed his last, and knew that there had been a peaceful look on his face as he died. But now, as we laid the two white cards on the still breast, the savant suddenly touched my arm, and pointing to the dead man's face, now frightfully distorted, whispered: —

"See, even in death It followed him. Let us close the coffin quickly."

1896

MARK TWAIN

TOM SAWYER, DETECTIVE

Unlike the rather dark story of "A Thumb-print and What Came of It," "Tom Sawyer, Detective" is a typically humorous tall tale involving the teenagers with whom Mark Twain enjoyed his greatest successes, the eponymous character and Huckleberry Finn, who narrates the story. It is a sequel to the more famous *Adventures of Tom Sawyer* (1876), *Adventures of Huckleberry Finn* (1884), and *Tom Sawyer Abroad* (1894) and is the last major work in which either character plays a role, though Twain attempted two further adventures of the young friends, *Huck Finn and Tom Sawyer Among the Indians* and *Tom Sawyer's Conspiracy,* neither of which were completed.

Like most of Twain's other mystery and detective stories, this is a parody of the genre, which was beginning to enjoy great popularity. It features several of the elements found in the earlier books about Tom and Huck, such as a desire to escape school and work, the quest for adventure, an insatiable curiosity, a hint of supernatural occurrences, and a use of vernacular language that wasn't always quite precise.

Twain claimed that the story was largely based on true incidents, as he wrote in a footnote to the first page:

> Strange as the incidents of this story are, they are not inventions, but facts — even to the public confession of the accused. I take them from an old-time Swedish criminal trial, change the actors, and transfer the scenes to America. I have added some details, but only a couple of them are important ones.

In spite of the disclaimer, Twain was accused of plagiarizing the plot from *The Vicar of Weilby,* a Danish story by Steen Blicher, a charge denied by Twain. The story was filmed in 1938; it was directed by Louis King and starred Billy Cook as Tom Sawyer and Donald O'Connor as Huckleberry Finn.

"Tom Sawyer, Detective" was first published as a serial in *Harper's New Monthly Magazine,* June-November 1896. It was first published in book form in *Tom Sawyer Abroad, Tom Sawyer, Detective, and Other Stories* (New York: Harper & Brothers, 1896).

• • •

CHAPTER I: AN INVITATION FOR TOM AND HUCK

WELL, IT WAS the next spring after me and Tom Sawyer set our old nigger Jim free, the time he was chained up for a runaway slave down there on Tom's uncle Silas's farm in Arkansaw. The frost was working out of the ground, and out of the air, too, and it was getting closer and closer onto barefoot time every day; and next it would be marble time, and next mumblety-peg, and next tops and hoops, and next kites, and then right away it would be summer and going in a-swimming. It just makes a boy homesick to look ahead like that and see how far off summer is. Yes, and it sets him to sighing and saddening around, and there's something the matter with him, he don't know what. But anyway, he gets out by himself and mopes and thinks; and mostly he hunts for a lonesome place high up on the hill in the edge of the woods, and sets there and looks away off on the big Mississippi down there a-reaching miles and miles around the points where the timber looks smoky and dim it's so far off and still, and everything's so solemn it seems like everybody you've loved is dead and gone, and you 'most wish you was dead and gone too, and done with it all.

Don't you know what that is? It's spring fever. That is what the name of it is. And when you've got it, you want—oh, you don't quite know what it is you *do* want, but it just fairly makes your heart ache, you want it so! It seems to you that mainly what you want is to get away; get away from the same old tedious things you're so used to seeing and so tired of, and see something new. That is the idea; you want to go and be a wanderer; you want to go wandering far away to strange countries where everything is mysterious and wonderful and romantic. And if you can't do that, you'll put up with considerable less; you'll go anywhere you *can* go, just so as to get away, and be thankful of the chance, too.

Well, me and Tom Sawyer had the spring fever, and had it bad, too; but it warn't any use to think about Tom trying to get away, because, as he said, his aunt Polly wouldn't let him quit school and go traipsing off somers wasting time; so we was pretty blue. We was setting on the front steps one day about sundown talking this way, when out comes his aunt Polly with a letter in her hand and says:

"Tom, I reckon you've got to pack up and go down to Arkansaw—your aunt Sally wants you."

I 'most jumped out of my skin for joy. I reckoned Tom would fly at his aunt and hug her head off; but if you believe me he set there like a rock, and never said a word. It made me fit to cry to see him act so foolish, with such a noble chance as this opening up. Why, we might lose it if he didn't speak up and show he was thankful and grateful. But he set there and studied and studied till I was that distressed I didn't know what to do; then he says, very ca'm, and I could 'a' shot him for it:

"Well," he says, "I'm right down sorry, Aunt Polly, but I reckon I got to be excused — for the present."

His aunt Polly was knocked so stupid and so mad at the cold impudence of it that she couldn't say a word for as much as a half a minute, and this gave me a chance to nudge Tom and whisper:

"Ain't you got any sense? Sp'iling such a noble chance as this and throwing it away?"

But he warn't disturbed. He mumbled back:

"Huck Finn, do you want me to let her *see* how bad I want to go? Why, she'd begin to doubt, right away, and imagine a lot of sicknesses and dangers and objections, and first you know she'd take it all back. You lemme alone; I reckon I know how to work her."

Now I never would 'a' thought of that. But he was right. Tom Sawyer was always right — the levelest head I ever see, and always *at* himself and ready for anything you might spring on him. By this time his aunt Polly was all straight again, and she let fly. She says:

"You'll be excused! *You* will! Well, I never heard the like of it in all my days! The idea of you talking like that to *me!* Now take yourself off and pack your traps; and if I hear another word out of you about what you'll be excused from and what you won't, I lay *I'll* excuse you — with a hickory!"

She hit his head a thump with her thimble as we dodged by, and he let on to be whimpering as we struck for the stairs. Up in his room he hugged me, he was so out of his head for gladness because he was going traveling. And he says:

"Before we get away she'll wish she hadn't let me go, but she won't know any way to get around it now. After what she's said, her pride won't let her take it back."

Tom was packed in ten minutes, all except what his aunt and Mary would finish up for him; then we waited ten more for her to get cooled down and sweet and gentle again; for Tom said it took her ten minutes to unruffle in times when half of her feathers was up, but twenty when they was all up, and this was one of the times when they was all up. Then we went down, being in a sweat to know what the letter said.

She was setting there in a brown study, with it laying in her lap. We set down, and she says:

"They're in considerable trouble down there, and they think you and Huck'll be a kind of diversion for them — 'comfort,' they say. Much of that they'll get out of you and Huck Finn, I reckon. There's a neighbor named Brace Dunlap that's been wanting to marry their Benny for three months, and at last they told him point blank and once for all, he *couldn't;* so he has soured on them, and they're worried about it. I reckon he's somebody they think they better be on the good side of, for they've tried to please him by hiring his no-account brother to help on the farm when they can't hardly afford it, and don't want him around anyhow. Who are the Dunlaps?"

"They live about a mile from Uncle Silas's place, Aunt Polly — all the farmers live about a mile apart down there — and Brace Dunlap is a long sight richer than any of the others, and owns a whole grist of niggers. He's a widower, thirty-six years old, without any children, and is proud of his money and overbearing, and everybody is a little afraid of him. I judge he thought he could have any girl he wanted, just for the asking, and it must have set him back a good deal when he found he couldn't get Benny. Why, Benny's only half as old as he is, and just as sweet and lovely as — well, you've seen her. Poor old Uncle Silas — why, it's pitiful, him trying to curry favor that way — so hard pushed and poor, and yet hiring that useless Jubiter Dunlap to please his ornery brother."

"What a name — Jubiter! Where'd he get it?"

"It's only just a nickname. I reckon they've forgot his real name long before this. He's twenty-seven, now, and has had it ever since the first time he ever went in swimming. The school teacher seen a round brown mole the size of a dime on his left leg above his knee, and four little bits of moles around it, when he was naked, and he said it 'minded him of Jubiter and his moons; and the children thought it was funny, and so they got to calling him Jubiter, and he's Jubiter yet. He's tall, and lazy, and sly, and sneaky, and ruther cowardly, too, but kind of good-natured, and wears long brown hair and no beard, and hasn't got a cent, and Brace boards him for nothing, and gives him his old clothes to wear, and despises him. Jubiter is a twin."

"What's t'other twin like?"

"Just exactly like Jubiter — so they say; used to was, anyway, but he hain't been seen for seven years. He got to robbing when he was nineteen or twenty, and they jailed him; but he broke jail and got away — up North here, somers. They used to hear about him robbing and burglaring now and then, but that was years ago. He's dead now. At least that's what they say. They don't hear about him any more."

"What was his name?"

"Jake."

There wasn't anything more said for a considerable while; the old lady was thinking. At last she says:

"The thing that is mostly worrying your aunt Sally is the tempers that that man Jubiter gets your uncle into."

Tom was astonished, and so was I. Tom says:

"Tempers? Uncle Silas? Land, you must be joking! I didn't know he *had* any temper."

"Works him up into perfect rages, your aunt Sally says; says he acts as if he would really hit the man, sometimes."

"Aunt Polly, it beats anything I ever heard of. Why, he's just as gentle as mush."

"Well, she's worried, anyway. Says your uncle Silas is like a changed man, on account of all this quarreling. And the neighbors talk about it, and lay all the blame on your uncle, of course, because he's a preacher and hain't got any business to quarrel. Your aunt Sally says he hates to go into the pulpit he's so ashamed; and the people have begun to cool toward him, and he ain't as popular now as he used to was."

"Well, ain't it strange? Why, Aunt Polly, he was always so good and kind and moony and absent-minded and chuckle-headed and lovable —why, he was just an angel! What *can* be the matter of him, do you reckon?"

CHAPTER II: JAKE DUNLAP

We had powerful good luck; because we got a chance in a stern-wheeler from away North which was bound for one of them bayous or one-horse rivers away down Louisiana way, and so we could go all the way down the Upper Mississippi and all the way down the Lower Mississippi to that farm in Arkansaw without having to change steam-boats at St. Louis; not so very much short of a thousand miles at one pull.

A pretty lonesome boat; there warn't but few passengers, and all old folks, that set around, wide apart, dozing, and was very quiet. We was four days getting out of the "upper river," because we got aground so much. But it warn't dull—couldn't be for boys that was traveling, of course.

From the very start me and Tom allowed that there was somebody sick in the stateroom next to ourn, because the meals was always toted in there by the waiters. By and by we asked about it—Tom did—and the waiter said it was a man, but he didn't look sick.

"Well, but *ain't* he sick?"

"I don't know; maybe he is, but 'pears to me he's just letting on."

"What makes you think that?"

"Because if he was sick he would pull his clothes off *some* time or other—don't you reckon he would? Well, this one don't. At least he don't ever pull off his boots, anyway."

"The mischief he don't! Not even when he goes to bed?"

"No."

It was always nuts for Tom Sawyer—a mystery was. If you'd lay out a mystery and a pie before me and him, you wouldn't have to say take your choice; it was a thing that would regulate itself. Because in my nature I have always run to pie, whilst in his nature he has always run to mystery. People are made different. And it is the best way. Tom says to the waiter:

"What's the man's name?"

"Phillips."

"Where'd he come aboard?"

"I think he got aboard at Elexandria, up on the Iowa line."

"What do you reckon he's a-playing?"

"I hain't any notion—I never thought of it."

I says to myself, here's another one that runs to pie.

"Anything peculiar about him?—the way he acts or talks?"

"No—nothing, except he seems so scary, and keeps his doors locked night and day both, and when you knock he won't let you in till he opens the door a crack and sees who it is."

"By jiminy, it's int'resting! I'd like to get a look at him. Say—the next time you're going in there, don't you reckon you could spread the door and—"

"No, indeedy! He's always behind it. He would block that game."

Tom studied over it, and then he says:

"Looky here. You lend me your apern and let me take him his breakfast in the morning. I'll give you a quarter."

The boy was plenty willing enough, if the head steward wouldn't mind. Tom says that's all right, he reckoned he could fix it with the head steward; and he done it. He fixed it so as we could both go in with aperns on and toting vittles.

He didn't sleep much, he was in such a sweat to get in there and find out the mystery about Phillips; and moreover he done a lot of guessing about it all night, which warn't no use, for if you are going to find out the facts of a thing, what's the sense in guessing out what ain't the facts and wasting ammunition? I didn't lose no sleep. I wouldn't give a dern to know what's the matter of Phillips, I says to myself.

Well, in the morning we put on the aperns and got a couple of trays of truck, and Tom he knocked on the door. The man opened it a crack, and then he let us in and shut it quick. By Jackson, when we got a sight of him, we 'most dropped the trays! and Tom says:

"Why, Jubiter Dunlap, where'd *you* come from?"

Well, the man was astonished, of course; and first off he looked like he didn't know whether to be scared, or glad, or both, or which, but finally he settled down to being glad; and then his color come back, though at first his face had turned pretty white. So we got to talking together while he et his breakfast. And he says:

"But I aint Jubiter Dunlap. I'd just as soon tell you who I am, though, if you'll swear to keep mum, for I ain't no Phillips, either."

Tom says:

"We'll keep mum, but there ain't any need to tell who you are if you ain't Jubiter Dunlap."

"Why?"

"Because if you ain't him you're t'other twin, Jake. You're the spit'n image of Jubiter."

"Well, I *am* Jake. But looky here, how do you come to know us Dunlaps?"

Tom told about the adventures we'd had down there at his uncle Silas's last summer, and when he see that there warn't anything about his folks — or him either, for that matter — that we didn't know, he opened out and talked perfectly free and candid. He never made any bones about his own case; said he'd been a hard lot, was a hard lot yet, and reckoned he'd be a hard lot plumb to the end. He said of course it was a dangerous life, and —

He give a kind of gasp, and set his head like a person that's listening. We didn't say anything, and so it was very still for a second or so, and there warn't no sounds but the screaking of the woodwork and the chug-chugging of the machinery down below.

Then we got him comfortable again, telling him about his people, and how Brace's wife had been dead three years, and Brace wanted to marry Benny and she shook him, and Jubiter was working for Uncle

Silas, and him and Uncle Silas quarreling all the time — and then he let go and laughed.

"Land!" he says, "it's like old times to hear all this tittle-tattle, and does me good. It's been seven years and more since I heard any. How do they talk about me these days?"

"Who?"

"The farmers — and the family."

"Why, they don't talk about you at all — at least only just a mention, once in a long time."

"The nation!" he says, surprised; "why is that?"

"Because they think you are dead long ago."

"No! Are you speaking true? — honor bright, now." He jumped up, excited.

"Honor bright. There ain't anybody thinks you are alive."

"Then I'm saved, I'm saved, sure! I'll go home. They'll hide me and save my life. You keep mum. Swear you'll keep mum — swear you'll never, never tell on me. Oh, boys, be good to a poor devil that's being hunted day and night, and dasn't show his face! I've never done you any harm; I'll never do you any, as God is in the heavens; swear you'll be good to me and help me save my life."

We'd 'a' swore it if he'd been a dog; and so we done it. Well, he couldn't love us enough for it or be grateful enough, poor cuss; it was all he could do to keep from hugging us.

We talked along, and he got out a little hand-bag and begun to open it, and told us to turn our backs. We done it, and when he told us to turn again he was perfectly different to what he was before. He had on blue goggles and the naturalest-looking long brown whiskers and mustashes you ever see. His own mother wouldn't 'a' knowed him. He asked us if he looked like his brother Jubiter, now.

"No," Tom said; "there ain't anything left that's like him except the long hair."

"All right, I'll get that cropped close to my head before I get there; then him and Brace will keep my secret, and I'll live with them as being a stranger, and the neighbors won't ever guess me out. What do you think?"

Tom he studied awhile, then he says:

"Well, of course me and Huck are going to keep mum there, but if you don't keep mum yourself there's going to be a little bit of a risk — it ain't much, maybe, but it's a little. I mean, if you talk, won't people notice that your voice is just like Jubiter's; and mightn't it make them think of the twin they reckoned was dead, but maybe after all was hid all this time under another name?"

"By George," he says, "you're a sharp one! You're perfectly right. I've got to play deef and dumb when there's a neighbor around. If I'd 'a' struck for home and forgot that little detail— However, I wasn't striking for home. I was breaking for any place where I could get away from these fellows that are after me; then I was going to put on this disguise and get some different clothes, and—"

He jumped for the outside door and laid his ear against it and listened, pale and kind of panting. Presently he whispers:

"Sounded like cocking a gun! Lord, what a life to lead!"

Then he sunk down in a chair all limp and sick-like, and wiped the sweat off of his face.

CHAPTER III: A DIAMOND ROBBERY

FROM THAT TIME out, we was with him 'most all the time, and one or t'other of us slept in his upper berth. He said he had been so lonesome, and it was such a comfort to him to have company, and somebody to talk to in his troubles. We was in a sweat to find out what his secret was, but Tom said the best way was not to seem anxious, then likely he would drop into it himself in one of his talks, but if we got to asking questions he would get suspicious and shet up his shell. It turned out just so. It warn't no trouble to see that he *wanted* to talk about it, but always along at first he would scare away from it when he got on the very edge of it, and go to talking about something else. The way it come about was this: He got to asking us, kind of indifferent like, about the passengers down on deck. We told him about them. But he warn't satisfied; we warn't particular enough. He told us to describe them better. Tom done it. At last, when Tom was describing one of the roughest and raggedest ones, he gave a shiver and a gasp and says:

"Oh, lordy, that's one of them! They're aboard sure—I just knowed it. I sort of hoped I had got away, but I never believed it. Go on."

Presently when Tom was describing another mangy, rough deck passenger, he give that shiver again and says:

"That's him!—that's the other one. If it would only come a good black stormy night and I could get ashore. You see, they've got spies on me. They've got a right to come up and buy drinks at the bar yonder forrard, and they take that chance to bribe somebody to keep watch on me

— porter or boots or somebody. If I was to slip ashore without anybody seeing me, they would know it inside of an hour."

So then he got to wandering along, and pretty soon, sure enough, he was telling! He was poking along through his ups and downs, and when he come to that place he went right along. He says:

"It was a confidence game. We played it on a julery-shop in St. Louis. What we was after was a couple of noble big di'monds as big as hazelnuts, which everybody was running to see. We was dressed up fine, and we played it on them in broad daylight. We ordered the di'monds sent to the hotel for us to see if we wanted to buy, and when we was examining them we had paste counterfeits all ready, and *them* was the things that went back to the shop when we said the water wasn't quite fine enough for twelve thousand dollars."

"Twelve — thousand — dollars!" Tom says. "Was they really worth all that money, do you reckon?"

"Every cent of it."

"And you fellows got away with them?"

"As easy as nothing. I don't reckon the julery people know they've been robbed yet. But it wouldn't be good sense to stay around St. Louis, of course, so we considered where we'd go. One was for going one way, one another, so we throwed up, heads or tails, and the Upper Mississippi won. We done up the di'monds in a paper and put our names on it and put it in the keep of the hotel clerk, and told him not to ever let either of us have it again without the others was on hand to see it done; then we went down-town, each by his own self — because I reckon maybe we all had the same notion. I don't know for certain, but I reckon maybe we had."

"What notion?" Tom says.

"To rob the others."

"What — one take everything, after all of you had helped to get it?"

"Cert'nly."

It disgusted Tom Sawyer, and he said it was the orneriest, low-downest thing he ever heard of. But Jake Dunlap said it warn't unusual in the profession. Said when a person was in that line of business he'd got to look out for his own intrust, there warn't nobody else going to do it for him. And then he went on. He says:

"You see, the trouble was, you couldn't divide up two di'monds amongst three. If there'd been three — But never mind about that, there *warn't* three. I loafed along the back streets studying and studying. And

I says to myself, I'll hog them di'monds the first chance I get, and I'll have a disguise all ready, and I'll give the boys the slip, and when I'm safe away I'll put it on, and then let them find me if they can. So I got the false whiskers and the goggles and this countrified suit of clothes, and fetched them along back in a hand-bag; and when I was passing a shop where they sell all sorts of things, I got a glimpse of one of my pals through the window. It was Bud Dixon. I was glad, you bet. I says to myself, I'll see what he buys. So I kept shady, and watched. Now what do you reckon it was he bought?"

"Whiskers?" said I.

"No."

"Goggles?"

"No."

"Oh, keep still, Huck Finn, can't you, you're only just hendering all you can. What *was* it he bought, Jake?"

"You'd never guess in the world. It was only just a screwdriver—just a wee little bit of a screwdriver."

"Well, I declare! What did he want with that?"

"That's what *I* thought. It was curious. It clean stumped me. I says to myself, what can he want with that thing? Well, when he come out I stood back out of sight, and then tracked him to a second-hand slop-shop and see him buy a red flannel shirt and some old ragged clothes—just the ones he's got on now, as you've described. Then I went down to the wharf and hid my things aboard the up-river boat that we had picked out, and then started back and had another streak of luck. I seen our other pal lay in *his* stock of old rusty second-handers. We got the di'monds and went aboard the boat.

"But now we was up a stump, for we couldn't go to bed. We had to set up and watch one another. Pity, that was; pity to put that kind of a strain on us, because there was bad blood between us from a couple of weeks back, and we was only friends in the way of business. Bad anyway, seeing there was only two di'monds betwixt three men. First we had supper, and then tramped up and down the deck together smoking till most midnight; then we went and set down in my stateroom and locked the doors and looked in the piece of paper to see if the di'monds was all right, then laid it on the lower berth right in full sight; and there we set, and set, and by and by it got to be dreadful hard to keep awake. At last Bud Dixon he dropped off. As soon as he was snoring a good regular gait that was likely to last, and had his chin on his breast and looked permanent, Hal Clayton nodded towards the di'monds and then towards the outside door, and I understood. I reached and got the paper, and then we stood up and waited perfectly still; Bud never stirred; I turned the key of the outside door very soft and slow, then turned the knob the same way, and we went tiptoeing out onto the guard, and shut the door very soft and gentle.

"There warn't nobody stirring anywhere, and the boat was slipping along, swift and steady, through the big water in the smoky moonlight. We never said a word, but went straight up onto the hurricane-deck and plumb back aft, and set down on the end of the skylight. Both of us knowed what that meant, without having to explain to one another. Bud Dixon would wake up and miss the swag, and would come straight for us, for he ain't afeard of anything or anybody, that man ain't. He would come, and we would heave him overboard, or get killed trying. It made me shiver, because I ain't as brave as some people, but if I showed the white feather — well, I knowed better than do that. I kind of hoped the boat would land somers, and we could skip ashore and not have to run the risk of this row, I was so scared of Bud Dixon, but she was an upper-river tub and there warn't no real chance of that.

"Well, the time strung along and along, and that fellow never come! Why, it strung along till dawn begun to break, and still he never come. 'Thunder,' I says, 'what do you make out of this? — ain't it suspicious?' 'Land!' Hal says, 'do you reckon he's playing us? — open the paper!' I done it, and by gracious there warn't anything in it but a couple of little pieces of loaf-sugar! *That's* the reason he could set there and snooze all night so comfortable. Smart? Well, I reckon! He had had them two papers all fixed and ready, and he had put one of them in place of t'other right under our noses.

"We felt pretty cheap. But the thing to do, straight off, was to make a plan; and we done it. We would do up the paper again, just as it was, and slip in, very elaborate and soft, and lay it on the bunk again, and let on *we* didn't know about any trick, and hadn't any idea he was a-laughing at us behind them bogus snores of his'n; and we would stick by him, and the first night we was ashore we would get him drunk and search him, and get the di'monds; and *do* for him, too, if it warn't too risky. If we got the swag, we'd *got* to do for him, or he would hunt us down and do for us, sure. But I didn't have no real hope. I knowed we could get him drunk — he was always ready for that — but what's the good of it? You might search him a year and never find —

"Well, right there I catched my breath and broke off my thought! For an idea went ripping through my head that tore my brains to rags — and land, but I felt gay and good! You see, I had had my boots off, to unswell my feet, and just then I took up one of them to put it on, and I catched a glimpse of the heel- bottom, and it just took my breath away. You remember about that puzzlesome little screwdriver?"

"You bet I do," says Tom, all excited.

"Well, when I catched that glimpse of that boot heel, the idea that went smashing through my head was, *I* know where he's hid the di'monds! You look at this boot heel, now. See, it's bottomed with a steel plate, and the plate is fastened on with little screws. Now there wasn't a screw about that feller anywhere but in his boot heels; so, if he needed a screwdriver, I reckoned I knowed why."

"Huck, ain't it bully!" says Tom.

"Well, I got my boots on, and we went down and slipped in and laid the paper of sugar on the berth, and sat down soft and sheepish and went to listening to Bud Dixon snore. Hal Clayton dropped off pretty soon, but I didn't; I wasn't ever so wide awake in my life. I was spying out from under the shade of my hat brim, searching the floor for leather. It took me a long time, and I begun to think maybe my guess was wrong, but at last I struck it. It laid over by the bulkhead, and was nearly the color of the carpet. It was a little round plug about as thick as the end of your little finger, and I says to myself there's a di'mond in the nest you've come from. Before long I spied out the plug's mate.

"Think of the smartness and coolness of that blatherskite! He put up that scheme on us and reasoned out what we would do, and we went ahead and done it perfectly exact, like a couple of pudd'nheads. He set there and took his own time to unscrew his heel-plates and cut out his plugs and stick in the di'monds and screw on his plates again. He allowed we would steal the bogus swag and wait all night for him to come up and get drownded, and by George it's just what we done! I think it was powerful smart."

"You bet your life it was!" says Tom, just full of admiration.

CHAPTER IV: THE THREE SLEEPERS

WELL, ALL DAY we went through the humbug of watching one another, and it was pretty sickly business for two of us and hard to act out, I can tell you. About night we landed at one of them little Missouri towns high up toward Iowa, and had supper at the tavern, and got a room upstairs with a cot and a double bed in it, but I dumped my bag under a deal table in the dark hall while we was moving along it to bed, single file, me last, and the landlord in the lead with a tallow candle. We had up a lot of whisky, and went to playing high-low-jack for dimes, and as soon as the whisky begun to take hold of Bud we stopped drinking, but we didn't let him stop. We loaded him till he fell out of his chair and laid there snoring.

"We was ready for business now. I said we better pull our boots off, and his'n too, and not make any noise, then we could pull him and haul him around and ransack him without any trouble. So we done it. I set my boots and Bud's side by side, where they'd be handy. Then we stripped him and searched his seams and his pockets and his socks and the inside of his boots, and everything, and searched his bundle. Never found any di'monds. We found the screwdriver, and Hal says, 'What do you reckon he wanted with that?' I said I didn't know; but when he wasn't looking I hooked it. At last Hal he looked beat and discouraged, and said we'd got to give it up. That was what I was waiting for. I says:

" 'There's one place we hain't searched.'

" 'What place is that?' he says.

" 'His stomach.'

" 'By gracious, I never thought of that! *Now* we're on the homestretch, to a dead moral certainty. How'll we manage?'

" 'Well,' I says, 'just stay by him till I turn out and hunt up a drug-store, and I reckon I'll fetch something that'll make them di'monds tired of the company they're keeping.'

"He said that's the ticket, and with him looking straight at me I slid myself into Bud's boots instead of my own, and he never noticed. They was just a shade large for me, but that was considerable better than being too small. I got my bag as I went a-groping through the hall, and in about a minute I was out the back way and stretching up the river road at a five-mile gait.

"And not feeling so very bad, neither — walking on di'monds don't have no such effect. When I had gone fifteen minutes I says to myself, there's more'n a mile behind me, and everything quiet. Another five minutes and I says there's considerable more land behind me now, and there's a man back there that's begun to wonder what's the trouble. Another five and I says to myself he's getting real uneasy — he's walking the floor now. Another five, and I says to myself, there's two mile and a half behind me, and he's *awful* uneasy — beginning to cuss, I reckon. Pretty soon I says to myself, forty minutes gone — he *knows* there's something up! Fifty minutes — the truth's a-busting on him now! he is reckoning I found the di'monds whilst we was searching, and shoved them in my pocket and never let on — yes, and he's starting out to hunt for me. He'll hunt for new tracks in the dust, and they'll as likely send him down the river as up.

"Just then I see a man coming down on a mule, and before I thought I jumped into the bush. It was stupid! When he got abreast he stopped and waited a little for me to come out; then he rode on again. But I didn't feel gay any more. I says to myself I've botched my chances by that; I surely have, if he meets up with Hal Clayton.

"Well, about three in the morning I fetched Elexandria and see this stern-wheeler laying there, and was very glad, because I felt perfectly safe, now, you know. It was just daybreak. I went aboard and got this stateroom and put on these clothes and went up in the pilot-house — to watch, though I didn't reckon there was any need of it. I set there and played with my di'monds and waited and waited for the boat to start, but she didn't. You see, they was mending her machinery, but I didn't know anything about it, not being very much used to steamboats.

"Well, to cut the tale short, we never left there till plumb noon; and long before that I was hid in this stateroom; for before breakfast I see a man coming, away off, that had a gait like Hal Clayton's, and it made me just sick. I says to myself, if he finds out I'm aboard this boat, he's got me like a rat in a trap. All he's got to do is to have me watched, and wait — wait till I slip ashore, thinking he is a thousand miles away, then slip after me and dog me to a good place and make me give up the di'monds, and then he'll — oh, I know what he'll do! Ain't it awful — awful! And now to think the *other* one's aboard, too! Oh, ain't it hard luck, boys — ain't it hard! But you'll help save me, *won't* you? — oh, boys, be good to a poor devil that's being hunted to death, and save me — I'll worship the very ground you walk on!"

We turned in and soothed him down and told him we would plan for him and help him, and he needn't be so afeard; and so by and by he got to feeling kind of comfortable again, and unscrewed his heel-plates and held up his di'monds this way and that, admiring them and loving them; and when the light struck into them they *was* beautiful, sure; why, they seemed to kind of bust, and snap fire out all around. But all the same I judged he was a fool. If I had been him I would 'a' handed the di'monds to them pals and got them to go ashore and leave me alone. But he was made different. He said it was a whole fortune and he couldn't bear the idea.

Twice we stopped to fix the machinery and laid a good while, once in the night; but it wasn't dark enough, and he was afeard to skip. But the third time we had to fix it there was a better chance. We laid up at a country woodyard about forty mile above Uncle Silas's place a little after one at night, and it was thickening up and going to storm. So Jake he laid for a chance to slide. We begun to take in wood. Pretty soon the rain come a-drenching down, and the wind blowed hard. Of course every boat-hand fixed a gunny sack and put it on like a bonnet, the way they do when they are toting wood, and we got one for Jake, and he slipped down aft with his hand-bag and come tramping forrard just like the rest, and walked ashore with them, and when we see him pass out of the light of the torch-basket and get swallowed up in the dark, we got our breath again and just felt grateful and splendid. But it wasn't for long. Somebody told, I reckon; for in about eight or ten minutes them two pals come tearing forrard as tight as they could jump and darted ashore and was gone. We waited plumb till dawn for them to come back, and kept hoping they would, but they never did. We was awful sorry and low-spirited. All the hope we had was that Jake had got such a start that they couldn't get on his track, and he would get to his brother's and hide there and be safe.

He was going to take the river road, and told us to find out if Brace and Jubiter was to home and no strangers there, and then slip out about sundown and tell him. Said he would wait for us in a little bunch of sycamores right back of Tom's uncle Silas's tobacker field on the river road, a lonesome place.

We set and talked a long time about his chances, and Tom said he was all right if the pals struck up the river instead of down, but it wasn't likely, because maybe they knowed where he was from; more likely they would go right, and dog him all day, him not suspecting, and kill him when it come dark, and take the boots. So we was pretty sorrowful.

CHAPTER V: A TRAGEDY IN THE WOODS

We didn't get done tinkering the machinery till away late in the afternoon, and so it was so close to sundown when we got home that we never stopped on our road, but made a break for the sycamores as tight as we could go, to tell Jake what the delay was, and have him wait till we could go to Brace's and find out how things was there. It was getting pretty dim by the time we turned the corner of the woods, sweat-ing and panting with that long run, and see the sycamores thirty yards ahead of us; and just then we see a couple of men run into the bunch and heard two or three terrible screams for help. "Poor Jake is killed, sure," we says. We was scared through and through, and broke for the tobacker field and hid there, trembling so our clothes would hardly stay on; and just as we skipped in there, a couple of men went tearing by, and into the bunch they went, and in a second out jumps four men and took out up the road as tight as they could go, two chasing two.

We laid down, kind of weak and sick, and listened for more sounds, but didn't hear none for a good while but just our hearts. We was thinking of that awful thing laying yonder in the sycamores, and it seemed like being that close to a ghost, and it give me the cold shudders. The moon come a-swelling up out of the ground, now, powerful big and round and bright, behind a comb of trees, like a face looking through prison bars, and the black shadders and white places begun to creep around, and it was miserable quiet and still and night-breezy and graveyardy and scary. All of a sudden Tom whispers:

"Look! — what's that?"

"Don't!" I says. "Don't take a person by surprise that way. I'm 'most ready to die, anyway, without you doing that."

"Look, I tell you. It's something coming out of the sycamores."

"Don't, Tom!"

"It's terrible tall!"

"Oh, lordy-lordy! let's —"

"Keep still — it's a-coming this way."

He was so excited he could hardly get breath enough to whisper. I had to look. I couldn't help it. So now we was both on our knees with our chins on a fence rail and gazing — yes, and gasping, too. It was coming down the road — coming in the shadder of the trees, and you couldn't see it good; not till it was pretty close to us; then it stepped into a bright splotch of moonlight and we sunk right down in our tracks — it was Jake Dunlap's ghost! That was what we said to ourselves.

We couldn't stir for a minute or two; then it was gone. We talked about it in low voices. Tom says:

"They're mostly dim and smoky, or like they're made out of fog, but this one wasn't."

"No," I says; "I seen the goggles and the whiskers perfectly plain."

"Yes, and the very colors in them loud countrified Sunday clothes — plaid breeches, green and black —"

"Cotton velvet westcot, fire-red and yaller squares —"

"Leather straps to the bottoms of the breeches legs and one of them hanging unbuttoned —"

"Yes, and that hat —"

"What a hat for a ghost to wear!"

You see it was the first season anybody wore that kind — a black sitff-brim stove-pipe, very high, and not smooth, with a round top — just like a sugar-loaf.

"Did you notice if its hair was the same, Huck?"

"No — seems to me I did, then again it seems to me I didn't."

"I didn't either; but it had its bag along, I noticed that."

"So did I. How can there be a ghost-bag, Tom?"

"Sho! I wouldn't be as ignorant as that if I was you, Huck Finn. Whatever a ghost has, turns to ghost-stuff. They've got to have their things, like anybody else. You see, yourself, that its clothes was turned to ghost-stuff. Well, then, what's to hender its bag from turning, too? Of course it done it."

That was reasonable. I couldn't find no fault with it. Bill Withers and his brother Jack come along by, talking, and Jack says:

"What do you reckon he was toting?"

"I dunno; but it was pretty heavy."

"Yes, all he could lug. Nigger stealing corn from old Parson Silas, I judged."

"So did I. And so I allowed I wouldn't let on to see him."

"That's me, too."

Then they both laughed, and went on out of hearing. It showed how unpopular old Uncle Silas had got to be now. They wouldn't 'a' let a nigger steal anybody else's corn and never done anything to him.

We heard some more voices mumbling along towards us and getting louder, and sometimes a cackle of a laugh. It was Lem Beebe and Jim Lane. Jim Lane says:

"Who? — Jubiter Dunlap?"

"Yes."

"Oh, I don't know. I reckon so. I seen him spading up some ground along about an hour ago, just before sundown — him and the parson. Said he guessed he wouldn't go to-night, but we could have his dog if we wanted him."

"Too tired, I reckon."

"Yes — works so hard!"

"Oh, you bet!"

They cackled at that, and went on by. Tom said we better jump out and tag along after them, because they was going our way and it wouldn't be comfortable to run across the ghost all by ourselves. So we done it, and got home all right.

That night was the second of September—a Saturday. I sha'n't ever forget it. You'll see why, pretty soon.

CHAPTER VI: PLANS TO SECURE THE DIAMONDS

We tramped along behind Jim and Lem till we come to the back stile where old Jim's cabin was that he was captivated in, the time we set him free, and here come the dogs piling around us to say howdy, and there was the lights of the house, too; so we warn't afeard any more, and was going to climb over, but Tom says:

"Hold on; set down here a minute. By George!"

"What's the matter?" says I.

"Matter enough!" he says. "Wasn't you expecting we would be the first to tell the family who it is that's been killed yonder in the sycamores, and all about them rapscallions that done it, and about the di'monds they've smouched off of the corpse, and paint it up fine, and have the glory of being the ones that knows a lot more about it than anybody else?"

"Why, of course. It wouldn't be you, Tom Sawyer, if you was to let such a chance go by. I reckon it ain't going to suffer none for lack of paint," I says, "when you start in to scollop the facts."

"Well, now," he says, perfectly ca'm, "what would you say if I was to tell you I ain't going to start in at all?"

I was astonished to hear him talk so. I says:

"I'd say it's a lie. You ain't in earnest, Tom Sawyer?"

"You'll soon see. Was the ghost barefooted?"

"No, it wasn't. What of it?"

"You wait—I'll show you what. Did it have its boots on?"

"Yes. I seen them plain."

"Swear it?"

"Yes, I swear it."

"So do I. Now do you know what that means?"

"No. What does it mean?"

"Means that them thieves *didn't get the di'monds.*"

"Jiminy! What makes you think that?"

"I don't only think it, I know it. Didn't the breeches and goggles and whiskers and hand-bag and every blessed thing turn to ghost-stuff? Everything it had on turned, didn't it? It shows that the reason its boots turned too was because it still had them on after it started to go ha'nting around, and if that ain't proof that them blatherskites didn't get the boots, I'd like to know what you'd *call* proof."

Think of that now. I never see such a head as that boy had. Why, *I* had eyes and I could see things, but they never meant nothing to me. But Tom Sawyer was different. When Tom Sawyer seen a thing it just got up on its hind legs and *talked* to him — told him everything it knowed. *I* never see such a head.

"Tom Sawyer," I says, "I'll say it again as I've said it a many a time before: I ain't fitten to black your boots. But that's all right — that's neither here nor there. God Almighty made us all, and some He gives eyes that's blind, and some He gives eyes that can see, and I reckon it ain't none of our lookout what He done it for; it's all right, or He'd 'a' fixed it some other way. Go on — I see plenty plain enough, now, that them thieves didn't get way with the di'monds. Why didn't they, do you reckon?"

"Because they got chased away by them other two men before they could pull the boots off of the corpse."

"That's so! I see it now. But looky here, Tom, why ain't we to go and tell about it?"

"Oh, shucks, Huck Finn, can't you see? Look at it. What's a-going to happen? There's going to be an inquest in the morning. Them two men will tell how they heard the yells and rushed there just in time to not save the stranger. Then the jury'll twaddle and twaddle and twaddle, and finally they'll fetch in a verdict that he got shot or stuck or busted over the head with something, and come to his death by the inspiration of God. And after they've buried him they'll auction off his things for to pay the expenses, and then's *our* chance."

"How, Tom?"

"Buy the boots for two dollars!"

Well, it 'most took my breath.

"My land! Why, Tom, *we'll* get the di'monds!"

"You bet. Some day there'll be a big reward offered for them — a thousand dollars, sure. That's our money! Now we'll trot in and see the folks. And mind you we don't know anything about any murder, or any di'monds, or any thieves — don't you forget that."

I had to sigh a little over the way he had got it fixed. *I'd* 'a' *sold* them di'monds — yes, sir — for twelve thousand dollars; but I didn't say anything. It wouldn't done any good. I says:

"But what are we going to tell your aunt Sally has made us so long getting down here from the village, Tom?"

"Oh, I'll leave that to you," he says. "I reckon you can explain it somehow."

He was always just that strict and delicate. He never would tell a lie himself.

We struck across the big yard, noticing this, that, and t'other thing that was so familiar, and we so glad to see it again, and when we got to the roofed big passageway betwixt the double log house and the kitchen part, there was everything hanging on the wall just as it used to was, even to Uncle Silas's old faded green baize working-gown with the hood to it, and raggedy white patch between the shoulders that always looked like somebody had hit him with a snowball; and then we lifted the latch and walked in. Aunt Sally she was just a-ripping and a-tearing around, and the children was huddled in one corner, and the old man he was huddled in the other and praying for help in time of need. She jumped for us with joy and tears running down her face and give us a whacking box on the ear, and then hugged us and kissed us and boxed us again, and just couldn't seem to get enough of it, she was so glad to see us; and she says:

"Where *have* you been a-loafing to, you good-for-nothing trash! I've been that worried about you I didn't know what to do. Your traps has been here *ever* so long, and I've had supper cooked fresh about four times so as to have it hot and good when you come, till at last my patience is just plumb wore out, and I declare I — I — why I could skin you alive! You must be starving, poor things! — set down, set down, everybody; don't lose no more time."

It was good to be there again behind all that noble corn-pone and spareribs, and everything that you could ever want in this world. Old Uncle Silas he peeled off one of his bulliest old-time blessings, with as many layers to it as an onion, and whilst the angels was hauling in the slack of it I was trying to study up what to say about what kept us so long. When our plates was all loadened and we'd got a-going, she asked me, and I says:

"Well, you see, — er — Mizzes —"

"Huck Finn! Since when am I Mizzes to you? Have I ever been stingy of cuffs or kisses for you since the day you stood in this room and I took you for Tom Sawyer and blessed God for sending you to me, though you told me four thousand lies and I believed every one of them like a simpleton? Call me Aunt Sally — like you always done."

So I done it. And I says:

"Well, me and Tom allowed we would come along afoot and take a smell of the woods, and we run across Lem Beebe and Jim Lane, and they asked us to go with them blackberrying to-night, and said they could borrow Jubiter Dunlap's dog, because he had told them just that minute—"

"Where did they see him?" says the old man; and when I looked up to see how *he* come to take an intrust in a little thing like that, his eyes was just burning into me, he was that eager. It surprised me so it kind of throwed me off, but I pulled myself together again and says:

"It was when he was spading up some ground along with you, towards sundown or along there."

He only said, "Um," in a kind of a disappointed way, and didn't take no more intrust. So I went on. I says:

"Well, then, as I was a-saying—"

"That'll do, you needn't go no furder." It was Aunt Sally. She was boring right into me with her eyes, and very indignant. "Huck Finn," she says, "how'd them men come to talk about going a-blackberrying in September—in *this* region?"

I see I had slipped up, and I couldn't say a word. She waited, still a-gazing at me, then she says:

"And how'd they come to strike that idiot idea of going a-blackberrying in the night?"

"Well, m'm, they—er—they told us they had a lantern, and—"

"Oh, *shet* up—do! Looky here; what was they going to do with a dog? —hunt blackberries with it?"

"I think, m'm, they—"

"Now, Tom Sawyer, what kind of a lie are you fixing *your* mouth to contribit to this mess of rubbage? Speak out—and I warn you before you begin, that I don't believe a word of it. You and Huck's been up to something you no business to—*I* know it perfectly well; *I* know you, *both* of you. Now you explain that dog, and them blackberries, and the lantern, and the rest of that rot—and mind you talk as straight as a string—do you hear?"

Tom he looked considerable hurt, and says, very dignified:

"It is a pity if Huck is to be talked to that way, just for making a little bit of a mistake that anybody could make."

"What mistake has he made?"

"Why, only the mistake of saying blackberries when of course he meant strawberries."

"Tom Sawyer, I lay if you aggravate me a little more, I'll—"

"Aunt Sally, without knowing it—and of course without intending it—you are in the wrong. If you'd 'a' studied natural history the way you ought, you would know that all over the world except just here in Arkansaw they *always* hunt strawberries with a dog—and a lantern—"

But she busted in on him there and just piled into him and snowed him under. She was so mad she couldn't get the words out fast enough, and she gushed them out in one everlasting freshet. That was what Tom Sawyer was after. He allowed to work her up and get her started and then leave her alone and let her burn herself out. Then she would be so aggravated with that subject that she wouldn't say another word about it, nor let anybody else. Well, it happened just so. When she was tuckered out and had to hold up, he says, quite ca'm:

"And yet, all the same, Aunt Sally—"

"Shet up!" she says, "I don't want to hear another word out of you."

So we was perfectly safe, then, and didn't have no more trouble about that delay. Tom done it elegant.

CHAPTER VII: A NIGHT'S VIGIL

BENNY SHE WAS looking pretty sober, and she sighed some, now and then; but pretty soon she got to asking about Mary, and Sid, and Tom's aunt Polly, and then Aunt Sally's clouds cleared off and she got in a good humor and joined in on the questions and was her lovingest best self, and so the rest of the supper went along gay and pleasant. But the old man he didn't take any hand hardly, and was absent-minded and restless, and done a considerable amount of sighing; and it was kind of heartbreaking to see him so sad and troubled and worried.

By and by, a spell after supper, come a nigger and knocked on the door and put his head in with his old straw hat in his hand bowing and scraping, and said his Marse Brace was out at the stile and wanted his brother, and was getting tired waiting supper for him, and would Marse Silas please tell him where he was? I never see Uncle Silas speak up so sharp and fractious before. He says:

"Am *I* his brother's keeper?" And then he kind of wilted together, and looked like he wished he hadn't spoken so, and then he says, very gentle: "But you needn't say that, Billy; I was took sudden and irritable, and I ain't very well these days, and not hardly responsible. Tell him he ain't here."

And when the nigger was gone he got up and walked the floor, backwards and forwards, mumbling and muttering to himself and plowing his hands through his hair. It was real pitiful to see him. Aunt Sally she whispered to us and told us not to take notice of him, it embarrassed him. She said he was always thinking and thinking, since these troubles come on, and she allowed he didn't more'n about half know what he was about when the thinking spells was on him; and she said he walked in his sleep considerable more now than he used to, and sometimes wandered around over the house and even outdoors in his sleep, and if we catched him at it we must let him alone and not disturb him. She said she reckoned it didn't do him no harm, and may be it done him good. She said Benny was the only one that was much help to him these days. Said Benny appeared to know just when to try to soothe him and when to leave him alone.

So he kept on tramping up and down the floor and muttering, till by and by he begun to look pretty tired; then Benny she went and snuggled up to his side and put one hand in his and one arm around his waist and walked with him; and he smiled down on her, and reached down and kissed her; and so, little by little the trouble went out of his face and she persuaded him off to his room. They had very petting ways together, and it was uncommon pretty to see.

Aunt Sally she was busy getting the children ready for bed; so by and by it got dull and tedious, and me and Tom took a turn in the moonlight, and fetched up in the watermelon-patch and et one, and had a good deal of talk. And Tom said he'd bet the quarreling was all Jubiter's fault, and he was going to be on hand the first time he got a chance, and see; and if it was so, he was going to do his level best to get Uncle Silas to turn him off.

And so we talked and smoked and stuffed watermelons much as two hours, and then it was pretty late, and when we got back the house was quiet and dark, and everybody gone to bed.

Tom he always seen everything, and now he see that the old green baize work-gown was gone, and said it wasn't gone when he went out; so he allowed it was curious, and then we went up to bed.

We could hear Benny stirring around in her room, which was next to ourn, and judged she was worried a good deal about her father and couldn't sleep. We found we couldn't, neither. So we set up a long time, and smoked and talked in a low voice, and felt pretty dull and downhearted. We talked the murder and the ghost over and over again, and got so creepy and crawly we couldn't get sleepy nohow and noway.

By and by, when it was away late in the night and all the sounds was late sounds and solemn, Tom nudged me and whispers to me to look, and I done it, and there we see a man poking around in the yard like he didn't know just what he wanted to do, but it was pretty dim and we couldn't see him good. Then he started for the stile, and as he went over it the moon came out strong, and he had a long-handled shovel over his shoulder, and we see the white patch on the old work-gown. So Tom says:

"He's a-walking in his sleep. I wish we was allowed to follow him and see where he's going to. There, he's turned down by the tobacker field. Out of sight now. It's a dreadful pity he can't rest no better."

We waited a long time, but he didn't come back any more, or if he did he come around the other way; so at last we was tuckered out and went to sleep and had nightmares, a million of them. But before dawn we was awake again, because meantime a storm had come up and been raging, and the thunder and lightning was awful, and the wind was a-thrashing the trees around, and the rain was driving down in slanting sheets, and the gullies was running rivers. Tom says:

"Looky here, Huck, I'll tell you one thing that's mighty curious. Up to the time we went out last night the family hadn't heard about Jake Dunlap being murdered. Now the men that chased Hal Clayton and Bud Dixon away would spread the thing around in a half an hour, and every neighbor that heard it would shin out and fly around from one farm to t'other and try to be the first to tell the news. Land, they don't have such a big thing as that to tell twice in thirty year! Huck, it's mighty strange; I don't understand it."

So then he was in a fidget for the rain to let up, so we could turn out and run across some of the people and see if they would say anything about it to us. And he said if they did we must be horribly surprised and shocked.

We was out and gone the minute the rain stopped. It was just broad day then. We loafed along up the road, and now and then met a person and stopped and said howdy, and told them when we come, and how we left the folks at home, and how long we was going to stay, and all that, but none of them said a word about that thing; which was just astonishing, and no mistake. Tom said he believed if we went to the sycamores we would find that body laying there solitary and alone, and not a soul around. Said he believed the men chased the thieves so far into the woods that the thieves prob'ly seen a good chance and turned on them at last, and maybe they all killed each other, and so there wasn't anybody left to tell.

First we knowed, gabbling along that away, we was right at the sycamores. The cold chills trickled down my back and I wouldn't budge another step, for all Tom's persuading. But he couldn't hold in; he'd *got* to see if the boots was safe on that body yet. So he crope in — and the next minute out he come again with his eyes bulging he was so excited, and says:

"Huck, it's gone!"

I *was* astonished! I says:

"Tom, you don't mean it."

"It's gone, sure. There ain't a sign of it. The ground is trampled some, but if there was any blood it's all washed away by the storm, for it's all puddles and slush in there."

At last I give in, and went and took a look myself; and it was just as Tom said — there wasn't a sign of a corpse.

"Dern it," I says, "the di'monds is gone. Don't you reckon the thieves slunk back and lugged him off, Tom?"

"Looks like it. It just does. Now where'd they hide him, do you reckon?"

"I don't know," I says, disgusted, "and what's more I don't care. They've got the boots, and that's all *I* cared about. He'll lay around these woods a long time before *I* hunt him up."

Tom didn't feel no more intrust in him neither, only curiosity to know what come of him; but he said we'd lay low and keep dark and it wouldn't be long till the dogs or somebody rousted him out.

We went back home to breakfast ever so bothered and put out and disappointed and swindled. I warn't ever so down on a corpse before.

CHAPTER VIII: TALKING WITH THE GHOST

IT WARN'T VERY cheerful at breakfast. Aunt Sally she looked old and tired and let the children snarl and fuss at one another and didn't seem to notice it was going on, which wasn't her usual style; me and Tom had a plenty to think about without talking; Benny she looked like she hadn't had much sleep, and whenever she'd lift her head a little and steal a look towards her father you could see there was tears in her eyes; and as for the old man, his things stayed on his plate and got cold without him knowing they was there, I reckon, for he was thinking and thinking all the time, and never said a word and never et a bite.

By and by when it was stillest, that nigger's head was poked in at the door again, and he said his Marse Brace was getting powerful uneasy about Marse Jubiter, which hadn't come home yet, and would Marse Silas please —

He was looking at Uncle Silas, and he stopped there, like the rest of his words was froze; for Uncle Silas he rose up shaky and steadied himself leaning his fingers on the table, and he was panting, and his eyes was set on the nigger, and he kept swallowing, and put his other hand up to his throat a couple of times, and at last he got his words started, and says:

"Does he—does he—think—*what* does he think! Tell him—tell him—" Then he sunk down in his chair limp and weak, and says, so as you could hardly hear him: "Go away—go away!"

The nigger looked scared and cleared out, and we all felt—well, I don't know how we felt, but it was awful, with the old man panting there, and his eyes set and looking like a person that was dying. None of us could budge; but Benny she slid around soft, with her tears running down, and stood by his side, and nestled his old gray head up against her and begun to stroke it and pet it with her hands, and nodded to us to go away, and we done it, going out very quiet, like the dead was there.

Me and Tom struck out for the woods mighty solemn, and saying how different it was now to what it was last summer when we was here and everything was so peaceful and happy and everybody thought so much of Uncle Silas, and he was so cheerful and simple-hearted and pudd'n-headed and good—and now look at him. If he hadn't lost his mind he wasn't muck short of it. That was what we allowed.

It was a most lovely day now, and bright and sunshiny; and the further and further we went over the hills towards the prairie the lovelier and lovelier the trees and flowers got to be and the more it seemed strange and somehow wrong that there had to be trouble in such a world as this. And then all of a sudden I catched my breath and grabbed Tom's arm, and all my livers and lungs and things fell down into my legs.

"There it is!" I says. We jumped back behind a bush shivering, and Tom says:

"'Sh!—don't make a noise."

It was setting on a log right in the edge of a little prairie, thinking. I tried to get Tom to come away, but he wouldn't, and I dasn't budge by myself. He said we mightn't ever get another chance to see one, and he was going to look his fill at this one if he died for it. So I looked too, though it give me the fantods to do it. Tom he *had* to talk, but he talked low. He says:

"Poor Jakey, it's got all its things on, just as he said he would. *Now* you see what we wasn't certain about—its hair. It's not long now the way it was: it's got it cropped close to its head, the way he said he would. Huck, I never see anything look any more naturaler than what It does."

"Nor I neither," I says; "I'd recognize it anywheres."

"So would I. It looks perfectly solid and genuwyne, just the way it done before it died."

So we kept a-gazing. Pretty soon Tom says:

"Huck, there's something mighty curious about this one, don't you know? *It* oughtn't to be going around in the daytime."

"That's so, Tom — I never heard the like of it before."

"No, sir, they don't ever come out only at night — and then not till after twelve. There's something wrong about this one, now you mark my words. I don't believe it's got any right to be around in the daytime. But don't it look natural! Jake was going to play deef and dumb here, so the neighbors wouldn't know his voice. Do you reckon it would do that if we was to holler at it?"

"Lordy, Tom, don't talk so! If you was to holler at it I'd die in my tracks."

"Don't you worry, I ain't going to holler at it. Look, Huck, it's a-scratching its head — don't you see?"

"Well, what of it?"

"Why, this. What's the sense of it scratching its head? There ain't anything there to itch; its head is made out of fog or something like that, and can't itch. A fog can't itch; any fool knows that."

"Well, then, if it don't itch and can't itch, what in the nation is it scratching it for? Ain't it just habit, don't you reckon?"

"No, sir, I don't. I ain't a bit satisfied about the way this one acts. I've a blame good notion it's a bogus one — I have, as sure as I'm a-sitting here. Because, if it — Huck!"

"Well, what's the matter now?"

"You can't see the bushes through it!"

"Why, Tom, it's so, sure! It's as solid as a cow. I sort of begin to think —"

"Huck, it's biting off a chaw of tobacker! By George, *they* don't chaw — they hain't got anything to chaw *with*. Huck!"

"I'm a-listening."

"It ain't a ghost at all. It's Jake Dunlap his own self!"

"Oh your granny!" I says.

"Huck Finn, did we find any corpse in the sycamores?"

"No."

"Or any sign of one?"

"No."

"Mighty good reason. Hadn't ever been any corpse there."

"Why, Tom, you know we heard —"

"Yes, we did—heard a howl or two. Does that prove anybody was killed? 'Course it don't. And we seen four men run, then this one come walking out and we took it for a ghost. No more ghost than you are. It was Jake Dunlap his own self, and it's Jake Dunlap now. He's been and got his hair cropped, the way he said he would, and he's playing himself for a stranger, just the same as he said he would. Ghost? Hum!—he's as sound as a nut."

Then I see it all, and how we had took too much for granted. I was powerful glad he didn't get killed, and so was Tom, and we wondered which he would like the best—for us to never let on to know him, or how? Tom reckoned the best way would be to go and ask him. So he started; but I kept a little behind, because I didn't know but it might be a ghost, after all. When Tom got to where he was, he says:

"Me and Huck's mighty glad to see you again, and you needn't be afeared we'll tell. And if you think it'll be safer for you if we don't let on to know you when we run across you, say the word and you'll see you can depend on us, and would ruther cut our hands off than get you into the least little bit of danger."

First off he looked surprised to see us, and not very glad, either; but as Tom went on he looked pleasanter, and when he was done he smiled, and nodded his head several times, and made signs with his hands, and says:

"Goo-goo—goo-goo," the way deef and dummies does.

Just then we see some of Steve Nickerson's people coming that lived t'other side of the prairie, so Tom says:

"You do it elegant; I never see anybody do it better. You're right; play it on us, too; play it on us same as the others; it'll keep you in practice and prevent you making blunders. We'll keep away from you and let on we don't know you, but any time we can be any help, you just let us know."

Then we loafed along past the Nickersons, and of course they asked if that was the new stranger yonder, and where'd he come from, and what was his name, and which communion was he, Babtis' or Methodis', and which politics, Whig or Democrat, and how long is he staying, and all them other questions that humans always asks when a stranger comes, and animals does, too. But Tom said he warn't able to make anything out of deef and dumb signs, and the same with goo-gooing. Then we watched them go and bullyrag Jake; because we was pretty uneasy for him. Tom said it would take him days to get so he wouldn't forget he was a deef and dummy sometimes, and speak out before he thought.

When we had watched long enough to see that Jake was getting along all right and working his signs very good, we loafed along again, allowing to strike the schoolhouse about recess time, which was a three-mile tramp.

I was so disappointed not to hear Jake tell about the row in the sycamores, and how near he come to getting killed, that I couldn't seem to get over it, and Tom he felt the same, but said if we was in Jake's fix we would want to go careful and keep still and not take any chances.

The boys and girls was all glad to see us again, and we had a real good time all through recess. Coming to school the Henderson boys had come across the new deef and dummy and told the rest; so all the scholars was chuck-full of him and couldn't talk about anything else, and was in a sweat to get a sight of him because they hadn't ever seen a deef and dummy in their lives, and it made a powerful excitement.

Tom said it was tough to have to keep mum now; said we would be heroes if we could come out and tell all we knowed; but after all, it was still more heroic to keep mum, there warn't two boys in a million could do it. That was Tom Sawyer's idea about it, and I reckoned there warn't anybody could better it.

CHAPTER IX: FINDING OF JUBITER DUNLAP

IN THE NEXT two or three days Dummy he got to be powerful popular. He went associating around with the neighbors, and they made much of him, and was proud to have such a rattling curiosity among them. They had him to breakfast, they had him to dinner, they had him to supper; they kept him loaded up with hog and hominy, and warn't ever tired staring at him and wondering over him, and wishing they knowed more about him, he was so uncommon and romantic. His signs warn't no good; people couldn't understand them and he prob'ly couldn't himself, but he done a sight of goo-gooing, and so everybody was satisfied, and admired to hear him do it. He toted a piece of slate around, and a pencil; and people wrote questions on it and he wrote answers; but there warn't anybody could read his writing but Brace Dunlap. Brace said he couldn't read it very good, but he could manage to dig out the meaning most of the time. He said Dummy said he belonged away off somers and used to be well off, but got busted by swindlers which he had trusted, and was poor now, and hadn't any way to make a living.

Everybody praised Brace Dunlap for being so good to that stranger.

He let him have a little log cabin all to himself, and had his niggers take care of it, and fetch him all the vittles he wanted.

Dummy was at our house some, because old Uncle Silas was so afflicted himself, these days, that anybody else that was afflicted was a comfort to him. Me and Tom didn't let on that we had knowed him before, and he didn't let on that he had knowed us before. The family talked their troubles out before him the same as if he wasn't there, but we reckoned it wasn't any harm for him to hear what they said. Generly he didn't seem to notice, but sometimes he did.

Well, two or three days went along, and everybody got to getting uneasy about Jubiter Dunlap. Everybody was asking everybody if they had any idea what had become of him. No, they hadn't, they said: and they shook their heads and said there was something powerful strange about it. Another and another day went by; then there was a report got around that p'raps he was murdered. You bet it made a big stir! Everybody's tongue was clacking away after that. Saturday two or three gangs turned out and hunted the woods to see if they could run across his remainders. Me and Tom helped, and it was noble good times and exciting. Tom he was so brimful of it he couldn't eat nor rest. He said if we could find that corpse we would be celebrated, and more talked about than if we got drownded.

The others got tired and give it up; but not Tom Sawyer — that warn't his style. Saturday night he didn't sleep any, hardly, trying to think up a plan; and towards daylight in the morning he struck it. He snaked me out of bed and was all excited, and says:

"Quick, Huck, snatch on your clothes — I've got it! Bloodhound!"

In two minutes we was tearing up the river road in the dark towards the village. Old Jeff Hooker had a bloodhound, and Tom was going to borrow him. I says:

"The trail's too old, Tom — and besides, it's rained, you know."

"It don't make any difference, Huck. If the body's hid in the woods anywhere around the hound will find it. If he's been murdered and buried, they wouldn't bury him deep, it ain't likely, and if the dog goes over the spot he'll scent him, sure. Huck, we're going to be celebrated, sure as you're born!"

He was just a-blazing; and whenever he got afire he was most likely to get afire all over. That was the way this time. In two minutes he had got it all ciphered out, and wasn't only just going to find the corpse — no, he was going to get on the track of that murderer and hunt *him* down, too; and not only that, but he was going to stick to him till —

"Well," I says, "you better find the corpse first; I reckon that's a-plenty for to-day. For all we know, there *ain't* any corpse and nobody hain't been murdered. That cuss could 'a' gone off somers and not been killed at all."

That graveled him, and he says:

"Huck Finn, I never see such a person as you to want to spoil everything. As long as *you* can't see anything hopeful in a thing, you won't let anybody else. What good can it do you to throw cold water on that corpse and get up that selfish theory that there ain't been any murder? None in the world. I don't see how you can act so. I wouldn't treat you like that, and you know it. Here we've got a noble good opportunity to make a ruputation, and—"

"Oh, go ahead," I says. "I'm sorry, and I take it all back. I didn't mean nothing. Fix it any way you want it. *He* ain't any consequence to me. If he's killed, I'm as glad of it as you are; and if he—"

"I never said anything about being glad; I only—"

"Well, then, I'm as *sorry* as you are. Any way you druther have it, that is the way *I* druther have it. He—"

"There ain't any druthers *about* it, Huck Finn; nobody said anything about druthers. And as for—"

He forgot he was talking, and went tramping along, studying. He begun to get excited again, and pretty soon he says:

"Huck, it'll be the bulliest thing that ever happened if we find the body after everybody else has quit looking, and then go ahead and hunt up the murderer. It won't only be an honor to us, but it'll be an honor to Uncle Silas because it was us that done it. It'll set him up again, you see if it don't."

But Old Jeff Hooker he throwed cold water on the whole business when we got to his blacksmith shop and told him what we come for.

"You can take the dog," he says, "but you ain't a-going to find any corpse, because there ain't any corpse to find. Everybody's quit looking, and they're right. Soon as they come to think, they knowed there warn't no corpse. And I'll tell you for why. What does a person kill another person *for*, Tom Sawyer?—answer me that."

"Why, he—er—"

"Answer up! You ain't no fool. What does he kill him *for?*"

"Well, sometimes it's for revenge, and—"

"Wait. One thing at a time. Revenge, says you; and right you are. Now who ever had anything agin that poor trifling no-account? Who do you reckon would want to kill *him?*—that rabbit!"

Tom was stuck. I reckon he hadn't thought of a person having to have a *reason* for killing a person before, and now he sees it warn't likely any-body would have that much of a grudge against a lamb like Jubiter Dun-lap. The blacksmith says, by and by:

"The revenge idea won't work, you see. Well, then, what's next? Rob-bery? B'gosh, that must 'a' been it, Tom! Yes, sirree, I reckon we've struck it this time. Some feller wanted his gallus-buckles, and so he—"

But it was so funny he busted out laughing, and just went *on* laughing and laughing and laughing till he was 'most dead, and Tom looked so put out and cheap that I knowed he was ashamed he had come, and he wished he hadn't. But old Hooker never let up on him. He raked up ev-erything a person ever could want to kill another person about, and any fool could see they didn't any of them fit this case, and he just made no end of fun of the whole business and of the people that had been hunt-ing the body; and he said:

"If they'd had any sense they'd 'a' knowed the lazy cuss slid out be-cause he wanted a loafing spell after all this work. He'll come pottering back in a couple of weeks, and then how'll you fellers feel? But, laws bless you, take the dog, and go and hunt his remainders. Do, Tom."

Then he busted out, and had another of them forty-rod laughs of hisn. Tom couldn't back down after all this, so he said, "All right, un-chain him"; and the blacksmith done it, and we started home and left that old man laughing yet.

It was a lovely dog. There ain't any dog that's got a lovelier disposi-tion than a bloodhound, and this one knowed us and liked us. He ca-pered and raced around ever so friendly, and powerful glad to be free and have a holiday; but Tom was so cut up he couldn't take any intrust in him, and said he wished he'd stopped and thought a minute before he ever started on such a fool errand. He said old Jeff Hooker would tell everybody, and we'd never hear the last of it.

So we loafed along home down the back lanes, feeling pretty glum and not talking. When we was passing the far corner of our tobacker field we heard the dog set up a long howl in there, and we went to the place and he was scratching the ground with all his might, and every now and then canting up his head sideways and fetching another howl.

It was a long square, the shape of a grave; the rain had made it sink down and show the shape. The minute we come and stood there we looked at one another and never said a word. When the dog had dug down only a few inches he grabbed something and pulled it up, and it was an arm and a sleeve. Tom kind of gasped out, and says:

"Come away, Huck — it's found."

I just felt awful. We struck for the road and fetched the first men that come along. They got a spade at the crib and dug out the body, and you never see such an excitement. You couldn't make anything out of the face, but you didn't need to. Everybody said:

"Poor Jubiter; it's his clothes, to the last rag!"

Some rushed off to spread the news and tell the justice of the peace and have an inquest, and me and Tom lit out for the house. Tom was all afire and 'most out of breath when we come tearing in where Uncle Silas and Aunt Sally and Benny was. Tom sung out:

"Me and Huck's found Jubiter Dunlap's corpse all by ourselves with a bloodhound, after everybody else had quit hunting and given it up; and if it hadn't 'a' been for us it never *would* 'a' been found; and he *was* murdered too — they done it with a club or something like that; and I'm going to start in and find the murderer, next, and I bet I'll do it!"

Aunt Sally and Benny sprung up pale and astonished, but Uncle Silas fell right forward out of his chair onto the floor and groans out:

"Oh, my God, you've found him *now!*"

CHAPTER X: THE ARREST OF UNCLE SILAS

THEM AWFUL WORDS froze us solid. We couldn't move hand or foot for as much as half a minute. Then we kind of come to, and lifted the old man up and got him into his chair, and Benny petted him and kissed him and tried to comfort him, and poor old Aunt Sally she done the same; but, poor things, they was so broke up and scared and knocked out of their right minds that they didn't hardly know what they was about. With Tom it was awful; it 'most petrified him to think maybe he had got his uncle into a thousand times more trouble than ever, and maybe it wouldn't ever happened if he hadn't been so ambitious to get celebrated, and let the corpse alone the way the others done. But pretty soon he sort of come to himself again and says:

"Uncle Silas, don't you say another word like that. It's dangerous, and there ain't a shadder of truth in it."

Aunt Sally and Benny was thankful to hear him say that, and they said the same; but the old man he wagged his head sorrowful and hopeless, and the tears run down his face, and he says:

"No — I done it; poor Jubiter, I done it!"

It was dreadful to hear him say it. Then he went on and told about it, and said it happened the day me and Tom come — along about sundown. He said Jubiter pestered him and aggravated him till he was so mad he just sort of lost his mind and grabbed up a stick and hit him over the head with all his might, and Jubiter dropped in his tracks. Then he was scared and sorry, and got down on his knees and lifted his head up, and begged him to speak and say he wasn't dead; and before long he come to, and when he see who it was holding his head, he jumped like he was 'most scared to death, and cleared the fence and tore into the woods, and was gone. So he hoped he wasn't hurt bad.

"But laws," he says, "it was only just fear that gave him that last little spurt of strength, and of course it soon played out and he laid down in the bush, and there wasn't anybody to help him, and he died."

Then the old man cried and grieved, and said he was a murderer and the mark of Cain was on him, and he had disgraced his family and was going to be found out and hung. But Tom said:

"No, you ain't going to be found out. You *didn't* kill him. *One* lick wouldn't kill him. Somebody else done it."

"Oh, yes," he says, "I done it—nobody else. Who else had anything against him? Who else *could* have anything against him?"

He looked up kind of like he hoped some of us could mention somebody that could have a grudge against that harmless no-account, but of course it warn't no use—he *had* us; we couldn't say a word. He noticed that, and he saddened down again, and I never see a face so miserable and so pitiful to see. Tom had a sudden idea, and says:

"But hold on!—somebody *buried* him. Now who—"

He shut off sudden. I knowed the reason. It give me the cold shudders when he said them words, because right away I remembered about us seeing Uncle Silas prowling around with a long-handled shovel away in the night that night. And I knowed Benny seen him, too, because she was talking about it one day. The minute Tom shut off he changed the subject and went to begging Uncle Silas to keep mum, and the rest of us done the same, and said he *must,* and said it wasn't his business to tell on himself, and if he kept mum nobody would ever know; but if it was found out and any harm come to him it would break the family's hearts and kill them, and yet never do anybody any good. So at last he promised. We was all of us more comfortable, then, and went to work to cheer up the old man. We told him all he'd got to do was to keep still, and it wouldn't be long till the whole thing would blow over and be forgot. We all said there wouldn't anybody ever suspect Uncle Silas, nor ever dream of such a thing, he being so good and kind, and having such a good character; and Tom says, cordial and hearty, he says:

"Why, just look at it a minute; just consider. Here is Uncle Silas, all these years a preacher — at his own expense; all these years doing good with all his might and every way he can think of — at his own expense, all the time; always been loved by everybody, and respected; always been peaceable and minding his own business, the very last man in this whole deestrict to touch a person, and everybody knows it. Suspect *him?* Why, it ain't any more possible than — "

"By authority of the State of Arkansaw, I arrest you for the murder of Jubiter Dunlap!" shouts the sheriff at the door.

It was awful. Aunt Sally and Benny flung themselves at Uncle Silas, screaming and crying, and hugged him and hung to him, and Aunt Sally said go away, she wouldn't ever give him up, they shouldn't have him, and the niggers they come crowding and crying to the door and — well, I couldn't stand it; it was enough to break a person's heart; so I got out.

They took him up to the little one-horse jail in the village, and we all went along to tell him good-bye; and Tom was feeling elegant, and says to me, "We'll have a most noble good time and heaps of danger some dark night getting him out of there, Huck, and it'll be talked about everywheres and we will be celebrated"; but the old man busted that scheme up the minute he whispered to him about it. He said no, it was his duty to stand whatever the law done to him, and he would stick to the jail plumb through to the end, even if there warn't no door to it. It disappointed Tom and graveled him a good deal, but he had to put up with it.

But he felt responsible and bound to get his uncle Silas free; and he told Aunt Sally, the last thing, not to worry, because he was going to turn in and work night and day and beat this game and fetch Uncle Silas out innocent; and she was very loving to him and thanked him and said she knowed he would do his very best. And she told us to help Benny take care of the house and the children, and then we had a good-bye cry all around and went back to the farm, and left her there to live with the jailer's wife a month till the trial in October.

CHAPTER XI: TOM SAWYER DISCOVERS THE MURDERERS

WELL, THAT WAS a hard month on us all. Poor Benny, she kept up the best she could, and me and Tom tried to keep things cheerful there at the house, but it kind of went for nothing, as you may say. It was the same up at the jail. We went up every day to see the old people, but it was awful dreary, because the old man warn't sleeping much, and was walking in his sleep considerable and so he got to looking fagged and miserable, and his mind got shaky, and we all got afraid his troubles would break him down and kill him. And whenever we tried to persuade him to feel cheerfuler, he only shook his head and said if we only knowed what it was to carry around a murderer's load in your heart we wouldn't talk that way. Tom and all of us kept telling him it *wasn't* murder, but just accidental killing, but it never made any difference — it was murder, and he wouldn't have it any other way. He actu'ly begun to come out plain and square towards trial time and acknowledge that he *tried* to kill the man. Why, that was awful, you know. It made things seem fifty times as dreadful, and there warn't no more comfort for Aunt Sally and Benny. But he promised he wouldn't say a word about his murder when others was around, and we was glad of that.

Tom Sawyer racked the head off of himself all that month trying to plan some way out for Uncle Silas, and many's the night he kept me up 'most all night with this kind of tiresome work, but he couldn't seem to get on the right track no way. As for me, I reckoned a body might as well give it up, it all looked so blue and I was so downhearted; but he wouldn't. He stuck to the business right along, and went on planning and thinking and ransacking his head.

So at last the trial come on, towards the middle of October, and we was all in the court. The place was jammed, of course. Poor old Uncle Silas, he looked more like a dead person than a live one, his eyes was so hollow and he looked so thin and so mournful. Benny she set on one side of him and Aunt Sally on the other, and they had veils on, and was full of trouble. But Tom he set by our lawyer, and had his finger in everywheres, of course. The lawyer let him, and the judge let him. He 'most took the business out of the lawyer's hands sometimes; which was well enough, because that was only a mud-turtle of a back-settlement lawyer and didn't know enough to come in when it rains, as the saying is.

They swore in the jury, and then the lawyer for the prostitution got up and begun. He made a terrible speech against the old man, that made him moan and groan, and made Benny and Aunt Sally cry. The way *he* told about the murder kind of knocked us all stupid. it was so different from the old man's tale. He said he was going to prove that Uncle Silas was *seen* to kill Jubiter Dunlap by two good witnesses, and done it deliberate, and *said* he was going to kill him the very minute he hit him with the club; and they seen him hide Jubiter in the bushes, and they seen that Jubiter was stone-dead. And said Uncle Silas come later and lugged

Jubiter down into the tobacker field, and two men seen him do it. And said Uncle Silas turned out, away in the night, and buried Jubiter, and a man seen him at it.

I says to myself, poor old Uncle Silas has been lying about it because he reckoned nobody seen him and he couldn't bear to break Aunt Sally's heart and Benny's; and right he was: as for me, I would 'a' lied the same way, and so would anybody that had any feeling, to save them such misery and sorrow which *they* warn't no ways responsible for. Well, it made our lawyer look pretty sick; and it knocked Tom silly, too, for a little spell, but then he braced up and let on that he warn't worried — but I knowed he *was,* all the same. And the people — my, but it made a stir amongst them!

And when that lawyer was done telling the jury what he was going to prove, he set down and begun to work his witnesses.

First, he called a lot of them to show that there was bad blood betwixt Uncle Silas and the diseased; and they told how they had heard Uncle Silas threaten the diseased, at one time and another, and how it got worse and worse and everybody was talking about it, and how diseased got afraid of his life, and told two or three of them he was certain Uncle Silas would up and kill him some time or another.

Tom and our lawyer asked them some questions; but it warn't no use, they stuck to what they said.

Next, they called up Lem Beebe, and he took the stand. It come into my mind, then, how Lem and Jim Lane had come along talking, that time, about borrowing a dog or something from Jubiter Dunlap; and that brought up the blackberries and the lantern; and that brought up Bill and Jack Withers, and how *they* passed by, talking about a nigger stealing Uncle Silas's corn; and that fetched up our old ghost that come along about the same time and scared us so — and here *he* was too, and a privileged character, on accounts of his being deef and dumb and a stranger, and they had fixed him a chair inside the railing, where he could cross his legs and be comfortable, whilst the other people was all in a jam so they couldn't hardly breathe. So it all come back to me just the way it was that day; and it made me mournful to think how pleasant it was up to then, and how miserable ever since.

> *Lem Beebe,* sworn, said: "I was a-coming along, that day, second of September, and Jim Lane was with me, and it was towards sundown, and we heard loud talk, like quarreling, and we was very close, only the hazel bushes between (that's along the fence); and we heard a voice say, 'I've told you more'n once I'd kill you,' and knowed it was this prisoner's voice;

> and then we see a club come up above the bushes and down out of sight again, and heard a smashing thump and then a groan or two: and then we crope soft to where we could see, and there laid Jupiter Dunlap dead, and this prisoner standing over him with the club; and the next he hauled the dead man into a clump of bushes and hid him, and then we stooped low, to be out of sight, and got away."

Well, it was awful. It kind of froze everybody's blood to hear it, and the house was 'most as still whilst he was telling it as if there warn't nobody in it. And when he was done, you could hear them gasp and sigh, all over the house, and look at one another the same as to say, "Ain't it perfectly terrible—ain't it awful!"

Now happened a thing that astonished me. All the time the first witnesses was proving the bad blood and the threats and all that, Tom Sawyer was alive and laying for them; and the minute they was through, he went for them, and done his level best to catch them in lies and spile their testimony. But now, how different. When Lem first begun to talk, and never said anything about speaking to Jubiter or trying to borrow a dog off of him, he was all alive and laying for Lem, and you could see he was getting ready to cross-question him to death pretty soon, and then I judged him and me would go on the stand by and by and tell what we heard him and Jim Lane say. But the next time I looked at Tom I got the cold shivers. Why, he was in the brownest study you ever see—miles and miles away. He warn't hearing a word Lem Beebe was saying; and when he got through he was still in that brown study, just the same. Our lawyer joggled him, and then he looked up startled, and says, "Take the witness if you want him. Lemme alone—I want to think."

Well, that beat me. I couldn't understand it. And Benny and her mother—oh, they looked sick, they was so troubled. They shoved their veils to one side and tried to get his eye, but it warn't any use, and I couldn't get his eye either. So the mud-turtle he tackled the witness, but it didn't amount to nothing; and he made a mess of it.

Then they called up Jim Lane, and he told the very same story over again, exact. Tom never listened to this one at all, but set there thinking and thinking, miles and miles away. So the mud-turtle went in alone again and come out just as flat as he done before. The lawyer for the prostitution looked very comfortable, but the judge looked disgusted. You see, Tom was just the same as a regular lawyer, nearly, because it was Arkansaw law for a prisoner to choose anybody he wanted to help his lawyer, and Tom had had Uncle Silas shove him into the case, and now he was botching it and you could see the judge didn't like it much. All that the mud-turtle got out of Lem and Jim was this: he asked them:

"Why didn't you go and tell what you saw?"

"We was afraid we would get mixed up in it ourselves. And we was just starting down the river a-hunting for all the week besides; but as soon as we come back we found out they'd been searching for the body, so then we went and told Brace Dunlap all about it."

"When was that?"

"Saturday night, September 9th."

The judge he spoke up and says:

"Mr. Sheriff, arrest these two witnesses on suspicions of being accessionary after the fact to the murder."

The lawyer for the prostitution jumps up all excited, and says:

"Your honor! I protest against this extraordi —"

"Set down!" says the judge, pulling his bowie and laying it on his pulpit. "I beg you to respect the Court."

So he done it. Then he called Bill Withers.

> *Bill Withers,* sworn, said: "I was coming along about sundown, Saturday, September 2d, by the prisoner's field, and my brother Jack was with me and we seen a man toting off something heavy on his back and allowed it was a nigger stealing corn; we couldn't see distinct; next we made out that it was one man carrying another; and the way it hung, so kind of limp, we judged it was somebody that was drunk; and by the man's walk we said it was Parson Silas, and we judged he had found Sam Cooper drunk in the road, which he was always trying to reform him, and was toting him out of danger."

It made the people shiver to think of poor old Uncle Silas toting off the diseased down to the place in his tobacker field where the dog dug up the body, but there warn't much sympathy around amongst the faces, and I heard one cuss say "'Tis the coldest-blooded work I ever struck, lugging a murdered man around like that, and going to bury him like a' animal, and him a preacher at that."

Tom he went on thinking, and never took no notice; so our lawyer took the witness and done the best he could, and it was plenty poor enough.

Then Jack Withers he come on the stand and told the same tale, just like Bill done.

And after him comes Brace Dunlap, and he was looking very mournful, and most crying; and there was a rustle and a stir all around, and everybody got ready to listen, and lots of the women folks said, "Poor cretur, poor cretur," and you could see a many of them wiping their eyes.

Brace Dunlap, sworn, said: "I was in considerable trouble a long time about my poor brother, but I reckoned things warn't near so bad as he made out, and I couldn't make myself believe anybody would have the heart to hurt a poor harmless cretur like that" — [by jings, I was sure I seen Tom give a kind of a faint little start, and then look disappointed again] — "and you know I *couldn't* think a preacher would hurt him — it warn't natural to think such an onlikely thing — so I never paid much attention, and now I sha'n't ever, ever forgive myself; for if I had 'a' done different, my poor brother would be with me this day, and not laying yonder murdered, and him so harmless." He kind of broke down there and choked up, and waited to get his voice; and people all around said the most pitiful things, and women cried; and it was very still in there, and solemn, and old Uncle Silas, poor thing, he give a groan right out so everybody heard him. Then Brace he went on, "Saturday, September 2d, he didn't come home to supper. By and by I got a little uneasy, and one of my niggers went over to this prisoner's place, but come back and said he warn't there. So I got uneasier and uneasier, and couldn't rest. I went to bed, but I couldn't sleep; and turned out, away late in the night, and went wandering over to this prisoner's place and all around about there a good while, hoping I would run across my poor brother, and never knowing he was out of his troubles and gone to a better shore —" So he broke down and choked up again, and most all the women was crying now. Pretty soon he got another start and says: "But it warn't no use; so at last I went home and tried to get some sleep, but couldn't. Well, in a day or two everybody was uneasy, and they got to talking about this prisoner's threats, and took to the idea, which I didn't take no stock in, that my brother was murdered; so they hunted around and tried to find his body, but couldn't and give it up. And so I reckoned he was gone off somers to have a little peace, and would come back to us when his troubles was kind of healed. But late Saturday night, the 9th, Lem Beebe and Jim Lane come to my house and told me all — told me the whole awful 'sassination, and my heart was broke. And *then* I remembered something that hadn't took no hold of me at the time, because reports said this prisoner had took to walking in his sleep and doing all kind of things of no consequence, not knowing what he was about. I will tell you what that thing was that come back into my memory. Away late that awful Saturday night when I was wandering around about this prisoner's place, grieving and troubled, I was down by the corner of the tobacker field and I heard a sound like digging in a gritty soil; and I crope nearer and peeped through the vines that hung on the rail fence and seen this prisoner *shoveling* — shoveling with a

> long-handled shovel—heaving earth into a big hole that was most filled up; his back was to me, but it was bright moonlight and I knowed him by his old green baize work-gown with a splattery white patch in the middle of the back like somebody had hit him with a snowball. *He was burying the man he'd murdered!*"

And he slumped down in his chair crying and sobbing, and 'most everybody in the house busted out wailing, and crying, and saying, "Oh, it's awful—awful—horrible!" and there was a most tremendous excitement, and you couldn't hear yourself think; and right in the midst of it up jumps old Uncle Silas, white as a sheet, and sings out:

"It's true, every word—I murdered him in cold blood!"

By Jackson, it petrified them! People rose up wild all over the house, straining and staring for a better look at him, and the judge was hammering with his mallet and the sheriff yelling "Order—order in the court—order!"

And all the while the old man stood there a-quaking and his eyes a-burning, and not looking at his wife and daughter, which was clinging to him and begging him to keep still, but pawing them off with his hands and saying he *would* clear his black soul from crime, he *would* heave off this load that was more than he could bear, and he *wouldn't* bear it another hour! And then he raged right along with his awful tale, everybody a-staring and gasping, judge, jury, lawyers, and everybody, and Benny and Aunt Sally crying their hearts out. And by George, Tom Sawyer never looked at him once! Never once—just set there gazing with all his eyes at something else, I couldn't tell what. And so the old man raged right along, pouring his words out like a stream of fire:

"I killed him! I am guilty! But I never had the notion in my life to hurt him or harm him, spite of all them lies about my threatening him, till the very minute I raised the club—then my heart went cold!—then the pity all went out of it, and I struck to kill! In that one moment all my wrongs come into my mind; all the insults that that man and the scoundrel his brother, there, had put upon me, and how they laid in together to ruin me with the people, and take away my good name, and *drive* me to some deed that would destroy me and my family that hadn't ever done *them* no harm, so help me God! And they done it in a mean revenge—for why? Because my innocent pure girl here at my side wouldn't marry that rich, insolent, ignorant coward, Brace Dunlap, who's been sniveling here over a brother he never cared a brass farthing for—" [I see Tom give a jump and look glad *this* time, to a dead certainty]—"and in that moment I've told you about, I forgot my God and remembered only my heart's bitterness, God forgive me, and I struck to kill. In one second I was miserably sorry—oh, filled with remorse; but I thought of my poor family, and I *must* hide what I'd done for their sakes; and I did hide that corpse in the bushes; and presently I carried it to the tobacker field; and in the deep night I went with my shovel and buried it where—"

Up jumps Tom and shouts:

"*Now,* I've got it!" and waves his hand, oh, ever so fine and starchy, towards the old man, and says:

"Set down! A murder *was* done, but you never had no hand in it!"

Well, sir, you could 'a' heard a pin drop. And the old man he sunk down kind of bewildered in his seat and Aunt Sally and Benny didn't know it, because they was so astonished and staring at Tom with their mouths open and not knowing what they was about. And the whole house the same. *I* never seen people look so helpless and tangled up, and I hain't ever seen eyes bug out and gaze without a blink the way theirn did. Tom says, perfectly ca'm:

"Your honor, may I speak?"

"For God's sake, yes—go on!" says the judge, so astonished and mixed up he didn't know what he was about hardly.

Then Tom he stood there and waited a second or two—that was for to work up an "effect," as he calls it—then he started in just as ca'm as ever, and says:

"For about two weeks now there's been a little bill sticking on the front of this courthouse offering two thousand dollars reward for a couple of big di'monds—stole at St. Louis. Them di'monds is worth twelve thousand dollars. But never mind about that till I get to it. Now about this murder. I will tell you all about it—how it happened—who done it—every *de*tail."

You could see everybody nestle now, and begin to listen for all they was worth.

"This man here, Brace Dunlap, that's been sniveling so about his dead brother that *you* know he never cared a straw for, wanted to marry that young girl there, and she wouldn't have him. So he told Uncle Silas he would make him sorry. Uncle Silas knowed how powerful he was, and how little chance he had against such a man, and he was scared and worried, and done everything he could think of to smooth him over and get him to be good to him: he even took his no-account brother Jubiter on the farm and give him wages and stinted his own family to pay them; and Jubiter done everything his brother could contrive to insult Uncle Silas, and fret and worry him, and try to drive Uncle Silas into doing him a hurt, so as to injure Uncle Silas with the people. And it done it. Everybody turned against him and said the meanest kind of things about him, and it gradu'ly broke his heart — yes, and he was so worried and distressed that often he warn't hardly in his right mind.

"Well, on that Saturday that we've had so much trouble about, two of these witnesses here, Lem Beebe and Jim Lane, come along by where Uncle Silas and Jubiter Dunlap was at work — and that much of what they've said is true, the rest is lies. They didn't hear Uncle Silas say he would kill Jubiter; they didn't hear no blow struck; they didn't see no dead man, and they didn't see Uncle Silas hide anything in the bushes. Look at them now — how they set there, wishing they hadn't been so handy with their tongues; anyway, they'll wish it before I get done.

"That same Saturday evening Bill and Jack Withers *did* see one man lugging off another one. That much of what they said is true, and the rest is lies. First off they thought it was a nigger stealing Uncle Silas's corn — you notice it makes them look silly, now, to find out somebody overheard them say that. That's because they found out by and by who it was that was doing the lugging, and *they* know best why they swore here that they took it for Uncle Silas by the gait — which it *wasn't,* and they knowed it when they swore to that lie.

"A man out in the moonlight *did* see a murdered person put under ground in the tobacker field — but it wasn't Uncle Silas that done the burying. He was in his bed at that very time.

"Now, then, before I go on, I want to ask you if you've ever noticed this: that people, when they're thinking deep, or when they're worried, are most always doing something with their hands, and they don't know it, and don't notice what it is their hands are doing. Some stroke their chins; some stroke their noses; some stroke up *under* their chin with their hand; some twirl a chain, some fumble a button, then there's some that draws a figure or a letter with their finger on their cheek, or under their chin or on their under lip. That's *my* way. When I'm restless, or worried, or thinking hard, I draw capital V's on my cheek or on my under lip or under my chin, and never anything *but* capital V's — and half the time I don't notice it and don't know I'm doing it."

That was odd. That is just what I do; only I make an O. And I could see people nodding to one another, same as they do when they mean *"That's so."*

"Now, then, I'll go on. That same Saturday — no, it was the night before—there was a steamboat laying at Flagler's Landing, forty miles above here, and it was raining and storming like the nation. And there was a thief aboard, and he had them two big di'monds that's advertised out here on this courthouse door; and he slipped ashore with his hand-bag and struck out into the dark and the storm, and he was a-hoping he could get to this town all right and be safe. But he had two pals aboard the boat, hiding, and he knowed they was going to kill him the first chance they got and take the di'monds; because all three stole them, and then this fellow he got hold of them and skipped.

"Well, he hadn't been gone more'n ten minutes before his pals found it out, and they jumped ashore and lit out after him. Prob'ly they burnt matches and found his tracks. Anyway, they dogged along after him all day Saturday and kept out of his sight; and towards sundown he come to the bunch of sycamores down by Uncle Silas's field, and he went in there to get a disguise out of his hand-bag and put it on before he showed himself here in the town—and mind you he done that just a little after the time that Uncle Silas was hitting Jubiter Dunlap over the head with a club—for he *did* hit him.

"But the minute the pals see that thief slide into the bunch of sycamores, they jumped out of the bushes and slid in after him.

"They fell on him and clubbed him to death.

"Yes, for all he screamed and howled so, they never had no mercy on him, but clubbed him to death. And two men that was running along the road heard him yelling that way, and they made a rush into the sycamore bunch—which was where they was bound for, anyway—and when the pals saw them they lit out and the two new men after them a-chasing them as tight as they could go. But only a minute or two—then these two new men slipped back very quiet into the sycamores.

"*Then* what did they do? I will tell you what they done. They found where the thief had got his disguise out of his carpet-sack to put on; so one of them strips and puts on that disguise."

Tom waited a little here, for some more "effect"—then he says, very deliberate:

"The man that put on that dead man's disguise was—*Jubiter Dunlap!*"

"Great Scott!" everybody shouted, all over the house, and old Uncle Silas he looked perfectly astonished.

"Yes, it was Jubiter Dunlap. Not dead, you see. Then they pulled off the dead man's boots and put Jubiter Dunlap's old ragged shoes on the corpse and put the corpse's boots on Jubiter Dunlap. Then Jubiter Dunlap stayed where he was, and the other man lugged the dead body off in the twilight; and after midnight he went to Uncle Silas's house, and took his old green work-robe off of the peg where it always hangs in the passage betwixt the house and the kitchen and put it on, and stole the long-handled shovel and went off down into the tobacker field and buried the murdered man."

He stopped, and stood half a minute. Then —

"And who do you reckon the murdered man *was?* It was — *Jake* Dunlap, the long-lost burglar!"

"Great Scott!"

"And the man that buried him was — *Brace* Dunlap, his brother!"

"Great Scott!"

"And who do you reckon is this mowing idiot here that's letting on all these weeks to be a deef and dumb stranger? It's — *Jubiter* Dunlap!"

My land, they all busted out in a howl, and you never see the like of that excitement since the day you was born. And Tom he made a jump for Jubiter and snaked off his goggles and his false whiskers, and there was the murdered man, sure enough, just as alive as anybody! And Aunt Sally and Benny they went to hugging and crying and kissing and smothering old Uncle Silas to that degree he was more muddled and confused and mushed up in his mind than he ever was before, and that is saying considerable. And next, people begun to yell:

"Tom Sawyer! Tom Sawyer! Shut up everybody, and let him go on! Go on, Tom Sawyer!"

Which made him feel uncommon bully, for it was nuts for Tom Sawyer to be a public character that-away, and a hero, as he calls it. So when it was all quiet, he says:

"There ain't much left, only this. When that man there, Bruce Dunlap, had most worried the life and sense out of Uncle Silas till at last he plumb lost his mind and hit this other blatherskite, his brother, with a club, I reckon he seen his chance. Jubiter broke for the woods to hide, and I reckon the game was for him to slide out, in the night, and leave the country. Then Brace would make everybody believe Uncle Silas killed him and hid his body somers; and that would ruin Uncle Silas and drive *him* out of the country — hang him, maybe; I dunno. But when they found their dead brother in the sycamores without knowing him, because he was so battered up, they see they had a better thing; disguise *both* and bury Jake and dig him up presently all dressed up in Jubiter's clothes, and hire Jim Lane and Bill Withers and the others to swear to some handy lies — which they done. And there they set, now, and I told them they would be looking sick before I got done, and that is the way they're looking now.

"Well, me and Huck Finn here, we come down on the boat with the thieves, and the dead one told us all about the di'monds, and said the others would murder him if they got the chance; and we was going to help him all we could. We was bound for the sycamores when we heard them killing him in there; but we was in there in the early morning after the storm and allowed nobody hadn't been killed, after all. And when we see Jubiter Dunlap here spreading around in the very same disguise Jake told us *he* was going to wear, we thought it was Jake his own self — and he was goo-gooing deef and dumb, and *that* was according to agreement.

"Well, me and Huck went on hunting for the corpse after the others quit, and we found it. And was proud, too; but Uncle Silas he knocked us crazy by telling us *he* killed the man. So we was mighty sorry we found the body, and was bound to save Uncle Silas's neck if we could; and it was going to be tough work, too, because he wouldn't let us break him out of prison the way we done with our old nigger Jim.

"I done everything I could the whole month to think up some way to save Uncle Silas, but I couldn't strike a thing. So when we come into court to-day I come empty, and couldn't see no chance anywheres. But by and by I had a glimpse of something that set me thinking — just a little wee glimpse — only that, and not enough to make sure; but it set me thinking hard — and *watching,* when I was only letting on to think; and by and by, sure enough, when Uncle Silas was piling out that stuff about *him* killing Jubiter Dunlap, I catched that glimpse again, and this time I jumped up and shut down the proceedings, because I *knowed* Jubiter Dunlap was a-setting here before me. I knowed him by a thing which I seen him do — and I remembered it. I'd seen him do it when I was here a year ago."

He stopped then, and studied a minute — laying for an "effect" — I knowed it perfectly well. Then he turned off like he was going to leave the platform, and says, kind of lazy and indifferent:

"Well, I believe that is all."

Why, you never heard such a howl! — and it come from the whole house:

"What *was* it you seen him do? Stay where you are, you little devil! You think you are going to work a body up till his mouth's a-watering and stop there? What *was* it he done?"

That was it, you see — he just done it to get an "effect"; you couldn't 'a' pulled him off of that platform with a yoke of oxen.

"Oh, it wasn't anything much," he says. "I seen him looking a little excited when he found Uncle Silas was actu'ly fixing to hang himself for a murder that warn't ever done; and he got more and more nervous and worried, I a-watching him sharp but not seeming to look at him — and all of a sudden his hands begun to work and fidget, and pretty soon his left crept up and *his finger drawed a cross on his cheek,* and then I *had* him!"

Well, then they ripped and howled and stomped and clapped their hands till Tom Sawyer was that proud and happy he didn't know what to do with himself.

And then the judge he looked down over his pulpit and says:

"My boy, did you *see* all the various details of this strange conspiracy and tragedy that you've been describing?"

"No, your honor, I didn't see any of them."

"Didn't see any of them! Why, you've told the whole history straight through, just the same as if you'd seen it with your eyes. How did you manage that?"

Tom says, kind of easy and comfortable:

"Oh, just noticing the evidence and piecing this and that together, your honor; just an ordinary little bit of detective work; anybody could 'a' done it."

"Nothing of the kind! Not two in a million could 'a' done it. You are a very remarkable boy."

Then they let go and give Tom another smashing round, and he — well, he wouldn't 'a' sold out for a silver mine. Then the judge says:

"But are you certain you've got this curious history straight?"

"Perfectly, your honor. Here is Brace Dunlap — let him deny his share of it if he wants to take the chance; I'll engage to make him wish he hadn't said anything . . . Well, you see *he's* pretty quiet. And his brother's pretty quiet, and them four witnesses that lied so and got paid for it, they're pretty quiet. And as for Uncle Silas, it ain't any use for him to put in his oar, I wouldn't believe him under oath!"

Well, sir, that fairly made them shout; and even the judge he let go and laughed. Tom he was just feeling like a rainbow. When they was done laughing he looks up at the judge and says:

"Your honor, there's a thief in this house."

"A thief?"

"Yes, sir. And he's got them twelve-thousand-dollar di'monds on him."

By gracious, but it made a stir! Everybody went shouting:

"Which is him? which is him? p'int him out!"

And the judge says:

"Point him out, my lad. Sheriff, you will arrest him. Which one is it?"

Tom says:

"This late dead man here — Jubiter Dunlap."

Then there was another thundering let-go of astonishment and excitement; but Jubiter, which was astonished enough before, was just fairly putrified with astonishment this time. And he spoke up, about half crying, and says:

"Now *that's* a lie. Your honor, it ain't fair; I'm plenty bad enough without that. I done the other things — Brace he put me up to it, and persuaded me, and promised he'd make me rich, some day, and I done it, and I'm sorry I done it, and I wisht I hadn't; but I hain't stole no di'monds, and I hain't *got* no di'monds; I wisht I may never stir if it ain't so. The sheriff can search me and see."

Tom says:

"Your honor, it wasn't right to call him a thief, and I'll let up on that a little. He did steal the di'monds, but he didn't know it. He stole them from his brother Jake when he was laying dead, after Jake had stole them from the other thieves; but Jubiter didn't know he was stealing them; and he's been swelling around here with them a month; yes, sir, twelve thousand dollars' worth of di'monds on him — all that riches, and going around here every day just like a poor man. Yes, your honor, he's got them on him now."

The judge spoke up and says:

"Search him, sheriff."

Well, sir, the sheriff he ransacked him high and low, and everywhere: searched his hat, socks, seams, boots, everything — and Tom he stood there quiet, laying for another of them effects of hisn. Finally the sheriff he give it up, and everybody looked disappointed, and Jubiter says:

"There, now! what'd I tell you?"

And the judge says:

"It appears you were mistaken this time, my boy."

Then Tom took an attitude and let on to be studying with all his might, and scratching his head. Then all of a sudden he glanced up chipper, and says:

"Oh, now I've got it! I'd forgot."

Which was a lie, and I knowed it. Then he says:

"Will somebody be good enough to lend me a little small screw-driver? There was one in your brother's hand-bag that you smouched, Jubiter. but I reckon you didn't fetch it with you."

"No, I didn't. I didn't want it, and I give it away."

"That's because you didn't know what it was for."

Jubiter had his boots on again, by now, and when the thing Tom wanted was passed over the people's heads till it got to him, he says to Jubiter:

"Put up your foot on this chair." And he kneeled down and begun to unscrew the heel-plate, everybody watching; and when he got that big di'mond out of that boot-heel and held it up and let it flash and blaze and squirt sunlight everwhichaway, it just took everybody's breath; and Jubiter he looked so sick and sorry you never see the like of it. And when Tom held up the other di'mond he looked sorrier than ever. Land! he was thinking how he would 'a' skipped out and been rich and independent in a foreign land if he'd only had the luck to guess what the screwdriver was in the carpet-bag for.

Well, it was a most exciting time, take it all around, and Tom got cords of glory. The judge took the di'monds, and stood up in his pulpit, and cleared his throat, and shoved his spectacles back on his head, and says:

"I'll keep them and notify the owners; and when they send for them it will be a real pleasure to me to hand you the two thousand dollars, for you've earned the money — yes, and you've earned the deepest and most sincerest thanks of this community besides, for lifting a wronged and innocent family out of ruin and shame, and saving a good and honorable man from a felon's death, and for exposing to infamy and the punishment of the law a cruel and odious scoundrel and his miserable creatures!"

Well, sir, if there'd been a brass band to bust out some music, then, it would 'a' been just the perfectest thing I ever see, and Tom Sawyer he said the same.

Then the sheriff he nabbed Brace Dunlap and his crowd, and by and by next month the judge had them up for trial and jailed the whole lot. And everybody crowded back to Uncle Silas's little old church, and was ever so loving and kind to him and the family and couldn't do enough for them; and Uncle Silas he preached them the blamedest jumbledest idiotic sermons you ever struck, and would tangle you up so you couldn't find your way home in daylight; but the people never let on but what they thought it was the clearest and brightest and elegantest sermons that ever was; and they would set there and cry, for love and pity; but, by George, they give me the jimjams and the fantods and caked up what brains I had, and turned them solid; but by and by they loved the old man's intellects back into him again, and he was as sound in his skull as ever he was, which ain't no flattery, I reckon. And so the whole family was as happy as birds, and nobody could be gratefuler and lovinger than what they was to Tom Sawyer; and the same to me, though I hadn't done nothing. And when the two thousand dollars come, Tom give half of it to me, and never told anybody so, which didn't surprise me, because I knowed him.

1896

MELVILLE DAVISSON POST

THE CORPUS DELICTI

The technical skill that MELVILLE DAVISSON POST (1869–1930) brought to his short stories helped make him the most commercially successful magazine writer of his time. Born in West Virginia, he practiced criminal and corporate law for eleven years before devoting himself to writing full-time. He died at the age of sixty-one after falling from a horse. He played an important role in the development of the detective story, and while his name may not be familiar to any but the most devoted readers of detective fiction, he was regarded as the best American mystery short story writer of the early twentieth century by no less an authority than Ellery Queen.

It is difficult to create a memorable character, but Post succeeded in doing it twice. The more likely to be remembered today is Uncle Abner, the backwoods protector of the innocent in Virginia during Thomas Jefferson's presidency. Not a member of a police force, Abner, known for his integrity and sense of justice, believed that evil would be defeated because of the omnipresence of God. His cases were collected in *Uncle Abner: Master of Mysteries* (1918).

A more conventional figure and undoubtedly of greater significance is Randolph Mason, a brilliant but utterly unscrupulous lawyer. Born in Virginia but practicing in New York, Mason recognizes that there is little correlation between justice and the law. In the past, criminals had tried to avoid capture, but in the Mason stories the paramount concern is the avoidance of punishment. He explains his amoral philosophy in one of his stories:

> No man who has followed my advice has ever committed a crime. Crime is a technical word. It is the law's term for certain acts which it is pleased to define and punish with a penalty. What the law permits is right, else it would prohibit it. What the law prohibits is wrong, because it punishes it. The word moral is a purely metaphysical one.

The Mason stories were all based on genuine legal loopholes, eventually bringing about numerous changes to criminal procedure.

Erle Stanley Gardner, who created the very moral lawyer Perry Mason, so admired Post's short stories that he named his own detective after Post's.

"The Corpus Delicti" was first published in *The Strange Schemes of Randolph Mason* (New York: G. P. Putnam, 1896).

• • •

I.

THAT MAN MASON," said Samuel Walcott, "is the mysterious member of this club. He is more than that; he is the mysterious man of New York."

"I was much surprised to see him," answered his companion, Marshall St. Clair, of the great law firm of Seward, St. Clair & De Muth. "I had lost track of him since he went to Paris as counsel for the American stockholders of the Canal Company. When did he come back to the States?"

"He turned up suddenly in his ancient haunts about four months ago," said Walcott, "as grand, gloomy, and peculiar as Napoleon ever was in his palmiest days. The younger members of the club call him 'Zanona Redivivus.' He wanders through the house usually late at night, apparently without noticing anything or anybody. His mind seems to be deeply and busily at work, leaving his bodily self to wander as it may happen. Naturally, strange stories are told of him; indeed, his individuality and his habit of doing some unexpected thing, and doing it in such a marvelously original manner that men who are experts at it look on in wonder, cannot fail to make him an object of interest.

"He has never been known to play at any game whatever, and yet one night he sat down to the chess table with old Admiral Du Brey. You know the Admiral is the great champion since he beat the French and English officers in the tournament last winter. Well, you also know that the conventional openings at chess are scientifically and accurately determined. To the utter disgust of Du Brey, Mason opened the game with an unheard-of attack from the extremes of the board. The old Admiral stopped and, in a kindly patronizing way, pointed out the weak and absurd folly of his move and asked him to begin again with some one of the safe openings. Mason smiled and answered that if one had a head that he could trust he should use it; if not, then it was the part of wisdom to follow blindly the dead forms of some man who had a head. Du Brey was naturally angry and set himself to demolish Mason as quickly as possible. The game was rapid for a few moments. Mason lost piece after piece. His opening was broken and destroyed and its utter folly apparent to the lookers-on. The Admiral smiled and the game seemed all one-sided, when, suddenly, to his utter horror, Du Brey found that his king was in a trap. The foolish opening had been only a piece of shrewd strategy. The old Admiral fought and cursed and sacrificed his pieces, but it was of no use. He was gone. Mason checkmated him in two moves and arose wearily.

"'Where in Heaven's name, man,' said the old Admiral, thunderstruck, 'did you learn that masterpiece?'

"'Just here,' replied Mason. 'To play chess, one should know his opponent. How could the dead masters lay down rules by which you could be beaten, sir? They had never seen you'; and thereupon he turned and left the room. Of course, St. Clair, such a strange man would soon become an object of all kinds of mysterious rumors. Some are true and some are not. At any rate, I know that Mason is an unusual man with a gigantic intellect. Of late he seems to have taken a strange fancy to me. In fact, I seem to be the only member of the club that he will talk with, and I confess that he startles and fascinates me. He is an original genius, St. Clair, of an unusual order."

"I recall vividly," said the younger man, "that before Mason went to Paris he was considered one of the greatest lawyers of this city and he was feared and hated by the bar at large. He came here, I believe, from Virginia and began with the high-grade criminal practice. He soon became famous for his powerful and ingenious defenses. He found holes in the law through which his clients escaped, holes that by the profession at large were not suspected to exist, and that frequently astonished the judges. His ability caught the attention of the great corporations. They tested him and found in him learning and unlimited resources. He pointed out methods by which they could evade obnoxious statutes, by which they could comply with the apparent letter of the law and yet violate its spirit, and advised them well in that most important of all things, just how far they could bend the law without breaking it. At the time he left for Paris he had a vast clientage and was in the midst of a brilliant career. The day he took passage from New York, the bar lost sight of him. No matter how great a man may be, the wave soon closes over him in a city like this. In a few years Mason was forgotten. Now only the older practitioners would recall him, and they would do so with hatred and bitterness. He was a tireless, savage, uncompromising fighter, always a recluse."

"Well," said Walcott, "he reminds me of a great world-weary cynic, transplanted from some ancient mysterious empire. When I come into the man's presence I feel instinctively the grip of his intellect. I tell you,

St. Clair, Randolph Mason is the mysterious man of New York."

At this moment a messenger boy came into the room and handed Mr. Walcott a telegram. "St. Clair," said that gentleman, rising, "the directors of the Elevated are in session, and we must hurry." The two men put on their coats and left the house.

Samuel Walcott was not a club man after the manner of the Smart Set, and yet he was in fact a club man. He was a bachelor in the latter thirties, and resided in a great silent house on the avenue. On the street he was a man of substance, shrewd and progressive, backed by great wealth. He had various corporate interests in the larger syndicates, but the basis and foundation of his fortune was real estate. His houses on the avenue were the best possible property, and his elevator row in the importers' quarter was indeed a literal gold mine. It was known that, many years before, his grandfather had died and left him the property, which, at that time, was of no great value. Young Walcott had gone out into the gold-fields and had been lost sight of and forgotten. Ten years afterward he had turned up suddenly in New York and taken possession of his property, then vastly increased in value. His speculations were almost phenomenally successful, and, backed by the now enormous value of his real property, he was soon on a level with the merchant princes. His judgment was considered sound, and he had the full confidence of his business associates for safety and caution. Fortune heaped up riches around him with a lavish hand. He was unmarried and the halo of his wealth caught the keen eye of the matron with marriageable daughters. He was invited out, caught by the whirl of society, and tossed into its maelstrom. In a measure he reciprocated. He kept horses and a yacht. His dinners at Delmonico's and the club were above reproach. But with all he was a silent man with a shadow deep in his eyes, and seemed to court the society of his fellows, not because he loved them, but because he either hated or feared solitude. For years the strategy of the matchmaker had gone gracefully afield, but Fate is relentless. If she shields the victim from the traps of men, it is not because she wishes him to escape, but because she is pleased to reserve him for her own trap. So it happened that, when Virginia St. Clair assisted Mrs. Miriam Steuvisant at her midwinter reception, this same Samuel Walcott fell deeply and hopelessly and utterly in love, and it was so apparent to the beaten generals present, that Mrs. Miriam Steuvisant applauded herself, so to speak, with encore after encore. It was good to see this courteous, silent man literally at the feet of the young debutante. He was there of right. Even the mothers of marriageable daughters admitted that. The young girl was brown-haired, brown-eyed, and tall enough, said the experts, and of the blue blood royal, with all the grace, courtesy, and inbred genius of such princely heritage.

Perhaps it was objected by the censors of the Smart Set that Miss St. Clair's frankness and honesty were a trifle old-fashioned, and that she was a shadowy bit of a Puritan; and perhaps it was of these same qualities that Samuel Walcott received his hurt. At any rate the hurt was there and deep, and the new actor stepped up into the old time-worn, semi-tragic drama, and began his role with a tireless, utter sincerity that was deadly dangerous if he lost.

II.

PERHAPS A WEEK after the conversation between St. Clair and Walcott, Randolph Mason stood in the private writing-room of the club with his hands behind his back.

He was a man apparently in the middle forties; tall and reasonably broad across the shoulders; muscular without being either stout or lean. His hair was thin and of a brown color, with erratic streaks of gray. His forehead was broad and high and of a faint reddish color. His eyes were restless inky black, and not over-large. The nose was big and muscular and bowed. The eyebrows were black and heavy, almost bushy. There were heavy furrows, running from the nose downward and outward to the corners of the mouth. The mouth was straight and the jaw was heavy, and square.

Looking at the face of Randolph Mason from above, the expression in repose was crafty and cynical; viewed from below upward, it was savage and vindictive, almost brutal; while from the front, if looked squarely in the face, the stranger was fascinated by the animation of the man and at once concluded that his expression was fearless and sneering. He was evidently of Southern extraction and a man of unusual power.

A fire smoldered on the hearth. It was a crisp evening in the early fall, and with that far-off touch of melancholy which ever heralds the coming winter, even in the midst of a city. The man's face looked tired and ugly. His long white hands were clasped tight together. His entire figure and face wore every mark of weakness and physical exhaustion; but his eyes contradicted. They were red and restless.

In the private dining-room the dinner party was in the best of spirits. Samuel Walcott was happy. Across the table from him was Miss Virginia St. Clair, radiant, a tinge of color in her cheeks. On either side,

Mrs. Miriam Steuvisant and Marshall St. Clair were brilliant and light-hearted. Walcott looked at the young girl and the measure of his worship was full. He wondered for the thousandth time how she could possibly love him and by what earthly miracle she had come to accept him, and how it would be always to have her across the table from him, his own table in his own house.

They were about to rise from the table when one of the waiters entered the room and handed Walcott an envelope. He thrust it quickly into his pocket. In the confusion of rising the others did not notice him, but his face was ash white and his hands trembled violently as he placed the wraps around the bewitching shoulders of Miss St. Clair.

"Marshall," he said, and despite the powerful effort his voice was hollow, "you will see the ladies safely cared for, I am called to attend a grave matter."

"All right, Walcott," answered the young man, with cheery good nature, "you are too serious, old man, trot along."

"The poor dear," murmured Mrs. Steuvisant, after Walcott had helped them to the carriage and turned to go up the steps of the club, — "The poor dear is hard hit, and men are such funny creatures when they are hard hit."

Samuel Walcott, as his fate would, went direct to the private writing-room and opened the door. The lights were not turned on and in the dark he did not see Mason motionless by the mantel-shelf. He went quickly across the room to the writing-table, turned on one of the lights, and, taking the envelope from his pocket, tore it open. Then he bent down by the light to read the contents. As his eyes ran over the paper, his jaw fell. The skin drew away from his cheekbones and his face seemed literally to sink in. His knees gave way under him and he would have gone down in a heap had it not been for Mason's long arms that closed around him and held him up. The human economy is ever mysterious. The moment the new danger threatened, the latent power of the man as an animal, hidden away in the centers of intelligence, asserted itself. His hand clutched the paper and, with a half slide, he turned in Mason's arms. For a moment he stared up at the ugly man whose thin arms felt like wire ropes.

"You are under the dead-fall, aye," said Mason. "The cunning of my enemy is sublime."

"Your enemy?" gasped Walcott. "When did you come into it? How in God's name did you know it? How your enemy?"

Mason looked down at the wide bulging eyes of the man.

"Who should know better than I?" he said. "Haven't I broken through all the traps and plots that she could set?"

"She? She trap you?" The man's voice was full of horror.

"The old schemer," muttered Mason. "The cowardly old schemer, to strike in the back; but we can beat her. She did not count on my helping you — I, who know her so well."

Mason's face was red, and his eyes burned. In the midst of it all he dropped his hands and went over to the fire. Samuel Walcott arose, panting, and stood looking at Mason, with his hands behind him on the table. The naturally strong nature and the rigid school in which the man had been trained presently began to tell. His composure in part returned and he thought rapidly. What did this strange man know? Was he simply making shrewd guesses, or had he some mysterious knowledge of this matter? Walcott could not know that Mason meant only Fate, that he believed her to be his great enemy. Walcott had never before doubted his own ability to meet any emergency. This mighty jerk had carried him off his feet. He was unstrung and panic-stricken. At any rate this man had promised help. He would take it. He put the paper and envelope carefully into his pocket, smoothed out his rumpled coat, and going over to Mason touched him on the shoulder.

"Come," he said, "if you are to help me we must go."

The man turned and followed him without a word. In the hall Mason put on his hat and overcoat, and the two went out into the street. Walcott hailed a cab, and the two were driven to his house on the avenue. Walcott took out his latchkey, opened the door, and led the way into the library. He turned on the light and motioned Mason to seat himself at the table. Then he went into another room and presently returned with a bundle of papers and a decanter of brandy. He poured out a glass of the liquor and offered it to Mason. The man shook his head. Walcott poured the contents of the glass down his own throat. Then he set the decanter down and drew up a chair on the side of the table opposite Mason.

"Sir," said Walcott, in a voice deliberate, indeed, but as hollow as a sepulcher, "I am done for. God has finally gathered up the ends of the net, and it is knotted tight."

"Am I not here to help you?" said Mason, turning savagely. "I can beat Fate. Give me the details of her trap."

He bent forward and rested his arms on the table. His streaked gray hair was rumpled and on end, and his face was ugly. For a moment Walcott did not answer. He moved a little into the shadow; then he spread the bundle of old yellow papers out before him.

"To begin with," he said, "I am a living lie, a gilded crime-made sham, every bit of me. There is not an honest piece anywhere. It is all lie. I am a liar and a thief before men. The property which I possess is not mine, but stolen from a dead man. The very name which I bear is not my own, but is the bastard child of a crime. I am more than all that—I am a murderer; a murderer before the law; a murderer before God; and worse than a murderer before the pure woman whom I love more than anything that God could make."

He paused for a moment and wiped the perspiration from his face.

"Sir," said Mason, "this is all drivel, infantile drivel. What you are is of no importance. How to get out is the problem, how to get out."

Samuel Walcott leaned forward, poured out a glass of brandy and swallowed it.

"Well," he said, speaking slowly, "my right name is Richard Warren. In the spring of 1879 I came to New York and fell in with the real Samuel Walcott, a young man with a little money and some property which his grandfather had left him. We became friends, and concluded to go to the far west together. Accordingly we scraped together what money we could lay our hands on, and landed in the gold-mining regions of California. We were young and inexperienced, and our money went rapidly. One April morning we drifted into a little shack camp, away up in the Sierra Nevadas, called Hell's Elbow. Here we struggled and starved for perhaps a year. Finally, in utter desperation, Walcott married the daughter of a Mexican gambler, who ran an eating house and a poker joint. With them we lived from hand to mouth in a wild God-forsaken way for several years. After a time the woman began to take a strange fancy to me. Walcott finally noticed it, and grew jealous.

"One night, in a drunken brawl, we quarreled, and I killed him. It was late at night, and, beside the woman, there were four of us in the poker room,—the Mexican gambler, a half-breed devil called Cherubim Pete, Walcott, and myself. When Walcott fell, the half-breed whipped out his weapon, and fired at me across the table; but the woman, Nina San Croix, struck his arm, and, instead of killing me, as he intended, the bullet mortally wounded her father, the Mexican gambler. I shot the half-breed through the forehead, and turned round, expecting the woman to attack me. On the contrary, she pointed to the window, and bade me wait for her on the cross-trail below.

"It was fully three hours later before the woman joined me at the place indicated. She had a bag of gold dust, a few jewels that belonged to her father, and a package of papers. I asked her why she had stayed behind so long, and she replied that the men were not killed outright, and that she had brought a priest to them and waited until they had died. This was the truth, but not all the truth. Moved by superstition or foresight, the woman had induced the priest to take down the sworn statements of the two dying men, seal it, and give it to her. This paper she brought with her. All this I learned afterwards. At the time I knew nothing of this damning evidence.

"We struck out together for the Pacific coast. The country was lawless. The privations we endured were almost past belief. At times the woman exhibited cunning and ability that were almost genius; and through it all, often in the very fingers of death, her devotion to me never wavered. It was doglike, and seemed to be her only object on earth. When we reached San Francisco, the woman put these papers into my hands." Walcott took up the yellow package, and pushed it across the table to Mason.

"She proposed that I assume Walcott's name, and that we come boldly to New York and claim the property. I examined the papers, found a copy of the will by which Walcott inherited the property, a bundle of correspondence, and sufficient documentary evidence to establish his identity beyond the shadow of a doubt. Desperate gambler as I now was, I quailed before the daring plan of Nina San Croix. I urged that I, Richard Warren, would be known, that the attempted fraud would be detected and would result in investigation, and perhaps unearth the whole horrible matter.

"The woman pointed out how much I resembled Walcott, what vast changes ten years of such life as we had led would naturally be expected to make in men, how utterly impossible it would be to trace back the fraud to Walcott's murder at Hell's Elbow, in the wild passes of the Sierra Nevadas. She bade me remember that we were both outcasts, both crime-branded, both enemies of man's law and God's; that we had nothing to lose; we were both sunk to the bottom. Then she laughed, and said that she had not found me a coward until now, but that if I had turned chicken-hearted, that was the end of it, of course. The result was, we sold the gold dust and jewels in San Francisco, took on such evidences of civilization as possible, and purchased passage to New York on the best steamer we could find.

"I was growing to depend on the bold gambler spirit of this woman,

Nina San Croix; I felt the need of her strong, profligate nature. She was of a queer breed and a queerer school. Her mother was the daughter of a Spanish engineer, and had been stolen by the Mexican, her father. She herself had been raised and educated as best might be in one of the monasteries along the Rio Grande, and had there grown to womanhood before her father, fleeing into the mountains of California, carried her with him.

"When we landed in New York I offered to announce her as my wife, but she refused, saying that her presence would excite comment and perhaps attract the attention of Walcott's relatives. We therefore arranged that I should go alone into the city, claim the property, and announce myself as Samuel Walcott, and that she should remain under cover until such time as we would feel the ground safe under us.

"Every detail of the plan was fatally successful. I established my identity without difficulty and secured the property. It had increased vastly in value, and I, as Samuel Walcott, soon found myself a rich man. I went to Nina San Croix in hiding and gave her a large sum of money, with which she purchased a residence in a retired part of the city, far up in the northern suburb. Here she lived secluded and unknown while I remained in the city, living here as a wealthy bachelor.

"I did not attempt to abandon the woman, but went to her from time to time in disguise and under cover of the greatest secrecy. For a time everything ran smooth, the woman was still devoted to me above everything else, and thought always of my welfare first and seemed content to wait so long as I thought best. My business expanded. I was sought after and consulted and drawn into the higher life of New York, and more and more felt that the woman was an albatross on my neck. I put her off with one excuse after another. Finally she began to suspect me and demanded that I should recognize her as my wife. I attempted to point out the difficulties. She met them all by saying that we should both go to Spain, there I could marry her and we could return to America and drop into my place in society without causing more than a passing comment.

"I concluded to meet the matter squarely once for all. I said that I would convert half of the property into money and give it to her, but that I would not marry her. She did not fly into a storming rage as I had expected, but went quietly out of the room and presently returned with two papers, which she read. One was the certificate of her marriage to Walcott duly authenticated; the other was the dying statement of her father, the Mexican gambler, and of Samuel Walcott, charging me with murder. It was in proper form and certified by the Jesuit priest.

"'Now,' she said, sweetly, when she had finished, 'which do you prefer, to recognize your wife, or to turn all the property over to Samuel Walcott's widow and hang for his murder?'

"I was dumbfounded and horrified. I saw the trap that I was in and I consented to do anything she should say if she would only destroy the papers. This she refused to do. I pleaded with her and implored her to destroy them. Finally she gave them to me with a great show of returning confidence, and I tore them into bits and threw them into the fire.

"That was three months ago. We arranged to go to Spain and do as she said. She was to sail this morning and I was to follow. Of course I never intended to go. I congratulated myself on the fact that all trace of evidence against me was destroyed and that her grip was now broken. My plan was to induce her to sail, believing that I would follow. When she was gone I would marry Miss St. Clair, and if Nina San Croix should return I would defy her and lock her up as a lunatic. But I was reckoning like an infernal ass, to imagine for a moment that I could thus hoodwink such a woman as Nina San Croix.

"Tonight I received this." Walcott took the envelope from his pocket and gave it to Mason. "You saw the effect of it; read it and you will understand why. I felt the death hand when I saw her writing on the envelope."

Mason took the paper from the envelope. It was written in Spanish, and ran:

> Greeting to RICHARD WARREN.
>
> The great Señor does his little Nina injustice to think she would go away to Spain and leave him to the beautiful American. She is not so thoughtless. Before she goes, she shall be, Oh so very rich! and the dear Señor shall be, Oh so very safe! The Archbishop and the kind Church hate murderers.
>
> NINA SAN CROIX.
>
> Of course, fool, the papers you destroyed were copies.
>
> N. SAN C.

To this was pinned a line in a delicate aristocratic hand saying that the Archbishop would willingly listen to Madam San Croix's statement if she would come to him on Friday morning at eleven.

"You see," said Walcott, desperately, "there is no possible way out. I know the woman — when she decides to do a thing that is the end of it. She has decided to do this."

Mason turned around from the table, stretched out his long legs, and thrust his hands deep into his pockets. Walcott sat with his head down, watching Mason hopelessly, almost indifferently, his face blank and sunken. The ticking of the bronze clock on the mantel shelf was loud, painfully loud. Suddenly Mason drew his knees in and bent over, put both his bony hands on the table, and looked at Walcott.

"Sir," he said, "this matter is in such shape that there is only one thing to do. This growth must be cut out at the roots, and cut out quickly. This is the first fact to be determined, and a fool would know it. The second fact is that you must do it yourself. Hired killers are like the grave and the daughters of the horse leech, — they cry always, 'Give, Give.' They are only palliatives, not cures. By using them you swap perils. You simply take a stay of execution at best. The common criminal would know this. These are the facts of your problem. The master plotters of crime would see here but two difficulties to meet:

"A practical method for accomplishing the body of the crime.

"A cover for the criminal agent.

"They would see no farther, and attempt to guard no farther. After they had provided a plan for the killing, and a means by which the killer could cover his trail and escape from the theater of the homicide, they would believe all the requirements of the problems met, and would stop. The greatest, the very giants among them, have stopped here and have been in great error.

"In every crime, especially in the great ones, there exists a third element, preeminently vital. This third element the master plotters have either overlooked or else have not had the genius to construct. They plan with rare cunning to baffle the victim. They plan with vast wisdom, almost genius, to baffle the trailer. But they fail utterly to provide any plan for baffling the punisher. Ergo, their plots are fatally defective and often result in ruin. Hence the vital necessity for providing the third element — the *escape ipso jure.*"

Mason arose, walked around the table, and put his hand firmly on Samuel Walcott's shoulder. "This must be done tomorrow night," he continued; "you must arrange your business matters tomorrow and announce that you are going on a yacht cruise, by order of your physician, and may not return for some weeks. You must prepare your yacht for a voyage, instruct your men to touch at a certain point on Staten Island, and wait until six o'clock day after tomorrow morning. If you do not come aboard by that time, they are to go to one of the South American ports and remain until further orders. By this means your absence for an indefinite period will be explained. You will go to Nina San Croix in the disguise which you have always used, and from her to the yacht, and by this means step out of your real status and back into it without leaving traces. I will come here tomorrow evening and furnish you with everything that you shall need and give you full and exact instructions in every particular. These details you must execute with the greatest care, as they will be vitally essential to the success of my plan."

Through it all Walcott had been silent and motionless. Now he arose, and in his face there must have been some premonition of protest, for Mason stepped back and put out his hand. "Sir," he said, with brutal emphasis, "not a word. Remember that you are only the hand, and the hand does not think." Then he turned around abruptly and went out of the house.

III.

THE PLACE WHICH Samuel Walcott had selected for the residence of Nina San Croix was far up in the northern suburb of New York. The place was very old. The lawn was large and ill-kept; the house, a square old-fashioned brick, was set far back from the street, and partly hidden by trees. Around it all was a rusty iron fence. The place had the air of genteel ruin, such as one finds in the Virginias.

On a Thursday of November, about three o'clock in the afternoon, a little man, driving a dray, stopped in the alley at the rear of the house. As he opened the back gate an old negro woman came down the steps from the kitchen and demanded to know what he wanted. The drayman asked if the lady of the house was in. The old negro answered that she was asleep at this hour and could not be seen.

"That is good," said the little man, "now there won't be any row. I brought up some cases of wine which she ordered from our house last week and which the Boss told me to deliver at once, but I forgot it until today. Just let me put it in the cellar now, Auntie, and don't say a word to the lady about it and she won't ever know that it was not brought up on time."

The drayman stopped, fished a silver dollar out of his pocket, and gave it to the old negro. "There now, Auntie," he said, "my job depends upon the lady not knowing about this wine; keep it mum."

"Dat's all right, honey," said the old servant, beaming like a May morning. "De cellar door is open, carry it all in and put it in de back part and nobody ain't never going to know how long it has been in dar."

The old negro went back into the kitchen and the little man began to unload the dray. He carried in five wine cases and stowed them away in the back part of the cellar as the old woman had directed. Then, after having satisfied himself that no one was watching, he took from the dray two heavy paper sacks, presumably filled with flour, and a little bundle wrapped in an old newspaper; these he carefully hid behind the wine cases in the cellar. After a while he closed the door, climbed on his dray, and drove off down the alley.

About eight o'clock in the evening of the same day, a Mexican sailor dodged in the front gate and slipped down to the side of the house. He stopped by the window and tapped on it with his finger. In a moment a woman opened the door. She was tall, lithe, and splendidly proportioned, with a dark Spanish face and straight hair. The man stepped inside. The woman bolted the door and turned round.

"Ah," she said, smiling, "it is you, Señor? How good of you!"

The man started. "Whom else did you expect?" he said quickly.

"Oh!" laughed the woman, "perhaps the Archbishop."

"Nina!" said the man, in a broken voice that expressed love, humility, and reproach. His face was white under the black sunburn.

For a moment the woman wavered. A shadow flitted over her eyes, then she stepped back. "No," she said, "not yet."

The man walked across to the fire, sank down in a chair, and covered his face with his hands. The woman stepped up noiselessly behind him and leaned over the chair. The man was either in great agony or else he was a superb actor, for the muscles of his neck twitched violently and his shoulders trembled.

"Oh," he muttered, as though echoing his thoughts, "I can't do it, I can't!"

The woman caught the words and leaped up as though some one had struck her in the face. She threw back her head. Her nostrils dilated and her eyes flashed.

"You can't do it!" she cried. "Then you do love her! You shall do it! Do you hear me? You shall do it! You killed him! You got rid of him! but you shall not get rid of me. I have the evidence, all of it. The Archbishop will have it tomorrow. They shall hang you! Do you hear me? They shall hang you!"

The woman's voice rose, it was loud and shrill. The man turned slowly round without looking up, and stretched out his arms toward the woman. She stopped and looked down at him. The fire glittered for a moment and then died out of her eyes, her bosom heaved and her lips began to tremble. With a cry she flung herself into his arms, caught him around the neck, and pressed his face up close against her cheek.

"Oh! Dick, Dick," she sobbed, "I do love you so! I can't live without you! Not another hour, Dick! I do want you so much, so much, Dick!"

The man shifted his right arm quickly, slipped a great Mexican knife out of his sleeve, and passed his fingers slowly up the woman's side until he felt the heart beat under his hand, then he raised the knife, gripped the handle tight, and drove the keen blade into the woman's bosom. The hot blood gushed out over his arm, and down on his leg. The body, warm and limp, slipped down in his arms. The man got up, pulled out the knife, and thrust it into a sheath at his belt, unbuttoned the dress, and slipped it off of the body. As he did this a bundle of papers dropped upon the floor; these he glanced at hastily and put into his pocket. Then he took the dead woman up in his arms, went out into the hall, and started to go up the stairway. The body was relaxed and heavy, and for that reason difficult to carry. He doubled it up into an awful heap, with the knees against the chin, and walked slowly and heavily up the stairs and out into the bathroom. There he laid the corpse down on the tiled floor. Then he opened the window, closed the shutters, and lighted the gas. The bathroom was small and contained an ordinary steel tub, porcelain lined, standing near the window and raised about six inches above the floor. The sailor went over to the tub, pried up the metal rim of the outlet with his knife, removed it, and fitted into its place a porcelain disk which he took from his pocket; to this disk was attached a long platinum wire, the end of which he fastened on the outside of the tub. After he had done this he went back to the body, stripped off its clothing, put it down in the tub and began to dismember it with the great Mexican knife. The blade was strong and sharp as a razor. The man worked rapidly and with the greatest care.

When he had finally cut the body into as small pieces as possible, he replaced the knife in its sheath, washed his hands, and went out of the bathroom and downstairs to the lower hall. The sailor seemed perfectly familiar with the house. By a side door he passed into the cellar. There he lighted the gas, opened one of the wine cases, and, taking up all the bottles that he could conveniently carry, returned to the bathroom. There he poured the contents into the tub on the dismembered body, and then returned to the cellar with the empty bottles, which he replaced in the wine cases. This he continued to do until all the cases but one were emptied and the bathtub was more than half full of liquid. This liquid was sulfuric acid.

When the sailor returned to the cellar with the last empty wine bottles, he opened the fifth case, which really contained wine, took some of it out, and poured a little into each of the empty bottles in order to remove any possible odor of the sulfuric acid. Then he turned out the gas and brought up to the bathroom with him the two paper flour sacks and the little heavy bundle. These sacks were filled with nitrate of soda. He set them down by the door, opened the little bundle, and took out two long rubber tubes, each attached to a heavy gas burner, not unlike the ordinary burners of a small gas stove. He fastened the tubes to two of the gas jets, put the burners under the tub, turned the gas on full, and lighted it. Then he threw into the tub the woman's clothing and the papers which he had found on her body, after which he took up the two heavy sacks of nitrate of soda and dropped them carefully into the sulfuric acid. When he had done this he went quickly out of the bathroom and closed the door.

The deadly acids at once attacked the body and began to destroy it; as the heat increased, the acids boiled and the destructive process was rapid and awful. From time to time the sailor opened the door of the bathroom cautiously, and, holding a wet towel over his mouth and nose, looked in at his horrible work. At the end of a few hours there was only a swimming mass in the tub. When the man looked at four o'clock, it was all a thick murky liquid. He turned off the gas quickly and stepped back out of the room. For perhaps half an hour he waited in the hall; finally, when the acids had cooled so that they no longer gave off fumes, he opened the door and went in, took hold of the platinum wire and, pulling the porcelain disk from the stopcock, allowed the awful contents of the tub to run out. Then he turned on the hot water, rinsed the tub clean, and replaced the metal outlet. Removing the rubber tubes, he cut them into pieces, broke the porcelain disk, and, rolling up the platinum wire, washed it all down the sewer pipe.

The fumes had escaped through the open window; this he now closed and set himself to putting the bathroom in order, and effectually removing every trace of his night's work. The sailor moved around with the very greatest degree of care. Finally, when he had arranged everything to his complete satisfaction, he picked up the two burners, turned out the gas, and left the bathroom, closing the door after him. From the bathroom he went directly to the attic, concealed the two rusty burners under a heap of rubbish, and then walked carefully and noiselessly down the stairs and through the lower hall. As he opened the door and stepped into the room where he had killed the woman, two police officers sprang out and seized him. The man screamed like a wild beast taken in a trap and sank down.

"Oh! oh!" he cried, "it was no use! it was no use to do it!" Then he recovered himself in a manner and was silent. The officers handcuffed him, summoned the patrol, and took him at once to the station house. There he said he was a Mexican sailor and that his name was Victor Ancona; but he would say nothing further. The following morning he sent for Randolph Mason and the two were long together.

IV.

THE OBSCURE DEFENDANT charged with murder has little reason to complain of the law's delays. The morning following the arrest of Victor Ancona, the newspapers published long sensational articles, denounced him as a fiend, and convicted him. The grand jury, as it happened, was in session. The preliminaries were soon arranged and the case was railroaded into trial. The indictment contained a great many counts, and charged the prisoner with the murder of Nina San Croix by striking, stabbing, choking, poisoning, and so forth.

The trial had continued for three days and had appeared so overwhelmingly one-sided that the spectators who were crowded in the courtroom had grown to be violent and bitter partisans, to such an extent that the police watched them closely. The attorneys for the People were dramatic and denunciatory, and forced their case with arrogant confidence. Mason, as counsel for the prisoner, was indifferent and listless. Throughout the entire trial he had sat almost motionless at the table, his gaunt form bent over, his long legs drawn up under his chair, and his weary, heavy-muscled face, with its restless eyes, fixed and staring out over the heads of the jury, was like a tragic mask. The bar, and even the judge, believed that the prisoner's counsel had abandoned his case.

The evidence was all in and the People rested. It had been shown that Nina San Croix had resided for many years in the house in which the prisoner was arrested; that she had lived by herself, with no other companion than an old negro servant; that her past was unknown, and that she received no visitors, save the Mexican sailor, who came to her house at long intervals. Nothing whatever was shown tending to explain who the prisoner was or whence he had come. It was shown that on Tuesday preceding the killing the Archbishop had received a communication from Nina San Croix, in which she said she desired to make a statement of the greatest import, and asking for an audience. To this the Archbishop replied that he would willingly grant her a hearing if she would come to him at eleven o'clock on Friday morning. Two policemen testified that about eight o'clock on the night of Thursday they had noticed the prisoner slip into the gate of Nina San Croix's residence and go down to the side of the house, where he was admitted; that his appearance and seeming haste had attracted their attention; that they had concluded that it was some clandestine amour, and out of curiosity had both slipped down to the house and endeavored to find a position from which they could see into the room, but were unable to do so, and were about to go back to the street when they heard a woman's voice cry out in, great anger: "I know that you love her and that you want to get rid of me, but you shall not do it! You murdered him, but you shall not murder me! I have all the evidence to convict you of murdering him! The Archbishop will have it tomorrow! They shall hang you! Do you hear me? They shall hang you for his murder!" that thereupon one of the policemen proposed that they should break into the house and see what was wrong, but the other had urged that it was only the usual lovers' quarrel and if they should interfere they would find nothing upon which a charge could be based and would only be laughed at by the chief; that they had waited and listened for a time, but hearing nothing further had gone back to the street and contented themselves with keeping a strict watch on the house.

The People proved further, that on Thursday evening Nina San Croix had given the old negro domestic a sum of money and dismissed her, with the instruction that she was not to return until sent for. The old woman testified that she had gone directly to the house of her son, and later had discovered that she had forgotten some articles of clothing which she needed; that thereupon she had returned to the house and had gone up the back way to her room,—this was about eight o'clock; that while there she had heard Nina San Croix's voice in great passion and remembered that she had used the words stated by the policemen; that these sudden, violent cries had frightened her greatly and she had bolted the door and been afraid to leave the room; shortly thereafter, she had heard heavy footsteps ascending the stairs, slowly and with great difficulty, as though some one were carrying a heavy burden; that therefore her fear had increased and that she had put out the light and hidden under the bed. She remembered hearing the footsteps moving about upstairs for many hours, how long she could not tell. Finally, about half-past four in the morning, she crept out, opened the door, slipped downstairs, and ran out into the street. There she had found the policemen and requested them to search the house.

The two officers had gone to the house with the woman. She had opened the door and they had had just time to step back into the shadow when the prisoner entered. When arrested, Victor Ancona had screamed with terror, and cried out, "It was no use! it was no use to do it!"

The Chief of Police had come to the house and instituted a careful search. In the room below, from which the cries had come, he found a dress which was identified as belonging to Nina San Croix and which she was wearing when last seen by the domestic, about six o'clock that evening. This dress was covered with blood, and had a slit about two inches long in the left side of the bosom, into which the Mexican knife, found on the prisoner, fitted perfectly. These articles were introduced in evidence, and it was shown that the slit would be exactly over the heart of the wearer, and that such a wound would certainly result in death. There was much blood on one of the chairs and on the floor. There was also blood on the prisoner's coat and the leg of his trousers, and the heavy Mexican knife was also bloody. The blood was shown by the experts to be human blood.

The body of the woman was not found, and the most rigid and tireless search failed to develop the slightest trace of the corpse, or the manner of its disposal. The body of the woman had disappeared as completely as though it had vanished into the air.

When counsel announced that he had closed for the People, the judge turned and looked gravely down at Mason. "Sir," he said, "the evidence for the defense may now be introduced."

Randolph Mason arose slowly and faced the judge.

"If your Honor please," he said, speaking slowly and distinctly, "the defendant has no evidence to offer." He paused while a murmur of astonishment ran over the courtroom. "But, if your Honor please," he continued, "I move that the jury be directed to find the prisoner not guilty."

The crowd stirred. The counsel for the People smiled. The judge looked sharply at the speaker over his glasses. "On what ground?" he said curtly.

"On the ground," replied Mason, "that the *corpus delicti* has not been proven."

"Ah!" said the judge, for once losing his judicial gravity.

Mason sat down abruptly. The senior counsel for the prosecution was on his feet in a moment.

"What!" he said, "the gentleman bases his motion on a failure to establish the *corpus delicti?* Does he jest, or has he forgotten the evidence? The term '*corpus delicti*' is technical, and means the body of the crime, or the substantial fact that a crime has been committed. Does anyone doubt it in this case? It is true that no one actually saw the prisoner kill the decedent, and that he has so successfully hidden the body that it has not been found, but the powerful chain of circumstances, clear and close-linked, proving motive, the criminal agency, and the criminal act, is overwhelming.

"The victim in this case is on the eve of making a statement that would prove fatal to the prisoner. The night before the statement is to be made he goes to her residence. They quarrel. Her voice is heard, raised high in the greatest passion, denouncing him, and charging that he is a murderer, that she has the evidence and will reveal it, that he shall be hanged, and that he shall not be rid of her. Here is the motive for the crime, clear as light. Are not the bloody knife, the bloody dress, the bloody clothes of the prisoner, unimpeachable witnesses to the criminal act? The criminal agency of the prisoner has not the shadow of a possibility to obscure it. His motive is gigantic. The blood on him, and his despair when arrested, cry 'Murder! murder!' with a thousand tongues.

"Men may lie, but circumstances cannot. The thousand hopes and fears and passions of men may delude, or bias the witness. Yet it is beyond the human mind to conceive that a clear, complete chain of concatenated circumstances can be in error. Hence it is that the greatest jurists have declared that such evidence, being rarely liable to delusion or fraud, is safest and most powerful. The machinery of human justice cannot guard against the remote and improbable doubt. The inference is persistent in the affairs of men. It is the only means by which the human mind reaches the truth. If you forbid the jury to exercise it, you bid them work after first striking off their hands. Rule out the irresistible inference, and the end of justice is come in this land; and you may as well leave the spider to weave his web through the abandoned courtroom."

The attorney stopped, looked down at Mason with a pompous sneer, and retired to his place at the table. The judge sat thoughtful and motionless. The jurymen leaned forward in their seats.

"If your Honor please," said Mason, rising, "this is a matter of law, plain, clear, and so well settled in the State of New York that even counsel for the People should know it. The question before your Honor is simple. If the *corpus delicti,* the body of the crime, has been proven, as required by the laws of the commonwealth, then this case should go to the jury. If not, then it is the duty of this Court to direct the jury to find the prisoner not guilty. There is here no room for judicial discretion. Your Honor has but to recall and apply the rigid rule announced by our courts prescribing distinctly how the *corpus delicti* in murder must be proven.

"The prisoner here stands charged with the highest crime. The law demands, first, that the crime, as a fact, be established. The fact that the victim is indeed dead must first be made certain before anyone can be convicted for her killing, because, so long as there remains the remotest doubt as to the death, there can be no certainty as to the criminal agent, although the circumstantial evidence indicating the guilt of the accused may be positive, complete, and utterly irresistible. In murder, the *corpus delicti,* or body of the crime, is composed of two elements:

"Death, as a result.

"The criminal agency of another as the means.

It is the fixed and immutable law of this State, laid down in the leading case of Ruloff v. The People, and binding upon this Court, that both components of the *corpus delicti* shall not be established by circumstantial evidence. There must be direct proof of one or the other of these two component elements of the *corpus delicti.* If one is proven by direct evidence, the other may be presumed; but both shall not be presumed from circumstances, no matter how powerful, how cogent, or how completely overwhelming the circumstances may be. In other words, no man can be convicted of murder in the State of New York, unless the body of the victim be found and identified, or there be direct proof that the prisoner did some act adequate to produce death, and did it in such a manner as to account for the disappearance of the body."

The face of the judge cleared and grew hard. The members of the bar were attentive and alert; they were beginning to see the legal escape open up. The audience were puzzled; they did not yet understand. Mason turned to the counsel for the People. His ugly face was bitter with contempt.

"For three days," he said, "I have been tortured by this useless and expensive farce. If counsel for the People had been other than play-actors, they would have known in the beginning that Victor Ancona could not be convicted for murder, unless he were confronted in this courtroom with a living witness, who had looked into the dead face of Nina San

Croix; or, if not that, a living witness who had seen him drive the dagger into her bosom.

"I care not if the circumstantial evidence in this case were so strong and irresistible as to be overpowering; if the judge on the bench, if the jury, if every man within sound of my voice, were convinced of the guilt of the prisoner to the degree of certainty that is absolute; if the circumstantial evidence left in the mind no shadow of the remotest improbable doubt; yet, in the absence of the eyewitness, this prisoner cannot be punished, and this Court must compel the jury to acquit him."

The audience now understood, and they were dumbfounded. Surely this was not the law. They had been taught that the law was common sense, and this, — this was anything else.

Mason saw it all, and grinned. "In its tenderness," he sneered, "the law shields the innocent. The good law of New York reaches out its hand and lifts the prisoner out of the clutches of the fierce jury that would hang him."

Mason sat down. The room was silent. The jurymen looked at each other in amazement. The counsel for the People arose. His face was white with anger, and incredulous.

"Your Honor," he said, "this doctrine is monstrous. Can it be said that, in order to evade punishment, the murderer has only to hide or destroy the body of the victim, or sink it into the sea? Then, if he is not seen to kill, the law is powerless and the murderer can snap his finger in the face of retributive justice. If this is the law, then the law for the highest crime is a dead letter. The great commonwealth winks at murder and invites every man to kill his enemy, provided he kill him in secret and hide him. I repeat, your Honor," — the man's voice was now loud and angry and rang through the courtroom — "that this doctrine is monstrous!"

"So said Best, and Story, and many another," muttered Mason, "and the law remained."

"The Court," said the judge, abruptly, "desires no further argument."

The counsel for the People resumed his seat. His face lighted up with triumph. The Court was going to sustain him.

The judge turned and looked down at the jury. He was grave, and spoke with deliberate emphasis.

"Gentlemen of the jury," he said, "the rule of Lord Hale obtains in this State and is binding upon me. It is the law as stated by counsel for the prisoner: that to warrant conviction of murder there must be direct proof either of the death, as of the finding and identification of the corpse, or of criminal violence adequate to produce death, and exerted in such a manner as to account for the disappearance of the body; and it is only when there is direct proof of the one that the other can be established by circumstantial evidence. This is the law, and cannot now be departed from. I do not presume to explain its wisdom. Chief-Justice Johnson has observed, in the leading case, that it may have its probable foundation in the idea that where direct proof is absent as to both the fact of the death and of criminal violence capable of producing death, no evidence can rise to the degree of moral certainty that the individual is dead by criminal intervention, or even lead by direct inference to this result; and that, where the fact of death is not certainly ascertained, all inculpatory circumstantial evidence wants the key necessary for its satisfactory interpretation, and cannot be depended on to furnish more than probable results. It may be, also, that such a rule has some reference to the dangerous possibility that a general preconception of guilt, or a general excitement of popular feeling, may creep in to supply the place of evidence, if, upon other than direct proof of death or a cause of death, a jury are permitted to pronounce a prisoner guilty.

"In this case the body has not been found and there is no direct proof of criminal agency on the part of the prisoner, although the chain of circumstantial evidence is complete and irresistible in the highest degree. Nevertheless, it is all circumstantial evidence, and under the laws of New York the prisoner cannot be punished. I have no right of discretion. The law does not permit a conviction in this case, although every one of us may be morally certain of the prisoner's guilt. I am, therefore, gentlemen of the jury, compelled to direct you to find the prisoner not guilty."

"Judge," interrupted the foreman, jumping up in the box, "we cannot find that verdict under our oath; we know that this man is guilty."

"Sir," said the judge, "this is a matter of law in which the wishes of the jury cannot be considered. The clerk will write a verdict of not guilty, which you, as foreman, will sign."

The spectators broke out into a threatening murmur that began to grow and gather volume. The judge rapped on his desk and ordered the bailiffs promptly to suppress any demonstration on the part of the audience. Then he directed the foreman to sign the verdict prepared by the clerk. When this was done he turned to Victor Ancona; his face was hard and there was a cold glitter in his eyes.

"Prisoner at the bar," he said, "you have been put to trial before this tribunal on a charge of cold-blooded and atrocious murder. The evidence produced against you was of such powerful and overwhelming character that it seems to have left no doubt in the minds of the jury, nor indeed in the mind of any person present in this courtroom.

"Had the question of your guilt been submitted to these twelve arbiters, a conviction would certainly have resulted and the death penalty would have been imposed. But the law, rigid, passionless, even-eyed, has thrust in between you and the wrath of your fellows and saved you from it. I do not cry out against the impotency of the law; it is perhaps as wise as imperfect humanity could make it. I deplore, rather, the genius of evil men who, by cunning design, are enabled to slip through the fingers of this law. I have no word of censure or admonition for you, Victor Ancona. The law of New York compels me to acquit you. I am only its mouthpiece, with my individual wishes throttled. I speak only those things which the law directs I shall speak.

"You are now at liberty to leave this courtroom, not guiltless of the crime of murder, perhaps, but at least rid of its punishment. The eyes of men may see Cain's mark on your brow, but the eyes of the Law are blind to it."

When the audience fully realized what the judge had said they were amazed and silent. They knew as well as men could know, that Victor Ancona was guilty of murder, and yet he was now going out of the courtroom free. Could it happen that the law protected only against the blundering rogue? They had heard always of the boasted completeness of the law which magistrates from time immemorial had labored to perfect, and now when the skillful villain sought to evade it, they saw how weak a thing it was.

V.

THE WEDDING MARCH of Lohengrin floated out from the Episcopal Church of St. Mark, clear and sweet, and perhaps heavy with its paradox of warning. The theater of this coming contract before high heaven was a wilderness of roses worth the taxes of a county. The high caste of Manhattan, by the grace of the checkbook, were present, clothed in Parisian purple and fine linen, cunningly and marvelously wrought.

Over in her private pew, ablaze with jewels, and decked with fabrics from the deft hand of many a weaver, sat Mrs. Miriam Steuvisant as imperious and self-complacent as a queen. To her it was all a kind of triumphal procession, proclaiming her ability as a general. With her were a choice few of the *genus homo,* which obtains at the five-o'clock teas, instituted, say the sages, for the purpose of sprinkling the holy water of Lethe.

"Czarina," whispered Reggie Du Puyster, leaning forward, "I salute you. The ceremony *sub jugum* is superb."

"Walcott is an excellent fellow," answered Mrs. Steuvisant; "not a vice, you know, Reggie."

"Aye, Empress," put in the others, "a purist taken in the net. The clean-skirted one has come to the altar. Vive la vertu!"

Samuel Walcott, still sunburned from his cruise, stood before the chancel with the only daughter of the blue-blooded St. Clairs. His face was clear and honest and his voice firm. This was life and not romance. The lid of the sepulcher had closed and he had slipped from under it. And now, and ever after, the hand red with murder was clean as any.

The minister raised his voice, proclaiming the holy union before God, and this twain, half pure, half foul, now by divine ordinance one flesh, bowed down before it. No blood cried from the ground. The sunlight of high noon streamed down through the window panes like a benediction.

Back in the pew of Mrs. Miriam Steuvisant, Reggie Du Puyster turned down his thumb. "Habet!" he said.

1897

L. FRANK BAUM

THE SUICIDE OF KIAROS

Yes, *that* L(YMAN) FRANK BAUM (1856–1919), the man who created the most magical and popular series of fairy tales ever written by an American, beginning with *The Wonderful Wizard of Oz* in 1900.

Although born to a wealthy family that made its fortune in the oil business, Baum went out on his own in search of a career, first as a journalist, then as a poultry farmer. When the family fell on hard times, he struggled to earn a living for himself, his wife, and their four children. In addition to journalistic pieces for newspapers and magazines, he wrote short stories and, in 1897, a successful children's book, *Mother Goose in Prose,* followed two years later by *Father Goose: His Book,* which became a bestseller. His next book was *The Wonderful Wizard of Oz,* the publication of which he financed himself, launching one of the most successful careers in American literature. He wrote sixty more books, mostly for young readers, including seventeen additional Oz books (a couple of which were published posthumously and one of which, *The Royal Book of Oz,* was credited to him but was written entirely by Ruth Plumly Thompson, who wrote more Oz novels than Baum — nineteen). Many of the Oz novels were filmed, though none as successfully as the 1939 film *The Wizard of Oz,* with its iconic portrayals of Dorothy by Judy Garland (though the studio's first choice had been Shirley Temple), the Cowardly Lion by Bert Lahr, the Scarecrow by Ray Bolger, and the Tin Man by Frank Haley.

Like all of Baum's books for young readers, the Oz novels offered positive, optimistic views that assured children that they could be successful by embracing the traditional American virtues of integrity, self-reliance, candor, and courage. It is therefore especially shocking to accept the notion that the same person who wrote those books could have written the following story, which is as diametrically opposite to those sentiments as it is possible for anything to be. It is one of the darkest stories in this book.

"The Suicide of Kiaros" was first published in a now-forgotten literary magazine, *The White Elephant,* in its issue of September 1897.

• • •

I.

Mr. Felix Marston, cashier for the great mercantile firm of Van Alsteyne & Traynor, sat in his little private office with a balance sheet before him and a frown upon his handsome face. At times he nervously ran his slim fingers through the mass of dark hair that clustered over his forehead, and the growing expression of annoyance upon his features fully revealed his disquietude.

The world knew and admired Mr. Marston, and a casual onlooker would certainly have decided that something had gone wrong with the firm's financial transactions; but Mr. Marston knew himself better than the world did, and grimly realized that although something had gone very wrong indeed, it affected himself in an unpleasantly personal way.

The world's knowledge of the popular young cashier included the following items: He had entered the firm's employ years before in an inferior position, and by energy, intelligence, and business ability, had worked his way up until he reached the post he now occupied, and became his employers' most trusted servant. His manner was grave, earnest, and dignified; his judgment, in business matters, clear and discerning. He had no intimate friends, but was courteous and affable to all he met, and his private life, so far as it was known, was beyond all reproach.

Mr. Van Alsteyne, the head of the firm, conceived a warm liking for Mr. Marston, and finally invited him to dine at his house. It was there the young man first met Gertrude Van Alsteyne, his employer's only child, a beautiful girl and an acknowledged leader in society. Attracted by the man's handsome face and gentlemanly bearing, the heiress encouraged him to repeat his visit, and Marston followed up his advantage so skillfully that within a year she had consented to become his wife. Mr. Van Alsteyne did not object to the match. His admiration for the young man deepened, and he vowed that upon the wedding day he would transfer one-half his interest in the firm to his son-in-law.

Therefore the world, knowing all this, looked upon Mr. Marston as one of fortune's favorites, and predicted a great future for him. But Mr. Marston, as I said, knew himself more intimately than did the world, and now, as he sat looking upon that fatal trial balance, he muttered in an undertone:

"Oh, you fool — you fool!"

Clear-headed, intelligent man of the world though he was, one vice had mastered him. A few of the most secret, but most dangerous gambling dens knew his face well. His ambition was unbounded, and before he had even dreamed of being able to win Miss Van Alsteyne as his bride, he had figured out several ingenious methods of winning a fortune at the green table. Two years ago he had found it necessary to "borrow" a sum of money from the firm to enable him to carry out these clever methods. Having, through some unforeseen calamity, lost the money, another sum had to be abstracted to allow him to win back enough to even the accounts. Other men have attempted this before; their experiences are usually the same. By a neat juggling of figures, the books of the firm had so far been made to conceal his thefts, but now it seemed as if fortune, in pushing him forward, was about to hurl him down a precipice.

His marriage to Gertrude Van Alsteyne was to take place in two weeks, and as Mr. Van Alsteyne insisted upon keeping his promise to give Marston an interest in the business, the change in the firm would necessitate a thorough overhauling of the accounts, which meant discovery and ruin to the man who was about to grasp a fortune and a high social position — all that his highest ambition had ever dreamed of attaining.

It is no wonder that Mr. Marston, brought face to face with his critical position, denounced himself for his past folly, and realized his helplessness to avoid the catastrophe that was about to crush him.

A voice outside interrupted his musings and arrested his attention.

"It is Mr. Marston I wish to see."

The cashier thrust the sheet of figures within a drawer of the desk, hastily composed his features, and opened the glass door beside him.

"Show Mr. Kiaros this way," he called, after a glance at his visitor. He had frequently met the person who now entered his office, but he could not resist a curious glance as the man sat down upon a chair and spread his hands over his knees. He was short and thick-set in form, and both oddly and carelessly dressed, but his head and face were most venerable in appearance. Flowing locks of pure white graced a forehead whose height and symmetry denoted unusual intelligence, and a full beard of the same purity reached full to his waist. The eyes were full and dark, but not piercing in character, rather conveying in their frank glance kindness and benevolence. A round cap of some dark material was worn upon his head, and this he deferentially removed as he seated himself, and said:

"For me a package of value was consigned to you, I believe?"

Marston nodded gravely. "Mr. Williamson left it with me," he replied.

"I will take it," announced the Greek, calmly; "twelve thousand dollars it contains."

Marston started. "I knew it was money," he said, "but was not aware of the amount. This is it, I think."

He took from the huge safe a packet, corded and sealed, and handed it to his visitor. Kiaros took a pen-knife from his pocket, cut the cords, and removed the wrapper, after which he proceeded to count the contents.

Marston listlessly watched him. Twelve thousand dollars. That would be more than enough to save him from ruin, if only it belonged to him instead of this Greek money-lender.

"The amount, it is right," declared the old man, rewrapping the parcel of notes. "You have my thanks, sir. Good afternoon," and he rose to go.

"Pardon me, sir," said Marston, with a sudden thought; "it is after banking hours. Will it be safe to carry this money with you until morning?"

"Perfectly," replied Kiaros; "I am never molested, for I am old, and few know my business. My safe at home large sums often contains. The money I like to have near me, to accommodate my clients."

He buttoned his coat tightly over the packet, and then in turn paused to look at the cashier.

"Lately you have not come to me for favors," he said.

"No," answered Marston, arousing from a slight reverie; "I have not needed to. Still, I may be obliged to visit you again soon."

"Your servant I am pleased to be," said Kiaros, with a smile, and turning abruptly he left the office.

Marston glanced at his watch. He was engaged to dine with his betrothed that evening, and it was nearly time to return to his lodgings to dress. He attended to one or two matters in his usual methodical way, and then left the office for the night, relinquishing any further duties to his assistant. As he passed through the various business offices on his way out, he was greeted respectfully by his fellow-employees, who already regarded him a member of the firm.

II.

ALMOST FOR THE first time during their courtship, Miss Van Alsteyne was tender and demonstrative that evening, and seemed loath to allow him to leave the house when he pleaded a business engagement and arose to go. She was a stately beauty, and little given to emotional ways, therefore her new mood affected him greatly, and as he walked away he realized, with a sigh, how much it would cost him to lose so dainty and charming a bride.

At the first corner he paused and examined his watch by the light of the street lamp. It was nine o'clock. Hailing the first passing cab, he directed the man to drive him to the lower end of the city, and leaning back upon the cushions, he became occupied in earnest thought.

The jolting of the cab over a rough pavement finally aroused him, and looking out he signaled the driver to stop.

"Shall I wait, sir?" asked the man, as Marston alighted and paid his fare.

"No."

The cab rattled away, and the cashier retraced his way a few blocks and then walked down a side street that seemed nearly deserted, so far as he could see in the dim light. Keeping track of the house numbers, which were infrequent and often nearly obliterated, he finally paused before a tall, brick building, the lower floors of which seemed occupied as a warehouse.

"Two eighty-six," he murmured; "this must be the place. If I remember right there should be a stairway at the left—ah, here it is."

There was no light at the entrance, but having visited the place before, under similar circumstances, Marston did not hesitate, but began mounting the stairs, guiding himself in the darkness by keeping one hand upon the narrow rail. One flight—two—three—four!

"His room should be straight before me," he thought, pausing to regain his breath; "yes, I think there is a light shining under the door."

He advanced softly, knocked, and then listened. There was a faint sound from within, and then a slide in the upper panel of the door was pushed aside, permitting a strong ray of lamp-light to strike Marston full in the face.

"Oho!" said a calm voice, "Mr. Marston has honored me. To enter I entreat you."

The door was thrown open and Kiaros stood before him, with a smile upon his face, gracefully motioning him to advance. Marston returned the old man's courteous bow, and entering the room, took a seat near the table, at the same time glancing at his surroundings.

The room was plainly but substantially furnished. A small safe stood in a corner at his right, and near it was the long table, used by Kiaros as a desk. It was littered with papers and writing material, and behind it was a high-backed, padded easy-chair, evidently the favorite seat of the Greek, for after closing the door he walked around the table and sat within the big chair, facing his visitor.

The other end of the room boasted a fireplace, with an old-fashioned mantel bearing an array of curiosities. Above it was a large clock, and at one side stood a small bookcase containing a number of volumes printed in the Greek language. A small alcove, containing a couch, occupied the remaining side of the small apartment, and it was evident these cramped quarters constituted Kiaros' combined office and living rooms.

"So soon as this I did not expect you," said the old man, in his grave voice.

"I am in need of money," replied Marston, abruptly, "and my interview with you this afternoon reminded me that you have sometimes granted me an occasional loan. Therefore, I have come to negotiate with you."

Kiaros nodded, and studied with his dark eyes the composed features of the cashier.

"A satisfactory debtor you have ever proved," said he, "and to pay me with promptness never failed. How much do you require?"

"Twelve thousand dollars."

In spite of his self-control, Kiaros started as the young man coolly stated this sum.

"Impossible!" he ejaculated, moving uneasily in his chair.

"Why is it impossible?" demanded Marston. "I know you have the money."

"True; I deny it not," returned Kiaros, dropping his gaze before the other's earnest scrutiny; "also to lend money is my business. But see — I will be frank with you Mr. Marston — I cannot take the risk. You are cashier for hire; you have no property; security for so large a sum you cannot give. Twelve thousand dollars! It is impossible!"

"You loaned Williamson twelve thousand," persisted Marston; doggedly.

"Mr. Williamson secured me."

Marston rose from his chair and began slowly pacing up and down before the table, his hands clasped tightly behind him and an impatient frown contracting his features. The Greek watched him calmly.

"Perhaps you have not heard, Mr. Kiaros," he said, at length, "that within two weeks I am to be married to Mr. Van Alsteyne's only daughter."

"I had not heard."

"And at the same time I am to receive a large interest in the business as a wedding gift from my father-in-law."

"To my congratulations you are surely entitled."

"Therefore my need is only temporary. I shall be able to return the money within thirty days, and I am willing to pay you well for the accommodation."

"A Jew I am not," returned Kiaros, with a slight shrug, "and where I lend I do not rob. But so great a chance I cannot undertake. You are not yet married, a partner in the firm not yet. To die, to quarrel with the lady, to lose Mr. Van Alsteyne's confidence, would leave me to collect the sum wholly unable. I might a small amount risk — the large amount is impossible."

Marston suddenly became calm, and resumed his chair with a quiet air, to Kiaros' evident satisfaction.

"You have gambled?" asked the Greek, after a pause.

"Not lately. I shall never gamble again. I owe no gambling debts; this money is required for another purpose."

"Can you not do with less?" asked Kiaros; "an advance I will make of one thousand dollars; not more. That sum is also a risk, but you are a man of discretion; in your ability I have confidence."

Marston did not reply at once. He leaned back in his chair, and seemed to be considering the money-lender's offer. In reality there passed before his mind the fate that confronted him, the scene in which he posed as a convicted felon; he saw the collapse of his great ambitions, the ruin of those schemes he had almost brought to fruition. Already he felt the reproaches of the man he had robbed, the scorn of the proud woman who had been ready to give him her hand, the cold sneers of those who gloated over his downfall. And then he bethought himself, and drove the vision away, and thought of other things.

Kiaros rested his elbow upon the table, and toyed with a curious-looking paper-cutter. It was made of pure silver, in the shape of a dagger; the blade was exquisitely chased, and bore a Greek motto. After a time Kiaros looked up and saw his guest regarding the paper-cutter.

"It is a relic most curious," said he, "from the ruins of Missolonghi rescued, and by a friend sent to me. All that is Greek I love. Soon to my country I shall return, and that is why I cannot risk the money I have in a lifetime earned."

Still Marston did not reply, but sat looking thoughtfully at the table. Kiaros was not impatient. He continued to play with the silver dagger, and poised it upon his finger while he awaited the young man's decision.

"I think I shall be able to get along with the thousand dollars," said Marston at last, his collected tone showing no trace of the disappointment Kiaros had expected. "Can you let me have it now?"

"Yes. As you know, the money is in my safe. I will make out the note."

He quietly laid down the paper-cutter and drew a notebook from a drawer of the table. Dipping a pen in the inkwell, he rapidly filled up the note and pushed it across the table to Marston.

"Will you sign?" he asked, with his customary smile.

Marston drew his chair close to the table and examined the note.

"You said you would not rob me!" he demurred.

"The commission it is very little," replied Kiaros, coolly. "A Jew much more would have exacted."

Marston picked up the pen, dashed off his name, and tossed the paper towards Kiaros. The Greek inspected it carefully, and rising from his chair, walked to the safe and drew open the heavy door. He placed the note in one drawer, and from another removed an oblong tin box, which he brought to the table. Reseating himself, he opened this box and drew out a large packet of banknotes.

Marston watched him listlessly as he carefully counted out one thousand dollars.

"The amount is, I believe, correct," said Kiaros, after a second count; "if you will kindly verify it I shall be pleased."

Marston half arose and reached out his hand, but he did not take the money. Instead, his fingers closed over the handle of the silver dagger, and with a swift, well-directed blow he plunged it to the hilt in the breast of the Greek. The old man lay back in his chair with a low moan, his form quivered once or twice and then became still, while a silence that suddenly seemed oppressive pervaded the little room.

III.

FELIX MARSTON SAT down in his chair and stared at the form of Kiaros. The usually benevolent features of the Greek were horribly convulsed, and the dark eyes had caught and held a sudden look of terror. His right hand, resting upon the table, still grasped the bundle of banknotes. The handle of the silver dagger glistened in the lamplight just above the heart, and a dark-colored fluid was slowly oozing outward and discoloring the old man's clothing and the point of his snowy beard.

Marston drew out his handkerchief and wiped the moisture from his forehead. Then he arose, and going to his victim, carefully opened the dead hand and removed the money. In the tin box was the remainder of the twelve thousand dollars the Greek had that day received. Marston wrapped it all in a paper and placed it in his breast pocket. Then he went to the safe, replaced the box in its drawer, and found the note he had just signed. This he folded and placed carefully in his pocketbook. Returning to the table, he stood looking down upon the dead man.

"He was a very good fellow, old Kiaros," he murmured; "I am sorry I had to kill him. But this is no time for regrets; I must try to cover all traces of my crime. The reason most murderers are discovered is because they become terrified, are anxious to get away, and so leave clues behind them. I have plenty of time. Probably no one knows of my visit here to-night, and as the old man lives quite alone, no one is likely to come here before morning."

He looked at his watch. It was a few minutes after ten o'clock.

"This ought to be a case of suicide," he continued, "and I shall try to make it look that way."

The expression of Kiaros' face first attracted his attention. That look of terror was incompatible with suicide. He drew a chair beside the old man and began to pass his hands over the dead face to smooth out the contracted lines. The body was still warm, and with a little perseverance, Marston succeeded in relaxing the drawn muscles until the face gradually resumed its calm and benevolent look.

The eyes, however, were more difficult to deal with, and it was only after repeated efforts that Marston was able to draw the lids over them, and hide their startled and horrified gaze. When this was accomplished, Kiaros looked as peaceful as if asleep, and the cashier was satisfied with his progress. He now lifted the Greek's right hand and attempted to clasp the fingers over the handle of the dagger, but they fell away limply.

"Rigor mortis has not yet set in," reflected Marston, "and I must fasten the hand in position until it does. Had the man himself dealt the blow, the tension of the nerves of the arm would probably have forced the fingers to retain their grip upon the weapon." He took his handkerchief and bound the fingers over the hilt of the dagger, at the same time altering the position of the head and body to better suit the assumption of suicide.

"I shall have to wait some time for the body to cool," he told himself, and then he considered what might be done in the meantime.

A box of cigars stood upon the mantel. Marston selected one and lit it. Then he returned to the table, turned up the lamp a trifle, and began searching in the drawers for specimens of the Greek's handwriting. Having secured several of these he sat down and studied them for a few minutes, smoking collectedly the while, and taking care to drop the ashes in a little tray that Kiaros had used for that purpose. Finally he drew a sheet of paper towards him, and carefully imitating the Greek's sprawling chirography, wrote as follows:

> My money I have lost. To live longer I cannot. To die I am therefore resolved.
> KIAROS.

"I think that will pass inspection," he muttered, looking at the paper approvingly, and comparing it again with the dead man's writing. "I must avoid all risks, but this forgery is by far too clever to be detected." He placed the paper upon the table before the body of the Greek, and then rearranged the papers as he had found them.

Slowly the hours passed away. Marston rose from his chair at intervals and examined the body. At one o'clock rigor mortis began to set in, and a half hour later Marston removed the handkerchief, and was pleased to find the hand retained its grasp upon the dagger. The position of the dead body was now very natural indeed, and the cashier congratulated himself upon his success.

There was but one task remaining for him to accomplish. The door must be found locked upon the inside. Marston searched until he found a piece of twine, one end of which he pinned lightly to the top of the table, a little to the left of the inkwell. The other end of the twine he carried to the door, and passed it through the slide in the panel. Withdrawing the key from the lock of the door, he now approached the table for the last time, taking a final look at the body, and laying the end of his cigar upon the tray. The theory of suicide had been excellently carried out; if only the key could be arranged for, he would be satisfied. Reflecting thus, he leaned over and blew out the light.

It was very dark, but he had carefully considered the distance beforehand, and in a moment he had reached the hallway and softly closed and locked the door behind him. Then he withdrew the key, found the end of the twine which projected through the panel, and running this through the ring of the key, he passed it inside the panel, and allowed the key to slide down the cord until a sharp click told him it rested upon the table within. A sudden jerk of the twine now unfastened the end which had been pinned to the table, and he drew it in and carefully placed it in his pocket. Before closing the door of the panel, Marston lighted a match, and satisfied himself the key was lying in the position he had wished. He breathed more freely then and closed the panel.

A few minutes later he had reached the street, and after a keen glance up and down, he stepped boldly from the doorway and walked away.

To his surprise, he now felt himself trembling with nervousness, and despite his endeavors to control himself, it required all of his four-mile walk home to enable him to regain his wonted composure.

He let himself in with his latchkey, and made his way noiselessly to his room. As he was a gentleman of regular habits, the landlady never bothered herself to keep awake watching for his return.

IV.

Mr. Marston appeared at the office the next morning in an unusually good humor, and at once busied himself with the regular routine of duties.

As soon as he was able, he retired to his private office and began to revise the books and make out a new trial balance. The exact amount he had stolen from the firm was put into the safe, the false figures were replaced with correct ones, and by noon the new balance sheet proved that Mr. Marston's accounts were in perfect condition.

Just before he started for luncheon a clerk brought him the afternoon paper. "What do you think, Mr. Marston?" he said. "Old Kiaros has committed suicide."

"Indeed! Do you mean the Kiaros who was here yesterday?" inquired Marston, as he put on his coat.

"The very same. It seems the old man lost his money in some unfortunate speculation, and so took his own life. The police found him in his room this morning, stabbed to the heart. Here is the paper, sir, if you wish to see it."

"Thank you," returned the cashier, in his usual quiet way. "I will buy one when I go out," and without further comment he went to luncheon.

But he purchased a paper, and while eating read carefully the account of Kiaros' suicide. The report was reassuring; no one seemed to dream the Greek was the victim of foul play.

The verdict of the coroner's jury completed his satisfaction. They found that Kiaros had committed suicide in a fit of despondency. The Greek was buried and forgotten, and soon the papers teemed with sensational accounts of the brilliant wedding of that estimable gentleman,

Mr. Felix Marston, to the popular society belle, Miss Gertrude Van Alsteyne. The happy pair made a bridal trip to Europe, and upon their return Mr. Marston was installed as an active partner in the great firm of Van Alsteyne, Traynor & Marston.

This was twenty years ago. Mr. Marston to-day has an enviable record as an honorable and highly respected man of business, although some consider him a trifle too cold and calculating.

His wife, although she early discovered the fact that he had married her to further his ambition, has found him reserved and undemonstrative, but always courteous and indulgent to both herself and her children.

He holds his head high and looks every man squarely in the eye, and he is very generally envied, since everything seems to prosper in his hands.

Kiaros and his suicide are long since forgotten by the police and the public. Perhaps Marston recalls the Greek at times. He told me this story when he lay upon what he supposed was his death-bed.

1897

ROBERT W. CHAMBERS

THE PURPLE EMPEROR

Although Robert W(illiam) Chambers produced fiction of all kinds, including adventure, mystery, and romance, he was regarded by critics and such contemporaries as H. P. Lovecraft (whose work he heavily influenced) as a major writer of supernatural fiction, whose talent shone most brightly in that genre. His finest work almost certainly was *The King in Yellow* (1895), a collection of short stories connected by a fictional work titled *The King in Yellow* that drives everyone who reads it insane.

Another of his works remembered today, if largely unread, is *The Tracer of Lost Persons* (1906), significant for having inspired one of the most popular radio programs of that medium's golden age, *Mr. Keen, Tracer of Lost Persons,* a crime drama that ran from 1937 to 1955. With 1,690 episodes broadcast nationally, it is easily the longest-running private detective series with a namesake character; the closest competitors are *Nick Carter, Master Detective* (726 episodes) and *The Adventures of Sherlock Holmes* (657 episodes). The show's background song was "Someday I'll Find You." The program was so well known that it became a popular parody for the iconic radio comedians Bob and Ray, who regularly featured skits involving "Mr. Trace, Keener than Most Persons."

One of the most successful writers of his era, with best-selling novels and numerous stories written for the highest-paying magazines, Chambers largely abandoned supernatural fiction for the romance story, though he also produced a good deal of mystery fiction, notably the stories in *The Mystery of Choice* (1897) and such novels as *In Secret* (1919), *The Moonlit Way* (1919), *The Mystery Lady* (1925), and *Secret Service Operator 13* (1934), which served as the basis for the 1934 MGM film titled *Operator 13* (released in England as *Spy 13*), a Civil War story of a Union spy (played by Marion Davies) impersonating a black maid whose mission becomes complicated when she falls in love with a Confederate officer (played by Gary Cooper).

"The Purple Emperor" was originally published in *The Mystery of Choice* (New York: Appleton, 1897).

• • •

Un souvenir heureux est peut-être, sur terre,
Plus vrai que le bonheur.

—A. de Musset.

I.

THE PURPLE EMPEROR watched me in silence. I cast again, spinning out six feet more of waterproof silk, and, as the line hissed through the air far across the pool, I saw my three flies fall on the water like drifting thistledown. The Purple Emperor sneered.

"You see," he said, "I am right. There is not a trout in Brittany that will rise to a tailed fly."

"They do in America," I replied.

"Zut! for America!" observed the Purple Emperor.

"And trout take a tailed fly in England," I insisted sharply.

"Now do I care what things or people do in England?" demanded the Purple Emperor.

"You don't care for anything except yourself and your wriggling caterpillars," I said, more annoyed than I had yet been.

The Purple Emperor sniffed. His broad, hairless, sunburnt features bore that obstinate expression which always irritated me. Perhaps the manner in which he wore his hat intensified the irritation, for the flapping brim rested on both ears, and the two little velvet ribbons which hung from the silver buckle in front wiggled and fluttered with every trivial breeze. His cunning eyes and sharp-pointed nose were out of all keeping with his fat red face. When he met my eye, he chuckled.

"I know more about insects than any man in Morbihan—or Finistère either, for that matter," he said.

"The Red Admiral knows as much as you do," I retorted.

"He doesn't," replied the Purple Emperor angrily.

"And his collection of butterflies is twice as large as yours," I added, moving down the stream to a spot directly opposite him.

"It is, is it?" sneered the Purple Emperor. "Well, let me tell you, Monsieur Darrel, in all his collection he hasn't a specimen, a single specimen, of that magnificent butterfly, Apatura Iris, commonly known as the 'Purple Emperor.'"

"Everybody in Brittany knows that," I said, casting across the sparkling water; "but just because you happen to be the only man who ever captured a 'Purple Emperor' in Morbihan, it doesn't follow that you are an authority on sea-trout flies. Why do you say that a Breton sea-trout won't touch a tailed fly?"

"It's so," he replied.

"Why? There are plenty of May-flies about the stream."

"Let 'em fly!" snarled the Purple Emperor, "you won't see a trout touch 'em."

My arm was aching, but I grasped my split bamboo more firmly, and, half turning, waded out into the stream and began to whip the ripples at the head of the pool. A great green dragon-fly came drifting by on the summer breeze and hung a moment above the pool, glittering like an emerald.

"There's a chance! Where is your butterfly net?" I called across the stream.

"What for? That dragon-fly? I've got dozens—Anax Junius, Drury, characteristic, anal angle of posterior wings, in male, round; thorax marked with—"

"That will do," I said fiercely. "Can't I point out an insect in the air without this burst of erudition? Can you tell me, in simple everyday French, what this little fly is—this one, flitting over the eel grass here beside me? See, it has fallen on the water."

"Huh!" sneered the Purple Emperor, "that's a Linnobia annulus."

"What's that?" I demanded.

Before he could answer there came a heavy splash in the pool, and the fly disappeared.

"He! he! he!" tittered the Purple Emperor. "Didn't I tell you the fish knew their business? That was a sea-trout. I hope you don't get him."

He gathered up his butterfly net, collecting box, chloroform bottle, and cyanide jar. Then he rose, swung the box over his shoulder, stuffed the poison bottles into the pockets of his silver-buttoned velvet coat, and lighted his pipe. This latter operation was a demoralizing spectacle, for the Purple Emperor, like all Breton peasants, smoked one of those microscopical Breton pipes which requires ten minutes to find, ten minutes to fill, ten minutes to light, and ten seconds to finish. With true Breton stolidity he went through this solemn rite, blew three puffs of smoke into the air, scratched his pointed nose reflectively, and waddled away, calling back an ironical "Au revoir, and bad luck to all Yankees!"

I watched him out of sight, thinking sadly of the young girl whose life he made a hell upon earth—Lys Trevec, his niece. She never admitted it, but we all knew what the black-and-blue marks meant on her soft, round arm, and it made me sick to see the look of fear come into her eyes when the Purple Emperor waddled into the café of the Groix Inn.

It was commonly said that he half-starved her. This she denied. Marie Joseph and 'Fine Lelocard had seen him strike her the day after the Pardon of the Birds because she had liberated three bullfinches which he had limed the day before. I asked Lys if this were true, and she refused to speak to me for the rest of the week. There was nothing to do about it. If the Purple Emperor had not been avaricious, I should never have seen Lys at all, but he could not resist the thirty francs a week which I offered him; and Lys posed for me all day long, happy as a linnet in a pink thorn hedge. Nevertheless, the Purple Emperor hated me, and constantly threatened to send Lys back to her dreary flax-spinning. He was suspicious, too, and when he had gulped down the single glass of cider which proves fatal to the sobriety of most Bretons, he would pound the long, discolored oaken table and roar curses on me, on Yves Terrec, and on the Red Admiral. We were the three objects in the world which he most hated: me, because I was a foreigner, and didn't care a rap for him and his butterflies; and the Red Admiral, because he was a rival entomologist.

He had other reasons for hating Terrec.

The Red Admiral, a little wizened wretch, with a badly adjusted glass eye and a passion for brandy, took his name from a butterfly which predominated in his collection. This butterfly, commonly known to amateurs as the "Red Admiral," and to entomologists as Vanessa Atalanta, had been the occasion of scandal among the entomologists of France and Brittany. For the Red Admiral had taken one of these common insects, dyed it a brilliant yellow by the aid of chemicals, and palmed it off on a credulous collector as a South African species, absolutely unique. The fifty francs which he gained by this rascality were, however, absorbed in a suit for damages brought by the outraged amateur a month later; and when he had sat in the Quimperlé jail for a month, he reappeared in the little village of St. Gildas soured, thirsty, and burning for revenge. Of course we named him the Red Admiral, and he accepted the name with suppressed fury.

The Purple Emperor, on the other hand, had gained his imperial title legitimately, for it was an undisputed fact that the only specimen of that beautiful butterfly, Apatura Iris, or the Purple Emperor, as it is called by amateurs — the only specimen that had ever been taken in Finistère or in Morbihan — was captured and brought home alive by Joseph Marie Gloanec, ever afterward to be known as the Purple Emperor.

When the capture of this rare butterfly became known the Red Admiral nearly went crazy. Every day for a week he trotted over to the Groix Inn, where the Purple Emperor lived with his niece, and brought his microscope to bear on the rare newly captured butterfly, in hopes of detecting a fraud. But this specimen was genuine, and he leered through his microscope in vain.

"No chemicals there, Admiral," grinned the Purple Emperor; and the Red Admiral chattered with rage.

To the scientific world of Brittany and France the capture of an Apatura Iris in Morbihan was of great importance. The Museum of Quimper offered to purchase the butterfly, but the Purple Emperor, though a hoarder of gold, was a monomaniac on butterflies, and he jeered at the Curator of the Museum. From all parts of Brittany and France letters of inquiry and congratulation poured in upon him. The French Academy of Sciences awarded him a prize, and the Paris Entomological Society made him an honorary member. Being a Breton peasant, and a more than commonly pig-headed one at that, these honors did not disturb his equanimity; but when the little hamlet of St. Gildas elected him mayor, and, as is the custom in Brittany under such circumstances, he left his thatched house to take up an official life in the little Groix Inn, his head became completely turned. To be mayor in a village of nearly one hundred and fifty people! It was an empire! So he became unbearable, drinking himself viciously drunk every night of his life, maltreating his niece, Lys Trevec, like the barbarous old wretch that he was, and driving the Red Admiral nearly frantic with his eternal harping on the capture of Apatura Iris. Of course he refused to tell where he had caught the butterfly. The Red Admiral stalked his footsteps, but in vain.

"He! he! he!" nagged the Purple Emperor, cuddling his chin over a glass of cider; "I saw you sneaking about the St. Gildas spinny yesterday morning. So you think you can find another Apatura Iris by running after me? It won't do, Admiral, it won't do, d'ye see?"

The Red Admiral turned yellow with mortification and envy, but the next day he actually took to his bed, for the Purple Emperor had brought home not a butterfly but a live chrysalis, which, if successfully hatched, would become a perfect specimen of the invaluable Apatura Iris. This was the last straw. The Red Admiral shut himself up in his little stone cottage, and for weeks now he had been invisible to everybody except 'Fine Lelocard who carried him a loaf of bread and a mullet or langouste every morning.

The withdrawal of the Red Admiral from the society of St. Gildas excited first the derision and finally the suspicion of the Purple Emperor. What deviltry could he be hatching? Was he experimenting with chemicals again, or was he engaged in some deeper plot, the object of which was to discredit the Purple Emperor? Roux, the postman, who carried the mail on foot once a day from Bannalec, a distance of fifteen miles each way, had brought several suspicious letters, bearing English stamps, to the Red Admiral, and the next day the Admiral had been observed at his window grinning up into the sky and rubbing his hands together. A night or two after this apparition the postman left two packages at the Groix Inn for a moment while he ran across the way to drink a glass of cider with me. The Purple Emperor, who was roaming about the café, snooping into everything that did not concern him, came upon the packages and examined the postmarks and addresses. One of the packages was square and heavy, and felt like a book. The other was also square, but very light, and felt like a pasteboard box. They were both addressed to the Red Admiral, and they bore English stamps.

When Roux, the postman, came back, the Purple Emperor tried to pump him, but the poor little postman knew nothing about the contents of the packages, and after he had taken them around the corner to the cottage of the Red Admiral the Purple Emperor ordered a glass of cider, and deliberately fuddled himself until Lys came in and tearfully supported him to his room. Here he became so abusive and brutal that Lys called to me, and I went and settled the trouble without wasting any words. This also the Purple Emperor remembered, and waited his chance to get even with me.

That had happened a week ago, and until to-day he had not deigned to speak to me.

Lys had posed for me all the week, and today being Saturday, and I lazy, we had decided to take a little relaxation, she to visit and gossip with her little black-eyed friend Yvette in the neighboring hamlet of St. Julien, and I to try the appetites of the Breton trout with the contents of my American fly book.

I had thrashed the stream very conscientiously for three hours, but not a trout had risen to my cast, and I was piqued. I had begun to believe that there were no trout in the St. Gildas stream, and would probably have given up had I not seen the sea-trout snap the little fly which the Purple Emperor had named so scientifically. That set me thinking. Probably the Purple Emperor was right, for he certainly was an expert in everything that crawled and wriggled in Brittany. So I matched, from my American fly book, the fly that the sea-trout had snapped up, and withdrawing the cast of three, knotted a new leader to the silk and slipped a fly on the loop. It was a queer fly. It was one of those unnamable experiments which fascinate anglers in sporting stores and which generally prove utterly useless. Moreover, it was a tailed fly, but of course I easily remedied that with a stroke of my penknife. Then I was all ready, and I stepped out into the hurrying rapids and cast straight as an arrow to the spot where the sea-trout had risen. Lightly as a plume the fly settled on the bosom of the pool; then came a startling splash, a gleam of silver, and the line tightened from the vibrating rod-tip to the shrieking reel. Almost instantly I checked the fish, and as he floundered for a moment, making the water boil along his glittering sides, I sprang to the bank again, for I saw that the fish was a heavy one and I should probably be in for a long run down the stream. The five-ounce rod swept in a splendid circle, quivering under the strain. "Oh, for a gaff-hook!" I said aloud, for I was now firmly convinced that I had a salmon to deal with, and no sea-trout at all.

Then as I stood, bringing every ounce to bear on the sulking fish, a lithe, slender girl came hurriedly along the opposite bank calling out to me by name.

"Why, Lys!" I said, glancing up for a second, "I thought you were at St. Julien with Yvette."

"Yvette has gone to Bannalec. I went home and found an awful fight going on at the Groix Inn, and I was so frightened that I came to tell you."

The fish dashed off at that moment, carrying all the line my reel held, and I was compelled to follow him at a jump. Lys, active and graceful as a young deer, in spite of her Pont-Aven sabots, followed along the opposite bank until the fish settled in a deep pool, shook the line savagely once or twice, and then relapsed into the sulks.

"Fight at the Groix Inn?" I called across the water. "What fight?"

"Not exactly fight," quavered Lys, "but the Red Admiral has come out of his house at last, and he and my uncle are drinking together and disputing about butterflies. I never saw my uncle so angry, and the Red Admiral is sneering and grinning. Oh, it is almost wicked to see such a face!"

"But Lys," I said, scarcely able to repress a smile, "your uncle and the Red Admiral are always quarreling and drinking."

"I know — oh, dear me! — but this is different, Monsieur Darrel. The Red Admiral has grown old and fierce since he shut himself up three weeks ago, and — oh, dear! I never saw such a look in my uncle's eyes before. He seemed insane with fury. His eyes — I can't speak of it — and then Terrec came in."

"Oh," I said more gravely, "that was unfortunate. What did the Red Admiral say to his son?"

Lys sat down on a rock among the ferns, and gave me a mutinous glance from her blue eyes.

Yves Terrec, loafer, poacher, and son of Louis Jean Terrec, otherwise the Red Admiral, had been kicked out by his father, and had also been forbidden the village by the Purple Emperor, in his majestic capacity of mayor. Twice the young ruffian had returned: once to rifle the bedroom of the Purple Emperor — an unsuccessful enterprise — and another time to rob his own father. He succeeded in the latter attempt, but was never caught, although he was frequently seen roving about the forests and moors with his gun. He openly menaced the Purple Emperor; vowed that he would marry Lys in spite of all the gendarmes in Quimperlé; and these same gendarmes he led many a long chase through briar-filled swamps and over miles of yellow gorse.

What he did to the Purple Emperor — what he intended to do — disquieted me but little; but I worried over his threat concerning Lys. During the last three months this had bothered me a great deal; for when Lys came to St. Gildas from the convent the first thing she captured was my heart. For a long time I had refused to believe that any tie of blood linked this dainty blue-eyed creature with the Purple Emperor. Although she dressed in the velvet-laced bodice and blue petticoat of Finistère, and wore the bewitching white coif of St. Gildas, it seemed like a pretty masquerade. To me she was as sweet and as gently bred as many a maiden of the noble Faubourg who danced with her cousins at a Louis XV fête champêtre. So when Lys said that Yves Terrec had returned openly to St. Gildas, I felt that I had better be there also.

"What did Terrec say, Lys?" I asked, watching the line vibrating above the placid pool.

The wild rose color crept into her cheeks. "Oh," she answered, with a little toss of her chin, "you know what he always says."

"That he will carry you away?"

"Yes."

"In spite of the Purple Emperor, the Red Admiral, and the gendarmes?"

"Yes."

"And what do you say, Lys?"

"I? Oh, nothing."

"Then let me say it for you."

Lys looked at her delicate pointed sabots, the sabots from Pont-Aven, made to order. They fitted her little foot. They were her only luxury.

"Will you let me answer for you, Lys?" I asked.

"You, Monsieur Darrel?"

"Yes. Will you let me give him his answer?"

"Mon Dieu, why should you concern yourself, Monsieur Darrel?"

The fish lay very quiet, but the rod in my hand trembled.

"Because I love you, Lys."

The wild rose color in her cheeks deepened; she gave a gentle gasp, then hid her curly head in her hands.

"I love you, Lys."

"Do you know what you say?" she stammered.

"Yes, I love you."

She raised her sweet face and looked at me across the pool.

"I love you," she said, while the tears stood like stars in her eyes. "Shall I come over the brook to you?"

II.

THAT NIGHT YVES Terrec left the village of St. Gildas vowing vengeance against his father, who refused him shelter.

I can see him now, standing in the road, his bare legs rising like pillars of bronze from his straw-stuffed sabots, his short velvet jacket torn and soiled by exposure and dissipation, and his eyes, fierce, roving, bloodshot—while the Red Admiral squeaked curses on him, and hobbled away into his little stone cottage.

"I will not forget you!" cried Yves Terrec, and stretched out his hand toward his father with a terrible gesture. Then he whipped his gun to his cheek and took a short step forward, but I caught him by the throat before he could fire, and a second later we were rolling in the dust of the Bannalec road. I had to hit him a heavy blow behind the ear before he would let go, and then, rising and shaking myself, I dashed his muzzle-loading fowling piece to bits against a wall, and threw his knife into the river. The Purple Emperor was looking on with a queer light in his eyes. It was plain that he was sorry Terrec had not choked me to death.

"He would have killed his father," I said, as I passed him, going toward the Groix Inn.

"That's his business," snarled the Purple Emperor. There was a deadly light in his eyes. For a moment I thought he was going to attack me; but he was merely viciously drunk, so I shoved him out of my way and went to bed, tired and disgusted.

The worst of it was I couldn't sleep, for I feared that the Purple Emperor might begin to abuse Lys. I lay restlessly tossing among the sheets until I could stay there no longer. I did not dress entirely; I merely slipped on a pair of chaussons and sabots, a pair of knickerbockers, a jersey, and a cap. Then, loosely tying a handkerchief about my throat, I went down the worm-eaten stairs and out into the moonlit road. There was a candle flaring in the Purple Emperor's window, but I could not see him.

"He's probably dead drunk," I thought, and looked up at the window where, three years before, I had first seen Lys.

"Asleep, thank Heaven!" I muttered, and wandered out along the road. Passing the small cottage of the Red Admiral, I saw that it was dark, but the door was open. I stepped inside the hedge to shut it, thinking, in case Yves Terrec should be roving about, his father would lose whatever he had left.

Then after fastening the door with a stone, I wandered on through the dazzling Breton moonlight. A nightingale was singing in a willow swamp below, and from the edge of the mere, among the tall swamp grasses, myriads of frogs chanted a bass chorus.

When I returned, the eastern sky was beginning to lighten, and across the meadows on the cliffs, outlined against the paling horizon, I saw a seaweed gatherer going to his work among the curling breakers on the coast. His long rake was balanced on his shoulder, and the sea wind carried his song across the meadows to me:

St. Gildas!
St. Gildas!
Pray for us,
Shelter us,
Us who toil in the sea.

Passing the shrine at the entrance of the village, I took off my cap and knelt in prayer to Our Lady of Faöuet; and if I neglected myself in that prayer, surely I believed Our Lady of Faöuet would be kinder to Lys. It is said that the shrine casts white shadows. I looked, but saw only the moonlight. Then very peacefully I went to bed again, and was only awakened by the clank of sabers and the trample of horses in the road below my window.

"Good gracious!" I thought, "it must be eleven o'clock, for there are the gendarmes from Quimperlé."

I looked at my watch; it was only half-past eight, and as the gendarmes made their rounds every Thursday at eleven, I wondered what had brought them out so early to St. Gildas.

"Of course," I grumbled, rubbing my eyes, "they are after Terrec," and I jumped into my limited bath.

Before I was completely dressed I heard a timid knock, and opening my door, razor in hand, stood astonished and silent. Lys, her blue eyes wide with terror, leaned on the threshold.

"My darling!" I cried, "what on earth is the matter?" But she only clung to me, panting like a wounded sea gull. At last, when I drew her into the room and raised her face to mine, she spoke in a heart-breaking voice:

"Oh, Dick! they are going to arrest you, but I will die before I believe one word of what they say. No, don't ask me," and she began to sob desperately.

When I found that something really serious was the matter, I flung on my coat and cap, and, slipping one arm about her waist, went down the stairs and out into the road. Four gendarmes sat on their horses in front of the café door; beyond them, the entire population of St. Gildas gaped, ten deep.

"Hello, Durand!" I said to the brigadier, "what the devil is this I hear about arresting me?"

"It's true, mon ami," replied Durand with sepulchral sympathy. I looked him over from the tip of his spurred boots to his sulfur-yellow saber belt, then upward, button by button, to his disconcerted face.

"What for?" I said scornfully. "Don't try any cheap sleuth work on me! Speak up, man, what's the trouble?"

The Purple Emperor, who sat in the doorway staring at me, started to speak, but thought better of it and got up and went into the house. The gendarmes rolled their eyes mysteriously and looked wise.

"Come, Durand," I said impatiently, "what's the charge?"

"Murder," he said in a faint voice.

"What!" I cried incredulously. "Nonsense! Do I look like a murderer? Get off your horse, you stupid, and tell me who's murdered."

Durand got down, looking very silly, and came up to me, offering his hand with a propitiatory grin.

"It was the Purple Emperor who denounced you! See, they found your handkerchief at his door—"

"Whose door, for Heaven's sake?" I cried.

"Why, the Red Admiral's!"

"The Red Admiral's? What has he done?"

"Nothing—he's only been murdered."

I could scarcely believe my senses, although they took me over to the little stone cottage and pointed out the blood-spattered room. But the horror of the thing was that the corpse of the murdered man had disappeared, and there only remained a nauseating lake of blood on the stone floor, in the center of which lay a human hand. There was no doubt as to whom the hand belonged, for everybody who had ever seen the Red Admiral knew that the shriveled bit of flesh which lay in the thickening blood was the hand of the Red Admiral. To me it looked like the severed claw of some gigantic bird.

"Well," I said, "there's been murder committed. Why don't you do something?"

"What?" asked Durand.

"I don't know. Send for the Commissaire."

"He's at Quimperlé. I telegraphed."

"Then send for a doctor, and find out how long this blood has been coagulating."

"The chemist from Quimperlé is here; he's a doctor."

"What does he say?"

"He says that he doesn't know."

"And who are you going to arrest?" I inquired, turning away from the spectacle on the floor.

"I don't know," said the brigadier solemnly; "you are denounced by the Purple Emperor, because he found your handkerchief at the door when he went out this morning."

"Just like a pig-headed Breton!" I exclaimed, thoroughly angry. "Did he not mention Yves Terrec?"

"No."

"Of course not," I said. "He overlooked the fact that Terrec tried to shoot his father last night, and that I took away his gun. All that counts for nothing when he finds my handkerchief at the murdered man's door."

"Come into the café," said Durand, much disturbed, "we can talk it over, there. Of course, Monsieur Darrel, I have never had the faintest idea that you were the murderer!"

The four gendarmes and I walked across the road to the Groix Inn and entered the café. It was crowded with Bretons, smoking, drinking, and jabbering in half a dozen dialects, all equally unsatisfactory to a civilized ear; and I pushed through the crowd to where little Max Fortin, the chemist of Quimperlé, stood smoking a vile cigar.

"This is a bad business," he said, shaking hands and offering me the mate to his cigar, which I politely declined.

"Now, Monsieur Fortin," I said, "it appears that the Purple Emperor found my handkerchief near the murdered man's door this morning, and so he concludes"—here I glared at the Purple Emperor—"that I am the assassin. I will now ask him a question," and turning on him suddenly, I shouted, "What were you doing at the Red Admiral's door?"

The Purple Emperor started and turned pale, and I pointed at him triumphantly.

"See what a sudden question will do. Look how embarrassed he is, and yet I do not charge him with murder; and I tell you, gentlemen, that man there knows as well as I do who was the murderer of the Red Admiral!"

"I don't!" bawled the Purple Emperor.

"You do," I said. "It was Yves Terrec."

"I don't believe it," he said obstinately, dropping his voice.

"Of course not, being pig-headed."

"I am not pig-headed," he roared again, "but I am mayor of St. Gildas, and I do not believe that Yves Terrec killed his father."

"You saw him try to kill him last night?"

The mayor grunted.

"And you saw what I did."

He grunted again.

"And," I went on, "you heard Yves Terrec threaten to kill his father. You heard him curse the Red Admiral and swear to kill him. Now the father is murdered and his body is gone."

"And your handkerchief?" sneered the Purple Emperor.

"I dropped it, of course."

"And the seaweed gatherer who saw you last night lurking about the Red Admiral's cottage," grinned the Purple Emperor.

I was startled at the man's malice.

"That will do," I said. "It is perfectly true that I was walking on the Bannalec road last night, and that I stopped to close the Red Admiral's door, which was ajar, although his light was not burning. After that I went up the road to the Dinez Woods, and then walked over by St. Julien, whence I saw the seaweed gatherer on the cliffs. He was near enough for me to hear what he sang. What of that?"

"What did you do then?"

"Then I stopped at the shrine and said a prayer, and then I went to bed and slept until Brigadier Durand's gendarmes awoke me with their clatter."

"Now, Monsieur Darrel," said the Purple Emperor, lifting a fat finger and shooting a wicked glance at me, "Now, Monsieur Darrel, which did you wear last night on your midnight stroll — sabots or shoes?"

I thought a moment. "Shoes — no, sabots. I just slipped on my chaussons and went out in my sabots."

"Which was it, shoes or sabots?" snarled the Purple Emperor.

"Sabots, you fool."

"Are these your sabots?" he asked, lifting up a wooden shoe with my initials cut on the instep.

"Yes," I replied.

"Then how did this blood come on the other one?" he shouted, and held up a sabot, the mate to the first, on which a drop of blood had spattered.

"I haven't the least idea," I said calmly; but my heart was beating very fast and I was furiously angry.

"You blockhead!" I said, controlling my rage, "I'll make you pay for this when they catch Yves Terrec and convict him. Brigadier Durand, do your duty if you think I am under suspicion. Arrest me, but grant me one favor. Put me in the Red Admiral's cottage, and I'll see whether I can't find some clue that you have overlooked. Of course, I won't disturb anything until the Commissaire arrives. Bah! You all make me very ill."

"He's hardened," observed the Purple Emperor, wagging his head.

"What motive had I to kill the Red Admiral?" I asked them all scornfully. And they all cried:

"None! Yves Terrec is the man!"

Passing out of the door I swung around and shook my finger at the Purple Emperor.

"Oh, I'll make you dance for this, my friend," I said; and I followed Brigadier Durand across the street to the cottage of the murdered man.

III.

THEY TOOK ME at my word and placed a gendarme with a bared saber at the gateway by the hedge.

"Give me your parole," said poor Durand, "and I will let you go where you wish." But I refused, and began prowling about the cottage looking for clues. I found lots of things that some people would have considered most important, such as ashes from the Red Admiral's pipe, footprints in a dusty vegetable bin, bottles smelling of Pouldu cider, and dust — oh, lots of dust! — but I was not an expert, only a stupid, everyday amateur; so I defaced the footprints with my thick shooting boots, and I declined to examine the pipe ashes through a microscope, although the Red Admiral's microscope stood on the table close at hand.

At last I found what I had been looking for, some long wisps of straw, curiously depressed and flattened in the middle, and I was certain I had found the evidence that would settle Yves Terrec for the rest of his life. It was plain as the nose on your face. The straws were sabot straws, flattened where the foot had pressed them, and sticking straight out where they projected beyond the sabot. Now nobody in St. Gildas used straw in sabots except a fisherman who lived near St. Julien, and the straw in his sabots was ordinary yellow wheat straw! This straw, or rather these straws, were from the stalks of the red wheat which only grows inland, and which, everybody in St. Gildas knew, Yves Terrec wore in his sabots. I was perfectly satisfied; and when, three hours later, a hoarse shouting from the Bannalec road brought me to the window, I was not surprised to see Yves Terrec, bloody, disheveled, hatless, with his strong arms bound behind him, walking with bent head between two mounted gendarmes. The crowd around him swelled every minute, crying: "Parricide! parricide! Death to the murderer!" As he passed my window I saw great clots of mud on his dusty sabots, from the heels of which projected wisps of red wheat straw. Then I walked back into the Red Admiral's study, determined to find what the microscope would show on the wheat straws. I examined each one very carefully, and then, my eyes aching, I rested my chin on my hand and leaned back in the chair. I had not been as fortunate as some detectives, for there was no evidence that the straws had ever been used in a sabot at all. Furthermore, directly across the hallway stood a carved Breton chest, and now I noticed for the first time that, from beneath the closed lid, dozens of similar red wheat straws projected, bent exactly as mine were bent by the lid.

I yawned in disgust. It was apparent that I was not cut out for a detective, and I bitterly pondered over the difference between clues in real life and clues in a detective story. After a while I rose, walked over to the chest and opened the lid. The interior was wadded with the red wheat straws, and on this wadding lay two curious glass jars, two or three small vials, several empty bottles labeled chloroform, a collecting jar of cyanide of potassium, and a book. In a farther corner of the chest were some letters bearing English stamps, and also the torn coverings of two parcels, all from England, and all directed to the Red Admiral under his proper name of "Sieur Louis Jean Terrec, St. Gildas, par Moëlan, Finistère."

All these traps I carried over to the desk, shut the lid of the chest, and sat down to read the letters. They were written in commercial French, evidently by an Englishman.

Freely translated, the contents of the first letter were as follows:

LONDON, June 12, 1894.

DEAR MONSIEUR (*sic*): Your kind favor of the 19th inst. received and contents noted. The latest work on the Lepidoptera of England is Blowzer's How to Catch British Butterflies, with notes and tables, and an introduction by Sir Thomas Sniffer. The price of this work (in one volume, calf) is £5 or 125 francs of French money. A post-office order will receive our prompt attention. We beg to remain,

Yours, etc.,
FRADLEY & TOOMER,
470 Regent Square, London, S.W.

The next letter was even less interesting. It merely stated that the money had been received and the book would be forwarded. The third engaged my attention, and I shall quote it, the translation being a free one:

DEAR SIR: Your letter of the 1st of July was duly received, and we at once referred it to Mr. Fradley himself. Mr. Fradley being much interested in your question, sent your letter to Professor Schweineri, of the Berlin Entomological Society, whose note Blowzer refers to on page 630, in his How to Catch British Butterflies. We have just received an answer from Professor Schweineri, which we translate into French — (see enclosed slip). Professor Schweineri begs to present to you two jars of cythyl, prepared under his own supervision. We forward the same to you. Trusting that you will find everything satisfactory, we remain,

Yours sincerely,
FRADLEY & TOOMER.

The enclosed slip read as follows:

> Messrs. FRADLEY & TOOMER,
>
> GENTLEMEN: Cythaline, a complex hydrocarbon, was first used by Professor Schnoot, of Antwerp, a year ago. I discovered an analogous formula about the same time and named it cythyl. I have used it with great success everywhere. It is as certain as a magnet. I beg to present you three small jars, and would be pleased to have you forward two of them to your correspondent in St. Gildas with my compliments. Blowzer's quotation of me, on page 630 of his glorious work, How to Catch British Butterflies, is correct.
>
> Yours, etc.
> HEINRICH SCHWEINERI,
> P.H.D., D.D., D.S., M.S.

When I had finished this letter I folded it up and put it into my pocket with the others. Then I opened Blowzer's valuable work, *How to Catch British Butterflies,* and turned to page 630.

Now, although the Red Admiral could only have acquired the book very recently, and although all the other pages were perfectly clean, this particular page was thumbed black, and heavy pencil marks enclosed a paragraph at the bottom of the page. This is the paragraph:

> Professor Schweineri says: "Of the two old methods used by collectors for the capture of the swift-winged, high-flying Apatura Iris, or Purple Emperor, the first, which was using a long-handled net, proved successful once in a thousand times; and the second, the placing of bait upon the ground, such as decayed meat, dead cats, rats, etc., was not only disagreeable, even for an enthusiastic collector, but also very uncertain. Once in five hundred times would the splendid butterfly leave the tops of his favorite oak trees to circle about the fetid bait offered. I have found cythyl a perfectly sure bait to draw this beautiful butterfly to the ground, where it can be easily captured. An ounce of cythyl placed in a yellow saucer under an oak tree, will draw to it every Apatura Iris within a radius of twenty miles. So, if any collector who possesses a little cythyl, even though it be in a sealed bottle in his pocket — if such a collector does not find a single Apatura Iris fluttering close about him within an hour, let him be satisfied that the Apatura Iris does not inhabit his country."

When I had finished reading this note I sat for a long while thinking hard. Then I examined the two jars. They were labeled *"Cythyl."* One was full, the other *nearly full.* "The rest must be on the corpse of the Red Admiral," I thought, "no matter if it is in a corked bottle — "

I took all the things back to the chest, laid them carefully on the straw, and closed the lid. The gendarme sentinel at the gate saluted me respectfully as I crossed over to the Groix Inn. The inn was surrounded by an excited crowd, and the hallway was choked with gendarmes and peasants. On every side they greeted me cordially, announcing that the real murderer was caught; but I pushed by them without a word and ran upstairs to find Lys. She opened her door when I knocked and threw both arms about my neck. I took her to my breast and kissed her. After a moment I asked her if she would obey me no matter what I commanded, and she said she would, with a proud humility that touched me.

"Then go at once to Yvette in St. Julien," I said. "Ask her to harness the dog-cart and drive you to the convent in Quimperlé. Wait for me there. Will you do this without questioning me, my darling?"

She raised her face to mine. "Kiss me," she said innocently; the next moment she had vanished.

I walked deliberately into the Purple Emperor's room and peered into the gauze-covered box which held the chrysalis of Apatura Iris. It was as I expected. The chrysalis was empty and transparent, and a great crack ran down the middle of its back, but, on the netting inside the box, a magnificent butterfly slowly waved its burnished purple wings; for the chrysalis had given up its silent tenant, the butterfly symbol of immortality. Then a great fear fell upon me. I know now that it was the fear of the Black Priest, but neither then nor for years after did I know that the Black Priest had ever lived on earth. As I bent over the box I heard a confused murmur outside the house which ended in a furious shout of "Parricide!" and I heard the gendarmes ride away behind a wagon which rattled sharply on the flinty highway. I went to the window. In the wagon sat Yves Terrec, bound and wild-eyed, two gendarmes at either side of him, and all around the wagon rode mounted gendarmes whose bared sabers scarcely kept the crowd away.

"Parricide!" they howled. "Let him die!"

I stepped back and opened the gauze-covered box. Very gently but firmly I took the splendid butterfly by its closed fore wings and lifted it unharmed between my thumb and forefinger. Then, holding it concealed behind my back, I went down into the café.

Of all the crowd that had filled it, shouting for the death of Yves Terrec, only three persons remained seated in front of the huge empty fireplace. They were the Brigadier Durand, Max Fortin, the chemist of Quimperlé, and the Purple Emperor. The latter looked abashed when I entered, but I paid no attention to him and walked straight to the chemist.

"Monsieur Fortin," I said, "do you know much about hydrocarbons?"

"They are my specialty," he said, astonished.

"Have you ever heard of such thing as cythyl?"

"Schweineri's cythyl? Oh, yes! We use it in perfumery."

"Good!" I said. "Has it an odor?"

"No — and yes. One is always aware of its presence, but nobody can affirm it has an odor. It is curious," he continued, looking at me, "it is very curious you should have asked me that, for all day I have been imagining I detected the presence of cythyl."

"Do you imagine so now?" I asked.

"Yes, more than ever."

I sprang to the front door and tossed out the butterfly. The splendid creature beat the air for a moment, flitted uncertainly hither and thither, and then, to my astonishment, sailed majestically back into the café and alighted on the hearthstone. For a moment I was nonplussed, but when my eyes rested on the Purple Emperor I comprehended in a flash.

"Lift that hearthstone!" I cried to the Brigadier Durand; "pry it up with your scabbard!"

The Purple Emperor suddenly fell forward in his chair, his face ghastly white, his jaw loose with terror.

"What is cythyl?" I shouted, seizing him by the arm; but he plunged heavily from his chair, face downward on the floor, and at the moment a cry from the chemist made me turn. There stood the Brigadier Durand, one hand supporting the hearthstone, one hand raised in horror. There stood Max Fortin, the chemist, rigid with excitement, and below, in the hollow bed where the hearthstone had rested, lay a crushed mass of bleeding human flesh, from the midst of which stared a cheap glass eye. I seized the Purple Emperor and dragged him to his feet.

"Look!" I cried; "look at your old friend, the Red Admiral!" but he only smiled in a vacant way, and rolled his head muttering, "Bait for butterflies! Cythyl! Oh, no, no, no! You can't do it, Admiral, d'ye see. I alone own the Purple Emperor! I alone am the Purple Emperor!"

And the same carriage that bore me to Quimperlé to claim my bride, carried him to Quimper, gagged and bound, a foaming, howling lunatic.

This, then, is the story of the Purple Emperor. I might tell you a pleasanter story if I chose; but concerning the fish that I had hold of, whether it was a salmon, a grilse, or a sea-trout, I may not say, because I have promised Lys, and she has promised me, that no power on earth shall wring from our lips the mortifying confession that the fish escaped.

1898

EDWARD BELLAMY

AT PINNEY'S RANCH

The second best-selling American novel of the nineteenth century (after Harriet Beecher Stowe's *Uncle Tom's Cabin*) was *Looking Backward* (1888), by EDWARD BELLAMY (1850–1898). It remains charmingly readable today, as Bellamy's style was simple, straightforward, and idealistic. Although it is frequently described as a Utopian socialist work, its espousal of pure state capitalism with complete nationalization of all private industry has more in common with a totalitarian state similar to fascism. Bellamy claimed to have written *Looking Backward* as a depiction of "enlightened self-interest and wholesale common sense," a "literary fantasy, a fairy tale of social felicity" rather than a call to political activism, but it did, in fact, serve as a rallying point for groups called Bellamy Clubs, which led to the Nationalist Party, eventually drawing the author himself to the cause. *Looking Backward* sold more than a million copies before the turn of the century. Bellamy was encouraged to write a sequel and did, a decade later, but *Equality* (1897) was more a sociological tract than a novel.

Bellamy was involved in several careers, passing the bar exam (although never practicing), then becoming a newspaper editor, but he wanted to be a writer and in 1873 began a magazine serial, *The Duke of Stockbridge*. He never completed the novel; it was published posthumously with an ending produced by a different author. Two early novels, *Dr. Heidenhoff's Process* (1880) and *Miss Ludington's Sister* (1884), were concerned with psychic phenomena, in which he was extremely interested, as the present story illustrates. Curiously, another of his short stories, "Two Days' Solitary Imprisonment," has an almost identical premise to that of "At Pinney's Ranch," with both of the protagonists reeling with guilt about being unfairly suspected of having committed a murder. The latter story was selected for this collection as it is slightly more believable than the former — though barely.

"At Pinney's Ranch" was first published in the author's collection *The Blindman's World and Other Stories* (Boston: Houghton Mifflin, 1898).

• • •

John Lansing first met Mary Hollister at the house of his friend Pinney, whose wife was her sister. She had soft gray eyes, a pretty color in her cheeks, rosy lips, and a charming figure. In the course of the evening somebody suggested mind-reading as a pastime, and Lansing, who had some powers, or supposed powers, in that direction, although he laughed at them himself, experimented in turn with the ladies. He failed with nearly every subject until it came Mary Hollister's turn. As she placed her soft palm in his, closed her eyes, and gave herself up to his influence, he knew that he should succeed with her, and so he did. She proved a remarkably sympathetic subject, and Lansing was himself surprised, and the spectators fairly thrilled, by the feats he was able to perform by her aid. After that evening he met her often, and there was more equally remarkable mind-reading; and then mind-reading was dropped for heart-reading, and the old, old story they read in each other's hearts had more fascination for them than the new science. Having once discovered that their hearts beat in unison, they took no more interest in the relation of their minds.

The action proper of this story begins four years after their marriage, with a very shocking event, — nothing less than the murder of Austin Flint, who was found dead one morning in the house in which he lived alone. Lansing had no hand in the deed, but he might almost as well have had; for, while absolutely guiltless, he was caught in one of those nets of circumstance which no foresight can avoid, whereby innocent men are sometimes snared helplessly, and delivered over to a horrid death. There had been a misunderstanding between him and the dead man, and only a couple of days before the murder, they had exchanged blows on the street. When Flint was found dead, in the lack of any other clue, people thought of Lansing. He realized that this was so, and remained silent as to a fact which otherwise he would have testified to at the inquest, but which he feared might now imperil him. He had been at Austin Flint's house the night of the murder, and might have committed it, so far as opportunity was concerned. In reality, the motive of his visit was anything but murderous. Deeply chagrined by the scandal of the fight, he had gone to Flint to apologize, and to make up their quarrel. But he knew very well that nobody would believe that this was his true object in seeking his enemy secretly by night, while the admission of the visit would complete a circumstantial evidence against him stronger than had often hanged men. He believed that no one but the dead man knew of the call, and that it would never be found out. He had not told his wife of it at the time, and still less afterward, on account of the anxiety she would feel at his position.

Two weeks passed, and he was beginning to breathe freely in the assurance of safety, when, like a thunderbolt from a cloud that seems to have passed over, the catastrophe came. A friend met him on the street one day, and warned him to escape while he could. It appeared that he had been seen to enter Flint's house that night. His concealment of the fact had been accepted as corroborating evidence of his guilt, and the police, who had shadowed him from the first, might arrest him at any moment. The conviction that he was guilty, which the friend who told him this evidently had, was a terrible comment on the desperateness of his position. He walked home as in a dream. His wife had gone out to a neighbor's. His little boy came to him, and clambered on his knee. "Papa, what makes your face so wet?" he asked, for there were great drops on his forehead. Then his wife came in, her face white, her eyes full of horror. "Oh, John!" she exclaimed. "They say you were at Mr. Flint's that night, and they are going to arrest you. Oh, John, what does it mean? Why don't you speak? I shall go mad, if you do not speak. You were not there! Tell me that you were not there!" The ghastly face he raised to hers might well have seemed to confess everything. At least she seemed to take it so, and in a fit of hysterical weeping sank to the floor, and buried her face in her hands upon a chair. The children, alarmed at the scene, began to cry. It was growing dark, and as he looked out of the window, Lansing saw an officer and a number of other persons approaching the house. They were coming to arrest him. Animal terror, the instinct of self-preservation, seized upon his faculties, stunned and demoralized as he was by the suddenness with which this calamity had come upon him. He opened the door and fled, with a score of men and boys yelling in pursuit. He ran wildly, blindly, making incredible leaps and bounds over obstacles. As men sometimes do in nightmares, he argued with himself, as he ran, whether this could possibly be a waking experience, and inclined to think that it could not. It must be a dream. It was too fantastically horrible to be anything else.

Presently he saw just before him the eddying, swirling current of the river, swollen by a freshet. Still half convinced that he was in a nightmare, and, if he could but shake it off, should awake in his warm bed, he plunged headlong in, and was at once swirled out of sight of his pursuers beneath the darkening sky. A blow from a floating object caused him to throw up his arms, and, clutching something solid, he clambered upon a shed carried away by the freshet from an up-river farm. All night he drifted with the swift current, and in the morning landed in safety thirty miles below the village from which he had fled for life.

So John Lansing, for no fault whatever except an error of judgment, if even it was that, was banished from home, and separated from his family almost as hopelessly as if he were dead. To return would be to meet an accusation of murder to which his flight had added overwhelming weight. To write to his wife might be to put the officers of the law, who doubtless watched her closely, upon his scent.

Under an assumed name he made his way to the far West, and, joining the rush to the silver mines of Colorado, was among the lucky ones. At the end of three years he was a rich man. What he had made the money for, he could not tell, except that the engrossment of the struggle had helped him to forget his wretchedness. Not that he ever did forget it. His wife and babies, from whose embraces he had been so suddenly torn, were always in his thoughts. Above all, he could not forget the look of horror in his wife's eyes in that last terrible scene. To see her again, and convince her, if not others, that he was innocent, was a need which so grew upon him that, at the end of three years, he determined to take his life in his hand and return home openly. This life of exile was not worth living.

One day, in the course of setting his affairs in order for his return, he was visiting a mining camp remote from the settlements, when a voice addressed him by his old name, and looking around he saw Pinney. The latter's first words, as soon as his astonishment and delight had found some expression, assured Lansing that he was no longer in danger. The murderer of Austin Flint had been discovered, convicted, and hanged two years previous. As for Lansing, it had been taken for granted that he was drowned when he leaped into the river, and there had been no further search for him. His wife had been broken-hearted ever since, but she and the children were otherwise well, according to the last letters received by Pinney, who, with his wife, had moved out to Colorado a year previous.

Of course Lansing's only idea now was to get home as fast as steam could carry him; but they were one hundred miles from the railroad, and the only communication was by stage. It would get up from the railroad the next day, and go back the following morning. Pinney took Lansing out to his ranch, some miles from the mining camp, to pass the interval. The first thing he asked Mrs. Pinney was if she had a photograph of his wife. When she brought him one, he durst not look at it before his hosts. Not till he had gone to his room and locked the door did he trust himself to see again the face of his beloved Mary.

That evening Mrs. Pinney told him how his wife and children had fared in his absence. Her father had helped them at first, but after his death Mary had depended upon needlework for support, finding it hard to make the two ends meet.

Lansing groaned at hearing this, but Mrs. Pinney comforted him. It was well worth while having troubles, she said, if they could be made up to one, as all Mary's would be to her when she saw her husband.

The upcoming stage brought the mail, and next day Pinney rode into camp to get his weekly newspaper, and engage a passage down the next morning for Lansing. The day dragged terribly to the latter, who stayed at the ranch. He was quite unfit for any social purpose, as Mrs. Pinney, to whom a guest in that lonely place was a rare treat, found to her sorrow, though indeed she could not blame him for being poor company. He passed hours, locked in his room, brooding over Mary's picture. The rest of the day he spent wandering about the place, smiling and talking to himself like an imbecile, as he dreamed of the happiness so soon to crown his trials. If he could have put himself in communication with Mary by telegraph during this period of waiting, it would have been easier to get through, but the nearest telegraph station was at the railroad. In the afternoon he saddled a horse and rode about the country, thus disposing of a couple of hours.

When he came back to the house, he saw that Pinney had returned, for his horse was tethered to a post of the front piazza. The doors and windows of the living-room were open, and as he reached the front door, he heard Pinney and his wife talking in agitated tones.

"Oh, how could God let such an awful thing happen?" she was exclaiming, in a voice broken by hysterical sobbing. "I'm sure there was never anything half so horrible before. Just as John was coming home to her, and she worshiping him so, and he her! Oh, it will kill him! Who is going to tell him? Who can tell him?"

"He must not be told to-day," said Pinney's voice. "We must keep it from him at least for to-day."

Lansing entered the room. "Is she dead?" he asked quietly. He could not doubt, from what he had overheard, that she was.

"God help him! He'll have to know it now," exclaimed Pinney.

"Is she dead?" repeated Lansing.

"No, she isn't dead."

"Is she dying, then?"

"No, she is well."

"It's the children, then?"

"No," answered Pinney. "They are all right."

"Then, in God's name, what is it?" demanded Lansing, unable to conceive what serious evil could have happened to him, if nothing had befallen his wife and babies.

"We can't keep it from him now," said Pinney to his wife. "You'll have to give him her letter."

"Can't you tell me what it is? Why do you keep me in suspense?" asked Lansing, in a voice husky with a dread he knew not of what.

"I can't, man. Don't ask me!" groaned Finney. "It's better that you should read it."

Mrs. Finney's face expressed an agony of compassion as, still half clutching it, she held out a letter to Lansing. "John, oh, John," she sobbed; "remember, she's not to blame! She doesn't know."

The letter was in his wife's handwriting, addressed to Mrs. Pinney, and read as follows:

> You will be surprised by what I am going to tell you. You, who know how I loved John, must have taken it for granted that I would never marry again. Not that it could matter to him. Too well I feel the gulf between the dead and living to fancy that his peace could be troubled by any of the weaknesses of mortal hearts. Indeed, he often used to tell me that, if he died, he wanted me to marry again, if ever I felt like doing so; but in those happy days I was always sure that I should be taken first. It was he who was to go first, though, and now it is for the sake of his children that I am going to do what I never thought I could. I am going to marry again. As they grow older and need more, I find it impossible for me to support them, though I do not mind how hard I work, and would wear my fingers to the bone rather than take any other man's name after being John's wife. But I cannot care for them as they should be cared for. Johnny is now six, and ought to go to school, but I cannot dress him decently enough to send him. Mary has outgrown all her clothes, and I cannot get her more. Her feet are too tender to go bare, and I cannot buy her shoes. I get less and less sewing since the new dressmaker came to the village, and soon shall have none. We live, oh so plainly! For myself I should not care, but the children are growing and need better food. They are John's children, and for their sake I have brought myself to do what I never could have done but for them. I have promised to marry Mr. Whitcomb. I have not deceived him as to why alone I marry him. He has promised to care for the children as his own, and to send Johnny to college, for I know his father would have wanted him to go. It will be a very quiet wedding, of

course. Mr. Whitcomb has had some cards printed to send to a few friends, and I enclose one to you. I cannot say that I wish you could be present, for it will be anything but a joyful day to me. But when I meet John in heaven, he will hold me to account for the children he left me, and this is the only way by which I can provide for them. So long as it is well with them, I ought not to care for myself.

Your sister,
MARY LANSING.

The card announced that the wedding would take place at the home of the bride, at six o'clock on the afternoon of the 27th of June.

It was June 27 that day, and it was nearly five o'clock. "The Lord help you!" ejaculated Pinney, as he saw, by the ashen hue which overspread Lansing's face, that the full realization of his situation had come home to him. "We meant to keep it from you till to-morrow. It might be a little easier not to know it till it was over than now, when it is going on, and you not able to lift a finger to stop it."

"Oh, John," cried Mrs. Pinney once more; "remember, she doesn't know!" and, sobbing hysterically, she fled from the room, unable to endure the sight of Lansing's face.

He had fallen into a chair, and was motionless, save for the slow and labored breathing which shook his body. As he sat there in Pinney's ranch this pleasant afternoon, the wife whom he worshiped never so passionately as now, at their home one thousand miles away, was holding another man by the hand, and promising to be his wife.

It was five minutes to five by the clock on the wall before him. It therefore wanted but five minutes of six, the hour of the wedding, at home, the difference in time being just an hour. In the years of his exile, by way of enhancing the vividness of his dreams of home, he had calculated exactly the difference in time from various points in Colorado, so that he could say to himself, "Now Mary is putting the babies to bed"; "Now it is her own bedtime"; "Now she is waking up"; or "Now the church-bells are ringing, and she is walking to church." He was accustomed to carry these two standards of time always in his head, reading one by the other, and it was this habit, bred of doting fondness, which now would compel him to follow, as if he were a spectator, minute by minute, each step of the scene being enacted so far away.

People were prompt at weddings. No doubt already the few guests were arriving, stared at by the neighbors from their windows. The complacent bridegroom was by this time on his way to the home of the bride, or perhaps knocking at the door. Lansing knew him well, an elderly, well-to-do furniture-maker, who had been used to express a fatherly admiration for Mary. The bride was upstairs in her chamber, putting the finishing touches to her toilet; or, at this very moment, it might be, was descending the stairs to take the bridegroom's arm and go in to be married.

Lansing gasped. The mountain wind was blowing through the room, but he was suffocating.

Pinney's voice, seeming to come from very far away, was in his ears. "Rouse yourself, for God's sake! Don't give it all up that way. I believe there's a chance yet. Remember the mind-reading you used to do with her. You could put almost anything into her mind by just willing it there. That's what I mean. Will her to stop what she is doing now. Perhaps you may save her yet. There's a chance you may do it. I don't say there's more than a chance, but there's that. There's a bare chance. That's better than giving up. I've heard of such things being done. I've read of them. Try it, for God's sake! Don't give up."

At any previous moment of his life the suggestion that he could, by mere will power, move the mind of a person a thousand miles away, so as to reverse a deliberate decision, would have appeared to Lansing as wholly preposterous as no doubt it does to any who read these lines. But a man, however logical he may be on land, will grasp at a straw when drowning, as if it were a log. Pinney had no need to use arguments or adjurations to induce Lansing to adopt his suggestion. The man before him was in no mood to balance probabilities against improbabilities. It was enough that the project offered a chance of success, albeit infinitesimal; for on the other hand there was nothing but an intolerable despair, and a fate that truly seemed more than flesh and blood could bear.

Lansing had sprung to his feet while Pinney was speaking. "I'm going to try it, and may God Almighty help me!" he cried, in a terrible voice.

"Amen!" echoed Pinney.

Lansing sank into his chair again, and sat leaning slightly forward, in a rigid attitude. The expression of his eyes at once became fixed. His features grew tense, and the muscles of his face stood out. As if to steady the mental strain by a physical one, he had taken from the table a horseshoe which had lain there, and held it in a convulsive grip.

Pinney had made this extraordinary suggestion in the hope of diverting Lansing's mind for a moment from his terrible situation, and with not so much faith even as he feigned that it would be of any practical avail. But now, as he looked upon the ghastly face before him, and realized the tremendous concentration of purpose, the agony of will, which it expressed, he was impressed that it would not be marvelous if some marvel should be the issue. Certainly, if the will really had any such power as Lansing was trying to exert, as so many theorists maintained, there could never arise circumstances better calculated than these to call forth a supreme assertion of the faculty. He went out of the room on tiptoe, and left his friend alone to fight this strange and terrible battle with the powers of the air for the honor of his wife and his own.

There was little enough need of any preliminary effort on Lansing's part to fix his thoughts upon Mary. It was only requisite that to the intensity of the mental vision, with which he had before imagined her, should be added the activity of the will, turning the former mood of despair into one of resistance. He knew in what room of their house the wedding party must now be gathered, and was able to represent to himself the scene there as vividly as if he had been present. He saw the relatives assembled; he saw Mr. Davenport, the minister, and, facing him, the bridal couple, in the only spot where they could well stand, before the fireplace. But from all the others, from the guests, from the minister, from the bridegroom, he turned his thoughts, to fix them on the bride alone. He saw her as if through the small end of an immensely long telescope, distinctly, but at an immeasurable distance. On this face his mental gaze was riveted, as by conclusive efforts his will strove to reach and move hers against the thing that she was doing. Although his former experiments in mental phenomena had in a measure familiarized him with the mode of addressing his powers to such an undertaking as this, yet the present effort was on a scale so much vaster that his will for a time seemed appalled, and refused to go out from him, as a bird put forth from a ship at sea returns again and again before daring to essay the distant flight to land. He felt that he was gaining nothing. He was as one who beats the air. It was all he could do to struggle against the influences that tended to deflect and dissipate his thoughts. Again and again a conviction of the uselessness of the attempt, of the madness of imagining that a mere man could send a wish, like a voice, across a continent, laid its paralyzing touch upon his will, and nothing but a sense of the black horror which failure meant enabled him to throw it off. If he but once admitted the idea of failing, all was lost. He must believe that he could do this thing, or he surely could not. To question it was to surrender his wife; to despair was to abandon her to her fate. So, as a wrestler strains against a mighty antagonist, his will strained and tugged in supreme stress against the impalpable obstruction of space, and, fighting despair with despair, doggedly held to its purpose, and sought to keep his faculties unremittingly streaming to one end. Finally, as this tremendous effort, which made minutes seem hours, went on, there came a sense of efficiency, the feeling of achieving something. From this consciousness was first born a faith, no longer desperate, but rational, that he might succeed, and with faith came an instantaneous tenfold multiplication of force. The overflow of energy lost the tendency to dissipation and became steady. The will appeared to be getting the mental faculties more perfectly in hand, if the expression may be used, not only concentrating but fairly fusing them together by the intensity with which it drove them to their object. It was time. Already, perhaps, Mary was about to utter the vows that would give her to another. Lansing's lips moved. As if he were standing at her side, he murmured with strained and labored utterance ejaculations of appeal and adjuration.

Then came the climax of the stupendous struggle. He became aware of a sensation so amazing that I know not if it can be described at all — a sensation comparable to that which comes up the mile-long sounding-line, telling that it touches bottom. Fainter far, as much finer as is mind than matter, yet not less unmistakable, was the thrill which told the man, agonizing on that lonely mountain of Colorado, that the will which he had sent forth to touch the mind of another, a thousand miles away, had found its resting-place, and the chain between them was complete. No longer projected at random into the void, but as if it sent along an established medium of communication, his will now seemed to work upon hers, not uncertainly and with difficulty, but as if in immediate contact. Simultaneously, also, its mood changed. No more appealing, agonizing, desperate, it became insistent, imperious, dominating. For only a few moments it remained at this pitch, and then, the mental tension suddenly relaxing, he aroused to a perception of his surroundings, of which toward the last he had become oblivious. He was drenched with perspiration and completely exhausted. The iron horseshoe which he had held in his hands was drawn halfway out.

Thirty-six hours later, Lansing, accompanied by Pinney, climbed down from the stage at the railroad station. During the interval Lansing had neither eaten nor slept. If at moments in that time he was able to indulge the hope that his tremendous experiment had been successful, for the main part the overwhelming presumption of common sense and common experience against such a notion made it seem childish folly to entertain it.

At the station was to be sent the dispatch, the reply to which would determine Mary's fate and his own. Pinney signed it, so that, if the worst were true, Lansing's existence might still remain a secret; for of going back to her in that case, to make her a sharer of his shame, there was no thought on his part. The dispatch was addressed to Mr. Davenport, Mary's minister, and merely asked if the wedding had taken place.

They had to wait two hours for the answer. When it came, Lansing was without on the platform, and Pinney was in the office. The operator mercifully shortened his suspense by reading the purport of the message from the tape: "The dispatch in answer to yours says that the wedding did not take place."

Pinney sprang out upon the platform. At sight of Lansing's look of ghastly questioning, the tears blinded him, and he could not speak, but the wild exultation of his face and gestures was speech enough.

The second day following, Lansing clasped his wife to his breast, and this is the story she told him, interrupted with weepings and shudderings and ecstatic embraces of reassurance. The reasons which had determined her, in disregard of the dictates of her own heart, to marry again, have been sufficiently intimated in her letter to Mrs. Pinney. For the rest, Mr. Whitcomb was a highly respectable man, whom she esteemed and believed to be good and worthy. When the hour set for the marriage arrived, and she took her place by his side before the minister and the guests, her heart indeed was like lead, but her mind calm and resolved. The preliminary prayer was long, and it was natural, as it went on, that her thoughts should go back to the day when she had thus stood by another's side. She had ado to crowd back the scalding tears, as she contrasted her present mood of resignation with the mingling of virginal timidity and the abandon of love in her heart that other day. Suddenly, seeming to rise out of this painful contrast of the past and the present, a feeling of abhorrence for the act to which she was committed possessed her mind. She had all along shrunk from it, as any sensitive woman might from a marriage without love, but there had been nothing in that shrinking to compare in intensity with this uncontrollable aversion which now seized upon her to the idea of holding a wife's relation to the man by her side. It had all at once come over her that she could not do it. Nevertheless she was a sensible and rational woman as well as a sweet and lovely one. Whatever might be the origin of this sudden repugnance, she knew it had none in reason. She was fulfilling a promise which she had maturely considered, and neither in justice to herself nor the man to whom she had given it could she let a purely hysterical attack like this prevent its consummation. She called reason and common sense to her aid, and resolutely struggled to banish the distressing fancies that assailed her. The moisture stood out upon her forehead with the severity of the conflict, which momentarily increased. At last the minister ended his prayer, of which she had not heard a word. The bridal pair were bidden to take each other by the hand. As the bridegroom's fingers closed around hers, she could not avoid a shudder as at a loathsome contact. It was only by a supreme effort of self-control that she restrained from snatching her hand away with a scream. She did not hear what the minister went on to say. Every faculty was concentrated on the struggle, which had now become one of desperation, to repress an outbreak of the storm that was raging within. For, despite the shuddering protest of every instinct and the wild repulsion with which every nerve tingled, she was determined to go through the ceremony. But though the will in its citadel still held out, she knew that it could not be for long. Each wave of emotion that it withstood was higher, stronger, than the last. She felt that it was going, going. She prayed that the minister might be quick, while yet she retained a little self-command, and give her an opportunity to utter some binding vow which should make good her solemn engagement, and avert the scandal of the outbreak on the verge of which she was trembling.

"Do you," said the minister to Mr. Whitcomb, "take this woman whom you hold by the hand to be your wife, to honor, protect, and love while you live?"

"I do," replied the bridegroom promptly.

"Do you," said the minister, looking at Mary, "take the man whom you hold by the hand to be your husband, to love and honor while you live?"

Mary tried to say "Yes," but at the effort there surged up against it an opposition that was almost tangible in its overpowering force. No longer merely operating upon her sensibilities, the inexplicable influence that was conquering her now seized on her physical functions, and laid its interdict upon her tongue. Three times she strove to throw off the incubus, to speak, but in vain. Great drops were on her forehead; she was deadly pale, and her eyes were wild and staring; her features twitched as in a spasm, while she stood there struggling with the invisible power that sealed her lips. There was a sudden movement among the spectators; they were whispering together. They saw that something was wrong.

"Do you thus promise?" repeated the minister, after a pause.

"Nod, if you can't speak," murmured the bridegroom. His words were the hiss of a serpent in her ears. Her will resisted no longer; her soul was wholly possessed by unreasoning terror of the man and horror of the marriage.

"No! no! no!" she screamed in piercing tones, and snatching her hand from the bridegroom, she threw herself upon the breast of the astonished minister, sobbing wildly as she clung to him, "Save me, save me! Take me away! I can't marry him — I can't! Oh, I can't!"

The wedding broke up in confusion, and that is the way, if you choose to think so, that John Lansing, one thousand miles away, saved his wife from marrying another man.

"If you choose to think so," I say, for it is perfectly competent to argue that the influence to which Mary Lansing yielded was merely an hysterical attack, not wholly strange at such a moment in the case of a woman devoted to her first husband, and reluctantly consenting to second nuptials. On this theory, Lansing's simultaneous agony at Pinney's ranch in Colorado was merely a coincidence; interesting, perhaps, but unnecessary to account for his wife's behavior. That John and Mary Lansing should reject with indignation this simple method of accounting for their great deliverance is not at all surprising in view of the common proclivity of people to be impressed with the extraordinary side of circumstances which affect themselves; nor is there any reason why their opinion of the true explanation of the facts should be given more weight than another's. The writer, who has merely endeavored to put this story into narrative form, has formed no opinion on it which is satisfactory to himself, and therefore abstains from any effort to influence the reader's judgment.

1898

STEPHEN CRANE

THE BLUE HOTEL

One of America's first great realist and naturalist novelists, STEPHEN CRANE (1871–1900) is best known for *The Red Badge of Courage* (1895), a powerful Civil War novel, and his first book, *Maggie: A Girl of the Streets* (1893), which provided a sympathetic portrait of a prostitute and life in New York City's ghetto in the Bowery.

Crane began writing at an early age, publishing articles by the time he was sixteen, and was a prolific short story writer whose work is taught in most American literature courses. In little more than a decade of professional writing, he produced five novels, three short story collections, two volumes of war stories, two collections of poetry, and scores of stories uncollected at the time of his death. His most famous story, "The Open Boat," is largely based on his own life. The tale of four men lost on a lifeboat in the Atlantic Ocean paralleled his experience while working as a war correspondent during the Spanish-American War, when a ship that was taking him to Cuba sank and he and others spent nearly two days adrift in a dinghy. The debilitating heat and deprivations contributed to his death at the age of twenty-eight.

His other most widely read stories include "The Bride Comes to Yellow Sky," "The Monster," and "The Blue Hotel," which is far more complex than it seems at first reading. While apparently the story of a man, the unnamed "Swede," who fears that he's going to be killed in the western town to which he has just traveled, it is also a tale of fear, overblown bravado, and, ultimately, cowardice.

Crane was enormously influential to other American writers, notably Ernest Hemingway, whose *A Farewell to Arms* clearly owes so much to *The Red Badge of Courage*. In 1936, in *The Green Hills of Africa*, Hemingway wrote that "the good writers are Henry James, Stephen Crane, and Mark Twain. That's not the order they're good in. There is no order for good writers."

"The Blue Hotel" was first published in the November 26, 1898, issue of *Collier's Weekly;* it was first published in book form in Crane's short story collection *The Monster and Other Stories* (New York: Harper & Brothers, 1899).

• • •

I

THE PALACE HOTEL at Fort Romper was painted a light blue, a shade that is on the legs of a kind of heron, causing the bird to declare its position against any background. The Palace Hotel, then, was always screaming and howling in a way that made the dazzling winter landscape of Nebraska seem only a gray swampish hush. It stood alone on the prairie, and when the snow was falling the town two hundred yards away was not visible. But when the traveler alighted at the railway station he was obliged to pass the Palace Hotel before he could come upon the company of low clapboard houses which composed Fort Romper, and it was not to be thought that any traveler could pass the Palace Hotel without looking at it. Pat Scully, the proprietor, had proved himself a master of strategy when he chose his paints. It is true that on clear days, when the great trans-continental expresses, long lines of swaying Pullmans, swept through Fort Romper, passengers were overcome at the sight, and the cult that knows the brown-reds and the subdivisions of the dark greens of the East expressed shame, pity, horror, in a laugh. But to the citizens of this prairie town, and to the people who would naturally stop there, Pat Scully had performed a feat. With this opulence and splendor, these creeds, classes, egotisms, that streamed through Romper on the rails day after day, they had no color in common.

As if the displayed delights of such a blue hotel were not sufficiently enticing, it was Scully's habit to go every morning and evening to meet the leisurely trains that stopped at Romper and work his seductions upon any man that he might see wavering, gripsack in hand. One morning, when a snow-crusted engine dragged its long string of freight cars and its one passenger coach to the station, Scully performed the marvel of catching three men. One was a shaky and quick-eyed Swede, with a great shining cheap valise; one was a tall bronzed cowboy, who was on his way to a ranch near the Dakota line; one was a little silent man from the East, who didn't look it, and didn't announce it. Scully practically made them prisoners. He was so nimble and merry and kindly that each probably felt it would be the height of brutality to try to escape. They trudged off over the creaking board sidewalks in the wake of the eager little Irishman. He wore a heavy fur cap squeezed tightly down on his head. It caused his two red ears to stick out stiffly, as if they were made of tin.

At last, Scully, elaborately, with boisterous hospitality, conducted them through the portals of the blue hotel. The room which they entered was small. It seemed to be merely a proper temple for an enormous stove, which, in the center, was humming with godlike violence. At various points on its surface the iron had become luminous and glowed yellow from the heat. Beside the stove Scully's son Johnnie was playing High-Five with an old farmer who had whiskers both gray and sandy. They were quarreling. Frequently the old farmer turned his face toward a box of sawdust — colored brown from tobacco juice — that was behind the stove, and spat with an air of great impatience and irritation. With a loud flourish of words Scully destroyed the game of cards, and bustled his son upstairs with part of the baggage of the new guests. He himself conducted them to three basins of the coldest water in the world. The cowboy and the Easterner burnished themselves fiery red with this water, until it seemed to be some kind of a metal polish. The Swede, however, merely dipped his fingers gingerly and with trepidation. It was notable that throughout this series of small ceremonies the three travelers were made to feel that Scully was very benevolent. He was conferring great favors upon them. He handed the towel from one to the other with an air of philanthropic impulse.

Afterwards they went to the first room, and, sitting about the stove, listened to Scully's officious clamor at his daughters, who were preparing the midday meal. They reflected in the silence of experienced men who tread carefully amid new people. Nevertheless, the old farmer, stationary, invincible in his chair near the warmest part of the stove, turned his face from the sawdust box frequently and addressed a glowing commonplace to the strangers. Usually he was answered in short but adequate sentences by either the cowboy or the Easterner. The Swede said nothing. He seemed to be occupied in making furtive estimates of each man in the room. One might have thought that he had the sense of silly suspicion which comes to guilt. He resembled a badly frightened man.

Later, at dinner, he spoke a little, addressing his conversation entirely to Scully. He volunteered that he had come from New York, where for ten years he had worked as a tailor. These facts seems to strike Scully as fascinating, and afterwards he volunteered that he had lived at Romper for fourteen years. The Swede asked about the crops and the price of labor. He seemed barely to listen to Scully's extended replies. His eyes continued to rove from man to man.

Finally, with a laugh and a wink, he said that some of these Western communities were very dangerous; and after his statement he straightened his legs under the table, tilted his head, and laughed again, loudly.

It was plain that the demonstration had no meaning to the others. They looked at him wondering and in silence.

II

As the men trooped heavily back into the front room, the two little windows presented views of a turmoiling sea of snow. The huge arms of the wind were making attempts — mighty, circular, futile — to embrace the flakes as they sped. A gate-post like a still man with a blanched face stood aghast amid this profligate fury. In a hearty voice Scully announced the presence of a blizzard. The guests of the blue hotel, lighting their pipes, assented with grunts of lazy masculine contentment. No island of the sea could be exempt in the degree of this little room with its humming stove. Johnnie, son of Scully, in a tone which defined his opinion of his ability as a card-player, challenged the old farmer of both gray and sandy whiskers to a game of High-Five. The farmer agreed with a contemptuous and bitter scoff. They sat close to the stove, and squared their knees under a wide board. The cowboy and the Easterner watched the game with interest. The Swede remained near the window, aloof, but with a countenance that showed signs of an inexplicable excitement.

The play of Johnnie and the gray-beard was suddenly ended by another quarrel. The old man arose while casting a look of heated scorn at his adversary. He slowly buttoned his coat, and then stalked with fabulous dignity from the room. In the discreet silence of all other men the Swede laughed. His laughter rang somehow childish. Men by this time had begun to look at him askance, as if they wished to inquire what ailed him.

A new game was formed jocosely. The cowboy volunteered to become the partner of Johnnie, and they all then turned to ask the Swede to throw in his lot with the little Easterner. He asked some questions about the game, and learning that it wore many names, and that he had played it when it was under an alias, he accepted the invitation. He strode toward the men nervously, as if he expected to be assaulted. Finally, seated, he gazed from face to face and laughed shrilly. This laugh was so strange that the Easterner looked up quickly, the cowboy sat intent and with his mouth open, and Johnnie paused, holding the cards with still fingers.

Afterwards there was a short silence. Then Johnnie said: "Well, let's get at it. Come on now!" They pulled their chairs forward until their knees were bunched under the board. They began to play, and their interest in the game caused the others to forget the manner of the Swede.

The cowboy was a board-whacker. Each time that he held superior cards he whanged them, one by one, with exceeding force, down upon the improvised table, and took the tricks with a glowing air of prowess and pride that sent thrills of indignation into the hearts of his opponents. A game with a board-whacker in it is sure to become intense. The countenances of the Easterner and the Swede were miserable whenever the cowboy thundered down his aces and kings, while Johnnie, his eyes gleaming with joy, chuckled and chuckled.

Because of the absorbing play none considered the strange ways of the Swede. They paid strict heed to the game. Finally, during a lull caused by a new deal, the Swede suddenly addressed Johnnie: "I suppose there have been a good many men killed in this room." The jaws of the others dropped and they looked at him.

"What in hell are you talking about?" said Johnnie.

The Swede laughed again his blatant laugh, full of a kind of false courage and defiance. "Oh, you know what I mean all right," he answered.

"I'm a liar if I do!" Johnnie protested. The card was halted, and the men stared at the Swede. Johnnie evidently felt that as the son of the proprietor he should make a direct inquiry. "Now, what might you be drivin' at, mister?" he asked. The Swede winked at him. It was a wink full of cunning. His fingers shook on the edge of the board. "Oh, maybe you think I have been to nowheres. Maybe you think I'm a tenderfoot?"

"I don't know nothin' about you," answered Johnnie, "and I don't give a damn where you've been. All I got to say is that I don't know what you're driving at. There hain't never been nobody killed in this room."

The cowboy, who had been steadily gazing at the Swede, then spoke. "What's wrong with you, mister?"

Apparently it seemed to the Swede that he was formidably menaced. He shivered and turned white near the corners of his mouth. He sent an appealing glance in the direction of the little Easterner. During these moments he did not forget to wear his air of advanced pot-valor. "They say they don't know what I mean," he remarked mockingly to the Easterner.

The latter answered after prolonged and cautious reflection. "I don't understand you," he said, impassively.

The Swede made a movement then which announced that he thought he had encountered treachery from the only quarter where he had expected sympathy, if not help. "Oh, I see you are all against me. I see—"

The cowboy was in a state of deep stupefaction. "Say," he cried, as he tumbled the deck violently down upon the board. "Say, what are you gittin' at, hey?"

The Swede sprang up with the celerity of a man escaping from a snake on the floor. "I don't want to fight!" he shouted. "I don't want to fight!"

The cowboy stretched his long legs indolently and deliberately. His hands were in his pockets. He spat into the sawdust box. "Well, who the hell thought you did?" he inquired.

The Swede backed rapidly towards a corner of the room. His hands were out protectingly in front of his chest, but he was making an obvious struggle to control his fright. "Gentlemen," he quavered, "I suppose I am going to be killed before I can leave this house! I suppose I am going to be killed before I can leave this house!" In his eyes was the dying-swan look. Through the windows could be seen the snow turning blue in the shadow of dusk. The wind tore at the house and some loose thing beat regularly against the clap-boards like a spirit tapping.

A door opened, and Scully himself entered. He paused in surprise as he noted the tragic attitude of the Swede. Then he said, "What's the matter here?"

The Swede answered him swiftly and eagerly: "These men are going to kill me."

"Kill you!" ejaculated Scully. "Kill you! What are you talkin'?"

The Swede made the gesture of a martyr.

Scully wheeled sternly upon his son. "What is this, Johnnie?"

The lad had grown sullen. "Damned if I know," he answered. "I can't make no sense to it." He began to shuffle the cards, fluttering them together with an angry snap. "He says a good many men have been killed in this room, or something like that. And he says he's goin' to be killed here too. I don't know what ails him. He's crazy, I shouldn't wonder."

Scully then looked for explanation to the cowboy, but the cowboy simply shrugged his shoulders.

"Kill you?" said Scully again to the Swede. "Kill you? Man, you're off your nut."

"Oh, I know," burst out the Swede. "I know what will happen. Yes, I'm crazy—yes. Yes, of course, I'm crazy—yes. But I know one thing—" There was a sort of sweat of misery and terror upon his face. "I know I won't get out of here alive."

The cowboy drew a deep breath, as if his mind was passing into the last stages of dissolution. "Well, I'm dog-goned," he whispered to himself.

Scully wheeled suddenly and faced his son. "You've been troublin' this man!"

Johnnie's voice was loud with its burden of grievance. "Why, good Gawd, I ain't done nothin' to 'im."

The Swede broke in. "Gentlemen, do not disturb yourselves. I will leave this house. I will go away because" — he accused them dramatically with his glance — "because I do not want to be killed."

Scully was furious with his son. "Will you tell me what is the matter, you young divil? What's the matter, anyhow? Speak out!"

"Blame it!" cried Johnnie in despair, "don't I tell you I don't know. He — he says we want to kill him, and that's all I know. I can't tell what ails him."

The Swede continued to repeat: "Never mind, Mr. Scully, never mind. I will leave this house. I will go away, because I do not wish to be killed. Yes, of course, I am crazy — yes. But I know one thing! I will go away. I will leave this house. Never mind, Mr. Scully, never mind. I will go away."

"You will not go 'way," said Scully. "You will not go 'way until I hear the reason of this business. If anybody has troubled you I will take care of him. This is my house. You are under my roof, and I will not allow any peaceable man to be troubled here." He cast a terrible eye upon Johnnie, the cowboy, and the Easterner.

"Never mind, Mr. Scully; never mind. I will go away. I do not wish to be killed." The Swede moved towards the door, which opened upon the stairs. It was evidently his intention to go at once for his baggage.

"No, no," shouted Scully peremptorily; but the white-faced man slid by him and disappeared. "Now," said Scully severely, "what does this mane?"

Johnnie and the cowboy cried together: "Why, we didn't do nothin' to 'im!"

Scully's eyes were cold. "No," he said, "you didn't?"

Johnnie swore a deep oath. "Why, this is the wildest loon I ever see. We didn't do nothin' at all. We were jest sittin' here playin' cards and he —"

The father suddenly spoke to the Easterner. "Mr. Blanc," he asked, "what has these boys been doin'?"

The Easterner reflected again. "I didn't see anything wrong at all," he said at last, slowly.

Scully began to howl. "But what does it mane?" He stared ferociously at his son. "I have a mind to lather you for this, me boy."

Johnnie was frantic. "Well, what have I done?" he bawled at his father.

III

"I THINK YOU ARE tongue-tied," said Scully finally to his son, the cowboy, and the Easterner, and at the end of this scornful sentence he left the room.

Upstairs the Swede was swiftly fastening the straps of his great valise. Once his back happened to be half turned towards the door, and hearing a noise there, he wheeled and sprang up, uttering a loud cry. Scully's wrinkled visage showed grimly in the light of the small lamp he carried. This yellow effulgence, streaming upward, colored only his prominent features, and left his eyes, for instance, in mysterious shadow. He resembled a murderer.

"Man, man!" he exclaimed, "have you gone daffy?"

"Oh, no! Oh, no!" rejoined the other. "There are people in this world who know pretty nearly as much as you do — understand?"

For a moment they stood gazing at each other. Upon the Swede's deathly pale cheeks were two spots brightly crimson and sharply edged, as if they had been carefully painted. Scully placed the light on the table and sat himself on the edge of the bed. He spoke ruminatively. "By cracky, I never heard of such a thing in my life. It's a complete muddle. I can't for the soul of me think how you ever got this idea into your head." Presently he lifted his eyes and asked: "And did you sure think they were going to kill you?"

The Swede scanned the old man as if he wished to see into his mind. "I did," he said at last. He obviously suspected that this answer might precipitate an outbreak. As he pulled on a strap his whole arm shook, the elbow wavering like a bit of paper.

Scully banged his hand impressively on the foot-board of the bed. "Why, man, we're goin' to have a line of ilictric street-cars in this town next spring."

" 'A line of electric street-cars,' " repeated the Swede stupidly.

"And," said Scully, "there's a new railroad goin' to be built down from Broken Arm to here. Not to mintion the four churches and the smashin' big brick schoolhouse. Then there's the big factory, too. Why, in two years Romper'll be a met-tro-*pol*-is."

Having finished the preparation of his baggage, the Swede straightened himself. "Mr. Scully," he said with sudden hardihood, "how much do I owe you?"

"You don't owe me anythin'," said the old man angrily.

"Yes, I do," retorted the Swede.

He took seventy-five cents from his pocket and tendered it to Scully; but the latter snapped his fingers in disdainful refusal. However, it happened that they both stood gazing in a strange fashion at three silver pieces in the Swede's open palm.

"I'll not take your money," said Scully at last. "Not after what's been goin' on here." Then a plan seemed to strike him. "Here," he cried, picking up his lamp and moving towards the door. "Here! Come with me a minute."

"No," said the Swede, in overwhelming alarm.

"Yes," urged the old man. "Come on! I want you to come and see a picter—just across the hall—in my room."

The Swede must have concluded that his hour was come. His jaw dropped and his teeth showed like a dead man's. He ultimately followed Scully across the corridor, but he had the step of one hung in chains.

Scully flashed the light high on the wall of his own chamber. There was revealed a ridiculous photograph of a little girl. She was leaning against a balustrade of gorgeous decoration, and the formidable bang to her hair was prominent. The figure was as graceful as an upright sled-stake, and, withal, it was of the hue of lead. "There," said Scully tenderly, "that's the picter of my little girl that died. Her name was Carrie. She had the purtiest hair you ever saw! I was that fond of her, she—"

Turning then, he saw that the Swede was not contemplating the picture at all, but, instead, was keeping keen watch on the gloom in the rear.

"Look, man!" cried Scully heartily. "That's the picter of my little gal that died. Her name was Carrie. And then here's the picter of my oldest boy, Michael. He's a lawyer in Lincoln an' doin' well. I gave that boy a grand eddycation, and I'm glad for it now. He's a fine boy. Look at 'im now. Ain't he bold as blazes, him there in Lincoln, an honored an' respicted gintleman. An honored an' respicted gintleman," concluded Scully with a flourish. And so saying, he smote the Swede jovially on the back.

The Swede faintly smiled.

"Now," said the old man, "there's only one more thing." He dropped suddenly to the floor and thrust his head beneath the bed. The Swede could hear his muffled voice. "I'd keep it under me piller if it wasn't for that boy Johnnie. Then there's the old woman— Where is it now? I never put it twice in the same place. Ah, now come out with you!"

Presently he backed clumsily from under the bed, dragging with him an old coat rolled into a bundle. "I've fetched him," he muttered. Kneeling on the floor, he unrolled the coat and extracted from its heart a large yellow-brown whiskey bottle.

His first maneuver was to hold the bottle up to the light. Reassured, apparently, that nobody had been tampering with it, he thrust it with a generous movement towards the Swede.

The weak-kneed Swede was about to eagerly clutch this element of strength, but he suddenly jerked his hand away and cast a look of horror upon Scully.

"Drink," said the old man affectionately. He had arisen to his feet, and now stood facing the Swede.

There was a silence. Then again Scully said: "Drink!"

The Swede laughed wildly. He grabbed the bottle, put it to his mouth, and as his lips curled absurdly around the opening and his throat worked, he kept his glance, burning with hatred, upon the old man's face.

IV

After the departure of Scully the three men, with the cardboard still upon their knees, preserved for a long time an astounded silence. Then Johnnie said: "That's the dod-dangest Swede I ever see."

"He ain't no Swede," said the cowboy scornfully.

"Well, what is he then?" cried Johnnie. "What is he then?"

"It's my opinion," replied the cowboy deliberately, "he's some kind of a Dutchman." It was a venerable custom of the country to entitle as Swedes all light-haired men who spoke with a heavy tongue. In consequence the idea of the cowboy was not without its daring. "Yes, sir," he repeated. "It's my opinion this feller is some kind of a Dutchman."

"Well, he says he's a Swede, anyhow," muttered Johnnie sulkily. He turned to the Easterner: "What do you think, Mr. Blanc?"

"Oh, I don't know," replied the Easterner.

"Well, what do you think makes him act that way?" asked the cowboy.

"Why, he's frightened!" The Easterner knocked his pipe against a rim of the stove. "He's clear frightened out of his boots."

"What at?" cried Johnnie and cowboy together.

The Easterner reflected over his answer.

"What at?" cried the others again.

"Oh, I don't know, but it seems to me this man has been reading dime-novels, and he thinks he's right out in the middle of it — the shootin' and stabbin' and all."

"But," said the cowboy, deeply scandalized, "this ain't Wyoming, ner none of them places. This is Nebrasker."

"Yes," added Johnnie, "an' why don't he wait till he gits *out West?*"

The traveled Easterner laughed. "It isn't different there even — not in these days. But he thinks he's right in the middle of hell."

Johnnie and the cowboy mused long.

"It's awful funny," remarked Johnnie at last.

"Yes," said the cowboy. "This is a queer game. I hope we don't git snowed in, because then we'd have to stand this here man bein' around with us all the time. That wouldn't be no good."

"I wish pop would throw him out," said Johnnie.

Presently they heard a loud stamping on the stairs, accompanied by ringing jokes in the voice of old Scully, and laughter, evidently from the Swede. The men around the stove stared vacantly at each other. "Gosh!" said the cowboy. The door flew open, and old Scully, flushed and anecdotal, came into the room. He was jabbering at the Swede, who followed him, laughing bravely. It was the entry of two roysterers from a banquet hall.

"Come now," said Scully sharply to the three seated men, "move up and give us a chance at the stove." The cowboy and the Easterner obediently sidled their chairs to make room for the newcomers. Johnnie, however, simply arranged himself in a more indolent attitude, and then remained motionless.

"Come! Git over, there," said Scully.

"Plenty of room on the other side of the stove," said Johnnie.

"Do you think we want to sit in the draft?" roared the father.

But the Swede here interposed with a grandeur of confidence. "No, no. Let the boy sit where he likes," he cried in a bullying voice to the father.

"All right! All right!" said Scully deferentially. The cowboy and the Easterner exchanged glances of wonder.

The five chairs were formed in a crescent about one side of the stove. The Swede began to talk; he talked arrogantly, profanely, angrily. Johnnie, the cowboy, and the Easterner maintained a morose silence, while old Scully appeared to be receptive and eager, breaking in constantly with sympathetic ejaculations.

Finally the Swede announced that he was thirsty. He moved in his chair, and said that he would go for a drink of water.

"I'll git it for you," cried Scully at once.

"No," said the Swede contemptuously. "I'll get it for myself." He arose and stalked with the air of an owner off into the executive parts of the hotel.

As soon as the Swede was out of hearing Scully sprang to his feet and whispered intensely to the others. "Upstairs he thought I was tryin' to poison 'im."

"Say," said Johnnie, "this makes me sick. Why don't you throw 'im out in the snow?"

"Why, he's all right now," declared Scully. "It was only that he was from the East and he thought this was a tough place. That's all. He's all right now."

The cowboy looked with admiration upon the Easterner. "You were straight," he said, "You were on to that there Dutchman."

"Well," said Johnnie to his father, "he may be all right now, but I don't see it. Other time he was scared, but now he's too fresh."

Scully's speech was always a combination of Irish brogue and idiom, Western twang and idiom, and scraps of curiously formal diction taken from the story-books and newspapers. He now hurled a strange mass of language at the head of his son. "What do I keep? What do I keep? What do I keep?" he demanded in a voice of thunder. He slapped his knee impressively, to indicate that he himself was going to make reply, and that all should heed. "I keep a hotel," he shouted. "A hotel, do you mind? A guest under my roof has sacred privileges. He is to be intimidated by none. Not one word shall he hear that would prijudice him in favor of goin' away. I'll not have it. There's no place in this here town where they can say they iver took in a guest of mine because he was afraid to stay here." He wheeled suddenly upon the cowboy and the Easterner. "Am I right?"

"Yes, Mr. Scully," said the cowboy, "I think you're right."

"Yes, Mr. Scully," said the Easterner, "I think you're right."

V

AT SIX-O'CLOCK SUPPER, the Swede fizzed like a fire-wheel. He sometimes seemed on the point of bursting into riotous song, and in all his madness he was encouraged by old Scully. The Easterner was incased in reserve; the cowboy sat in wide-mouthed amazement, forgetting to eat, while Johnnie wrathily demolished great plates of food. The daughters of the house, when they were obliged to replenish the biscuits, approached as warily as Indians, and, having succeeded in their purpose, fled with ill-concealed trepidation. The Swede domineered the whole feast, and he gave it the appearance of a cruel bacchanal. He seemed to have grown suddenly taller; he gazed, brutally disdainful, into every face. His voice rang through the room. Once when he jabbed out harpoon-fashion with his fork to pinion a biscuit, the weapon nearly impaled the hand of the Easterner which had been stretched quietly out for the same biscuit.

After supper, as the men filed towards the other room, the Swede smote Scully ruthlessly on the shoulder. "Well, old boy, that was a good square meal." Johnnie looked hopefully at his father; he knew that shoulder was tender from an old fall; and indeed it appeared for a moment as if Scully was going to flame out over the matter, but in the end he smiled a sickly smile and remained silent. The others understood from his manner that he was admitting his responsibility for the Swede's new viewpoint.

Johnnie, however, addressed his parent in an aside. "Why don't you license somebody to kick you downstairs?" Scully scowled darkly by way of reply.

When they were gathered about the stove, the Swede insisted on another game of High-Five. Scully gently deprecated the plan at first, but the Swede turned a wolfish glare upon him. The old man subsided, and the Swede canvassed the others. In his tone there was always a great threat. The cowboy and the Easterner both remarked indifferently that they would play. Scully said that he would presently have to go to meet the 6.58 train, and so the Swede turned menacingly upon Johnnie. For a moment their glances crossed like blades, and then Johnnie smiled and said, "Yes, I'll play."

They formed a square, with the little board on their knees. The Easterner and the Swede were again partners. As the play went on, it was noticeable that the cowboy was not board-whacking as usual. Meanwhile,

Scully, near the lamp, had put on his spectacles and, with an appearance curiously like an old priest, was reading a newspaper. In time he went out to meet the 6.58 train, and, despite his precautions, a gust of polar wind whirled into the room as he opened the door. Besides scattering the cards, it chilled the players to the marrow. The Swede cursed frightfully. When Scully returned, his entrance disturbed a cozy and friendly scene. The Swede again cursed. But presently they were once more intent, their heads bent forward and their hands moving swiftly. The Swede had adopted the fashion of board-whacking.

Scully took up his paper and for a long time remained immersed in matters which were extraordinarily remote from him. The lamp burned badly, and once he stopped to adjust the wick. The newspaper as he turned from page to page rustled with a slow and comfortable sound. Then suddenly he heard three terrible words: "You are cheatin'!"

Such scenes often prove that there can be little of dramatic import in environment. Any room can present a tragic front; any room can be comic. This little den was now hideous as a torture-chamber. The new faces of the men themselves had changed it upon the instant. The Swede held a huge fist in front of Johnnie's face, while the latter looked steadily over it into the blazing orbs of his accuser. The Easterner had grown pallid; the cowboy's jaw had dropped in that expression of bovine amazement which was one of his important mannerisms. After the three words, the first sound in the room was made by Scully's paper as it floated forgotten to his feet. His spectacles had also fallen from his nose, but by a clutch he had saved them in air. His hand, grasping the spectacles, now remained poised awkwardly and near his shoulder. He stared at the card-players.

Probably the silence was while a second elapsed. Then, if the floor had been suddenly twitched out from under the men, they could not have moved quicker. The five had projected themselves headlong towards a common point. It happened that Johnnie, in rising to hurl himself upon the Swede, had stumbled slightly because of his curiously instinctive care for the cards and the board. The loss of the moment allowed time for the arrival of Scully, and also allowed the cowboy time to give the Swede a great push which sent him staggering back. The men found tongue together, and hoarse shouts or rage, appeal, or fear burst from every throat. The cowboy pushed and jostled feverishly at the Swede, and the Easterner and Scully clung wildly to Johnnie; but, through the smoky air, above the swaying bodies of the peace-compellers, the eyes of the two warriors ever sought each other in glances of challenge that were at once hot and steely.

Of course the board had been overturned, and now the whole company of cards was scattered over the floor, where the boots of the men trampled the fat and painted kings and queens as they gazed with their silly eyes at the war that was waging above them.

Scully's voice was dominating the yells. "Stop now! Stop, I say! Stop, now—"

Johnnie, as he struggled to burst through the rank formed by Scully and the Easterner, was crying, "Well, he says I cheated! He says I cheated! I won't allow no man to say I cheated! If he says I cheated, he's a —!"

The cowboy was telling the Swede, "Quit, now! Quit, d'ye hear—"

The screams of the Swede never ceased: "He did cheat! I saw him! I saw him—"

As for the Easterner, he was importuning in a voice that was not heeded: "Wait a moment, can't you? Oh, wait a moment. What's the good of a fight over a game of cards? Wait a moment—"

In this tumult no complete sentences were clear. "Cheat"—"Quit"—"He says"—these fragments pierced the uproar and rang out sharply. It was remarkable that whereas Scully undoubtedly made the most noise, he was the least heard of any of the riotous band.

Then suddenly there was a great cessation. It was as if each man had paused for breath, and although the room was still lighted with the anger of men, it could be seen that there was no danger of immediate conflict, and at once Johnnie, shouldering his way forward, almost succeeded in confronting the Swede. "What did you say I cheated for? What did you say I cheated for? I don't cheat and I won't let no man say I do!"

The Swede said, "I saw you! I saw you!"

"Well," cried Johnnie, "I'll fight any man what says I cheat!"

"No, you won't," said the cowboy. "Not here."

"Ah, be still, can't you?" said Scully, coming between them.

The quiet was sufficient to allow the Easterner's voice to be heard. He was repeating, "Oh, wait a moment, can't you? What's the good of a fight over a game of cards? Wait a moment!"

Johnnie, his red face appearing above his father's shoulder, hailed the Swede again. "Did you say I cheated?"

The Swede showed his teeth. "Yes."

"Then," said Johnnie, "we must fight."

"Yes, fight," roared the Swede. He was like a demoniac. "Yes, fight! I'll show you what kind of a man I am! I'll show you who you want to fight! Maybe you think I can't fight! Maybe you think I can't! I'll show you, you skin, you card-sharp! Yes, you cheated! You cheated! You cheated!"

"Well, let's git at it, then, mister," said Johnnie coolly.

The cowboy's brow was beaded with sweat from his efforts in intercepting all sorts of raids. He turned in despair to Scully. "What are you goin' to do now?"

A change had come over the Celtic visage of the old man. He now seemed all eagerness; his eyes glowed.

"We'll let them fight," he answered stalwartly. "I can't put up with it any longer. I've stood this damned Swede till I'm sick. We'll let them fight."

VI

The men prepared to go out-of-doors. The Easterner was so nervous that he had great difficulty in getting his arms into the sleeves of his new leather coat. As the cowboy drew his fur cap down over his ears his hands trembled. In fact, Johnnie and old Scully were the only ones who displayed no agitation. These preliminaries were conducted without words.

Scully threw open the door. "Well, come on," he said. Instantly a terrific wind caused the flame of the lamp to struggle at its wick, while a puff of black smoke sprang from the chimney-top. The stove was in mid-current of the blast, and its voice swelled to equal the roar of the storm. Some of the scarred and bedabbled cards were caught up from the floor and dashed helplessly against the farther wall. The men lowered their heads and plunged into the tempest as into a sea.

No snow was falling, but great whirls and clouds of flakes, swept up from the ground by the frantic winds, were streaming southward with the speed of bullets. The covered land was blue with the sheen of an unearthly satin, and there was no other hue save where, at the low black railway station — which seemed incredibly distant — one light gleamed like a tiny jewel. As the men floundered into a thigh-deep drift, it was known that the Swede was bawling out something. Scully went to him, put a hand on his shoulder, and projected an ear. "What's that you say?" he shouted.

"I say," bawled the Swede again, "I won't stand much show against this gang. I know you'll all pitch on me."

Scully smote him reproachfully on the arm. "Tut, man!" he yelled.

The wind tore the words from Scully's lips and scattered them far a-lee.

"You are all a gang of—" boomed the Swede, but the storm also seized the remainder of this sentence.

Immediately turning their backs upon the wind, the men had swung around a corner to the sheltered side of the hotel. It was the function of the little house to preserve here, amid this great devastation of snow, an irregular V-shape of heavily incrusted grass, which crackled beneath the feet. One could imagine the great drifts piled against the windward side. When the party reached the comparative peace of this spot it was found that the Swede was still bellowing.

"Oh, I know what kind of a thing this is! I know you'll all pitch on me. I can't lick you all!"

Scully turned upon him panther fashion. "You'll not have to whip all of us. You'll have to whip my son Johnnie. An' the man what troubles you durin' that time will have me to dale with."

The arrangements were swiftly made. The two men faced each other, obedient to the harsh commands of Scully, whose face, in the subtly luminous gloom, could be seen set in the austere impersonal lines that are pictured on the countenances of the Roman veterans. The Easterner's teeth were chattering, and he was hopping up and down like a mechanical toy. The cowboy stood rock-like.

The contestants had not stripped off any clothing. Each was in his ordinary attire. Their fists were up, and they eyed each other in a calm that had the elements of leonine cruelty in it.

During this pause, the Easterner's mind, like a film, took lasting impressions of three men—the iron-nerved master of the ceremony; the Swede, pale, motionless, terrible; and Johnnie, serene yet ferocious, brutish yet heroic. The entire prelude had in it a tragedy greater than the tragedy of action, and this aspect was accentuated by the long, mellow cry of the blizzard, as it sped the tumbling and wailing flakes into the black abyss of the south.

"Now!" said Scully.

The two combatants leaped forward and crashed together like bullocks. There was heard the cushioned sound of blows, and of a curse squeezing out from between the tight teeth of one.

As for the spectators, the Easterner's pent-up breath exploded from him with a pop of relief, absolute relief from the tension of the preliminaries. The cowboy bounded into the air with a yowl. Scully was immovable as from supreme amazement and fear at the fury of the fight which he himself had permitted and arranged.

For a time the encounter in the darkness was such a perplexity of flying arms that it presented no more detail than would a swiftly revolving wheel. Occasionally a face, as if illumined by a flash of light, would shine out, ghastly and marked with pink spots. A moment later, the men might have been known as shadows, if it were not for the involuntary utterance of oaths that came from them in whispers.

Suddenly a holocaust of warlike desire caught the cowboy, and he bolted forward with the speed of a broncho. "Go it, Johnnie; go it! Kill him! Kill him!"

Scully confronted him. "Kape back," he said; and by his glance the cowboy could tell that this man was Johnnie's father.

To the Easterner there was a monotony of unchangeable fighting that was an abomination. This confused mingling was eternal to his sense, which was concentrated in a longing for the end, the priceless end. Once the fighters lurched near him, and as he scrambled hastily backward, he heard them breathe like men on the rack.

"Kill him, Johnnie! Kill him! Kill him! Kill him!" The cowboy's face was contorted like one of those agony masks in museums.

"Keep still," said Scully icily.

Then there was a sudden loud grunt, incomplete, cut short, and Johnnie's body swung away from the Swede and fell with sickening heaviness to the grass. The cowboy was barely in time to prevent the mad Swede from flinging himself upon his prone adversary. "No, you don't," said the cowboy, interposing an arm. "Wait a second."

Scully was at his son's side. "Johnnie! Johnnie, me boy!" His voice had a quality of melancholy tenderness. "Johnnie? Can you go on with it?" He looked anxiously down into the bloody, pulpy face of his son.

There was a moment of silence, and then Johnnie answered in his ordinary voice, "Yes, I — it — yes."

Assisted by his father he struggled to his feet. "Wait a bit now till you git your wind," said the old man.

A few paces away the cowboy was lecturing the Swede. "No, you don't! Wait a second!"

The Easterner was plucking at Scully's sleeve. "Oh, this is enough," he pleaded. "This is enough! Let it go as it stands. This is enough!"

"Bill," said Scully, "git out of the road." The cowboy stepped aside. "Now." The combatants were actuated by a new caution as they advanced towards collision. They glared at each other, and then the Swede aimed a lightning blow that carried with it his entire weight. Johnnie was evidently half stupid from weakness, but he miraculously dodged, and his fist sent the over-balanced Swede sprawling.

The cowboy, Scully and the Easterner burst into a cheer that was like a chorus of triumphant soldiery, but before its conclusion the Swede had scuffled agilely to his feet and come in berserk abandon at his foe. There was another perplexity of flying arms, and Johnnie's body again swung away and fell, even as a bundle might fall from a roof. The Swede instantly staggered to a little wind-waved tree and leaned upon it, breathing like an engine, while his savage and flame-lit eyes roamed from face to face as the men bent over Johnnie. There was a splendor of isolation in his situation at this time which the Easterner felt once when, lifting his eyes from the man on the ground, he beheld that mysterious and lonely figure, waiting.

"Are you any good yet, Johnnie?" asked Scully in a broken voice.

The son gasped and opened his eyes languidly. After a moment he answered, "No — I ain't — any good — any — more." Then, from shame and bodily ill, he began to weep, the tears furrowing down through the bloodstains on his face. "He was too — too — too heavy for me."

Scully straightened and addressed the waiting figure. "Stranger," he said, evenly, "it's all up with our side." Then his voice changed into that vibrant huskiness which is commonly the tone of the most simple and deadly announcements. "Johnnie is whipped."

Without replying, the victor moved off on the route to the front door of the hotel.

The cowboy was formulating new and unspellable blasphemies. The Easterner was startled to find that they were out in a wind that seemed to come direct from the shadowed arctic floes. He heard again the wail of the snow as it was flung to its grave in the south. He knew now that all this time the cold had been sinking into him deeper and deeper, and he wondered that he had not perished. He felt indifferent to the condition of the vanquished man.

"Johnnie, can you walk?" asked Scully.

"Did I hurt — hurt him any?" asked the son.

"Can you walk, boy? Can you walk?"

Johnnie's voice was suddenly strong. There was a robust impatience in it. "I asked you whether I hurt him any!"

"Yes, yes, Johnnie," answered the cowboy consolingly; "he's hurt a good deal."

They raised him from the ground, and as soon as he was on his feet he went tottering off, rebuffing all attempts at assistance. When the party rounded the corner they were fairly blinded by the pelting of the snow. It burned their faces like fire. The cowboy carried Johnnie through the drift to the door. As they entered some cards again rose from the floor and beat against the wall.

The Easterner rushed to the stove. He was so profoundly chilled that he almost dared to embrace the glowing iron. The Swede was not in the room. Johnnie sank into a chair, and, folding his arms on his knees, buried his face in them. Scully, warming one foot and then the other at the rim of the stove, muttered to himself with Celtic mournfulness. The cowboy had removed his fur cap, and with a dazed and rueful air he was now running one hand through his tousled locks. From overhead they could hear the creaking of boards, as the Swede tramped here and there in his room.

The sad quiet was broken by the sudden flinging open of a door that led towards the kitchen. It was instantly followed by an inrush of women. They precipitated themselves upon Johnnie amid a chorus of lamentation. Before they carried their prey off to the kitchen, there to be bathed and harangued with a mixture of sympathy and abuse which is a feat of their sex, the mother straightened herself and fixed old Scully with an eye of stern reproach. "Shame be upon you, Patrick Scully!" she cried, "Your own son, too. Shame be upon you!"

"There, now! Be quiet, now!" said the old man weakly.

"Shame be upon you, Patrick Scully!" The girls rallying to this slogan, sniffed disdainfully in the direction of those trembling accomplices, the cowboy and the Easterner. Presently they bore Johnnie away, and left the three men to dismal reflection.

VII

"I'D LIKE TO fight this here Dutchman myself," said the cowboy, breaking a long silence.

Scully wagged his head sadly. "No, that wouldn't do. It wouldn't be right. It wouldn't be right."

"Well, why wouldn't it?" argued the cowboy. "I don't see no harm in it."

"No," answered Scully with mournful heroism. "It wouldn't be right. It was Johnnie's fight, and now we mustn't whip the man just because he whipped Johnnie."

"Yes, that's true enough," said the cowboy; "but—he better not get fresh with me, because I couldn't stand no more of it."

"You'll not say a word to him," commanded Scully, and even then they heard the tread of the Swede on the stairs. His entrance was made theatric. He swept the door back with a bang and swaggered to the middle of the room. No one looked at him. "Well," he cried, insolently, at Scully, "I s'pose you'll tell me now how much I owe you?"

The old man remained stolid. "You don't owe me nothin'."

"Huh!" said the Swede, "huh! Don't owe 'im nothin'."

The cowboy addressed the Swede. "Stranger, I don't see how you come to be so gay around here."

Old Scully was instantly alert. "Stop!" he shouted, holding his hand forth, fingers upward. "Bill, you shut up!"

The cowboy spat carelessly into the sawdust box. "I didn't say a word, did I?" he asked.

"Mr. Scully," called the Swede, "how much do I owe you?" It was seen that he was attired for departure, and that he had his valise in his hand.

"You don't owe me nothin'," repeated Scully in his same imperturbable way.

"Huh!" said the Swede. "I guess you're right. I guess if it was any way at all, you'd owe me somethin'. That's what I guess." He turned to the cowboy. " 'Kill him! Kill him! Kill him!' " he mimicked, and then guffawed victoriously. " 'Kill him!' " He was convulsed with ironical humor.

But he might have been jeering the dead. The three men were immovable and silent, staring with glassy eyes at the stove.

The Swede opened the door and passed into the storm, giving one derisive glance backward at the still group.

As soon as the door was closed, Scully and the cowboy leaped to their feet and began to curse. They trampled to and fro, waving their arms and smashing into the air with their fists. "Oh, but that was a hard minute! Him there leerin' and scoffin'! One bang at his nose was worth forty dollars to me that minute! How did you stand it, Bill?"

"How did I stand it?" cried the cowboy in a quivering voice. "How did I stand it? Oh!"

The old man burst into sudden brogue. "I'd loike to take that Swade," he wailed, "and hould 'im down on a shtone flure and bate 'im to a jelly wid a shtick!"

The cowboy groaned in sympathy. "I'd like to git him by the neck and ha-ammer him"—he brought his hand down on a chair with a noise like a pistol-shot—"hammer that there Dutchman until he couldn't tell himself from a dead coyote!"

"I'd bate 'im until he—"

"I'd show *him* some things —"

And then together they raised a yearning, fanatic cry. "Oh-o-oh! if we only could —"

"Yes!"

"Yes!"

"And then I'd —"

"O-o-oh!"

VIII

THE SWEDE, TIGHTLY gripping his valise, tacked across the face of the storm as if he carried sails. He was following a line of little naked gasping trees, which he knew must mark the way of the road. His face, fresh from the pounding of Johnnie's fists, felt more pleasure than pain in the wind and the driving snow. A number of square shapes loomed upon him finally, and he knew them as the houses of the main body of the town. He found a street and made travel along it, leaning heavily upon the wind whenever, at a corner, a terrific blast caught him.

He might have been in a deserted village. We picture the world as thick with conquering and elate humanity, but here, with the bugles of the tempest pealing, it was hard to imagine a peopled earth. One viewed the existence of man then as a marvel, and conceded a glamour of wonder to these lice which were caused to cling to a whirling, fire-smote, ice-locked, disease-stricken, space-lost bulb. The conceit of man was explained by this storm to be the very engine of life. One was a coxcomb not to die in it. However, the Swede found a saloon.

In front of it an indomitable red light was burning, and the snowflakes were made blood-color as they flew through the circumscribed territory of the lamp's shining. The Swede pushed open the door of the saloon and entered. A sanded expanse was before him, and at the end of it four men sat about a table drinking. Down one side of the room extended a radiant bar, and its guardian was leaning upon his elbows listening to the talk of the men at the table. The Swede dropped his valise upon the floor, and, smiling fraternally upon the barkeeper, said, "Gimme some whiskey, will you?" The man placed a bottle, a whiskey-glass, and glass of ice-thick water upon the bar. The Swede poured himself an abnormal portion of whiskey and drank it in three gulps. "Pretty bad night," remarked the bartender indifferently. He was making the pretension of blindness, which is usually a distinction of his class; but it could have been seen that he was furtively studying the half-erased bloodstains on the face of the Swede. "Bad night," he said again.

"Oh, it's good enough for me," replied the Swede hardily, as he poured himself some more whiskey. The barkeeper took his coin and maneuvered it through its reception by the highly nickeled cash-machine. A bell rang; a card labeled "20 cts." had appeared.

"No," continued the Swede, "this isn't too bad weather. It's good enough for me."

"So?" murmured the barkeeper languidly.

The copious drams made the Swede's eyes swim, and he breathed a trifle heavier. "Yes, I like this weather. I like it. It suits me." It was apparently his design to impart a deep significance to these words.

"So?" murmured the bartender again. He turned to gaze dreamily at the scroll-like birds and bird-like scrolls which had been drawn with soap upon the mirrors back of the bar.

"Well, I guess I'll take another drink," said the Swede presently. "Have something?"

"No, thanks; I'm not drinkin'," answered the bartender. Afterwards he asked, "How did you hurt your face?"

The Swede immediately began to boast loudly. "Why, in a fight. I thumped the soul out of a man down here at Scully's hotel."

The interest of the four men at the table was at last aroused.

"Who was it?" said one.

"Johnnie Scully," blustered the Swede. "Son of the man what runs it. He will be pretty near dead for some weeks, I can tell you. I made a nice thing of him, I did. He couldn't get up. They carried him in the house. Have a drink?"

Instantly the men in some subtle way incased themselves in reserve. "No, thanks," said one. The group was of curious formation. Two were prominent local business men; one was the district-attorney; and one was a professional gambler of the kind known as "square." But a scrutiny of the group would not have enabled an observer to pick the gambler from the men of more reputable pursuits. He was, in fact, a man so delicate in manner, when among people of fair class, and so judicious in his choice of victims, that in the strictly masculine part of the town's life he had come to be explicitly trusted and admired. People called him a thoroughbred. The fear and contempt with which his craft was regarded was undoubtedly the reason that his quiet dignity shone conspicuous above the quiet dignity of men who might be merely hatters, billiard-markers, or grocery clerks. Beyond an occasional unwary traveler, who came by rail, this gambler was supposed to prey solely upon reckless and senile farmers, who, when flush with good crops, drove into town in all the pride and confidence of an absolutely invulnerable stupidity. Hearing at times in circuitous fashion of the despoilment of such a farmer, the important men of Romper invariably laughed in contempt of the victim, and if they thought of the wolf at all, it was with a kind of pride at the knowledge that he would never dare think of attacking their wisdom and courage. Besides, it was popular that this gambler had a real wife and two real children in a neat cottage in a suburb, where he led an exemplary home life, and when any one even suggested a discrepancy in his character, the crowd immediately vociferated descriptions of this virtuous family circle. Then men who led exemplary home lives, and men who did not lead exemplary home lives, all subsided in a bunch, remarking that there was nothing more to be said.

However, when a restriction was placed upon him — as, for instance, when a strong clique of members of the new Pollywog Club refused to permit him, even as a spectator, to appear in the rooms of the organization — the candor and gentleness with which he accepted the judgment disarmed many of his foes and made his friends more desperately partisan. He invariably distinguished between himself and a respectable Romper man so quickly and frankly that his manner actually appeared to be a continual broadcast compliment.

And one must not forget to declare the fundamental fact of his entire position in Romper. It is irrefutable that in all affairs outside of his business, in all matters that occur eternally and commonly between man and man, this thieving card-player was so generous, so just, so moral, that, in a contest, he could have put to flight the consciences of nine-tenths of the citizens of Romper.

And so it happened that he was seated in this saloon with the two prominent local merchants and the district-attorney.

The Swede continued to drink raw whiskey, meanwhile babbling at the barkeeper and trying to induce him to indulge in potations. "Come on. Have a drink. Come on. What — no? Well, have a little one then. By gawd, I've whipped a man to-night, and I want to celebrate. I whipped him good, too. Gentlemen," the Swede cried to the men at the table, "have a drink?"

"Ssh!" said the barkeeper.

The group at the table, although furtively attentive, had been pretending to be deep in talk, but now a man lifted his eyes towards the Swede and said shortly, "Thanks. We don't want any more."

At this reply the Swede ruffled out his chest like a rooster. "Well," he exploded, "it seems I can't get anybody to drink with me in this town. Seems so, don't it? Well!"

"Ssh!" said the barkeeper.

"Say," snarled the Swede, "don't you try to shut me up. I won't have it. I'm a gentleman, and I want people to drink with me. And I want 'em to drink with me now. *Now*—do you understand?" He rapped the bar with his knuckles.

Years of experience had calloused the bartender. He merely grew sulky. "I hear you," he answered.

"Well," cried the Swede, "listen hard then. See those men over there? Well, they're going to drink with me, and don't you forget it. Now you watch."

"Hi!" yelled the barkeeper, "this won't do!"

"Why won't it?" demanded the Swede. He stalked over to the table, and by chance laid his hand upon the shoulder of the gambler. "How about this?" he asked, wrathfully. "I asked you to drink with me."

The gambler simply twisted his head and spoke over his shoulder. "My friend, I don't know you."

"Oh, hell!" answered the Swede, "come and have a drink."

"Now, my boy," advised the gambler kindly, "take your hand off my shoulder and go 'way and mind your own business." He was a little slim man, and it seemed strange to hear him use this tone of heroic patronage to the burly Swede. The other men at the table said nothing.

"What? You won't drink with me, you little dude? I'll make you then! I'll make you!" The Swede had grasped the gambler frenziedly at the throat, and was dragging him from his chair. The other men sprang up. The barkeeper dashed around the corner of his bar. There was a great tumult, and then was seen a long blade in the hand of the gambler. It shot forward, and a human body, this citadel of virtue, wisdom, power, was pierced as easily as if it had been a melon. The Swede fell with a cry of supreme astonishment.

The prominent merchants and the district-attorney must have at once tumbled out of the place backward. The bartender found himself hanging limply to the arm of a chair and gazing into the eyes of a murderer.

"Henry," said the latter, as he wiped his knife on one of the towels that hung beneath the bar-rail, "you tell 'em where to find me. I'll be home, waiting for 'em." Then he vanished. A moment afterward the barkeeper was in the street dinning through the storm for help, and, moreover, companionship.

The corpse of the Swede, alone in the saloon, had its eyes fixed upon a dreadful legend that dwelt atop of the cash-machine. "This registers the amount of your purchase."

IX

MONTHS LATER, THE cowboy was frying pork over the stove of a little ranch near the Dakota line, when there was a quick thud of hoofs outside, and presently the Easterner entered with the letters and the papers.

"Well," said the Easterner at once, "the chap that killed the Swede has got three years. Wasn't much, was it?"

"He has? Three years?" The cowboy poised his pan of pork, while he ruminated upon the news. "Three years. That ain't much."

"No. It was a light sentence," replied the Easterner as he unbuckled his spurs. "Seems there was a good deal of sympathy for him in Romper."

"If the bartender had been any good," observed the cowboy thoughtfully, "he would have gone in and cracked that there Dutchman on the head with a bottle in the beginnin' of it and stopped all this here murderin'."

"Yes, a thousand things might have happened," said the Easterner tartly.

The cowboy returned his pan of pork to the fire, but his philosophy continued. "It's funny, ain't it? If he hadn't said Johnnie was cheatin' he'd be alive this minute. He was an awful fool. Game played for fun, too. Not for money. I believe he was crazy."

"I feel sorry for that gambler," said the Easterner.

"Oh, so do I," said the cowboy. "He don't deserve none of it for killin' who he did."

"The Swede might not have been killed if everything had been square."

"Might not have been killed?" exclaimed the cowboy. "Everythin' square? Why, when he said that Johnnie was cheatin' and acted like such a jackass? And then in the saloon he fairly walked up to git hurt?" With these arguments the cowboy browbeat the Easterner and reduced him to rage.

"You're a fool!" cried the Easterner viciously. "You're a bigger jackass than the Swede by a million majority. Now let me tell you one thing. Let me tell you something. Listen! Johnnie *was* cheating!"

"Johnnie," said the cowboy blankly. There was a minute of silence, and then he said robustly, "Why, no. The game was only for fun."

"Fun or not," said the Easterner, "Johnnie was cheating. I saw him. I know it. I saw him. And I refused to stand up and be a man. I let the Swede fight it out alone. And you — you were simply puffing around the place and wanting to fight. And then old Scully himself! We are all in it! This poor gambler isn't even a noun. He is kind of an adverb. Every sin is the result of a collaboration. We, five of us, have collaborated in the murder of this Swede. Usually there are from a dozen to forty women really involved in every murder, but in this case it seems to be only five men — you, I, Johnnie, old Scully, and that fool of an unfortunate gambler came merely as a culmination, the apex of a human movement, and gets all the punishment."

The cowboy, injured and rebellious, cried out blindly into this fog of mysterious theory. "Well, I didn't do anythin', did I?"

1899

EDITH WHARTON

A CUP OF COLD WATER

Although EDITH (NEWBOLD) WHARTON, née Jones (1862–1937), is most famous as a writer of literary, mainstream works than of what in lesser hands would ordinarily be called genre fiction, there can be little doubt that some of her most enduring works are her ghost and supernatural stories, as is the case with her friend and major literary influence, Henry James, whose most widely read book these days may well be the subtle ghost story *The Turn of the Screw.*

Wharton was the first woman to win the Pulitzer Prize, her novel *The Age of Innocence* (1920) taking the honor. *Old New York* (1924), a collection of four novellas, inspired the play *The Old Maid,* by Zoë Atkins, which won the Pulitzer Prize in 1935. The following story, admittedly, stretches the definition of a "mystery" story somewhat, but it is not unlike the work of several authors whose works are categorized in that genre. It is the tale of a con man and thief who, not surprisingly, finds himself caught up in events that spiral out of his control — someone not so different from other crooks (both in real life and in literature), who often discover that they are no longer masters of their own futures.

Born to enormous wealth in New York City, Wharton rebelled against her privileged life among high society in New York, Paris, and Newport, Rhode Island, by writing fiction, which her family regarded as an eccentricity that was best ignored and never discussed. Her earliest stories were written for *Scribner's Magazine,* and when the editor requested a serial novel "in six months," she wrote her first big bestseller for him, *The House of Mirth* (1905). Six years later she published what many regard as her masterpiece, *Ethan Frome* (1911), and she ultimately wrote forty-seven books. "A Cup of Cold Water," like so many of her stories, reflects her disdain for the social milieu in which she was expected to live. It is fraught with suspense, although the "crime" of which the heroine is guilty is really the least of her troubles.

"A Cup of Cold Water" was first published in Wharton's short story collection *The Greater Inclination* (New York: Charles Scribner's Sons, 1899).

• • •

I

It was three o'clock in the morning, and the cotillion was at its height, when Woburn left the over-heated splendor of the Gildermere ballroom, and after a delay caused by the determination of the drowsy footman to give him a ready-made overcoat with an imitation astrachan collar in place of his own unimpeachable Poole garment, found himself breasting the icy solitude of the Fifth Avenue. He was still smiling, as he emerged from the awning, at his insistence in claiming his own overcoat: it illustrated, humorously enough, the invincible force of habit. As he faced the wind, however, he discerned a providence in his persistency, for his coat was fur-lined, and he had a cold voyage before him on the morrow.

It had rained hard during the earlier part of the night, and the carriages waiting in triple line before the Gildermeres' door were still domed by shining umbrellas, while the electric lamps extending down the avenue blinked Narcissus-like at their watery images in the hollows of the sidewalk. A dry blast had come out of the north, with pledge of frost before daylight, and to Woburn's shivering fancy the pools in the pavement seemed already stiffening into ice. He turned up his coat-collar and stepped out rapidly, his hands deep in his coat-pockets.

As he walked he glanced curiously up at the ladder-like door-steps which may well suggest to the future archaeologist that all the streets of New York were once canals; at the spectral tracery of the trees about St. Luke's, the fretted mass of the Cathedral, and the mean vista of the long side-streets. The knowledge that he was perhaps looking at it all for the last time caused every detail to start out like a challenge to memory, and lit the brown-stone house-fronts with the glamour of sword-barred Edens.

It was an odd impulse that had led him that night to the Gildermere ball; but the same change in his condition which made him stare wonderingly at the houses in the Fifth Avenue gave the thrill of an exploit to the tame business of ball-going. Who would have imagined, Woburn mused, that such a situation as his would possess the priceless quality of sharpening the blunt edge of habit?

It was certainly curious to reflect, as he leaned against the doorway of Mrs. Gildermere's ball-room, enveloped in the warm atmosphere of the accustomed, that twenty-four hours later the people brushing by him with looks of friendly recognition would start at the thought of having seen him and slur over the recollection of having taken his hand!

And the girl he had gone there to see: what would she think of him? He knew well enough that her trenchant classifications of life admitted no overlapping of good and evil, made no allowance for that incalculable interplay of motives that justifies the subtlest casuistry of compassion. Miss Talcott was too young to distinguish the intermediate tints of the moral spectrum; and her judgments were further simplified by a peculiar concreteness of mind. Her bringing-up had fostered this tendency and she was surrounded by people who focused life in the same way. To the girls in Miss Talcott's set, the attentions of a clever man who had to work for his living had the zest of a forbidden pleasure; but to marry such a man would be as unpardonable as to have one's carriage seen at the door of a cheap dress-maker. Poverty might make a man fascinating; but a settled income was the best evidence of stability of character. If there were anything in heredity, how could a nice girl trust a man whose parents had been careless enough to leave him unprovided for?

Neither Miss Talcott nor any of her friends could be charged with formulating these views; but they were implicit in the slope of every white shoulder and in the ripple of every yard of imported tulle dappling the foreground of Mrs. Gildermere's ball-room. The advantages of line and color in veiling the crudities of a creed are obvious to emotional minds; and besides, Woburn was conscious that it was to the cheerful materialism of their parents that the young girls he admired owed that fine distinction of outline in which their skillfully-rippled hair and skillfully-hung draperies cooperated with the slimness and erectness that came of participating in the most expensive sports, eating the most expensive food and breathing the most expensive air. Since the process which had produced them was so costly, how could they help being costly themselves? Woburn was too logical to expect to give no more for a piece of old Sèvres than for a bit of kitchen crockery; he had no faith in wonderful bargains, and believed that one got in life just what one was willing to pay for. He had no mind to dispute the taste of those who preferred the rustic simplicity of the earthen crock; but his own fancy inclined to the piece of *pâte tendre* which must be kept in a glass case and handled as delicately as a flower.

It was not merely by the external grace of these drawing-room ornaments that Woburn's sensibilities were charmed. His imagination was touched by the curious exoticism of view resulting from such conditions. He had always enjoyed listening to Miss Talcott even more than looking at her. Her ideas had the brilliant bloom and audacious irrelevance of those tropical orchids which strike root in air. Miss Talcott's opinions had no connection with the actual; her very materialism had the grace of artificiality. Woburn had been enchanted once by seeing her helpless before a smoking lamp: she had been obliged to ring for a servant because she did not know how to put it out.

Her supreme charm was the simplicity that comes of taking it for granted that people are born with carriages and country-places: it never occurred to her that such congenital attributes could be matter for self-consciousness, and she had none of the *nouveau riche* prudery which classes poverty with the nude in art and is not sure how to behave in the presence of either.

The conditions of Woburn's own life had made him peculiarly susceptible to those forms of elegance which are the flower of ease. His father had lost a comfortable property through sheer inability to go over his agent's accounts; and this disaster, coming at the outset of Woburn's school-days, had given a new bent to the family temperament. The father characteristically died when the effort of living might have made it possible to retrieve his fortunes; and Woburn's mother and sister, embittered by this final evasion, settled down to a vindictive war with circumstances. They were the kind of women who think that it lightens the burden of life to throw over the amenities, as a reduced housekeeper puts away her knick-knacks to make the dusting easier. They fought mean conditions meanly; but Woburn, in his resentment of their attitude, did not allow for the suffering which had brought it about: his own tendency was to overcome difficulties by conciliation rather than by conflict. Such surroundings threw into vivid relief the charming figure of Miss Talcott. Woburn instinctively associated poverty with bad food, ugly furniture, complaints and recriminations: it was natural that he should be drawn toward the luminous atmosphere where life was a series of peaceful and good-humored acts, unimpeded by petty obstacles. To spend one's time in such society gave one the illusion of unlimited credit; and also, unhappily, created the need for it.

It was here in fact that Woburn's difficulties began. To marry Miss Talcott it was necessary to be a rich man: even to dine out in her set involved certain minor extravagances. Woburn had determined to marry her sooner or later; and in the meanwhile to be with her as much as possible.

As he stood leaning in the doorway of the Gildermere ball-room, watching her pass him in the waltz, he tried to remember how it had begun. First there had been the tailor's bill; the fur-lined overcoat with cuffs and collar of Alaska sable had alone cost more than he had spent on his clothes for two or three years previously. Then there were theater tickets; cab fares; florist's bills; tips to servants at the country houses where he went because he knew that she was invited; the *Omar Khayyám* bound by Sullivan that he sent her at Christmas; the contributions to her pet charities; the reckless purchases at fairs where she had a stall. His whole way of life had imperceptibly changed and his year's salary was gone before the second quarter was due.

He had invested the few thousand dollars which had been his portion of his father's shrunken estate: when his debts began to pile up, he took a flyer in stocks and after a few months of varying luck his little patrimony disappeared. Meanwhile his courtship was proceeding at an inverse ratio to his financial ventures. Miss Talcott was growing tender and he began to feel that the game was in his hands. The nearness of the goal exasperated him. She was not the girl to wait and he knew that it must be now or never. A friend lent him five thousand dollars on his personal note and he bought railway stocks on margin. They went up and he held them for a higher rise: they fluctuated, dragged, dropped below the level at which he had bought, and slowly continued their uninterrupted descent. His broker called for more margin; he could not respond and was sold out.

What followed came about quite naturally. For several years he had been cashier in a well-known banking-house. When the note he had given his friend became due it was obviously necessary to pay it and he used the firm's money for the purpose. To repay the money thus taken, he increased his debt to his employers and bought more stocks; and on these operations he made a profit of ten thousand dollars. Miss Talcott rode in the Park, and he bought a smart hack for seven hundred, paid off his tradesmen, and went on speculating with the remainder of his profits. He made a little more, but failed to take advantage of the market and lost all that he had staked, including the amount taken from the firm. He increased his over-draft by another ten thousand and lost that; he over-drew a farther sum and lost again. Suddenly he woke to the fact that he owed his employers fifty thousand dollars and that the partners were to make their semi-annual inspection in two days. He realized then that within forty-eight hours what he had called borrowing would become theft.

There was no time to be lost: he must clear out and start life over again somewhere else. The day that he reached this decision he was to have met Miss Talcott at dinner. He went to the dinner, but she did not appear: she had a headache, his hostess explained. Well, he was not to have a last look at her, after all; better so, perhaps. He took leave early and on his way home stopped at a florist's and sent her a bunch of violets. The next morning he got a little note from her: the violets had done her head so much good — she would tell him all about it that evening at the Gildermere ball. Woburn laughed and tossed the note into the fire. That evening he would be on board ship: the examination of the books was to take place the following morning at ten.

Woburn went down to the bank as usual; he did not want to do anything that might excite suspicion as to his plans, and from one or two questions which one of the partners had lately put to him he divined that he was being observed. At the bank the day passed uneventfully. He discharged his business with his accustomed care and went uptown at the usual hour.

In the first flush of his successful speculations he had set up bachelor lodgings, moved by the temptation to get away from the dismal atmosphere of home, from his mother's struggles with the cook and his sister's curiosity about his letters. He had been influenced also by the wish for surroundings more adapted to his tastes. He wanted to be able to give little teas, to which Miss Talcott might come with a married friend. She came once or twice and pronounced it all delightful: she thought it *so* nice to have only a few Whistler etchings on the walls and the simplest crushed levant for all one's books.

To these rooms Woburn returned on leaving the bank. His plans had taken definite shape. He had engaged passage on a steamer sailing for Halifax early the next morning; and there was nothing for him to do before going on board but to pack his clothes and tear up a few letters. He threw his clothes into a couple of portmanteaux, and when these had been called for by an expressman he emptied his pockets and counted up his ready money. He found that he possessed just fifty dollars and seventy-five cents; but his passage to Halifax was paid, and once there he could pawn his watch and rings. This calculation completed, he unlocked his writing-table drawer and took out a handful of letters. They were notes from Miss Talcott. He read them over and threw them into the fire. On his table stood her photograph. He slipped it out of its frame and tossed it on top of the blazing letters. Having performed this rite, he got into his dress-clothes and went to a small French restaurant to dine.

He had meant to go on board the steamer immediately after dinner; but a sudden vision of introspective hours in a silent cabin made him call for the evening paper and run his eye over the list of theaters. It would be as easy to go on board at midnight as now.

He selected a new vaudeville and listened to it with surprising freshness of interest; but toward eleven o'clock he again began to dread the approaching necessity of going down to the steamer. There was something peculiarly unnerving in the idea of spending the rest of the night in a stifling cabin jammed against the side of a wharf.

He left the theater and strolled across to the Fifth Avenue. It was now nearly midnight and a stream of carriages poured up town from the opera and the theaters. As he stood on the corner watching the familiar spectacle it occurred to him that many of the people driving by him in smart broughams and C-spring landaus were on their way to the Gildermere ball. He remembered Miss Talcott's note of the morning and wondered if she were in one of the passing carriages; she had spoken so confidently of meeting him at the ball. What if he should go and take a last look at her? There was really nothing to prevent it. He was not likely to run across any member of the firm: in Miss Talcott's set his social standing was good for another ten hours at least. He smiled in anticipation of her surprise at seeing him, and then reflected with a start that she would not be surprised at all.

His meditations were cut short by a fall of sleety rain, and hailing a hansom he gave the driver Mrs. Gildermere's address.

As he drove up the avenue he looked about him like a traveler in a strange city. The buildings which had been so unobtrusively familiar stood out with sudden distinctness: he noticed a hundred details which had escaped his observation. The people on the sidewalks looked like strangers: he wondered where they were going and tried to picture the lives they led; but his own relation to life had been so suddenly reversed that he found it impossible to recover his mental perspective.

At one corner he saw a shabby man lurking in the shadow of the side street; as the hansom passed, a policeman ordered him to move on. Farther on, Woburn noticed a woman crouching on the door-step of a handsome house. She had drawn a shawl over her head and was sunk in the apathy of despair or drink. A well-dressed couple paused to look at her. The electric globe at the corner lit up their faces, and Woburn saw the lady, who was young and pretty, turn away with a little grimace, drawing her companion after her.

The desire to see Miss Talcott had driven Woburn to the Gildermeres', but once in the ball-room he made no effort to find her. The people about him seemed more like strangers than those he had passed in the street. He stood in the doorway, studying the petty maneuvers of the women and the resigned amenities of their partners. Was it possible that these were his friends? These mincing women, all paint and dye and whalebone, these apathetic men who looked as much alike as the figures that children cut out of a folded sheet of paper? Was it to live among such puppets that he had sold his soul? What had any of these people done that was noble, exceptional, distinguished? Who knew them by name even, except their tradesmen and the society reporters? Who were they, that they should sit in judgment on him?

The bald man with the globular stomach, who stood at Mrs. Gildermere's elbow surveying the dancers, was old Boylston, who had made his pile in wrecking railroads; the smooth chap with glazed eyes, at whom a pretty girl smiled up so confidingly, was Collerton, the political lawyer, who had been mixed up to his own advantage in an ugly lobbying transaction; near him stood Brice Lyndham, whose recent failure had ruined his friends and associates, but had not visibly affected the welfare of his large and expensive family. The slim fellow dancing with Miss Gildermere was Alec Vance, who lived on a salary of five thousand a year, but whose wife was such a good manager that they kept a brougham and victoria and always put in their season at Newport and their spring trip to Europe. The little ferret-faced youth in the corner was Regie Colby, who wrote the *Entre-Nous* paragraphs in the *Social Searchlight:* the women were charming to him and he got all the financial tips he wanted from their husbands and fathers.

And the women? Well, the women knew all about the men, and flattered them and married them and tried to catch them for their daughters. It was a domino-party at which the guests were forbidden to unmask, though they all saw through each other's disguises.

And these were the people who, within twenty-four hours, would be agreeing that they had always felt there was something wrong about Woburn! They would be extremely sorry for him, of course, poor devil; but there are certain standards, after all—what would society be without standards? His new friends, his future associates, were the suspicious-looking man whom the policeman had ordered to move on, and the drunken woman asleep on the door-step. To these he was linked by the freemasonry of failure.

Miss Talcott passed him on Collerton's arm; she was giving him one of the smiles of which Woburn had fancied himself sole owner. Collerton was a sharp fellow; he must have made a lot in that last deal; probably she would marry him. How much did she know about the transaction?

She was a shrewd girl and her father was in Wall Street. If Woburn's luck had turned the other way she might have married him instead; and if he had confessed his sin to her one evening, as they drove home from the opera in their new brougham, she would have said that really it was of no use to tell her, for she never *could* understand about business, but that she did entreat him in future to be nicer to Regie Colby. Even now, if he made a big strike somewhere, and came back in ten years with a beard and a steam yacht, they would all deny that anything had been proved against him, and Mrs. Collerton might blush and remind him of their friendship. Well—why not? Was not all morality based on a convention? What was the staunchest code of ethics but a trunk with a series of false bottoms? Now and then one had the illusion of getting down to absolute right or wrong, but it was only a false bottom—a removable hypothesis—with another false bottom underneath. There was no getting beyond the relative.

The cotillion had begun. Miss Talcott sat nearly opposite him: she was dancing with young Boylston and giving him a Woburn-Collerton smile. So young Boylston was in the syndicate too!

Presently Woburn was aware that she had forgotten young Boylston and was glancing absently about the room. She was looking for someone, and meant the someone to know it: he knew that *Lost-Chord* look in her eyes.

A new figure was being formed. The partners circled about the room and Miss Talcott's flying tulle drifted close to him as she passed. Then the favors were distributed; white skirts wavered across the floor like thistle-down on summer air; men rose from their seats and fresh couples filled the shining *parquet.*

Miss Talcott, after taking from the basket a Legion of Honor in red enamel, surveyed the room for a moment; then she made her way through the dancers and held out the favor to Woburn. He fastened it in his coat, and emerging from the crowd of men about the doorway, slipped his arm about her. Their eyes met; hers were serious and a little sad. How fine and slender she was! He noticed the little tendrils of hair about the pink convolution of her ear. Her waist was firm and yet elastic; she breathed calmly and regularly, as though dancing were her natural motion. She did not look at him again and neither of them spoke.

When the music ceased they paused near her chair. Her partner was waiting for her and Woburn left her with a bow.

He made his way down-stairs and out of the house. He was glad that he had not spoken to Miss Talcott. There had been a healing power in their silence. All bitterness had gone from him and he thought of her now quite simply, as the girl he loved.

At Thirty-fifth Street he reflected that he had better jump into a car and go down to his steamer. Again there rose before him the repulsive vision of the dark cabin, with creaking noises overhead, and the cold wash of water against the pier: he thought he would stop in a café and take a drink. He turned into Broadway and entered a brightly-lit café; but when he had taken his whisky and soda there seemed no reason for lingering. He had never been the kind of man who could escape difficulties in that way. Yet he was conscious that his will was weakening; that he did not mean to go down to the steamer just yet. What did he mean to do? He began to feel horribly tired and it occurred to him that a few hours' sleep in a decent bed would make a new man of him. Why not go on board the next morning at daylight?

He could not go back to his rooms, for on leaving the house he had taken the precaution of dropping his latch-key into his letter-box; but he was in a neighborhood of discreet hotels and he wandered on till he came to one which was known to offer a dispassionate hospitality to luggageless travelers in dress-clothes.

II

HE PUSHED OPEN the swinging door and found himself in a long corridor with a tessellated floor, at the end of which, in a brightly-lit enclosure of plate-glass and mahogany, the night-clerk dozed over a copy of the *Police Gazette*. The air in the corridor was rich in reminiscences of yesterday's dinners, and a bronzed radiator poured a wave of dry heat into Woburn's face.

The night-clerk, roused by the swinging of the door, sat watching Woburn's approach with the unexpectant eye of one who has full confidence in his capacity for digesting surprises. Not that there was anything surprising in Woburn's appearance; but the night-clerk's callers were given to such imaginative flights in explaining their luggageless arrival in the small hours of the morning, that he fared habitually on fictions which would have staggered a less experienced stomach. The night-clerk, whose unwrinkled bloom showed that he throve on this high-seasoned diet, had a fancy for classifying his applicants before they could frame their explanations.

"This one's been locked out," he said to himself as he mustered Woburn.

Having exercised his powers of divination with his accustomed accuracy he listened without stirring an eye-lid to Woburn's statement; merely replying, when the latter asked the price of a room, "Two-fifty."

"Very well," said Woburn, pushing the money under the brass lattice, "I'll go up at once; and I want to be called at seven."

To this the night-clerk proffered no reply, but stretching out his hand to press an electric button, returned apathetically to the perusal of the *Police Gazette.* His summons was answered by the appearance of a man in shirt-sleeves, whose rumpled head indicated that he had recently risen from some kind of makeshift repose; to him the night-clerk tossed a key, with the brief comment, "Ninety-seven"; and the man, after a sleepy glance at Woburn, turned on his heel and lounged toward the staircase at the back of the corridor.

Woburn followed and they climbed three flights in silence. At each landing Woburn glanced down the long passage-way lit by a lowered gas-jet, with a double line of boots before the doors, waiting, like yesterday's deeds, to carry their owners so many miles farther on the morrow's destined road. On the third landing the man paused, and after examining the number on the key, turned to the left, and slouching past three or four doors, finally unlocked one and preceded Woburn into a room lit only by the upward gleam of the electric globes in the street below.

The man felt in his pockets; then he turned to Woburn. "Got a match?" he asked.

Woburn politely offered him one, and he applied it to the gas-fixture which extended its jointed arm above an ash dressing-table with a blurred mirror fixed between two standards. Having performed this office with an air of detachment designed to make Woburn recognize it as an act of supererogation, he turned without a word and vanished down the passageway.

Woburn, after an indifferent glance about the room, which seemed to afford the amount of luxury generally obtainable for two dollars and a half in a fashionable quarter of New York, locked the door and sat down at the ink-stained writing-table in the window. Far below him lay the pallidly-lit depths of the forsaken thoroughfare. Now and then he heard the jingle of a horse-car and the ring of hoofs on the freezing pavement, or saw the lonely figure of a policeman eclipsing the illumination of the plate-glass windows on the opposite side of the street. He sat thus for a long time, his elbows on the table, his chin between his hands, till at length the contemplation of the abandoned sidewalks, above which the electric globes kept Stylites-like vigil, became intolerable to him, and he drew down the window-shade, and lit the gas-fixture beside the dressing-table. Then he took a cigar from his case, and held it to the flame.

The passage from the stinging freshness of the night to the stale overheated atmosphere of the Haslemere Hotel had checked the preternaturally rapid working of his mind, and he was now scarcely conscious of thinking at all. His head was heavy, and he would have thrown himself on the bed had he not feared to oversleep the hour fixed for his departure. He thought it safest, instead, to seat himself once more by the table, in the most uncomfortable chair that he could find, and smoke one cigar after another till the first sign of dawn should give an excuse for action.

He had laid his watch on the table before him, and was gazing at the hour-hand, and trying to convince himself by so doing that he was still wide awake, when a noise in the adjoining room suddenly straightened him in his chair and banished all fear of sleep.

There was no mistaking the nature of the noise; it was that of a woman's sobs. The sobs were not loud, but the sound reached him distinctly through the frail door between the two rooms; it expressed an utter abandonment to grief; not the cloud-burst of some passing emotion, but the slow down-pour of a whole heaven of sorrow.

Woburn sat listening. There was nothing else to be done; and at least his listening was a mute tribute to the trouble he was powerless to relieve. It roused, too, the drugged pulses of his own grief: he was touched by the chance propinquity of two alien sorrows in a great city throbbing with multifarious passions. It would have been more in keeping with the irony of life had he found himself next to a mother singing her child to sleep: there seemed a mute commiseration in the hand that had led him to such neighborhood.

Gradually the sobs subsided, with pauses betokening an effort at self-control. At last they died off softly, like the intermittent drops that end a day of rain.

"Poor soul," Woburn mused, "she's got the better of it for the time. I wonder what it's all about?"

At the same moment he heard another sound that made him jump to his feet. It was a very low sound, but in that nocturnal silence which gives distinctness to the faintest noises, Woburn knew at once that he had heard the click of a pistol.

"What is she up to now?" he asked himself, with his eye on the door between the two rooms; and the brightly-lit keyhole seemed to reply with a glance of intelligence. He turned out the gas and crept to the door, pressing his eye to the illuminated circle.

After a moment or two of adjustment, during which he seemed to himself to be breathing like a steam-engine, he discerned a room like his own, with the same dressing-table flanked by gas-fixtures, and the same table in the window. This table was directly in his line of vision; and beside it stood a woman with a small revolver in her hands. The lights being behind her, Woburn could only infer her youth from her slender silhouette and the nimbus of fair hair defining her head. Her dress seemed dark and simple, and on a chair under one of the gas-jets lay a jacket edged with cheap fur and a small traveling-bag. He could not see the other end of the room, but something in her manner told him that she was alone. At length she put the revolver down and took up a letter that lay on the table. She drew the letter from its envelope and read it over two or three times; then she put it back, sealing the envelope, and placing it conspicuously against the mirror of the dressing-table.

There was so grave a significance in this dumb-show that Woburn felt sure that her next act would be to return to the table and take up the revolver; but he had not reckoned on the vanity of woman. After putting the letter in place she still lingered at the mirror, standing a little sideways, so that he could now see her face, which was distinctly pretty, but of a small and inelastic mold, inadequate to the expression of the larger emotions. For some moments she continued to study herself with the expression of a child looking at a playmate who has been scolded; then she turned to the table and lifted the revolver to her forehead.

A sudden crash made her arm drop, and sent her darting backward to the opposite side of the room. Woburn had broken down the door, and stood torn and breathless in the breach.

"Oh!" she gasped, pressing closer to the wall.

"Don't be frightened," he said; "I saw what you were going to do and I had to stop you."

She looked at him for a moment in silence, and he saw the terrified flutter of her breast; then she said, "No one can stop me for long. And besides, what right have you —"

"Everyone has the right to prevent a crime," he returned, the sound of the last word sending the blood to his forehead.

"I deny it," she said passionately. "Everyone who has tried to live and failed has the right to die."

"Failed in what?"

"In everything!" she replied. They stood looking at each other in silence.

At length he advanced a few steps.

"You've no right to say you've failed," he said, "while you have breath to try again." He drew the revolver from her hand.

"Try again—try again? I tell you I've tried seventy times seven!"

"What have you tried?"

She looked at him with a certain dignity.

"I don't know," she said, "that you've any right to question me—or to be in this room at all—" and suddenly she burst into tears.

The discrepancy between her words and action struck the chord which, in a man's heart, always responds to the touch of feminine unreason. She dropped into the nearest chair, hiding her face in her hands, while Woburn watched the course of her weeping.

At last she lifted her head, looking up between drenched lashes.

"Please go away," she said in childish entreaty.

"How can I?" he returned. "It's impossible that I should leave you in this state. Trust me—let me help you. Tell me what has gone wrong, and let's see if there's no other way out of it."

Woburn had a voice full of sensitive inflections, and it was now trembling with profoundest pity. Its note seemed to reassure the girl, for she said, with a beginning of confidence in her own tones, "But I don't even know who you are."

Woburn was silent: the words startled him. He moved nearer to her and went on in the same quieting tone.

"I am a man who has suffered enough to want to help others. I don't want to know any more about you than will enable me to do what I can for you. I've probably seen more of life than you have, and if you're willing to tell me your troubles perhaps together we may find a way out of them."

She dried her eyes and glanced at the revolver.

"That's the only way out," she said.

"How do you know? Are you sure you've tried every other?"

"Perfectly sure, I've written and written, and humbled myself like a slave before him, and she won't even let him answer my letters. Oh, but you don't understand"— she broke off with a renewal of weeping.

"I begin to understand—you're sorry for something you've done?"

"Oh, I've never denied that—I've never denied that I was wicked."

"And you want the forgiveness of someone you care about?"

"My husband," she whispered.

"You've done something to displease your husband?"

"To displease him? I ran away with another man!" There was a dismal exultation in her tone, as though she were paying Woburn off for having underrated her offense.

She had certainly surprised him; at worst he had expected a quarrel over a rival, with a possible complication of mother-in-law. He wondered how such helpless little feet could have taken so bold a step; then he remembered that there is no audacity like that of weakness.

He was wondering how to lead her to completer avowal when she added forlornly, "You see there's nothing else to do."

Woburn took a turn in the room. It was certainly a narrower strait than he had foreseen, and he hardly knew how to answer; but the first flow of confession had eased her, and she went on without farther persuasion.

"I don't know how I could ever have done it; I must have been downright crazy. I didn't care much for Joe when I married him — he wasn't exactly handsome, and girls think such a lot of that. But he just laid down and worshipped me, and I *was* getting fond of him in a way; only the life was so dull. I'd been used to a big city — I come from Detroit — and Hinksville is such a poky little place; that's where we lived; Joe is telegraph-operator on the railroad there. He'd have been in a much bigger place now, if he hadn't — well, after all, he behaved perfectly splendidly about *that*.

"I really was getting fond of him, and I believe I should have realized in time how good and noble and unselfish he was, if his mother hadn't been always sitting there and everlastingly telling me so. We learned in school about the Athenians hating some man who was always called just, and that's the way I felt about Joe. Whenever I did anything that wasn't quite right his mother would say how differently Joe would have done it. And she was forever telling me that Joe didn't approve of this and that and the other. When we were alone he approved of everything, but when his mother was round he'd sit quiet and let her say he didn't. I knew he'd let me have my way afterwards, but somehow that didn't prevent my getting mad at the time.

"And then the evenings were so long, with Joe away, and Mrs. Glenn (that's his mother) sitting there like an image knitting socks for the heathen. The only caller we ever had was the Baptist minister, and he never took any more notice of me than if I'd been a piece of furniture. I believe he was afraid to before Mrs. Glenn."

She paused breathlessly, and the tears in her eyes were now of anger.

"Well?" said Woburn gently.

"Well—then Arthur Hackett came along; he was traveling for a big publishing firm in Philadelphia. He was awfully handsome and as clever and sarcastic as anything. He used to lend me lots of novels and magazines, and tell me all about society life in New York. All the girls were after him, and Alice Sprague, whose father is the richest man in Hinksville, fell desperately in love with him and carried on like a fool; but he wouldn't take any notice of her. He never looked at anybody but me." Her face lit up with a reminiscent smile, and then clouded again. "I hate him now," she exclaimed, with a change of tone that startled Woburn. "I'd like to kill him—but he's killed me instead.

"Well, he bewitched me so I didn't know what I was doing; I was like somebody in a trance. When he wasn't there I didn't want to speak to anybody; I used to lie in bed half the day just to get away from folks; I hated Joe and Hinksville and everything else. When he came back the days went like a flash; we were together nearly all the time. I knew Joe's mother was spying on us, but I didn't care. And at last it seemed as if I couldn't let him go away again without me; so one evening he stopped at the back gate in a buggy, and we drove off together and caught the eastern express at River Bend. He promised to bring me to New York." She paused, and then added scornfully, "He didn't even do that!"

Woburn had returned to his seat and was watching her attentively. It was curious to note how her passion was spending itself in words; he saw that she would never kill herself while she had any one to talk to.

"That was five months ago," she continued, "and we traveled all through the southern states, and stayed a little while near Philadelphia, where his business is. He did things real stylishly at first. Then he was sent to Albany, and we stayed a week at the Delavan House. One afternoon I went out to do some shopping, and when I came back he was gone. He had taken his trunk with him, and hadn't left any address; but in my traveling-bag I found a fifty-dollar bill, with a slip of paper on which he had written, 'No use coming after me; I'm married.' We'd been together less than four months, and I never saw him again.

"At first I couldn't believe it. I stayed on, thinking it was a joke—or that he'd feel sorry for me and come back. But he never came and never wrote me a line. Then I began to hate him, and to see what a wicked fool I'd been to leave Joe. I was so lonesome—I thought I'd go crazy. And I kept thinking how good and patient Joe had been, and how badly I'd used him, and how lovely it would be to be back in the little parlor at Hinksville, even with Mrs. Glenn and the minister talking about free-will and predestination. So at last I wrote to Joe. I wrote him the humblest letters you ever read, one after another; but I never got any answer.

"Finally I found I'd spent all my money, so I sold my watch and my rings — Joe gave me a lovely turquoise ring when we were married — and came to New York. I felt ashamed to stay alone any longer in Albany; I was afraid that some of Arthur's friends, who had met me with him on the road, might come there and recognize me. After I got here I wrote to Susy Price, a great friend of mine who lives at Hinksville, and she answered at once, and told me just what I had expected — that Joe was ready to forgive me and crazy to have me back, but that his mother wouldn't let him stir a step or write me a line, and that she and the minister were at him all day long, telling him how bad I was and what a sin it would be to forgive me. I got Susy's letter two or three days ago, and after that I saw it was no use writing to Joe. He'll never dare go against his mother and she watches him like a cat. I suppose I deserve it — but he might have given me another chance! I know he would if he could only see me."

Her voice had dropped from anger to lamentation, and her tears again overflowed.

Woburn looked at her with the pity one feels for a child who is suddenly confronted with the result of some unpremeditated naughtiness.

"But why not go back to Hinksville," he suggested, "if your husband is ready to forgive you? You could go to your friend's house, and once your husband knows you are there you can easily persuade him to see you."

"Perhaps I could — Susy thinks I could. But I can't go back; I haven't got a cent left."

"But surely you can borrow money? Can't you ask your friend to forward you the amount of your fare?"

She shook her head.

"Susy ain't well off; she couldn't raise five dollars, and it costs twenty-five to get back to Hinksville. And besides, what would become of me while I waited for the money? They'll turn me out of here to-morrow; I haven't paid my last week's board, and I haven't got anything to give them; my bag's empty; I've pawned everything."

"And don't you know anyone here who would lend you the money?"

"No; not a soul. At least I do know one gentleman; he's a friend of Arthur's, a Mr. Devine; he was staying at Rochester when we were there. I met him in the street the other day, and I didn't mean to speak to him, but he came up to me, and said he knew all about Arthur and how meanly he had behaved, and he wanted to know if he couldn't help me

— I suppose he saw I was in trouble. He tried to persuade me to go and stay with his aunt, who has a lovely house right round here in Twenty-fourth Street; he must be very rich, for he offered to lend me as much money as I wanted."

"You didn't take it?"

"No," she returned; "I daresay he meant to be kind, but I didn't care to be beholden to any friend of Arthur's. He came here again yesterday, but I wouldn't see him, so he left a note giving me his aunt's address and saying she'd have a room ready for me at any time."

There was a long silence; she had dried her tears and sat looking at Woburn with eyes full of helpless reliance.

"Well," he said at length, "you did right not to take that man's money; but this isn't the only alternative," he added, pointing to the revolver.

"I don't know any other," she answered wearily. "I'm not smart enough to get employment; I can't make dresses or do type-writing, or any of the useful things they teach girls now; and besides, even if I could get work I couldn't stand the loneliness. I can never hold my head up again — I can't bear the disgrace. If I can't go back to Joe I'd rather be dead."

"And if you go back to Joe it will be all right?" Woburn suggested with a smile.

"Oh," she cried, her whole face alight, "if I could only go back to Joe!"

They were both silent again; Woburn sat with his hands in his pockets gazing at the floor. At length his silence seemed to rouse her to the unwontedness of the situation, and she rose from her seat, saying in a more constrained tone, "I don't know why I've told you all this."

"Because you believed that I would help you," Woburn answered, rising also; "and you were right; I'm going to send you home."

She colored vividly. "You told me I was right not to take Mr. Devine's money," she faltered.

"Yes," he answered, "but did Mr. Devine want to send you home?"

"He wanted me to wait at his aunt's a little while first and then write to Joe again."

"I don't — I want you to start tomorrow morning; this morning, I mean. I'll take you to the station and buy your ticket, and your husband can send me back the money."

"Oh, I can't — I can't — you mustn't —" she stammered, reddening and paling. "Besides, they'll never let me leave here without paying."

"How much do you owe?"

"Fourteen dollars."

"Very well; I'll pay that for you; you can leave me your revolver as a pledge. But you must start by the first train; have you any idea at what time it leaves the Grand Central?"

"I think there's one at eight."

He glanced at his watch.

"In less than two hours, then; it's after six now."

She stood before him with fascinated eyes.

"You must have a very strong will," she said. "When you talk like that you make me feel as if I had to do everything you say."

"Well, you must," said Woburn lightly. "Man was made to be obeyed."

"Oh, you're not like other men," she returned; "I never heard a voice like yours; it's so strong and kind. You must be a very good man; you remind me of Joe; I'm sure you've got just such a nature; and Joe is the best man I've ever seen."

Woburn made no reply, and she rambled on, with little pauses and fresh bursts of confidence.

"Joe's a real hero, you know; he did the most splendid thing you ever heard of. I think I began to tell you about it, but I didn't finish. I'll tell you now. It happened just after we were married; I was mad with him at the time, I'm afraid, but now I see how splendid he was. He'd been telegraph operator at Hinksville for four years and was hoping that he'd get promoted to a bigger place; but he was afraid to ask for a raise. Well, I was very sick with a bad attack of pneumonia and one night the doctor said he wasn't sure whether he could pull me through. When they sent word to Joe at the telegraph office he couldn't stand being away from me another minute. There was a poor consumptive boy always hanging round the station; Joe had taught him how to operate, just to help him along; so he left him in the office and tore home for half an hour, knowing he could get back before the eastern express came along.

"He hadn't been gone five minutes when a freight-train ran off the rails about a mile up the track. It was a very still night, and the boy heard the smash and shouting, and knew something had happened. He couldn't tell what it was, but the minute he heard it he sent a message over the wires like a flash, and caught the eastern express just as it was pulling out of the station above Hinksville. If he'd hesitated a second, or made any mistake, the express would have come on, and the loss of life would have been fearful. The next day the Hinksville papers were full of Operator Glenn's presence of mind; they all said he'd be promoted. That was early in November and Joe didn't hear anything from the company till the first of January. Meanwhile the boy had gone home to his father's farm out in the country, and before Christmas he was dead. Well, on New Year's day Joe got a notice from the company saying that his pay was to be raised, and that he was to be promoted to a big junction near Detroit, in recognition of his presence of mind in stopping the eastern express. It was just what we'd both been pining for and I was nearly wild with joy; but I noticed Joe didn't say much. He just telegraphed for leave, and the next day he went right up to Detroit and told the directors there what had really happened. When he came back he told us they'd suspended him; I cried every night for a week, and even his mother said he was a fool. After that we just lived on at Hinksville, and six months later the company took him back; but I don't suppose they'll ever promote him now."

Her voice again trembled with facile emotion.

"Wasn't it beautiful of him? Ain't he a real hero?" she said. "And I'm sure you'd behave just like him; you'd be just as gentle about little things, and you'd never move an inch about big ones. You'd never do a mean action, but you'd be sorry for people who did; I can see it in your face; that's why I trusted you right off."

Woburn's eyes were fixed on the window; he hardly seemed to hear her. At length he walked across the room and pulled up the shade. The electric lights were dissolving in the gray alembic of the dawn. A milk-cart rattled down the street and, like a witch returning late from the Sabbath, a stray cat whisked into an area. So rose the appointed day.

Woburn turned back, drawing from his pocket the roll of bills which he had thrust there with so different a purpose. He counted them out, and handed her fifteen dollars.

"That will pay for your board, including your breakfast this morning," he said. "We'll breakfast together presently if you like; and meanwhile suppose we sit down and watch the sunrise. I haven't seen it for years."

He pushed two chairs toward the window, and they sat down side by side. The light came gradually, with the icy reluctance of winter; at last a red disk pushed itself above the opposite house-tops and a long cold gleam slanted across their window. They did not talk much; there was a silencing awe in the spectacle.

Presently Woburn rose and looked again at his watch.

"I must go and cover up my dress-coat," he said, "and you had better put on your hat and jacket. We shall have to be starting in half an hour."

As he turned away she laid her hand on his arm.

"You haven't even told me your name," she said.

"No," he answered; "but if you get safely back to Joe you can call me Providence."

"But how am I to send you the money?"

"Oh—well, I'll write you a line in a day or two and give you my address; I don't know myself what it will be; I'm a wanderer on the face of the earth."

"But you must have my name if you mean to write to me."

"Well, what is your name?"

"Ruby Glenn. And I think—I almost think you might send the letter right to Joe's—send it to the Hinksville station."

"Very well."

"You promise?"

"Of course I promise."

He went back into his room, thinking how appropriate it was that she should have an absurd name like Ruby. As he re-entered the room, where the gas sickened in the daylight, it seemed to him that he was returning to some forgotten land; he had passed, with the last few hours, into a wholly new phase of consciousness. He put on his fur coat, turning up the collar and crossing the lapels to hide his white tie. Then he put his cigar-case in his pocket, turned out the gas, and, picking up his hat and stick, walked back through the open doorway.

Ruby Glenn had obediently prepared herself for departure and was standing before the mirror, patting her curls into place. Her eyes were still red, but she had the happy look of a child that has outslept its grief. On the floor he noticed the tattered fragments of the letter which, a few hours earlier, he had seen her place before the mirror.

"Shall we go down now?" he asked.

"Very well," she assented; then, with a quick movement, she stepped close to him, and putting her hands on his shoulders lifted her face to his.

"I believe you're the best man I ever knew," she said, "the very best—except Joe."

She drew back blushing deeply, and unlocked the door which led into the passage-way. Woburn picked up her bag, which she had forgotten, and followed her out of the room. They passed a frowzy chambermaid, who stared at them with a yawn. Before the doors the row of boots still waited; there was a faint new aroma of coffee mingling with the smell of vanished dinners, and a fresh blast of heat had begun to tingle through the radiators.

In the unventilated coffee-room they found a waiter who had the melancholy air of being the last survivor of an exterminated race, and who reluctantly brought them some tea made with water which had not boiled, and a supply of stale rolls and staler butter. On this meager diet they fared in silence, Woburn occasionally glancing at his watch; at length he rose, telling his companion to go and pay her bill while he called a hansom. After all, there was no use in economizing his remaining dollars.

In a few moments she joined him under the portico of the hotel. The hansom stood waiting and he sprang in after her, calling to the driver to take them to the Forty-second Street station.

When they reached the station he found a seat for her and went to buy her ticket. There were several people ahead of him at the window, and when he had bought the ticket he found that it was time to put her in the train. She rose in answer to his glance, and together they walked down the long platform in the murky chill of the roofed-in air. He followed her into the railway carriage, making sure that she had her bag, and that the ticket was safe inside it; then he held out his hand, in its pearl-colored evening glove: he felt that the people in the other seats were staring at them.

"Good-bye," he said.

"Good-bye," she answered, flushing gratefully. "I'll never forget—never. And you *will* write, won't you? Promise!"

"Of course, of course," he said, hastening from the carriage.

He retraced his way along the platform, passed through the dismal waiting-room and stepped out into the early sunshine. On the sidewalk outside the station he hesitated awhile; then he strolled slowly down Forty-second Street and, skirting the melancholy flank of the Reservoir, walked across Bryant Park. Finally he sat down on one of the benches near the Sixth Avenue and lit a cigar.

The signs of life were multiplying around him; he watched the cars roll by with their increasing freight of dingy toilers, the shop-girls hurrying to their work, the children trudging schoolward, their small vague noses red with cold, their satchels clasped in woolen-gloved hands. There is nothing very imposing in the first stirring of a great city's activities; it is a slow reluctant process, like the waking of a heavy sleeper; but to Woburn's mood the sight of that obscure renewal of humble duties was more moving than the spectacle of an army with banners.

He sat for a long time, smoking the last cigar in his case, and murmuring to himself a line from Hamlet—the saddest, he thought, in the play—

For every man hath business and desire.

Suddenly an unpremeditated movement made him feel the pressure of Ruby Glenn's revolver in his pocket; it was like a devil's touch on his arm, and he sprang up hastily. In his other pocket there were just four dollars and fifty cents; but that didn't matter now. He had no thought of flight.

For a few minutes he loitered vaguely about the park; then the cold drove him on again, and with the rapidity born of a sudden resolve he began to walk down the Fifth Avenue towards his lodgings. He brushed past a maid-servant who was washing the vestibule and ran up stairs to his room. A fire was burning in the grate and his books and photographs greeted him cheerfully from the walls; the tranquil air of the whole room seemed to take it for granted that he meant to have his bath and breakfast and go down town as usual.

He threw off his coat and pulled the revolver out of his pocket; for some moments he held it curiously in his hand, bending over to examine it as Ruby Glenn had done; then he laid it in the top drawer of a small cabinet, and locking the drawer threw the key into the fire.

After that he went quietly about the usual business of his toilet. In taking off his dress-coat he noticed the Legion of Honor which Miss Talcott had given him at the ball. He pulled it out of his buttonhole and tossed it into the fire-place. When he had finished dressing he saw with surprise that it was nearly ten o'clock. Ruby Glenn was already two hours nearer home.

Woburn stood looking about the room of which he had thought to take final leave the night before; among the ashes beneath the grate he caught sight of a little white heap which symbolized to his fancy the remains of his brief correspondence with Miss Talcott. He roused himself from this unseasonable musing and with a final glance at the familiar setting of his past, turned to face the future which the last hours had prepared for him.

He went down stairs and stepped out of doors, hastening down the street towards Broadway as though he were late for an appointment. Every now and then he encountered an acquaintance, whom he greeted with a nod and smile; he carried his head high, and shunned no man's recognition.

At length he reached the doors of a tall granite building honeycombed with windows. He mounted the steps of the portico, and passing through the double doors of plate-glass, crossed a vestibule floored with mosaic to another glass door on which was emblazoned the name of the firm.

This door he also opened, entering a large room with wainscoted subdivisions, behind which appeared the stooping shoulders of a row of clerks.

As Woburn crossed the threshold a gray-haired man emerged from an inner office at the opposite end of the room.

At sight of Woburn he stopped short.

"Mr. Woburn!" he exclaimed; then he stepped nearer and added in a low tone: "I was requested to tell you when you came that the members of the firm are waiting; will you step into the private office?"

1899

NICHOLAS CARTER

THE DETECTIVE'S PRETTY NEIGHBOR

The ever-young NICK CARTER has appeared in more detective novels than any other character in American literature, with more than 1,500 books devoted to his adventures, beginning with *The Old Detective's Star Pupil; or, The Mysterious Crime of Madison Square* in the September 18, 1886, issue of the *New York Weekly.* The creator of the private detective was Ormond G. Smith, the son of one of the founders of the publishing company Street & Smith. He provided the outline to John Russell Coryell, who wrote the story and two others, after which the series was continued by a score of writers, the most prolific of whom was Frederick Van Rensselaer Dey, who wrote more than 1,000 novels.

In an early story, the All-American detective was described this way:

> Giants were like children in his grasp. He could fell an ox with one blow of his small, compact fist. Old Slim Carter had made the physical development of his son one of the studies of his life. Only one of his studies, however. Young Nick's mind was stored with knowledge—knowledge of a peculiar sort. His gray eyes, had, like an Indian's, been trained to take in minutest details fresh for use. His rich, full voice could run the gamut of sounds, from an old woman's broken, querulous squeak to the deep, hoarse notes of a burly ruffian. And his handsome face could, in an instant, be transformed into any one of a hundred types of unrecognizable ugliness. He was a master of disguise, and could so transform himself that even old Slim could not recognize him. And his intellect, naturally keen as a razor blade, had been incredibly sharpened by the judicious cultivation of the astute old man.

Carter remained popular as a radio hero in the 1940s, had several films made of his adventures (three of which starred Walter Pidgeon), and moved from dime novels to pulp magazines to a paperback series of more than 260 adventures of a grown-up espionage agent known as the Killmaster.

"The Detective's Pretty Neighbor" was first published in *The Detective's*

Pretty Neighbor and Other Stories, Magnet Detective Library No. 89 (New York: Street & Smith, Publishers, 1899.

• • •

CHAPTER I: A GLASSFUL OF PRUSSIC ACID

It is often said of Nick Carter that he knows in advance just how a case is coming out.

Headquarters men who have no other superstitions will declare their belief that some mysterious instinct supplies Nick with the criminal's name at the start, and that he really has nothing to do but arrest his man and prepare his evidence.

They have long ceased to be jealous of Nick's infallibility, and now they are trying to account for it.

Nothing amuses the famous detective so much as to be told of these queer fancies.

Quite recently the present writer repeated one of these fairy stories to Nick, and then asked him flatly if there was anything at all in it.

"Nothing whatever," he replied, laughing. "I follow a train of reasoning, and am often astonished to find where it leads me. This talk of a mysterious instinct is all nonsense. Why, only a few days ago I got hold of a case which fooled me completely. No countryman, opening a packet of sawdust after a visit to the city, was ever more surprised than I was by the outcome of the Keane poisoning case."

The great detective then proceeded to relate the facts in this strange affair. Although it was an occurrence absolutely unique in criminal records, it did not get over five lines in any newspaper, and no mention whatever was made of poison.

It appears that the little, old-fashioned house two doors east of Nick's, on the same side of the street, had been vacant for some years, up to October 1, 1893.

Then it was rented by Dr. Elisha Keane, a thin and withered old fellow, with a young and very pretty wife.

It was rumored in the neighborhood that Dr. Keane had left a large and lucrative practice in St. Paul solely to please his wife, who did not like the cold climate.

He was said to be rich, but a good deal of a miser, as was shown by his renting so poor and mean a house.

How these stories got about it would puzzle even Nick himself to tell, but they were circulated, and they acted as an advertisement.

The result was that Dr. Keane picked up a fair practice in a few months. Those who employed him invariably spoke well of him.

In the course of the winter Dr. Keane was so unfortunate as to have himself for a patient. He fell on his own doorstep and broke his ankle.

In spite of his medical skill he could not make the ankle strong again; and he was thereafter obliged to wear an artificial support cunningly devised by himself.

Such are the important facts about Dr. Keane. Nick paid little attention to his new neighbors, and their life was so quiet that the detective was very far from supposing that they would ever furnish him with a criminal case.

One morning, however, there was a loud ring at Nick's doorbell. It was a little before five o'clock and the detective was wrapped in a profound slumber.

The sound of the bell aroused him, and a few seconds later there was a sharp rap on his bedroom door.

Nick called, "Come in," and springing from the bed, enveloped himself in a great bathrobe.

Instantly there entered Dr. Keane, pallid, haggard, a pitiable spectacle. He sank into a chair. The attendant who had shown him to Nick's room, obeying a sign from the detective, withdrew.

"Dr. Keane!" exclaimed Nick. "What has happened?"

The miserable man buried his face in his hands. Tears ran between his bony fingers.

Age looks never so old as in the fresh light of morning, and Dr. Keane's emaciated form, lying limp in the chair, looked like a worn-out garment which his spirit had flung down there.

"Come, sir," said Nick kindly; "let me hear what has happened."

"My wife!" groaned the wretched man.

"What of her?"

"Dead! dead!"

"I knew that she was ill," said Nick; "but did not suppose that there was any danger."

"Murdered!" whispered Dr. Keane, as if he was afraid to hear the word.

Now, if any person supposes that because Nick Carter is always outwardly calm, he has no-heart in his bosom, that person is very much mistaken.

When the detective heard that this lovely, golden-haired creature, whom he had often seen tripping along the street as merrily as a schoolgirl, had been stricken down by violence, he was deeply moved by pity and anger.

If the dastardly assassin could have looked into Nick's heart at that moment he might have felt a strong impulse to take his own miserable life as the only means of escaping the law's hand.

"Murdered!" echoed Nick. "Can that be possible? Tell me how the deed was done."

While speaking these words the detective sprang into his dressing room and hastily clothed himself.

The door was open and he heard the rambling, broken narrative of the unhappy old man.

"I had been with a patient all night," said Dr. Keane. "Mr. Henry Lee — you may know him; he lives on West Tenth Street — was dangerously ill.

"It was not until four o'clock that we could pronounce him out of danger. Dr. Ransom was with me, and we worked hard all night.

"At last, worn out with exertions far beyond my strength, I left the house for my own home.

"I was so weary that I could hardly ascend the stairs to our bedroom, which is on the second floor at the front. I must have been a long time on the stairs. At last I reached the door and pushed it open.

"The morning light had not found its way into the room, for the heavy curtains were drawn to.

"The night lamp in a corner was more bright than usual. It showed me every visible thing in the room.

"But there was something invisible which made its presence known.

"A penetrating and deadly odor came to my nostrils — the odor of prussic acid.

"Then, in a flash, I saw the little stand beside the bed, with its glasses and vials of medicine; and beyond, on the pillow, her face!"

Dr. Keane's voice had sunk to a hoarse whisper, but Nick had now returned to the room. He heard every word.

The doctor spoke very slowly, as if the effort necessary to put his hideous story into words was too much for his strength.

So the detective had had time to fully clothe himself when the narration had proceeded thus far.

"Her face," repeated Nick. "You read the terrible truth in her face?"

"Yes; it was rigid and white as marble, except —"

He trembled so violently at the recollection of his horror that he could not continue, until Nick had said:

"The scar made by the acid?"

"Yes; the terrible black stain across her lips. I could not endure the sight of it."

"Yet you examined her to assure yourself that there was no hope?"

"I did. The sight of that terrible scar repelled me, but a stronger impulse urged me forward.

"Yet I knew in an instant that she was dead. The great quantity of the poison was evident from its vapor in the room, and a few drops would have been enough — indeed a single drop of the strong acid is fatal."

"How was the poison administered?"

"It must have been put into a little bottle which stood on the table by her bedside.

"This contained medicine which was to be used in case she awoke with a headache — which has happened almost every night during her illness."

"But the odor?" asked Nick. "Why did she not notice it?"

This medicine, replied the doctor, was to be added to another which stood ready in a glass. In order to get the effect, it was necessary to pour it in very quickly, and drink the portion from the glass while the violent bubbling resulting from the mixture was in progress.

"She would, therefore, have acted so quickly that the odor would not have been perceived, especially as it would have been somewhat disguised by the natural pungency of the medicine."

"And you are sure that the poison was in the small bottle?"

"Yes."

"Of course it would be only necessary to smell it."

"Certainly."

"So much for the method of the crime. Now for the criminal. Have you any suspicions?"

"Mr. Carter, I am so terribly affected, so utterly prostrated by this awful sorrow, that I scarcely know what I am saying. Perhaps I may do injustice to someone if I state my suspicions now. Let me wait till I am calmer."

"As you wish. Now let us go to your house. I must examine the scene of this crime."

CHAPTER II: ALPHONSE MARTEL

NICK ASSISTED Dr. Keane to arise, and held him by the arm as they descended the stairs.

The old man seemed feeble, and the weakness of his injured ankle, despite the ingeniously contrived support, made walking difficult for him.

However, with Nick's help he made fair progress, and in a few minutes they stood before the doctor's door.

His trembling fingers made the key rattle on the outer plate of the lock. Nick took the key from his hand, and at the same instant released his hold upon the other's arm.

No sooner had he done so than the doctor sank down upon the step with a groan.

Nick stooped beside him.

"My ankle gave way under me," said the doctor. "The support has become loosened."

"I will replace it," said Nick.

He found that this task would occupy a considerable time, but he did not especially regret this.

Apparently there was nothing to be lost by so short a delay, and, on the other hand, the cool morning air would do much to restore Dr. Keane, who was almost in a condition of collapse.

The detective, therefore, made the doctor sit down on the doorstep, and proceeded in a leisurely manner to adjust the complicated mechanism of the support.

Meanwhile he utilized the minutes in asking necessary questions.

"You suspect someone," Nick began. "Tell me who it is."

"My suspicion is founded wholly on this," replied the doctor; "there is only one person in the world, so far as I know, who had, or thought he had, any cause of resentment against my wife."

"And who was that?"

"A young man who assisted me in a certain chemical work this winter."

"His name?"

"Alphonse Martel."

"Was he in the house last night?"

"No; I discharged him from my employ yesterday morning."

"For what reason?"

"Dishonesty."

"He had stolen from you?"

"From my wife."

"What had he taken?"

"Some jewelry. She had been missing it, a piece at a time, for two weeks. We suspected a servant, and watched her closely, but without result.

"We never thought of Martel, for, so far as we knew, he had no access to the room from which the jewels were taken.

"Neither of us ever saw him go near it, whereas the servant was in that room every day.

"Day before yesterday we discharged the servant. Martel knew nothing about it.

"About noon of yesterday my wife told me that another article of jewelry was missing.

"She had seen it since the girl left the house. There was absolutely nobody who could be suspected except Martel.

"I accused him. He turned white as a sheet, but he denied everything.

"My wife would have had him arrested, but I thought that another plan would be more likely to result in the recovery of the jewelry.

"The articles were not of great value, but my wife prized them highly as keepsakes. Some of them were presents I had made her.

"I suggested that we allow Martel to go, with the understanding that if the jewels were returned to us by evening nothing more should be said; but if not, the police should be notified.

"At six o'clock the stolen property had not been returned, and my wife insisted on sending word to headquarters.

"An officer was sent out to find Martel, but was not successful. He came to our house about eight o'clock to report that Martel had vacated his lodgings, and that there was a rumor that he intended to skip to France."

"To France?" said Nick. "There's a French liner to sail this morning."

"True; and the police would be watching her; but shortly after the officer called, a messenger boy brought all the missing articles in a little box.

"The boy said that a young man had given him the box, and had sent this verbal message: 'Keep to your agreement.'

"I understood that to mean that we were expected to withdraw the complaint, and I sent to headquarters to notify them that we would not prosecute."

"How much was the jewelry worth?"

"About three hundred dollars."

"That's queer. A man doesn't skip the country for three hundred dollars. Was this fellow smart?"

"He was exceedingly smart—much too smart for me. He deceived me entirely about the robberies."

"This is unusual. I don't like the looks of this story about going to France. Are you sure this fellow hasn't got away with something more valuable than the jewelry?"

"I never thought of that. It may be so. If this fiend murdered my wife, he must have been in the house after I went to Mr. Lee's. Doubtless he plundered the house; but you will understand I gave no thought to such things in the presence of my dead wife."

"True; but now we must think of them. What had you of value in the house?"

"A large sum of money in my safe."

"How much?"

"Sixteen thousand dollars and more. Perhaps nearer seventeen thousand. I cannot recall the exact sum."

"There isn't a minute to be lost," said Nick. "We must examine that safe."

He raised Dr. Keane and opened the door. They entered the hall. The safe stood in a recess in the wall at the rear.

It was an old-fashioned, useless affair, opening with a key. A modern burglar would think no more of it than if it were made of cheese.

"I have not the key," said Dr. Keane, fumbling in his pockets. "I will go upstairs and get it. But no, I cannot. It is in that room. I — I dare not —"

"There is no need," said Nick.

He flung open the door of the safe. It was not locked.

Dr. Keane got down upon his knees and peered into the safe.

"Everything is gone!" he said.

"That would seem to settle it," rejoined Nick.

"The two crimes hang together. No person in the world, except myself and Martel, knew that there was a large sum in this safe."

"How did he happen to know it?"

"He came upon me suddenly last Monday morning when I was putting an envelope containing ten one-thousand-dollar bills into the safe. I had marked the amount on the outside of the envelope. He must have seen it.

"The fellow had a noiseless way of getting about the house which should have made me suspect him at the start. On that occasion he stood right at my elbow before I knew he was anywhere near."

Nick glanced at his watch. "The Normandie sails at six," he said, "and I must make sure that Martel does not go with her. I shall have to go to the pier myself."

"Can you reach it in time?"

"Without doubt."

"But you have no carriage."

"I shall run for it."

"Do not let him escape you."

"Don't be alarmed about that. Now give me his description."

"He is of medium height and rather slender. His face is exceedingly handsome. He has large brown eyes and a very clear skin. His teeth are small and regular. They look as if they were false, but they are not. The eyetooth on the right side has a large gold filling on the back of it."

"That's all I need. Now for your part.

"Summon help at once from my house. Ask for Chick and Patsy.

"Let Patsy come to the pier. Chick will take charge in this house. And, Dr. Keane, let me say this, which may be a comfort to you:

"I shall devote myself to a special branch of this case, the capture of Martel. To my assistant, Chick, will fall the decisive work in this house. And when he has taken hold of it, the murderer may abandon hope. Whether he is Martel, or any other of the myriad scoundrels who infest the earth, he is lost.

"It is not my habit to boast of the prowess of my friend and assistant, but in this case my sympathy for you prompts me to throw off reserve.

"Your desire for vengeance must be very nearly all that is left to you. It shall be gratified.

"There is no refuge for this murderer but in the grave."

CHAPTER III: ON THE FRENCH LINER

NICK LOOKED STEADILY into the old physician's face as he spoke the words which promised full revenge for this cowardly murder.

There seemed to be an answering gleam in the other's eyes. Dr. Keane was rousing from the stupor which had been upon him since his dreadful discovery that morning.

New strength and resolution came to him at the sound of Nick's words.

A moment later the detective was in the street, running with incredible speed toward the French liner's pier.

The last preparations for sailing were made. In a few minutes the lines would be cast off, and the great ship would move out into the river.

Nick knew that he must do quick work. He was determined to search the big steamer thoroughly, even if he should be obliged to go down the bay in her, and come back in a tug.

As Nick hurried toward the gangway, he saw one of Police Inspector McLaughlin's men disguised as a baggage handler standing near, and evidently keeping a sharp eye on all who went aboard the ship.

To this officer Nick made himself known.

"You are after Martel, I suppose," said Nick.

"Yes, but I'm afraid I shan't get him this morning."

"He hasn't shown up, eh?"

"No; but I had a dead straight tip that he was to go."

"You want him for the Keane affair?"

"Yes; are you on to it?"

Nick was a good deal more "on to it" than the other man, but he did not say so. It was not his purpose to impart information, but to receive it.

"Tell me what you know of it," said Nick.

"Why, it's this way: Martel is accused of taking some jewelry belonging to Mrs. Keane, but in my opinion that doesn't really cut any figure in the case. Martel has a bigger job than that, or I'm a farmer."

"Why do you think so?"

"Because Martel is a thief, and a mighty slick one. He robbed the druggist who employed him before Keane got hold of him.

"The druggist had him arrested for some petty larceny—a few cents out of the cash drawer or something of that kind that could hardly be taken into court—but back of that was a big haul.

"In my opinion that druggist lost thousands, but Martel managed to get some hold over him. The arrest was only a bluff, and it didn't go. Martel and the druggist had a talk, and the druggist evidently weakened. He withdrew his charge.

"That's the kind of Frenchman Monsieur Martel is, and when I find such a man making preparations to skip the country very quietly, I know there's something beside three gold rings and two little diamonds in the case.

"Keane withdraws his charge just as the druggist did. They've both been stuck for big money, and the man who did it is too smart to be at large."

"Do you think Martel has a hold on Keane?"

"I'm nearly sure of it. How else can we account for Keane's conduct? When a man presses a charge one minute, and withdraws it in a hurry the next, why, there's a reason, and nobody on earth knows that better than you do. Mr. Carter, I'm not such a chump as to try to teach you anything."

"I'm obliged to you for your information," said Nick. "Is there anything more?"

"Yes; there's one very peculiar thing. I hardly understand it. Would you believe that Keane hired that man, knowing him to be a thief?"

"Is that so?"

"No doubt of it. Keane went to the druggist and asked about Martel. The druggist told him that the fellow was an habitual thief, and a dangerous rascal generally. Then Keane went right off and hired him."

"How did Keane get hold of Martel's name in the first place?"

"I don't know, unless he saw a little paragraph in the papers."

"Giving a hint of this druggist's affair?"

"Yes."

"You mean that Keane was deliberately hunting for a crook?"

"It may be."

Could Keane have hired Martel to poison the woman? Was the money in the safe a bait? These were the questions which rushed through Nick's mind. It seemed incredible.

Martel was almost certain to be captured. Keane must know that, and if the Frenchman was arrested there was scarcely a chance that he would carry his secret to the death chamber of a prison.

The risks involved seemed too great. If Keane was playing such a game, it was the most desperate one which Nick had ever encountered.

To hire a murderer was no new thing; but for the principal in such an affair to put the police at once upon the track of his agent, and betray that agent from the start, was sheer madness.

Nick could not believe that Keane had done so foolish a thing. And yet why had he hired a man whom he knew to be dishonest?

"I'm almost ready to give up hope of catching my man here," said the Central Office man, "and yet I felt sure of him."

"How did you get the tip?"

"From a woman."

"One who had learned that Martel was going to desert her, I suppose."

"Exactly so."

"That is generally a good source of information."

"None better."

"You think she is giving you a straight story?"

"I haven't a doubt of it."

"Where is she?"

"On board the steamer."

"Acting in your interest?"

"Yes. She is making sure that Martel is not aboard. When she satisfies herself of that, she will come ashore. If she suspects that he is there, but is not sure, she will signal to me from the upper deck."

"She may be playing a game."

"I've thought of that. At the last minute, if she says he isn't there, I'm going to try a bluff."

"Arrest her?"

"Yes."

"Suppose she doesn't squeal?"

"Then I'll search the ship anyway. That is, that was my plan. Of course, since you are here I put the whole matter in your hands."

"I don't see how you could do better than carry out your design. You can't lose anything by it. If the woman is straight she can help you. If she isn't, you'll search the vessel, and that's all you could have done in any case."

"That was my idea."

"Isn't it nearly time the woman appeared?"

"I should say so. Ah, there she is!"

He directed Nick's attention to a young and stylishly dressed woman who had just come to the rail above the gangway.

The woman put her hand to the right side of her head with a somewhat peculiar movement.

"That's the signal," said the officer. "It means that she is in doubt."

"Then let's go aboard and talk with her."

"Can this be a plan to get me out of the way while the fellow slips aboard?"

"I think not, but at any rate, we'll balk it. You go on the upper deck where she is, and I'll wait here. When you get there, you'll command the gangway. Then I'll join you."

"Good."

In a couple of minutes the officer appeared beside the woman.

Nick then left his post and proceeded at once to the upper deck.

"Miss Laselle," said the officer, "this gentleman is Mr. Nick Carter, the famous detective. He is now in charge of the case."

"I am glad to see you, Mr. Carter," said the woman, speaking with a slight French accent. "You will not let this man escape me."

"No danger of that," said Nick.

"She is afraid that he is aboard, although she has found no trace of him," said the headquarters officer.

"Why do you believe him to be here?" asked Nick.

"Because I am sure that he had planned to sail on this steamer."

"What do you propose to do?"

"She has suggested a plan which looks to me good," said the police officer. "She proposes to sail on the steamer if I can furnish the necessary funds.

"She believes that Martel is here, and she is sure that she can spot him before voyage is over. Of course we shall cable to have the vessel searched on the other side, and she can point out the man to the French police."

"A shrewd scheme," said Nick.

"There is an assistant steward aboard," said the woman, "who was a friend to Martel. His manner when I questioned him confirmed my suspicion that Martel is hidden on the vessel."

"And if the money is furnished you, you will take the voyage?" said Nick.

"Yes, gladly. Do you approve of the plan?"

"No," said Nick slowly; "I do not. Martel will not sail on this steamer. Come; the lines will be cast off in another minute. We must go ashore."

"And abandon the pursuit?" exclaimed Miss Laselle.

"No; far from it. We will go and put Martel behind the bars."

"What do you mean?"

"I mean that this farce is played out. Alphonse Martel, you are my prisoner!"

Miss Laselle turned deadly pale. The man from headquarters uttered a cry of astonishment.

"There's no doubt about it," said Nick. "He makes a very pretty woman, but he opens his mouth too wide when he talks. He shows that peculiar gold filling in his eyetooth."

"Caught, for a thousand dollars to a doughnut!" exclaimed the police officer.

Martel collapsed.

"Of what am I accused?" he stammered. "Who brings a charge against me?"

"Dr. Keane is your accuser," said Nick.

"Those jewels?"

"Oh, no; a much graver crime."

Every trace of color left Martel's face. Even his lips looked white.

"Do you admit your guilt?" asked Nick.

"What is the use of denying it?" said Martel, almost in a whisper. "I am guilty."

CHAPTER IV: NO REFUGE BUT THE GRAVE

TAKE HIM TO headquarters," said Nick to the officer.

"What is the exact charge?" whispered the other in Nick's ear.

"Murder!" returned Nick in the same tone.

The officer was amazed.

"Question him on your way to headquarters," whispered Nick, "concerning the murder of Mrs. Keane by prussic acid poisoning. Let me know what he says about it."

"He has already admitted his guilt."

"True, but I wish to know the details. I am going to Keane's house now."

Martel had been in a sort of stupor from which he was aroused by the heavy hand of the officer on his shoulder.

The prisoner made no resistance.

Nick hurried away from the pier. He was anxious to return to Dr. Keane's house as soon as possible. There was one point which needed explanation. Why had not Patsy appeared?

It was possible, of course, that Dr. Keane, in his agitation, had not delivered Nick's message aright.

Yet Nick wondered that Chick had not sent Patsy in any case.

It was a little after seven o'clock when Nick reached Dr. Keane's house.

All was quiet. He noted the heavy curtains at the windows of Mrs. Keane's room, and he wondered that Chick had not let in more light.

He rang the bell, and there was no answer. Again he tried, but without success.

Could the house be empty? There was every indication that only the corpse was within.

In a second Nick had picked the lock.

Coming from the dazzling daylight into the dim hall, Nick was blinded for a few seconds.

Then he saw clearly, and the sight that met his eyes was the first of the complete surprises in this case.

On the lower steps of the stairway leading to the floor above was the body of Dr. Keane.

His face was sunken, white and ghastly.

A surprising quantity of blood was gathered in a pool at the dead man's feet.

By his side, on the step, was a shining implement of surgery.

Nick examined the body, to make sure that the man was quite dead. There was no doubt of that.

He had opened the carotid artery.

As Nick rose from the dead man's side, he heard a noise of wheels without.

A carriage had dashed up to the curb.

Opening the door, Nick admitted a policeman in uniform, who announced at once that he came with a hurried message from the officer whom Nick had left in charge of Martel.

"The man denies all knowledge of the murder," said the policeman. Garrison, the Central Office man, picked me up on the street and sent me to you.

"He says you ought to know Martel's story at once. It seems that Martel admits having robbed Keane by forgery. He drew the doctor's balance from two banks.

"But as to the murder, he professes absolute ignorance. He accuses Keane of the deed, and says that he knows that Mrs. Keane was insured for a large amount in her husband's favor.

"Garrison believes that Martel speaks the truth. He told me to put myself under your orders. If you desire it, Garrison will bring Martel up here, so that you can question him."

"It won't be necessary," said Nick. "There is the answer to all questions."

He pointed to the body of the suicide.

There was a piece of paper on the stairs. It was a leaf torn from the doctor's diary.

On it was scrawled a dying message and confession.

It was rambling and incoherent, but the story was this:

Keane had killed his wife for the insurance money. She was the third victim of his deadly avarice. He had hired Martel as his assistant, knowing that the man was a criminal, and expecting to put the crime onto him. The jewelry had been stolen by the doctor himself in order to make his wife accuse Martel, and thus raise a presumption of resentment as a motive for the murder. There had been no money in the safe. That was another trick.

Knowing that he was to be out all night with a patient, Dr. Keane had left the bottle of prussic acid by his wife's bedside. On coming home he had found her dead, as he had expected.

And then, as he wrote, for the first time in his wicked life, remorse had overwhelmed him. Terror of discovery had shaken all his nerves.

It was with the greatest possible effort that he carried out his plan of going to Nick's house.

Afterward the manner of the detective, and especially his closing words, had completed the wreck of Keane's determination.

He had not dared to summon Chick. He had not even dared to look again into his wife's room.

On the first occasion he had not dared approach her side. The blackened lips seemed to be moving in the utterance of curses upon him.

And so, a prey to utter panic terror, he had taken his own life to cheat the law.

"You said," were the last words of the message, "that there was no refuge but the grave. I seek that refuge."

Nick read this terrible confession aloud, and even the policeman, hardened by the sight of many crimes, was nearly overcome by this.

There was such dread in every word of that last writing; it gave so awful a picture of a life's remorse concentrated into a few heartrending moments, that Nick was ready to declare it the most fearful cry of conscience which had ever come to him.

The thought of this wretched old man who had bartered his soul for money, and dared not wait for the miserable pay, alone with the dead in that house, and seeking the last refuge of the hunted criminal, was infinitely terrible.

Nick drew a long breath, and then with a firm step ascended the stairs.

In the upper hall, as he turned, was a door to the right, which evidently led to Mrs. Keane's apartment.

Nick pushed it open. The policeman, trembling with excitement, looked over the detective's shoulder.

It was a pretty room, decked out with all the resources of feminine good taste.

There were bright pictures and many little ornaments such as a woman loves to surround herself with.

There was the bed in the corner, and the small table with its glasses and vials much disturbed.

All these things came to Nick in a flash, but they were of small moment to the main purpose.

In the bed, sitting up, and not stretched dead upon her pillow, was the golden-haired young wife of the physician.

She had a glass raised to her lips, and Nick could see that the liquid within it was bubbling and seething.

"Stop!" cried Nick, in horror. "It is poisoned!"

He was too late. The beautiful head was already thrown back to drink off the potion. It passed her lips.

She dropped the empty glass, and uttered a piercing scream.

Never in all the great detective's experience had he known such a moment as that.

The whole case was clear to him in a flash.

Dr. Keane's fears had deceived him. He had returned expecting to find his wife dead, and had found her sleeping. He feared to examine more closely, for something in her attitude had suggested death, and he had leaped to the conclusion that the poison had done its work.

And now, right under the eyes of the detective, the deadly draft had been drunk off. Could that be possible?

The sickening vapor of the fatal acid could be perceived in the room, but not strongly.

As Nick sprang toward the bed, his only hope was in that. Could there have been less of the acid than the doctor had supposed? Might the wronged wife still be saved?

She lay perfectly still upon the pillows. Faintly about her lips could be seen a dark discoloration. Surely the acid had done its work.

Nick was beside her in a moment. As he bent over her, he was surprised to see the dark stain disappear.

And then he saw the cause.

That stain was a shadow!

The night lamp, still burning in the corner, cast the shadow of a vial on the table directly on her face.

Nick had interrupted it, and the illusion had vanished.

The woman was only fainting. The sight of two strangers invading her bedroom was enough to account for that.

The detective seized the glass from which she had drunk. A strong aromatic odor was exhaled from it, but there was no suggestion of prussic acid.

And yet the deadly vapor could be perceived in the room.

Nick's quick eye glanced at the table. He marked the disarray of the vials.

One had fallen to the floor and was broken.

He seized it. The odor of prussic acid was so strong upon it that it made Nick's head throb with that peculiar terrible shock which those who know the infernal acid cannot fail to recognize.

"It is as plain as day!" cried Nick, speaking aloud in the extremity of his joy. "In her sleep she upset the bottle with the poison.

"It was spilled and gave forth the odor which Dr. Keane recognized. That and the shadow on her face and the terror of his guilty soul deceived him, so that he thought her dead.

"She slept well. She had just awakened. Her head ached from the vapor in the room.

"She looked for the medicine which she was accustomed to take to relieve a headache. She saw the broken vial.

"But there was more of it in the closet. She secured it, and was just in the act of taking a harmless draft when we entered."

And so it proved. The young woman was quickly brought to her senses, and she subsequently confirmed, as far as possible, the theory Nick had formed.

She had not wakened during the night. Her sleep had saved her life. She must have had a sort of nightmare, in which she had struck the table and broken some of the vials, the poison one, happily, among them.

Her horror, when the truth was told to her, was intense, for she had really loved the wretched old man who had plotted to take her life.

And this is the end of the story. The money which Martel had stolen was recovered and paid to Mrs. Keane.

Martel was sentenced to a long term in prison, but he was not disposed to regard his fate as hard. He had escaped a much more serious charge which the old physician's plot had nearly fastened upon him.

1899

ELLEN GLASGOW

A POINT IN MORALS

The justly respected realism in the work of the noted southern writer ELLEN (ANDERSON GHOLSON) GLASGOW (1873–1945) is so believable that it takes a second thought to accept the notion that casual shipboard acquaintances would calmly discuss the life and death of a human being as if it had no more significance than the morality of stepping on an ant. This story is somewhat unusual for Glasgow as it has a varied cast of characters from different backgrounds. It is her portrayal of southern life, among both its aristocracy and its lower social levels, with a particular emphasis on the relationship between women and the men in their lives, that won Glasgow accolades in the 1920s and 1930s as one of the enduring leaders of the literary renaissance of the South. In 1940 she was awarded the Howells Medal for fiction by the American Academy of Arts and Letters, and her 1942 novel, *In This Our Life,* won the Pulitzer Prize for fiction. While she is recognized as an important regional writer, her sophisticated ghost stories have been frequently anthologized and are much read today. "A Point in Morals" is a mystery that invites the reader to make some decisions. How many murderers are there in the story? And would you have done what the alienist (psychologist) did?

Born in Richmond, Virginia, Glasgow was a rather frail child and dropped out of school at the age of nine, after which she taught herself by reading her father's substantial library. She lived briefly in New York, where she began and then maintained a lengthy, long-distance affair with a married man (as recounted in her posthumous autobiography, *The Woman Within,* 1954), but soon returned to her birthplace, where she continued to live and write, very much in solitude, in an old gray stone house in the middle of the city.

"A Point in Morals" was first published in the May 1899 issue of *Harper's New Monthly Magazine 98;* it was first collected in Glasgow's short story collection *The Shadowy Third and Other Stories* (New York: Doubleday, Page, 1923).

• • •

THE QUESTION SEEMS to be—" began the Englishman. He looked up and bowed to a girl in a yachting-cap who had just come in from deck and was taking the seat beside him. "The question seems to be —" The girl was having some difficulty in removing her coat, and he turned to assist her.

"In my opinion," broke in a well-known alienist on his way to a convention in Vienna, "the question is simply whether or not civilization, in placing an exorbitant value upon human life, is defeating its own aims." He leaned forward authoritatively, and spoke with a half-foreign precision of accent.

"You mean that the survival of the fittest is checkmated," remarked a young journalist traveling in the interest of a New York daily, "that civilization should practice artificial selection, as it were?"

The alienist shrugged his shoulders deprecatingly. "My dear sir," he protested, "I don't mean anything. It is the question that means something."

"Well, as I was saying," began the Englishman again, reaching for the salt and upsetting a spoonful, "the question seems to be whether or not, under any circumstances, the saving of a human life may become positively immoral."

"Upon that point —" began the alienist; but a young lady in a pink blouse who was seated on the Captain's right interrupted him.

"How could it?" she asked. "At least I don't see how it could; do you, Captain?"

"There is no doubt," remarked the journalist, looking up from a conversation he had drifted into with a lawyer from one of the Western States, "that the more humane spirit pervading modern civilization has not worked wholly for good in the development of the species. Probably, for instance, if we had followed the Spartan practice of exposing unhealthy infants, we should have retained something of the Spartan hardihood. Certainly if we had been content to remain barbarians both our digestions and our nerves would have been the better for it, and melancholia would perhaps have been unknown. But, at the same time, the loss of a number of the more heroic virtues is overbalanced by an increase of the softer ones. Notably, human life has never before been regarded so sacredly."

"On the other side," observed the lawyer, lifting his hand to adjust his eyeglasses, and pausing to brush a crumb from his coat, "though it may all be very well to be philanthropic to the point of pauperizing half a community and of growing squeamish about capital punishment, the whole thing sometimes takes a disgustingly morbid turn. Why, it seems as if criminals were the real American heroes! Only last week I visited a man sentenced to death for the murder of his two wives, and, by Jove, the jailer was literally besieged by women sympathizers. I counted six bunches of heliotrope in his cell, and at least fifty notes."

"Oh, but that is a form of nervous hysteria!" said the girl in the yachting-cap, "and must be considered separately. Every sentiment has its fanatics — philanthropy as well as religion. But we don't judge a movement by a few overwrought disciples."

"That is true," said the Englishman, quietly. He was a middle-aged man, with an insistently optimistic countenance, and a build suggestive of general solidity. "But to return to the original proposition. I suppose we will all accept as a fundamental postulate the statement that the highest civilization is the one in which the highest value is placed upon individual life —"

"And happiness," added the girl in the yachting cap.

"And happiness," assented the Englishman.

"And yet," commented the lawyer, "I think that most of us will admit that such a society, where life is regarded as sacred because it is valuable to the individual, and not because it is valuable to the state, tends to the non-production of heroes —"

"That the average will be higher and the exception lower," observed the journalist. "In other words, that there will be a general elevation of the mass, accompanied by a corresponding lowering of the few."

"On the whole, I think our system does very well," said the Englishman, carefully measuring the horseradish he was placing upon his oysters. "A mean between two extremes is apt to be satisfactory in results. If we don't produce a Marcus Aurelius or a Seneca, neither do we produce a Nero or a Phocas. We may have lost patriotism, but we have gained cosmopolitanism, which is better. If we have lost chivalry, we have acquired decency; and if we have ceased to be picturesque, we have become cleanly, which is considerably more to be desired."

"I have never felt the romanticism of the Middle Ages," remarked the girl in the yachting-cap. "When I read of the glories of the Crusaders, I can't help remembering that a knight wore a single garment for a lifetime, and hacked his horse to pieces for a whim. Just as I never think of that chivalrous brute, Richard the Lion-Hearted, that I don't see him chopping off the heads of his three thousand prisoners."

"Oh, I don't think that any of us are sighing for a revival of the Middle Ages," returned the journalist. "The worship of the past has usually for its devotees people who have only known the present —"

"Which is as it should be," commented the lawyer. "If man was confined to the worship of the knowable, all the world would lapse into atheism."

"Just as the great lovers of humanity were generally hermits," added the girl in the yachting-cap. "I had an uncle who used to say that he never really loved mankind until he went to live in the wilderness."

"I think we are drifting from the point," said the alienist, helping himself to potatoes. "Was it not — can the saving of a human life ever prove to be an immoral act? I once held that it could."

"Did you act upon it?" asked the lawyer, with rising interest. "I maintain that no proposition can be said to exist until it is acted upon. Otherwise it is in merely an embryonic state —"

The alienist laid down his fork and leaned forward. He was a notable-looking man of some thirty-odd years, who had made a sudden leap into popularity through several successful cases. He had a nervous, muscular face, with singularly penetrating eyes, and hair of a light sandy color. His hands were white and well shaped.

"It was some years ago," he said, bending a scintillant glance around the table. "If you will listen —"

There followed a stir of assent, accompanied by a nod from the young lady upon the Captain's right. "I feel as if it would be a ghost story," she declared.

"It is not a story at all," returned the alienist, lifting his wineglass and holding it against the light. "It is merely a fact."

Then he glanced swiftly around the table as if challenging attention.

"As I said," he began, slowly, "it was some few years ago. Just what year does not matter, but at that time I had completed a course at Heidelberg, and expected shortly to set out with an exploring party for South Africa. It turned out afterwards that I did not go, but for the purpose of the present story it is sufficient that I intended to do so, and had made my preparations accordingly. At Heidelberg I had lived among a set of German students who were permeated with the metaphysics of Schopenhauer, von Hartmann, and the rest, and I was pretty well saturated myself. At that age I was an ardent disciple of pessimism. I am still a disciple, but my ardor has abated — which is not the fault of pessimism, but the virtue of middle age —"

"A man is usually called conservative when he has passed the twenties," interrupted the journalist, "yet it is not that he grows more conservative, but that he grows less radical —"

"Rather that he grows less in every direction," added the Englishman, "except in physical bulk."

The alienist accepted the suggestions with an inclination, and continued. "One of my most cherished convictions," he said, "was to the effect that every man is the sole arbiter of his fate. As Schopenhauer has it, '*that there is nothing to which a man has a more unassailable title than to his own life and person.*' Indeed, that particular sentence had become a kind of motto with our set, and some of my companions even went so far as to preach the proper ending of life with the ending of the power of individual usefulness."

He paused to help himself to salad.

"I was in Scotland at the time, where I had spent a fortnight with my parents, in a small village on the Kyles of Bute. While there I had been treating an invalid cousin who had acquired the morphine habit, and who, under my care, had determined to uproot it. Before leaving I had secured from her the amount of the drug which she had in her possession — some thirty grains — done up in a sealed package, and labeled by a London chemist. As I was in haste, I put it in my bag, thinking that I would add it to my case of medicines when I reached Leicester, where I was to spend the night with an old schoolmate. I took the boat at Tighnabruaich, the small village, found a local train at Gourock to reach Glasgow with one minute in which to catch the first express to London. I made the change and secured a first-class smoking-compartment, which I at first thought to be vacant, but when the train had started a man came from the dressing-room and took the seat across from me. At first I paid no heed to him, but upon looking up once or twice and finding his eyes upon me, I became unpleasantly conscious of his presence. He was thin almost to emaciation, and yet there was a muscular suggestion of physical force about him which it was difficult to account for, since he was both short and slight. His clothes were shabby, but well made, and his cravat had the appearance of having been tied in haste or by nervous fingers. There was a trace of sensuality about the mouth, over which he wore a drooping yellow mustache tinged with gray, and he was somewhat bald upon the crown of his head, which lent a deceptive hint of intellectuality to his uncovered forehead. As he crossed his legs I saw that his boots were carefully blacked, and that they were long and slender, tapering to a decided point."

"I have always held," interpolated the lawyer, "that to judge a man's character you must read his feet."

The alienist sipped his claret and took up his words:

"After passing the first stop I remembered a book at the bottom of my bag, and, unfastening the strap, in my search for the book I laid a number of small articles upon the seat beside me, among them the sealed package bearing the morphine label and the name of the London chemist. Having found the book, I turned to replace the articles, when I noticed that the man across from me was gazing attentively at the labeled package. For a moment his expression startled me, and I stared back at him from across my open bag, into which I had dropped the articles. There was in his eyes a curious mixture of passion and repulsion, and, beyond it all, the look of a hungry hound when he sees food. Thinking that I had chanced upon a victim of the opium craving, I closed the bag, placed it in the net above my head, and opened my book.

"For a while we rode in silence. Nothing was heard except the noise of the train and the clicking of our bags as they jostled each other in the receptacle above. I remember these details very vividly, because since then I have recalled the slightest fact in connection with the incident. I knew that the man across from me drew a cigar from his case, felt in his pocket for an instant, and then turned to me for a match. At the same time I experienced the feeling that the request veiled a larger purpose, and that there were matches in the pocket into which he thrust his fingers.

"But, as I complied with his request, he glanced indifferently out of the window, and following his gaze, I saw that we were passing a group of low-lying hills flecked with stray patches of heather, and that across the hills a flock of sheep were filing, followed by a peasant girl in a short skirt. It was the last faint suggestion of the Highlands.

"The man across from me leaned out, looking back upon the neutral sky, the sparse patches of heather, and the flock of sheep.

" 'What a tone the heather gives to a landscape!' he remarked, and his voice sounded forced and affected.

"I bowed without replying, and as he turned from the window, and I sat upon the back seat in the draft of cinders, I bent forward to lower the sash. In a moment he spoke again:

" 'Do you go to London?'

" 'To Leicester,' I answered, laying the book aside, impelled by a sudden interest. 'Why do you ask?'

"He flushed nervously.

" 'I — oh, nothing,' he answered, and drew from me.

"Then, as if with swift determination, he reached forward and lifted the book I had laid upon the seat. It was a treatise of von Hartmann's in German.

"'I had judged that you were a physician,' he said—'a student, perhaps, from a German university?'

"'I am.'

"He paused for an instant, and then spoke in absent-minded reiteration, 'So you don't go on to London?'

"'No,' I returned, impatiently; 'but can I do anything for you?'

"He handed me the book, regarding me resolutely as he did so.

"'Are you a sensible man?'

"I bowed.

"'And a philosopher?'

"'In amateur fashion.'

"With fevered energy he went on more quickly, 'You have in your possession,' he said, 'something for which I would give my whole fortune.' He laid two half-sovereigns and some odd silver in the palm of his hand. 'This is all I possess,' he continued, 'but I would give it gladly.'

"I looked at him curiously.

"'You mean the morphia?' I demanded.

"He nodded. 'I don't ask you to give it to me,' he said; 'I only ask—'

"I interrupted him. 'Are you in pain?'

"He laughed softly, and I really believe he felt a tinge of amusement. 'It is a question of expediency,' he explained. 'If you happen to be a moralist—'

"He broke off. 'What of it?' I inquired.

"He settled himself in his corner, resting his head against the cushions.

"'You get out at Leicester,' he said, recklessly. 'I go on to London, where Providence, represented by Scotland Yard, is awaiting me.'

"I started. 'For what?'

"'They call it murder, I believe,' he returned; 'but what they call it matters very little. I call it justifiable homicide—that also matters very little. The point is—I will arrive, they will be there before me. That is settled. Every station along the road is watched.'

"I glanced out of the window.

"'But you came from Glasgow,' I suggested.

"'Worse luck! I waited in the dressing-room until the train started. I hoped to have the compartment alone, but—' He leaned forward and lowered the window-shade. 'If you don't object,' he said, apologetically; 'I find the glare trying. It is a question for a moralist,' he repeated. 'Indeed, I may call myself a question for a moralist,' and he smiled again with that ugly humor. 'To begin with the beginning, the question is bred in the bone and it's out in the blood.' He nodded at my look of surprise. 'You are an American,' he continued, 'and so am I. I was born in Washington some thirty years ago. My father was a politician of note, whose honor was held to be unimpeachable — which was a mistake. His name doesn't matter, but he became very wealthy through judicious speculations — in votes and other things. My mother has always suffered from an incipient hysteria, which developed shortly before my birth.' He wiped his forehead with his pocket-handkerchief, and knocked the ashes from his cigar with a flick of his finger. 'The motive for this is not far to seek,' he said, with a glance at my traveling-bag. He had the coolest bravado I have ever met. 'As a child,' he went on, 'I gave great promise. Indeed, we moved to England that I might be educated at Oxford. My father considered the atmospheric ecclesiasticism to be beneficial. But while at college I got into trouble with a woman, and I left. My father died, his fortune burst like a bubble, and my mother moved to the country. I was put into a banking office, but I got into more trouble with women — this time two of them. One was a low variety actress, and I married her. I didn't want to do it. I tried not to, but I couldn't help it, and I did it. A month later I left her. I changed my name and went to Belfast, where I resolved to become an honest man. It was a tough job, but I labored and I succeeded — for a time. The variety actress began looking for me, but I escaped her, and have escaped her so far. That was eight years ago. And several years after reaching Belfast I met another woman. She was different. I fell ill of fever in Ireland, and she nursed me. She was a good woman, with a broad Irish face, strong hands, and motherly shoulders. I was weak and she was strong, and I fell in love with her. I tried to tell her about the variety actress, but somehow I couldn't, and I married her.' He shot the stump of his cigar through the opposite window and lighted another, this time drawing the match from his pocket. 'She is an honest woman,' he said — 'as honest as the day. She believes in me. It would kill her to know about the variety actress — and all the others. There is one child, a girl — a freckle-faced mite just like her mother — and another is coming.'

"'She knows nothing of this affair?'

"'Not a blamed thing. She is the kind of woman who is good because she can't help herself. She enjoys it. I never did. My mother is different, too. She would die if other people knew of this; my wife would die if she knew of it herself. Well, I got tired, and I wanted money, so I left her and went to Dublin. I changed my name and got a clerkship in a shipping office. My wife thinks I went to America to get work, and if she never hears of me she'll probably think no worse. I did intend going to America, but somehow I didn't. I got in with a man who signed somebody's name to a check and got me to present it. Then we quarreled about the money, and the man threw the job on me and the affair came out. But before they arrested me I ran him down and shot him. I was ridding the world of a damned traitor.'

"He raised the shade with a nervous hand, but the sun flashed into his eyes, and he lowered it.

"'I suppose I'd hang for it,' he said; 'there isn't much doubt of that. If I waited I'd hang for it, but I am not going to wait. I am going to die. It is the only thing left, and I am going to do it.'

"'And how?'

"'Before this train reaches London,' he replied, 'I am a dead man. There are two ways. I might say three, except that a pitch from the carriage might mean only a broken leg. But there is this —' He drew a vial from his pocket and held it to the light. It contained an ounce or so of carbolic acid.

"'One of the most corrosive of irritants,' I observed.

"'And there is — your package.'

"My first impulse prompted me to force the vial from him. He was a slight man, and I could have overcome him with but little exertion. But the exertion I did not make. I should as soon have thought, when my rational humor reasserted itself, of knocking a man down on Broadway and robbing him of his watch. The acid was as exclusively his property as the clothes he wore, and equally his life was his own. Had he declared his intention to hurl himself from the window I might not have made way for him, but I should certainly not have obstructed his passage.

"But the morphia was mine, and that I should assist him was another matter, so I said,

"'The package belongs to me.'

"'And you will not exchange?'

"'Certainly not.'

"He answered, almost angrily:

"'Why not be reasonable? You admit that I am in a mess of it?'

"'Readily.'

"'You also admit that my life is morally my own?'

"'Equally.'

"'That its continuance could in no wise prove to be of benefit to society?'

"'I do.'

"'That for all connected with me it would be better that I should die unknown and under an assumed name than that I should end upon the scaffold, my wife and mother wrecked for life, my children discovered to be illegitimate?'

"'Yes.'

"'Then you admit also that the best I can do is to kill myself before reaching London?'

"'Perhaps.'

"'So you will leave me the morphine when you get off at Leicester?'

"'No.'

"He struck the window-sill impatiently with the palm of his hand.

"'And why not?'

"I hesitated an instant.

"'Because, upon the whole, I do not care to be the instrument of your self-destruction.'

"'Don't be a fool!' he retorted. 'Speak honestly, and say that because of a little moral shrinkage on your part you prefer to leave a human being to a death of agony. I don't like physical pain. I am like a woman about it, but it is better than hanging, or life-imprisonment, or any jury finding.'

"I became exhortatory.

"'Why not face it like a man and take your chances? Who knows—'

"'I have had my chances,' he returned. 'I have squandered more chances than most men ever lay eyes on—and I don't care. If I had the opportunity, I'd squander them again. It is the only thing chances are made for.'

"'What a scoundrel you are!' I exclaimed.

"'Well, I don't know,' he answered; 'there have been worse men. I never said a harsh word to a woman, and I never hit a man when he was down—'

"I blushed. 'Oh, I didn't mean to hit you,' I responded.

"He took no notice.

"'I like my wife,' he said. 'She is a good woman, and I'd do a good deal to keep her and the children from knowing the truth. Perhaps I'd kill myself even if I didn't want to. I don't know, but I am tired—damned tired.'

"'And yet you deserted her.'

"'I did. I tried not to, but I couldn't help it. If I was free to go back to her to-morrow, unless I was ill and wanted nursing, I'd see that she had grown shapeless, and that her hands were coarse.' He stretched out his own, which were singularly white and delicate. 'I believe I'd leave her in a week,' he said.

"Then with an eager movement he pointed to my bag.

" 'That is the ending of the difficulty,' he added, 'otherwise I swear that before the train gets to London I will swallow this stuff, and die like a rat.'

" 'I admit your right to die in any manner you choose, but I don't see that it is my place to assist you. It is an ugly job.'

" 'So am I,' he retorted, grimly. 'At any rate, if you leave the train with that package in your bag it will be cowardice — sheer cowardice. And for the sake of your cowardice you will damn me to this — ' He touched the vial.

" 'It won't be pleasant,' I said, and we were silent.

"I knew that the man had spoken the truth. I was accustomed to lies, and had learned to detect them. I knew, also, that the world would be well rid of him and his kind. Why I should preserve him for death upon the gallows I did not see. The majesty of the law would be in no way ruffled by his premature departure; and if I could trust that part of his story, the lives of innocent women and children would, in the other case, suffer considerably. And even if I and my unopened bag alighted at Leicester, I was sure that he would never reach London alive. He was a desperate man, this I read in his set face, his dazed eyes, his nervous hands. He was a poor devil, and I was sorry for him as it was. Why, then, should I contribute, by my refusal to comply with his request, an additional hour of agony to his existence? Could I, with my pretence of philosophic latitudinarianism, alight at my station, leaving him to swallow the acid and die like a rat in a cage before the journey was over? I remembered that I had once seen a guinea-pig die from the effects of carbolic acid, and the remembrance sickened me suddenly.

"As I sat there listening to the noise of the slackening train, which was nearing Leicester, I thought of a hundred things. I thought of Schopenhauer and von Hartmann. I thought of the dying guinea-pig. I thought of the broad-faced Irish wife and the two children.

"Then 'Leicester' flashed before me, and the train stopped. I rose, gathered my coat and rug, and lifted the volume of von Hartmann from the seat. The man remained motionless in the corner of the compartment, but his eyes followed me.

"I stooped, opened my bag, and laid the chemist's package upon the seat. Then I stepped out, closing the door after me." As the speaker finished, he reached forward, selected an almond from the stand of nuts, fitted it carefully between the crackers, and cracked it slowly.

The young lady upon the Captain's right shook herself with a shudder.

"What a horrible story!" she exclaimed; "for it is a story, after all, and not a fact."

"A point, rather," suggested the Englishman; "but is that all?"

"All of the point," returned the alienist. "The next day I saw in the *Times* that a man, supposed to be James Morganson, who was wanted for murder, was found dead in a first-class smoking-compartment of the Midland Railway, Coroner's verdict, 'Death resulting from an overdose of morphia, taken with suicidal intent.'"

The journalist dropped a lump of sugar in his cup and watched it attentively.

"I don't think I could have done it," he said. "I might have left him with his carbolic. But I couldn't have deliberately given him his death-potion."

"But as long as he was going to die," responded the girl in the yachting-cap, "it was better to let him die painlessly."

The Englishman smiled. "Can a woman ever consider the ethical side of a question when the sympathetic one is visible?" he asked.

The alienist cracked another almond. "I was sincere," he said. "Of that there is no doubt. I thought I did right. The question is — did I do right?"

"It would have been wiser," began the lawyer, argumentatively, "since you were stronger than he, to take the vial from him, and to leave him to the care of the law."

"But the wife and children," replied the girl in the yachting-cap. "And hanging is so horrible!"

"So is murder," responded the lawyer, dryly.

The young lady on the Captain's right laid her napkin upon the table and rose. "I don't know what was right," she said, "but I do know that in your place I should have felt like a murderer."

The alienist smiled half cynically. "So I did," he answered; "but there is such a thing, my dear young lady, as a conscientious murderer."

1899

JACK LONDON

A THOUSAND DEATHS

Born John Chaney, Jack London (1876–1916) was the illegitimate son of an itinerant astrologer; eight months after his birth, his mother married John London. Growing up in poverty in California's Bay Area, he went on the road as a hobo, riding freight trains and going to jail for a month of hard labor, which helped give him both understanding of and sympathy for the working-class poor as well as distaste for the drudgery of that sort of life. He became enamored of socialism after reading *The Communist Manifesto,* though he was so eager to be rich that he joined the gold rush to the Klondike region in Yukon, Canada, in 1896. He returned to Oakland without having mined an ounce of gold but with the background for the classic American novel *The Call of the Wild* (1903), which became one of the best-selling novels of the early twentieth century, with more than one and a half million copies sold in his lifetime.

London began to sell stories to *Overland Monthly, The Black Cat,* and *Atlantic Monthly* in the 1890s. Books soon followed. He was hired as a journalist by Hearst to report the Russo-Japanese War for the unheard-of fee of $4,000, became an international best-selling author, earning over $1 million, and by 1913 was called the highest-paid, best-known, and most popular writer in the world. Among the books that remain read to this day are such adventure classics as *The Sea Wolf* (1904) and *White Fang* (1905) and the autobiographical *Martin Eden* (1909). He had become a heavy drinker while still a teenager, and alcoholism, illness, financial woes, and overwork probably induced him to commit suicide at the age of forty, though the official cause of death was listed as uremic poisoning.

Though best known for his adventure fiction, London excelled at many literary genres, including crime fiction. The present story is a strange and compelling mixture of science, adventure, and crime fiction and is one of very few stories involving multiple murders — of the same victim!

"A Thousand Deaths" was first published in the May 1899 issue of *The Black Cat.*

• • •

I HAD BEEN IN the water about an hour, and cold, exhausted, with a terrible cramp in my right calf, it seemed as though my hour had come. Fruitlessly struggling against the strong ebb tide, I had beheld the maddening procession of the water-front lights slip by, but now I gave up attempting to breast the stream and contended myself with the bitter thoughts of a wasted career, now drawing to a close.

It had been my luck to come of good, English stock, but of parents whose account with the bankers far exceeded their knowledge of child-nature and the rearing of children. While born with a silver spoon in my mouth, the blessed atmosphere of the home circle was to me unknown. My father, a very learned man and a celebrated antiquarian, gave no thought to his family, being constantly lost in the abstractions of his study; while my mother, noted far more for her good looks than her good sense, sated herself with the adulation of the society in which she was perpetually plunged. I went through the regular school and college routine of a boy of the English bourgeoisie, and as the years brought me increasing strength and passions, my parents suddenly became aware that I was possessed of an immortal soul, and endeavored to draw the curb. But it was too late; I perpetrated the wildest and most audacious folly, and was disowned by my people, ostracized by the society I had so long outraged, and with the thousand pounds my father gave me, with the declaration that he would neither see me again nor give me more, I took a first-class passage to Australia.

Since then my life had been one long peregrination — from the Orient to the Occident, from the Arctic to the Antarctic — to find myself at last, an able seaman at thirty, in the full vigor of my manhood, drowning in San Francisco bay because of a disastrously successful attempt to desert my ship.

My right leg was drawn up by the cramp, and I was suffering the keenest agony. A slight breeze stirred up a choppy sea, which washed into my mouth and down my throat, nor could I prevent it. Though I still contrived to keep afloat, it was merely mechanical, for I was rapidly becoming unconscious. I have a dim recollection of drifting past the sea-wall, and of catching a glimpse of an upriver steamer's starboard light; then everything became a blank.

I heard the low hum of insect life, and felt the balmy air of a spring morning fanning my cheek. Gradually it assumed a rhythmic flow, to whose soft pulsations my body seemed to respond. I floated on the gentle bosom of a summer's sea, rising and falling with dreamy pleasure on each crooning wave. But the pulsations grew stronger; the humming, louder; the waves, larger, fiercer — I was dashed about on a stormy sea. A great agony fastened upon me. Brilliant, intermittent sparks of light flashed athwart my inner consciousness; in my ears there was the sound of many waters; then a sudden snapping of an intangible something, and I awoke.

The scene, of which I was protagonist, was a curious one. A glance sufficed to inform me that I lay on the cabin floor of some gentleman's yacht, in a most uncomfortable posture. On either side, grasping my arms and working them up and down like pump handles, were two peculiarly clad, dark-skinned creatures. Though conversant with most aboriginal types, I could not conjecture their nationality. Some attachment had been fastened about my head, which connected my respiratory organs with the machine I shall next describe. My nostrils, however, had been closed, forcing me to breathe through my mouth. Foreshortened by the obliquity of my line of vision, I beheld two tubes, similar to small hosing but of different composition, which emerged from my mouth and went off at an acute angle from each other. The first came to an abrupt termination and lay on the floor beside me; the second traversed the floor in numerous coils, connecting with the apparatus I have promised to describe.

In the days before my life had become tangential, I had dabbled not a little in science, and, conversant with the appurtenances and general paraphernalia of the laboratory, I appreciated the machine I now beheld. It was composed chiefly of glass, the construction being of that crude sort which is employed for experimentative purposes. A vessel of water was surrounded by an air chamber, to which was fixed a vertical tube, surmounted by a globe. In the center of this was a vacuum gauge. The water in the tube moved upwards and downwards, creating alternate inhalations and exhalations, which were in turn communicated to me through the hose. With this, and the aid of the men who pumped my arms so vigorously, had the process of breathing been artificially carried on, my chest rising and falling and my lungs expanding and contracting, till nature could be persuaded to again take up her wonted labor.

As I opened my eyes the appliance about my head, nostrils and mouth was removed. Draining a stiff three fingers of brandy, I staggered to my feet to thank my preserver, and confronted — my father. But long years of fellowship with danger had taught me self-control, and I waited to see if he would recognize me. Not so; he saw in me no more than a runaway sailor and treated me accordingly.

Leaving me to the care of the blackies, he fell to revising the notes he had made on my resuscitation. As I ate of the handsome fare served up to me, confusion began on deck, and from the chanteys of the sailors and the rattling of blocks and tackles I surmised that we were getting under way. What a lark! Off on a cruise with my recluse father into the wide Pacific! Little did I realize, as I laughed to myself, which side the joke was to be on. Aye, had I known, I would have plunged overboard and welcomed the dirty fo'c'sle from which I had just escaped.

I was not allowed on deck till we had sunk the Farallones and the last pilot boat. I appreciated this forethought on the part of my father and made it a point to thank him heartily, in my bluff seaman's manner. I could not suspect that he had his own ends in view, in thus keeping my presence secret to all save the crew. He told me briefly of my rescue by his sailors, assuring me that the obligation was on his side, as my appearance had been most opportune. He had constructed the apparatus for the vindication of a theory concerning certain biological phenomena, and had been waiting for an opportunity to use it.

"You have proved it beyond all doubt," he said; then added with a sigh, "But only in the small matter of drowning." But, to take a reef in my yarn—he offered me an advance of two pounds on my previous wages to sail with him, and this I considered handsome, for he really did not need me. Contrary to my expectations, I did not join the sailor's mess, for'ard, being assigned to a comfortable stateroom and eating at the captain's table. He had perceived that I was no common sailor, and I resolved to take this chance for reinstating myself in his good graces. I wove a fictitious past to account for my education and present position, and did my best to come in touch with him. I was not long in disclosing a predilection for scientific pursuits, nor he in appreciating my aptitude. I became his assistant, with a corresponding increase in wages, and before long, as he grew confidential and expounded his theories, I was as enthusiastic as himself.

The days flew quickly by, for I was deeply interested in my new studies, passing my waking hours in his well-stocked library, or listening to his plans and aiding him in his laboratory work. But we were forced to forego many enticing experiments, a rolling ship not being exactly the proper place for delicate or intricate work. He promised me, however, many delightful hours in the magnificent laboratory for which we were bound. He had taken possession of an uncharted South Sea island, as he said, and turned it into a scientific paradise.

We had not been on the island long before I discovered the horrible mare's nest I had fallen into. But before I describe the strange things which came to pass, I must briefly outline the causes which culminated in as startling an experience as ever fell to the lot of man.

Late in life, my father had abandoned the musty charms of antiquity and succumbed to the more fascinating ones embraced under the general head of biology. Having been thoroughly grounded during his youth in the fundamentals, he rapidly explored all the higher branches as far as the scientific world had gone, and found himself on the no man's land of the unknowable. It was his intention to pre-empt some of this unclaimed territory, and it was at this stage of his investigations that we had been thrown together. Having a good brain, though I say it myself, I had mastered his speculations and methods of reasoning, becoming almost as mad as himself. But I should not say this. The marvelous results we afterwards obtained can only go to prove his sanity. I can but say that he was the most abnormal specimen of cold-blooded cruelty I have ever seen.

After having penetrated the dual mysteries of physiology and psychology, his thought had led him to the verge of a great field, for which, the better to explore, he began studies in higher organic chemistry, pathology, toxicology and other sciences and sub-sciences rendered kindred as accessories to his speculative hypotheses. Starting from the proposition that the direct cause of the temporary and permanent arrest of vitality was due to the coagulation of certain elements and compounds in the protoplasm, he had isolated and subjected these various substances to innumerable experiments. Since the temporary arrest of vitality in an organism brought coma, and a permanent arrest death, he held that by artificial means this coagulation of the protoplasm could be retarded, prevented, and even overcome in the extreme states of solidification. Or, to do away with the technical nomenclature, he argued that death, when not violent and in which none of the organs had suffered injury, was merely suspended vitality; and that, in such instances, life could be induced to resume its functions by the use of proper methods. This, then, was his idea: To discover the method — and by practical experimentation prove the possibility — of renewing vitality in a structure from which life had seemingly fled. Of course, he recognized the futility of such endeavor after decomposition had set in; he must have organisms which but the moment, the hour, or the day before, had been quick with life. With me, in a crude way, he had proved this theory. I was really drowned, really dead, when picked from the water of San Francisco bay—but the vital spark had been renewed by means of his aerotherapeutical apparatus, as he called it.

Now to his dark purpose concerning me. He first showed me how completely I was in his power. He had sent the yacht away for a year, retaining only his two blackies, who were utterly devoted to him. He then made an exhaustive review of his theory and outlined the method of proof he had adopted, concluding with the startling announcement that I was to be his subject.

I had faced death and weighed my chances in many a desperate venture, but never in one of this nature. I can swear I am no coward, yet this proposition of journeying back and forth across the borderland of death put the yellow fear upon me. I asked for time, which he granted, at the same time assuring me that but the one course was open—I must submit. Escape from the island was out of the question; escape by suicide was not to be entertained, though really preferable to what it seemed I must undergo; my only hope was to destroy my captors. But this latter was frustrated through the precautions taken by my father. I was subjected to a constant surveillance, even in my sleep being guarded by one or the other of the blacks.

Having pleaded in vain, I announced and proved that I was his son. It was my last card, and I had played all my hopes upon it. But he was inexorable; he was not a father but a scientific machine. I wonder yet how it ever came to pass that he married my mother or begat me, for there was not the slightest grain of emotion in his make-up. Reason was all in all to him, nor could he understand such things as love or sympathy in others, except as petty weaknesses which should be overcome. So he informed me that in the beginning he had given me life, and who had better right to take it away than he? Such, he said, was not his desire, however; he merely wished to borrow it occasionally, promising to return it punctually at the appointed time. Of course, there was a liability of mishaps, but I could do no more than take the chances, since the affairs of men were full of such.

The better to insure success, he wished me to be in the best possible condition, so I was dieted and trained like a great athlete before a decisive contest. What could I do? If I had to undergo the peril, it were best to be in good shape. In my intervals of relaxation he allowed me to assist in the arranging of the apparatus and in the various subsidiary experiments. The interest I took in all such operations can be imagined. I mastered the work as thoroughly as he, and often had the pleasure of seeing some of my suggestions or alterations put into effect. After such events I would smile grimly, conscious of officiating at my own funeral.

He began by inaugurating a series of experiments in toxicology. When all was ready, I was killed by a stiff dose of strychnine and allowed to lie dead for some twenty hours. During that period my body was dead, absolutely dead. All respiration and circulation ceased; but the frightful part of it was, that while the protoplasmic coagulation proceeded, I retained consciousness and was enabled to study it in all its ghastly details.

The apparatus to bring me back to life was an air-tight chamber, fitted to receive my body. The mechanism was simple — a few valves, a rotary shaft and crank, and an electric motor. When in operation, the interior atmosphere was alternately condensed and rarefied, thus communicating to my lungs an artificial respiration without the agency of the hosing previously used. Though my body was inert, and, for all I knew, in the first stages of decomposition, I was cognizant of everything that transpired. I knew when they placed me in the chamber, and though all my senses were quiescent, I was aware of hypodermic injections of a compound to react upon the coagulatory process. Then the chamber was closed and the machinery started. My anxiety was terrible; but the circulation became gradually restored, the different organs began to carry on their respective functions, and in an hour's time I was eating a hearty dinner.

It cannot be said that I participated in this series, nor in the subsequent ones, with much verve; but after two ineffectual attempts of escape, I began to take quite an interest. Besides, I was becoming accustomed. My father was beside himself at his success, and as the months rolled by his speculations took wilder and yet wilder flights. We ranged through the three great classes of poisons, the neurotics, the gaseous and the irritants, but carefully avoided some of the mineral irritants and passed the whole group of corrosives. During the poison regime I became quite accustomed to dying, and had but one mishap to shake my growing confidence. Scarifying a number of lesser blood vessels in my arm, he introduced a minute quantity of that most frightful of poisons, the arrow poison, or curare. I lost consciousness at the start, quickly followed by the cessation of respiration and circulation, and so far had the solidification of the protoplasm advanced, that he gave up all hope. But at the last moment he applied a discovery he had been working upon, receiving such encouragement as to redouble his efforts.

In a glass vacuum, similar but not exactly like a Crookes' tube, was placed a magnetic field. When penetrated by polarized light, it gave no phenomena of phosphorescence nor the rectilinear projection of atoms, but emitted non-luminous rays, similar to the X-ray. While the X-ray could reveal opaque objects hidden in dense mediums, this was possessed of far subtler penetration. By this he photographed my body, and found on the negative an infinite number of blurred shadows, due to the chemical and electric motions still going on. This was an infallible proof that the rigor mortis in which I lay was not genuine; that is, those mysterious forces, those delicate bonds which held my soul to my body, were still in action. The resultants of all other poisons were unapparent, save those of mercurial compounds, which usually left me languid for several days.

Another series of delightful experiments was with electricity. We verified Tesla's assertion that high currents were utterly harmless by passing 100,000 volts through my body. As this did not affect me, the current was reduced to 2,500, and I was quickly electrocuted. This time he ventured so far as to allow me to remain dead, or in a state of suspended vitality, for three days. It took four hours to bring me back.

Once, he super-induced lockjaw; but the agony of dying was so great that I positively refused to undergo similar experiments. The easiest deaths were by asphyxiation, such as drowning, strangling, and suffocation by gas; while those by morphine, opium, cocaine and chloroform, were not at all hard.

Another time, after being suffocated, he kept me in cold storage for three months, not permitting me to freeze or decay. This was without my knowledge, and I was in a great fright on discovering the lapse of time. I became afraid of what he might do with me when I lay dead, my alarm being increased by the predilection he was beginning to betray towards vivisection. The last time I was resurrected, I discovered that he had been tampering with my breast. Though he had carefully dressed and sewed the incisions up, they were so severe that I had to take to my bed for some time. It was during this convalescence that I evolved the plan by which I ultimately escaped.

While feigning unbounded enthusiasm in the work, I asked and received a vacation from my moribund occupation. During this period I devoted myself to laboratory work, while he was too deep in the vivisection of the many animals captured by the blacks to take notice of my work.

It was on these two propositions that I constructed my theory: First, electrolysis, or the decomposition of water into its constituent gases by means of electricity; and, second, by the hypothetical existence of a force, the converse of gravitation, which Astor has named "apergy." Terrestrial attraction, for instance, merely draws objects together but does not combine them; hence, apergy is merely repulsion. Now, atomic or molecular attraction not only draws objects together but integrates them; and it was the converse of this, or a disintegrative force, which I wished to not only discover and produce, but to direct at will. Thus, the molecules of hydrogen and oxygen reacting on each other, separate, and create new molecules containing both elements and forming water. Electrolysis causes these molecules to split up and resume their original condition, producing the two gases separately. The force I wished to find must not only do this with two, but with all elements, no matter in what compounds they exist. If I could then entice my father within its radius, he would be instantly disintegrated and sent flying to the four quarters, a mass of isolated elements.

It must not be understood that this force, which I finally came to control, annihilated matter; it merely annihilated form. Nor, as I soon discovered, had it any effect on inorganic structure; but to all organic form it was absolutely fatal. This partiality puzzled me at first, though had I stopped to think deeper I would have seen through it. Since the number of atoms in organic molecules is far greater than in the most complex mineral molecules, organic compounds are characterized by their instability and the ease with which they are split up by physical forces and chemical reagents.

By two powerful batteries, connected with magnets constructed specially for this purpose, two tremendous forces were projected. Considered apart from each other, they were perfectly harmless; but they accomplished their purpose by focusing at an invisible point in mid-air. After practically demonstrating its success, besides narrowly escaping being blown into nothingness, I laid my trap. Concealing the magnets, so that their force made the whole space of my chamber doorway a field of death, and placing by my couch a button by which I could throw on the current from the storage batteries, I climbed into bed.

The blackies still guarded my sleeping quarters, one relieving the other at midnight. I turned on the current as soon as the first man arrived. Hardly had I begun to doze, when I was aroused by a sharp, metallic tinkle. There, on the mid-threshold, lay the collar of Dan, my father's St. Bernard. My keeper ran to pick it up. He disappeared like a gust of wind, his clothes falling to the floor in a heap. There was a slight whiff of ozone in the air, but since the principal gaseous components of his body were hydrogen, oxygen and nitrogen, which are equally colorless and odorless, there was no other manifestation of his departure. Yet when I shut off the current and removed the garments, I found a deposit of carbon in the form of animal charcoal; also other powders, the isolated, solid elements of his organism, such as sulfur, potassium and iron. Resetting the trap, I crawled back to bed. At midnight I got up and removed the remains of the second black, and then slept peacefully till morning.

I was awakened by the strident voice of my father, who was calling to me from across the laboratory. I laughed to myself. There had been no one to call him and he had overslept. I could hear him as he approached my room with the intention of rousing me, and so I sat up in bed, the better to observe his translation—perhaps apotheosis were a better term. He paused a moment at the threshold, then took the fatal step. Puff! It was like the wind sighing among the pines. He was gone. His clothes fell in a fantastic heap on the floor. Besides ozone, I noticed the faint, garlic-like odor of phosphorus. A little pile of elementary solids lay among his garments. That was all. The wide world lay before me. My captors were no more.